THE WHITE COMPANY
AND SIR NIGEL

• THE BARNES & NOBLE LIBRARY OF ESSENTIAL READING •

THE WHITE COMPANY
AND SIR NIGEL

Sir Arthur Conan Doyle

Introduction by Douglas Elliott

BARNES & NOBLE BOOKS

NEW YORK

THE BARNES & NOBLE
LIBRARY OF ESSENTIAL READING

Introduction and Suggested Reading Copyright © 2005 by Barnes & Noble Books

The White Company was first published in book format in 1891 and *Sir Nigel* in 1906

This edition published by Barnes & Noble Publishing, Inc.

Cover Design by Stacey May

2005 Barnes & Noble Publishing, Inc.

ISBN 0-7607-6890-0

Printed and bound in the United States of America

3 5 7 9 10 8 6 4 2

CONTENTS

INTRODUCTION

SIR Arthur Conan Doyle's two novels of adventure in the fourteenth century, *The White Company* and *Sir Nigel,* seamlessly blend real history and imaginative fiction into spirited, fast-paced narratives that draw us in, eager witnesses to the medieval soldier's life. Eclipsed in popularity by his Sherlock Holmes stories, they have nonetheless found a lasting readership. Never out of print since their first publications in 1891 and 1906—more than fifty editions of *The White Company* were printed during Conan Doyle's lifetime alone—they remain memorable for their accessible style, nonstop action, gentle humor, larger-than-life characters, and vibrant imagery. *The White Company* follows the mustering of English troops in 1366-7 as they march to defend the ousted king of Spain against the usurper's army. Seen through the eyes of young Alleyne Edricson, raised in a monastery and now experiencing the secular world for the first time as squire to the valiant knight Sir Nigel Loring, this is history painted on a very personal level. Along the way, Alleyne encounters all manner of characters, noble and peasant, honorable and venal, master and victim, who populate a world of both beauty and horror. The early life of Loring himself is told in *Sir Nigel.* We travel with him as his first encounters with danger in battle-torn France transform an undisciplined youth into a warrior and knight. Conan Doyle fervently believed that these works would shine a clear new light on a dramatic era in English history and for over one hundred years his many readers have agreed with him.

Born in 1859 in Edinburgh, Arthur Conan Doyle is primarily known today for his tales of the ultimate Victorian consulting detective, Sherlock Holmes. He also earned fame during his lifetime for his science-fiction adventure, *The Lost World,* his humorous short stories about Napoleon's soldier, Brigadier Gerard, and his historical novels, including *Micah Clarke* (1889), *The Refugees* (1893), *The White Company,* and *Sir Nigel.* The latter two, he declared, were his most satisfying works and his greatest literary achievements. Until his death in 1930, he remained by degrees bemused, puzzled, and angered that the public should constantly be asking him about Holmes while apparently ignoring his historical fiction.

The Middle Ages had long been a subject of fascination for Conan Doyle. As a boy, he had been entertained and taught by his mother with stories from medieval history and tales of his forebears, traced back five hundred years to their Anglo-Norman and Irish-Catholic roots. Following the many branches of the family tree also meant understanding the science of heraldry, which the young Arthur embraced under his mother's enthusiastic tutelage. And he had learned from her to admire and practice the ideals of chivalry: loyalty, bravery, humility, and respect for all, especially for the poor and for women.

With such an upbringing it is not surprising that Conan Doyle's literary preferences tended toward stories of medieval adventure, knighthood, and chivalry. Among his earliest favorites were Sir Walter Scott's *Ivanhoe* (1819) and Charles Reade's *The Cloister and the Hearth (1861),* both set in the period.

After completing his medical degree at the University of Edinburgh, Conan Doyle settled in Southsea, a seaside suburb of Portsmouth, and established a medical practice while submitting for publication, with mixed results, a stream of stories and novels, including Holmes' first appearance, *A Study in Scarlet* (1887). With the modest success of his first historical novel, *Micah Clarke,* set in the mid-eighteenth century, Conan Doyle decided to attempt another more ambitious one, a story that would reflect his love of the Middle Ages. He chose the mid-fourteenth century, a period he believed to be "the splendid dawn of modern England."

In the spring of 1889, Conan Doyle moved into a rented cottage in the New Forest of Hampshire where he read a considerable stack of books about the period. All that summer he researched, returning to Southsea in the autumn with volumes of notes to begin writing the novel, which he finished in July 1890. He remembered the final moment clearly more than thirty years later: "As I wrote the last words of *The White Company* I felt a wave of exultation and with a cry of 'That's done it!' I hurled my inky pen across the room, where it left a black smudge upon the duck's egg wall-paper. I knew in my heart that the book would live and that it would illuminate our national traditions."

The White Company appeared as a serial through 1891 in England in the prestigious *Cornhill Magazine* and was published in book form later that year in England and America. It was generally well received. "As brisk and lively as could be wished," wrote *The Athaneum. The Saturday Review* assured its readers that the book "will be devoured with eagerness by all healthy-minded Britons who love adventure." Even American reviewers were caught up in the patriotic frenzy. "We Americans cannot but share the pride of our English cousins in the heroic deeds of our common ancestors," enthused San Francisco's *Overland Monthly.*

It would be fifteen years before Conan Doyle would complete a companion work to *The White Company.* Written in the summer and fall of 1905, *Sir Nigel* was published late the following year. The events of the story begin seventeen years earlier than those of *The White Company.* Now confident in his writer's voice, he introduced a personal note: In Dame Ermyntrude, Nigel Loring's mother, Conan Doyle gives us a loving portrait of his own mother, whose teachings and stories had started him on his journey to the fourteenth century.

Critics were also kind to *Sir Nigel. The Daily Mail* thought that it "should take its place on the shelves near to the immortal company of Sir Walter Scott."

Though these two novels have fallen under the shadow of the great detective, they have nonetheless remained popular and influential. Winston Churchill wrote, "The works I like even more than the detective stories are the great historical novels which, like Sherlock Holmes, have certainly found a permanent place in English literature." Author Kurt Vonnegut, Jr., recalled reading *The White Company* as a child. Anthony Burgess wrote that the book is "vivid, always plausible, never lacking in life."

For atmosphere, language, and history, Conan Doyle relied heavily upon the great chronicler of the fourteenth century, Jean Froissart, whose *Chronicles* is packed with brave knights' exploits, passages of arms, diplomatic maneuverings between states, and great battles between colorful armies. Froissart's historical accuracy is generally disparaged, but as a portrait of the manners, styles, and speech of the time, the *Chronicles* is a goldmine.

For further contemporary color, Conan Doyle called upon two fourteenth-century pioneers of the English language, Geoffrey Chaucer (c. 1343 - 1400) and William Langland (c. 1330 - c. 1387). Chaucer is well known to us for his *Canterbury Tales*, which gives us a taste of the rich stew of fourteenth-century life. Langland was the author of the alliterative poem *The Vision of Piers Plowman*, a monument of early English poetic art with its great themes of truth and honor.

Conan Doyle assumes a great deal of historical knowledge on the part of his readers, plunging right into each narrative with very little exposition. For the English reader of 1891, this was probably a reasonable approach, but in the twenty-first century such details have fallen out of common knowledge, so a brief historical backgrounder is in order.

Life and events in England and France during this period revolved around the Hundred Years' War, actually a series of wars between the two countries. The conflict was rooted in the desire of the English monarch to possess the crown of France, or at least a large portion of its territory known as Aquitaine (or Guyenne), and the French king's corresponding efforts to remove English rule from the area. Apart from isolated French raids on southern English seaports, the war was waged exclusively on French soil. It is generally considered to have erupted in 1337 with mutual declarations by Edward III of England and Philip VI of France.

England entered the war as the underdog, but soon proved itself by decisively winning a series of important battles: a naval encounter at Sluys (1340) and land battles at Crécy (1346) and Poitiers (1356). Poitiers was particularly significant for both sides in that one of the captured nobles was King John of France, who had succeeded Philip VI in 1350. Among the deciding factors in these victories was a new weapon of which the English alone were masters and against which defense was extremely difficult: the longbow.

Medieval soldiers were as much motivated by greed as by patriotism: Every combatant, from the wealthiest knight to the humblest spearsman, could hope to greatly improve his material life by returning home laden with plunder. Ransom was another source of revenue for the invading armies. Captured barons and local politicians could be held for payment or released on the promise that an appropriate ransom would be paid. Lowlier citizens and men-at-arms whose standing did not make them ransom-worthy were simply killed.

From about 1347, Edward himself spent relatively little time engaged in the direct management of the war, leaving the task of campaigning to his son, Edward, Prince of Wales, who would be known in future centuries as the Black Prince.

The war was driven into hiatus between 1348 and 1350 by the arrival of the Black Death, bubonic and pneumonic plague which killed as much as one-third of the European population and made maintaining an army unrealistic for either side. During this period of relative peace, there were still excuses for the two nations to continue their bickering, not least of which was supporting rival claimants to the dukedom of Brittany in northwestern France. The many bloody skirmishes spawned by this dispute, and the resumption of full-blown hostilities leading to the battle of Poitiers itself, form much of the story of *Sir Nigel*.

After Poitiers in 1356, the prince immediately released his troops, who found themselves far from home with no source of income. Accustomed to the rewards of plunder, they formed the so-called Free Companies and proceeded to ravage the French countryside. In Paris, the government was powerless to protect the peasantry from the depredations of the Companies. Anger smoldered into flame in 1358 in a vicious peasant uprising called the *Jacquerie,* after the derisive name *Jacque* used by the nobles to refer to the typical peasant.

In 1360 the war was halted again by the treaty of Brétigny and two years later Edward III ceded Aquitaine to the Prince of Wales, who would hold court in its capitol, Bordeaux, for seven years. Once again, though there was no open warfare between England and France during this period, there were still opportunities for battle. The Spanish crown was contested by Pedro the Cruel, king of Castile, and his illegitimate brother Don Enrique (Henry) of Trastamare. Pedro was supported by the English, Henry by the French. As *The White Company* opens in the spring of 1366, armies are forming in southern France and northern Spain, and history is shepherding them inexorably toward their collision at the battle of Najera (Navarette) the following year.

In England, meanwhile, Edward III had achieved a stable central government and was in the process of repairing a longstanding national division. After William of Normandy had conquered England in 1066, his French-speaking barons had established rule over the local Saxons who spoke Old English. By Edward's time, the rift between master and serf had closed somewhat and, though the king himself barely spoke English, there was considerable interaction between the two groups and the Saxon language was being transformed into Middle English.

In England, as elsewhere in Europe, the nobility (and those who aspired to it) shared a great chivalric ideal. The fourteenth-century knight saw himself as the moral descendent of the mythical King Arthur: defender of the faith, upholder of justice, champion of the oppressed. The ideals of chivalry—prowess, honor, loyalty, courtesy, and courtly love — governed relationships, war, politics, indeed life itself, and provided some hope of order in a chaotic, brutal, and often arbitrary world.

But in spite of this unifying standard, real power was still largely fragmented, held by bickering local barons with no central source of order, so the Church emerged as a central civilizing influence in a society that desperately needed one. A commoner could not aspire to a position of nobility; his only paths to material improvement lay in joining his lord's army or taking holy orders. The Church would take in a young man, educate him in languages, art, and sciences, and train him to assume a position of respect in the community.

There was an actual White Company. It was formed out of the Free Companies in eastern France and was recruited as a mercenary army to fight in Italy in 1361. It finally broke up in 1364, two years before the story of *The White Company* opens. There was also a real Sir Nigel (or Neil or Nele) Loring. Knighted for bravery at Sluys, he was one of the original twenty-five knights of the Order of the Garter founded by Edward III in 1348. He became chamberlain (household manager) to the Black Prince following the battle of Poitiers, fought at the prince's side and was sent by him on important diplomatic missions.

Conan Doyle's aim in writing these novels was to reveal the everyday life of this period of English history, to make it accessible by wrapping it in an engaging story, and to celebrate the chivalric ideal. He felt that earlier authors such as Scott had concentrated on the maneuverings of the upper classes and the grand sweep of armies, at the expense of telling the human experience of the humble soldier, particularly the English archer. He shows us the beginnings of the new movements for social justice emerging in France and England. And he wanted us to know that in the midst of an ocean of misery and cruelty there flourished tiny islands of enlightenment and beauty, exemplified by the delicate works of stained glass that were among the highest achievements of the period's art. Conan Doyle was never less than enthusiastic in any of his writings, and every page of these stories pulses with life and glows with his love of the times.

Arthur Conan Doyle was certain that his two medieval novels "would illuminate our national traditions" and was disappointed that they became known as simple boys' adventures, playing second fiddle to Sherlock Holmes. Yet creating an adventure that can still quicken the pulse and fire the imagination after over a century is no small feat in itself. What a bonus, then, that Conan Doyle has been able to weave into these engaging stories a wealth of detail that shines a brilliant light on the fourteenth century, making it accessible to a new generation of readers.

Douglas Elliott has been writing about the life and works of Arthur Conan Doyle for over twenty-five years. He is the author of *The Curious Incident of the Missing Link: Arthur Conan Doyle and Piltdown Man* and the co-editor of *The Annotated White Company*.

TO THE HOPE OF THE FUTURE

THE REUNION OF THE
ENGLISH-SPEAKING RACES

THIS LITTLE CHRONICLE OF OUR
COMMON ANCESTRY IS INSCRIBED

SOUTH NORWOOD
SEPTEMBER 29, 1891

CHAPTER I

HOW THE BLACK SHEEP CAME FORTH
FROM THE FOLD

THE great bell of Beaulieu was ringing. Far away through the forest might be heard its musical clangour and swell. Peat-cutters on Blackdown and fishers upon the Exe heard the distant throbbing rising and falling upon the sultry summer air. It was a common sound in those parts—as common as the chatter of the jays and the booming of the bittern. Yet the fishers and the peasants raised their heads and looked questions at each other, for the Angelus had already gone and Vespers was still far off. Why should the great bell of Beaulieu toll when the shadows were neither short nor long?

All round the Abbey the monks were trooping in. Under the long green-paved avenues of gnarled oaks and of lichened beeches the white-robed brothers gathered to the sound. From the vineyard and the vinepress, from the bouvary or ox-farm, from the marl-pits and salterns, even from the distant ironworks of Sowley and the outlying grange of St Leonard's, they had all turned their steps homewards. It had been no sudden call. A swift messenger had the night before sped round to the outlying dependencies of the Abbey and had left the summons for every monk to be back in the cloisters by the third hour after noontide. So urgent a message had not been issued within the memory of old lay-brother Athanasius, who had cleaned the Abbey knocker since the year after the Battle of Bannockburn.

A stranger who knew nothing either of the Abbey or of its immense resources might have gathered from the appearance of the brothers some conception of the varied duties which they were called upon to perform, and of the busy widespread life which centred in the old monastery. As they swept gravely in by twos and by threes, with bended heads and muttering lips, there were few who did not bear upon them some signs of their daily toil. Here were two with wrists and sleeves all spotted with the ruddy grape juice. There again was a bearded brother with a broad-headed axe and a bundle of faggots upon his shoulders, while beside him walked another with the shears under his arm and the white wool still clinging to his whiter gown. A long straggling troop bore spades and mattocks, while the two rearmost of all staggered along under a huge basket of fresh-caught carp—for the morrow was Friday, and there were fifty platters to be filled and as many sturdy trenchermen behind them. Of all the throng there was scarce one who was not labour-stained and weary, for Abbot Berghersh was a hard man to himself and to others.

Meanwhile, in the broad and lofty chamber set apart for occasions of import, the Abbot himself was pacing impatiently backwards and forwards, with his long white nervous hands clasped in front of him. His thin thought-worn features and sunken haggard cheeks bespoke one who had indeed beaten down that inner foe whom every man must face, but had none the less suffered sorely in the contest. In crushing his passions he had wellnigh crushed himself. Yet, frail as was his person, there gleamed out ever and anon from under his drooping brows a flash of fierce energy, which recalled to men's minds that he came of a fighting stock, and that even now his twin brother, Sir Bartholomew Berghersh, was one of the most famous of those stern warriors who had planted the Cross of St George before the gates of Paris. With lips compressed and clouded brow, he strode up and down the oaken floor, the very genius and impersonation of asceticism, while the great bell still thundered and clanged above his head. At last the uproar died away in three last, measured throbs, and ere their echo had ceased the Abbot struck a small gong which summoned a lay-brother to his presence. "Have the brethren come?" he asked, in the Anglo-French dialect used in religious houses.

"They are here," the other answered, with his eyes cast down, and his hands crossed upon his chest.

"All?"

"Two-and-thirty of the seniors and fifteen of the novices, most holy father. Brother Mark of the Spicarium is sore smitten with a fever and could not come. He said that—"

"It boots not what he said. Fever or no, he should have come at my call. His spirit must be chastened, as must that of many more in this Abbey. You yourself, brother Francis, have twice raised your voice, so that it hath come to my ears, when the reader in the refectory hath been dealing with the lives of God's most blessed saints. What hast thou to say?"

The lay-brother stood meek and silent, with his arms still crossed in front of him.

"One thousand Aves and as many Credos, said standing with arms outstretched before the shrine of the Virgin, may help thee to remember that the Creator hath given us two ears and but one mouth, as a token that there is twice the work for one as for the other. Where is the master of the novices?"

"He is without, most holy father."

"Send him hither."

The sandalled feet clattered over the wooden floor, and the iron-bound door creaked upon its hinges. In a few moments it opened again to admit a short square monk with a heavy, composed face and authoritative manner.

"You have sent for me, holy father?"

"Yes, brother Jerome, I wish that this matter be disposed of with as little scandal as may be; and yet it is needful that the example should be a public one." The Abbot spoke in Latin now, as a language which was more fitted by its age and solemnity to convey the thoughts of two high dignitaries of the order.

5

"It would perchance be best that the novices be not admitted," suggested the master. "This mention of a woman may turn their minds from their pious meditations to worldly and evil thoughts."

"Woman! Woman!" groaned the Abbot. "Well has the holy Chrysostom termed them *radix malorum*. From Eve downwards, what good hath come from any of them? Who brings the plaint?"

"It is brother Ambrose."

"A holy and devout young man."

"A light and a pattern to every novice."

"Let the matter be brought to an issue, then, according to our old-time monastic habit. Bid the chancellor and the sub-chancellor lead in the brothers according to age, together with brother John the accused and brother Ambrose the accuser."

"And the novices?"

"Let them bide in the north alley of the cloisters. Stay! Bid the sub-chancellor send out to them Thomas the lector to read unto them from the 'Gesta beati Benedicti.' It may save them from foolish and pernicious babbling."

The Abbot was left to himself once more, and bent his thin grey face over his illuminated breviary. So he remained while the senior monks filed slowly and sedately into the chamber, seating themselves upon the long oaken benches which lined the wall on either side. At the further end, in two high chairs as large as that of the Abbot, though hardly as elaborately carved, sat the master of the novices and the chancellor, the latter a broad and portly priest, with dark mirthful eyes and a thick outgrowth of crisp black hair all round his tonsured head. Between them stood a lean white-faced brother who appeared to be ill at ease, shifting his feet from side to side and tapping his chin nervously with the long parchment roll which he held in his hand. The Abbot, from his point of vantage, looked down on the two lines of faces, placid and sun-browned for the most part, with the large bovine eyes and unlined features which told of their easy, unchanging existence. Then he turned his eager, fiery gaze upon the pale-faced monk who faced him.

"This plaint is thine, as I learn, brother Ambrose," said he. "May the holy Benedict, patron of our house, be present this day and aid us in our findings. How many counts are there?"

"Three, most holy father," the brother answered in a low and quavering voice.

"Have you set them forth according to rule?"

"They are here set down, most holy father, upon a cantle of sheepskin."

"Let the sheepskin be handed to the chancellor. Bring in brother John, and let him hear the plaints which have been urged against him."

At this order a lay-brother swung open the door, and two other lay-brothers entered, leading between them a young novice of the order. He was a man of huge stature, dark-eyed and red-headed, with a peculiar half humorous, half defiant expression upon his bold, well-marked features. His cowl was thrown back upon his shoulders, and his gown, unfastened at the top, disclosed a round sinewy neck, ruddy and corded like the bark of the fir. Thick muscular arms, covered with a reddish down, protruded from the wide sleeves of his habit, while his white skirt, looped up upon one side, gave a glimpse of a huge knotty leg, scarred and torn with the scratches of brambles. With a bow to the Abbot, which had in it perhaps more pleasantry than reverence, the novice strode across to the carved prie-dieu which had been set apart for him, and stood silent and erect with his hand upon the gold bell which was used in the private orisons of the Abbot's own household. His dark eyes glanced rapidly over the assembly, and finally settled with a grim and menacing twinkle upon the face of his accuser.

The chancellor rose, and having slowly unrolled the parchment scroll, proceeded to read it out in a thick and pompous voice, while a subdued rustle and movement among the brothers bespoke the interest with which they followed the proceedings.

Charges brought upon the second Thursday after the feast of the Assumption, in the year of our Lord thirteen hundred and sixty-six, against brother John, formerly known as Hordle John, or

John of Hordle, but now a novice in the holy monastic order of the Cistercians. Read upon the same day at the Abbey of Beaulieu in the presence of the most reverend Abbot Berghersh and of the assembled order.

The charges against the said brother John are the following, namely, to wit:

"First, that on the above-mentioned feast of the Assumption, small beer having been served to the novices in the proportion of one quart to each four, the said brother John did drain the pot at one draught to the detriment of brother Paul, brother Porphyry, and brother Ambrose, who could scarce eat their none-meat of salted stock-fish, on account of their exceeding dryness."

At this solemn indictment the novice raised his hand and twitched his lip, while even the placid senior brothers glanced across at each other and coughed to cover their amusement. The Abbot alone sat grey and immutable, with a drawn face and a brooding eye.

"Item, that having been told by the master of the novices that he should restrict his food for two days to a single three-pound loaf of bran and beans, for the greater honouring and glorifying of St Monica, mother of the holy Augustine, he was heard by brother Ambrose and others to say that he wished twenty thousand devils would fly away with the said Monica, mother of the holy Augustine, or any other saint who came between a man and his meat. Item, that upon brother Ambrose reproving him for this blasphemous wish, he did hold the said brother face downwards over the piscatorium or fishpond for a space during which the said brother was able to repeat a Pater and four Aves for the better fortifying of his soul against impending death."

There was a buzz and murmur among the white-frocked brethren at this grave charge; but the Abbot held up his long quivering hand. "What then?" said he.

"Item, that between Nones and Vespers on the feast of James the Less the said brother John was observed upon the Brockenhurst road, near the spot which is known as Hatchett's Pond, in converse with a person of the other sex, being a maiden of the name of Mary Sowley, the daughter of the King's verderer. Item, that after sundry japes and jokes the said brother John did lift up the said Mary Sowley and did take, carry, and convey her across a stream, to the infinite relish of the devil and the exceeding detriment of his own soul, which scandalous and wilful falling away was witnessed by three members of our order."

A dead silence throughout the room, with a rolling of heads and upturning of eyes, bespoke the pious horror of the community. The Abbot drew his grey brows low over his fiercely questioning eyes.

"Who can vouch for this thing?" he asked.

"That can I," answered the accuser. "So too can brother Porphyry, Who was with me, and brother Mark of the Spicarium, who hath been so much stirred and inwardly troubled by the sight that he now lies in a fever through it."

"And the woman?" asked the Abbot. 'Did she not break into lamentation and woe that a brother should so demean himself?'

"Nay, she smiled sweetly upon him and thanked him. I can vouch it, and so can brother Porphyry."

"Canst thou?" cried the Abbot, in a high tempestuous tone. "Canst thou so? Hast forgotten that the five-and-thirtieth rule of the order is that in the presence of a woman the face should be ever averted and the eyes cast down? Hast forgot it, I say? If your eyes were upon your sandals, how came ye to see this smile of which ye prate? A week in your cells, false brethren, a week of rye-bread and lentils, with double Lauds and double Matins, may help ye to a remembrance of the laws under which ye live."

At this sudden outflame of wrath the two witnesses sank their faces on to their chests, and sat as men crushed. The Abbot turned his angry eyes away from them and bent them upon the accused, who met his searching gaze with a firm and composed face.

"What hast thou to say, brother John, upon these weighty things which are urged against thee?"

"Little enough, good father, little enough," said the novice, speaking English with a broad West Saxon drawl. The brothers, who were English to a man, pricked up their ears, at the sound of the homely and yet unfamiliar speech: but the Abbot flushed red with anger, and struck his hand upon the oaken arm of his chair.

"What talk is this?" he cried. "Is this a tongue to be used within the walls of an old and well-famed monastery? But grace and learning have ever gone hand in hand, and when one is lost it is needless to look for the other."

"I know not about that," said brother John. "I know only that the words come kindly to my mouth, for it was the speech of my fathers before me. Under your favour I shall either use it now or hold my peace."

The Abbot patted his foot and nodded his head, as one who passes a point but does not forget it.

"For the matter of the ale," continued brother John, "I had come in hot from the fields and had scarce got the taste of the thing before mine eye lit upon the bottom of the pot. It may be, too, that I spoke somewhat shortly concerning the bran and the beans, the same being poor provender and unfitted for a man of my inches. It is true also that I did lay my hands upon this jack-fool of a brother Ambrose, though, as you can see, I did him little scathe. As regards the maid, too, it is true that I did heft her over the stream, she having on her hosen and shoon, whilst I had but my wooden sandals, which could take no hurt from the water. I should have thought shame upon my manhood, as well as my monkhood, if I had held back my hand from her." He glanced around as he spoke, with the half-amused look which he had worn during the whole proceedings.

"There is no need to go further," said the Abbot. "He has confessed to all. It only remains for me to portion out the punishment which is due to his evil conduct."

He rose and the two long lines of brothers followed his example, looking sideways with scared faces at the angry prelate.

"John of Hordle," he thundered, "you have shown yourself during the two months of your novitiate to be a recreant monk, and one who is unworthy to wear the white garb which is the outer symbol of the spotless spirit. That dress shall therefore be stripped from thee, and thou shalt be cast into the outer world without benefit of clerkship, and without lot or part in the graces and blessings of those who dwell under the care of the blessed Benedict. Thou shalt come back neither to Beaulieu nor to any of the granges of Beaulieu, and thy name shall be struck off the scrolls of the order."

The sentence appeared a terrible one to the older monks, who had become so used to the safe and regular life of the Abbey that they would have been as helpless as children in the outer world. From their pious oasis they looked dreamily out at the desert of life —a place full of stormings and strivings, comfortless, restless, and overshadowed by evil. The young novice, however, appeared to have other thoughts, for his eyes sparkled and his smile broadened. It needed but that to add fresh fuel to the fiery mood of the prelate.

"So much for thy spiritual punishment," he cried. "But it is to the grosser feelings that we must turn in such natures as thine, and as thou art no longer under the shield of holy Church there is the less difficulty. Ho there! lay-brothers—Francis, Naomi, Joseph— seize him and bind his arms! Drag him forth, and let the foresters and the porters scourge him from the precincts!"

As the three brothers advanced towards him to carry out the Abbot's direction the smile faded from the novice's face, and he glanced right and left with his fierce brown eyes, like a bull at a baiting. Then, with a sudden deep-chested shout, he tore up the heavy oaken prie-dieu, and poised it to strike, taking two steps backward the while, that none might take him at a vantage.

"By the black rood of Waltham!" he roared, "if any knave among you lays a finger-end upon the edge of my gown, I will crush his skull like a filbert!" With his thick knotted arms, his thundering voice, and his bristle of red hair, there was something so repellent in the man that the three brothers flew back at the very glare of him; and the two rows of white monks strained away from him like poplars in a tempest. The Abbot only sprang forward with shining eyes; but the chancellor and the master hung upon either arm and wrested him back out of danger's way.

"He is possessed of a devil!" they shouted. "Run, brother Ambrose, brother Joachim! Call Hugh of the Mill, and Woodman Wat, and Raoul with his arbalest and bolts. Tell them that we are in fear of our lives! Run, run! for the love of the Virgin!"

But the novice was a strategist as well as a man of action. Springing forward, he hurled his unwieldy weapon at brother Ambrose, and, as desk and monk clattered on to the floor together, he sprang through the open door and down the winding stair. Sleepy old brother Athanasius, at the porter's cell, had a fleeting vision of twinkling feet and flying skirts; but before he had time to rub his eyes the recreant had passed the lodge, and was speeding as fast as his sandals could patter along the Lyndhurst road.

CHAPTER II

HOW ALLEYNE EDRICSON CAME
OUT INTO THE WORLD

NEVER had the peaceful atmosphere of the old Cistercian house been so rudely ruffled. Never had there been insurrection so sudden, so short, and so successful. Yet the Abbot Berghersh was a man of too firm a grain to allow one bold outbreak to imperil the settled order of his great household. In a few hot and bitter words, he compared their false brother's exit to the expulsion of our first parents from the garden, and more than hinted that unless a reformation occurred some others of the community might find themselves in the same evil and perilous case. Having thus pointed the moral and reduced his flock to a fitting state of docility, he dismissed them once more to their labours and withdrew himself to his own private chamber, there to seek spiritual aid in the discharge of the duties of his high office.

The Abbot was still on his knees, when a gentle tapping at the door of his cell broke in upon his orisons. Rising in no very good humour at the interruption, he gave the word to enter; but his look of impatience softened down into a pleasant and paternal smile as his eye fell upon his visitor.

He was a thin-faced, yellow-haired youth, rather above the middle size, comely and well shapen, with straight lithe figure and eager boyish features. His clear, pensive grey eyes, and quick delicate expression, spoke of a nature which had unfolded far from the boisterous joys and sorrows of the world. Yet there was a set of the mouth and a prominence of the chin which relieved him of any trace of effeminacy. Impulsive he might be, enthusiastic, sensitive, with something sympathetic and adaptive in his disposition; but an observer of nature's tokens would have confidently pledged himself that there was native firmness and strength underlying his gentle, monk-bred ways.

The youth was not clad in monastic garb, but in lay attire, though his jerkin, cloak, and hose were all of a sombre hue, as befitted one who dwelt in sacred precincts. A broad leather strap hanging from his shoulder supported a scrip or satchel such as travellers were wont to carry. In one hand he grasped a thick staff pointed and shod with metal, while in the other he held his coif or bonnet, which bore in its front a broad pewter medal stamped with the image of Our Lady of Rocamadour.

"Art ready, then, fair son?" said the Abbot. "This is indeed a day of comings and of goings. It is strange that in one twelve hours the Abbey should have cast off its foulest weed, and should now lose what we are fain to look upon as our choicest blossom."

"You speak too kindly, father," the youth answered. "If I had my will I should never go forth, but should end my days here in Beaulieu. It hath been my home as far back as my mind can carry me, and it is a sore thing for me to have to leave it."

"Life brings many a cross," said the Abbot gently. "Who is without them? Your going forth is a grief to us as well as to yourself. But there is no help. I had given my foreword and sacred promise to your father, Edric the Franklin, that at the age of twenty you should be sent out into the world to see for yourself how you liked the savour of it. Seat thee upon the settle, Alleyne, for you may need rest ere long."

The youth sat down as directed, but reluctantly and with diffidence. The Abbot stood by the narrow window, and his long black shadow fell slantwise across the rush-strewn floor.

"Twenty years ago," he said, "your father, the Franklin of Minstead, died, leaving to the Abbey three hides of rich land in the hundred of Malwood, and leaving to us also his infant son on condition that we should rear him until he came to man's estate. This he did partly because your mother was dead, and partly because your elder brother, now Socman of Minstead, had already given sign of that fierce and rude nature which would make him no fit companion for you. It was his desire and request, however, that you should not remain in the cloisters, but should at a ripe age return into the world."

"But, father," interrupted the young man, "it is surely true that I am already advanced several degrees in clerkship?"

"Yes, fair son, but not so far as to bar you from the garb you now wear or the life which you must now lead. You have been porter?"

"Yes, father."

"Exorcist?"

"Yes, father."

"Reader?"

"Yes, father."

"Acolyte?"

"Yes, father."

"But have sworn no vows of constancy or chastity?"

"No, father."

"Then you are free to follow a worldly life. But let me hear, ere you start, what gifts you take away with you from Beaulieu. Some I already know. There is the playing of the citole and the rebec. Our choir will be dumb without you. You carve too?"

The youth's pale face flushed with the pride of the skilled workman. "Yes, holy father," he answered. "Thanks to good brother Bartholomew, I carve in wood and in ivory, and can do something also in silver, and in bronze. From brother Francis I learned to paint on vellum, on glass, and on metal, with a knowledge of those pigments and essences which can preserve the colour against damp or a biting air. Brother Luke hath given me some skill in damask work, and in enamelling of shrines, tabernacles, diptychs and triptychs. For the rest, I know a little of the making of covers, the cutting of precious stones, and the fashioning of instruments."

"A goodly list, truly," cried the superior with a smile. "What clerk of Cambrig or of Oxenford could say as much? But of thy reading—hast not so much to show there, I fear?"

"No, father, it hath been slight enough. Yet, thanks to our good chancellor, I am not wholly unlettered. I have read Ockham, Bradwardine, and other of the schoolmen, together with the learned Duns Scotus and the book of the holy Aquinas."

"But of the things of this world, what have you gathered from your reading? From this high window you may catch a glimpse over the wooded point and the smoke of Bucklershard, of the mouth of the Exe, and the shining sea. Now, I pray you, Alleyne, if a man were to take a ship and spread sail across yonder waters, where might he hope to arrive?"

The youth pondered, and drew a plan amongst the rushes with the point of his staff. "Holy father," said he, "he would come upon those parts of France which are held by the King's Majesty. But if he tended to the south he might reach Spain and the Barbary States. To his north would be Flanders and the country of the Eastlanders and of the Muscovites."

"True. And how if, after reaching the King's possessions, he still journeyed on to the eastward?"

"He would then come upon that part of France which is still in dispute, and he might hope to reach the famous city of Avignon, where dwells our blessed father, the prop of Christendom."

"And then?"

"Then he would pass through the land of the Almains and the great Roman Empire, and so to the country of the Huns and of the Lithuanian pagans, beyond which lie the great city of Constantine and the kingdom of the unclean followers of Mahmoud."

"And beyond that, fair son?"

"Beyond that is Jerusalem and the Holy Land, and the great river which hath its source in the Garden of Eden."

"And then?"

"Nay, good father, I cannot tell. Methinks the end of the world is not far from there."

"Then we can still find something to teach thee, Alleyne," said the Abbot complaisantly. "Know that many strange nations lie betwixt there and the end of the world. There is the country of the Amazons, and the country of the dwarfs, and the country of the fair but evil women who slay with beholding, like the basilisk. Beyond that again is the kingdom of Prester John and of the Great Cham. These things I know for very sooth, for I had them from that pious Christian and valiant knight, Sir John de Mandeville, who stopped twice at Beaulieu on his way to and from Southampton, and discoursed to us concerning what he had seen from the reader's desk in the refectory, until there was many a good brother who got neither bit nor sup, so stricken were they by his strange tales."

"I would fain know, father," asked the young, man, "what there may be at the end of the world?"

"There are some things," replied the Abbot gravely, "into which it was never intended that we should inquire. But you have a long road before you. Whither will you first turn?"

"To my brother's at Minstead. If he be indeed an ungodly and violent man, there, is the more need that I should seek him out and see whether I cannot turn him to better ways."

The Abbot shook his head. "The Socman of Minstead hath earned an evil name over the countryside," he said. "If you must go to him, see at least that he doth not turn you from the narrow path upon which you have learned to tread. But you are in God's keeping, and Godward should you ever look in danger and in trouble. Above all, shun the snares of women, for they are ever set for the foolish feet of the young. Kneel down, my child, and take an old man's blessing."

Alleyne Edricson bent his head while the Abbot poured out his heartfelt supplication that Heaven would watch over this young soul, now going forth into the darkness and danger of the world. It was no mere form for either of them. To them the outside life of mankind did indeed seem to be one of violence and of sin, beset with physical and still more with spiritual danger. Heaven, too, was very near to them in those days. God's direct agency was to be seen in the thunder and the rainbow, the whirlwind and the lightning. To the believer, clouds of angels and confessors, and martyrs, armies of the sainted and the saved, were ever stooping over their struggling brethren upon earth, raising, encouraging, and supporting them. It was then with a lighter heart and a stouter courage that the young man turned from the Abbot's room, while the latter, following him to the stair-head, finally commended him to the protection of the holy Julian, patron of travellers.

Underneath, in the porch of the Abbey, the monks had gathered to give him a last God-speed. Many had brought some parting token by which he should remember them. There was brother Bartholomew with a crucifix of rare carved ivory, and brother Luke with a white-backed psalter adorned with golden bees, and brother Francis with the "Slaying of the Innocents" most daintily set forth upon vellum. All these were duly packed away deep in the traveller's scrip, and above them old pippin-faced brother Athanasius had placed a parcel of simnel bread and rammel cheese, with a small flask of the famous blue-sealed Abbey wine. So, amid hand-shakings and laughings and blessing, Alleyne Edricson turned his back upon Beaulieu.

At the turn of the road he stopped and gazed back. There was the widespread building which he knew so well, the Abbot's house, the long church, the cloisters with their line of arches, all bathed and mellowed in the evening sun. There too was the broad sweep of the River Exe, the old stone well, the canopied niche of the Virgin, and, in the centre of all, the cluster of white-robed figures who waved their hands to him. A sudden mist swam up before the young man's eyes, and he turned away upon his journey with a heavy heart and a choking throat.

CHAPTER III

HOW HORDLE JOHN COZENED
THE FULLER OF LYMINGTON

IT is not, however, in the nature of things that a lad of twenty, with young life glowing in his veins and all the wide world before him, should spend his first hours of freedom in mourning for what he had left. Long ere Alleyne was out of sound of the Beaulieu bells he was striding sturdily along, swinging his staff and whistling as merrily as the birds in the thicket. It was an evening to raise a man's heart. The sun shining slantwise through the trees threw delicate traceries across the road, with bars of golden light between. Away in the distance, before and behind, the green boughs, now turning in places to a coppery redness, shot their broad arches across the track. The still summer air was heavy with the resinous smell of the great forest. Here and there a tawny brook prattled out from among the underwood and lost itself again in the ferns and brambles upon the further side. Save the dull piping of insects and the sough of the leaves, there was silence everywhere — the sweet restful silence of nature.

And yet there was no want of life — the whole wide wood was full of it. Now it was a lithe, furtive stoat which shot across the path upon some fell errand of its own; then it was a wild cat which squatted upon the outlying branch of an oak and peeped at the traveller with a yellow and dubious eye. Once it was a wild sow which scuttled out of the bracken, with two young sounders at her heels; and once a lordly red staggard walked daintily out from among the tree-trunks and looked around him with the fearless gaze of one who lived under the king's own high protection. Alleyne gave his staff a merry flourish, however, and the red deer bethought him that the king was far off, so bounded away whence he came.

The youth had now journeyed considerably beyond the furthest domains of the Abbey. He was the more surprised therefore when, on coming round a turn in the path, he perceived a man clad in the familiar garb of the order, and seated in a clump of heather by the roadside. Alleyne had known every brother well, but this was a face which was new to him — a face which was very red and puffed, working this way and that, as though the man were sore perplexed in his mind. Once he shook both hands furiously in the air, and twice he sprang from his seat and hurried down the road. When he rose, however, Alleyne observed that his robe was much too long and loose for him in every direction, trailing upon the ground and bagging about his ankles, so that even with trussed-up skirts he could make little progress. He ran once, but the long gown clogged him so that he slowed down into a shambling walk, and finally plumped into the heather once more.

"Young friend," said he, when Alleyne was abreast of him, "I fear from thy garb that thou canst know little of the Abbey of Beaulieu."

"Then you are in error, friend," the clerk answered, "for I have spent all my days within its walls."

"Hast so indeed?" cried he. "Then perhaps canst tell me the name of a great loathly lump of a brother wi' freckled face an' a hand like a spade. His eyes were black an' his hair was red an' his voice like the parish bull. I trow that there cannot be two alike in the same cloisters."

"That surely can be no other than brother John," said Alleyne. "I trust he has done you no wrong, that you should be so hot against him."

"Wrong, quotha?" cried the other, jumping out of the heather. "Wrong! why he hath stolen every plack of clothing off my back, if that be a wrong, and hath left me here in this sorry frock of white

falding, so that I have shame to go back to my wife, lest she think I
have donned her old kirtle. Harrow and alas that ever I should
have met him!"

"But how came this?" asked the young clerk, who could scarce
keep from laughter at the sight of the hot little man so swathed in
the great white cloak.

"It came in this way," he said, sitting down once more: "I was
passing this way, hoping to reach Lymington ere nightfall, when I
came on this red-headed knave seated even where we are sitting
now. I uncovered and louted as I passed, thinking that he might be
a holy man at his orisons, but he called to me and asked if I had
heard speak of the new indulgence in favour of the Cistercians.
"Not I," I answered. "Then the worse for thy soul," said he; and with
that he broke into a long tale how that on account of the virtues of
the Abbot Berghersh it had been decreed by the Pope that whoever should wear the habit of a monk of Beaulieu for as long as he
might say the seven psalms of David should be assured of the kingdom of Heaven. When I heard this I prayed him on my knees that
he would give me the use of his gown, which after many con-
tentions he at last agreed to do, on my paying him three marks
towards the regilding of the image of Laurence the martyr. Having
stripped his robe, I had no choice but to let him have the wearing
of my good leathern jerkin and hose, for, as he said, it was chilling
to the blood and unseemly to the eye to stand frockless whilst I
made my orisons. He had scarce got them on, and it was a sore
labour, seeing that my inches will scarce match my girth—he had
scarce got them on, I say, and I not yet at the end of the second
psalm, when he, bade me do honour to my new dress, and with that
set off down the road as fast as feet would carry him. For myself, I
could no more run than if I had been sewn in a sack; so here I sit,
and here I am like to sit, before I set eyes upon my clothes again."

"Nay, friend, take it not so sadly," said Alleyne, clapping the disconsolate one upon the shoulder. "Canst change thy robe for a
jerkin once more at the Abbey, unless perchance you have a friend
near at hand."

"That have I," he answered, "and close; but I care not to go nigh him in this plight, for his wife hath a gibing tongue, and would spread the tale until I could not show my face in any market from Fordingbridge to Southampton. But if you, fair sir, out of your kind charity, would be pleased to go a matter of two bow-shots out of your way, you would do me such a service as I could scarce repay."

"With all my heart," said Alleyne readily.

"Then take this pathway on the left, I pray thee, and then the deer-track which passes on the right. You will then see under a great beech-tree the hut of a charcoal-burner. Give him my name, good sir, the name of Peter the Fuller, of Lymington, and ask him for a change of raiment, that I may pursue my journey without delay. There are reasons why he would be loth to refuse me."

Alleyne started off along the path indicated, and soon found the log-hut where the burner dwelt. He was away faggot-cutting in the forest; but his wife, a ruddy, bustling dame, found the needful garments and tied them into a bundle. While she busied herself in finding and folding them Alleyne Edricson stood by the open door looking in at her with much interest and some distrust, for he had never been so nigh to a woman before. She had round red arms, a dress of some sober woollen stuff, and a brass brooch the size of a cheese-cake stuck in the front of it.

"Peter the Fuller!" she kept repeating. "Marry come up! if I were Peter the Fuller's wife, I would teach him better than to give his clothes to the first knave who asks for them. But he was always a poor, fond, silly creature, was Peter, though we are beholden to him for helping to bury our second son, Wat, who was a 'prentice to him at Lymington in the year of the Black Death. But who are you, young sir?"

"I am a clerk on my road from Beaulieu to Minstead."

"Aye, indeed! Hast been brought up at the Abbey then. I could read it from thy reddened cheek and downcast eye. Hast learned from the monks, I trow, to fear a woman as thou wouldst a lazar-house. Out upon them, that they should dishonour their own mothers by such teaching! A pretty world it would be with all the women out of it."

"Heaven forefend that such a thing should come to pass!" said Alleyne.

"Amen and amen! But thou art a pretty lad, and the prettier for thy modest ways. It is easy to see from thy cheek that thou hast not spent thy days in the rain and the heat and the wind, as my poor Wat hath been forced to do."

"I have indeed seen little of life, good dame."

"Wilt find nothing in it to pay thee for the loss of thy own freshness. Here are the clothes, and Peter can leave them when next he comes this way. Holy Virgin! see the dust upon thy doublet. It were easy to see that there is no woman to tend to thee. So!—that is better. Now buss me, boy."

Alleyne stooped and kissed her, for the kiss was the common salutation of the age, and, as Erasmus long afterwards remarked, more used in England than in any other country. Yet it sent the blood to his temples again, and he wondered, as he turned away, what the Abbot Berghersh would have answered to so frank an invitation. He was still tingling from this new experience when he came out upon the high road and saw a sight which drove all other thoughts from his mind.

Some way down from where he had left him the unfortunate Peter was stamping and raving tenfold worse than before. Now, however, instead of the great white cloak, he had no clothes on at all, save a short woollen shirt and a pair of leather shoes. Far down the road a long-legged figure was running, with a bundle under one arm and the other hand to his side, like a man who laughs until he is sore.

"See him!" yelled Peter. "Look to him! You shall be my witness. He shall see Winchester gaol for this. See where he goes with my cloak under his arm!"

"Who then!" cried Alleyne.

"Who but that cursed brother John! He hath not left me clothes enough to make a gallybagger. The double thief hath cozened me out of my gown."

"Stay though, my friend, it was his gown," objected Alleyne.

"It boots not. He hath them all—gown, jerkin, hosen, and all. Gramercy to him that he left me the shirt and the shoon! I doubt not that he will be back for them anon."

"But how came this?" asked Alleyne, open-eyed with astonishment.

"Are those the clothes? For dear charity's sake, give them to me. Not the Pope himself shall have these from me though he sent the whole college of cardinals to ask it. How came it? Why, you had scarce gone ere this loathly John came running back again, and when I oped mouth to reproach him, he asked me whether it was indeed likely that a man of prayer would leave his own godly raiment in order to take a layman's jerkin. He had, he said, but gone for a while that I might be the freer for my devotions. On this I plucked off the gown, and he with much show of haste did begin to undo his points; but when I threw his frock down he clipped it up and ran off all untrussed, leaving me in this sorry plight. He laughed so the while, like a great croaking frog, that I might have caught him, had my breath not been as short as his legs were long."

The young man listened to this tale of wrong with all the seriousness that he could maintain; but at the sight of the pursy red-faced man and the dignity with which he bore him, the laughter came so thick upon him that he had to lean up against a tree-trunk. The fuller looked sadly and gravely at him; but finding that he still laughed, he bowed with much mock politeness and stalked onwards in his borrowed clothes. Alleyne watched him until he was small in the distance, and then, wiping the tears from his eyes, he set off briskly once more upon his journey.

CHAPTER IV

HOW THE BAILIFF OF SOUTHAMPTON
SLEW THE TWO MASTERLESS MEN

THE road along which he travelled was scarce as populous as most other roads in the kingdom, and far less so than those which lie between the larger towns. Yet from time to time Alleyne met other wayfarers, and more than once was overtaken by strings of pack-mules and horsemen journeying in the same direction as himself. Once a begging friar came limping along in a brown habit, imploring him in a most dolorous voice to give him a single groat to buy bread wherewith to save himself from impending death. Alleyne passed him swiftly by, for he had learned from the monks to have no love for the wandering friars, and, besides, there was a great half-gnawed mutton-bone sticking out of his pouch to prove him a liar. Swiftly as he went, however, he could not escape the curse of the four blessed Evangelists which the mendicant howled behind him. So dreadful were his execrations that the frightened lad thrust his fingers into his ear-holes, and ran until the fellow was but a brown smirch upon the yellow road.

Further on, at the edge of the woodland, he came upon a chapman and his wife, who sat upon a fallen tree. He had put his pack down as a table, and the two of them were devouring a great pasty, and washing it down with some drink from a stone jar. The chapman broke a rough jest as he passed, and the woman called shrilly to Alleyne to come and join them, on which the man, turning suddenly from mirth to wrath, began to belabour her with his cudgel. Alleyne hastened on, lest he make more mischief, and his heart was heavy as lead within him. Look where he would, he seemed to see nothing but injustice and violence, and the hardness of man to man.

But even as he brooded sadly over it, and pined for the sweet peace of the Abbey, he came on an open space dotted with holly-bushes, where was the strangest sight that he had yet chanced upon. Near to the pathway lay a long clump of greenery, and from behind this there stuck straight up into the air four human legs clad in parti-coloured hosen, yellow and black. Strangest of all was it when a brisk tune struck suddenly up and the four legs began to kick and twitter in time to the music. Walking on tiptoe round the bushes, he stood in amazement to see two men bounding about on their heads while they played, the one a viol and the other a pipe, as merrily and as truly as though they were seated in choir. Alleyne crossed himself as he gazed at this unnatural sight, and could scarce hold his ground with a steady face, when the two dancers, catching sight of him, came bouncing in his direction. A spear's length from him they each threw a somersault into the air, and came down upon their feet with smirking faces and their hands over their hearts.

"A guerdon—a guerdon, my knight of the staring eyes!" cried one.

"A gift, my prince!" shouted the other. "Any trifle will serve—a purse of gold, or even a jewelled goblet."

Alleyne thought of what he had read of demoniac possession— the jumpings, the twitchings, the wild talk. It was in his mind to repeat over the exorcism proper to such attacks; but the two burst out a-laughing at his scared face, and, turning on to their heads once more, clapped their heels in derision.

"Hast never seen tumblers before?" asked the elder, a black-browed swarthy man, as brown and supple as a hazel-twig. "Why shrink from us, then, as though we were the spawn of the Evil One?"

"Why shrink, my honey-bird? Why so afeard, my sweet cinna-mon?" exclaimed the other, a loosely-jointed lanky youth with a dancing roguish eye.

"Truly, sirs, it is a new sight to me," the clerk answered. "When I saw your four legs above the bush I could scarce credit my own eyes. Why is it that you do this thing?"

"A dry question to answer," cried the younger, coming back on to his feet. "A most husky question, my fair bird! But how? A flask, a flask!—by all that is wonderful!" He shot out his hand as he spoke, and plucking Alleyne's bottle out of his scrip, he deftly knocked the neck off, and poured the half of it down his throat. The rest he handed to his comrade, who drank the wine, and then, to the clerk's increasing amazement, made a show of swallowing the bottle, with such skill that Alleyne seemed to see it vanish down his throat. A moment later, however, he flung it over his head, and caught it bottom downwards upon the calf of his left leg.

"We thank you for the wine, kind sir," he said, "and for the ready courtesy wherewith you offered it. Touching your question, we may tell you that we are strollers and jugglers, who, having performed with much applause at Winchester fair, are now on our way to the great Michaelmas market at Ringwood. As our art is a very fine and delicate one, however, we cannot let a day go by without exercising ourselves in it, to which end we choose some quiet and sheltered spot, where we may break our journey. Here you find us; and we cannot wonder that you, who are new to tumbling, should be astounded, since many great barons, earls, marshals, and knights, who have wandered as far as the Holy Land, are of one mind in saying that they have never seen a more noble or gracious performance. If you will be pleased to sit upon that stump, we will now continue our exercise."

Alleyne sat down willingly as directed, with two great bundles on either side of him which contained the strollers' dresses—doublets of flame-coloured silk and girdles of leather, spangled with brass and tin. The jugglers were on their heads once more, bounding about with rigid necks, playing the while in perfect time and tune. It chanced that out of one of the bundles there stuck the end of what the clerk saw to be a cittern, so, drawing it forth, he tuned it up and twanged a harmony to the merry lilt which the dancers played. On that they dropped their own instruments, and putting their hands to the ground they hopped about faster and faster, ever shouting to him to play more briskly, until at last for very weariness all three had to stop.

"Well played, sweet poppet!" cried the younger. "Hast a rare touch on the strings."

"How knew you the tune?" asked the other.

"I knew it not. I did but follow the notes I heard."

Both opened their eyes at this, and stared at Alleyne with as much amazement as he had shown at them.

"You have a fine trick of ear, then," said one. "We have long wished to meet such a man. Wilt join us and jog on to Ring-wood? Thy duties shall be light, and thou shalt have twopence a day and meat for supper every night."

"With as much beer as you can put away," said the other, "and a flask of Gascon wine on Sabbaths."

"Nay, it may not be. I have other work to do. I have tarried with you over long," quoth Alleyne, and resolutely set forth upon his journey once more. They ran behind him some little way, offering him first fourpence and then sixpence a day; but he only smiled and shook his head until at last they fell away from him. Looking back, he saw that the smaller had mounted on the younger's shoulders, and that they stood so, some ten feet high, waving their adieus to him. He waved back to them, and then hastened on, the lighter of heart for having fallen in with these strange men of pleasure.

Alleyne had gone no great distance for all the many small passages that had befallen him. Yet to him, used as he was to a life of such quiet that the failure of a brewing, or the altering of an anthem, had seemed to be of the deepest import, the quick changing play of the lights and shadows of life was strangely startling and interesting. A gulf seemed to divide this brisk, uncertain existence from the old steady round of work and of prayer which he had left behind him. The few hours that had passed since he saw the Abbey tower stretched out in his memory until they outgrew whole months of the stagnant life of the cloister. As he walked and munched the soft bread from his scrip, it seemed strange to him to feel that it was still warm from the ovens of Beaulieu.

When he passed Penerley, where were three cottages and a barn, he reached the edge of the tree country, and found the great barren heath of Blackdown stretching in front of him, all pink with heather and bronzed with the fading ferns. On the left the woods were still thick, but the road edged away from them and wound over the open. The sun lay low in the west upon a purple cloud, whence it threw a mild chastening light over the wild moorland and glittered on the fringe of forest, turning the withered leaves into flakes of dead gold, the brighter for the black depths behind them. To the seeing eye decay is as fair as growth, and death as life. The thought stole into Alleyne's heart as he looked upon the autumnal country-side and marvelled at its beauty. He had little time to dwell upon it, however, for there were still six good miles between him and the nearest inn. He sat down by the roadside to partake of his bread and cheese, and then with a lighter strip he hastened upon his way.

There appeared to be more wayfarers on the down than in the forest. First he passed two Dominicans in their long black dresses, who swept by him with downcast looks and pattering lips, without so much as a glance at him. Then there came a grey friar, or minorite, with a good paunch upon him, walking slowly and looking about him with the air of a man who was at peace with himself and with all men. He stopped Alleyne to ask him whether it were not true that there was a hostel somewhere in those parts which was especially famous for the stewing of eels. The clerk having made answer that he had heard the eels of Sowley well spoken of, the friar sucked in his lip and hurried forward. Close at his heels came three labourers walking abreast, with spade and mattock over their shoulders. They sang some rude chorus right tunefully as they walked, but their English was so coarse and rough that to the ears of a cloister-bred man it sounded like a foreign and barbarous tongue. One of them carried a young bittern which they had caught upon the moor, and they offered it to Alleyne for a silver groat. Very glad he was to get safely past them, for, with their bristling red beards and their fierce blue eyes, they were uneasy men to bargain with upon a lonely moor.

Yet it is not always the burliest and the wildest who are the most to be dreaded. The workers looked hungrily at him, and then jogged onwards upon their way in slow lumbering Saxon style. A worse man to deal with was a wooden-legged cripple who came hobbling down the path, so weak and so old to all appearance that a child need not stand in fear of him. Yet when Alleyne had passed him, of a sudden, out of pure devilment, he screamed out a curse at him, and sent a jagged flint-stone hurtling past his ear. So horrid was the causeless rage of the crooked creature, that the clerk came over a cold thrill, and took to his heels until he was out of shot from stone or word. It seemed to him that in this country of England there was no protection for a man save that which lay in the strength of his own arm and the speed of his own foot. In the cloisters he had heard vague talk of the law—the mighty law which was higher than prelate or baron, yet no sign could he see of it. What was the benefit of a law written fair upon parchment, he wondered, if there were no officers to enforce it? As it fell out, however, he had that very evening, ere the sun had set, a chance of seeing how stern was the grip of the English law when it did happen to seize the offender.

A mile or so out upon the moor the road takes a very sudden dip into a hollow, with a peat-coloured stream running swiftly down the centre of it. To the right of this stood, and stands to this day, an ancient barrow, or burying mound, covered deeply in a bristle of heather and bracken. Alleyne was plodding down the slope upon one side, when he saw an old dame coming towards him upon the other, limping with weariness and leaning heavily upon a stick. When she reached the edge of the stream she stood helpless, looking to right and to left for some ford. Where the path ran down a great stone had been fixed in the centre of the brook, but it was too far from the bank for her aged and uncertain feet. Twice she thrust forward at it, and twice she drew back, until at last, giving it up in despair, she sat herself down by the brink and wrung her hands wearily. There she still sat when Alleyne reached the crossing.

"Come, mother," quoth he, "it is not so very perilous a passage."

"Alas! good youth," she answered, "I have a humour in the eyes, and though I can see that there is a stone there, I can by no means be sure as to where it lies."

"That is easily amended," said he cheerily, and picking her lightly up, for she was much worn with time, he passed across with her. He could not but observe, however, that as he placed her down her knees seemed to fail her, and she could scarcely prop herself up with her staff.

"You are weak, mother," said he. "Hast journeyed far, I wot."

"From Wiltshire, friend," said she, in a quavering voice; "three days have I been on the road. I go to my son, who is one of the king's regarders at Brockenhurst. He has ever said that he would care for me in mine old age."

"And rightly, too, mother, since you cared for nun in his youth. But when have you broken fast?"

"At Lyndenhurst; but, alas! my money is at an end, and I could but get a dish of bran-porridge from the nunnery. Yet I trust that I may be able to reach Brockenhurst tonight, where I may have all that heart can desire; for, oh, sir! but my son is a fine man, with a kindly heart of his own, and it is as good as food to me to think that he should have a doublet of Lincoln-green to his back and be the king's own paid man."

"It is a long road to Brockenhurst," said Alleyne; "but here is such bread and cheese as I have left, and here, too, is a penny which may help you to supper. May God be with you!"

"May God be with you, young man!" she cried. "May He make your heart as glad as you have made mine!" She turned away, still mumbling blessings, and Alleyne saw her short figure and her long shadow stumbling slowly up the slope.

He was moving away himself, when his eyes lit upon a strange sight, and one which sent a tingling through his skin. Out of the tangled scrub on the old overgrown barrow two human faces were looking at him; the sinking sun glimmered full upon them, showing up every line and feature. The one was an oldish man with a thin beard, a crooked nose, and a broad red smudge from a birthmark over his temple; the other was a negro, a thing rarely met in England at that day, and rarer still in the quiet southland parts. Alleyne had read of such folk, but had never seen one before, and could scarce take his eyes from the fellow's broad pouting lip and shining teeth. Even as he gazed, however, the two came writhing out from among the heather, and came down towards him with such a guilty, slinking carriage, that the clerk felt that there was no good in them, and hastened onwards upon his way.

He had not gained the crown of the slope, when he heard a sudden scuffle behind him, and a feeble voice bleating for help. Looking round, there was the old dame down upon the roadway, with her red wimple flying on the breeze, while the two rogues, black and white, stooped over her, wresting away from her the penny and such other poor trifles as were worth the taking. At the sight of her thin limbs struggling in weak resistance, such a glow of fierce anger passed over Alleyne as set his head in a whirl. Dropping his scrip, he bounded over the stream once more, and made for the two villains, with his staff whirled over his shoulder, and his grey eyes blazing with fury.

The robbers, however, were not disposed to leave their victim until they had worked their wicked will upon her. The black man, with the woman's crimson scarf tied round his swarthy head, stood forward in the centre of the path, with a long dull-coloured knife in his hand, while the other, waving a ragged cudgel, cursed at Alleyne and dared him to come on. His blood was fairly aflame, however, and he needed no such challenge. Dashing at the black man, he smote at him with such good will that he let his knife tinkle into the roadway, and hopped howling to a safer distance. The second rogue, however, made of sterner stuff, rushed in upon the clerk, and clipped him round the waist with a grip like a bear, shouting the while to his comrade to come round and stab him in the back. At this the negro took heart of grace, and, picking up his dagger again, he came stealing with prowling step and murderous eye, while the two swayed backwards and forwards, staggering this way and that. In the very midst of the scuffle, however, while Alleyne braced himself to feel the cold blade between his shoulders, there came a sudden scurry of hoofs, and the black man yelled with terror, and ran for his life through the heather. The man with the birth-mark, too, struggled to break away, and Alleyne heard his teeth chatter and felt his limbs grow limp to his hand. At this sign of coming aid the clerk held on the tighter, and at last was able to pin his man down and glance behind him to see whence all the noise was coming.

Down the slanting road there was riding a big burly man, clad in a tunic of purple velvet and driving a great black horse as hard as it could gallop. He leaned well over its neck as he rode, and made a heaving with his shoulders at every bound as though he were lifting the steed instead of it carrying him. In the rapid glance Alleyne saw that he had white doeskin gloves, a curling white feather in his flat velvet cap, and a broad gold-embroidered baldric across his bosom. Behind him rode six others, two and two, clad in sober brown jerkins, with the long yellow staves of their bows thrusting out from behind their right shoulders. Down the hill they thundered, over the brook, and up to the scene of the contest.

"Here is one!" said the leader, springing down from his reeking horse, and seizing the white rogue by the edge of his jerkin. "This is one of them. I know him by that devil's touch upon his brow. Where are your cords, Peterkin? So! Bind him hand and foot. His last hour has come. And you, young man, who may you be?"

"I am a clerk, sir, travelling from Beaulieu."

"A clerk!" cried the other. "Art from Oxenford or from Cambridge? Hast thou a letter from the chancellor of thy college, giving thee a permit to beg? Let me see thy letter." He had a stern square face, with bushy side-whiskers, and a very questioning eye.

"I am from Beaulieu Abbey, and I have no need to beg," said Alleyne, who was all of a tremble now that the ruffle was over.

"The better for thee," the other answered. "Dost thou know who I am?"

"No, sir, I do not."

"I am the law!"—nodding his head solemnly. "I am the law of England and the mouthpiece of his most gracious and royal majesty, Edward the Third."

Alleyne louted low to the king's representative.

"Truly you came in good time, honoured sir," said he. "A moment later and they would have slain me."

"But there should be another one," cried the man in the purple coat. "There should be a black man. A shipman with St Anthony's fire, and a black man who had served him as cook—those are the pair that we are in chase of."

"The black man fled over to that side," said Alleyne pointing towards the barrow.

"He could not have gone far, sir bailiff," cried one of the archers, unslinging his bow. "He is in hiding somewhere for he knew well, black paynim as he is, that our horses' four legs could outstrip his two."

"Then we shall have him," said the other. "It shall never be said whilst I am Bailiff of Southampton, that any waster, riever, drawlatch or murtherer came scathless away from me and my posse. Leave that rogue lying. Now stretch out in line, my merry ones, with arrow on string, and I shall show you such sport as only the king can give. You on the left, Howett, and Thomas of Redbridge upon the right. So! Beat high and low among the heather, and a pot of wine to the lucky marksman."

As it chanced, however, the searchers had not far to seek. The negro had burrowed down into his hiding-place upon the barrow, where he might have lain snug enough, had it not been for the red gear upon his head. As he raised himself to look over the bracken at his enemies, the staring colour caught the eye of the bailiff, who broke into a long screeching whoop and spurred forward sword in hand. Seeing himself discovered, the man rushed out from his hiding-place, and bounded at the top of his speed down the line of archers, keeping a good hundred paces to the front of them. The two who were on either side of Alleyne bent their bows as calmly as though they were shooting at the popinjay at a village fair.

"Seven yards windage, Hal," said one, whose hair was streaked with grey.

"Five," replied the other, letting loose his string. Alleyne gave a gulp in his throat, for the yellow streak seemed to pass through the man; but he still ran forward.

"Seven you jack-fool," growled the first speaker, and his bow twanged like a harpstring. The black man sprang high up into the air, and shot but both his arms and his legs, coming down all asprawl among the heather. "Right under the blade bone!", quoth the archer, sauntering forward for his arrow.

"The old hound is the best when all is said," quoth the Bailiff of Southampton, as they made back for the roadway. "That means a quart of the best malmsey in Southampton this very night, Matthew Atwood. Art sure that he is dead?"

"Dead as Pontius Pilate, worshipful sir."

"It is well. Now, as to the other knave. There are trees and to spare over yonder, but we have scarce leisure to make for them. Draw thy sword, Thomas of Redbridge, and hew me his head from his shoulders."

"A boon, gracious sir, a boon!" cried the condemned man.

"What then?" asked the bailiff.

"I will confess to my crime. It was indeed I and the black cook, both from the ship *La Rose de Gloire*, of Southampton, who did set upon the Flanders merchant and rob him of his spicery and his mercery, for which, as we well know, you hold a warrant against us."

"There is little merit in this confession," quoth the bailiff sternly. "Thou hast done evil within my bailiwick, and must die."

"But, sir," urged Alleyne, who was white to the lips at these bloody doings, "he hath not yet come to trial."

"Young clerk," said the bailiff, "you speak of that of which you know nothing. It is true that he hath not come to trial, but the trial hath come to him. He hath fled the law and is beyond its pale. Touch not that which is no concern of thine. But what is this boon, rogue, which you would crave?"

"I have in my shoe, most worshipful sir, a strip of wood which belonged once to the bark wherein the blessed Paul was dashed up against the island of Melita. I bought it for two rose nobles from a shipman who came from the Levant. The boon I crave is that you will place it in my hands and let me die grasping it. In this manner, not only shall my own eternal salvation be secured, but thine also, for I shall never cease to intercede for thee."

At the command of the bailiff they plucked off the fellow's shoe, and there sure enough at the side of the instep, wrapped in a piece of fine sendal, lay a long dark splinter of wood. The archers doffed caps at the sight of it, and the bailiff crossed himself devoutly as he handed it to the robber.

"If it should chance," he said, "that through the surpassing merits of the blessed Paul your sin-stained soul should gain a way into paradise, I trust that you will not forget that intercession which you have promised. Bear in mind, too, that it is Herward the Bailiff for whom you pray, and not Herward the Sheriff, who is my uncle's son. Now, Thomas, I pray you despatch, for we have a long ride before us and sun has already set."

Alleyne gazed upon the scene — the portly velvet-clad official, the knot of hard-faced archers with their hands to the bridles of their horses, the thief with his arms trussed back and his doublet turned down upon his shoulders. By the side of the track the old dame was standing, fastening her red wimple once more round her head. Even as he looked one of the archers drew his sword with a sharp whirr of steel and stepped up to the lost man. The clerk hurried away in horror; but ere he had gone many paces, he heard a sudden, sullen thump, with a choking, whistling sound at the end of it. A minute later the bailiff and four of his men rode past him on their journey back to Southampton, the other two having been chosen as grave-diggers. As they passed, Alleyne saw that one of the men was wiping his sword-blade upon the mane of his horse. A deadly sickness came over him at the sight, and sitting down by the wayside he burst out a-weeping, with his nerves all in a jangle. It was a terrible world, thought he, and it was hard to know which were the more to be dreaded, the knaves or the men of the law.

CHAPTER V

HOW A STRANGE COMPANY GATHERED
AT THE "PIED MERLIN"

THE night had already fallen, and the moon was shining between the rifts of ragged drifting clouds, before Alleyne Edricson, footsore and weary from the unwonted exercise, found himself in front of the forest inn which stood upon the outskirts of Lyndhurst. The building was long and low, standing back a little from the road, with two flambeaux blazing on either side of the door as a welcome to the traveller. From one window there thrust forth a long pole with a bunch of greenery tied to the end of it—a sign that liquor was to be sold within. As Alleyne walked up to it he perceived that it was rudely fashioned out of beams of wood, with twinkling lights all over where the glow from within shone through the chinks. The roof was poor and thatched; but in strange contrast to it there ran all along under the eaves a line of wooden shields, most gorgeously painted with chevron, bend, saltire, and every heraldic device. By the door a horse stood tethered, the ruddy glow beating strongly upon his brown head and patient eyes, while his body stood back in the shadow.

Alleyne stood still in the roadway for a few minutes reflecting upon what he should do. It was, he knew, only a few miles further to Minstead, where his brother dwelt. On the other hand, he had never seen his brother since childhood, and the reports which had come to his ears concerning him were seldom to his advantage. By all accounts he was a hard and a bitter man. It might be an evil start to come to his door so late and claim the shelter of his roof.

Better to sleep here at this inn and then travel on to Minstead in the morning. If his brother would take him in, well and good. He would bide with him for a time and do what he might to serve him. If, on the other hand, he should have hardened his heart against him, he could only go on his way and do the best he might by his skill as a craftsman and a scrivener. At the end of a year he would be free to return to the cloisters, for such had been his father's bequest. A monkish upbringing, one year in the world after the age of twenty, and then a free selection one way or the other—it was a strange course which had been marked out for him. Such as it was, however, he had no choice but to follow it, and if he were to begin by making a friend of his brother he had best wait until morning before he knocked at his dwelling.

The rude plank door was ajar, but as Alleyne approached it there came from within such a gust of rough laughter and clatter of tongues that he stood irresolute upon the threshold. Summoning courage, however, and reflecting that it was a public dwelling, in which he had as much right as any other man, he pushed it open and stepped into the common room.

Though it was an autumn evening and somewhat warm, a huge fire of heaped billets of wood crackled and sparkled in a broad, open grate, some of the smoke escaping up a rude chimney, but the greater part rolling out into the room, so that the air was thick with it, and a man coming from without could scarce catch his breath. On this fire a great caldron bubbled and simmered, giving forth a rich and promising smell. Seated round it were a dozen or so folk, of all ages and conditions, who set up such a shout as Alleyne entered that he stood peering at them through the smoke, uncertain what this riotous greeting might portend.

"A rouse! A rouse!" cried one rough-looking fellow in a tattered jerkin. "One more round of mead or ale and the score to the last comer."

"'Tis the law of the 'Pied Merlin'," shouted another. "Ho, there, Dame Eliza! Here is fresh custom come to the house, and not a drain for the company."

"I will take your orders, gentles; I will assuredly take your orders," the landlady answered, bustling in with her hands full of leathern drinking-cups. "What is it that you drink then? Beer for the lads of the forest, mead for the gleeman, strong waters for the tinker, and wine for the rest. It is an old custom of the house, young sir. It has been the use at the 'Pied Merlin' this many a year back that the company should drink to the health of the last comer. Is it your pleasure to humour it?"

"Why, good dame," said Alleyne, "I would not offend the customs of your house, but it is only sooth when I say that my purse is a thin one. As far as two pence will go, however, I shall be right glad to do my part."

"Plainly said and bravely spoken, my sucking friar," roared a deep voice, and a heavy hand fell upon Alleyne's shoulder. Looking up, he saw beside him his former cloister companion, the renegade monk, Hordle John.

"By the thorn of Glastonbury! ill days are coming upon Beaulieu," said he. "Here they have got rid in one day of the only two men within their walls—for I have had mine eyes upon thee, youngster, and I know that for all thy baby-face there is the making of a man in thee. Then there is the Abbot, too. I am no friend of his, nor he of mine; but he has warm blood in his veins. He is the only man left among them. The others, what are they?"

"They are holy men," Alleyne answered gravely.

"Holy men? Holy cabbages! Holy bean-pods! What do they do but live and suck in sustenance and grow fat? If that be holiness, I could show you hogs in this forest who are fit to head the Calendar. Think you it was for such a life that this good arm was fixed upon my shoulder, or that head placed upon your neck? There is work in the world, man, and it is not by hiding behind stone walls that we shall do it."

"Why, then, did you join the brothers?" asked Alleyne.

"A fair enough question; but it is as fairly answered. I joined them because Margery Alspaye, of Bolder, married Crooked Thomas of Ringwood, and left a certain John of Hordle in the cold, for that he was a ranting, roving blade who was not to be trusted in wedlock. That was why, being fond and hot-headed, I left the world; and that is why, having had time to take thought, I am right glad to find myself back in it once more. Ill betide the day that ever I took off my yeoman's jerkin to put on the white gown!"

Whilst he was speaking the landlady came in again, bearing a broad platter, upon which stood all the beakers and flagons charged to the brim with the brown ale or the ruby wine. Behind her came a maid with a high pile of wooden plates, and a great sheaf of spoons, one of which she handed round to each of the travellers. Two of the company, who were dressed in the weather-stained green doublet of foresters, lifted the big pot off the fire, and a third with a huge pewter ladle served out a portion of steaming collops to each guest. Alleyne bore his share and his ale-mug away with him to a retired trestle in the corner, where he could sup in peace and watch the strange scene, which was so different to those silent and well-ordered meals to which he was accustomed.

The room was not unlike a stable. The low ceiling, smoke-blackened and dingy, was pierced by several square trapdoors with rough-hewn ladders leading up to them. The walls of bare unpainted planks were studded here and there with great wooden pins, placed at irregular intervals and heights, from which hung overtunics, wallets, whips, bridles, and saddles. Over the fireplace were suspended six or seven shields of wood, with coats-of-arms rudely daubed upon them, which showed by their varying degrees of smokiness and dirt that they had been placed there at different periods. There was no furniture, save a single long dresser covered with coarse crockery, and a number of wooden benches and trestles, the legs of which sank deeply into the soft clay floor, while the only light, save that of the fire, was furnished by three torches stuck in sockets on the wall, which flickered and crackled, giving forth a strong resinous odour. All this was novel and strange to the cloister-bred youth; but most interesting of all was the motley circle of guests who sat eating their collops round the blaze. They were a humble group of wayfarers, such as might have been found that night in any inn through the length and breadth of England; but to him they represented that vague world against which he had been so frequently and so earnestly warned. It did not seem to him from what he could see of it to be such a very wicked place after all.

Three or four of the men round the fire were evidently underkeepers and verderers from the forest, sunburned and bearded, with the quick restless eye and lithe movements of the deer among which they lived. Close to the corner of the chimney sat a middle-aged gleeman, clad in a faded garb of Norwich cloth, the tunic of which was so outgrown that it did but fasten at the neck and at the waist. His face was swollen and coarse, and its watery protruding eyes spoke of a life which never wandered very far from the wine-pot. A gilt harp, blotched with many stains and with two of its strings missing, was tucked under one of his arms, while with the other he scooped greedily at his platter. Next to him sat two other men of about the same age, one with a trimming of fur to his coat, which gave him a dignity which was evidently dearer to him than his comfort, for he still drew it around him in spite of the hot glare of the faggots. The other, clad in a dirty russet suit with a long sweeping doublet, had a cunning foxy face with keen twinkling eyes and a peaky beard. Next to him sat Hordle John, and beside him three other rough unkempt fellows with tangled beards and matted hair —free labourers from the adjoining farms, where small patches of freehold property had been suffered to remain scattered about in the heart of the royal demesne. The company was completed by a peasant in a rude dress of undyed sheepskin, with the old-fashioned galligaskins about his legs, and a gaily dressed young man with striped cloak jagged at the edges and parti-coloured hosen, who looked about him with high disdain upon his face, and held a blue smelling-flask to his nose with one hand, while he brandished a busy spoon with the other. In the corner a very fat man was lying all asprawl upon a truss, snoring stertorously, and evidently in the last stage of drunkenness.

"That is Wat the Limner," quoth the landlady, sitting down beside Alleyne, and pointing with the ladle to the sleeping man. "That is he who paints the signs and the tokens. Alack and alas that ever I should have been fool enough to trust him! Now, young man, what manner of a bird would you suppose a pied merlin to be—that being the proper sign of my hostel?"

"Why," said Alleyne, "a merlin is a bird of the same form as an eagle or a falcon. I can well remember that learned brother Bartholomew, who is deep in all secrets of Nature, pointed one out to me as we walked together near Vinney Ridge."

"A falcon, or an eagle, quotha? And pied, that is of two several colours. So any man would say except this barrel of lies. He came to me, look you, saying that if I would furnish him with a gallon of ale, wherewith to strengthen himself as he worked, and also the pigments and a board, he would paint for me a noble pied merlin which I might hang along with the blazonry over my door. I, poor simple fool, gave him the ale and all that he cared, leaving him alone too, because he said that a man's mind must be left untroubled when he had great work to do. When I came back the gallon jar was empty, and he lay as you see him, with the board in front of him with this sorry device." She raised up a panel which was leaning against the wall, and showed a rude painting of a scraggy and angular fowl, with very long legs and a spotted body.

"Was that," she asked, "like the bird which thou hast seen?"

Alleyne shook his head, smiling.

"No, nor any other bird that ever wagged a feather. It is most like a plucked pullet which has died of the spotted fever. And scarlet, too! What would the gentles, Sir Nicholas Borhunte, or Sir Bernard Brocas, of Roche Court, say if they saw such a thing—or, perhaps, even the king's own majesty himself, who often has ridden past this way, and who loves his falcons as he loves his sons? It would be the downfall of my house."

"The matter is not past mending," said Alleyne. "I pray you, good dame, to give me those three pigment-pots and the brush, and I shall try whether I cannot better this painting."

Dame Éliza looked doubtfully at him, as though fearing some other stratagem, but, as he made no demand for ale, she finally brought the paints, and watched him as he smeared on his background, talking the while about folk round the fire.

"The four forest lads must be jogging soon," she said. "They bide at Emery Down, a mile or more from here. Yeomen-prickers they are, who tend to the king's hunt. The gleeman is called Floyting Will. He comes from the north country, but for many years he hath gone the round of the forest from Southampton to Christchurch. He drinks much and pays little; but it would make your ribs crackle to hear him sing the 'Jest of Hendy Tobias.' Mayhap he will sing it when the ale has warmed him."

"Who are those next to him?" asked Alleyne, much interested. "He of the fur mantle has a wise and reverent face."

"He is a seller of pills and salves, very learned in humours, and rheums, and fluxes, and all manner of ailments. He wears, as you perceive, the vernicle of Sainted Luke, the first physician, upon his sleeve. May good St Thomas of Kent grant that it may be long before either I or mine need his help! He is here tonight for herbergage, as are the others, except the foresters. His neighbour is a tooth-drawer. That bag at his girdle is full of the teeth that he drew at Winchester fair. I warrant that there are more sound ones than sorry, for he is quick at his work and a trifle dim in the eye. The lusty man next him with the red head I have not seen before. The four on this side are all workers, three of them in the service of the bailiff of Sir Baldwin Redvers, and the other, he with the sheepskin is, as I hear, a villein from the midlands who hath run from his master. His year and day are well-nigh up, when he will be a free man."

"And the other?" asked Alleyne in a whisper. "He is surely some very great man, for he looks as though he scorned those who were about him."

The landlady looked at him in a motherly way and shook her head. "You have had no great truck with the world," she said, "or you would have learned that it is the small men and not the great who hold their noses in the air. Look at those shields upon my walls and under my eaves. Each of them is the device of some noble lord or gallant knight who hath slept under my roof at one time or another. Yet milder men or easier to please I have never seen: eating my bacon and drinking my wine with a merry face, and paying my score with some courteous word or jest which was dearer to me than my profit. Those are the true gentles. But your chapman or your bearward will swear that there is a lime in the wine, and water in the ale, and fling off at the last with a curse instead of a blessing. This youth is a scholar from Cambrig, where men are wont to be blown out by a little knowledge, and lose the use of their hands in learning the laws of the Romans. But I must away to lay down the beds. So may the saints keep you and prosper you in your undertaking!"

Thus left to himself, Alleyne drew his panel of wood where the light of one of the torches would strike full upon it, and worked away with all the pleasure of the trained craftsman, listening the while to the talk which went on round the fire. The peasant in the sheepskins, who had sat glum and silent all evening, had been so heated by his flagon of ale that he was talking loudly and angrily with clenched hands and flashing eyes.

"Sir Humphrey Tennant of Ashby may till his own fields for me," he cried. "The castle has thrown its shadow upon the cottage over long. For three hundred years my folk have swinked and sweated, day in and day out, to keep the wine on the lord's table and the harness on the lord's back. Let him take off his plates and delve himself, if delving must be done."

"A proper spirit, my fair son!" said one of the free labourers. "I would that all men were of thy way of thinking."

"He would have sold me with his acres," the other cried, in a voice which was hoarse with passion. "'The man, the woman, and their litter'—so ran the words of the dotard bailiff. Never a bullock on the farm was sold more lightly. Ha! he may wake some black night to find the flames licking about his ears—for fire is a good friend to the poor man, and I have seen a smoking heap of ashes where overnight there stood just such another castlewick as Ashby."

"This is a lad of metal!" shouted another of the labourers. "He dares to give tongue to what all men think. Are we not all from Adam's loins, all with flesh and blood, and with the same mouth that must needs have food and drink? Where all this difference, then, between the ermine cloak arid the leathern tunic, if what they cover is the same?"

"Aye, Jenkin," said another, "our foeman is under the stole and the vestments as much as under the helmet and plate of proof. We have as much to fear from the tonsure as from the hauberk. Strike at the noble and the priest shrieks, strike at the priest and the noble lays his hand upon glaive. They are twin thieves who live upon our labour."

"It would take a clever man to live upon thy labour, Hugh," remarked one of the foresters, "seeing that the half of thy time is spent in swilling mead at the 'Pied Merlin'."

"Better that than stealing the deer that thou art placed to guard, like some folk I know."

"If you dare open that swine's mouth against me," shouted the woodman, "I'll crop your ears for you before the hangman has the doing of it, thou long-jawed lack-brain."

"Nay, gentles, gentles!" cried Dame Eliza, in a sing-song, heedless voice, which showed that such bickerings were nightly things among her guests. "No brawling or brabbling, gentles! Take heed of the good name of the house."

"Besides, if it comes to the cropping of ears, there are other folk who may say their say," quoth the third labourer. "We are all freemen, and I trow that a yeoman's cudgel is as good as a forester's knife. By St Anselm! it would be an evil day if we had to bend to our masters' servants as well as to our masters."

"No man is my master save the king," the woodman answered. "Who is there, save a false traitor, who would refuse to serve the English king?"

"I know not about the English king," said the man Jenkin. "What sort of English king is it who cannot lay his tongue to a word of English? You mind last year when he came down to Mallwood, with his inner marshal and his outer marshal, his justiciar, his seneschal, and his four-and-twenty guardsmen. One noontide I was by Franklin Swinton's gate, when up he rides with a yeoman-pricker at his heels. 'Ouvre,' he cried, 'ouvre,' or some such word, making sign for me to open the gate; and then 'Merci,' as though he were adrad of me. And you talk of an English king!"

"I do not marvel at it," cried the Cambrig scholar, speaking in the high drawling voice which was common among his class. "It is not a tongue for men of sweet birth arid delicate upbringing. It is a foul, snorting, snarling manner of speech. For myself, I swear by the learned Polycarp that I have most ease with Hebrew, and after that perchance with Arabian."

"I will not hear a word against old King Ned," cried Hordle John in a voice like a bull. "What if he is fond of a bright eye and a saucy face? I know one of his subjects who could match him at that. If he cannot speak like an Englishman, I trow that he can fight like an Englishman; and he was hammering at the gates of Paris while ale-house topers were grutching and grumbling at home."

This loud speech, coming from a man of so formidable an appearance, somewhat daunted the disloyal party, and they fell into a sudden silence, which enabled Alleyne to hear something of the talk which was going on in the farther corner between the physician, the tooth-drawer, and the gleeman.

"A raw rat," the man of drugs was saying, "that is what it is ever my use to order for the plague—a raw rat with its paunch cut open."

"Might it not be broiled, most learned sir?" asked the tooth-drawer. "A raw rat sounds a most sorry and cheerless dish."

"Not to be eaten," cried the physician, in high disdain. "Why should any man eat such a thing?"

"Why indeed?" asked the gleeman, taking a long drain at his tankard.

"It is to be placed on the sore or swelling. For the rat, mark you, being a foul-living creature, hath a natural drawing or affinity for all foul things, so that the noxious humours pass from the man into the unclean beast."

"Would that cure the black death, master?" asked Jenkin.

"Aye, truly would it, my fair son."

"Then I am right glad that there were none who knew of it. The black death is the best friend that ever the common folk had in England."

"How that then?" asked Hordle John.

"Why, friend, it is easy so see that you have not worked with your hands, or you would not need to ask. When half the folk in the country were dead it was then that the other half could pick and choose who they would work for, and for what wage. That is why I say that the murrain was the best friend that the borel folk ever had."

"True, Jenkin," said another workman, "but it is not all good that is brought by it either. We well know that through it corn land has been turned into pasture, so that flocks of sheep with per-chance a single shepherd wander now where once a hundred men had work and wage."

"There is no great harm in that," remarked the tooth-drawer, "for the sheep give many folk their living. There is not only the herd, but the shearer and brander, and then the dresser, the curer, the dyer, the fuller, the webster, the merchant, and a score of others."

"If it come to that," said one of the foresters, "the tough meat of them will wear folks' teeth out, and there is a trade for the man who can draw them."

A general laugh followed this sally at the dentist's expense, in the midst of which the gleeman placed his battered harp upon his knee, and began to pick out a melody upon the frayed strings.

"Elbow room for Floyting Will!" cried the woodmen. "Twang us a merry lilt."

"Aye, aye, the 'Lasses of Lancaster'," one suggested.

"Or 'St Simeon and the Devil'."

"Or the 'Jest of Hendy Tobias'."

To all these suggestions the jongleur made no response, but sat with his eye fixed abstractedly upon the ceiling, as one who calls words to his mind. Then, with a sudden sweep across the strings, he broke out into a song so gross and so foul that ere he had finished a verse the pure-minded lad sprang to his feet with the blood tingling in his face.

"How can you sing such things?" he cried. "You, too, an old man who should be an example to others."

The wayfarers all gazed in the utmost astonishment at the interruption.

"By the holy Dicon of Hampole! our silent clerk has found his tongue," said one of the woodmen. "What is amiss with the song then? How has it offended your baby-ship?"

"A milder and better mannered song hath never been heard within these walls," cried another. "What sort of talk is this for a public inn?"

"Shall it be a litany, my good clerk?" shouted the third, "or would a hymn be good enough to serve?"

The jongleur had put down his harp in high dudgeon. "Am I to be preached to by a child?" he cried, staring across at Alleyne with an inflamed and angry countenance. "Is a hairless infant to raise his tongue against me, when I have sung in every fair from Tweed to Trent, and have twice been named aloud by the High Court of the Minstrels at Beverley? I shall sing no more tonight."

"Nay, but you will so," said one of the labourers. "Hi! Dame Eliza, bring a stoup of your best to Will to clear his throat. Go forward with thy song, and if our girl-faced clerk does not love it he can take to the road and go whence he came."

"Nay, but not too fast," broke in Hordle John. "There are two words in this matter. It may be that my little comrade has been over quick in reproof, he having gone early into the cloisters and seen little of the rough ways and words of the world. Yet there is truth in what he says, for, as you know well, the song was not of the cleanest. I shall stand by him, therefore, and he shall neither be put out on the road, nor shall his ears be offended indoors."

"Indeed, your high and mighty grace," sneered one of the yeomen, "have you in sooth so ordained?"

"By the Virgin!" said a second, "I think that you may both chance to find yourselves upon the road before long."

"And so belaboured as to be scarce able to crawl along it," cried a third.

"Nay, I shall go! I shall go!" said Alleyne hurriedly, as Hordle John began to slowly roll up his sleeve, and bare an arm like a leg of mutton. "I would not have you brawl about me."

"Hush, lad!" he whispered, "I count them not a fly. They may find they have more tow on their distaff than they know how to spin. Stand thou clear and give me space."

Both the foresters and the labourers had risen from their bench, and Dame Eliza and the travelling doctor had flung themselves between the two parties with soft words and soothing gestures, when the door of the "Pied Merlin" was flung violently open, and the attention of the company was drawn from their own quarrel to the new-comer who had burst so unceremoniously upon them.

CHAPTER VI

HOW SAMKIN AYLWARD WAGERED
HIS FEATHER-BED

He was a middle-sized man, of most massive and robust build, with an arching chest and extraordinary breadth of shoulder. His shaven face was as brown as a hazel-nut, tanned and dried by the weather, with harsh well-marked features, which were not improved by a long white scar which stretched from the corner of his left nostril to the angle of the jaw. His eyes were bright and searching, with something of menace and of authority in their quick glitter, and his mouth was firm set and hard, as befitted one who was wont to set his face against danger. A straight sword by his side and a painted long-bow jutting over his shoulder proclaimed his profession, while his scarred brigandine of chainmail and his dinted steel cap showed that he was no holiday soldier, but one who was even now fresh from the wars. A white surcoat with the lion of St George in red upon the centre covered his broad breast, while a sprig of new-plucked broom at the side of his headgear gave a touch of gaiety and grace to his grim war-worn equipment.

"Ha!" he cried, blinking like an owl in the sudden glare. "Good even to you, camarades! Holà! a woman, by my soul!" and in an instant he had clipped Dame Eliza round the waist and was kissing her violently. His eye happening to wander upon the maid, however, he instantly abandoned the mistress and danced off after the other, who scurried in confusion up one of the ladders, and dropped the heavy trap-door upon her pursuer. He then turned back and saluted the landlady once more with the utmost relish and satisfaction.

"La petite is frightened," said he. "Ah, c'est l'amour, l'amour! Curse this trick of French, which will stick to my throat. I must wash it out with some good English ale. By my hilt! camarades, there is no drop of French blood in my body, and I am a true English bowman, Samkin Aylward by name, once of Crooks-bury; and I tell you, mes amis, that it warms my very heartroots to set my feet on the dear old land once more. When I came off the galley at Hythe, this very day, I down on my bones, and I kissed the good brown earth, as I kiss thee now, ma belle, for it was eight long years since I had seen it. The very smell of it seemed life to me. But where are my six rascals? Holà, there! En avant!"

At the order, six men, dressed as common drudges, marched solemnly into the room, each bearing a huge bundle upon his head. They formed in military line, while the soldier stood in front of them with stem eyes, checking off their several packages.

"Number one—a French feather-bed with the two counter-panes of white sendal," said he.

"Here, worthy sir," answered the first of the bearers, laying a great package down in the corner.

"Number two—seven ells of red Turkey cloth and nine ells of cloth of gold. Put it down by the other. Good dame, I prythee give each of these men a bottrine of wine or a jack of ale. Three—a full piece of white Genoan velvet with twelve ells of purple silk. Thou rascal, there is dirt on the hem! Thou hast brushed it against some wall, coquin!"

"Not I, most worthy sir," cried the carrier, shrinking away from the fierce eyes of the bowman.

"I say yes, dog! By the three kings! I have seen a man gasp out his last breath for less. Had you gone through the pain and unease that I have done to earn these things you would be at more care. I swear by my ten finger-bones that there is not one of them that hath not cost its weight in French blood! Four—an incense boat, an ewer of silver, a gold buckle and a cope worked in pearls. I found them, camarades, at the Church of St Denis in the harrying of Narbonne, and I took them away with me lest they fall into the hands of the wicked. Five—a cloak of fur turned up with minever, a gold goblet with stand and cover, and a box of rose-coloured sugar. See that you lay them together. Six—a box of monies, three pounds of Limousine gold-work, a pair of boots, silver tagged, and, lastly, a store of naping linen. So, the tally is complete! Here is a groat apiece and you may go."

"Go whither, worthy sir?" asked one of the carriers.

"Whither? To the devil if ye will. What is it to me? Now, ma belle, to supper. A pair of cold capons, a mortress of brawn, or what you will, with a flask or two of the right Gascony. I have crowns in my pouch, my sweet, and I mean to spend them. Bring in wine while the food is dressing. Buvons, my brave lads! you shall each empty a stoup with me."

Here was an offer which the company in an English inn at that or any other date are slow to refuse. The flagons were regathered, and came back with the white foam dripping over their edges. Two of the woodmen and three of the labourers drank their portions off hurriedly and trooped off together, for their homes were distant and the hour late. The others, however, drew closer, leaving the place of honour to the right of the gleeman to the free-handed new-comer. He had thrown off his steel cap and his brigandine, and had placed them with his sword, quiver and his painted longbow, on the top of his varied heap of plunder in the corner. Now, with his thick and somewhat bowed legs stretched in front of the blaze, his green jerkin thrown open, and a great quart pot held in his corded fist, he looked the picture of comfort and of good-fellowship. His hard-set face had softened, and the thick crop of crisp brown curls which had been hidden by his helmet grew low upon his massive neck. He might have been forty years of age, though hard toil and harder pleasure had left their grim marks upon his features. Alleyne had ceased painting his pied merlin, and sat, brush in hand, staring with open eyes at a type of man so strange and so unlike any whom he had met. Men had been good or had been bad in his catalogue, but here was a man who was fierce one instant and gentle the next, with a curse on his lips and a smile in his eye. What was to be made of such a man as that?

It chanced that the soldier looked up and saw the questioning glance which the young clerk threw upon him. He raised his flagon and drank to him, with a merry flash of his white teeth.

"A toi, mon garçon!" he cried. "Hast surely never seen a man-at-arms, that thou shouldst stare so?"

"I never have," said Alleyne frankly, "though I have oft heard talk of their deeds."

"By my hilt!" cried the other, "if you were to cross the narrow sea you would find them as thick as bees at a tee-hole. Couldst not shoot a bolt down any street of Bordeaux I warrant, but you would pink archer, squire or knight. There are more breastplates than gaberdines to be seen, I promise you."

"And where got you all those pretty things?" asked Hordle John, pointing at the heap in the corner.

"Where there is as much more waiting for any brave lad to pick it up. Where a good man can always earn a good wage, and where he need look upon no man as his paymaster, but just reach his hand out and help himself. Aye, it is a goodly and a proper life. And here I drink to mine old comrades, and the saints be with them! A rouse all together, mes enfants, under pain of my displeasure! To Sir Claude Latour and the White Company!"

"Sir Claude Latour and the White Company!" shouted the travellers, draining off their goblets.

"Well quaffed, mes braves! It is for me to fill your cups again, since you have drained them to my dear lads of the white jerkin. Holà! mon ange, bring wine and ale. How runs the old stave?—"

We'll drink all together
To the grey goose feather
And the land where the grey goose flew.

He roared out the catch in a harsh unmusical voice, and ended with a shout of laughter. "I trust that I am a better bowman than a minstrel," said he.

"Methinks I have some remembrance of the lilt," remarked the gleeman, running his finger over the strings. "Hoping that it will give thee no offence, most holy sir"—with a vicious snap at Alleyne—"and with the kind permit of the company, I will even venture upon it."

Many a time in the after days Alleyne Edricson seemed to see that scene, for all that so many which were stranger and more stirring were soon to crowd upon him. The fat, red-faced gleeman, the listening group, the archer with upraised finger beating in time to the music, and the huge sprawling figure of Hordle John, all thrown into red light and black shadow by the flickering fire in the centre—memory was to come often lovingly back to it.

At the time he was lost in admiration at the deft way in which the jongleur disguised the loss of his two missing strings, and the lusty, hearty fashion in which he trolled out his little ballad of the outland bowmen, which ran in some such fashion as this:

What of the bow?
    The bow was made in England:
Of true wood, of yew-wood,
    The wood of English bows;
      So men who are free
      Love the old yew-tree
And the land where the yew-tree grows.

What of the cord?
    The cord was made in England:
A rough cord, a tough cord,
    A cord that bowmen love;
      So we'll drain our jacks
      To the English flax
And the land where the hemp was wove.

What of the shaft?
    The shaft was cut in England:
A long shaft, a strong shaft,
    Barbed and trim and true;
        So we'll drink all together
        To the grey goose feather
And the land where the grey goose flew.

What of the men?
    The men were bred in England:
The bowmen—the yeomen—
    The lads of dale and fell.
        Here's to you—and to you!
        To the hearts that are true
And the land where the true hearts dwell.

"Well sung, by my hilt!" shouted the archer in high delight. "Many a night have I heard that song, both in the old wartime and after, in the days of the White Company, when Black Simon of Norwich would lead the stave, and four hundred of the best bowmen that ever drew string would come roaring in upon the chorus. I have seen old John Hawkwood, the same who has led half the Company into Italy, stand laughing in his beard as he heard it, until his plates rattled again. But to get the full smack of it ye must yourselves be English bowmen, and be far off upon an outland soil."

Whilst the song had been singing Dame Eliza and the maid had placed a board across two trestles, and had laid upon it the knife, the spoon, the salt, the tranchoir of bread, and finally the smoking dish which held the savoury supper. The archer settled himself to it like one who had known what it was to find good food scarce; but his tongue still went as merrily as his teeth.

"It passes me," he cried, "how all you lusty fellows can bide scratching your backs at home when there are such doings over the seas. Look at me—what have I to do? It is but the eye to the

56

cord, the cord to the shaft, and the shaft to the mark. There is the whole song of it. It is but what you do yourselves for pleasure upon a Sunday evening at the parish village butts."

"And the wage?" asked a labourer.

"You see what the wage brings," he answered. "I eat of the best, and I drink deep. I treat my friend, and I ask no friend to treat me. I clap a silk gown on my girl's back. Never a knight's lady shall be better betrimmed and betrinketed. How of all that, mon garçon? And how of the heap of trifles that you can see for yourselves in yonder corner? They are from the South French, every one, upon whom I have been making war. By my hilt! camarades, I think that I may let my plunder speak for itself."

"It seems indeed to be a goodly service," said the tooth-drawer.

"Tête bleu! yes, indeed. Then there is the chance of a ransom. Why, look you, in the affair at Brignais, some four years back, when the companies slew James of Bourbon, and put his army to the sword, there was scarce a man of ours who had not count, baron, or knight. Peter Karsdale, who was but a common country lout newly brought over, with the English fleas still hopping under his doublet, laid his great hands upon the Sieur Amaury de Chatonville, who owns half Picardy, and had five thousand crowns out of him, with horse and harness. 'Tis true that a French wench took it all off Peter as quick as the Frenchman paid it; but what then? By the twang of string! it would be a bad thing if money was not made to be spent; and how better than on woman—eh, ma belle?"

"It would indeed be a bad thing if we had not our brave archers to bring wealth and kindly customs into the country," quoth Dame Eliza, on whom the soldier's free and open ways had made a deep impression.

"A toi, ma chérie!" said he, with his hand over his heart. "Holà! there is la petite peeping from behind the door. A toi, aussi, ma petite! Mon Dieu! but the lass has a good colour!"

"There is one thing, fair sir," said the Cambridge student in his piping voice, "which I would fain that you would make more clear. As I understand it, there was a peace made at the town of Brétigny some six years back between our most gracious mon arch and the King of the French. This being so, it seems most passing strange that you should talk so loudly of war and of companies when there is no quarrel between the French and us."

"Meaning that I lie," said the archer, laying down his knife.

"May heaven forefend!" cried the student hastily. *"Magna est veritas sed rara,* which means in the Latin tongue that archers are all honourable men. I come to you seeking knowledge, for it is my trade to learn."

"I fear that you are yet a 'prentice to that trade," quoth the soldier, "for there is no child over the water but could answer what you ask. Know, then, that though there, may be peace between our own provinces and the French, yet within the marches of France there is always war, for the country is much divided against itself, and is furthermore harried by bands of flayers, skinners, Brabaçons, tard-venus, and the rest of them. When every man's grip is on his neighbour's throat, and every five-sous-piece of a baron is marching with tuck of drum to fight whom he will, it would be a strange thing if five hundred brave English boys could not pick up a living. Now that Sir John Hawkwood hath gone with the East Anglian lads and the Nottingham woodmen into the service of the Marquis of Montferrat to fight against the Lord of Milan, there are but ten-score of us left; yet I trust that I may be able to bring some back with me to fill the ranks of the White Company. By the tooth of Peter! it would be a bad thing if I could not muster many a Hampton-shire man who would be ready to strike in under the red flag of St George, and the more so if my old master Sir Nigel Loring, of Christchurch, should don hauberk once more and take the lead of us."

"Ah! you would indeed be in luck then," quoth a woodman, "for it is said that, setting aside the prince, and mayhap good old Sir John Chandos, there was not in the whole army a man of such tried courage."

"It is sooth, every word of it," the archer answered. "I have seen him with these two eyes on stricken fields and never did man carry himself better. Mon Dieu! yes, ye would not credit it to look at him, or to hearken to his soft voice, but for, clear twenty years, there was not skirmish, onfall, sally, bushment, escalado, or battle, but Sir Nigel was in the heart of it. I go now to Christchurch with a letter to him from Sir Claude Latour, to ask him if he will take the place of Sir John Hawkwood; and there is the more chance that he will if I bring one or two likely men at my heels. What say you, woodman: wilt leave the bucks to loose a shaft at a nobler mark?"

The forester shook his head. "I have a wife and child at Emery Down," quoth he. "I would not leave them for such a venture."

"You then, young sir?" asked the archer.

"Nay, I am a man of peace," said Alleyne Edricson. "Besides, I have other work to do."

"Peste!" growled the soldier, striking his flagon on the board until the dishes danced again. "What, in the name of the devil, hath come over the folk? Why sit ye all moping by the fireside, like crows round a dead horse, when there is man's work to be done within a few short leagues of ye? Out upon you all, as a set of laggards and hang-backs! By my hilt! I believe that the men of England are all in France already, and that what is left behind are in sooth the women dressed up in their paltocks and hosen."

"Archer," quoth Hordle John, "you have lied more than once and more than twice; for which, and also because I see much in you to mislike, I am sore tempted to lay you upon your back."

"By my hilt! then, I have found a man at last!" shouted the bowman. "And, 'fore God, you are a better man than I take you for if you can lay me on my back, mon garçon. I have won the ram more times than there are toes to my feet, and for seven long years I have found no man in the Company who could make my jerkin dusty."

"We have had enough bobance and boasting," said Hordle John, rising and throwing off his doublet. "I will show you that there are better men left in England than ever went thieving to France."

"Pasques Dieu!" cried the archer, loosening his jerkin, and eyeing his foeman over with the keen glance of one who is a judge of manhood. "I have only once before seen such a body of a man. By your leave, my red-headed friend, I should be right sorry to exchange buffets with you; and I will allow that there is no man in the Company who would pull against you on a rope; so let that be a salve to your pride. On the other hand, I should judge that you have led a life of ease for some months back, and that my muscle is harder than your own. I am ready to wager upon myself against you, if you are not afeard."

"Afeard, thou lurden!" growled big John. "I never saw the face yet of the man that I was afeard of. Come out, and we shall see who is the better man."

"But the wager?"

"I have nought to wager. Come out for the love and the lust of the thing."

"Nought to wager!" cried the soldier. "Why, you have that which I covet above all things. It is that big body of thine that I am after. See, now, mon garçon. I have a French feather-bed there, which I have been at pains to keep these years back. I had it at the sacking of Issodun, and the king himself hath not such a bed. If you throw me, it is thine; but, if I throw you, then you are under a vow to take bow and bill and hie with me to France, there to serve in the White Company as long as we be enrolled."

"A fair wager!" cried all the travellers, moving back their benches and trestles, so as to give fair field for the wrestlers.

"Then you may bid farewell to your bed, soldier," said Hordle John.

"Nay; I shall keep the bed, and I shall have you to France in spite of your teeth, and you shall live to thank me for it. How shall it be, then, mon enfant? Collar and elbow, or closelock, or catch how you can?"

"To the devil with your tricks," said John, opening and shutting his great red hands. "Stand forth, and let me clip thee."

"Shalt clip me as best you can, then," quoth the archer, moving out into the open, space, and keeping a most wary eye upon his opponent He had thrown off his green jerkin, and his chest was covered only by a pink sink jupon, or undershirt, cut low in the neck and sleeveless. Hordle John was stripped from his waist upwards, and his huge body, with his great muscles swelling out like the gnarled roots of an oak, towered high above the soldier. The other, however, though near a foot shorter, was a man of great strength; and there was a gloss upon his white skin which was wanting in the heavier limbs of the renegade monk. He was quick on his feet, too, and skilled at the game; so that it was clear, from the poise of head and shine of eye, that he counted the chances to be in his favour. It would have been hard that night, through the whole length of England, to set up a finer pair in face of each other.

Big John stood waiting in the centre with a sullen, menacing eye, and his red hair in a bristle, while the archer paced lightly and swiftly to the right and the left with crooked knee and hands advanced. Then, with a sudden dash, so swift that the eye could scarce follow it, he flew in upon his man and locked his leg round him. It was a grip that, between men of equal strength, would mean a fall; but Hordle John tore him off from him as he might a rat, and hurled him across the room, so that his head cracked up against the wooden wall.

"Ma foi!" cried the bowman, passing his fingers through his curls, "You were not far from the feather-bed then, mon gar. A little more, and this good hostel would have a new window."

Nothing daunted, he approached his man once more; but this time with more caution than before. With a quick feint he threw the other off his guard, and then, bounding upon him, threw his legs round his waist and his arms round his bull-neck, in the hope of bearing him to the ground with the sudden shock. With a bellow of rage, Hordle John squeezed him limp in his huge arms; and then, picking him up, cast him down upon the floor with a force which might well have splintered a bone or two, had not the archer with the most perfect coolness clung to the other's forearms to break his fall: As it was, he dropped upon his feet and kept his balance, thought it sent a jar through his frame which set every joint a-creaking. He bounded back from his perilous foeman; but the other, heated by the bout, rushed madly after him, and so gave the practised wrestler the very vantage for which he had planned. As big John flung himself upon him, the archer ducked under the great red hands that clutched for him, and, catching his man round the thighs, hurled him over his shoulder—helped as much by his own mad rush as by the trained strength of the heave. To Alleyne's eye, it was as if John had taken unto himself wings and flown. As he hurtled through the air, with giant limbs revolving, the lad's heart was in his mouth; for surely no man ever yet had such a fall and came scathless out of it. In truth, hardy as the man was, his neck had been assuredly broken had he not pitched head first on the very midriff of the drunken artist, who was slumbering so peacefully in the corner, all unaware of these stirring doings. The luckless limner, thus suddenly brought out from his dreams, sat up with a piercing yell, while Hordle John bounded back into the circle almost as rapidly as he had left it.

"One more fall, by all the saints!" he cried, throwing out his arms.

"Not I," quoth the archer, pulling on his clothes. "I have come well out of the business. I would sooner wrestle with the great bear of Navarre."

"It was a trick," cried John.

"Aye was it. By my ten finger-bones! it is a trick that will add a proper man to the ranks of the Company."

"Oh, for that," said the other, "I count it not a fly; for I had promised myself a good hour ago that I should go with thee, since the life seems to be a goodly and proper one. Yet I would fain have had the feather-bed."

"I doubt it not, mon ami," quoth the archer, going back to his tankard. "Here is to thee, lad, and may we be good comrades to each other! But holà! what is it that ails our friend of the wrathful face?"

The unfortunate limner had been sitting up, rubbing himself ruefully and staring about with a vacant gaze, which showed that he knew neither where he was nor what had occurred to him. Suddenly, however, a flash of intelligence had come over his sodden features, and he rose and staggered for the door. "'Ware the ale!" he said in a hoarse whisper, shaking a warning finger at the company. "Oh, holy Virgin, 'ware the ale!" and clapping his hands to his injury, he flitted off into the darkness, amid a shout of laughter, in which the vanquished joined as merrily as the victor. The remaining forester and the two labourers were also ready for the road, and the rest of the company turned to the blankets which Dame Eliza and the maid had laid out for them upon the floor. Alleyne, weary with the unwonted excitements of the day, was soon in a deep slumber, broken only by fleeting visions of twittering legs, cursing beggars, black robbers, and the many strange folk whom he had met at the "Pied Merlin."

CHAPTER VII

HOW THE THREE COMRADES JOURNEYED THROUGH THE WOODLANDS

At early dawn the country inn was all alive, for it was rare indeed that an hour of daylight would be wasted at a time when lighting was so scarce and dear. Indeed, early as it was when Dame Eliza began to stir, it seemed that others could be earlier still, for the door was ajar and the learned student of Cambridge had taken himself off, with a mind which was too intent upon the high things of antiquity to stoop to consider the fourpence which he owed for bed and board. It was the shrill outcry of the landlady when she found her loss, and the clucking of the hens, which had streamed in through the open door, that first broke in upon the slumbers of the tired wayfarers.

Once afoot, it was not long before the company began to disperse. A sleek mule with red trappings was brought round from some neighbouring shed for the physician, and he ambled away with much dignity upon his road to Southampton. The toothdrawer and the gleeman called for a cup of small ale apiece, and started off together for Ringwood Fair, the old jongleur looking very yellow in the eye and swollen in the face after his overnight potations. The archer, however, who had drunk more than any man in the room, was as merry as a grig, and having kissed the matron and chased the maid up the ladder once more, he went out to the brook, and came back with the water dripping from his face and hair.

"Holà! my man of peace," he cried to Alleyne, "whither are you bent this morning?"

"To Minstead," quoth he. "My brother Simon Edricson is socman there, and I go to bide with him for a while. I prythee, let me have my score, good dame."

"Score, indeed!" cried she, standing with upraised hands in front of the panel on which Alleyne had worked the night before. "Say, rather, what it is that I owe to thee, good youth. Aye, this is indeed a pied merlin, and with a leveret under its claws, as I am a living woman. By the rood of Waltham! but thy touch is deft and dainty."

"And see the red eye of it!" cried the maid.

"Aye, and the open beak."

"And the ruffled wing," added Hordle John.

"By my hilt!" cried the archer, "it is the very bird itself."

The young clerk flushed with pleasure at this chorus of praise, rude and indiscriminate indeed, and yet so much heartier and less grudging than any which he had ever heard from the critical brother Jerome or the short-spoken Abbot. There was, it would seem, great kindness as well as great wickedness in this world, of which he had heard so little that was good. His hostess would hear nothing of his paying either for bed or for board, while the archer and Hordle John placed a hand upon either shoulder and led him off to the board, where some smoking fish, a dish of spinach, and a jug of milk were kid out for their breakfast.

"I should not be surprised to learn, mon camarade," said the soldier, as he heaped a slice of the fish upon Alleyne's tranchoir of bread, "that you could read written things, since you are so ready with your brushes and pigments."

"It would be shame to the good brothers of Beaulieu if I could not," he answered, "seeing that I have been their clerk this ten years back."

The bowman looked at him with great respect. "Think of that!" said he. "And you with not a hair to your face, and a skin like a girl. I can shoot three hundred and fifty paces with my little popper there, and four hundred and twenty with the great war-bow; yet I can make nothing of this, nor read my own name if you were to set 'Sam Aylward' up against me. In the whole Company there was only one man who could read, and he fell down a well at the taking of Ventadour, which proves that the thing is not suited to a soldier, though most needful to a clerk."

"I can make some show at it," said big John; "though I was scarce long enough among the monks to catch the whole trick of it."

"Here, then, is something to try upon," quoth the archer, pulling a square of parchment from the inside of his tunic. It was tied securely with a broad band of purple silk, and firmly sealed at either end with a large red seal. John pored long and earnestly over the inscription upon the back, with his brows bent as one who bears up against great mental strain.

"Not having read much of late," he said, "I am loth to say too much about what this may be. Some might say one thing and some another, just as one bowman loves the yew, and a second will not shoot save with the ash. To me, by the length and the look of it, I should judge this to be a verse from one of the Psalms."

The bowman shook his head. "It is scarce likely," he said, "that Sir Claude Latour should send me all the way across seas with naught more weighty than a psalm-verse. You have clean overshot the butts this time, mon camarade. Give it to the little one. I will wager my feather-bed that he makes more sense of it."

"Why, it is written in the French tongue," said Alleyne, "and in a right clerkly hand. This is how it runs: 'A le moult puissant et moult honorable chevalier, Sir Nigel Loring de Christchurch, de sont très fidèle amis Sir Claude Latour, capitaine de la Compagnie blanche, châtelain de Biscar, grand seigneur de Montchâteau, vavaseur de la renommé Gaston, Comte de Foix, tenant les droits de la haute justice, de la milieu, et de la basse.' Which signifies in our speech: 'To the very powerful and very honourable knight, Sir Nigel Loring of Christchurch, from his very faithful friend Sir Claude Latour, captain of the White Company, chatelain of Biscar, grand lord of Montchâteau, and vassal to the renowned Gaston, Count of Foix, who holds the rights of the high justice, the middle and the low'."

"Look at that now!" cried the bowman in triumph. "That is just what he would have said."

"I can see now that it is even so," said John, examining the parchment again. "Though I scarce understand this high, middle, and low."

"By my hilt! you would understand it if you were Jacques Bonhomme. The low justice means that you may fleece him, and the middle that you may torture him, and the high that you may slay him. That is about the truth of it. But this is the letter which I am to take; and since the platter is clean it is time that we trussed up and were afoot. You come with me, mon gros Jean; and as to you, little one, where did you say that you journeyed?"

"To Minstead."

"Ah, yes, I know this forest-country well, though I was born myself in the Hundred of Eastbourne, in the Rape of Chichester, hard by the village of Midhurst. Yet I have not a word to say against the Hampton men, for there are no better comrades or truer archers in the whole Company than some who learned to loose the string in these very parts. We shall travel round with you to Minstead, lad, seeing that it is little out of our way."

"I am ready," said Alleyne, right pleased at the thought of such company upon the road.

"So am not I. I must store my plunder at this inn, since the hostess is an honest woman. Holà, ma chérie, I wish to leave with you my gold-work, my velvet, my silk, my feather-bed, my incense-boat, my ewer, my naping linen, and all the rest of it. I take only the money in a linen bag, and the box of rose-coloured sugar, which is a gift from my Captain to the Lady Loring. Wilt guard my treasure for me?"

"It shall be put in the safest loft, good archer. Come when you may, you shall find it ready for you."

"Now, there is a true friend!" cried the bowman, taking her hand. "There is a bonne amie! English land and English women, say I, and French wine and French plunder. I shall be back anon, mon ange. I am a lonely man, my sweeting, and I must settle some day when the wars are over and done. Mayhap you and I—Ah, méchanic, méchante! There is la petite peeping from behind the door. Now, John, the sun is over the trees; you must be brisker than this when the bugleman blows 'Bows and Bills'."

"I have been waiting this time back," said Hordle John gruffly.

"Then we must off. Adieu, ma vie! The two livres shall settle the score and buy some ribbons against the next kermesse. Do not forget Sam Aylward, for his heart shall ever be thine alone— and thine, ma petite! So, marchons, and may St Julian grant us good quarters elsewhere!"

The sun had risen over Ashurst and Denny woods, and was shining brightly, though the eastern wind had a sharp flavour to it, and the leaves were flickering thickly from the trees. In the High Street of Lyndhurst the wayfarers had to pick their way, for the little town was crowded with the guardsmen, grooms, and yeomen-prickers who were attached to the king's hunt. The king himself was staying at Castle Malwood, but several of his suite had been compelled to seek such quarters as they might find in the wooden or wattle-and-daub cottages of the village. Here and there a small escutcheon, peeping from a glassless window, marked the night's lodging of knight or baron. These coats-of-arms could be read, where a scroll would be meaningless, and the bowman, like most men of his age, was well versed in the common symbols of heraldry.

"There is the Saracen's head of Sir Bernard Brocas," quoth he. "I saw him last at the ruffle at Poictiers some ten years back, when he bore himself like a man. He is the master of the king's horse, and can sing a right jovial stave, though in that he cannot come nigh to Sir John Chandos, who is the first at the board or in the saddle. Three martlets on a field azure. That must be one of the Luttrells. By the crescent upon it, it should be the second son of old Sir Hugh, who had a bolt through his ankle at the in-taking of Romorantin, he having rushed into the fray ere his squire had time to clasp his solleret to his greave. There too is the hackle which is the old device of the De Brays. I have served under Sir Thomas de Bray, who was as jolly as a pie, and a lusty swordsman until he got too fat for his harness."

So the archer gossiped as the three wayfarers threaded their way among the stamping horses, the busy grooms, and the knots of pages and squires who disputed over the merits of their masters' horses and deerhounds. As they passed the old church, which stood upon a mound at the left-hand side of the village street, the door was flung open, and a stream of worshippers wound down the sloping path, coming from the morning mass, all chattering like a cloud of jays. Alleyne bent knee and doffed hat at the sight of the open door; but ere he had finished an ave, his comrades were out of sight round the curve of the path, and he had to run to overtake them.

"What!" he said, "not one word of prayer before God's own open house? How can ye hope for His blessing upon the day?"

"My friend," said Hordle John, "I have prayed so much during the last two months, not only during the day, but at matins, lauds, and the like, when I could scarce keep my head upon my shoulders for nodding, that I feel that I have somewhat over-prayed myself."

"How can a man have too much religion?" cried Alleyne earnestly. "It is the one thing that availeth. A man is but a beast as he lives from day to day, eating and drinking, breathing and sleeping. It is only when he raises himself, and concerns himself with the immortal spirit within him, that he becomes in very truth a man. Bethink ye how sad a thing it would be that the blood of the Redeemer should be spilled to no purpose."

"Bless the lad, if he doth not blush like any girl, and yet preach like the whole College of Cardinals," cried the archer.

"In truth I blush that anyone so weak and so unworthy as I should try to teach another that which he finds it so passing hard to follow himself."

"Prettily said, mon garçon. Touching that same slaying of the Redeemer, it was a bad business. A good padre in France read to us from a scroll the whole truth of the matter. The soldiers came upon Him in the garden. In truth, these Apostles of His may have been holy men, but they were of no great account as men-at-arms. There was one, indeed, Sir Peter, who smote out like a true man; but, unless he is belied, he did but clip a varlet's ear, which was no very knightly deed. By these ten finger-bones! had I been there, with Black Simon of Norwich, and but one score picked men of the Company, We had held them in play. Could we do no more, we had at least filled the false knight, Sir Judas, so full of English arrows that he would curse the day that ever he came on such an errand."

The young clerk smiled at his companion's earnestness. "Had He wished help," he said, "He could have summoned legions of archangels from heaven, so what need had He of your poor bow and arrow? Besides, bethink you of His own words—that those who live by the sword shall perish by the sword."

"And how could man die better?" asked the archer. "If I had my wish, it would be to fall so—not, mark you, in any mere skirmish of the Company, but in a stricken field, with the great lion banner waving over us and the red oriflamme in front, amid the shouting of my fellows and the twanging of the strings. But let it be sword, lance, or bolt that strikes me down: for I should think it shame to die from an iron ball from fire-crake or bombard or any such unsoldierly weapon which is only fitted to scare babes with its foolish noise and smoke."

"I have heard much even in the quiet cloisters of these new and dreadful engines," quoth Alleyne. "It is said, though I can scarce bring myself to believe it, that they will send a ball twice as far as a bowman can shoot his shaft, and with such force as to break through armour of proof."

"True enough, my lad. But while the armourer is thrusting in his devil's lust, and dropping his ball, and lighting his flambeau, I can very easily loose six shafts, or eight maybe, so he hath no great vantage after all. Yet I will not deny that at the intaking of a town it is well to have good store of bombards. I am told that at Calais they made lints in the wall that a man might put his head into. But surely, comrades, someone who is grievously hurt hath passed along this road before us."

All along the woodland track there did indeed run a scattered straggling trail of blood-marks, sometimes in single drops, and in other places in broad ruddy gouts, smudged over the dead leaves or crimsoning the white flint stones.

"It must be a stricken deer," said John.

"Nay, I am woodman enough to see that no deer hath passed this way this morning; and yet the blood is fresh. But hark to the sound!"

They stood listening all three with sidelong heads. Through the silence of the great forest there came a swishing, whistling sound, mingled with the most dolorous groans, and the voice of a man raised in a high quavering kind of song. The comrades hurried onwards eagerly, and topping the brow of a small rising they saw upon the other side the source from which these strange noises arose.

A tall man, much stooped in the shoulders, was walking slowly with bended head and clasped hands in the centre of the path. He was dressed from head to foot in a long white linen cloth, and a high white cap with a red cross printed upon it. His gown was turned back from his shoulders, and the flesh there was a sight to make a man wince, for it was all beaten to a pulp, and the blood was soaking into his gown and trickling down upon the ground. Behind him walked a smaller man, with his hair touched with grey, who was clad in the same white garb. He intoned a long whining rhyme in the French tongue, and at the end of every line he raised a thick cord, all jagged with pellets of lead, and smote his companion across the shoulders until the blood spurted again. Even as the three wayfarers stared, however, there was a sudden change, for the smaller man, having finished his song, loosened his own gown and handed the scourge to the other, who took up the stave once more and lashed his companion with all the strength of his bare and sinewy arm. So, alternately beating and beaten, they made their dolorous way through the beautiful woods and under the amber arches of the fading beech-trees, where the calm strength and majesty of Nature might serve to rebuke the foolish energies and misspent strivings of mankind.

Such a spectacle was new to Hordle John and to Alleyne Edricson; but the archer treated it lightly, as a common matter enough.

"These are the Beating Friars, otherwise called the Flagellants," quoth he. "I marvel that ye should have come upon none of them before, for across the water they are as common as gally-baggers. I have heard that there are no English among them, but that they are from France, Italy, and Bohemia. En avant, camarades! that we may have speech with them."

As they came up to them, Alleyne could hear the doleful dirge which the beater was chanting, bringing down his heavy whip at the end of each line, while the groans of the sufferer formed a sort of dismal chorus. It was in old French, and ran somewhat in this way:

Or avant, entre nous tous frères
Battons nos charognes bien fort
En remembrant la grant misère
De Dieu et sa piteuse mort,
Qui fut pris en la gent amère
Et vendus et trais à tort
Et bastu sa chair, vierge et dère
Au nom de ce battons plus fort.

Then at the end of the verse the scourge changed hands and the chanting began anew.

"Truly, holy fathers," said the archer in French as they came abreast of them, "you have beaten enough for today. The road is all spotted like a shambles at Martinmas. Why should ye mishandle yourselves thus?"

"C'est pour vos péchés—pour vos péchés," they droned, looking at the travellers with sad lack-lustre eyes, and then bent to their bloody work once more without heed to the prayers and persuasions which were addressed to them. Finding all remonstrance useless, the three comrades hastened on their way, leaving these strange travellers to their dreary task.

"Mort Dieu!" cried the bowman, "there is a bucketful or more of my blood over in France, but it was all spilled in hot fight, and I should think twice before I drew it drop by drop as these friars are doing. By my hilt! our young one here is as white as a Picardy cheese. What is amiss then, mon cher?"

"It is nothing," Alleyne answered. "My life has been too quiet. I am not used to such sights."

"Ma foi!" the other cried, "I have never yet seen a man who was so stout of speech and yet so weak of heart."

"Not so, friend," quoth big John, "it is not weakness of heart, for I know the lad well. His heart is as good as thine or mine, but he hath more in his pate than ever you will carry under that tin pot of thine, and as a consequence he can see further into things, so that they weigh upon him more."

"Surely to any man it is a sad sight," said Alleyne, "to see these holy men, who have done no sin themselves, suffering so for the sin of others. Saints are they, if in this age any may merit so high a name."

"I count them not a fly," cried Hordle John, "for who is the better for all their whipping and yowling? They are like other friars, I trow, when all is done. Let them leave their backs alone, and beat the pride out of their hearts."

"By the three kings! there is sooth in what you say," remarked the archer. "Besides, methinks if I were le bon Dieu, it would bring me little joy to see a poor devil cutting the flesh off his bones; and I should think that he had but a small opinion of me, that he should hope to please me by such provost-marshal work. No, by my hilt! I should look with a more loving eye upon a jolly archer who never harmed a fallen foe and never feared a hale one."

"Doubtless you mean no sin," said Alleyne. "If your words are wild, it is not for me to judge them. Can you not see that there are other foes in this world besides Frenchmen, and as much glory to be gained in conquering them? Would it not be a proud day for knight or squire if he could overthrow seven adversaries in the lists? Yet here are we in the lists of life, and there come the seven black champions against us: Sir Pride, Sir Covetousness, Sir Lust,

Sir Anger, Sir Gluttony, Sir Envy, and Sir Sloth. Let a man lay those seven low, and he shall have the prize of the day, from the hands of the fairest queen of beauty, even from the Virgin-Mother herself. It is for this that these men mortify their flesh, and to set us an example, who would pamper ourselves overmuch. I say again that they are God's own saints, and I bow my head to them."

"And so you shall, mon petit," replied the archer. "I have not heard a man speak better since old Dom Bertrand died, who was at one time chaplain to the White Company. He was a very valiant man, but at the battle of Brignais he was spitted through the body by a Hainault man-at-arms. For this we had an excommunication read against the man, when next we saw our holy father at Avignon; but as we had not his name, and knew nothing of him, save that he rode a dapple-grey roussin, I have feared sometimes that the blight may have settled upon the wrong man."

"Your Company has been, then, to bow knee before our holy father, the Pope Urban, the prop and centre of Christendom?" asked Alleyne, much interested. "Perchance you have yourself set eyes upon his august face?"

"Twice I saw him," said the archer. "He was a lean little rat of a man, with a scab on his chin. The first time we had five thousand crowns out of him, though he made much ado about it. The second time we asked ten thousand, but it was three days before we could come to terms, and I am of opinion myself that we might have done better by plundering the palace. His chamberlain and cardinals came forth, as I remember, to ask whether we would take seven thousand crowns with his blessing and a plenary absolution, or the ten thousand with his solemn ban by bell, book, and candle. We were all of one mind that it was best to have the ten thousand with the curse; but in some way they prevailed upon Sir John, so that we were blessed and shriven against our will. Perchance it is as well, for the Company were in need of it about that time."

The pious Alleyne was deeply shocked by this reminiscence. Involuntarily he glanced up and around to see if there were any trace of those opportune levin-flashes and thunderbolts which, in the "Acta Sanctorum," were wont so often to cut short the loose talk of the scoffer. The autumn sun streamed down as brightly as ever, and the peaceful red path still wound in front of them through the rustling yellow-tinted forest. Nature seemed to be too busy with her own concerns to heed the dignity of an outraged pontiff. Yet he felt a sense of weight and reproach within his breast, as though he had sinned himself in giving ear to such words. The teachings of twenty years cried out against such licence. It was not until he had thrown himself down before one of the many wayside crosses, and had prayed from his heart both for the archer and for himself, that the dark cloud rolled back again from his spirit.

CHAPTER VIII

THE THREE FRIENDS

ALLEYNE'S companions had passed on whilst he was at his orisons; but his young blood and the fresh morning air both invited him to a scamper. His staff in one hand and his scrip in the other, with springy step and floating locks, he raced along the forest path, as active and as graceful as a young deer. He had not far to go, however, for, on turning a corner, he came on a roadside cottage with a wooden fence-work around it, where stood big John and Aylward the bowman, staring at something within. As he came up with them he saw that two little lads, the one about nine years of age and the other somewhat older, were standing on the plot in front of the cottage, each holding out a round stick in their left hands, with their arms stiff and straight from the shoulder, as silent and still as two small statues. They were pretty blue-eyed yellow-haired lads, well made and sturdy, with bronzed skins, which spoke of a woodland life.

"Here are young chips from an old bow-stave!" cried the soldier in great delight. "This is the proper way to raise children. By my hilt! I could not have trained them better had I the ordering of it myself."

"What is it, then?" asked Hordle John. "They stand very stiff, and I trust that they have not been struck so."

"Nay, they are training their left arms, that they may have a steady grasp of the bow. So my own father trained me, and six days a week I held out his walking-staff till my arm was heavy as lead. Holà, mes enfants! how long will you hold out?"

"Until the sun is over the great lime-tree, good master," the elder answered.

"What would ye be, then? Woodmen? Verderers?"

"Nay, soldiers," they cried both together.

"By the beard of my father! but ye are whelps of the true breed. Why so keen, then, to be soldiers?"

"That we may fight the Scots," they answered. "Daddy will send us to fight the Scots."

"And why the Scots, my pretty lads? We have seen French and Spanish galleys no further away than Southampton, but I doubt that it will be some time before the Scots find their way to these parts."

"Our business is with the Scots," quoth the elder, "for it was the Scots who cut off daddy's string fingers and his thumbs."

"Ay, lads, it was that," said a deep voice from behind Alleyne's shoulder. Looking round, the wayfarers saw a gaunt, big-boned man, with sunken, cheeks and a sallow face, who had come up behind them. He held up his two hands as he spoke, and showed that the thumbs and two first fingers had been torn away from each of them.

"Ma foi, camarade!" cried Aylward. "Who hath served thee in so shameful a fashion?"

"It is easy to see, friend, that you were born far from the marches of Scotland," quoth the stranger, with a bitter smile. "North of Humber there is no man who would not know the handiwork of Devil Douglas, the black Lord James."

"And how fell you into his hands?" asked John.

"I am a man of the north country, from the town of Beverley and the wapentake of Holderness," he answered. "There was a day when, from Trent to Tweed, there was no better marksman than Robin Heathcot. Yet, as you see, he hath left me, as he hath left many another poor border archer, with no grip for bill or bow. Yet the king hath given me a living here in the southlands, and please God these two lads of mine will pay off a debt that hath been owing over long. What is the price of daddy's thumbs, boys?"

"Twenty Scottish lives," they answered together.

"And for the fingers?"

"Half a score."

"When they can bend my war-bow, and bring down a squirrel at a hundred paces, I send them to take service under Johnny Copeland, the Lord of the Marches and Governor of Carlisle. By my soul, I would give the rest of my fingers to see the Douglas within arrow-flight of them."

"May you live to see it," quoth the bowman. "And hark ye, mes enfants, take an old soldier's rede and lay your bodies to the bow, drawing from hip and thigh as much as from arm. Learn also, I pray you, to shoot with a dropping shaft; for though a bowman may at times be called upon to shoot straight and fast, yet it is more often that he has to do with a town-guard behind a wall, or an arbalestier with his mantlet raised, when you cannot hope to do him scath unless your shaft fall straight upon him from the clouds. I have not drawn string for two weeks, but I may be able to show ye how such shots should be made." He loosened his long bow, slung his quiver round to the front, and then glanced keenly round for a fitting mark. There was a yellow and withered stump some way off, seen under the drooping branches of a lofty oak. The archer measured the distance with his eye; and then, drawing three shafts, he shot them off with such speed that the first had not reached the mark ere the last was on the string. Each arrow passed high over the oak; and, of the three, two struck fair into the stump; while the third, caught in some wandering puff of wind, was driven a foot or two to one side.

"Good!" cried the north countryman. "Hearken to him, lads! He is a master bowman. Your dad says amen to every word he says."

"By my hilt!" said Aylward, "if I am to preach on bowmanship, the whole day long would scarce give me time for my sermon. We have marksmen in the Company who will notch with a shaft every crevice and joint of a man-at-arm's harness, from the clasp of his bassinet to the hinge of his greave. But, with your favour, friend, I must gather my arrows again, for while a shaft costs a penny, a poor man can scarce leave them sticking in wayside stumps. We must, then, on our road again, and I hope from my heart that you may train these two young goshawks here until they are ready for a cast even at such a quarry as you speak of."

Leaving the thumbless archer and his brood, the wayfarers struck through the scattered huts of Emery Down, and out on to the broad rolling heath covered deep in ferns and in heather, where droves of the half-wild black forest pigs were rooting about amongst the hillocks. The woods about this point fall away to the left and the right, while the road curves upwards and the wind sweeps keenly over the swelling uplands. The broad strips of bracken glowed red and yellow against the black peaty soil, and a queenly doe who grazed among them turned her white front and her great questioning eyes towards the wayfarers. Alleyne gazed in admiration at the supple beauty of the creature; but the archer's fingers played with his quiver, and his eyes glistened with the fell instinct which urges a man to slaughter.

"Tête Dieu!" he growled, "were this France, or even Guienne, we should have a fresh haunch for our none-meat. Law or no law, I have a mind to loose a bolt at her."

"I would break your stave across my knee first," cried John, laying his great hand upon the bow. "What! man, I am forest born, and I know what comes of it. In our own township of Hordle two have lost their eyes and one his skin for this very thing. On my troth, I felt no great love when I first saw you, but since then I have conceived over much regard for you to wish to see the verderer's flayer at work upon you."

"It is my trade to risk my skin," growled the archer; but none the less he thrust his quiver over his hip again and turned his face for the west.

As they advanced, the path still trended upwards, running from heath into copses of holly and yew, and so back into heath again. It was joyful to hear the merry whistle of blackbirds as they darted from one clump of greenery to the other. Now and again a peaty amber-coloured stream rippled across their way, with ferny overgrown banks, where the blue kingfisher flitted busily from side to side, or the grey and pensive heron, swollen with trout and dignity, stood ankle-deep among the sedges. Chattering jays and loud wood-pigeons flapped thickly overhead, while ever and anon the meas-ured tapping of Nature's carpenter, the great green wood-pecker, sounded from each wayside grove. On either side, as the path mounted, the long sweep of country broadened and expanded, sloping down on the one side through yellow forest and brown moor to the distant smoke of Lymington and the blue misty chan-nel which lay alongside the sky-line, while to the north the woods rolled away, grove topping grove, to where in the furthest distance the white spire of Salisbury stood out hard and clear against the cloudless sky. To Alleyne, whose days had been spent in the low-lying coast-land, the eager upland air and the wide free country-side gave a sense of life and of the joy of living which made his young blood tingle in his veins. Even the heavy John was not unmoved by the beauty of their road, while the bowman whistled lustily or sang snatches of French love songs in a voice which might have scared the most stout-hearted maiden that ever hearkened to serenade.

"I have a liking for that north countryman," he remarked presently. "He hath good power of hatred. Couldst see by his cheek and eye that he is as bitter as verjuice. I warm to a man who hath some gall in his liver."

"Ah me!" sighed Alleyne. "Would it not be better if he had some love in his heart?"

"I would not say nay to that. By my hilt! I shall never be said to be a traitor to the little king. Let a man love the sex. Pasques Dieu! they are made to be loved, les petites, from wimple down to shoe-string! I am right glad, mon garçon, to see that the good monks have trained thee so wisely and so well."

"Nay, I meant not worldly love, but rather that his heart should soften towards those who have wronged him."

The archer shook his head. "A man should love those of his own breed," said he. "But it is not in nature that an English-born man should love a Scot or a Frenchman. Ma foi! you have not seen a drove of Nithsdale raiders on their Galloway nags, or you would not speak of loving them. I would as soon take Beelzebub himself to my arms. I fear, mon gar, that they have taught thee but badly at Beaulieu, for surely a bishop knows more of what is right and what is ill than an abbot can do, and I myself with these very eyes saw the Bishop of Lincoln hew into a Scottish hobeler with a battle-axe, which was a passing strange way of showing him that he loved him."

Alleyne scarce saw his way to argue in the face of so decided an opinion on the part of a high dignitary of the Church. "You have borne arms against the Scots, then?" he asked.

"Yes, I have many times taken the field against them. Ma foi! it is rough soldiering, and a good school for one who would learn to be hardy and war-wise."

"I have heard that the Scots are good men of war," said Hordle John.

"For axemen and for spearmen I have not seen their match," the archer answered. "They can travel, too, with bag of meal and gridiron slung to their sword-belt, so that it is ill to follow them. There are scant crops, and few beeves in the borderland, where a man must reap his grain with sickle in one fist and brown bill in the other. On the other hand, they are the sorriest archers I have ever seen, and cannot so much as aim with the arbalest, to say nought of the long-bow. Again, they are mostly poor folk, even the nobles among them, so that there are few who can buy as good a brigandine of chain mail as that which I am wearing, and it is ill for them to stand up against our own knights, who carry the price of five Scotch farms upon their chest and shoulders. Man for man, with equal weapons, they are as worthy and valiant men as could be found in the whole of Christendom."

"And the French?" asked Alleyne, to whom the archer's light gossip had all the relish that the words of the man of action have for the recluse.

"The French are also very worthy men. We have had great good fortune in France, and it hath led to much bobance and camp-fire talk, but I have ever noticed that those who know the most have the least to say about it. I have seen Frenchmen fight both in open field, in the intaking and the defending of towns or castlewicks, in escalados, camisades, night forays, bushments, sallies, outfalls, and knightly spear-runnings. Their knights and squires, lad, are every whit as good as ours, and I could pick out a score of those who ride behind Du Guesclin who would hold the lists with sharpened lances against the best men in the army of England. On the other hand, their common folk are so crushed down with gabelle, and poll-tax, and every manner of cursed tallage, that the spirit has passed right out of them. It is a fool's plan to teach a man to be a cur in peace, and think that he will be a lion in war. Fleece them like sheep, and sheep they will remain. If the nobles had not conquered the poor folk it is like enough that we should not have conquered the nobles."

"But they must be sorry folk to bow down to the rich in such a fashion," said big John. "I am but a poor commoner of England myself, and yet I know something of charters, liberties, franchises, usages, privileges, customs and the like. If these be broken, then all men know that it is time to buy arrow-heads."

"Ay, but the men of the law are strong in France as well as the men of war. By my hilt! I hold that a man has more to fear there from the ink-pot of the one than from the iron of the other. There is ever some cursed sheepskin in their strong boxes to prove that the rich man should be richer and the poor man poorer. It would scarce pass in England, but they are quiet folk over the water."

"And what other nations have you seen in your travels, good sir?" asked Alleyne Edricson. His young mind hungered for plain facts of life, after the long course of speculation and of mysticism on which he had been trained.

"I have seen the Low-countryman in arms, and I have nought to say against him. Heavy and slow is he by nature, and is not to be brought into battle for the sake of a lady's eye-lash or the twang of a minstrel's string, like the hotter blood of the south. But, ma foi! lay hand on his wool-bales, or trifle with his velvet of Bruges, and out buzzes every stout burgher, like bees from the tee-hole, ready to lay on as though it were his one business in life. By Our Lady! they have shown the French at Courtrai and elsewhere that they are as deft in wielding steel as in welding it."

"And the men of Spain?"

"They too are very hardy soldiers, the more so as for many hundred years they have had to fight hard against the cursed followers of the black Mahound, who have pressed upon them from the south, and still, as I understand, hold the fairer half of the country. I had a turn with them upon the sea when they came over to Winchelsea, and the good queen with her ladies sat upon the cliffs looking down at us, as if it had been joust or tourney. By my hilt! it was a sight that was worth seeing, for all that was best in England was out on the water that day. We went forth in little ships and came back in great galleys— for, of fifty tall ships of Spain, over two score flew the Cross of St George ere the sun had set. But now, youngster, I have answered you freely, and I trow it is time that you answered me. Let things be plat and plain between us. I am a man who shoots straight at his mark. You saw the things I had with me at yonder hostel; name which you will, save only the box of rose-coloured sugar which I take to the Lady Loring, and you shall have it if you will but come with me to France."

"Nay," said Alleyne, "I would gladly come with ye to France or where else ye will, just to list to your talk, and because ye are the only two friends that I have in the whole wide world outside of the cloisters; but indeed it may not be, for my duty is towards my brother, seeing that father and mother are dead, and he my elder. Besides, when ye talk of taking me to France, ye do not conceive how useless I should be to you, seeing that neither by training nor by nature am I fitted for the wars, and there seems to be nought but strife in those parts."

"That comes from my fool's talk," cried the archer, "for being a man of no learning myself, my tongue turns to blades and targets even as my hand does. Know then that for every parchment in England there are twenty in France. For every statue, cut gem, shrine, carven screen, or what else might please the eye of a learned clerk, there are a good hundred to our one. At the spoiling of Carcassonne I have seen chambers stored with writings, though not one man in our Company could read them. Again, in Aries and Nîmes, and other towns that I could name, there are the great arches and fortalices still standing which were built of old by giant men who came from the south. Can I not see by your brightened eye how you would love to look upon these things? Come then with me, and, by these ten finger-bones! there is not One of them which you shall not see."

"I should indeed love to look upon them," Alleyne answered, "but I have come from Beaulieu for a purpose and I must be true to my service, even as thou art true to thine."

"Bethink you again, mon ami," quoth Aylward, "that you might do much good yonder, since there are three hundred men in the Company, and none who has ever a word of grace for them, and yet the Virgin knows that there was never a set of men who were in more need of it. Sickerly the one duty may balance the other. Your brother hath done without you this many a year, and, as I gather, he hath never walked as far as Beaulieu to see you during all that time, so he cannot be in any great need of you."

"Besides," said John, "the Socman of Minstead is a byeword through the forest, from Bramshaw Hill to Holmesley Walk. He is a drunken, brawling, perilous churl, as you may find to your cost."

"The more reason that I should strive to mend him," quoth Alleyne. "There is no need to urge me, friends, for my own wishes would draw me to France, and it would be a joy to me if I could go with you. But indeed and indeed it cannot be, so here I take my leave of you, for yonder square tower amongst the trees upon the right must surely be the church of Minstead, and I may reach it by this path through the woods."

"Well, God be with thee, lad!" cried the archer, pressing Alleyne to his heart. "I am quick to love, and quick to hate, and 'fore God I am loth to part."

"Would it not be well," said John, "that we should wait here, and see what manner of greeting you have from your brother? You may prove to be as welcome as the king's purveyor to the village dame."

"Nay, nay," he answered, "ye roust not bide for me, for where I go I stay."

"Yet it may be as well that you should know whither we go," said the archer. "We shall now journey south through the woods until we come out upon the Christchurch road, and so onwards, hoping tonight to reach the castle of Sir William Montacute, Earl of Salisbury, of which Sir Nigel Loring is constable. There we shall bide, and it is like enough that for a month or more you may find us there, ere we are ready for our viage back to France."

It was hard indeed for Alleyne to break away from these two new but hearty friends, and so strong was the combat between his conscience and his inclinations that he dared not look round, lest his resolution should slip away from him. It was not until he was deep among the tree trunks that he cast a glance backwards, when he found that he could still see through the branches on the road above him. The archer was standing with folded arms, his bow jutting from over his shoulder, and the sun gleaming brightly upon his head-piece and the links of his chain-mail. Beside him stood his giant recruit, still clad in the home-spun and ill-fitting garments of the fuller of Lymington, with arms and legs shooting out of his scanty garb. Even as Alleyne watched them they turned upon their heels and plodded off together upon their way.

CHAPTER IX

HOW STRANGE THINGS BEFELL
IN MINSTEAD WOOD

THE path which the young clerk had now to follow lay through a magnificent forest of the very heaviest timber, where the giant boles of oak and of beech formed long aisles in every direction, shooting up their huge branches to build the majestic arches of Nature's own cathedral. Beneath lay a broad carpet of the softest and greenest moss, flecked over with fallen leaves, but yielding pleasantly to the foot of the traveller. The track which guided him was one so seldom used that in places it lost itself entirely among the grass, to reappear as a reddish rut between the distant tree trunks. It was very still here in the heart of the woodlands. The gentle rustle of the branches and the distant cooing of pigeons were the only sounds which broke in upon the silence, save that once Alleyne heard afar off a merry call upon a hunting bugle and the shrill yapping of the hounds.

It was not without some emotion that he looked upon the scene around him, for, in spite of his secluded life, he knew enough of the ancient greatness of his own family to be aware that the time had been when they had held undisputed and paramount sway over all that tract of country. His father could trace his pure Saxon lineage back to that Godfrey Malf who had held the manors of Bisterne and of Minstead at the time when the Norman first set mailed foot upon English soil. The afforestation of the district, however, and its conversion into a royal demesne

86

had clipped off a large section of his estate, while other parts had been confiscated as a punishment for his supposed complicity in an abortive Saxon rising. The fate of the ancestor had been typical of that of his descendants. During three hundred years their domains had gradually contracted, sometimes through royal or feudal encroachment, and sometimes through such gifts to the Church as that with which Alleyne's father had opened the doors of Beaulieu Abbey to his younger son. The importance of the family had thus dwindled, but they still retained the old Saxon manor-house, with a couple of farms and a grove large enough to afford pannage to a hundred pigs — "sylva de centum porcis," as the old family parchments describe it. Above all, the owner of the soil could still hold his head high as the veritable Socman of Minstead — that is, as holding the land in free socage, with no feudal superior, and answerable to no man lower than the king. Knowing this, Alleyne felt some little glow of worldly pride as he looked for the first time upon the land with which so many generations of his ancestors had been associated. He pushed on the quicker, twirling his staff merrily, and looking out at every turn of the path for some sign of the old Saxon residence. He was suddenly arrested, however, by the appearance of a wild-looking fellow armed with a club, who sprang out from behind a tree and barred his passage. He was a rough, powerful peasant, with cap and tunic of untanned sheepskin, leather breeches, and galligaskins round legs and feet.

"Stand!" he shouted, raising his heavy cudgel to enforce the order. "Who are you who walk so freely through the wood? Whither would you go, and what is your errand?"

"Why should I answer your questions, my friend?" said Alleyne, standing on his guard.

"Because your tongue may save your pate. But where have I looked upon your face before?"

"No longer ago than last night at the 'Pied Merlin'," the clerk answered, recognizing the escaped serf who had been so outspoken as to his wrongs.

"By the Virgin! yes. You were the little clerk who sat so mum in the corner, and then cried fy on the gleeman. What hast in the scrip?"

"Nought of any price."

"How can I tell that, clerk? Let me see."

"Not I."

"Fool! I could pull you limb from limb like a pullet. What would you have? Hast forgot that we are alone, far from all men? How can your clerkship help you? Wouldst lose scrip and life too?"

"I will part with neither without a fight."

"A fight, quotha? A fight betwixt spurred cock and new-hatched chicken! Thy fighting days may soon be over."

"Hadst asked me in the name of charity I would have given freely," cried Alleyne. "As it stands, not one farthing shall you have with my free will, and when I see my brother, the Socman of Minstead, he will raise hue and cry from vill to vill, from hundred to hundred, until you are taken as a common robber and a scourge to the country."

The outlaw sank his club. "The Socman's brother!" he gasped. "Now by the keys of Peter! I had rather that hand withered and tongue was palsied ere I had struck or miscalled you. If you are the Socman's brother you are one of the right side, I warrant, for all your clerkly dress."

"His brother I am," replied Alleyne. "But even if I were not, is that reason why you should molest me on the king's ground?"

"I give not the pip of an apple for king or for noble," cried the serf passionately. "Ill have I had from them, and ill I shall repay them. I am a good friend to my friends, and, by the Virgin! an evil foeman to my foes."

"And therefore the worst of foemen to thyself," said Alleyne. "But I pray you since you seem to know him, to point out to me the shortest path to my brother's house."

The serf was about to reply, when the clear ringing call of a bugle burst from the wood close behind them, and Alleyne caught sight for an instant of the dun side and white breast of a lordly stag glancing swiftly betwixt the distant tree trunks. A minute later came the shaggy deerhounds, a dozen or fourteen of them, running on a hot scent, with nose to earth and tail in air. As they streamed past the silent forest around broke suddenly into loud life, with galloping of hoofs, crackling of brushwood, and the short sharp cries of the hunters. Close behind the pack rode a fourrier and a yeoman-pricker, whooping on the laggards and encouraging the leaders, in the shrill half-French jargon which was the language of venery and woodcraft. Alleyne was still gazing after them, listening to the loud "Hyke-a-Bayard! Hyke-a-Pomers! Hyke-a-Lebryt!" with which they called upon their favourite hounds, when a group of horsemen crashed out through the underwood at the very spot where the serf and he were standing.

The one who led was a man between fifty and sixty years of age, war-worn and weather-beaten, with a broad thoughtful forehead and eyes which shone brightly from under his fierce and overhung brows. His beard, streaked thickly with grey, bristled forward from his chin, and spoke of a passionate nature, while the long finely-cut face and firm mouth marked the leader of men. His figure was erect and soldierly, and he rode his horse with the careless grace of a man whose life had been spent in the saddle. In common garb, his masterful face and flashing eye would have marked him as one who was born to rule; but now, with his silken tunic powdered with golden fleurs-de-lys, his velvet mantle lined with the royal minever, and the lions of England stamped in silver upon his harness, none could fail to recognize the noble Edward, most warlike and powerful of all the long line of fighting monarchs who had ruled the Anglo-Norman race. Alleyne doffed his hat and bowed head at the sight of him, but the serf folded his hands and leaned them upon his cudgel, looking with little love at the knot of nobles and knights-in-waiting who rode behind the king.

"Ha!" cried Edward, reining up for an instant his powerful black steed, "Le cerf est passé? Non? Ici Brocas; tu parles Anglais."

"The deer, clowns?" said a hard-visaged, swarthy-faced man, who rode at the king's elbow. "If ye have headed it back, it is as much as your ears are worth."

SIR ARTHUR CONAN DOYLE

"It passed by the blighted beech there," said Alleyne, pointing, "and the hounds were hard at its heels."

"It is well," cried Edward, still speaking in French; for though he could understand English, he had never learned to express himself in so barbarous and unpolished a tongue. "By my faith, sirs," he continued, half turning in his saddle to address his escort, "unless my woodcraft is sadly at fault, it is a stag of six tines and the finest that we have roused this journey. A golden St Hubert to the man who is the first to sound the mort." He shook his bridle as he spoke, and thundered away, his knights lying low upon their horses and galloping as hard as whip and spur would drive them, in the hope of winning the king's prize. Away they drove down the long green glade—bay horses, black and grey, riders clad in every shade of velvet, fur, or silk, with glint of brazen horn and flash of knife and spear. One only lingered, the black-browed Baron Brocas, who, making a gambade which brought him within arms' sweep of the serf, slashed him across the face with his riding-whip. "Doff, dog, doff," he hissed, "when a monarch deigns to lower his eyes to such as you!"—then spurred through the underwood and was gone, with a gleam of steel shoes and flutter of dead leaves.

The villein took the cruel blow without wince or cry, as one to whom stripes are a birthright and an inheritance. His eyes flashed, however, and he shook his bony hand with a fierce wild gesture after the retreating figure.

"Black hound of Gascony," he muttered, "evil the day that you and those like you set foot in free England! I know thy kennel of Rochecourt. The night will come when I may do to thee and thine what you and yours have wrought upon mine and me. May God smite me if I fail to smite thee, thou French robber, with thy wife and thy child, and all that is under thy castle roof!"

"Forbear!" cried Alleyne. "Mix not God's name with these unhallowed threats! And yet it was a coward's blow, and one to stir the blood and loose the tongue of the most peaceful. Let me find some soothing simples and lay them on the weal to draw the sting."

"Nay, there is but one thing that can draw the sting, and that the future may bring to me. But, clerk, if you would see your brother you must go on, for there is a meeting today, and his merry men will await him ere the shadows turn from west to east. I pray you not to hold him back, for it would be an evil thing if all the stout lads were there and the leader a-missing. I would come with you, but sooth to say I am stationed here and may not move. The path over yonder, betwixt the oak and the thorn, should bring you out into his netherfield."

Alleyne lost no time in following the directions of the wild, masterless man, whom he left among the trees where he had found him. His heart was the heavier for the encounter, not only because all bitterness and wrath were abhorrent to his gentle nature, but also because it disturbed him to hear his brother spoken of as though he were a chief of outlaws or the leader of a party against the State. Indeed, of all the things which he had seen yet in the world to surprise him, there was none more strange than the hate which class appeared to bear to class. The talk of labourer, woodman, and villein in the inn had all pointed to the widespread mutiny, and now his brother's name was spoken as though he were the very centre of the universal discontent. In good truth, the commons throughout the length and breadth of the land were heart-weary of this fine game of chivalry which had been played so long at their expense. So long as knight and baron were a strength and a guard to the kingdom they might be endured; but now, when all men knew that the great battles in France had been won by English yeomen and Welsh stabbers, warlike fame, the only fame to which his class had ever aspired, appeared to have deserted the plateclad horseman. The sports of the lists had done much in days gone by to impress the minds of the people, but the plumed and unwieldy champion was no longer an object either of fear or reverence to men whose fathers and brothers had shot into the press at Crécy, or Poictiers, and seen the proudest chivalry in the world unable to make head against the weapons of disciplined peasants. Power had changed hands. The protector had become

the protected, and the whole fabric of the feudal system was tot-
tering to a fall. Hence the fierce mutterings of the lower classes
and the constant discontent, breaking out into local tumult and
outrage and culminating some years later in the great rising of
Tyler. What Alleyne saw and wondered at in Hampshire would
have appealed equally to the traveller in any other English county
from the Channel to the marches of Scotland.

He was following the track, his misgivings increasing with every
step which took him nearer to that home which he had never
seen, when of a sudden the trees began to thin and the sward to
spread out into a broad green lawn, where five cows lay in the sunshine and droves of black swine wandered unchecked. A brown
forest stream swirled down the centre of this clearing, with a rude
bridge flung across it, and on the other side was a second field
sloping up to a long, low-lying wooden house, with thatched roof
and open squares for windows. Alleyne gazed across at it with
flushed cheeks and sparkling eyes—for this, he knew, must be the
home of his fathers. A wreath of blue smoke floated up through a
hole in the thatch, and was the only sign of life in the place, save a
great black hound which lay sleeping chained to the doorpost. In
the yellow shimmer of the autumn sunshine it lay as peacefully
and as still as he had oft pictured it to himself in his dreams.

He was roused, however, from his pleasant reverie by the sound
of voices, and two people emerged from the forest some little way
to his right and moved across the field in the direction of the
bridge. The one was a man with yellow flowing beard and very long
hair of the same tint drooping over his shoulders; his dress of good
Norwich cloth and his assured bearing marked him as a man of
position, while the sombre hue of his clothes and the absence of all
ornament contrasted with the flash and glitter which had marked
the king's retinue. By his side walked a woman, tall and slight and
dark, with lithe graceful figure and clear-cut composed features.
Her jet-black hair was gathered back under a light pink coif, her
head poised proudly upon her neck, and her step long and springy,
like that of some wild tireless woodland creature. She held her left

hand in front of her, covered with a red velvet glove, and on the wrist a little brown falcon, very fluffy and bedraggled, which she smoothed and fondled as she walked. As she came out into the sunshine, Alleyne noticed that her light gown, slashed with pink, was all stained with earth and with moss upon one side from shoulder to hem. He stood in the shadow of an oak staring at her with parted lips, for this woman seemed to him to be the most beautiful and graceful creature that mind could conceive of. Such had he imagined the angels, and such he had tried to paint them in the Beaulieu missals; but here was something human, were it only in the battered hawk and discoloured dress, which sent a tingle and thrill through his nerves such as no dream of radiant and stainless spirit had ever yet been able to conjure up. Good, quiet, uncomplaining mother Nature, long slighted and miscalled, still bides her time and draws to her bosom the most errant of her children.

The two walked swiftly across the meadow to the narrow bridge, he in front and she a pace or two behind. There they paused, and stood for a few minutes face to face talking earnestly. Alleyne had read and had heard of love and of lovers. Such were these, doubtless — this golden-bearded man and the fair damsel with the cold proud face. Why else should they wander together in the woods, or be so lost in talk by rustic streams? And yet as he watched, uncertain whether to advance from the cover or to choose some other path to the house, he soon came to doubt the truth of this first conjecture. The man stood, tall and square, blocking the entrance to the bridge, and throwing out his hands as he spoke in a wild eager fashion, while the deep tones of his stormy voice rose at times into accents of menace and of anger. She stood fearlessly in front of him, still stroking her bird; but twice she threw a swift questioning glance over her shoulder, as one who is in search of aid. So moved was the young clerk by these mute appeals, that he came forth from the trees and crossed the meadow, uncertain what to do, and yet loth to hold back from one who might need his aid. So intent were they upon each other that neither took note of his approach; until, when he was close upon them, the man threw his arm roughly round the damsel's waist and drew her towards him, she straining her lithe supple figure away and striking fiercely at him, while the hooded hawk screamed with ruffled wings and pecked blindly in its mistress's defence. Bird and maid, however, had but little chance against their assailant, who, laughing loudly, caught her wrists in one hand while he drew her towards him with the other.

"The best rose has ever the longest thorns," said he. "Quiet, little one, or you may do yourself a hurt. Must pay Saxon toll on Saxon land, my proud Maude, for all your airs and graces."

"You boor!" she hissed. "You base underbred clod! Is this your care and your hospitality? I would rather wed a branded serf from my father's fields. Leave go, I say—Ah, good youth, Heaven has sent you. Make him loose me! By the honour of your mother, I pray you to stand by me and to make this knave loose me."

"Stand by you I will, and that blithely," said Alleyne. "Surely, sir, you should take shame to hold the damsel against her will."

The man turned a face upon him which was lion-like in its strength and in its wrath. With his tangle of golden hair, his fierce blue eyes, and his large, well-marked features, he was the most comely man whom Alleyne had ever seen; and yet there was something so sinister and so fell in his expression that child or beast might well have shrunk from him. His brows were drawn, his cheek flushed, and there was a mad sparkle in his eyes which spoke of a wild untamable nature.

"Young fool!" he cried, holding the woman still to his side, though every line of her shrinking figure spoke her abhorrence. "Do you keep your spoon in your own broth. I rede you to go on your way, lest worse befall you. This little wench has come with me, and with me she shall bide."

"Liar!" cried the woman; and, stooping her head, she suddenly bit fiercely into the broad brown hand which held her. He whipped it back with an oath, while she tore herself free and slipped behind Alleyne, cowering up against him like the trembling leveret who sees the falcon poising for the swoop above him.

"Stand off my land!" the man said fiercely, heedless of the blood which trickled freely from his fingers. "What have you to do here? By your dress you should be one of those cursed clerks who overrun the land like vile rats, poking and prying into other men's concerns, too caitiff to fight and too lazy to work. By the rood! if I had my will upon ye, I should nail you upon the abbey doors, as they hang vermin before their holes. Art neither man nor woman, young shaveling. Get thee back to thy fellows ere I lay hands upon you: for your foot is on my land, and I may slay you as a common drawlatch."

"Is this your land, then?" gasped Alleyne.

"Would you dispute it, dog? Would you wish by trick or quibble to juggle me out of these last acres? Know, baseborn knave, that you have dared this day to stand in the path of one whose race have been the advisers of kings and the leaders of hosts, ere ever this vile crew of Norman robbers came into the land, or such half-blood hounds as you were let loose to preach that the thief should have his booty and the honest man should sin if he strove to win back his own."

"You are the Socman of Minstead!"

"That am I; and the son of Edric the Socman, of the pure blood of Godfrey the thane, by the only daughter of the house of Aluric, whose forefathers held the white-horse banner at the fatal fight where our shield was broken and our sword shivered. I tell you, clerk, that my folk held this land from Bramshaw Wood to the Ringwood road; and by the soul of my father! it will be a strange thing if I am to be bearded upon the little that is left of it. Begone, I say, and meddle not with my affair."

"If you leave me now," whispered the woman, "then shame for ever upon your manhood."

"Surely, sir," said Alleyne, speaking in as persuasive and soothing a way as he could, "if your birth is gentle, there is more reason that your manners should be gentle too. I am well persuaded that you did but jest with this lady, and that you will now permit her to leave your land either alone or with me as a guide, if she should need one, through the wood. As to birth, it does not become me to boast, and there is sooth in what you say as to the unworthiness of clerks, but it is none the less true that I am as well born as you!"

"Dog!" cried the furious Socman, "there is no man in the south who can say as much."

"Yet can I," said Alleyne, smiling, "for indeed I also am the son of Edric the Socman, of the pure blood of Godfrey the thane, by the only daughter of Aluric of Brockenhurst. Surely, dear brother," he continued, holding out his hand, "you have a warmer greeting than this for me. There are but two boughs left upon this old Saxon trunk."

His elder brother dashed his hand aside with an oath, while an expression of malignant hatred passed over his passion-drawn features. "You are the young cub of Beaulieu, then?" said he. "I might have known it by the sleek face and the slavish manner, too monk-ridden and craven in spirit to answer back a rough word. Thy father, shaveling, with all his faults, had a man's heart; and there were few who could look him in the eyes on the day of his anger. But you! Look there, rat, oh yonder field where the cows graze, and on the other beyond, and on the orchard hard by the church. Do you know that all these were squeezed out of your dying father by greedy priests, to pay for your upbringing in the cloisters! I, the Socman, am shorn of my lands that you may snivel Latin and eat bread for which you never yet did hand's turn. You rob me first, and now you would come preaching and whining, in search may-hap of another field or two for your priestly friends. Knave! my dogs shall be set upon you; but, meanwhile, stand out of my path, and stop me at your peril!" As he spoke he rushed forward, and throwing the lad to one side, caught the woman's wrist; Alleyne, however, as active as a young deer-hound, sprang to her aid and seized her by the other arm, raising his iron-shod staff as he did so.

"You may say what you will to me," he said between his clenched teeth — "it may be no better than I deserve; but, brother or no, I swear by my hopes of salvation that I will break your arm if you do not leave hold of the maid."

There was a ring in his voice and a flash in his eyes which promised that the blow would follow quick at the heels of the word. For a moment the blood of the long line of hot-headed thanes was too strong for the soft whisperings of the doctrine of meekness and mercy. He was conscious of a fierce wild thrill through his nerves and a throb of mad gladness at his heart, as his real human self burst for an instant the bonds of custom and of teaching which had held it so long. The Socman sprang back, looking to left and to right for some stick or stone which might serve him for a weapon; but, finding none, he turned and ran at the top of his speed for the house, blowing the while upon a shrill whistle.

"Come!" gasped the woman. "Fly, friend, ere he come back."

"Nay, let him come!" cried Alleyne. "I shall not budge a foot for him or his dogs."

"Come, come!" she cried, tugging at his arm. "I know the man: he will kill you. Come, for the Virgin's sake, or for my sake, for I cannot go and leave you here."

"Come, then," said he; and they ran together to the cover of the woods. As they gained the edge of the brushwood, Alleyne, looking back, saw his brother come running out of the house again, with the sun gleaming upon his hair and his beard. He held something which flashed in his right hand, and he stooped at the threshold to unloose the black hound.

"This way!" the woman whispered in a low eager voice. "Through the bushes to that forked ash. Do not heed me: I can run as fast as you, I trow. Now into the stream—right in, over ankles, to throw the dog off, though I think it is but a common cur, like its master." As she spoke, she sprang herself into the shallow stream and ran swiftly up the centre of it, with the brown water bubbling over her feet, and her hand outstretched to ward off the clinging branches of bramble or sapling. Alleyne followed close at her heels, with his mind in a whirl at this black welcome and sudden shifting of all his plans and hopes. Yet, grave as were his thoughts, they would still turn to wonder as he looked at the twinkling feet of his guide and saw her lithe figure bend this way and that, dipping under boughs, springing over stones with a lightness and ease which made it no small task for him to keep up with her. At last, when he was almost out of breath, she suddenly threw herself down upon a mossy bank, between two hollybushes, and looked ruefully down at her own dripping feet and bedraggled skin.

"Holy Mary!" said she, "what shall I do? Mother will keep me to my chamber for a month, and make me work at the tapestry of the nine bold knights. She promised as much last week, when I fell into Wilverley bog, and yet she knows that I cannot abide needlework!"

Alleyne, still standing in the stream, glanced down at the graceful pink-and-white figure, the curve of raven-black hair, and the proud, sensitive face, which looked up frankly and confidingly at his own.

"We had best on," he said. "He may yet overtake us."

"Not so. We are well off his land now, nor can he tell in this great wood which way we have taken. But you—you had him at your mercy. Why did you not kill him?"

"Kill him! My brother!"

"And why not?"—with a quick gleam of her white teeth. "He would have killed you. I know him, and I read it in his eyes. Had I had your staff I would have tried—ay, and done it, too." She shook her clenched white hand as she spoke, and her lips tightened ominously.

"I am already sad in heart for what I have done," said he, sitting down on the bank, and sinking his face into his hands, "God help me!—all that is worst in me seemed to come uppermost. Another instant, and I had smitten him; the son of my own mother, the man whom I have longed to take to my heart. Alas! that I should still be so weak!"

"Weak!" she exclaimed, raising her black eyebrows. "I do not think that even my father himself, who is a hard judge of manhood, would call you that. But it is, as you may think, sir, a very pleasant thing for me to hear that you are grieved at what you have done, and I can but rede that we should go back together, and you should make your peace with the Socman by handing back your prisoner. It is a sad thing that so small a thing as a woman should come between two who are of one blood."

Simple Alleyne opened his eyes at this little spurt of feminine bitterness. "Nay, lady," said he, "that were worst of all. What man would be so caitiff and thrall as to fail you at your need? I have turned my brother against me, and now, alas! I appear to have given you offence also with my clumsy tongue. But indeed, lady, I am torn both ways, and can scarce grasp in my mind what it is that has befallen."

"Nor can I marvel at that," said she, with a little tinkling laugh. "You came in as the knight does in the jongleur's romances, between dragon and damsel, with small time for the asking of questions. Come," she went on, springing to her feet, and smoothing down her rumpled frock, "let us walk through the shaw together, and we may come upon Bertrand with the horses. If poor Troubadour had not cast a shoe, we should not have had this trouble. Nay, I must have your arm: for, though I speak lightly, now that all is happily over I am as frightened as my brave Roland. See how his chest heaves, and his dear feathers all awry—the little knight who could not have his lady mishandled." So she prattled on to her hawk, while Alleyne walked by her side, stealing a glance from time to time at this queenly and wayward woman. In silence they wandered together over the velvet turf and on through the broad Minstead woods, where the old lichen-draped beeches threw their circles of black shadow upon the sunlit sward.

"You have no wish, then, to hear my story?" said she, at last.

"If it pleases you to tell it me," he answered.

"Oh!" she cried, tossing her head, "if it is of so little interest to you, we had best let it bide."

"Nay," said he eagerly, "I would fain hear it."

"You have a right to know it, if you have lost a brother's favour through it. And yet—Ah, well, you are, as I understand, a clerk, so I must think of you as one step further in orders, and make you my father-confessor. Know then that this man has been a suitor for my hand, less as I think for my own sweet sake than because he hath ambition, and had it on his mind that he might improve his fortunes by dipping into my father's strong-box—though the Virgin knows that he would have found little enough therein. My father, however, is a proud man, a gallant knight and tried soldier of the oldest blood to whom this man's churlish birth and low descent—Oh, lackaday! I had forgot that he was of the same strain as yourself."

"Nay, trouble not for that," said Alleyne, "we are all from good mother Eve."

"Streams may spring from one source, and yet some be clear and some be foul," quoth she quickly. "But, to be brief over the matter, my father would have none of his wooing, nor in sooth would I. On that he swore a vow against us, and as he is known to be a perilous man, with many outlaws and others at his back, my father forbade that I should hawk or hunt in any part of the wood to the north of the Christchurch road. As it chanced, how-ever, this morning my little Roland here was loosed at a strong-winged heron, and page Bertrand and I rode on, with no thoughts but for the sport, until we found ourselves in Minstead woods. Small harm then, but that my horse Troubadour trod with a tender foot upon a sharp stick, rearing and throwing me to the ground. See to my gown, the third that I have befouled within the week. Woe worth me when Agatha the tirewoman sets eyes upon it."

"And what then, lady?" asked Alleyne.

"Why, then away ran Troubadour, for belike I spurred him in falling, and Bertrand rode after him as hard as hoofs could bear him. When I rose there was the Socman himself by my side, with the news that I was on his land, but with so many courteous words besides, and such gallant bearing, that he prevailed upon me to come to his house for shelter, there to wait until the page return. By the grace of the Virgin and the help of my patron St Magdalen, I stopped short ere I reached his door, though, as you saw, he strove to hale me up to it. And then—ah-h-h-h!"—she shivered and chattered like one in an ague-fit.

"What is it?" cried Alleyne, looking about in alarm.

"Nothing, friend, nothing! I was but thinking how I bit into his hand. Sooner would I bite living toad or poisoned snake. Oh, I shall loathe my lips for ever! But you—how brave you were, and how quick! How meek for yourself, and how bold for a stranger! If I were a man, I should wish to do what you have done."

"It was a small thing," he answered, with a tingle of pleasure at these sweet words of praise. "But you—what will you do?"

"There is a great oak near here, and I think that Bertrand will bring the horses there, for it is an old hunting-tryst of ours. Then hey for home, and no more hawking today! A twelve-mile gallop will dry feet and skirt."

"But your father?"

"Not one word shall I tell him. You do not know him; but I can tell you he is not a man to disobey as I have disobeyed him. He would avenge me, it is true, but it is not to him that I shall look for vengeance. Some day, perchance, in joust or in tourney, knight may wish to wear my colours, and then I shall tell him that if he does indeed crave my favour there is wrong unredressed, and the wronger the Socman of Minstead. So my knight shall find a venture such as bold knights love, and my debt shall be paid, and my father none the wiser, and one rogue the less in the world. Say, is not that a brave plan?"

"Nay, lady, it is a thought which is unworthy of you. How can such as you speak of violence and of vengeance? Are none to be gentle and kind, none to be piteous and forgiving? Alas! it is a hard, cruel world, and I would that I had never left my abbey cell. To hear such words from your lips is as though I heard an angel of grace preaching the devil's own creed."

She started from him as a young colt who first feels the bit. "Gramercy for your rede, young sir!" she said with a little curtsey. "As I understand your words, you are grieved that you ever met me, and look upon me as a preaching devil. Why, my father is a bitter man when he is wroth, but hath never called me such a name as that. It may be his right and duty, but certes it is none of thine. So it would be best, since you think so lowly of me, that you should take this path to the left while I keep on upon this one; for it is clear that I can be no fit companion for you." So saying, with downcast lids and a dignity which was somewhat marred by her bedraggled skirt, she swept off down the ruddy track, leaving Alleyne standing staring ruefully after her. He waited in vain for some backward glance or sign of relenting, but she walked on with a rigid neck until her dress was only a white flutter among the leaves. Then, with a sunken head and a heavy heart, he plodded wearily down the other path, wroth with himself for the rude and uncouth tongue which had given offence where so little was intended.

He had gone some way, lost in doubt and in self-reproach, his mind all tremulous with a thousand new-found thoughts and fears and wonderments, when of a sudden there was a light rustle of the leaves behind him, and, glancing round, there was this graceful, swift-footed creature, treading in his very shadow, with her proud head bowed, even as his was — the picture of humility and repentance.

"I shall not vex you, nor even speak," she said, "but I would fain keep with you while we are in the wood."

"Nay, you cannot vex me," he answered, all warm again at the very sight of her. "It was my rough words which vexed you; but I have been thrown among men all my life, and indeed, with all the will, I scarce know how to temper my speech to a lady's ear."

"Then unsay it," cried she quickly, "say that I was right to wish to have vengeance on the Socman."

"Nay, I cannot do that," he answered gravely.

"Then who is ungentle and unkind now?" she cried in triumph. "How stern and cold you are for one so young! Art surely no mere clerk, but bishop or cardinal at the least. Shouldst have crozier for staff and mitre for cap. Well, well, for your sake I will forgive the Socman and take vengeance on none but on my own wilful self who must needs run into danger's path. So will that please you, sir?"

"There spoke your true self," said he, "and you will find more pleasure in such forgiveness than in any vengeance."

She shook her head, as if by no means assured of it, and then with a sudden little cry, which had more of surprise than of joy in it, "Here is Bertrand with the horses!"

Down the glade there came a little green-clad page with laughing eyes, and long curls floating behind him. He sat perched on a high bay horse, and held on to the bridle of a spirited black palfrey, the hides of both glistening from a long run.

"I have sought you everywhere, dear Lady Maude," said he in a piping voice, springing down from his horse and holding the stirrup. "Troubadour galloped as far as Holmhill ere I could catch him. I trust that you had no hurt or scath?" He shot a questioning glance at Alleyne as he spoke.

"No, Bertrand," said she, "thanks to this courteous stranger. And now, sir," she continued, springing into her saddle, "it is not fit that I leave you without a word more. Clerk or no, you have acted this day as becomes a true knight. King Arthur and all his table could not have done more. It may be that, as some small return, my father or his kin may have power to advance your interest. He is not rich, but he is honoured and hath great friends. Tell me what is your purpose, and see if he may not aid it."

"Alas! lady, I have now no purpose. I have but two friends in the world, and they have gone to Christchurch, where it is likely I shall join them."

"And where in Christchurch?"

"At the castle which is held by the brave knight, Sir Nigel Loring, constable to the Earl of Salisbury."

To his surprise she burst out a-laughing, and, spurring her palfrey, dashed off down the glade, with her page riding behind her. Not one word did she say, but as she vanished amid the trees she half turned in her saddle and waved a last greeting. Long time he stood, half hoping that she might again come back to him; but the thud of the hoofs had died away, and there was no sound in all the woods but the gentle rustle and dropping of the leaves. At last he turned away and made his way back to the high road—another person from the light-hearted boy who had left it a short three hours before.

CHAPTER X

HOW HORDLE JOHN FOUND A MAN
WHOM HE MIGHT FOLLOW

IF he might not return to Beaulieu within the year, and if his brother's dogs were to be set upon him if he showed face upon Minstead land, then indeed he was adrift upon earth. North, south, east and west—he might turn where he would, but all was equally chill and cheerless. The Abbot had rolled ten silver crowns in a lettuce-leaf and hid them away in the bottom of his scrip, but that would be a sorry support for twelve long months. In all the darkness there was but the one bright spot of the sturdy comrades whom he had left that morning; if he could find them again all would be well. The afternoon was not very advanced, for all that had befallen him. When a man is afoot at cockcrow much may be done in the day. If he walked fast he might yet overtake his friends ere they reached their destination. He pushed on, therefore, now walking and now running. As he journeyed he bit into a crust which remained from his Beaulieu bread, and he washed it down with a draught from a woodland stream.

It was no easy or light thing to journey through this great forest, which was some twenty miles from east to west and a good sixteen from Bramshaw Woods in the north to Lymington in the south. Alleyne, however, had the good fortune to fall in with a woodman, axe upon shoulder, trudging along in the very direction that he wished to go. With his guidance he passed the fringe of Bolderwood Walk, famous for old ash and yew, through Mark

Ash, with its giant beech-trees, and on through the Knightwood groves, where the giant oak was already a great tree, but only one of many comely brothers. They plodded along together, the woodman and Alleyne, with little talk on either side, for their thoughts were as far asunder as the poles. The peasant's gossip had been of the hunt, of the bracken, of the grey-headed kites that had nested in Wood Fidley, and of the great catch of herring brought back by the boats of Pitt's Deep. The clerk's mind was on his brother, on his future — above all, on this strange, fierce, melting, beautiful woman who had broken so suddenly into his life, and as suddenly had passed out of it again. So *distrait* was he, and so random his answers, that the woodman took to whistling, and soon branched off upon the track to Burley, leaving Alleyne upon the main Christchurch road.

Down this he pushed as fast as he might, hoping at every turn and rise to catch sight of his companions of the morning. From Vinney Ridge to Rhinefield Walk the woods grow thick and dense up to the very edges of the track, but beyond the country opens up into broad dun-coloured moors, flecked with clumps of trees, and topping each other in long low curves up to the dark lines of forest in the furthest distance. Clouds of insects danced and buzzed in the golden autumn light, and the air was full of the piping of the song-birds. Long glinting dragon-flies shot across the path, or hung tremulous with gauzy wings and gleaming bodies. Once a white-necked sea eagle soared screaming high over the traveller's head, and again a flock of brown bustards popped up from among the bracken, and blundered away in their clumsy fashion, half running, half flying, with strident cry and whirr of wings.

There were folk, too, to be met upon the road — beggars and couriers, chapmen and tinkers — cheery fellows for the most part, with a rough jest and homely greeting for each other and for Alleyne. Near Shotwood he came upon five seamen, on their way from Poole to Southampton — rude red-faced men, who shouted at him in a jargon which he could scarce understand, and held out to him a great pot from which they had been drinking — nor would they let him pass until he had dipped pannikin in and taken a mouthful which set him coughing and choking, with the tears running down his cheeks. Further on he met a sturdy black-bearded man, mounted on a brown horse, with a rosary in his right hand and a long two-handed sword jangling against his stirrup-iron. By his black robe and the eight-pointed cross upon his sleeve, Alleyne recognized him as one of the Knights Hospipi-tallers of St John of Jerusalem, whose presbytery was at Baddesley. He held up two fingers as he passed, with a *"Benedic, fili mi!"* whereat Alleyne doffed hat and bent knee, looking with much reverence at one who had devoted his life to the overthrow of the infidel. Poor simple lad! he had not learned yet that what men are and what men profess to be are very wide asunder, and that the Knights of St John, having come into large part of the riches of the ill-fated Templars, were very much too comfortable to think of exchanging their palace for a tent, or the cellars of England for the thirsty deserts of Syria. Yet ignorance may be more precious than wisdom, for Alleyne as he walked on braced himself to a higher life by the thought of this other's sacrifice, and strengthened himself by his example, which he could scarce have done had he known that the Hospitaller's mind ran more upon malmsey than on Mamelukes, and on venison rather than victories.

As he pressed on the plain turned to woods once more in the region of Wilverley Walk, and a cloud swept up from the south with the sun shining through the chinks of it. A few great drops came pattering loudly down, and then in a moment the steady swish of a brisk shower, with the dripping and dropping of the leaves. Alleyne, glancing round for shelter, saw a thick and lofty holly-bush, so hollowed out beneath that no house could have been drier. Under this canopy of green two men were already squatted, who waved their hands to Alleyne that he should join them. As he approached he saw that they had five dried herrings laid out in front of them, with a great hunch of wheaten bread and a leathern flask full of milk, but instead of setting to at their food, they appeared to have forgotten all about it, and were disputing together with flushed faces and angry gestures. It was easy to see by their dress and manner that they were two of those wandering students who formed about this time so enormous a multitude in every country in Europe. The one was long and thin, with melancholy features, while the other was fat and sleek, with a loud voice and the air of a man who is not to be gainsaid.

"Come hither, good youth," he cried, "come hither. *Vultus ingenui puer.* Heed not the face of my good coz here. *Fænum habet in cornu,* as Dan Horace has it; but I warrant him harmless for all that."

"Stint your bull's bellowing!" exclaimed the other. "If it come to Horace, I have a line in my mind: *Loquaces si sapiat*—How doth it run? The English o't being that a man of sense should ever avoid a great talker. That being so, if all were men of sense, then thou wouldst be a lonesome man, coz."

"Alas! Dicon, I fear that your logic is as bad as your philosophy or your divinity—and God wot it would be hard to say a worse word than that for it. For, hark ye: granting, *propter argumentum,* that I am a talker, then the true reasoning runs that since all men of sense should avoid me, and thou hast not avoided me, but art at the present moment eating herrings with me under a hollybush, ergo you are no man of sense, which is exactly what I have been dinning into your long ears ever since I first clapped eyes on your sunken chops."

"Tut, tut!" cried the other. "Your tongue goes like the clapper of a mill-wheel. Sit down here, friend, and partake of this herring. Understand, first, however, that there are certain conditions attached to it."

"I had hoped," said Alleyne, falling into the humour of the twain, "that a tranchoir of bread and a draught of milk might be attached to it."

"Hark to him, hark to him!" cried the little fat man. "It is ever thus, Dicon! Wit, lad, is a catching thing, like the itch or the sweating sickness. I exude it around me; it is an aura. I tell you, coz, that no man can come within seventeen feet of me without catching a spark. Look at your own case. A duller man never stepped, and yet within the week you have said three things which might pass, and one thing the day we left Fordingbridge which I should hot have been ashamed of myself."

"Enough, rattlepate, enough!" said the other. "The milk you shall have and the bread also, friend, together with the herring, but you must hold the scales between us."

"If he holds the herring he holds the scales, my sapient brother," cried the fat man. "But I pray you, good youth, to tell us whether you are a learned clerk, and, if so, whether you have studied at Oxenford or at Paris."

"I have some small stock of learning," Alleyne answered, picking at his herring, "but I have been at neither of these places. I was bred amongst the Cistercian monks at Beaulieu Abbey."

"Pooh, pooh!" they cried both together. "What sort of an upbringing is that?"

"Non cuivis contingit adire Corinthum," quoth Alleyne.

"Come, brother Stephen, he hath some tincture of letters," said the melancholy man more hopefully. "He may be the better judge, since he hath no call to side with either of us. Now, attention, friend, and let your ears work as well as your nether jaw. *Judex damnatur*—you know the old saw. Here am I upholding the good fame of the learned Duns Scotus against the foolish quibblings and poor silly reasonings of Willie Ockham."

"While I," quoth the other loudly, "do maintain the good sense and extraordinary wisdom of that most learned William against the crack-brained fantasies of the muddy Scotchman, who hath hid such little wit as he has under so vast a pile of words, that it is like one drop of Gascony in a firkin of ditch-water. Solomon in his wisdom would not suffice to say what the rogue means."

"Certes, Stephen Hapgood, his wisdom doth not suffice," cried the other. "It is as though a mole cried out against the morning star, because he could not see it. But our dispute, friend, is concerning the nature of that subtle essence which we call thought. For I hold with the learned Scotus that thought is in very truth a thing, even as vapour or fumes, or many other substances which our gross bodily eyes are blind to. For, look you, that which produces a thing must be itself a thing, and if a man's thought may produce a written book, then must thought itself be a material thing, even as the book is. Have I expressed it? Do I make it plain?"

"Whereas I hold," shouted the, other, "with my revered preceptor, *doctor præclarus et excellentissimus,* that all things are but thought; for when thought is gone I prythee where are the things then? Here are trees about us, and I see them because I think I see them; but if I have swooned, or sleep, or am in wine, then my thought having gone forth from me, lo the trees go forth also. How now, coz, have I touched thee on the raw?"

Alleyne sat between them munching his bread while the twain disputed across his knees, leaning forward with flushed faces and darting hands, in all the heat of argument. Never had he heard such jargon of scholastic philosophy, such fine-drawn distinctions, such cross-fire of major and minor proposition, syllogism, attack and refutation. Question clattered upon answer like a sword on a buckler. The ancients, the fathers of the Church, the moderns, the Scriptures, the Arabians, were each sent hurtling against the other, while the rain still dripped and the dark holly-leaves glistened with the moisture. At last the fat man seemed to weary of it, for he set to work quietly upon his meal while his opponent, as proud as a rooster who is left unchallenged upon the midden, crowed away in a last long burst of quotation and deduction. Suddenly, however, his eyes dropped upon his food, and he gave a howl of dismay.

"You double thief!" he cried, "you have eaten my herrings, and I without bite or sup since morning."

"That," quoth the other complacently, "was my final argument, my crowning effort, or *peroratio,* as the orators have it. For, coz, since all thoughts are things, you have but to think a pair of herrings, and then conjure up a pottle of milk wherewith to wash them down."

"A brave piece of reasoning," cried the other, "and I know of but one reply to it." On which, leaning forward, he caught his comrade a rousing smack across his rosy cheek. "Nay, take it not amiss," he said, "since all things are but thoughts, then that also is but a thought, and may be disregarded."

This last argument, however, by no means commended itself to the pupil of Ockham, who plucked a great stick from the ground and signified his dissent by smiting the realist over the pate with it. By good fortune, the wood was so light and rotten that it went to a thousand splinters; but Alleyne thought it best to leave the twain to settle the matter at their leisure, the more so as the sun was shining brightly once more. Looking back down the pool-strewn road, he saw the two excited philosophers waving their hands and shouting at each other, but their babble soon became a mere drone in the distance, and a turn in the road hid them from his sight.

And now, after passing Holmesley Walk and the Wooton Heath, the forest began to shred out into scattered belts of trees, with gleam of cornfield and stretch of pasture-land between. Here and there by the wayside stood little knots of wattle-and-daub huts, with shock-haired labourers lounging by the doors and red-cheeked children sprawling in the roadway. Back among the groves he could see the high gable ends and thatched roofs of the franklins' houses, on whose fields these men found employment, or more often a thick dark column of smoke marked their position and hinted at the coarse plenty within. By these signs Alleyne knew that he was on the very fringe of the forest, and therefore no great way from Christchurch. The sun was lying low in the west and shooting its level rays across the long sweep of rich green country, glinting on the white-fleeced sheep, and throwing long shadows from the red kine who waded knee-deep in the juicy clover. Right glad was the traveller to see the high tower of Christchurch Priory gleaming in the mellow evening light, and gladder still when, on rounding a corner, he came upon his comrades of the morning seated astraddle upon a fallen tree. They had a flat space before them, on which they alternately threw little square pieces of bone, and were so intent upon their occupation that they never raised eye as he approached them. He observed with astonishment, as he drew near, that the archer's bow was on John's back, the archer's sword by John's side, and the steel cap laid upon the tree-trunk between them.

"Mort de ma vie!" Aylward shouted, looking down at the dice. "Never had I such cursed luck. A murrain on the bones! I have not thrown a good main since I left Navarre. A one and a three! En avant, camarade!"

"Four and three," cried Hordle John, counting on his great fingers, "that makes seven. Ho, archer, I have thy cap! Now have at thee for thy jerkin!"

"Mon Dieu!" he growled, "I am like to reach Christchurch in my shirt." Then suddenly glancing up, "Holà, by the splendour of heaven, here is our cher petit! Now, by my ten finger-bones! this is a rare sight to mine eyes." He sprang up and threw his arms round Alleyne's neck, while John, no less pleased, but more backward and Saxon in his habits, stood grinning and bobbing by the way-side, with his newly won steel cap stuck wrong side foremost upon his tangle of red hair.

"Hast come to stop?" cried the bowman, patting Alleyne all over in his delight. "Shall not get away from us again!"

"I wish no better," said he, with a pringling in the eyes at this hearty greeting.

"Well said, lad!" cried big John. "We three shall to the wars together, and the devil may fly away with the Abbot of Beaulieu! But your feet and hosen are all besmudged. Hast been in the water, or I am the more mistaken."

"I have in good sooth," Alleyne answered, and then as they journeyed on their way he told them the many things that had befallen him, his meeting with the villein, his sight of the king, his coming upon his brother, with all the tale of the black welcome and of the fair damsel. They strode on either side, each with an ear slanting towards him, but ere he had come to the end of his story the bow-man had spun round upon his heel, and was hastening back the way they had come, breathing loudly through his nose.

"What then?" asked Alleyne, trotting after him and gripping at his jerkin.

"I am back for Minstead, lad."

"And why, in the name of sense?"

"To thrust a handful of steel into the Socman. What! hale a demoiselle against her will, and then loose dogs at his own brother! Let me go!"

"Nenny, nenny!" cried Alleyne, laughing. "There was no scath done. Come back, friend"—and so, by mingled pushing and entreaties, they got his head round for Christchurch once more. Yet he walked with his chin upon his shoulder, until, catching sight of a maiden by a wayside well, the smiles came back to his face and peace to his heart.

"But you," said Alleyne, "there have been changes with you also. Why should not the workman carry his tools? Where are bow, and sword, and cap—and why so warlike, John?"

"It is a game which friend Aylward hath been a-teaching of me."

"And I found him an over-apt pupil," grumbled the bowman. "He hath stripped me as though I had fallen into the hands of the tardvenus. But, by my hilt! you must render them back to me, camarade, lest you bring discredit upon my mission, and I will pay you for them at armourers' prices."

"Take them back, man, and never heed the pay," said John. "I did but wish to learn the feel of them, since I am like to have such trinkets hung to my own girdle for some years to come."

"Ma foi, he was born for a free companion!" cried Aylward. "He hath the very trick of speech and turn of thought. I take them back then, and indeed it gives me unease not to feel my yew-stave tapping against my leg-bone. But see, mes garçons, on this side of the church rises the square and darkling tower of Earl Salisbury's castle, and even from here I seem to see on yonder banner the red roebuck of the Montacutes."

"Red upon white," said Alleyne, shading his eyes; "but whether roebuck or no is more than I could vouch. How black is the great tower, and how bright the gleam of arms upon the wall! See below the flag, how it twinkles like a star!"

"Aye, it is the steel head-piece of the watchman," remarked the archer. "But we must on, if we are to be there before the draw-bridge rises at the vespers bugle; for it is likely that Sir Nigel, being so renowned a soldier, may keep hard discipline within the walls, and let no man enter after sundown." So saying, he quickened his pace, and the three comrades were soon close to the straggling and broad-spread town which centred round the noble church and the frowning castle.

It chanced on that very evening that Sir Nigel Loring, having supped before sunset, as was his custom, and having himself seen that Pommers and Cadsand, his two warhorses, with the thirteen hacks, the five jennets, my lady's three palfreys, and the great dapple-grey roussin, had all their needs supplied, had taken his dogs for an evening breather. Sixty or seventy of them, large and small, smooth and shaggy — deer-hound, boar-hound, blood-hound, wolf-hound, mastiff, alaun, talbot, lurcher, terrier, spaniel — snapping, yelling and whining, with score of lolling tongues and waving tails, came surging down the narrow lane which leads from the Twynham kennels to the bank of Avon. Two russet-clad varlets, with loud halloo and cracking whips, walked thigh-deep amid the swarm, guiding, controlling, and urging. Behind came Sir Nigel himself, with Lady Loring upon his arm, the pair walking slowly and sedately, as befitted both their age and their condition, while they watched with a smile in their eyes the scrambling crowd in front of them. They paused, however, at the bridge, and, leaning their elbows upon the stonework, they stood looking down at their own faces in the glassy stream, and at the swift flash of speckled trout against the tawny gravel.

Sir Nigel was a slight man of poor stature, with soft lisping voice and gentle ways. So short was he that his wife, who was no very tall woman, had the better of him by the breadth of three fingers. His sight having been injured in his early wars by a basketful of lime which had been emptied over him when he led the Earl of Derby's stormers up the beach at Bergerac, he had contracted something of a stoop, with a blinking, peering expression of face.

His age was six-and-forty, but the constant practice of arms, together with a cleanly life, had preserved his activity and endurance unimpaired, so that from a distance he seemed to have the slight limbs and swift grace of a boy. His face, however, was tanned of a dull yellow tint, with a leathery poreless look, which spoke of rough outdoor doings, and the little pointed beard which he wore, in deference to the prevailing fashion, was streaked and shot with grey. His features were small, delicate, and regular, with clear-cut curving nose, and eyes which jutted forward from the lids. His dress was simple and yet spruce. A Flandrish hat of beevor, bearing in the band the token of Our Lady of Embrun, was drawn low upon the left side to hide that ear which had been partly shorn from his head by a Flemish man-at-arms in a camp broil before Tournay. His cote-hardie, or tunic, and trunk-hosen were of a purple plum colour, with long weepers which hung from either sleeve to below his knees. His shoes were of red leather, daintily pointed at the toes, but not yet prolonged to the extravagant lengths which the succeeding reign was to bring into fashion. A gold-embroidered belt of knighthood encircled his loins, with his arms, five roses gules on a field argent, cunningly worked upon the clasp. So stood Sir Nigel Loring upon the bridge of Avon, and talked lightly with his lady.

And, certes, had the two visages alone been seen, and the stranger been asked which were the more likely to belong to the bold warrior whose name was loved by the roughest soldiery of Europe, he had assuredly selected the lady's. Her face was square and strong, with thick brows, and the eyes of one who was accustomed to rule. Taller and broader than her husband, her flowing gown of sendal, and fur-lined tippet, could not conceal the full outlines of her figure. It was the age of martial women. The deeds of Black Agnes of Dunbar, of Lady Salisbury and of the Countess of Montfort, were still fresh in the public mind. With such examples before them, the wives of the English captains had become as warlike as their mates, and ordered their castles in their absence with the prudence and discipline of veteran seneschals. Right easy were the Montacutes of their Castle of Twynham, and little had they to dread from roving galley or French squadron while Lady Mary Loring had the ordering of it. There were men who said that of all the stern passages and daring deeds by which Sir Nigel Loring had proved the true temper of his courage, not the least was his wooing and winning of so high-mettled a dame.

"I tell you, my fair lord," she was saying, "that it is no fit training for a demoiselle: hawks and hounds, rotes and citoles, singing a French rondel, or reading the Gestes de Doon de Mayence, as I found her yesternight, pretending sleep, the artful, with the corner of the scroll thrusting forth from under her pillow. Lent her by Father Christopher of the Priory, forsooth — that is ever her answer. How shall all this help her when she has castle of her own to keep, with a hundred mouths all agape for beef and beer?"

"True, my sweet bird, true," answered the knight, picking a comfit from his gold drageoir. "The maid is like the young filly, which kicks heels and plunges for very lust of life. Give her time, dame, give her time."

"Well I know that my father would have given me, not time, but a good hazel-stick across my shoulders. Ma foi! I know not what the world is coming to, when young maids may flout their elders. I wonder that you do not correct her, my fair lord."

"Nay, my heart's comfort, I never raised hand to woman yet, and it would be a passing strange thing if I began upon my own flesh and blood. It was a woman's hand which cast this lime into mine eyes, and though I saw her stoop, and might well have stopped her ere she threw, I deemed it unworthy of my knighthood to hinder or balk one of her sex."

"The hussy!" cried Lady Loring, clenching her broad right hand. "I would I had been at the side of her!"

"And so would I, since you would have been the nearer me, my own. But I doubt not that you are right, and that Maude's wings need clipping, which I may leave in your hands when I am gone, for, in sooth, this peaceful life is not for me, and were it not for your gracious kindness and loving care I could not abide it a week. I hear that there is talk of warlike muster at Bordeaux once more, and by St Paul! it would be a new thing if the lions of England and the red pile of Chandos were to be seen in the field, and the roses of Loring were not waving by their side."

"Now woe worth me but I feared it!" cried she, with the colour all struck from her face. "I have noted your absent mind, your kindling eye, your trying and riveting of old harness. Consider, my sweet lord, that you have already won much honour, that we have seen but little of each other, that you bear upon your body the scars of over twenty wounds received in I know not how many bloody encounters. Have you not done enough for honour and the public cause?"

"My lady, when our liege lord the king at nigh threescore, and my Lord Chandos at threescore and ten, are blithe and ready to lay lance in rest for England's cause, it would ill beseem me to prate of service done. It is sooth that I have received seven-and-twenty wounds. There is the more reason that I should be thankful that I am still long of breath and sound in limb. I have also seen some bickering and scuffling. Six great land battles I count, with four upon the sea, and seven-and-fifty onfalls, skirmishes and bushments. I have held two-and-twenty towns, and I have been at the intaking of thirty-one. Surely then it would be bitter shame to me, and also to you, since my fame is yours, that I should now hold back if a man's work is to be done. Besides, bethink you how low is our purse, with bailiff and reeve ever croaking of empty farms and wasting lands. Were it not for this constableship which the Earl of Salisbury hath bestowed upon us we could scarce uphold the state which is fitting to our degree. Therefore, my sweeting, there is the more need that I should turn to where there is good pay to be earned and brave ransoms to be won."

"Ah, my dear lord," quoth she, with sad, weary eyes. "I thought that at last I had you to mine own self, even though your youth had been spent afar from my side. Yet my voice, as I know well, should speed you on to glory and renown, not hold you back when fame

is to be won. Yet what can I say?—for all men know that your valour needs the curb and not the spur. It goes to my heart that you
should ride forth now a mere knight bachelor, when there is no
noble in the land who has so good a claim to the square pennon,
save only that you have not the money to uphold it."

"And whose fault that, my sweet bird?" said he.

"No fault, my fair lord, but a virtue; for how many rich ransoms
have you won, and yet have scattered the crowns among page and
archer and varlet, until in a week you had not as much as would
buy food and forage. It is a most knightly largesse, and yet without
money how can man rise?"

"Dirt and dross!" cried he. "What matter rise or fall, so that duty
be done and honour gained! Banneret or bachelor, square pennon or forked, I would not give a denier for the difference, and
the less since Sir John Chandos, chosen flower of English chivalry,
is himself but a humble knight. But meanwhile fret not thyself, my
heart's dove, for it is like that there may be no war waged, and we
must await the news. But here are three strangers, and one, as I
take it, a soldier fresh from service. It is likely that he may give us
word of what is stirring over the water."

Lady Loring glancing up, saw in the fading light three companions walking abreast down the road, all grey with dust, and
stained with travel, yet chattering merrily between themselves. He
in the midst was young and comely, with boyish open face and
bright grey eyes, which glanced from right to left as though he
found the world around him both new and pleasing. To his right
walked a huge red-headed man with broad smile and merry twinkle, whose clothes seemed to be bursting and splitting at every
seam, as though he were some lusty chick who was breaking
bravely from his shell. On the other side, with his knotted hand
upon the young man's shoulder, came a stout and burly archer,
brown and fierce-eyed, with sword at belt and long yellow yew-
stave peeping over his shoulder. Hard face, battered headpiece,
dinted brigandine, with faded red lion of St George ramping on a
discoloured ground, all proclaimed as plainly as words that he was

indeed from the land of war. He looked keenly at Sir Nigel as he approached, and then, plunging his hand under his breast-plate, he stepped up to him with a rough uncouth bow to the lady.

"Your pardon, fair sir," said he, "but I fear you forget one who was once your humble friend and comrade."

"Nay, it is Samkin Aylward," cried the knight. "Often have I wondered what cheer you made, for it is indeed many years since I last set eyes upon your face."

"Aye, master; it is other days since we set forth together from Tilford with our faces towards the wars," said the archer.

"It is a great joy to see you once again. Rest awhile, and you shall come to the hall anon and tell us what is passing in France, for I have heard that it is likely that our pennons may flutter to the south of the great Spanish mountains ere another year be passed."

"There was talk of it in Bordeaux," answered the archer, "and I saw myself that the armourers and smiths were as busy as rats in a wheat-rick. But I bring you this letter from the valiant Gascon knight, Sir Claude Latour. And to you, lady," he added after a pause, "I bring from him this box of red sugar of Narbonne, with every courteous and knightly greeting which a gallant cavalier may make to a fair and noble dame."

This little speech had cost the blunt bowman much pains and planning; but he might have spared his breath, for the lady was quite as much absorbed as her lord in the letter, which they held between them, a hand on either corner, spelling it out very slowly, with drawn brows and muttering lips. As they read it, Alleyne, who stood with Hordle John a few paces back from their comrade, saw the lady catch her breath, while the knight laughed softly to himself.

"You see, dear heart," said he, "that they will not leave the old dog in his kennel when the game is afoot. And what of this White Company, Aylward?"

"Ah, sir, you speak of dogs," cried Aylward, "but there are a pack of lusty hounds who are ready for any quarry, if they have but a good huntsman to halloo them on. Sir, we have been in the wars together, and I have seen many a brave following, but never such a set of woodland boys as this. They do but want you at their head, and who will bar the way to them?"

"Pardieu!" said Sir Nigel, "if they are all like their messengers they are indeed men of whom a leader may be proud. What is the name of this giant behind you?"

"He is big John, of Hordle, a forest man, who hath now taken service in the Company."

"A proper figure of a man-at-arms," said the little knight. "Why, man, you are no chicken, yet I warrant him the stronger man. See to that great stone from the coping which hath fallen upon the bridge. Four of my lazy varlets strove this day to carry it hence. I would that you two could put them to shame by budging it, though I fear that I overtask you, for it is a grievous weight."

He pointed as he spoke to a huge rough-hewn block which lay by the roadside, deep sunken from its own weight in the reddish earth. The archer approached it, rolling back the sleeves of his jerkin, but with no very hopeful countenance, for indeed it was a mighty rock. John, however, put him aside with his left hand, and, stooping over the stone, he plucked it single-handed from its soft bed and swung it far into the stream. There it fell with mighty splash, one jagged end peaking out above the surface, while the waters bubbled and foamed with far-circling eddy.

"Good lack!" cried Sir Nigel and "Good lack!" cried his lady, while John stood laughing and wiping the caked dirt from his fingers.

"I have felt his arms round my ribs," said the bowman, "and they crackle yet at the thought of it. This other comrade of mine is a right learned clerk, for all that he is so young, hight Alleyne, the son of Edric, brother to the Socman of Minstead."

"Young man," quoth Sir Nigel sternly, "if you are of the same way of thought as your brother, you may not pass under portcullis of mine."

"Nay, fair sir," cried Aylward hastily, "I will be pledge for it that they have no thought in common; for this very day his brother hath set his dogs upon him, and driven him from his lands."

"And are you, too, of the White Company?" asked Sir Nigel. "Hast had small experience of war, if I may judge by your looks and bearing."

"I would fain to France with my friends here," Alleyne answered, "but I am a man of peace—a reader, exorcist, acolyte, and clerk."

"That need not hinder," quoth Sir Nigel.

"No, fair sir," cried the bowman joyously. "Why, I myself have served two terms with Arnold de Cervolles, he whom they called the archpriest. By my hilt! I have seen him ere now, with monk's gown trussed to his knees, over his sandals in blood in the forefront of the battle. Yet, ere the last string had twanged, he would be down on his four bones among the stricken, and have them all houseled and shriven, as quick as shelling peas. Ma foi! there were those who wished that he would have less care for their souls and a little more for their bodies!"

"It is well to have a learned clerk in every troop," said Sir Nigel. "By St Paul! there are men so caitiff that they think more of a scrivener's pen than of their lady's smile, and do their devoir in hopes that they may fill a line in a chronicle or make a tag to a jongleur's romance. I remember well that, at the siege of Retters, there was a little, sleek, fat clerk of the name of Chaucer, who was so apt at rondel, sirvente, or tonson, that no man dare give back a foot from the walls, lest he find it all set down in his rhymes and sung by every underling and varlet in the camp. But, my soul's bird, you hear me prate as though all were decided, when I have not yet taken counsel either with you or with my lady mother. Let us to the chamber, while these strangers find such fare as pantry and cellar may furnish."

"The night air strikes chill," said the lady, and turned down the road with her hand upon her lord's arm. The three comrades dropped behind and followed: Aylward much the lighter for having accomplished his mission, Alleyne full of wonderment at the humble bearing of so renowned a captain, and John loud with snorts and sneers, which spoke his disappointment and contempt.

"What ails the man?" asked Aylward in surprise.

"I have been cozened and bejaped," quoth he gruffly.

"By whom, Sir Samson the strong?"

"By thee, Sir Balaam the false prophet."

"By my hilt!" cried the archer, "though I be not Balaam, yet I hold converse with the very creature that spake to him. What is amiss, then, and how have I played you false?"

"Why, marry, did you not say, and Alleyne here will be my witness, that, if I would hie to the wars with you, you would place me under a leader who was second to none in all England for valour? Yet here you bring me to a shred of a man, peaky and ill-nourished, with eyes like a moulting owl, who must needs, forsooth, take counsel with his mother ere he buckle sword to girdle."

"Is that where the shoe galls?" cried the bowman, and laughed aloud. "I will ask you what you think of him three months hence, if we be all alive; for sure I am that—"

Aylward's words were interrupted by an extraordinary hubbub which broke out that instant some little way down the street in the direction of the Priory. There was deep-mouthed shouting of men, frightened shrieks of women, howling and barking of curs, and over all a sullen thunderous rumble, indescribably menacing and terrible. Round the corner of the narrow street there came rushing a brace of whining dogs with tails tucked under their legs, and after them a white-faced burgher, with outstretched hands and widespread fingers, his hair all abristle and his eyes glinting back from one shoulder to the other, as though some great terror were at his very heels. "Fly, my lady, fly!" he screeched, and whizzed past them like a bolt from bow; while close behind came lumbering a huge black bear, with red tongue lolling from his mouth, and a broken chain jangling behind him. To right and left the folk flew for arch and doorway. Hordle John caught up the Lady Loring as though she had been a feather, and sprang with her into an open porch; while Aylward, with a whirl of French oaths, plucked at his quiver and tried to unsling his bow. Alleyne, all unnerved at so strange and unwonted a sight, shrank up against a wall with his eyes fixed upon the frenzied creature, which came bounding along with ungainly speed, looking the larger in the uncertain light, its huge jaws agape, with blood and slaver trickling to the ground. Sir Nigel, alone unconscious to all appearance of the universal panic, walked with unfaltering step up the centre of the road, a silken handkerchief in one hand and his gold comfit-box in the other. It sent the blood cold through Alleyne's veins to see that as they came together—the man and the beast—the creature reared up, with eyes ablaze with fear and hate, and whirled its great paws above the knight to smite him to the earth. He, however, blinking with puckered eyes, reached up his kerchief, and flicked the beast twice across the snout with it. "Ah, saucy! saucy!" quoth he, with gentle chiding; on which the bear, uncertain and puzzled, dropped its fore legs to earth again, and waddling back, was soon swathed in ropes by the bearward and a crowd of peasants who had been in close pursuit.

A scared man was the keeper; for, having chained the brute to a stake while he drank a stoup of ale at the inn, it had been baited by stray curs until, in wrath and madness, it had plucked loose the chain, and smitten or bitten all who came in its path. Most scared of all was he to find that the creature had come nigh to harm the Lord and Lady of the castle, who had power to place him in the stretch-neck or to have the skin scourged from his shoulders. Yet, when he came with bowed head and humble entreaty for forgiveness, he was met with a handful of small silver from Sir Nigel, whose dame, however, was less charitably disposed, being much ruffled in her dignity by the manner in which she had been hustled from her lord's side. As they passed through the castle gate, John plucked at Aylward's sleeve, and the two fell behind.

"I must crave your pardon, comrade," said he, bluntly. "I was a fool not to know that a little rooster may be the gamest. I believe that this man is indeed a leader whom we may follow."

CHAPTER XI

HOW A YOUNG SHEPHERD
HAD A PERILOUS FLOCK

BLACK was the mouth of Twynham Castle, though a pair of torches burning at the further end of the gateway cast a red glare over the outer bailey, and sent a dim ruddy flicker through the rough-hewn arch, rising and falling with fitful brightness. Over the door the travellers could discern the escutcheon of the Montacutes, a roebuck gules on a field argent, flanked on either side by smaller shields which bore the red roses of the veteran constable. As they passed over the drawbridge Alleyne marked the gleam of arms in the embrasures to right and left, and they had scarce set foot upon the causeway ere a hoarse blare burst from a bugle, and with screech of hinge and clank of chain, the ponderous bridge swung up into the air, drawn by unseen hands. At the same instant the huge portcullis came rattling down from above, and shut off the fast fading light of day. Sir Nigel and his lady walked on in deep talk, while a fat understeward took charge of the three comrades, and led them to the buttery, where beef, bread, and beer were kept ever in readiness for the wayfarer. After a hearty meal and a dip in the trough to wash the dust from them, they strolled forth into the bailey, where the bowman peered about through the darkness at wall and at keep, with the carping eyes of one who has seen something of sieges, and is not lightly to be satisfied. To Alleyne and to John, however, it appeared to be as great and as stout a fortress as could be built by the hands of man.

Erected by Sir Baldwin de Redvers in the old fighting days of the twelfth century, when men thought much of war and little of comfort, Castle Twynham had been designed as a stronghold pure and simple, unlike those later and more magnificent structures where warlike strength had been combined with the magnificence of a palace. From the time of the Edwards such buildings as Conway and Caernarvon Castles, to say nothing of Royal Windsor, had shown that it was possible to secure luxury in peace as well as security in times of trouble. Sir Nigel's trust, however, still frowned above the smooth-flowing waters of the Avon, very much as the stern race of early Anglo-Normans had designed it. There were the broad outer and inner bailies, not paved, but sown with grass to nourish the sheep and cattle which might be driven in on sign of danger. All round were high and turreted walls, with at the corner a bare square-faced keep, gaunt and windowless, rearing up from a lofty mound, which made it almost inaccessible to an assailant. Against the bailey-walls were rows of frail wooden houses and leaning sheds, which gave shelter to the archers and men-at-arms who formed the garrison. The doors of these humble dwellings were mostly open, and against the yellow glare from within Alleyne could see the bearded fellows cleaning their harness, while their wives would come out for a gossip, with their needlework in their hands, and their long black shadows streaming across the yard. The air was full of the clack of their voices and the merry prattling of children, in strange contrast to the flash of arms and constant warlike challenge from the walls above.

"Methinks a company of school lads could hold this place against an army," quoth John.

"And so say I," said Alleyne.

"Nay, there you are wide of the clout," the bowman said gravely. "By my hilt! I have seen a stronger fortalice carried in a summer evening. I remember such a one in Picardy, with a name as long as a Gascon's pedigree. It was when I served under Sir Robert Knolles, before the days of the Company; and we came by good plunder at the sacking of it. I had myself a great silver bowl, with two goblets, and a plastron of Spanish steel. Pasques Dieu! there are some fine women over yonder! Mort de ma vie! see to that one in the doorway; I will go speak to her. But whom have we here?"

"Is there an archer here hight Sam Aylward?" asked a gaunt man-at-arms, clanking up to them across the courtyard.

"My name, friend," quoth the bowman.

"Then sure I have no need to tell thee mine," saith the other.

"By the rood! if it is not Black Simon of Norwich!" cried Aylward. "A mon coeur, camarade, à mon coeur! Ah, but I am blithe to see thee!" The two fell upon each other and hugged like bears.

"And where from, old blood and bones?" asked the bowman.

"I am in service here. Tell me, comrade, is it sooth that we shall have another fling at these Frenchmen? It is so rumoured in the guard-room, and that Sir Nigel will take the field once more."

"It is like enough, mon gar, as things go."

"Now may the Lord be praised!" cried the other. "This very night will I set apart a golden ouche to be offered on the shrine of my name-saint. I have pined for this, Aylward, as a young maid pines for her lover."

"Art so set on plunder then? Is the purse so light that there is not enough for a rouse? I have a bag at my belt, camarade, and you have but to put your fist into it for what you want. It was ever share and share between us."

"Nay, friend, it is not the Frenchman's gold, but the Frenchman's blood that I would have. I should not rest quiet in the grave, coz, if I had not another turn at them. For with us in France it has ever been fair and honest war—a shut fist for the man, but a bended knee for the woman. But how was it at Winchelsea when their galleys came down upon it some few years back? I had an old mother there, lad, who had come down thither from the Midlands to be nearer her son. They found her afterwards by her own hearthstone, thrust through by a Frenchman's bill. My second sister, my brother's wife, and her two children, they were but ash-heaps in the smoking ruins of their house. I will not say that we have not wrought great scath upon France, but women and children have been safe from us. And so, old friend, my heart is hot within me, and I long to hear the old battle-cry again, and, by God's truth, if Sir Nigel unfurls his pennon, here is one who will be right glad to feel the saddle-flaps under his knees."

"We have seen good work together, old war-dog," quoth Aylward; "and, by my hilt! we may hope to see more ere we die. But we are more like to hawk at the Spanish woodcock than at the French heron, though certes it is rumoured that Du Guesclin, with all the best lances of France, has taken service under the lions and towers of Castile. But, comrade, it is in my mind that there is some small matter of dispute still open between us."

"'Fore God, it is sooth," cried the other. "I had forgot it. The provost-marshal and his men tore us apart when last we met."

"On which, friend, we vowed that we should settle the point when next we come together. Hast thy sword, I see, and the moon throws glimmer enough for such old night-birds as we. On guard, mon gar! I have not heard clink of steel this month or more."

"Out from the shadow, then," said the other, drawing his sword. "A vow is a vow, and not lightly to be broken."

"A vow to the saints," cried Alleyne, "is indeed not to be set aside, but this is a devil's vow, and simple clerk as I am, I am yet the mouthpiece of the true Church when I say that it were mortal sin to fight on such a quarrel. What! shall two grown men carry malice for years, and fly like snarling curs at each other's throats?"

"No malice, my young clerk, no malice," quoth Black Simon. "I have not a bitter drop in my heart for mine old comrade; but the quarrel, as he hath told you, is still open and unsettled. Fall on, Aylward!"

"Not whilst I can stand between you," cried Alleyne, springing before the bowman. "It is shame and sin to see two Christian Englishmen turn swords against each other like the frenzied bloodthirsty paynim."

"And what is more," said Hordle John, suddenly appearing out of the buttery with the huge board upon which the pastry was rolled, "if either raise sword I shall flatten him like Shrovetide pan-cake. By the black rood! I shall drive him into the earth like a nail into a door, rather than see you do scath to each other."

"'Fore God, this is a strange way of preaching peace," cried Black Simon. "You may find the scath yourself, my lusty friend, if you raise your great cudgel to me. I had as lief have a castle draw-bridge drop upon my pate."

"Tell me, Aylward," said Alleyne earnestly, with hands out-stretched to keep the pair asunder, "what is the cause of quarrel, that we may see whether honourable settlement may not be arrived at?"

The bowman looked down at his feet and then up at the moon. "Parbleu!" he cried, "the cause of quarrel? Why, mon petit, it was years ago in Limousin, and how can I bear in mind what was the cause of it? Simon there hath it at the end of his tongue."

"Not I, in troth," replied the other; "I have had other things to think of. There was some sort of bickering over dice, or wine, or was it a woman, coz?"

"Pasques Dieu! but you have nicked it," cried Aylward. "It was indeed about a woman; and the quarrel must go forward, for I am still of the same mind as before."

"What of the woman, then?" asked Simon. "May the murrain strike me if I can call to mind aught about her."

"It was La Blanche Rose, maid at the sign of the 'Trois Corbeaux' at Limoges. Bless her pretty heart! Why, mon gar, I loved her."

"So did a many," quoth Simon. "I call her to mind now. On the very day that we fought over the little hussy, she went off with Evan ap Price, a long-legged Welsh dagsman. They have a hostel of their own now, somewhere on the banks of Garonne, where the landlord drinks so much of the liquor that there is little left for the customers."

"So ends our quarrel, then," said Aylward, sheathing his sword. "A Welsh dagsman, i' faith! C'était mauvais goût, camarade, and the more so when she had a jolly archer and a lusty man-at-arms to choose from."

"True, old lad. And it is as well that we can compose our differ-ences honourably, for Sir Nigel had been out at the first clash of steel; and he hath sworn that if there be quarrelling in the garri-son he would smite the right hand from the broilers. You know him of old, and that he is like to be as good as his word."

"Mort Dieu! yes. But there are ale, mead, and wine in the buttery, and the steward a merry rogue, who will not haggle over a quart or two. Buvons, mon gar, for it is not every day that two old friends come together."

The old soldiers and Hordle John strode off together in all good-fellowship. Alleyne had turned to follow them, when he felt a touch upon his shoulder, and found a young page by his side.

"The Lord Loring commands," said the boy, "that you will follow me to the great chamber, and await him there."

"But my comrades?"

"His commands were for you alone."

Alleyne followed the messenger to the east end of the courtyard, where a broad flight of steps led up to the doorway of the main hall, the outer wall of which is washed by the waters of the Avon. As designed at first, no dwelling had been allotted to the lord of the castle and his family but the dark and dismal basement story of the keep. A more civilised or more effeminate generation, however, had refused to be pent up in such a cellar, and the hall with its neighbouring chambers had been added for their accommodation. Up the broad steps Alleyne went, still following his boyish guide, until at the folding oak doors the latter paused, and ushered him into the main hall of the castle.

On entering the room the clerk looked round; but, seeing no one, he continued to stand, his cap in his hand, examining with the greatest interest a chamber which was so different to any to which he was accustomed. The days had gone by when a nobleman's hall was but a barn-like rush-strewn enclosure, the common lounge and eating room of every inmate of the castle. The Crusaders had brought back with them experiences of domestic luxuries, of Damascus carpets and rugs of Aleppo, which made them impatient of the hideous bareness and want of privacy which they found in their ancestral strongholds. Still stronger, however, had been the influence of the great French war; for, however well matched the nations might be in martial exercises, there could be no question but that our neighbours were infinitely superior to us in the arts of peace. A stream of returning knights, of wounded soldiers, and of unransomed French noblemen, had been for a quarter of a century continually pouring into England, every one of whom exerted an influence in the direction of greater domestic refinement; while shiploads of French furniture from Calais, Rouen, and other plundered towns had supplied our own artisans with models on which to shape their work. Hence, in most English castles, and in Castle Twynham among the rest, chambers were to be found which would seem to be not wanting either in beauty or in comfort.

In the great stone fireplace a log fire was spurting and crackling, throwing out a ruddy glare which, with the four bracket-lamps which stood at each corner of the room, gave a bright and lightsome air to the whole apartment. Above was a wreath-work of blazonry, extending up to the carved and corniced oaken roof; while on either side stood the high canopied chairs placed for the master of the house and for his most honoured guest. The walls were hung all round with most elaborate and brightly coloured tapestry representing the achievements of Sir Bevis of Hampton, and behind this convenient screen were stored the tables dormant and benches which would be needed for banquet or high festivity. The floor was of polished tiles, with a square of red and black diapered Flemish carpet in the centre; and many settees, cushions, folding chairs, and carved bancals littered all over it. At the further end was a long black buffet or dresser, thickly covered with gold cups, silver salvers, and other such valuables. All this Alleyne examined with curious eyes; but most interesting of all to him was a small ebony table at his very side, on which, by the side of a chessboard and the scattered chessmen, there lay an open manuscript written in a right clerkly hand, and set forth with brave flourishes and devices along the margins. In vain Alleyne bethought him of where he was, and of those laws of good breeding and decorum which should restrain him: those coloured capitals and black even lines drew his hand down to them as the loadstone draws the needle, until, almost before he knew it, he was standing with the romance of Garin de Montglane before his eyes, so absorbed in its contents as to be completely oblivious both of where he was and why he had come there.

He was brought back to himself, however, by a sudden little ripple of quick feminine laughter. Aghast, he dropped the manuscript among the chessmen and stared in bewilderment round the room. It was as empty and as still as ever. Again he stretched his hand out to the romance, and again came that roguish burst of merriment. He looked up at the ceiling, back at the closed door, and round at the stiff folds of motionless tapestry. Of a sudden, however, he caught a quick shimmer from the corner of a high-backed bancal in front of him, and, shifting a pace or two to the side, saw a white slender hand, which held a mirror of polished silver in such a way that the concealed observer could see without being seen. He stood irresolute, uncertain whether to advance or to take no notice; but, even as he hesitated, the mirror was whipped in, and a tall and stately young lady swept out from behind the oaken screen, with a dancing light of mischief in her eyes. Alleyne started with astonishment as he recognised the very maiden who had suffered from his brother's violence in the forest. She no longer wore her gay riding-dress, however, but was attired in a long sweeping robe of black velvet of Bruges, with delicate tracery of white lace at neck and at wrist, scarce to be seen against her ivory skin. Beautiful as she had seemed to him before, the lithe charm of her figure and the proud, free grace of her bearing were enhanced now by the rich simplicity of her attire.

"Ah, you start," said she, with the same sidelong look of mischief, "and I cannot marvel at it. Didst not look to see the distressed damozel again. Oh that I were a minstrel, that I might put it into rhyme, with the whole romance — the luckless maid, the wicked socman, and the virtuous clerk! So might our fame have gone down together for all time, and you be numbered with Sir Percival or Sir Galahad, or all the other rescuers of oppressed ladies."

"What I did," said Alleyne, "was too small a thing for thanks; and yet, if I may say it without offence, it was too grave and near a matter for mirth and raillery. I had counted on my brother's love, but

God has willed that it should be otherwise. It is a joy to me to see you again, lady, and to know that you have reached home in safety, if this be indeed your home."

"Yes, in sooth, Castle Twynham is my home, and Sir Nigel Loring my father. I should have told you so this morning, but you said that you were coming hither, so I bethought me that I might hold it back as a surprise to you. Oh dear, but it was brave to see you!" she cried, bursting out a-laughing once more, standing with her hand pressed to her side, and her half-closed eyes twinkling with amusement. "You drew back and came forward with your eyes upon my book there, like the mouse who sniffs the cheese and yet dreads the trap."

"I take shame," said Alleyne, "that I should have touched it."

"Nay, it warmed my very heart to see it. So glad was I that I laughed for very pleasure. My fine preacher can himself be tempted then, thought I; he is not made of another clay to the rest of us."

"God help me! I am the weakest of the weak," groaned Alleyne. "I pray that I may have more strength."

"And to what end?" she asked sharply. "If you are, as I understand, to shut yourself for ever in your cell within the four walls of an abbey, then of what use would it be were your prayer to be answered?"

"The use of my own salvation."

She turned from him with a pretty shrug and wave. "Is that all?" she said. "Then you are no better than Father Christopher and the rest of them. Your own, your own, ever your own! My father is the king's man, and when he rides into the press of fight he is not thinking ever of the saving of his own poor body; he recks little enough if he leave it on the field. Why then should you, who are soldier of the spirit, be ever moping and hiding in cell or in cave, with minds full of your own concerns, while the world, which you should be mending, is going on its way, and neither sees nor hears you? Were ye all as thoughtless of your own souls as the soldier is of his body, ye would be of more avail to the souls of others."

"There is sooth in what you say, lady," Alleyne answered, "and yet I scarce can see what you would have the clergy and the church to do."

"I would have them live as others, and do men's work in the world, preaching by their lives rather than their words. I would have them come forth from their lonely places, mix with the borel folks, feel the pains and the pleasures, the cares and the rewards the temptings and the stirrings of the common people. Let them toil, and swinken, and labour and plough the land, and take wives to themselves—"

"Alas! alas!" cried Alleyne aghast, "you have surely sucked this poison from the man Wicliffe, of whom I have heard such evil things."

"Nay, I know him not. I have learned it by looking from mine own chamber window and marking these poor monks of the priory, their weary life, their profitless round. I have asked myself if the best which can be done with virtue is to shut it within high walls as though it were some savage creature. If the good will lock themselves up, and if the wicked will still wander free, then alas for the world!"

Alleyne looked at her in amazement for her cheek was flushed, her eyes gleaming, and her whole pose full of eloquence and conviction. Yet in an instant she had changed again to her old expression of merriment leavened with mischief.

"Wilt do what I ask?" said she.

"What is it, lady?"

"Oh, most ungallant clerk! A true knight would never have asked, but would have vowed upon the instant. 'Tis but to bear me out in what I say to my father."

"In what?"

"In saying, if he ask, that it was south of the Christchurch road that I met you. I shall be shut up with the tirewomen else, and have a week of spindle and bodkin, when I would fain be galloping Troubadour up Wilverley Walk, or loosing little Roland at the Vinney Ridge herons."

"I shall not answer him if he asks."

"Not answer! But he will have an answer. Nay, but you must not fail me, or it will go ill with me."

"But, lady," cried poor Alleyne in great distress, "how can I say that it was to the south of the road when I know well that it was four miles to the north?"

"You will not say it?"

"Surely, you will not, too, when you know that it is not so?"

"Oh, I weary of your preaching!" she cried, and swept away with a toss of her beautiful head, leaving Alleyne as cast down and ashamed as though he had himself proposed some infamous thing. She was back again in an instant, however, in another of her varying moods.

"Look at that, my friend!" said she. "If you had been shut up in an abbey or in cell this day you could not have taught a wayward maiden to abide by the truth. Is it not so? What avail is the shepherd if he leave his sheep?"

"A sorry shepherd!" said Alleyne humbly. "But here is your noble father."

"And you shall see how worthy a pupil I am. Father, I am much beholden to this young clerk, who was of service to me and helped me this very morning in Minstead Woods, four miles to the north of the Christchurch road, where I had no call to be, you having ordered it otherwise." All this she reeled off in a loud voice, and then glanced with sidelong questioning eyes at Alleyne for his approval.

Sir Nigel, who had entered the room with a silvery-haired old lady upon his arm, stared aghast at this sudden burst of candour.

"Maude, Maude!" said he, shaking his head, "it is more hard for me to gain obedience from you than from the ten score drunken archers who followed me to Guienne. Yet, hush! little one, for your fair lady-mother will be here anon, and there is no need that she should know it. We will keep you from the provost-marshal this journey. Away to your chamber, sweeting, and keep a blithe face, for she who confesses is shriven. And now, fair mother," he continued when his daughter had gone, "sit you here by the fire, for your blood runs colder than it did. Alleyne Edricson, I would have a word with you, for I would fain that you should take service under me. And here in good time comes my lady, without whose counsel it is not my wont to decide aught of import; but, indeed, it was her own thought that you should come."

"For I have formed a good opinion of you, and can see that you are one who may be trusted," said the Lady Loring. "And in good sooth my dear lord hath need of such a one by his side, for he recks so little of himself that there should be one there to look to his needs and meet his wants. You have seen the cloisters: it were well that you should see the world too, ere you make choice for life between them."

"It was for that very reason that my father willed that I should come forth into the world at my twentieth year," said Alleyne.

"Then your father was a man of good counsel," said she, "and you cannot carry out his will better than by going on this path, where all that is noble and gallant in England will be your companions."

"You can ride?" asked Sir Nigel, looking at the youth with puckered eyes.

"Yes, I have ridden much at the abbey."

"Yet there is a difference betwixt a friar's hack and a warrior's destrier. You can sing and play?"

"On citole, flute, and rebeck."

"Good! You can read blazonry?"

"Indifferent well."

"Then read this," quoth Sir Nigel, pointing upwards to one of the many quarterings which adorned the wall over the fireplace.

"Argent," Alleyne answered, "a fess azure charged with three lozenges dividing three mullets sable. Over all, on an escutcheon of the first, a jambe gules."

"A jambe gules erased," said Sir Nigel, shaking his head solemnly. "Yet it is not amiss for a monk-bred man. I trust that you are lowly and serviceable?"

"I have served all my life, my lord."

"Canst carve too?"

"I have carved two days a week for the brethren."

"A model truly! Wilt make a squire of squires. But tell me, I pray, canst curl hair?"

"No, my lord, but I could learn."

"It is of import," said he, "for I love to keep my hair well ordered, seeing that the weight of my helmet for thirty years hath in some degree frayed it upon the top." He pulled off his velvet cap of maintenance as he spoke, and displayed a pate which was as bald as an egg, and shone bravely in the firelight. "You see," said he, whisking round, and showing one little strip where a line of scattered hairs, like the last survivors in some fatal field, still barely held their own against the fate which had fallen upon their comrades; "these locks need some little oiling and curling, for I doubt not that if you look slantwise at my head, when the light is good, you will yourself perceive that there are places where the hair is sparse."

"It is for you also to bear the purse," said the lady, "for my sweet lord is of so free and gracious a temper that he would give it gaily to the first who asked alms of him. All these things, with some knowledge of venerie, and of the management of horse, hawk, and hound, with the grace and hardihood and courtesy which are proper to your age, will make you a fit squire for Sir Nigel Loring."

"Alas! lady," Alleyne answered, "I know well the great honour that you have done me in deeming me worthy to wait upon so renowned a knight, yet I am so conscious of my own weakness that I scarce dare incur duties which I might be so ill-fitted to fulfil."

"Modesty and a humble mind," said she, "are the very first and rarest gifts in page or squire. Your words prove that you have these, and all the rest is but the work of use and of time. But there is no call for haste. Rest upon it for the night, and let your orisons ask for guidance in the matter. We knew your father well, and would fain help his son, though we have small cause to love your brother the socman, who is for ever stirring up strife in the county."

"We can scarce hope," said Sir Nigel, "to have all ready for our start before the feast of St Luke, for there is much to be done in the time. You will have leisure therefore, if it please you to take service under me, in which to learn your devoir. Bertrand, my daughter's page, is hot to go; but in sooth he is over young for such rough work as may be before us."

"And I have one favour to crave from you," added the lady of the castle, as Alleyne turned to leave their presence. "You have, as I understand, much learning which you have acquired at Beaulieu."

"Little enough, lady, compared with those who were my teachers."

"Yet enough for my purpose, I doubt not. For I would have you give an hour or two a day whilst you are with us in discoursing with my daughter, the Lady Maude; for she is somewhat backward, I fear, and hath no love for letters, save for these poor fond romances, which do but fill her empty head with dreams of enchanted maidens and of errant cavaliers. Father Christopher comes over after nones from the priory, but he is stricken with years and slow of speech, so that she gets small profit from his teaching. I would have you do what you can with her, and with Agatha my young tirewoman, and with Dorothy Pierpoint."

And so Alleyne found himself not only chosen as squire to a knight, but also as squire to three damozels, which was even further from the part which he had thought to play in the world. Yet he could but agree to do what he might, and so went forth from the castle hall with his face flushed and his head in a whirl at the thought of the strange and perilous paths which his feet were destined to tread.

CHAPTER XII

HOW ALLEYNE LEARNED MORE
THAN HE COULD TEACH

AND now there came a time of stir and bustle, of furbishing of arms and clang of hammer from all the southland counties. Fast spread the tidings from thorpe to thorpe and from castle to castle, that the old game was afoot once more, and the lions and lilies to be in the field with the early spring. Great news this for that fierce old country, whose trade for a generation had been war, her exports archers and her imports prisoners. For six years her sons had chafed under an unwonted peace. Now they flew to their arms as to their birthright. The old soldiers of Crécy, of Nogent, and of Poictiers were glad to think that they might hear the war-trumpet once more, and gladder still were the hot youth who had chafed for years under the martial tales of their sires. To pierce the great mountains of the south, to fight the tamers of the fiery Moors, to follow the greatest captain of the age, to find sunny cornfields and vineyards, when the marches of Picardy and Normandy were as bare and bleak as the Jedburgh forests—here was a golden prospect for a race of warriors. From sea to sea there was stringing of bows in the cottage and clang of steel in the castle.

Nor did it take long for every stronghold to pour forth its cavalry, and every hamlet its footmen. Through the late autumn and the early winter every road and country lane resounded with nakir and trumpet, with the neigh of the war horse and the clatter of marching men. From the Wrekin in the Welsh marches to the

Cotswolds in the west, or Butser in the south, there was no hilltop from which the peasant might not have seen the bright shimmer of arms, the toss and flutter of plume and of pensil. From bye-path, from woodland clearing, or from winding moor-side track these little rivulets of steel united in the larger roads to form a broader stream, growing ever fuller and larger as it approached the nearest or most commodious seaport. And there all day, and day after day, there was bustle and crowding and labour, while the great ships loaded up, and one after the other spread their white pinions and darted off to the open sea, amid the clash of cymbals and rolling of drums and lusty shouts of those who went and of those who waited. From Orwell to the Dart there was no port which did not send forth its little fleet, gay with streamer and bunting, as for a joyous festival. Thus in the season of the waning days the might of England put forth on to the waters.

In the ancient and populous county of Hampshire there was no lack of leaders or of soldiers for a service which promised either honour or profit. In the north the Saracen's head of the Brocas and the scarlet fish of the De Roches were waving over a strong body of archers from Holt, Woolmer, and Harewood forests. De Borhunte was up in the east, and Sir John de Montague in the west. Sir Luke de Ponynges, Sir Thomas West, Sir Maurice de Bruin, Sir Arthur Lipscombe, Sir Walter Ramsey, and stout Sir Oliver Buttesthorn were all marching south with levies from Andover, Alresford, Odiham, and Winchester, while from Sussex came Sir John Clinton, Sir Thomas Cheyne, and Sir John Fallislee, with a troop of picked men-at-arms, making for their port at South-ampton. Greatest of all the musters, however, was that at Twynham Castle, for the name and the fame of Sir Nigel Loring drew towards him the keenest and boldest spirits, all eager to serve under so valiant a leader. Archers from the New Forest and the Forest of Bere, billmen from the pleasant country which is watered by the Stour, the Avon, and the Itchen, young cavaliers from the ancient Hampshire houses, all were pushing for Christchurch to take serv-ice under the banner of the five scarlet roses.

And now, could Sir Nigel have shown the bachelles of land which the laws of rank required, he might well have cut his forked pennon into a square banner, and taken such a following into the field as would have supported the dignity of a banneret. But poverty was heavy upon him, his land was scant, his coffers empty, and the very castle which covered him the holding of another. Sore was his heart when he saw rare bowmen and war-hardened spearmen turned away from his gates, for the lack of the money which might equip and pay them. Yet the letter which Aylward had brought him gave him powers which he was not slow to use. In it Sir Claude Latour, the Gascon lieutenant of the White Company, assured him that there remained in his keeping enough to fit out a hundred archers and twenty men-at-arms, which, joined to the three hundred veteran companions already in France, would make a force which any leader might be proud to command. Carefully and sagaciously the veteran knight chose out his men from the swarm of volunteers. Many an anxious consultation he held with Black Simon, Sam Aylward, and other of his more experienced followers, as to who should come and who should stay. By All Saints' Day, however, ere the last leaves had fluttered to earth in the Wilverley and Holmesley glades, he had filled up his full numbers, and mustered under his banner as stout a following of Hampshire foresters as ever twanged their war-bows. Twenty men-at-arms, too, well mounted and equipped, formed the cavalry of the party, while young Peter Terlake of Fareham, and Walter Ford of Botley, the martial sons of martial sires, came at their own cost to wait upon Sir Nigel and to share with Alleyne Edricson the duties of his squireship.

Yet, even after the enrolment, there was much to be done ere the party could proceed upon its way. For armour, swords, and lances there was no need to take much forethought, for they were to be had both better and cheaper in Bordeaux than in England. With the long-bow, however, it was different. Yew staves indeed might be got in Spain, but it was well to take enough and to spare with them. Then three spare cords should be carried for each bow, with a great store of arrow-heads, besides the brigandines of chain mail, the wadded steel caps, and the brassarts or arm-guards, which were the proper equipment of the archer. Above all, the women for miles round were hard at work cutting the white surcoats which were the badge of the Company, and adorning them with the red lion of St George upon the centre of the breast. When all was completed and the muster called in the castle yard, the oldest soldier of the French wars was fain to confess that he had never looked upon a better-equipped or more warlike body of men, from the old knight with his silk jupon, sitting his great black warhorse in the front of them, to Hordle John, the giant recruit, who leaned carelessly upon a huge black bow-stave in the rear. Of the six score, fully half had seen service before, while a fair sprinkling were men who had followed the wars all their lives, and had a hand in those battles which had made the whole world ring with the fame and the wonder of the island infantry.

Six long weeks were taken in these preparations, and it was close on Martinmas ere all was ready for a start. Nigh two months had Alleyne Edricson been in Castle Twynham—months which were fated to turn the whole current of his life, to divert it from that dark and lonely bourne towards which it tended, and to guide it into freer and more sunlit channels. Already he had learned to bless his father for that wise provision which had made him seek to know the world ere he had ventured to renounce it.

For it was a very different place from that which he had pictured —very different from that which he had heard described when the master of the novices held forth to his charges upon the ravening wolves who lurked for them beyond the peaceful fold of Beaulieu. There was cruelty in it, doubtless, and lust and sin and sorrow; but were there not virtues to atone, robust positive virtues, which did not shrink from temptation, which held their own in all the rough blasts of the work-a-day world? How colourless by contrast appeared the sinlessness which came from inability to sin, the conquest which was attained by flying from the enemy! Monk-bred as he was, Alleyne had native shrewdness and a mind which was young enough to form new conclusions and to outgrow old ones. He could not fail to see that the men with whom he was thrown in contact, rough-tongued, fierce and quarrelsome as they were, were yet of deeper nature and of more service in the world than the ox-eyed brethren who rose and ate and slept from year's end to year's end in their own narrow stagnant circle of existence. Abbot Berghersh was a good man, but how was he better than this kindly knight, who lived as simple a life, held as lofty and inflexible an ideal of duty, and did with all his fearless heart whatever came to his hand to do? In turning from the service of the one to that of the other, Alleyne could not feel that he was lowering his aims in life. True that his gentle and thoughtful nature recoiled from the grim work of war, yet in those days of martial orders and militant brotherhoods there was no gulf fixed betwixt the priest and the soldier. The man of God and the man of the sword might without scandal be united in the same individual. Why then should he, a mere clerk, have scruples when so fair a chance lay in his way of carrying out the spirit as well as the letter of his father's provision? Much struggle it cost him, anxious spirit-questionings and midnight prayings, with many a doubt and a misgiving; but the issue was that ere he had been three days in Castle Twynham he had taken service under Sir Nigel, and had accepted horse and harness, the same to be paid for out of his share of the profits of the expedition. Henceforth for seven hours a day he strove in the tiltyard to qualify himself to be a worthy squire to so worthy a knight. Young, supple, and active, with all the pent energies from years of pure and healthy living, it was not long before he could manage his horse and his weapon well enough to earn an approving nod from critical men-at-arms, or to hold his own against Terlake and Ford, his fellow-servitors.

But were there no other considerations which swayed him from the cloisters towards the world? So complex is the human spirit that it can itself scarce discern the deep springs which impel it to action. Yet to Alleyne had been opened now a side of life of which he had been as innocent as a child, but one which was of such

SIR ARTHUR CONAN DOYLE

deep import that it could not fail to influence him in choosing his
path. A woman, in monkish precepts, had been the embodiment
and concentration of what was dangerous and evil—a focus
whence spread all that was to be dreaded and avoided. So defiling
was her presence that a true Cistercian might not raise his eyes to
her face or touch her finger-tips under ban of church and fear of
deadly sin. Yet here, day after day, for an hour after nones, and for
an hour before vespers, he found himself in close communion
with three maidens, all young, all fair, and all therefore doubly
dangerous from the monkish standpoint. Yet he found that in
their presence he was conscious of a quick sympathy, a pleasant
ease, a ready response to all that was most gentle and best in himself, which filled his soul with a vague and new-found joy.

And yet the Lady Maude Loring was no easy pupil to handle.
An older and more world-wise man might have been puzzled by
her varying moods, her sudden prejudices, her quick resentment
at all constraint and authority. Did a subject interest her, was there
space in it for either romance or imagination, she would fly
through it with her subtle active mind, leaving her two fellow-
students and even her teacher toiling behind her. On the other
hand, were there dull patience needed with steady toil and strain
of memory, no single fact could by any driving be fixed in her
mind. Alleyne might talk to her of the stories of old gods and
heroes, of gallant deeds and lofty aims, or he might hold forth
upon moon and stars, and let his fancy wander over the hidden
secrets of the universe, and he would have a rapt listener with
flushed cheeks and eloquent eyes, who could repeat after him the
very words which had fallen from his lips. But when it came to
almagest and astrolabe, the counting of figures and reckoning of
epicycles, away would go her thoughts to horse and hound, and a
vacant eye and listless face would warn the teacher that he had lost
his hold upon his scholar. Then he had but to bring out the old
romance book from the priory, with befingered cover of sheepskin and gold letters upon a purple ground, to entice her wayward
mind back to the paths of learning.

At times, too, when the wild fit was upon her, she would break into pertness and rebel openly against Alleyne's gentle firmness. Yet he would jog quietly on with his teachings, taking no heed to her mutiny, until suddenly she would be conquered by his patience, and break into self-revilings a hundred times stronger than her fault demanded. It chanced however that, on one of these mornings when the evil mood was upon her, Agatha the young tirewoman, thinking to please her mistress, began also to toss her head and make tart rejoinder to the teacher's questions. In an instant the Lady Maude had turned upon her two blazing eyes and a face which was blanched with anger.

"You would dare!" said she. "You would dare!"

The frightened tirewoman tried to excuse herself. "But, my fair lady," she stammered, "what have I done? I have said no more than I heard."

"You would dare!" repeated the lady in a choking voice. "You, a graceless baggage, a foolish lack-brain, with no thought above the hemming of shifts! And he so kindly, and hendy and long-suffering! You would—ha, you may well flee the room!"

She had spoken with a rising voice, and a clasping and opening of her long white fingers, so that it was no marvel that ere the speech was over the skirts of Agatha were whisking round the door and the click of her sobs to be heard dying swiftly away down the corridor.

Alleyne stared open-eyed at this tigress who had sprung so suddenly to his rescue. "There is no need for such anger," he said mildly. "The maid's words have done me no scath. It is you yourself who have erred."

"I know it," she cried. "I am a most wicked woman. But it is bad enough that one should misuse you. Ma foi! I will see that there is not a second one."

"Nay, nay, no one has misused me," he answered. "But the fault lies in your hot and bitter words. You have called her a baggage and a lack-brain, and I know not what."

"And you are he who taught me to speak the truth," she cried. "Now I have spoken it, and yet I cannot please you. Lack-brain she is, and lack-brain I shall call her."

Such was the sample of the sudden janglings which marred the peace of that little class. As the weeks passed, however, they became fewer and less violent, as Alleyne's firm and constant nature gained sway and influence over the Lady Maude. And yet, sooth to say, there were times when he had to ask himself whether it was not the Lady Maude who was gaining sway and influence over him. If she were changing, so was he. In drawing her up from the world, he was day by day being himself dragged down towards it. In vain he strove and reasoned with himself as to the madness of letting his mind rest upon Sir Nigel's daughter. What was he—a younger son, a penniless clerk, a squire unable to pay for his own harness—that he should dare to raise his eyes to the fairest maid in Hampshire? So spake reason; but, in spite of all, her voice was ever in his ears and her image in his heart. Stronger than reason, stronger than cloister teachings, stronger than all that might hold him back, was that old, old tyrant who will brook no rival in the kingdom of youth.

And yet it was a surprise and a shock to himself to find how deeply she had entered into his life; how completely those vague ambitions and yearnings which had filled his spiritual nature centred themselves now upon this thing of earth. He had scarce dared to face the change which had come upon him, when a few sudden chance words showed it all up hard and clear, like a lightning flash in the darkness.

He had ridden over to Poole, one November day, with his fellow-squire, Peter Terlake, in quest of certain yew-staves from Wat Swathling, the Dorsetshire armourer. The day for their departure had almost come, and the two youths spurred it over the lonely downs at the top of their speed on their homeward course, for evening had fallen and there was much to be done. Peter was a hard, wiry, brown-faced country-bred lad, who looked on the coming war as the schoolboy looks on his holidays. This day, however, he had been sombre and mute, with scarce a word a mile to bestow upon his comrade.

"Tell me, Alleyne Edricson," he broke out, suddenly, as they clattered along the winding track which leads over the Bournemouth hills, "Has it not seemed to you that of late the Lady Maude is paler and more silent than is her wont?"

"It may be so," the other answered shortly.

"And would rather sit distrait by her oriel than ride gaily to the chase as of old. Methinks, Alleyne, it is this learning which you have taught her that has taken all the life and sap from her. It is more than she can master, like a heavy spear to a light rider."

"Her lady-mother has so ordered it," said Alleyne.

"By our Lady! and withouten disrespect," quoth Terlake, "it is in my mind that her lady-mother is more fitted to lead a company to a storming than to have the upbringing of this tender and milk-white maid. Hark ye, lad Alleyne, to what I never told man or woman yet. I love the fair Lady Maude, and would give the last drop of my heart's blood to serve her." He spoke with a gasping voice, and his face flushed crimson in the moonlight.

Alleyne said nothing, but his heart seemed to turn to a lump of ice in his bosom.

"My father has broad acres," the other continued, "from Fareham Creek to the slope of the Portsdown Hill. There is filling of granges, hewing of wood, malting of grain, and herding of sheep as much as heart could wish, and I the only son. Sure am I that Sir Nigel would be blithe at such a match."

"But how of the lady?" asked Alleyne, with dry lips.

"Ah, lad, there lies my trouble. It is a toss of the head and a droop of the eyes if I say one word of what is in my mind. 'Twere as easy to woo the snow-dame that we shaped last winter in our castle yard. I did but ask her yesternight for her green veil, that I might bear it as a token or lambrequin upon my helm; but she flashed out at me that she kept it for a better man, and then all in a breath asked pardon for that she had spoke so rudely. Yet she would not take back the words either, nor would she grant the veil. Has it seemed to thee, Alleyne, that she loves anyone?"

"Nay, I cannot say," said Alleyne, with a wild throb of sudden hope in his heart.

"I have thought so, and yet I cannot name the man. Indeed, save myself, and Walter Ford, and you, who are half a clerk, and Father Christopher of the Priory, and Bertrand the page, who is there whom she sees?"

"I cannot tell," quoth Alleyne shortly: and the two squires rode on again, each intent upon his own thoughts.

Next day at morning lesson the teacher observed that his pupil was indeed looking pale and jaded, with listless eyes and a weary manner. He was heavy-hearted to note the grievous change in her.

"Your mistress, I fear, is ill, Agatha," he said to the tirewoman, when the Lady Maude had sought her chamber.

The maid looked aslant at him with laughing eyes. "It is not an illness that kills," quoth she.

"Pray God not!" he cried. "But tell me, Agatha, what it is that ails her."

"Methinks that I could lay my hand upon another who is smitten with the same trouble," she said, with the same sidelong look. "Canst not give a name to it, and thou so skilled in leechcraft?"

"Nay, save that she seems aweary."

"Well, bethink you that it is but three days ere you will all be gone, and Castle Twynham be as dull as the Priory. Is there not enough there to cloud a lady's brow?"

"In sooth, yes," he answered, "I had forgot that she is about to lose her father."

"Her father!" cried the tirewoman, with a little trill of laughter. "Oh, simple, simple!" And she was off down the passage like arrow from bow, while Alleyne stood gazing after her, betwixt hope and doubt, scarce daring to put faith in the meaning which seemed to underlie her words.

CHAPTER XIII

HOW THE WHITE COMPANY
SET FORTH TO THE WARS

ST Luke's day had come and had gone, and it was in the season of Martinmas, when the oxen are driven in to the slaughter, that the White Company was ready for its journey. Loud shrieked the brazen bugles from keep and from gateway, and merry was the rattle of the war-drum, as the men gathered in the outer bailey, with torches to light them, for the mom had not yet broken. Alleyne, from the window of the armoury, looked down upon the strange scene — the circles of yellow flickering light, the lines of stern and bearded faces, the quick shimmer of arms, and the lean heads of the horses. In front stood the bowmen, ten deep, with a fringe of under-officers, who paced hither and thither marshalling the ranks with curt precept or short rebuke. Behind were the little clump of steel-clad horsemen, their lances raised, with long pensils drooping down the oaken shafts. So silent and still were they, that they might have been metal-sheathed statues, were it not for the occasional quick impatient stamp of their chargers, or the rattle of chamfron against neck plates as they tossed and strained. A spear's length in front of them sat the spare and long-limbed figure of Black Simon, the Norwich fighting man, his fierce, deep-lined face framed in steel, and the silk guidon marked with the five scarlet roses slanting over his right shoulder. All round, in the edge of the circle of the light, stood the castle servants, the soldiers who were to form the garrison, and little knots of women, who sobbed in their aprons and called shrilly to their name-saints to watch over the Wat, or Will, or Peterkin who had turned his hand to the work of war.

The young squire was leaning forward, gazing at the stirring and martial scene, when he heard a short quick gasp at his shoulder, and there was the Lady Maude, with her hand to her heart, leaning up against the wall, slender and fair like a half-plucked lily. Her face was turned away from him, but he could see, by the sharp intake of her breath, that she was weeping bitterly.

"Alas! alas!" he cried, all unnerved at the sight, "why is it that you are so sad, lady?"

"It is the sight of these brave men," she answered, "and to think how many of them go and how few are like to find their way back. I have seen it before, when I was a little maid, in the year of the Prince's great battle. I remember then how they mustered in the bailey, even as they do now, and my lady-mother holding me in her arms at this very window that I might see the show."

"Please God, you will see them all back ere another year be out," said he.

She shook her head, looking round at him with flushed cheeks and eyes which sparkled in the lamp-light. "Oh, but I hate myself for being a woman!" she cried, with a stamp of her little foot. "What can I do that is good? Here I must bide, and talk and sew and spin, and spin and sew and talk. Ever the same dull round, with nothing at the end of it. And now you are going too, who could carry my thoughts out of these grey walls, and raise my mind above tapestry and distaffs. What can I do? I am of no more use or value than that broken bow-stave."

"You are of such value to me," he cried, in a whirl of hot passionate words, "that all else has become nought. You are my heart, my life, my one and only thought. Oh, Maude, I cannot live without you, I cannot leave you without a word of love. All is changed to me since I have known you. I am poor and lowly and all unworthy of you; but if great love may weigh down such defects, then mine may do it. Give me but one word of hope to take to the wars with me—but one. Ah, you shrink, you shudder! My wild words have frightened you."

Twice she opened her lips, and twice no sound came from them. At last she spoke in a hard and measured voice, as one who dare not trust herself to speak too freely.

"This is over-sudden," she said. "It is not so long since the world was nothing to you. You have changed once; perchance you may change again."

"Cruel!" he cried, "who hath changed me?"

"And then your brother," she continued with a little laugh, disregarding his question. "Methinks this hath become a family custom amongst the Edricsons. Nay, I am sorry; I did not mean a jibe. But indeed, Alleyne, this hath come suddenly upon me, and I scarce know what to say."

"Say some word of hope, however distant—some kind word that I may cherish in my heart."

"Nay, Alleyne, it were a cruel kindness, and you have been too good and true a friend to me that I should use you despitefully. There cannot be a closer link between us. It is madness to think of it. Were there no other reasons, it is enough that my father and your brother would both cry out against it."

"My brother, what has he to do with it? And your father—"

"Come, Alleyne, was it not you who would have me act fairly to all men, and, certes, to my father amongst them?"

"You say truly," he cried, "you say truly. But you do not reject me, Maude? You give me some ray of hope? I do not ask pledge or promise. Say only that I am not hateful to you—that on some happier day I may hear kinder words from you."

Her eyes softened upon him, and a kind answer was on her lips, when a hoarse shout, with the clatter of arms and stamping of steeds, rose up from the bailey below. At the sound her face set, her eyes sparkled, and she stood with flushed cheek and head thrown back—a woman's body but a soul of fire.

"My father hath gone down," she cried. "Your place is by his side. Nay, look not at me, Alleyne. It is no time for dallying. Win my father's love, and all may follow. It is when the brave soldier hath done his devoir that he hopes for his reward. Farewell, and may God be with you!" She held out her white, slim hand to him, but as he bent his lips over it she whisked it away and was gone, leaving in his outstretched hand the very green veil for which poor Peter Terlake had craved in vain. Again the hoarse cheering burst out from below, and he heard the clang of the rising portcullis. Pressing the veil to his lips, he thrust it into the bosom of his tunic, and rushed as fast as feet could bear him to arm himself and join the muster.

The raw morning had broken ere the hot spiced ale was served found and the last farewell spoken. A cold wind blew up from the sea and ragged clouds drifted swiftly across the sky. The Christchurch townsfolk stood huddled about the Bridge of Avon, the women pulling tight their shawls and the men swathing themselves in their gaberdines, while down the winding path from the castle came the van of the little army, their feet clanging on the hard frozen road. First came Black Simon with his banner, bestriding a lean and powerful dapple-grey charger, as hard and wiry and warwise as himself. After him, riding three abreast, were nine men-atarms, all picked soldiers, who had followed the French wars before, and knew the marches of Picardy as they knew the downs of their native Hampshire. They were armed to the teeth with lance, sword, and mace, with square shields notched at the upper right-hand corner to serve as a spear-rest. For defence each man wore a coat of interlaced leathern thongs strengthened at the shoulder, elbow and upper arm with slips of steel. Greaves and knee-pieces were also of leather backed by steel, and their gauntlets and shoes were of iron plates, craftily jointed. So, with jingle of arms and clatter of hoofs, they rode across the Bridge of Avon, while the burghers shouted lustily for the flag of the five roses and its gallant guard.

Close at the heels of the horses came two score archers, bearded and burly, their round targets on their backs and their long yellow bows, the most deadly weapon that the wit of man had yet devised, thrusting forth from behind their shoulders. From each man's girdle hung sword or axe, according to his humour, and over the right hip there jutted out the leathern quiver, with its bristle of goose, pigeon, and peacock feathers. Behind the bowmen strode two drummers beating their nakirs, and two trumpeters in parti-coloured clothes. After them came twenty-seven sumpter-horses carrying tent-poles, cloth, spare arms, spurs, wedges, cooking kettles, horseshoes, bags of nails, and the hundred other things which experience had shown to be needful in a harried and hostile country. A white mule with red trappings, led by a varlet, carried Sir Nigel's own napery and table comforts. Then came two score more archers, ten more men-at-arms, and finally a rearguard of twenty bowmen, with big John towering in the front rank and the veteran Aylward marching by his side, his battered harness and faded surcoat in strange contrast with the snow-white jupons and shining brigandines of his companions. A quick cross-fire of greetings and questions and rough West Saxon jests flew from rank to rank, or were bandied about betwixt the marching archers and the gazing crowd.

"Holà, Gaffer Higginson!" cried Aylward, as he spied the portly figure of the village innkeeper. "No more of thy nutbrown, mon gar. We leave it behind us."

"By St Paul, no!" cried the other. "You take it with you. Devil a drop have you left in the great kilderkin. It was time for you to go."

"If your cask is leer, I warrant your purse is full, gaffer," shouted Hordle John. "See that you lay in good store of the best for our home-coming."

"See that you keep your throat whole for the drinking of it, archer," cried a voice, and the crowd laughed at the rough pleasantry.

"If you will warrant the beer, I will warrant the throat," said John composedly.

"Close up the ranks!" cried Aylward. "En avant, mes enfants! Ah, by my finger-bones, there is my sweet Mary from the Priory Mill! Ma foi, but she is beautiful! Adieu, Mary, ma chérie. Mon coeur est toujours à toi. Brace your belt, Watkin, man, and swing your shoulders as a free companion should. By my hilt! your jerkins will be as dirty as mine ere you clap eyes on Hengistbury Head again."

The Company had marched to the turn of the road ere Sir Nigel Loring rode out from the gateway, mounted on Pommers, his great black war-horse, whose ponderous footfall on the wooden drawbridge echoed loudly from the gloomy arch which spanned it. Sir Nigel was still in his velvet dress of peace, with flat velvet cap of maintenance, and curling ostrich feather clasped in a golden brooch. To his three squires riding behind him it looked as though he bore the bird's egg as well as its feather, for the back of his bald pate shone like a globe of ivory. He bore no arms save the long and heavy sword which hung at his saddle-bow; but Terlake carried in front of him the high wivern-crested bassinet, Ford the heavy ash spear with swallow-tail pennon, while Alleyne was entrusted with the emblazoned shield. The Lady Loring rode her palfrey at her Lord's bridle-arm, for she would see him as far as the edge of the forest, and ever and anon she turned her hard-lined face up wistfully to him and ran a questioning eye over his apparel and appointments.

"I trust that there is nothing forgot," she said, beckoning to Alleyne to ride on her further side. "I trust him to you, Edricson. Hosen, shirts, cyclas, and under-jupons are in the brown basket on the left side of the mule. His wine he takes hot when the nights are cold, malvoisie or vernage, with as much spice as would cover the thumb-nail. See that he hath a change if he come back hot from the tilting. There is a goose-grease in a box, if the old scars ache at the turn of the weather. Let his blankets be dry and—"

"Nay, my heart's life," the little knight interrupted, "trouble not now about such matters. Why so pale and wan, Edricson? Is it not enow to make a man's heart dance to see this noble company, such valiant men-at-arms, such lusty archers? By St Paul! I should be ill to please if I were not blithe to see the red roses flying at the head of so noble a following!"

"The purse I have already given you, Edricson," continued the lady. "There are in it twenty-three marks, one noble, three shillings and fourpence, which is a great treasure for one man to carry. And I pray you to bear in mind, Edricson, that he hath two pair of shoes, those of red leather for common use, and the others with golden toe-chains, which he may wear should he chance to drink wine with the Prince or with Chandos."

"My sweet bird," said Sir Nigel, "I am right loth to part from you, but we are now at the fringe of the forest, and it is not right that I should take the chatelaine too far from her trust."

"But oh, my dear lord," she cried with a trembling lip, "let me bide with you for one furlong further—or one and a half, perhaps. You may spare me this out of the weary miles that you will journey alone."

"Come then, my heart's comfort," he answered. "But I must crave a gage from thee. It is my custom, dearling, and hath been since I have first known thee, to proclaim by herald in such camps, townships, or fortalices as I may chance to visit, that my ladylove being beyond compare the fairest and sweetest in Christendom, I should deem it great honour and kindly condescension if any cavalier would run three courses against me with sharpened lances, should he chance to have a lady whose claim he was willing to advance. I pray you then, my fair dove, that you will vouchsafe to me one of those doeskin gloves, that I may wear it as the badge of her whose servant I shall ever be."

"Alack and alas for the fairest and sweetest!" she cried. "Fair and sweet I would fain be for your dear sake, my lord, but old I am and ugly, and the knights would laugh should you lay lance in rest in such a cause."

"Edricson," quoth Sir Nigel, "you have young eyes, and mine are somewhat bedimmed. Should you chance to see a knight laugh, or smile, or even, look you, arch his brows, or purse his mouth, or in any way show surprise that I should uphold the Lady Mary, you will take particular note of his name, his coat-armour, and his lodging. Your glove, my life's desire!"

The Lady Mary Loring slipped her hand from her yellow leather gauntlet, and he, lifting it with dainty reverence, bound it to the front of his velvet cap.

"It is with mine other guardian angels," quoth he, pointing at the saints' medals which hung beside it. "And now, my dearest, you have come far enow. May the Virgin guard and prosper thee! One kiss!" He bent down from his saddle, and then striking spurs into his horse's sides, he galloped at top speed after his men, with his three squires at his heels. Half a mile further, where the road topped a hill, they looked back, and the Lady Mary on her white palfrey was still where they had left her. A moment later they were on the downward slope, and she had vanished from their view.

CHAPTER XIV

HOW SIR NIGEL SOUGHT
FOR A WAYSIDE VENTURE

FOR a time Sir Nigel was very moody and downcast, with bent brows and eyes upon the pommel of his saddle. Edricson and Terlake rode behind him in little better case, while Ford, a careless and light-hearted youth, grinned at the melancholy of his companions, and flourished his lord's heavy spear, making a point to right and a point to left, as though he were a paladin contending against a host of assailants. Sir Nigel happening, however, to turn himself in his saddle, Ford instantly became as stiff and as rigid as though he had been struck with a palsy. The four rode alone, for the archers had passed a curve in the road, though Alleyne could still hear the heavy clump, clump of their marching, or catch a glimpse of the sparkle of steel through the tangle of leafless branches.

"Ride by my side, friends, I entreat of you," said the knight, reining in his steed that they might come abreast of him. "For since it hath pleased you to follow me to the wars, it were well that you should know how you may best serve me. I doubt not, Terlake, that you will show yourself a worthy son of a valiant father, and you, Ford, of yours; and you, Edricson, that you are mindful of the old-time house from which all men know that you are sprung. And first I would have you bear very steadfastly in mind that our setting forth is by no means for the purpose of gaining spoil or exacting ransom, though it may well happen that such may come to us also. We go to France, and from thence, I trust, to Spain, in humble search of a field in which we may win advancement and perchance some small share of glory. For this purpose I would have you know that it is not my wont to let any occasion pass where it is in any way possible that honour may be gained. I would have you bear this in mind, and give great heed to it that you may bring me word of all cartels, challenges, wrongs, tyrannies, infamies, and wronging of damsels. Nor is any occasion too small to take note of, for I have known such trifles as the dropping of a gauntlet, or the flicking of a breadcrumb, when well and properly followed up, lead to a most noble spear-running. But, Edricson, do I not see a cavalier Who rides down yonder road amongst the nether shaw? It would be well, perchance, that you should give him greeting from me, and, should he be of gentle blood, it may be that he would care to exchange thrusts with me."

"Why, my lord," quoth Ford, standing in his stirrups and shading his eyes, "it is old Hob Davidson, the fat miller of Milton!"

"Ah, so it is, indeed," said Sir Nigel, puckering his cheeks, "but wayside ventures are not to be scorned, for I have seen no finer passages than are to be had from such chance meetings, when cavaliers are willing to advance themselves. I can well remember that two leagues from the town of Rheims I met a very valiant and courteous cavalier of France, with whom I had gentle and most honourable contention for upwards of an hour. It hath ever grieved me that I had not his name, for he smote upon me with a mace and went upon his way ere I was in condition to have much speech with him; but his arms were an allurion in chief above a fess azure. I was also on such an occasion thrust through the shoulder by Lyon de Montcourt, whom I met on the high road betwixt Libourne and Bordeaux. I met him but once, but I have never seen a man for whom I bear a greater love and esteem. And so also with the squire Le Bourg Capillet, who would have been a very valiant captain had he lived."

"He is dead, then?" asked Alleyne Edricson.

"Alas! it was my ill fate to slay him in a bickering which broke out in a field near the township of Tarbes. I cannot call to mind how the thing came about, for it was in the year of the Prince's ride through Languedoc, when there was much fine skirmishing to be had at barriers. By St Paul! I do not think that any honourable cavalier could ask for better chance of advancement than might be had by spurring forth before the army and riding to the gateways of Narbonne, or Bergerac, or Mont Giscar, where some courteous gentleman would ever be at wait to do what he might to meet your wish or ease you of your vow. Such a one at Ventadour ran three courses with me betwixt daybreak and sunrise, to the great exaltation of his lady."

"And did you slay him also, my lord?" asked Ford with reverence.

"I could never learn, for he was carried within the barrier, and as I had chanced to break the bone of my leg it was a great unease to me to ride or even to stand. Yet, by the goodness of heaven and the pious intercession of the valiant St George, I was able to sit my charger in the great battle which was no very long time afterwards. But what have we here? A very fair and courtly maiden, or I mistake."

It was indeed a tall and buxom country lass, with a basket of spinach leaves upon her head, and a great slab of bacon tucked under one arm. She bobbed a frightened curtsey as Sir Nigel swept his velvet hat from his head and reined up his great charger.

"God be with thee, fair maiden!" said he.

"God guard thee, my lord!" she answered, speaking in the broadest West Saxon speech, and balancing herself first on one foot and then on the other in her bashfulness.

"Fear not, my fair damsel," said Sir Nigel, "but tell me if perchance a poor and most unworthy knight can in any wise be of service to you. Should it chance that you have been used despitefully, it may be that I may obtain justice for you."

"Lawk no, kind sir," she answered, clutching her bacon the tighter, as though some design upon it might be hid under this knightly offer. "I be the milking wench o' fairmer Arnold, and he be as kind a maister as heart could wish."

"It is well," said he, and with a shake of the bridle rode on down the woodland path. "I would have you bear in mind," he continued to his squires, "that gentle courtesy is not, as is the base use of so many false knights, to be shown only to maidens of high degree, for there is no woman so humble that a true knight may not listen to her tale of wrong. But here comes a cavalier who is indeed in haste. Perchance it would be well that we should ask him whither he rides, for it may be that he is one who desires to advance himself in chivalry."

The bleak, hard, wind-swept road dipped down in front of them into a little valley, and then, writhing up the heathy slope upon the other side, lost itself among the gaunt pinetrees. Far away between the black lines of trunks the quick glitter of steel marked where the Company pursued its way. To the north stretched the tree country, but to the south, between two swelling downs, a glimpse might be caught of the cold grey shimmer of the sea, with the white fleck of a galley sail upon the distant sky-line. Just in front of the travellers a horseman was urging his steed up the slope, driving it on with whip and spur as one who rides for a set purpose. As he clattered up, Alleyne could see that the roan horse was grey with dust and flecked with foam, as though it had left many a mile behind it: The rider was a stern-faced man, hard of mouth and dry of eye, with a heavy sword clanking at his side, and a stiff white bundle swathed in linen balanced across the pommel of his saddle.

"The king's messenger!" he bawled as he came up to them. "The messenger of the king! Clear the causeway for the king's own man."

"Not so loudly, friend," quoth the little knight, reining his horse half round to bar the path. "I have myself been the king's man for thirty years and more, but I have not been wont to halloo about it on a peaceful highway."

"I ride in his service," cried the other, "and I carry that which belongs to him. You bar my path at your peril."

"Yet I have known the king's enemies to ride in his name," said Sir Nigel. "The foul fiend may lurk beneath a garment of light. We must have some sign or warrant of your mission."

"Then must I hew a passage," cried the stranger, with his shoulder braced round and his hand upon his hilt. "I am not to be stopped on the king's service by every gadabout."

"Should you be a gentleman of quarterings and coat-armour," lisped Sir Nigel, "I shall be very blithe to go further into the matter with you. If not, I have three very worthy squires, any one of whom would take the thing upon himself, and debate it with you in a very honourable way."

The man scowled from one to the other, and his hand stole away from his sword.

"You ask me for a sign," he said. "Here is a sign for you, since you must have one." As he spoke he whirled the covering from the object in front of him and showed to their horror that it was a newly severed human leg. "By God's tooth!" he continued, with a brutal laugh, "you ask me if I am a man of quarterings, and it is even so, for I am officer to the verderer's court at Lyndhurst. This thievish leg is to hang at Milton, and the other is already at Brockenhurst, as a sign to all men of what comes of being over fond of venison pasty."

"Faugh!" cried Sir Nigel. "Pass on the other side of the road, fellow, and let us have the wind of you. We shall trot our horses, my friends, across this pleasant valley, for, by Our Lady, a breath of God's fresh air is right welcome after such a sight."

"We hoped to snare a falcon," said he presently, "but we netted a carrion-crow. Ma foi! but there are men whose hearts are tougher than a boar's hide. For me, I have played the old game of war since ever I had hair on my chin, and I have seen ten thousand brave men in one day with their faces to the sky, but I swear by Him who made me that I cannot abide the work of the butcher."

"And yet, my fair lord," said Edricson, "there has, from what I hear, been much of such devil's work in France."

"Too much, too much," he answered. "But I have ever observed that the foremost in the field are they who would scorn to mishandle a prisoner! By St Paul! it is not they who carry the breach who are wont to sack the town, but the laggard knaves who come crowding in when a way has been cleared for them. But what is this among the trees?"

"It is a shrine of Our Lady," said Terlake, "and a blind beggar who lives by the alms of those who worship there."

"A shrine!" cried the knight, "Then let us put up an orison."
Pulling off his cap, and clasping his hands, he chaunted in a shrill
voice: "Benedictus dominus Deus meus, qui docet manus meas ad
proelium, et digitos meos ad bellum." A strange figure he seemed
to his three squires, perched on his huge horse, with his eyes
upturned and the wintry sun shimmering upon his bald head. "It
is a noble prayer," he remarked, putting on his hat again, "and it
was taught to me by the noble Chandos himself. But how fares it
with you, father? Methinks that I should have ruth upon you, seeing that I am myself like one who looks through a horn window
while his neighbours have the clear crystal. Yet, by St Paul! there is
a long stride between the man who hath a horn casement and him
who is walled in on every hand."

"Alas! fair sir," cried the blind old man, "I have not seen the
blessed blue of heaven this two score years, since a levin flash
burned the sight out of my head."

"You have been blind to much that is goodly and fair," quoth Sir
Nigel, "but you have also been spared much that is sorry and foul.
This very hour our eyes have been shocked with that which would
have left you unmoved. But, by St Paul! we must on, or our
Company will think that they have lost their captain somewhat early
in the venture. Throw the man my purse, Edricson, and let us go."

Alleyn, lingering behind, bethought him of the Lady Loring's
counsel, and reduced the noble gift which the knight had so freely
bestowed to a single penny, which the beggar with many mumbled
blessings thrust away into his wallet. Then, spurring his steed, the
young squire rode at the top of his speed after his companions,
and overtook them just at the spot where the trees fringe off into
the moor and the straggling hamlet of Hordle lies scattered on
either side of the winding and deeply rutted track. The Company
was already well nigh through the village; but as the knight and his
squires closed up upon them, they heard the clamour of a strident
voice, followed by a roar of deep-chested laughter from the ranks
of the archers. Another minute brought them up with the rearguard, where every man marched with his beard on his shoulder

and a face which was agrin with merriment. By the side of the column walked a huge red-headed bowman, with his hands thrown out in argument and expostulation, while close at his heels followed a little wrinkled woman, who poured forth a shrill volley of abuse, varied by an occasional thwack from her stick, given with all the force of her body, though she might have been beating one of the forest trees for all the effect that she seemed likely to produce.

"I trust, Aylward," said Sir Nigel gravely, as he rode up, "that this doth not mean that any violence hath been offered to women. If such a thing happened, I tell you that the man shall hang, though he were the best archer that ever wore brassart."

"Nay, my fair lord," Aylward answered with a grin, "it is violence which is offered to a man. He comes from Hordle, and this is his mother who hath come forth to welcome him."

"You rammucky lurden," she was howling, with a blow between each catch of her breath, "you shammocking yaping over-long good-for-nought. I will teach thee! I will baste thee! Aye, by my faith!"

"Whist, mother," said John, looking back at her from the tail of his eye. "I go to France as an archer to give blows and to take them."

"To France, quotha?" cried the old dame. "Bide here with me, and I shall warrant you more blows than you are like to get in France. If blows be what you seek, you need not go further than Hordle."

"By my hilt! the good dame speaks truth," said Aylward. "It seems to be the very home of them."

"What have you to say, you clean-shaved galleybagger?" cried the fiery dame, turning upon the archer. "Can I not speak with my own son but you must let your tongue clack? A soldier, quotha, and never a hair on his face. I have seen a better soldier with pap for food and swaddling clothes for harness."

"Stand to it, Aylward," cried the archers, amid a fresh burst of laughter.

"Do not thwart her, comrade," said big John. "She hath a proper spirit for her years and cannot abide to be thwarted. It is kindly and homely to me to hear her voice and to feel that she is behind me. But I must leave you now, mother, for the way is over-rough for your feet; but I will bring you back a silken gown, if there be one in France, or Spain, and I will bring Jinny a silver penny; so good-bye to you, and God have you in his keeping!" Whipping up the little woman, he lifted her lightly to his lips, and then, taking his place in the ranks again, marched on with the laughing Company.

"That was ever his way," she cried, appealing to Sir Nigel, who reined up his horse and listened with the gravest courtesy. "He would jog on his own road for all that I could do to change him. First he must be a monk forsooth, and all because a wench was wise enough to turn her back on him. Then he joins a rascally crew and must needs trapse off to the wars, and me with no one to bait the fire if I be out, or tend the cow if I be home. Yet I have been a good mother to him. Three hazel switches a day have I broke across his shoulders, and he takes no more notice than you have seen him today."

"Doubt not that he will come back to you both safe and prosperous, my fair dame," quoth Sir Nigel. "Meanwhile it grieves me that, as I have already given my purse to a beggar up the road, I—"

"Nay, my lord," said Alleyne, "I still have some monies remaining."

"Then I pray you to give them to the very worthy woman." He cantered on as he spoke, while Alleyn, having dispensed two more pence, left the old dame standing by the furthest cottage of Hordle with her shrill voice raised in blessings instead of revilings.

There were two cross-roads before they reached the Lymington Ford, and at each of them Sir Nigel pulled up his horse, and waited with many a curvet and gambade, craning his neck this way and that to see if fortune would send him a venture. Crossroads had, as he explained, been rare places for knightly spear-running, and in his youth it was no uncommon thing for a cavalier to abide for weeks at such a point, holding gentle debate with all comers, to his own advancement and the great honour of his lady. The times were changed, however, and the forest tracks wound away from them deserted and silent, with no trample of warhorse or clang of armour which might herald the approach of an adversary—so that Sir Nigel rode on his way disconsolate. At the Lymington river they splashed through the ford, and lay in the meadows on the further side to eat the bread and salt meat which they carried upon the sumpter horses. Then, ere the sun was up the slope of the heavens, they had deftly trussed up again, and were swinging merrily upon their way, two hundred feet moving like two.

There is a third cross-road where the track from Boldre runs down to the old fishing village of Pitt's Deep. Down this, as they came abreast of it, there walked two men, the one a pace or two behind the other. The cavaliers could not but pull up their horses to look at them, for a stranger pair were never seen journeying together. The first was a mis-shapen squalid man with cruel cunning eyes and a shock of tangled red hair, bearing in his hands a small unpainted cross, which he held high so that all men might see it. He seemed to be in the last extremity of fright, with a face the colour of clay and his limbs all ashake as one who hath an ague. Behind him, with his toe ever rasping upon the other's heels, there walked a very stern black-bearded man with a hard eye and a set mouth. He bore over his shoulder a great knotted stick with three jagged nails stuck in the head of it, and from time to time he whirled it up in the air with a quivering arm, as though he could scarce hold back from dashing his companion's brains out. So in silence they walked under the spread of the branches on the grass-grown path from Boldre.

"By St Paul!" quoth the knight, "but this is a passing strange sight, and perchance some very perilous and honourable venture may arise from it. I pray you, Edricson, to ride up to them and to ask them the cause of it."

There was no need, however, for him to move, for the twain came swiftly towards them until they were within a spear's length, when the man with the cross sat himself down sullenly upon a tussock of grass by the wayside, while the other stood beside him with his great cudgel still hanging over his head. So intent was he that he raised his eyes neither to knight nor squires, but kept them ever fixed with a savage glare upon his comrade.

"I pray you, friend," said Sir Nigel, "to tell us truthfully who you are, and why you follow this man with such bitter enmity."

"So long as I am within the pale of the king's law," the stranger answered, "I cannot see why I should render account to every passing wayfarer."

"You are no very shrewd reasoner, fellow," quoth the knight; "for if it be within the law for you to threaten him with your club, then it is also lawful for me to threaten you with my sword."

The man with the cross was down in an instant on his knees upon the ground, with hands clasped above him and his face shining with hope. "For dear Christ's sake, my fair lord," he cried in a crackling voice, "I have at my belt a bag with a hundred rose nobles, and I will give it to you freely if you will but pass your sword through this man's body."

"How, you foul knave?" exclaimed Sir Nigel hotly. "Do you think that a cavalier's arm is to be bought like a packman's ware? By St Paul! I have little doubt that this fellow hath some very good cause to hold you in hatred."

"Indeed, my fair sir, you speak sooth," quoth he with the club, while the other seated himself once more by the wayside. "For this man is Peter Peterson, a very noted rieve, drawlatch, and murtherer, who has wrought much evil for many years in the parts about Winchester. It was but the other day, upon the feast of the blessed Simon and Jude, that he slew my younger brother William in Bere Forest—for which, by the black thorn of Glastonbury! I shall have his heart's blood, though I walked behind him to the further end of the earth."

"But if this be indeed so," asked Sir Nigel, "why is it that you have come with him so far through the forest?"

"Because I am an honest Englishman, and will take no more than the law allows. For when the deed was done this foul and base wretch fled to sanctuary at St Cross, and I, as you may think, after him with all the posse. The Prior, however, hath so ordered that while he holds this cross no man may lay hand upon him without the ban of church, which heaven forefend from me or mine. Yet, if for an instant he lay the cross aside, or if he fail to journey to Pitt's Deep, where it is ordered that he shall take ship to outland parts, or if he take not the first ship, or if until the ship be ready he walk not every day into the sea as far as his loins, then he becomes out-law, and I shall forthwith dash out his brains."

At this the man on the ground snarled up at him like a rat, while the other clenched his teeth, and shook his club, and looked down at him with murder in his eyes. Knight and squires gazed from rogue to avenger, but as it was a matter which none could mend they tarried no longer, but rode upon their way. Alleyne, looking back, saw that the murderer had drawn bread and cheese from his scrip, and was silently munching it, with the protecting cross still hugged to his breast, while the other, black and grim, stood in the sunlit road and threw his dark shadow athwart him.

CHAPTER XV

HOW THE YELLOW COG SAILED
FORTH FROM LEPE

THAT night the Company slept at St Leonard's, in the great monastic barns and spicarium—ground well known both to Alleyne and to John, for they were almost within sight of the Abbey of Beaulieu. A strange thrill it gave to the young squire to see the well-remembered white dress once more, and to hear the measured tolling of the deep vespers bell. At early dawn they passed across the broad, sluggish, reed-girt stream—men, horses, and baggage in the flat ferry barges—and so journeyed on through the fresh morning air past Exbury to Lepe. Topping the heathy down, they came of a sudden full in sight of the old seaport —a cluster of houses, a trail of blue smoke, and a bristle of masts. To right and left the long blue curve of the Solent lapped in a fringe of foam upon the yellow beach. Some way out from the town a line of pessoners, creyers, and other small craft were rolling lazily on the gentle swell. Further out still lay a great merchant-ship, high ended, deep waisted, painted of a canary yellow, and towering above the fishing boats like a swan among ducklings.

"By St Paul!" said the knight, "our good merchant of South-ampton hath not played us false, for methinks I can see our ship down yonder. He said that she would be of great size and of a yellow shade."

"By my hilt, yes!" muttered Aylward, "she is yellow as a kite's claw, and would carry as many men as there are pips in a pomegranate."

"It is as well," remarked Terlake, "for methinks, my fair lord, that we are not the only ones who are waiting a passage to Gascony. Mine eye catches at times a flash and sparkle from among yonder houses which assuredly never came from shipman's jacket or the gaberdine of a burgher."

"I can also see it," said Alleyne, shading his eyes with his hand. "And I can see men-at-arms in yonder boats which ply betwixt the vessel and the shore. But methinks that we are very welcome here, for already they come forth to meet us."

A tumultuous crowd of fishermen, citizens, and women had indeed swarmed out from the northern gate, approached them up the side of the moor, waving their hands and dancing with joy, as though a great fear had been rolled back from their minds. At their head rode a very large and solemn man with a long chin and a drooping lip. He wore a fur tippet round his neck and a heavy gold chain over it, with a medallion which dangled in front of him.

"Welcome, most puissant and noble lord," he cried, doffing his bonnet to Black Simon. "I have heard of your lordship's valiant deeds, and in sooth they might be expected from your lordship's face and bearing. Is there any small matter in which I may oblige you?"

"Since you ask me," said the man-at-arms, "I would take it kindly if you could spare a link or two of the chain which hangs round your neck."

"What, the corporation chain!" cried the other in horror. "The ancient chain of the township of Lepe! This is but a sorry jest, Sir Nigel."

"What the plague did you ask me for, then?" said Simon. "But if it is Sir Nigel Loring with whom you would speak, that is he upon the black horse."

The Mayor of Lepe gazed with amazement on the mild face and slender frame of the famous warrior.

"Your pardon, my very gracious lord," he cried. "You see in me the mayor and chief magistrate of the ancient and powerful town of Lepe. I bid you very heartily welcome, and the more so as you are come at a moment when we are sore put to it for means of defence."

"Ha!" cried Sir Nigel, pricking up his ears.

"Yes, my lord, for the town being very ancient, and the walls as old as the town, it follows that they are very ancient too. But there is a certain villainous and bloodthirsty Norman pirate hight Tête-Noire, who, with a Genoan called Tito Caracci, commonly known as Spade-beard, hath been a mighty scourge upon these coasts. Indeed, my lord, they are very cruel and black-hearted men, graceless and ruthless, and if they should come to the ancient and powerful town of Lepe, then—"

"Then good-bye to the ancient and powerful town of Lepe," quoth Ford, whose lightness of tongue could at times rise above his awe of Sir Nigel.

The knight, however, was too much intent upon the matter in hand to give heed to the flippancy of his squire. "Have you then cause," he asked, "to think that these men are about to venture an attempt upon you?"

"They have come in two great galleys," answered the mayor, "with two bank of oars on either side, and great store of engines of war and men-at-arms. At Weymouth and at Portland they have murdered and ravished. Yesterday morning they were at Cowes, and we saw the smoke from the burning crofts. Today they lie at their ease near Freshwater, and we fear much lest they come upon us and do us a mischief."

"We cannot tarry," said Sir Nigel, riding towards the town, with the mayor upon his left side. "The Prince awaits us at Bordeaux, and we may not be behind the general muster. Yet I will promise you that on our way we shall find time to pass Freshwater and to prevail upon these rovers to leave you in peace."

"We are much beholden to you!" cried the mayor. "But I cannot see, my lord, how, without a war-ship, you may venture against these men. With your archers, however, you might well hold the town and do them great scath if they attempt to land."

"There is a very proper cog out yonder," said Sir Nigel. "It would be a very strange thing if any ship were not a war-ship when it had such men as these upon her decks. Certes, we shall do as I say, and that no later than this very day."

"My lord," said a rough-haired, dark-faced man, who walked by the knight's other stirrup, with his head sloped to catch all that he was saying. "By your leave, I have no doubt that you are skilled in land fighting and the marshalling of lances, but, by my soul! you will find it another thing upon the sea. I am the master-shipman of this yellow cog, and my name is Goodwin Hawtayne. I have sailed since I was as high as this staff, and I have fought against these Normans and against the Genoese, as well as the Scotch, the Bretons, the Spanish, and the Moors. I tell you, sir, that my ship is over light and over frail for such work, and it will but end in bur having our throats cut, or being sold as slaves to the Barbary heathen."

"I also have experienced one of two gentle and honourable ventures upon the sea," quoth Sir Nigel, "and I am right blithe to have so fair a task before us. I think, good master-shipman, that you and I may win great honour in this matter, and I can see very readily that you are a brave and stout man."

"I like it not," said the other sturdily. "In God's name, I like it not. And yet Goodwin Hawtayne is not the man to stand back when his fellows are for pressing forward. By my soul! be it sink or swim, I shall turn her beak into Freshwater Bay, and if good Master Witherton, of Southampton, like not my handling of his ship, then he may find another master-shipman."

They were close by the old north gate of the little town, and Alleyne, half turning in his saddle, looked back at the motley crowd who followed. The bowmen and men-at-arms had broken their ranks and were intermingled with the fishermen and citizens, whose laughing faces and hearty gestures bespoke the weight of care from which this welcome arrival had relieved them. Here and there among the moving throng of dark jerkins and of white surcoats were scattered dashes of scarlet or blue, the wimples or shawls of the women. Aylward, with a fishing lass on either arm, was vowing constancy alternately to her on the right and her on the left, while big John towered in the rear with a little chubby maiden enthroned upon his great shoulder, her soft white arm curled round his shining headpiece. So the throng moved on, until at the very gate it was brought to a stand by a wondrously fat man, who came darting forth from the town with rage in every feature of his rubicund face.

"How now, Sir Mayor?" he roared, in a voice like a bull, "How now, Sir Mayor? How of the clams and the scallops?"

"By Our Lady, my sweet Sir Oliver," cried the mayor, "I have had so much to think of, with these wicked villains so close upon us, that it had quite gone out of my head."

"Words, words!" shouted the other furiously. "Am I to be put off with words? I say to you again, how of the clams and scallops?"

"My fair sir, you flutter me," cried the mayor. "I am a peaceful trader, and I am not wont to be so shouted at upon so small a matter."

"Small!" shrieked the other. "Small! Clams and scallops! Ask me to your table to partake of the dainty of the town, and when I come a barren welcome and a bare board! Where is my spear-bearer?"

"Nay, Sir Oliver, Sir Oliver!" cried Sir Nigel, laughing. "Let your anger be appeased, since instead of this dish you come upon an old friend and comrade."

"By St Martin of Tours!" shouted the fat knight, his wrath all changed in an instant to joy, "if it is not my dear little game rooster of the Garonne. Ah, my sweet coz, I am right glad to see you. What days we have seen together!"

"Aye, by my faith," cried Sir Nigel, with sparkling eyes, "we have seen some valiant men, and we have shown our pennons in some noble skirmishes. By St Paul! We have had great joys in France."

"And sorrows also," quoth the other. "I have some sad memories of the land. Can you recall that which befell us at Libourne?"

"Nay, I cannot call to mind that we ever so much as drew sword at the place."

"Man, man," cried Sir Oliver, "your mind still runs on nought but blades and bassinets. Hast no space in thy frame for the softer joys? Ah, even now I can scarce speak of it unmoved. So noble a pie, such tender pigeons, and sugar in the gravy instead of salt! You were by my side that day, as were Sir Claude Latour and the Lord of Pommers."

"I remember it," said Sir Nigel, laughing, "and how you harried the cook down the street, and spoke of setting fire to the inn. By St Paul! most worthy mayor, my old friend is a perilous man, and I rede you that you may compose your difference with him on such terms as you may."

"The clams and scallops shall be ready within the hour," the mayor answered. "I had asked Sir Oliver Buttesthorn to do my humble board the honour to partake at it of the dainty upon which we take some little pride, but in sooth this alarm of pirates hath cast such a shadow on my wits that I am like one distrait. But I trust, Sir Nigel, that you will also partake of none-meat with me?"

"I have overmuch to do," Sir Nigel answered, "for we must be aboard, horse and man, as early as we may. How many do you muster, Sir Oliver?"

"Three-and-forty. The forty are drunk, and the three are but indifferent sober. I have them all safe upon the ship."

"They had best find their wits again, for I shall have work for every man of them ere the sun set. It is my intention, if it seems good to you, to try a venture against these Norman and Genoese rovers."

"They carry caviare and certain very noble spices from the Levant aboard of ships from Genoa," quoth Sir Oliver. "We may come to great profit through the business. I pray you, master-shipman, that when you go on board you pour a helmetful of sea-water over any of my rogues whom you may see there."

Leaving the lusty knight and the Mayor of Lepe, Sir Nigel led the Company straight down to the water's edge, where long lines of flat lighters swiftly bore them to their vessel. Horse after horse was slung by main force up from the barges, and after kicking and plunging in empty air was dropped into the deep waist of the yellow cog, where rows of stalls stood ready for their safe-keeping. Englishmen in those days were skilled and prompt in such matters, for it was not so long before that Edward had embarked as many as fifty thousand men in the port of Orwell, with their horses and their baggage, all in the space of four-and-twenty hours. So

urgent was Sir Nigel on the shore, and so prompt was Goodwin
Hawtayne on the cog, that Sir Oliver Buttesthorn had scarce swallowed his last scallop ere the peal of trumpet and clang of nakir
announced that all was ready and the anchor drawn. In the last
boat which left the shore the two commanders sat together in the
sheets, a strange contrast to one another, while under the feet of
the rowers was a litter of huge stones which Sir Nigel had ordered
to be carried to the cog. These once aboard, the ship set her broad
mainsail, purple in colour, with a golden St Christopher bearing
Christ upon his shoulder in the centre of it. The breeze blew, the
sail bellied, over heeled the portly vessel, and away she plunged
through the smooth blue rollers, amid the clang of the minstrels
on her poop and the shouting of the crowd who fringed the yellow
beach. To the left lay the green Island of Wight, with its long low
curving hills peeping over each other's shoulders to the sky-line;
to the right the wooded Hampshire coast as far as eye could reach;
above a steel-blue heaven, with a wintry sun shimmering down
upon them, and enough of frost to set the breath a-smoking.

"By St Paul!" said Sir Nigel gaily, as he stood upon the poop and
looked on either side of him, "it is a land which is very well worth
fighting for, but it were pity to go to France for what may be had at
home. Did you not spy a crooked man upon the beach?"

"Nay, I spied nothing," grumbled Sir Oliver, "for I was hurried
down with a clam stuck in my gizzard and an untasted goblet of
Cyprus on the board beside me."

"I saw him, my fair lord," said Terlake, "an old man with one
shoulder higher than the other."

"'Tis a sign of good fortune," quoth Sir Nigel "Our path was
also crossed by a woman and by a priest, so all should be well with
us. What say you, Edricson?"

"I cannot tell, my fair lord. The Romans of old were a very wise
people, yet, certes, they placed their faith in such matters. So, too,
did the Greeks, and divers other ancient peoples who were famed
for their learning. Yet of the moderns there are many who scoff
at all omens."

"There can be no manner of doubt about it," said Sir Oliver Buttesthorn. "I can well remember that in Navarre one day it thundered on the left out of a cloudless sky. We knew that ill would come of it, nor had we long to wait. Only thirteen days after, a haunch of prime venison was carried from my very tent door by the wolves, and on the same day two flasks of old vernage turned sour and muddy."

"You may bring my harness from below," said Sir Nigel to his squires, "and also, I pray you, bring up Sir Oliver's, and we shall don it here. Ye may then see to your own gear; for this day you will, I hope, make a very honourable entrance into the field of chivalry, and prove yourselves to be very worthy and valiant squires. And now, Sir Oliver, as to our dispositions: would it please you that I should order them or will you?"

"You, my cockerel, you. By our Lady! I am no chicken, but I cannot claim to know as much of war as the squire of Sir Walter Manny. Settle the matter to your own liking."

"You shall fly your pennon upon the fore part, then, and I upon the poop. For foreguard I shall give you your own forty men, with two score archers. Two score men, with my own men-at-arms and squires, may serve as a poop guard. Ten archers, with thirty shipmen, under the master may hold the waist while ten lie aloft with stones and arbalests. How like you that?"

"Good, by my faith, good! But here comes my harness, and I must to work, for I cannot slip into it as I was wont when I first set my face to the wars."

Meanwhile there had been bustle and preparation in all parts of the great vessel. The archers stood in groups about the decks, new-stringing their bows, and testing that they were firm at the nocks. Among them moved Aylward and other of the older soldiers, with a few whispered words of precept here and of warning there.

"Stand to it, my hearts of gold," said the old bowman as he passed from knot to knot. "By my hilt! we are in luck this journey. Bear in mind the old saying of the Company."

"What is that, Aylward?" cried several, leaning on their bows and laughing at him.

"'Tis the master-bowyer's rede: 'Every bow well bent. Every shaft well sent. Every stave well knocked. Every string well locked.' There, with that jingle in his head, a bracer on his left hand, a shooting glove on his right, and a farthing's-worth of wax in his girdle, what more doth a bowman need?"

"It would not be amiss," said Hordle John, "if under his girdle he had four farthings'-worth of wine!"

"Work first, wine afterwards, mon camarade. But it is time that we took our order, for methinks that between the Needle rocks and the Alum cliffs yonder I can catch a glimpse of the topmasts of the galleys. Hewett, Cook, Johnson, Cunningham, your men are of the poop-guard. Thornbury, Walters, Hackett, Baddlesmere, you are with Sir Oliver on the forecastle. Simon, you bide with your lord's banner; but ten men must go forward."

Quietly and promptly the men took their places, lying flat upon their faces on the deck, for such was Sir Nigel's order. Near the prow was planted Sir Oliver's spear, with his arms—a boar's head gules upon a field of gold. Close by the stern stood Black Simon with the pennon of the house of Loring. In the waist gathered the Southampton mariners, hairy and burly men, with their jerkins thrown off, their waists braced tight, swords, mallets, and pole-axes in their hands. Their leader, Goodwin Hawtayne, stood upon the poop and talked with Sir Nigel, casting his eye up sometimes at the swelling sail, and then glancing back at the two seamen who held the tiller.

"Pass the word," said Sir Nigel, "that no man shall stand to arms or draw his bowstring until my trumpeter shall sound. It would be well that we should seem to be a merchant-ship from Southampton and appear to flee from them."

"We shall see them anon," said the master-shipman. "Ha! said I not so? There they lie, the water-snakes, in Freshwater Bay; and mark the reek of smoke from yonder point, where they have been at their Devil's work. See how their shallops pull from the land! They have seen us and called their men aboard. Now they draw upon the anchor. See them like ants upon the forecastle! They stoop and heave like handy ship-men. But, my fair lord, these are no niefs. I doubt but we have taken in hand more than we can do. Each of these ships is a galeasse, and of the largest and swiftest make."

"I would I had your eyes," said Sir Nigel, blinking at the pirate galleys. "They seem very gallant ships, and I trust that we shall have much pleasance from our meeting with them. It would be well to pass the word that we should neither give nor take quarter this day. Have you perchance a priest or friar aboard this ship, Master Hawtayne?"

"No, my fair lord."

"Well, well, it is no great matter for my Company, for they were all houseled and shriven ere we left Twynham Castle; and Father Christopher of the Priory gave me his word that they were as fit to march to heaven as to Gascony. But my mind misdoubts me as to these Winchester men who have come with Sir Oliver, for they appear to be a very ungodly crew. Pass the word that the men kneel, and that the under-officers repeat to them the pater, the ave, and the credo."

With a clank of arms, the rough archers and seamen took to their knees with bent heads and crossed hands, listening to the hoarse mutter from the file-leaders. It was strange to mark the hush; so that the lapping of the water, the straining of the sail, and the creaking of the timbers grew louder of a sudden upon the ear. Many of the bowmen had drawn amulets and relics from their bosoms, while he who possessed some more than usually sanctified treasure passed it down the line of his comrades, that all might kiss and reap the virtue.

The yellow cog had now shot out from the narrow waters of the Solent, and was plunging and rolling on the long heave of the open channel. The wind blew freshly from the east, with a very keen edge to it; and the great sail bellied roundly out, laying the vessel over until the water hissed beneath her lee bulwarks. Broad land ungainly she floundered from wave to wave, dipping her round bows deeply into the blue rollers, and sending the white flakes of foam in a spatter over her decks. On her larboard quarter lay the two dark galleys, which had already hoisted sail, and were shooting out from Freshwater Bay in swift pursuit, their double line of oars giving them a vantage which could not fail to bring them up with any vessel which trusted to sails alone. High and bluff the English cog; long, black and swift the pirate galleys, like two fierce lean wolves which have seen a lordly and unsuspecting stag walk past their forest lair.

"Shall we turn, my fair lord, or shall we carry on?" asked the master-shipman, looking behind him with anxious eyes.

"Nay, we must carry on, and play the part of the helpless merchant."

"But your pennons? They will see that we have two knights with us."

"Yet it would not be to a knight's honour or good name to lower his pennon. Let them be, and they will think that we are a wine-ship for Gascony, or that we bear the wool-bales of some mercer of the Staple. Ma foi! but they are very swift! They swoop upon us like two goshawks on a heron. Is there not some symbol or device upon their sails?"

"That on the right," said Edricson, "appears to have the head of an Ethiop upon it."

"'Tis the badge of Tête-noire, the Norman," cried the seaman-mariner. "I have seen it before when, he harried us at Winchelsea. He is a wondrous large and strong man, with no ruth for man, woman, or beast. They say that he hath the strength of six; and, certes, he hath the crimes of six upon his soul. See, now, to the poor souls who swing at either end of his yard-arm!"

At each end of the yard there did indeed hang the dark figure of a man, jolting and lurching with hideous jerkings of its limbs at every plunge and swoop of the galley.

"By St Paul!" said Sir Nigel, "and by, the help of St George and Our Lady, it will be a very strange thing if our black-headed friend does not himself swing thence ere he be many hours older. But what is that upon the other galley?"

"It is the red cross of Genoa. This Spade-beard is a very noted captain, and it is his boast that there are no seamen and no archers in the world who can compare with those who serve the Doge Boccanegra."

"That we shall prove," said Goodwin Hawtayne, "but it would be well, ere they close with us, to raise up the mantlets and pavises as a screen against their bolts." He shouted a hoarse order, and his seamen worked swiftly and silently, heightening the bulwarks and strengthening them. The three ship's anchors were at Sir Nigel's command carried into the waist, and tied to the mast, with twenty feet of cable between, each under the care of four seamen. Eight others were stationed with leather water-bags to quench any fire-arrows which might come aboard, while others were sent up the mast, to lie along the yard and drop stones or shoot arrows as the occasion served.

"Let them be supplied with all that is heavy and weighty in the ship," said Sir Nigel.

"Then we must send them up Sir Oliver Buttesthorn," quoth Ford.

The knight looked at him with a face which struck the smile from his lips. "No squire of mine," he said, "shall ever make jest of a belted knight. And yet," he added, his eyes softening, "I know that it is but a boy's mirth, with no sting in it. Yet I should ill do my part towards your father if I did not teach you to curb your tongue-play."

"They will lay us aboard on either quarter, my lord," cried the master. "See how they stretch out from each other! The Norman hath a mangonel or a trabuch upon the forecastle. See, they bend to the levers! They are about to loose it."

"Aylward," cried the knight, "pick your three trustiest archers, and see if you cannot do something to hinder their aim. Methinks they are within long arrow flight."

"Seventeen score paces," said the archer, running his eye backwards and forwards. "By my ten finger-bones! it would be a strange thing if we could not notch a mark at that distance. Here, Watkin of Sowley, Arnold, Long Williams, let us show the rogues that they have English bowmen to deal with."

The three archers named stood at the further end of the poop, balancing themselves with feet widely spread and bows drawn, until the heads of the cloth-yard arrows were level with the centre of the stave. "You are the surer, Watkin," said Aylward, standing by them with shaft upon string. "Do you take the rogue with the red coif. You two bring down the man with the headpiece, and I will hold myself ready if you miss. Ma foi! they are about to loose her. Shoot, mes garçons, or you will be too late."

The throng of pirates had cleared away from the great wooden catapult, leaving two of their number to discharge it. One in a scarlet cap bent over it, steadying the jagged rock which was balanced on the spoon-shaped end of the long wooden lever. The other held the loop of the rope which would release the catch and send the unwieldy missile hurtling through the air. So for an instant they stood, showing hard and clear against the white sail behind them. The next, redcap had fallen across the stone with an arrow between his ribs; and the other, struck in the leg and in the throat, was writhing and spluttering upon the ground. As he toppled backwards he had loosed the spring, and the huge beam of wood, swinging round with tremendous force, cast the corpse of his comrade so close to the English ship that its mangled and distorted limbs grazed their very stern. As to the stone, it glanced off obliquely and fell midway between the vessels. A roar of cheering and of laughter broke from the rough archers and seamen at the sight, answered by a yell of rage from their pursuers.

"Lie low, mes enfants," cried Aylward, motioning with his left hand. "They will learn wisdom. They are bringing forward shield and mantlet. We shall have some pebbles about our ears ere long."

CHAPTER XVI

HOW THE YELLOW COG FOUGHT
THE TWO ROVER GALLEYS

THE three vessels had been sweeping swiftly westwards, the cog still well to the front, although the galleys were slowly drawing in upon either quarter. To the left was a hard sky-line unbroken by a sail. The island already lay like a cloud behind them, while right in front was St Alban's Head, with Portland looming mistily in the farthest distance. Alleyne stood by the tiller, looking backwards, the fresh wind full in his teeth, the crisp winter air tingling on his face and blowing his yellow curls from under his bassinet. His cheeks were flushed and his eyes shining, for the blood of a hundred fighting Saxon ancestors was beginning to stir in his veins.

"What was that?" he asked, as a hissing sharp-drawn voice seemed to whisper in his ear. The steersman smiled, and pointed with his foot to where a short heavy cross-bow quarrel stuck quivering in the boards. At the same instant the man stumbled forward upon his knee, and lay lifeless upon the deck, a bloodstained feather jutting out from his back. As Alleyne stooped to raise him, the air seemed to be alive with the sharp zip-zip of the bolts, and he could hear them pattering on the deck like apples at a tree-shaking.

"Raise two more mantlets by the poop-lanthorn," said Sir Nigel quietly.

"And another man to the tiller," cried the master-shipman.

"Keep them in play, Aylward, with ten of your men," the knight continued. "And let ten of Sir Oliver's bowmen do as much for the Genoese. I have no mind as yet to show them how much they have to fear from us."

Ten picked shots under Aylward stood in line across the broad deck, and it was a lesson to the young squires who had seen nothing of war to note how orderly and how cool were these old soldiers, how quick the command, and how prompt the carrying out, ten moving like one. Their comrades crouched beneath the bulwarks, with many a rough jest and many a scrap of criticism or advice. "Higher, Wat, higher!" "Put thy body into it; Will!" "Forget not the wind, Hal!" So ran the muttered chorus, while high above it rose the sharp twanging of the strings, the hiss of the shafts, and the short "Draw your arrow! Nick your arrow! Shoot wholly together!" from the master-bowman.

And now both mangonels were at work from the galleys, but so covered and protected that, save at the moment of discharge, no glimpse could be caught of them. A huge brown rock from the Genoese sang over their heads, and plunged sullenly into the slope of a wave. Another from the Norman whizzed into the waist, broke the back of a horse, and crashed its way through the side of the vessel. Two others, flying together, tore a great gap in the St Christopher upon the sail, and brushed three of Sir Oliver's men-at-arms from the forecastle. The master-shipman looked at the knight with a troubled face.

"They keep their distance from us," said he. "Our archery is over good, and they will not close. What defence can we make against the stones?"

"I think I may trick them," the knight answered cheerfully, and passed his order to the archers. Instantly five of them threw up their hands and fell prostrate upon the deck. One had already been slain by a bolt, so that there were but four upon their feet.

"That should give them heart," said Sir Nigel, eyeing the galleys, which crept along on either side with a slow measured swing of their great oars, the water swirling and foaming under their sharp stems.

"They still hold aloof," cried Hawtayne.

"Then down with two more," shouted their leader. "That will do. Ma foi! but they come to our lure like chicks to the fowler. To your arms, men! The pennon behind me, and the squires round the pennon. Stand fast with the anchors in the waist, and be ready for a cast. Now blow out the trumpets, and may God's benison be with the honest men!"

As he spoke a roar of voices and a roll of drums came from either galley, and the water was lashed into spray by the hurried beat of a hundred oars. Down they swooped, one on the right, one on the left, the sides and shrouds black with men and bristling with weapons. In heavy clusters they hung upon the forecastle all ready for a spring—faces white, faces brown, faces yellow, and faces black, fair Norsemen, swarthy Italians, fierce rovers from the Levant, and fiery Moors from the Barbary States, of all hues and countries, and marked solely by the common stamp of a wild-beast ferocity. Rasping up on either side, with oars trailing to save them from snapping, they poured in a living torrent with horrid yell and shrill whoop upon the defenceless merchantman.

But wilder yet was the cry, and shriller still the scream, when there rose up from the shadow of those silent bulwarks the long lines of the English bowmen, and the arrows whizzed in a deadly sleet among the unprepared masses upon the pirate decks. From the higher sides of the cog the bowmen could shoot straight down, at a range which was so short as to enable a cloth-yard shaft to pierce through mail-coats or to transfix a shield, though it were an inch thick of toughened wood. One moment Alleyne saw the galley's poop crowded with rushing figures, waving arms, exultant faces; the next it was a blood-smeared shambles, with bodies piled three deep upon each other, the living cowering behind the dead to shelter themselves from that sudden storm-blast of death. On either side the seamen whom Sir Nigel had chosen for the purpose had cast their anchors over the side of the galleys, so that the three vessels, locked in an iron grip, lurched heavily forward upon the swell.

And now set in a fell and fierce fight, one of a thousand of which no chronicler has spoken and no poet sung. Through all the centuries, and over all those southern waters, nameless men have fought in nameless places, their sole monument a protected coast and an unravaged country-side.

Fore and aft the archers had cleared the galleys' decks, but from either side the rovers had poured down into the waist, where the seamen and bowmen were pushed back and so mingled with their foes that it was impossible for their comrades above to draw string to help them. It was a wild chaos where axe and sword rose and fell, while Englishmen, Norman and Italian staggered and reeled on a deck which was cumbered with bodies and slippery with blood. The clang of blows, the cries of the stricken, the short deep shout of the islanders, and the fierce whoops of the rovers, rose together in a deafening tumult, while the breath of the panting men went up in the wintry air like the smoke from a furnace. The giant Tête-noire, towering above his fellows and clad from head to foot in plate of proof, led on his boarders, waving a huge mace in the air, with which he struck to the deck every man who opposed him. On the other side, Spade-beard, a dwarf in height, but of great breadth of shoulder and length of arm, had cut a road almost to the mast, with threescore Genoese men-at-arms close at his heels. Between these two formidable assailants the seamen were being slowly wedged more closely together, until they stood back to back under the mast with the rovers raging upon every side of them.

But help was close at hand. Sir Oliver Buttesthorn with his men-at-arms had swarmed down from the forecastle, while Sir Nigel, with his three squires, Black Simon, Aylward, Hordle John, and a score more, threw themselves from the poop and hurled themselves into the thickest of the fight. Alleyne, as in duty bound, kept his eyes fixed ever on his lord and pressed forward close at his heels. Often had he heard of Sir Nigel's prowess and skill with all knightly weapons, but all the tales that had reached his ears fell far short of the real quickness and coolness of the man. It was as if the devil was in him, for he sprang here and sprang there, now thrusting and now cutting, catching blows on his shield, turning them with his blade, stooping under the swing of an axe, springing over the sweep of a sword, so swift and so erratic that the man who braced himself for a blow at him might find him six paces off ere he could bring it down. Three pirates had fallen before him, and he had wounded Spade-beard in the neck, when the Norman giant sprang at him from the side with a slashing blow from his deadly mace. Sir Nigel stooped to avoid it, and at the same instant turned a thrust from the Genoese swordsman, but, his foot slipping in a pool of blood, he fell heavily to the boards. Alleyne sprang in front of the Norman, but his sword was shattered and he himself beaten to the boards by a second blow from the ponderous weapon. Ere the pirate chief could repeat it, however, John's iron grip fell upon his wrist, and he found that for once he was in the hands of a stronger man than himself. Fiercely he strove to disengage his weapon, but Hordle John bent his arm slowly back until, with a sharp crack, like a breaking stave, it turned limp in his grasp, and the mace dropped from the nerveless fingers. In vain he tried to pluck it up with the other hand. Back and back still his foeman bent him, until, with a roar of pain and of fury, the giant clanged his full length upon the boards, while the glimmer of a knife before the bars of his helmet warned him that short would be his shrift if he moved.

Cowed and disheartened by the loss of their leader, the Normans had given back and were now streaming over the bulwarks on to their own galley, dropping a dozen at a time on to her deck. But the anchor still held them in its crooked claw, and Sir Oliver with fifty men was hard upon their heels. Now, too, the archers had room to draw their bows once more, and great stones from the yard of the cog came thundering and crashing among the flying rovers. Here and there they rushed with wild screams and curses, diving under the sail, crouching behind booms, huddling into corners like rabbits when the ferrets are upon them, as helpless and as hopeless. They were stern days, and if the honest soldier, too poor for a ransom, had no prospect of mercy upon the battle-field, what ruth was there for sea-robbers, the enemies of human kind, taken in the very deed, with proofs of their crimes still swinging upon their yard-arm?

But the fight had taken a new and a strange turn upon the other side. Spade-beard and his men had given slowly back, hard pressed by Sir Nigel, Aylward, Black Simon, and the poop-guard. Foot by foot the Italian had retreated, his armour running blood at every joint, his shield split, his crest shorn, his voice fallen away to a mere gasping and croaking. Yet he faced his foemen with dauntless courage, dashing in, springing back, surefooted, steady-handed, with a point which seemed to menace three at once. Beaten back on to the deck of his own vessel, and closely followed by a dozen Englishmen, he disengaged himself from them, ran swiftly down the deck, sprang back into the cog once more, cut the rope which held the anchor, and was back in an instant among his crossbowmen. At the same time the Genoese sailors thrust with their oars against the side of the cog, and a rapidly widening rift appeared between the two vessels.

"By St George!" cried Ford, "we are cut off from Sir Nigel."

"He is lost," gasped Terlake. "Come, let us spring for it." The two youths jumped with all their strength to reach the departing galley. Ford's feet reached the edge of the bulwarks, and his hand clutching a rope he swung himself on board. Terlake fell short, crashed in among the oars, and bounded off into the sea. Alleyne, staggering to the side, was about to hurl himself after him, but Hordle John dragged him back by the girdle.

"You can scarce stand, lad, far less jump," said he. "See how the blood drips from your bassinet."

"My place is by the flag," cried Alleyne, vainly struggling to break from the other's hold.

"Bide here, man. You would need wings ere you could reach Sir Nigel's side."

The vessels were indeed so far apart now that the Genoese could use the full sweep of their oars, and draw away rapidly from the cog.

"My God, but it is a noble fight!" shouted big John, clapping his hands. "They have cleared the poop, and they spring into the waist. Well struck, my lord! Well struck, Aylward! See to Black Simon, how he storms among the shipmen! But this Spade-beard is a gallant warrior. He rallies his men upon the forecastle. He hath slain an archer. Ha! my lord is upon him. Look to it, Alleyne! See to the whirl and glitter of it!"

"By heaven, Sir Nigel is down!" cried the squire.

"Up!" roared John. "It was but a feint. He bears him back. He drives him to the side. Ah, by Our Lady, his sword is through him! They cry for mercy. Down goes the red cross, and up springs Simon with the scarlet roses!"

The death of the Genoese leader did indeed bring the resistance to an end. Amid a thunder of cheering from cog and from galleys the forked pennon fluttered upon the forecastle, and the galley, sweeping round, came slowly back, as the slaves who rowed it learned the wishes of their new masters.

The two knights had come aboard the cog, and the grapplings having been thrown off, the three vessels now moved abreast. Through all the storm and rush of the fight Alleyne had been aware of the voice of Goodwin Hawtayne, the master-shipman, with his constant "Hale the bowline! Veer the sheet!" and strange it was to him to see how swiftly the blood-stained sailors turned from the strife to the ropes and back. Now the cog's head was turned Francewards, and the shipman walked the deck, a peaceful master-mariner once more.

"There is sad scath done to the cog, Sir Nigel," said he. "Here is a hole in the side two ells across, the sail split through the centre, and the wood as bare as a friar's poll. In good sooth, I know not what I shall say to Master Witherton when I see the Itchen once more."

"By St Paul! it would be a very sorry thing if we suffered you to be the worse for this day's work," said Sir Nigel. "You shall take these galleys back with you, and Master Witherton may sell them. Then from the monies he shall take as much as may make good the damage, and the rest he shall keep until our homecoming, when every man shall have his share. An image of silver fifteen inches high I have vowed to the Virgin, to be placed in her chapel within the Priory, for that she was pleased to allow me to come upon this Spade-beard, who seemed to me from what I have seen of him to be a very sprightly and valiant gentleman. But how fares it with you, Edricson?"

"It is nothing, my fair lord," said Alleyne, who had now loosened his bassinet, which was cracked across by the Norman's blow. Even as he spoke, however, his head swirled round, and he fell to the deck with the blood gushing from his nose and mouth.

"He will come to anon," said the knight, stooping over him and passing his fingers through his hair. "I have lost one very valiant and gentle squire this day. I can ill afford to lose another. How many men have fallen?"

"I have pricked off the tally," said Aylward, who had come aboard with his lord. "There are seven of the Winchester men, eleven seamen, your squire, young Master Terlake, and nine archers!"

"And of the others?"

"They are all dead—save only the Norman knight who stands behind you. What would you that we should do with him?"

"He must hang on his own yard," said Sir Nigel. "It was my vow and must be done."

The pirate leader had stood by the bulwarks, a cord round his arms, and two stout archers on either side. At Sir Nigel's words he started violently, and his swarthy features blanched to a livid grey.

"How, Sir Knight?" he cried in broken English. "Que dites-vous? To hang, la mort du chien! To hang!"

"It is my vow," said Sir Nigel shortly. "From what I hear, you thought little enough of hanging others."

"Peasants, base roturiers," cried the other. "It is their fitting death. Mais Le Seigneur d'Andelys, avec le sang des rois dans ses veines! C'est incroyable!"

Sir Nigel turned upon his heel, while two seamen cast a noose over the pirate's neck. At the touch of the cord he snapped the bonds which bound him, dashed one of the archers to the deck, and, seizing the other round the waist, sprang with him into the sea.

"By my hilt, he is gone!" cried Aylward, rushing to the side. "They have sunk together like a stone."

"I am right glad of it," answered Sir Nigel; "for though it was against my vow to loose him, I deem that he has carried himself like a very gentle and débonnaire cavalier."

CHAPTER XVII

HOW THE YELLOW COG CROSSED THE BAR OF GIRONDE

FOR two days the yellow cog ran swiftly before a north-easterly wind, and on the dawn of the third the high land of Ushant lay like a mist upon the shimmering sky-line. There came a plump of rain towards mid-day and the breeze died down, but it freshened again before nightfall, and Goodwin Hawtayne veered his sheet and held her head for the south. Next morning they had passed Belle Isle, and ran through the midst of a fleet of transports returning from Guienne. Sir Nigel Loring and Sir Oliver Buttesthorn at once hung their shields over the side, and displayed their pennons as was the custom, noting with the keenest interest the answering symbols which told the names of the cavaliers who had been constrained by ill health or wounds to leave the prince at so critical a time.

That evening a great dun-coloured cloud banked up in the west, and an anxious man was Goodwin Hawtayne, for a third part of his crew had been slain and half of the remainder were aboard the galleys, so that, with an injured ship, he was little fit to meet such a storm as sweeps over those waters. All night it blew in short fitful puffs, heeling the great cog over until the water curled over her lee bulwarks. As the wind still freshened the yard was lowered halfway down the mast in the morning. Alleyne, wretchedly ill and weak, with his head still ringing from the blow which he had received, crawled up upon deck. Water-swept and aslant, it was preferable to the noisome, rat-haunted dungeons which served as cabins. There, clinging to the stout halliards of the sheet, he gazed with amazement at the long lines of black waves, each with its curling ridge of foam, racing in endless succession from out the inexhaustible west. A huge sombre cloud, flecked with livid blotches, stretched over the whole seaward sky-line, with long ragged streamers whirled out in front of it. Far behind them the two galleys laboured heavily, now sinking between the rollers until their yards were level with the waves, and again shooting up with a reeling scooping motion until every spar and rope stood out hard against the sky. On the left the low-lying land stretched in a dim haze, rising here and there into a darker blur which marked the higher capes and headlands. The land of France! Alleyne's eyes shone as he gazed upon it. The land of France! — the very words sounded as the call of a bugle in the ears of the youth of England. The land where their fathers had bled, the home of chivalry and of knightly deeds, the country of gallant men, of courtly women, of princely buildings, of the wise, the polished and the sainted. There it lay, so still and grey beneath the drifting wrack — the home of things noble and of things shameful — the theatre where a new name might be made or an old one marred. From his bosom to his lips came the crumpled veil, and he breathed a vow that if valour and goodwill could raise him to his lady's side, then death alone should not hold him back from her. His thoughts were still in the woods of Minstead and the old armoury of Twynham Castle, when the hoarse voice of the master-shipman brought them back once more to the Bay of Biscay.

"By my troth, young sir," he said, "you are as long in the face as the devil at a christening, and I cannot marvel at it, for I have sailed these waters since I was as high as this whinyard, and yet I never saw more sure promise of an evil night."

"Nay, I had other things upon my mind," the squire answered.

"And so has every man," cried Hawtayne, in an injured voice. "Let the shipman see to it. It is the master-shipman's affair. Put it all upon good Master Hawtayne! Never had I so much care since first I blew trumpet and showed cartel at the west gate of Southampton."

"What is amiss then?" asked Alleyne, for the man's words were as gusty as the weather.

"Amiss, quotha? Here am I with but half my mariners, and a hole in the ship, where that twenty-devil stone struck us, big enough to fit the fat widow of Northam through. It is well enough on this tack, but I would have you tell me what I am to do on the other. We are like to have salt water upon us until we be found pickled like herrings in an Easterling's barrels."

"What says Sir Nigel to it?"

"He is below pricking out the coat-armour of his mother's uncle. 'Pester me not with such small matters!' was all that I could get from him. Then there is Sir Oliver. 'Fry them in oil with a dressing of Gascony,' quoth he, and then swore at me because I had not been the cook. 'Walawa,' thought I, 'mad master, sober man'—so away forward to the archers. Harrow and alas! but they were worse than the others."

"Would they not help you then?"

"Nay, they sat tway and tway at a board, him that they call Aylward and the great red-headed man who snapped the Norman's arm-bone, and the black man from Norwich, and a score of others, rattling their dice in an archer's gauntlet for want of a box. 'The ship can scarce last much longer, my masters,' quoth I. 'That is your business, old swine's head,' cried the black galliard. 'Le Diable t'emporte!' says Aylward. 'A five, a four, and the main,' shouted the big man, with a voice like the flap of a sail. Hark to them now, young sir, and say if I speak not sooth."

As he spoke, there sounded high above the shriek of the gale arid the straining of the timbers a gust of oaths with a roar of deep-chested mirth from the gamblers in the forecastle.

"Can I be of avail?" asked Alleyne. "Say the word and the thing is done, if two hands may do it."

"Nay, nay, your head I can see is still totty, and i' faith little head would you have, had your bassinet not stood your friend. All that may be done is already carried out, for we have stuffed the gape with sails and corded it without and within. Yet when we hale our bowline and veer the sheet our lives will hang upon the breach remaining blocked. See how yonder headland looms upon us through the mist! We must tack within three arrow flights, or we may find a rock through our timbers. Now St Christopher be praised! here is Sir Nigel, with whom I may confer."

"I prythee that you will pardon me," said the knight, clutching his way along the bulwark. "I would not show lack of courtesy toward a worthy man, but I was deep in a matter of some weight, concerning which, Alleyne, I should be glad of your rede. It touches the question of dimidiation or impalement in the coat of mine uncle, Sir John Leighton of Shropshire, who took unto wife the widow of Sir Henry Oglander of Nunwell. The case has been much debated by pursuivants and kings-of-arms. But how is it with you, master-shipman?"

"Ill enough, my fair lord. The cog must go about anon, and I know not how we may keep the water out of her."

"Go call Sir Oliver!" said Sir Nigel, and presently the portly knight made his way all astraddle down the slippery deck.

"By my soul, master-shipman, this passes all patience!" he cried wrathfully. "If this ship of yours must needs dance and skip like a clown at a kermesse, then I pray you that you will put me into one of these galeasses. I had but sat down to a flask of malvoisie and a mortress of brawn, as is my use about this hour, when there comes a cherking, and I find my wine over my legs and the flask in my lap, and then as I stoop to clip it there comes another cursed cherk, and there is a mortress of brawn stuck fast to the nape of my neck. At this moment I have two pages coursing after it from side to side, like hounds behind a leveret. Never did living pig gambol more lightly. But you have sent for me, Sir Nigel?"

"I would fain have your rede, Sir Oliver, for Master Hawtayne hath fears that when we veer there may come danger from the hole in our side."

"Then do not veer," quoth Sir Oliver hastily. "And now, fair sir, I must hasten back to see how my rogues have fared with the brawn."

"Nay, but this win scarce suffice," cried the shipman. "If we do not veer we shall be upon the rocks within the hour."

"Then veer," said Sir Oliver, "There is my rede; and now, Sir Nigel, I must crave—"

At this instant, however, a startled shout rang out from two seamen upon the forecastle. "Rocks!" they yelled, stabbing into the air with their forefingers, "rocks beneath our very bows!" Through the belly of a great black wave, not one hundred paces to the front of them, there thrust forth a huge jagged mass of brown stone, which spouted spray as though it were some crouching monster, while a dull menacing boom and roar filled the air.

"Yare! Yare!" screamed Goodwin Hawtayne, flinging himself upon the long pole which served as a tiller. "Cut the halliard! Haul her over! Lay her two courses to the wind!"

Over swung the great boom, and the cog trembled and quivered within five spear-lengths of the breakers.

"She can scarce draw clear," cried Hawtayne, with his eyes from the sail to the seething line of foam. "May the holy Julian stand by us and the thrice-sainted Christopher!"

"If there be such peril, Sir Oliver," quoth Sir Nigel, "it would be very knightly and fitting that we should show our pennons. I pray you, Edricson, that you will command my guidon-bearer to put forward my banner."

"And sound the trumpets!" cried Sir Oliver. "In manus tuas, Domine! I am in the keeping of James of Compostella, to whose shrine I shall make pilgrimage, and in whose honour I vow that I will eat a carp each year upon his feast-day. Mon Dieu, but the waves roar! How is it with us now, master-shipman?"

"We draw! We draw!" cried Hawtayne, with his eyes still fixed upon the foam which hissed under the very bulge of the side. "Ah Holy Mother, be with us now!"

As he spoke the cog rasped along the edge of the reef, and a long white curling sheet of wood was planed off from her side from waist to poop by a jutting horn of the rock. At the same instant she lay suddenly over, the sail drew full, and she plunged seawards amid the shoutings of the seamen and the archers.

"The Virgin be praised!" cried the shipman, wiping his brow. "For this shall bell swing and candle burn when I see South-ampton Water once more. Cheerily, my hearts! Pull yarely on the bowline!"

"By my soul! I would rather have a dry death," quoth Sir Oliver. "Though, Mort Dieu! I have eaten so many fish that it were but justice that the fish should eat me. Now I must back to the cabin, for I have matters there which crave my attention."

"Nay, Sir Oliver, you had best bide with us, and still show your ensign," Sir Nigel answered; "for, if I understand the matter aright, we have but turned from one danger to the other."

"Good Master Hawtayne," cried the boatswain, rushing aft, "the water comes in upon us apace. The waves have driven in the sail wherewith we strove to stop the hole." As he spoke the seamen came swarming on to the poop and the forecastle to avoid the torrent which poured through the huge leak into the waist. High above the roar of the wind and the clash of the sea rose the shrill half-human cries of the horses, as they found the water rising rapidly around them.

"Stop it from without!" cried Hawtayne, seizing the end of the wet sail with which the gap had been plugged. "Speedily, my hearts, or we are gone!" Swiftly they rove ropes to the corners, and then, rushing forward to the bows they lowered them under the keel, and drew them tight in such a way that the sail should cover the outer face of the gap. The force of the rush of water was checked by this obstacle, but it still squirted plentifully from every side of it. At the sides the horses were above the belly, and in the centre a man from the poop could scarce touch the deck with a seven-foot spear. The cog lay lower in the water and the waves splashed freely over the weather bulwark.

"I fear that we can scare bide upon this tack," cried Hawtayne; "and yet the other will drive us on the rocks."

"Might we not haul down sail and wait for better times?" suggested Sir Nigel.

"Nay, we should drift upon the rocks. Thirty years have I been on the sea, and never yet in greater straits. Yet are we in the hands of the Saints."

"Of whom," cried Sir Oliver, "I look more particularly to Saint James of Compostella, who hath already befriended us this day, and on whose feast I hereby vow that I shall eat a second carp, if he will but interpose a second time."

The wrack had thickened to seaward, and the coast was but a blurred line. Two vague shadows in the offing showed where the galeasses rolled and tossed upon the great Atlantic rollers. Hawtayne looked wistfully in their direction. "If they would but lie closer we might find safety, even should the cog founder. You will bear me out with good Master Witherton of Southampton that I have done all that a shipman might. It would be well that you should doff camail and greaves, Sir Nigel, for, by the black rood, it is like enough that we shall have to swim for it."

"Nay," said the little knight, "it would be scarce fitting that a cavalier should throw off his harness for the fear of every puff of wind and puddle of water. I would rather that my Company should gather round me here on the poop, where we might abide together whatever God may be pleased to send. But, certes, Master Hawtayne, for all that my sight is none of the best, it is not the first time that I have seen that headland upon the left."

The seaman shaded his eyes with his hand, and gazed earnestly through the haze and spray. Suddenly he threw up his arms, and shouted aloud in his joy.

"'Tis the Point of La Tremblade!" he cried. "I had not thought that we were as far as Oléron. The Gironde lies before us, and once over the bar, and under shelter of the Tour de Cordouan, all will be well with us. Veer again, my hearts, and bring her to try with the main course!"

The sail swung round once more, and the cog, battered and torn and well-nigh water-logged, staggered in for this haven of refuge. A bluff cape to the north and a long spit to the south marked the mouth of the noble river, with a low-lying island of silted sand in the centre, all shrouded and curtained by the spume of the breakers. A line of broken water traced the dangerous bar, which in clear day and balmy weather has cracked the back of many a tall ship.

"There is a channel," said Hawtayne, "which was shown to me by the prince's own pilot. Mark yonder tree upon the bank, and see the tower which rises behind it. If these two be held in a line, even as we hold them now, it may be done, though our ship draws two good ells more than when she put forth."

"God speed you, Master Hawtayne!" cried Sir Oliver. "Twice have we come scathless out of peril, and now for the third time I commend me to the blessed James of Compostella, to whom I vow—"

"Nay, nay, old friend," whispered Sir Nigel. "You are like to bring a judgment upon us with these vows, which no living man could accomplish. Have I not already heard you vow to eat two carp in one day, and now you would venture upon a third?"

"I pray you that you will order the Company to lie down," cried Hawtayne, who had taken the tiller and was gazing ahead with a fixed eye. "In three minutes we shall either be lost or in safety."

Archers and seamen lay flat upon the deck, waiting in stolid silence for whatever fate might come. Hawtayne bent his weight upon the tiller, and crouched to see under the bellying sail. Sir Oliver and Sir Nigel stood erect with hands crossed in front of the poop. Down swooped the great cog into the narrow channel which was the portal to safety. On either bow roared the shallow bar. Right ahead one small lane of black swirling water marked the pilot's course. But true was the eye and firm the hand which guided. A dull scraping came from beneath, the vessel quivered and shook, at the waist, at the quarter, and behind sounded that grim roaring of the waters, and with a plunge the yellow cog was over the bar and speeding swiftly up the broad and tranquil estuary of the Gironde.

CHAPTER XVIII

HOW SIR NIGEL LORING PUT
A PATCH UPON HIS EYE

IT was on the morning of Friday, the eight-and-twentieth day of November, two days before the feast of St Andrew, that the cog and her two prisoners, after a weary tacking up the Gironde and the Garonne, dropped anchor at last in front of the noble city of Bordeaux. With wonder and admiration, Alleyne, leaning over the bulwarks, gazed at the forest of masts, the swarm of boats darting hither and thither on the bosom of the broad curving stream, and the grey crescent-shaped city which stretched with many a tower and minaret along the western shore. Never had he in his quiet life seen so great a town, nor was there in the whole of England, save London alone, one which might match it in size or in wealth. Here came the merchandise of all the fair countries which are watered by the Garonne and the Dordogne — the cloths of the south, the skins of Guienne, the wines of the Médoc — to be borne away to Hull, Exeter, Dartmouth, Bristol or Chester, in exchange for the wools and woolfels of England. Here too dwelt those famous smelters and welders who had made the Bordeaux steel the most trusty upon earth, and could give a temper to lance or to sword which might mean dear life to its owner. Alleyne could see the smoke of their forges reeking up in the clear morning air. The storm had died down now to a gentle breeze which wafted to his ears the long-drawn stirring bugle-calls which sounded from the ancient ramparts.

"Holà, mon petit!" said Aylward, coming up to where he stood. "Thou art a squire now, and like enough to win the golden spurs, while I am still the master-bowman, and master-bowman I shall abide. I dare scarce wag my tongue so freely with you as when we tramped together past Wilverley Chase, else I might be your guide now, for indeed I know every house in Bordeaux as a friar knows the beads on his rosary."

"Nay, Aylward," said Alleyne, laying his hand upon the sleeve of his companion's frayed jerkin, "you cannot think me so thrall as to throw aside an old friend because I have had some small share of good fortune. I take it unkind that you should have thought such evil of me."

"Nay, mon gar. 'Twas but a flight shot to see if the wind blew steady, though I were a rogue to doubt it."

"Why, had I not met you, Aylward, at the Lyndhurst inn, who can say where I had now been? Certes, I had not gone to Twynham Castle, nor become squire to Sir Nigel, nor met—" He paused abruptly and flushed to his hair, but the bowman was too busy with his own thoughts to notice his young companion's embarrassment.

"It was a good hostel, that of the 'Pied Merlin'," remarked Aylward. "By my ten finger-bones! when I hang bow on nail and change my brigandine for a tunic, I might do worse than take over the dame and her business."

"I thought," said Alleyne, "that you were betrothed to some one at Christchurch."

"To three," Aylward answered moodily, "to three. I fear I may not go back to Christchurch. I might chance to see hotter service in Hampshire than I have ever done in Gascony. But mark you now yonder lofty turret in the centre, which stands back from the river and hath a broad banner upon the summit. See the rising sun flashes full upon it and sparkles on the golden lions. 'Tis the royal banner of England, crossed by the prince's label. There he dwells in the Abbey of St Andrew, where he hath kept his court these years back. Beside it is the minster of the same saint, who hath the town under his very special care."

"And how of yon grey turret, on the left?"

"'Tis the fane of St Michael, as that upon the right is of St Remi. There, too, above the poop of yonder nief, you see the towers of St Croix and of Pey Berland. Mark also the mighty ramparts which are pierced by the three water-gates, and sixteen others to the landward side."

"And how is it, good Aylward, that there comes so much music from the town? I seem to hear a hundred trumpets, all calling in chorus."

"It would be strange else, seeing that all the great lords of England and of Gascony are within the walls, and each would have his trumpeter blow as loud as his neighbour, lest it might be thought that his dignity had been abated. Ma foi! they make as much louster as a Scotch army, where every man fills himself with girdle-cakes, and sits up all night to blow upon the toodle-pipe. See all along the banks how the pages water the horses, and there beyond the town how they gallop them over the plain! For every horse you see a belted knight hath herbergage in the town, for, as I learn, the men-at-arms and archers have already gone forward to Dax."

"I trust, Aylward," said Sir Nigel, coming upon deck, "that the men are ready for the land. Go tell them that the boats will be for them within the hour."

The archer raised his hand in salute, and hastened forward. In the meantime Sir Oliver had followed his brother knight, and the two paced the poop together, Sir Nigel in his plum-coloured velvet suit with flat cap of the same, adorned in front with the Lady Loring's glove and girt round with a curling ostrich feather. The lusty knight, on the other hand, was clad in the very latest mode, with côte-hardie, doublet, pourpoint, court-pie, and pal-tock of olive-green, picked out with pink and jagged at the edges. A red chaperon or cap, with long hanging cornette, sat daintily on the back of his black-curled head, while his gold-hued shoes were twisted up *à la poulaine,* as though the toes were shooting forth a tendril which might hope in time to entwine itself around his massive leg.

"Once more, Sir Oliver," said Sir Nigel, looking shorewards with sparkling eyes, "do we find ourselves at the gate of honour, the door which hath so often led us to all that is knightly and worthy. There flies the prince's banner, and it would be well that we haste ashore and pay our obeisance to him. The boats already swarm from the bank."

"There is a goodly hostel near the west gate, which is famed for the stewing of spiced pullets," remarked Sir Oliver. "We might take the edge of our hunger off ere we seek the prince, for though his tables are gay with damask and silver, he is no trencherman himself, and hath no sympathy for those who are his betters."

"His betters!"

"His betters before the tranchoir, lad. Sniff not treason where none is meant. I have seen him smile in his quiet way because I had looked for the fourth time towards the carving squire. And indeed to watch him dallying with a little gobbet of bread, or sipping his cup of thrice-watered wine, is enough to make a man feel shame at his own hunger. Yet war and glory, my good friend, though well enough in their way, will not serve to tighten such a belt as clasps my waist."

"How read you that coat which hangs over yonder galley, Alleyne?" asked Sir Nigel.

"Argent, a bend vert between cotises dancetté gules."

"It is a northern coat. I have seen it in the train of the Percies. From the shields, there is not one of these vessels which hath not knight or baron aboard. I would mine eyes were better. How read you this upon the left?"

"Argent and azure, a barry wavy of six."

"Ha, it is the sign of the Wiltshire Stourtons! And there beyond I see the red and silver of the Worsleys of Apulder-combe, who like myself are of Hampshire lineage. Close behind us is the moline cross of the gallant William Molyneux, and beside it the bloody chevrons of the Norfolk Woodhouses, with the annulets of the Musgrave of Westmoreland. By Saint Paul! it would be a very strange thing if so noble a company were to gather without some notable deed of arms arising from it. And here is our boat, Sir Oliver, so it seems best to me that we should go to the abbey with our squires, leaving Master Hawtayne to have his own way in the unloading."

The horses both of knights and squires were speedily lowered into a broad lighter, and reached the shore almost as soon as their masters. Sir Nigel bent his knee devoutly as he put foot on land, and taking a small black patch from his bosom he bound it tightly over his left eye.

"May the blessed George and the memory of my sweet ladylove raise high in my heart!" quoth he. "And as a token I vow that I will not take this patch from mine eye until I have seen something of this country of Spain, and done such a small deed as it lies in me to do. And this I swear upon the cross of my sword and upon the glove of my lady."

"In truth, you take me back twenty years, Nigel," quoth Sir Oliver, as they mounted and rode slowly through the watergate. "After Cadsand, I deem that the French thought that we were an army of the blind, for there was scarce a man who had not closed an eye for the greater love and honour of his lady. Yet it goes hard with you that you should darken one side, when with both open you can scarce tell a horse from a mule. In truth, friend, I think that you step over the line of reason in this matter."

"Sir Oliver Buttesthorn," said the little knight shortly, "I would have you to understand that, as blind as I am, I can yet see the path of honour very clearly, and that that is a road upon which I do not crave another man's guidance."

"By my soul," said Sir Oliver, "you are as tart as verjuice this morning! If you are bent upon a quarrel with me I must leave you to your humour and drop into the 'Tête d'Or' here, for I marked a varlet pass the door who bare a smoking dish, which had, methought, a most excellent smell."

"Nenny, nenny," cried his comrade, laying his hand upon his knee; "we have known each other over long to fall out, Oliver, like two raw pages at their first épreuves. You must come with me first to the prince, and then back to the hostel; though sure I am that it would grieve his heart that any gentle cavalier should turn from his board to a common tavern. But is not that my Lord Delewar who waves to us? Ha! my fair lord, God and Our Lady be with you! And there is Sir Robert Cheney. Good morrow, Robert! I am right glad to see you."

The two knights walked their horses abreast, while Alleyne and Ford, with John Norbury, who was squire to Sir Oliver, kept some paces behind them, a spear's length in front of Black Simon and of the Winchester guidon-bearer. Norbury, a lean, silent man, had been to those parts before, and sat his horse with a rigid neck; but the two young squires gazed eagerly to right or left, and plucked each other's sleeves to call attention to the many strange things on every side of them.

"See to the brave stalls!" cried Alleyne. "See to the noble armour set forth, and the costly taffeta—and oh, Ford, see to where the scrivener sits with the pigments and the ink-horns, and the rolls of sheepskin as white as the Beaulieu napery! Saw man ever the like before?"

"Nay, man, there are finer stalls in Cheapside," answered Ford, whose father had taken him to London on occasion of one of the Smithfield joustings. "I have seen a silversmith's booth there which would serve to buy either side of this street. But mark these houses, Alleyne, how they thrust forth upon the top. And see to the coats-of-arms at every window, and banner or pensil on the roof."

"And the churches!" cried Alleyne. "The Priory at Christchurch was a noble pile, but it was cold and bare, methinks, by one of these, with their frettings, and their carvings, and their traceries, as though some great ivy-plant of stone had curled and wantoned over the walls."

"And hark to the speech of the folk!" said Ford. "Was ever such a hissing and clacking? I wonder that they have not wit to learn English now that they have come under the English crown. By Richard of Hampole! there are fair faces amongst them. See the wench with the brown wimple! Out on you, Alleyne, that you would rather gaze upon dead stone than on living flesh!"

It was little wonder that the richness and ornament, not only of church and of stall, but of every private house as well, should have impressed itself upon the young squires. The town was now at the height of its fortunes. Besides its trade and its armourers, other causes had combined to pour wealth into it. War, which had wrought evil upon so many fair cities around, had brought nought but good to this one. As her French sisters decayed she increased, for here, from north, and from east, and from south, came the plunder to be sold and the ransom money to be spent. Through all her sixteen landward gates there had set for many years a double tide of empty-handed soldiers hurrying Francewards, and of enriched and laden bands who brought their spoils home. The prince's court, too, with its swarm of noble barons and wealthy knights, many of whom, in imitation of their master, had brought their ladies and their children from England, all helped to swell the coffers of the burghers. Now with this fresh influx of noblemen and cavaliers, food and lodgings were scarce to be had, and the prince was hurrying forward his forces to Dax in Gascony to relieve the overcrowding of his capital.

In front of the minster and abbey of St Andrew's was a large square crowded with priests, soldiers, women, friars, and burghers, who made it their common centre for sightseeing and gossip. Amid the knots of noisy and gesticulating townsfolk, many small parties of mounted knights and squires threaded their way towards the prince's quarters, where the huge iron-clamped doors were thrown back to show that he held audience within. Two score archers stood about the gateway, and beat back from time to time with their bow-staves the inquisitive and chattering crowd who swarmed found the portal. Two knights in full armour, with lances raised and closed vizors, sat their horses on either side, while in the centre, with two pages to tend upon him, there stood a noble-faced man in flowing purple gown, who pricked off upon a sheet of parchment the style and title of each applicant, marshalling them in their due order, and giving to each the place and facility which his rank demanded. His long white beard and searching eyes imparted to him an air of masterful dignity, which was increased by his tabardlike vesture and the heraldic barret cap with triple plume which bespoke his office.

"It is Sir William de Pakington, the prince's own herald and scrivener," whispered Sir Nigel, as they pulled up amid the line of knights who awaited admission. "Ill fares it with the man who should venture to deceive him. He hath by rote the name of every knight of France or of England, and all the tree of his family, with his kinships, coat-armour, marriages, augmentations, abatements, and I know not what beside. We may leave our horses here with the varlets, and push forward with our squires."

Following Sir Nigel's counsel, they pressed on upon foot until they were close to the prince's secretary, who was in high debate with a young and foppish knight, who was bent upon making his way past him.

"Mackworth!" said the king-at-arms. "It is in my mind, young sir, that you have not been presented before."

"Nay, it is but a day since I set foot in Bordeaux, but I feared lest the prince should think it strange that I had not waited upon him."

"The prince hath other things to think upon," quoth Sir William de Pakington, "but if you be a Mackworth you must be a Mackworth of Normanton, and indeed I see now that your coat is sable and ermine."

"I am a Mackworth of Normanton," the other answered, with some uneasiness of manner.

"Then must you be Sir Stephen Mackworth, for I learn that when old Sir Guy died he came in for the arms and the name, the war-cry and the profit."

"Sir Stephen is my elder brother, and I am Arthur, the second son," said the youth.

"In sooth and in sooth!" cried the king-at-arms with scornful eyes. "And pray, sir second son, where is the cadency mark which should mark your rank? Dare you to wear your brother's coat without the crescent which should stamp you as his cadet? Away to your lodgings, and come not nigh the prince until the armourer hath placed the true charge upon your shield." As the youth withdrew in confusion, Sir William's keen eye singled out the five red roses from amid the overlapping shields and cloud of pennons which faced him.

"Ha!" he cried, "there are charges here which are above counterfeit. The roses of Loring and the boar's head of Buttesthorn may stand back in peace, but, by my faith! they are not to be held back in war. Welcome, Sir Oliver, Sir Nigel! Chandos will be glad to his very heart-roots when he sees you. This way, my fair sirs. Your squires are doubtless worthy the fame of their masters. Down this passage, Sir Oliver! Edricson! Ha! one of the old strain of Hampshire Edricsons, I doubt not. And Ford, they are of a south Saxon stock, and of good repute. There are Norburys in Cheshire and in Wiltshire, and also, as I have heard, upon the borders. So, my fair sirs, and I shall see that you are shortly admitted."

He had finished his professional commentary by flinging open a folding-door, and ushering the party into a broad hall, which was filled with a great number of people who were waiting, like themselves, for an audience. The room was very spacious, lighted on one side by three arched and mullioned windows, while opposite was a huge fireplace in which a pile of faggots was blazing merrily. Many of the company had crowded round the flames, for the weather was bitterly cold; but the two knights seated themselves upon a bancal, with their squires standing behind them. Looking down the room, Alleyne marked that both floor and ceiling were of the richest oak, the latter spanned by twelve arching beams, which were adorned at either end by the lilies and the lions of the royal arms. On the further side was a small door, on each side of which stood men-at-arms. From time to time an elderly man in black with rounded shoulders and a long white wand in his hand came softly forth from this inner room, and beckoned to one or other of the company, who doffed cap and followed him.

The two knights were deep in talk, when Alleyne became aware of a remarkable individual who was walking round the room in their direction. As he passed each knot of cavaliers every head turned to look after him, and it was evident, from the bows and respectful salutations on all sides, that the interest which he excited was not due merely to his strange personal appearance. He was tall and as straight as a lance, though of a great age, for his hair, which curled from under his black velvet cap of maintenance, was as white as the new-fallen snow. Yet, from the swing of his stride and spring of his step, it was clear that he had not yet lost the fire and activity of his youth. His fierce hawklike face was clean shaven like that of a priest, save for a long thin wisp of white moustache which dropped down halfway to his shoulder. That he had been handsome might be easily judged from his high aquiline nose and clear-cut chin; but his features had been so distorted by the seams and scars of old wounds, and by the loss of one eye which had been torn from the socket, that there was little left to remind one of the dashing young knight who had been fifty years ago the fairest as well as the boldest of the English chivalry. Yet what knight was there in that hall of St Andrew's who would not have gladly laid down youth, beauty, and all that he possesed to win the fame of this man? For who could be named with Chandos, the stainless knight, the wise councillor, the valiant warrior, the hero of Crécy, of Winchelsea, of Poictiers, of Auray, and of as many other battles as there were years to his life?

"Ha, my little heart of gold!" he cried, darting forward suddenly and throwing his arms round Sir Nigel. "I heard that you were here, and have been seeking you."

"My fair and dear lord," said the knight, returning the warrior's embrace, "I have indeed come back to you, for where else shall I go that I may learn to be a gentle and a hardy knight?"

"By my troth," said Chandos with a smile, "it is very fitting that we should be companions, Nigel, for since you have tied up one of your eyes, and I have had the mischance to lose one of mine, we have but a pair between us. Ah, Sir Oliver! you were on the blind side of me and I saw you not. A wise woman hath made prophecy that this blind side will one day be the death of me. We shall go in to the prince anon; but in truth he hath much upon his hands, for what with Pedro, and the King of Majorca, and the King of Navarre, who is no two days of the same mind, and the Gascon barons, who are all chaffering for terms like so many hucksters, he hath an uneasy part to play. But how left you the Lady Loring?"

"She was well, my fair lord, and sent her service and greetings to you."

"I am ever her knight and slave. And your journey, I trust that it was pleasant?"

"As heart could wish. We had sight of two rover galleys, and even came to have some slight bickering with them."

"Ever in luck's way, Nigel!" quoth Sir John. "We must hear the tale anon. But I deem it best that ye should leave your squires and come with me, for, howsoe'er pressed the prince may be, I am very sure that he would be loth to keep two old comrades in arms upon the further side of the door. Follow close behind me, and I will forestall old Sir William, though I can scarce promise to roll forth your style and rank as is his wont." So saying, he led the way to the inner chamber, the two companions treading close at his heels, and nodding to right and left as they caught sight of familiar faces among the crowd.

CHAPTER XIX

HOW THERE WAS STIR AT THE ABBEY
OF ST ANDREW'S

THE prince's reception room, although of no great size, was fitted up with all the state and luxury which the fame and power of its owner demanded. A high daïs at the further end was roofed in by a broad canopy of scarlet velvet spangled with silver fleurs-de-lis, and supported at either corner by silver rods. This was approached by four steps carpeted with the same material, while all round were scattered rich cushions, Oriental mats, and costly rugs of fur. The choicest tapestries which the looms of Arras could furnish draped the walls whereon the battles of Judas Maccabæus were set forth, with the Jewish warriors in plate of proof, with crest and lance and banderole, as the naïve artists of the day were wont to depict them. A few rich settles and bancals, choicely carved and decorated with glazed leather hangings of the sort termed *or basané,* completed the furniture of the apartment, save that at one side of the daïs there stood a lofty perch, upon which a cast of three solemn Prussian gerfalcons sat, hooded and jesseled, as silent and motionless as the royal fowler who stood beside them.

In the centre of the daïs were two very high chairs with dorserets, which arched forwards over the heads of the occupants, the whole covered with light blue silk thickly powdered with golden stars. On that to the right sat a very tall and well-formed man with red hair, a livid face, and a cold blue eye, which had in it something peculiarly sinister and menacing. He lounged back in a careless position, and yawned repeatedly as though heartily weary of the proceedings, stopping from time to time to fondle a shaggy Spanish greyhound which lay stretched at his feet. On the other throne there was perched bolt upright, with prim demeanour, as though he felt himself to be upon his good behaviour, a little round, pippin-faced person, who smiled and bobbed to every one whose eye he chanced to meet. Between, and a little in front of them, on a humble charette or stool, sat a slim, dark young man, whose quiet attire and modest manner would scarce proclaim him to be the most noted prince in Europe. A jupon of dark blue cloth, tagged with buckles and pendants of gold, seemed but a sombre and plain attire amidst the wealth of silk and ermine and gilt tissue of fustian with which he was surrounded. He sat with his two hands clasped round his knee, his head slightly bent, and an expression of impatience and of trouble upon his clear well-chiselled features. Behind the thrones there stood two men in purple gowns, with ascetic, clean-shaven faces, and half a dozen other high dignitaries and office-holders of Aquitaine. Below on either side of the steps were forty or fifty barons, knights, and courtiers, ranged in a triple row to the right and the left, with a clear passage in the centre.

"There sits the prince," whispered Sir John Chandos as they entered. "He on the right is Pedro, whom we are about to put upon the Spanish throne. The other is Don James, whom we purpose with the aid of God to help to his throne in Majorca. Now follow me, and take it not to heart, if he be a little short in his speech, for indeed his mind is full of many very weighty concerns."

The prince, however, had already observed their entrance, and, springing to his feet, he had advanced with a winning smile and the light of welcome in his eyes.

"We do not need your good offices as herald here, Sir John," said he in a low but clear voice, "these valiant knights are very well known to me. Welcome to Aquitaine, Sir Nigel Loring and Sir Oliver Buttesthorn. Nay, keep your knee for my sweet father at Windsor. I would have your hands, my friends. We are like to give you some work to do ere you see the downs of Hampshire once more. Know you ought of Spain, Sir Oliver?"

"Nought, my sire, save that I have heard men say that there is a dish named an olla which is prepared there, though I have never been clear in my mind as to whether it was but a ragout such as is to be found in the south, or whether there is some seasoning such as fennel or garlic which is peculiar to Spain."

"Your doubts, Sir Oliver, shall soon be resolved," answered the prince, laughing heartily, as did many of the barons who surrounded them. "His Majesty here will doubtless order that you have this dish hotly seasoned when we are all safely in Castile."

"I will have a hotly seasoned dish for some folk I know of," answered Don Pedro with a cold smile.

"But my friend Sir Oliver can fight right hardily without either bite or sup," remarked the prince. "Did I not see him at Poictiers, when for two days we had not more than a crust of bread and a cup of foul water, yet carrying himself most valiantly? With my own eyes I saw him in the rout sweep the head from a knight of Picardy with one blow of his sword."

"The rogue got between me and the nearest French victual-wain," muttered Sir Oliver, amid a fresh titter from those who were near enough to catch his words.

"How many have you in your train?" asked the prince, assuming a graver mien.

"I have forty men-at-arms, sire," said Sir Oliver.

"And I have one hundred archers and a score of lances, but there are two hundred men who wait for me on this side of the water upon the borders of Navarre."

"And who are they, Sir Nigel?"

"They are a free company, sire, and they are called the White Company."

To the astonishment of the knight, his words provoked a burst of merriment from the barons round, in which the two kings and the prince were fain to join. Sir Nigel blinked mildly from one to the other, until at last, perceiving a stout black-bearded knight at his elbow, whose laugh rang somewhat louder than the others, he touched him lightly upon the sleeve.

"Perchance, my fair sir," he whispered, "there is some small vow of which I may relieve you. Might we not have some honourable debate upon the matter? Your gentle courtesy may perhaps grant me an exchange of thrusts."

"Nay, nay, Sir Nigel," cried the prince, "fasten not the offence upon Sir Robert Briquet, for we are one and all bogged in the same mire. Truth to say, our ears have just been vexed by the doings of the same Company, and I have even now made vow to hang the man who held the rank of captain over it. I little thought to find him among the bravest of my own chosen chieftains. But the vow is now nought, for, as you have never seen your Company, it would be a fool's act to blame you for their doings."

"My liege," said Sir Nigel, "it is a very small matter that I should be hanged, albeit the manner of death is somewhat more ignoble than I had hoped for. On the other hand, it would be a very grievous thing that you, the Prince of England and the flower of knighthood, should make a vow, whether in ignorance or no, and fail to bring it to fulfilment."

"Vex not your mind on that," the prince answered, smiling. "We have had a citizen from Montauban here this very day, who told us such a tale of sack and murder and pillage that it moved our blood; but our wrath was turned upon the man who was in authority over them, and not on him who had never set eyes upon them."

"My dear and honoured master," cried Sir Nigel, in great anxiety, "I fear me much that in your gentleness of heart you are straining this vow which you have taken. If there be so much as a shadow of doubt as to the form of it, it were a thousand times best—"

"Peace! peace!" cried the prince impatiently. "I am very well able to look to my own vows and their performance. We hope to see you both in the banquet-hall anon. Meanwhile you will attend upon us with our train." He bowed, and Chandos, plucking Sir Oliver by the sleeve, led them both away to the back of the press of courtiers.

"Why, little coz," he whispered, "you are very eager to have your neck in a noose. By my soul! had you asked as much from our new ally, Don Pedro, he had not baulked you. Between friends, there is overmuch of the hangman in him, and too little of the prince. But indeed this White Company is a rough band, and may take some handling ere you find yourself safe in your captaincy."

"I doubt not, with the help of St Paul, that I shall bring them to some order," Sir Nigel answered. "But there are many faces here which are new to me, though others have been before me since first I waited upon my dear master, Sir Walter. I pray you to tell me, Sir John, who are these priests upon the daïs?"

"The one is the Archbishop of Bordeaux, Nigel, and the other the Bishop of Agen."

"And the dark knight with grey-streaked beard? By my troth, he seems to be a man of much wisdom and valour."

"He is Sir William Felton, who, with my unworthy self, is the chief counsellor of the prince, he being high steward and I the seneschal of Aquitaine."

"And the knights upon the right, beside Don Pedro?"

"They are cavaliers of Spain who have followed him in his exile. The one at his elbow is Fernando de Castro, who is as brave and true a man as heart could wish. In front to the right are the Gascon lords. You may well tell them by their clouded brows, for there hath been some illwill of late betwixt the prince and them. The tall and burly man is the Captal de Buch, whom I doubt not that you know, for a braver knight never laid lance in rest. That heavy-faced cavalier who plucks his skirts and whispers in his ear is Lord Oliver de Clisson, known also as the Butcher. He it is who stirs up strife, and for ever blows the dying embers into flame. The man with the mole upon his cheek is the Lord Pommers, and his two brothers stand behind him, with the Lord Lesparre, Lord de Rosem, Lord de Mucident, Sir Perducas d'Albret, the Souldich de la Trane, and others. Further back are knights from Quercy, Limousin, Saintonge, Poitou, and Aquitaine, with the valiant Sir Guiscard d'Angle. That is he in the rose-coloured doublet with the ermine."

"And the knights upon this side?"

"They are all Englishmen, some of the household and others who, like yourself, are captains of companies. There is Lord Neville, Sir Stephen Cossington, and Sir Matthew Gourney, with Sir Walter Huet, Sir Thomas Banaster, and Sir Thomas Felton, who is the brother of the high steward. Mark well the man with the high nose and flaxen beard who hath placed his hand upon the shoulder of the dark hard-faced cavalier in the rust-stained jupon."

"Ay, by St Paul!" observed Sir Nigel, "they both bear the print of their armour upon their côtes-hardies. Methinks they are men who breathe freer in a camp than a court."

"There are many of us who do that, Nigel," said Chandos, "and the head of the court is, I dare warrant, among them. But of these two men the one is Sir Hugh Calverley, and the other is Sir Robert Knolles."

Sir Nigel and Sir Oliver craned their necks to have the clearer view of these famous warriors, the one a chosen leader of free companies, the other a man who by his fierce valour and energy had raised himself from the lowest ranks until he was second only to Chandos himself in the esteem of the army.

"He hath no light hand in war, hath Sir Robert," said Chandos. "If he passes through a country you may tell it for some years to come. I have heard that in the north it is still the use to call a house which hath but the two gable-ends left, without walls and roof, a Knolles' mitre."

"I have served under him," said Sir Nigel, "and I have hoped to be so honoured as to run a course with him. But hark, Sir John, what is amiss with the prince?"

Whilst Chandos had been conversing with the two knights a continuous stream of suitors had been ushered in, adventurers seeking to sell their swords, and merchants clamouring over some grievance, a ship detained for the carriage of troops, or a tun of sweet wine which had the bottom knocked out by a troop of thirsty archers. A few words from the prince disposed of each case, and if the applicant liked not the judgment, a quick glance from the prince's dark eyes sent him to the door with the grievance all gone out of him. The young ruler had sat listlessly upon his stool with the two puppet monarchs enthroned behind him, but of a sudden a dark shadow passed over his face, and he sprang to his feet in one of those gusts of passion which were the single blot upon his noble and generous character.

"How now, Don Martin de la Carra?" he cried. "How now, sirrah? What message do you bring to us from our brother of Navarre?"

The new-comer to whom this abrupt query had been addressed was a tall and exceedingly handsome cavalier who had just been ushered into the apartment. His swarthy cheek and raven black hair spoke of the fiery south, and he wore his long black coat swathed across his chest and over his shoulders in a graceful sweeping fashion, which was neither English nor French. With stately steps and many profound bows he advanced to the foot of the daïs before replying to the prince's question.

"My powerful and illustrious master," he began, "Charles, King of Navarre, Earl of Evreux, Count of Champagne, who also writeth himself Overlord of Beam, hereby sends his love and greetings to his dear cousin Edward, the Prince of Wales, Governor of Aquitaine, Grand Commander of—"

"Tush! tush! Don Martin!" interrupted the prince, who had been beating the ground with his foot impatiently during this stately preamble. "We already know our cousin's titles and style, and, certes, we know our own. To the point, man, and at once. Are the passes open to us, or does your master go back from his word pledged to me at Libourne no later than last Michaelmas?"

"It would ill become my gracious master, sire, to go back from promise given. He does but ask some delay and certain conditions and hostages—"

"Conditions! Hostages! Is he speaking to the Prince of England, or is it to the bourgeois provost of some half-captured town? Conditions, quotha? He may find much to mend in his own condition ere long. The passes are, then, closed to us?"

"Nay, sire—"

"They are open, then?"

"Nay, sire, if you would but—"

"Enough, enough, Don Martin," cried the prince. "It is a sorry sight to see so true a knight pleading in so false a cause. We know the doings of our Cousin Charles. We know that while with the right hand he takes our fifty thousand crowns for the holding of the passes open, he hath his left outstretched to Henry of Trastamare, or to the King of France, all ready to take as many more for the keeping them closed. I know our good Charles, and, by my blessed name-saint the Confessor, he shall learn that I know him. He sets his kingdom up to the best bidder, like some scullion farrier selling a glandered horse. He is—"

"My lord," cried Don Martin. "I cannot stand here to hear such words of my master. Did they come from other lips I should know better how to answer them."

Don Pedro frowned and curled his lip, but the prince smiled and nodded his approbation.

"Your bearing and your words, Don Martin, are such as I should have looked for in you," he remarked. "You will tell the king, your master, that he hath been paid his price, and that if he holds to his promise he hath my word for it that no scath shall come to his people, nor to their houses or gear. If, however, we have not his leave, I shall come close at the heels of this message without his leave, and bearing a key with me which shall open all that he may close." He stooped and whispered to Sir Robert Knolles and Sir Hugh Calverley, who smiled as men well pleased, and hastened from the room.

"Our Cousin Charles has had experience of our friendship," the prince continued, "and now, by the Saints! he shall feel a touch of our displeasure. I send now a message to our Cousin Charles which his whole kingdom may read. Let him take heed lest worse befall him. Where is my Lord Chandos? Ha, Sir John, I commend this worthy knight to your care. You will see that he hath refection, and such a purse of gold as may defray his charges, for indeed it is great honour to any court to have within it so noble and gentle a cavalier. How say you, sire?" he asked, turning to the Spanish refugee, while the herald of Navarre was conducted from the chamber by the old warrior.

"It is not our custom in Spain to reward pertness in a messenger," Don Pedro answered, patting the head of his greyhound. "Yet we have all heard the lengths to which your royal generosity runs."

"In sooth, yes," cried the King of Majorca.

"Who should know it better than we," said Don Pedro bitterly, "since we have had to fly to you in our trouble as to the natural protector of all who are weak?"

"Nay, nay, as brothers to a brother," cried the prince, with sparkling eyes. "We doubt not, with the help of God, to see you very soon restored to those thrones from which you have been so traitorously thrust."

"When that happy day comes," said Pedro, "then Spain shall be to you as Aquitaine, and, be your project what it may, you may ever count on every troop and every ship over which flies the banner of Castile."

"And," added the other, "upon every aid which the wealth and power of Majorca can bestow."

"Touching the hundred thousand crowns in which I stand your debtor," continued Pedro carelessly, "it can no doubt—"

"Not a word, sire, not a word!" cried the prince. "It is not now when you are in grief that I would vex your mind with such base and sordid matters. I have said once and for ever that I am yours with every bowstring of my army and every florin in my coffers."

"Ah! here is indeed a mirror of chivalry," said Don Pedro. "I think, Sir Fernando, since the prince's bounty is stretched so far, that we may make further use of his gracious goodness to the extent of fifty thousand crowns. Good Sir William Felton, here, will doubtless settle the matter with you."

The stout old English counsellor looked somewhat blank at this prompt acceptance of his master's bounty.

"If it please you, sire," he said, "the public funds are at their lowest, seeing that I have paid twelve thousand men of the companies, and the new taxes—the hearth tax and the wine tax—not yet come in. If you could wait until the promised help from England comes—"

"Nay, nay, my sweet cousin," cried Don Pedro. "Had we known that your own coffers were so low, or that this sorry sum could have weighed one way or the other, we had been loth indeed—"

"Enough, sire, enough!" said the prince, flushing with vexation. "If the public funds be, indeed, so backward, Sir William, there is still, I trust, my own private credit, which hath never been drawn upon for my own uses, but is now ready in the cause of a friend in adversity. Go, raise this money upon our own jewels, if nought else may serve, and see that it be paid over to Don Fernando."

"In security I offer—" cried Don Pedro.

"Tush! tush!" said the prince. "I am not a Lombard, sire. Your kingly pledge is my security, without bond or seal. But I have tidings for you, my lords and lieges, that our brother of Lancaster is on his way for our capital with four hundred lances and as many archers to aid us in our venture. When he hath come, and when our fair consort is recovered in her health, which I trust by the grace of God may be ere many weeks be past, we shall then join the army at Dax, and set our banners to the breeze once more."

A buzz of joy at the prospect of immediate action arose up from the group of warriors. The prince smiled at the martial ardour which shone upon every face around him.

"It will hearten you to know," he continued, "that I have sure advices that this Henry is a valiant leader, and that he has it in his power to make such a stand against us as promises to give us much honour and pleasure. Of his own people he hath brought together, as I learn, some fifty thousand, with twelve thousand of the French free companies, who are, as you know, very valiant and expert men-at-arms. It is certain, also, that the brave and worthy Bertrand du Guesclin hath ridden into France to the Duke of Anjou, and purposes to take back with him great levies from Picardy and Brittany. We hold Bertrand in high esteem, for he has oft before been at great pains to furnish us with an honourable encounter. What think you of it, my worthy Captal? He took you at Cocherel, and, by my soul! You will have the chance now to pay that score."

The Gascon warrior winced a little at the allusion, nor were his countrymen around him better pleased, for on the only occasion when they had encountered the arms of France without English aid they had met with a heavy defeat.

"There are some who say, sire," said the burly De Clisson, "that the score is already overpaid, for that without Gascon help Bertrand had not been taken at Auray, nor had King John been overborne at Poictiers."

"By heaven, but this is too much!" cried an English nobleman. "Methinks that Gascony is too small a cock to crow so lustily."

"The smaller cock, my Lord Audley, may have the longer spur," remarked the Captal de Buch.

"May have its comb clipped if it make overmuch noise," broke in an Englishman.

"By Our Lady of Rocmadour!" cried the Lord of Mucident, "this is more than I can abide. Sir John Charnell, you shall answer to me for those words!"

"Freely, my lord, and when you will," returned the Englishman carelessly.

"My Lord de Clisson," cried Lord Audley, "you look somewhat fixedly in my direction. By God's soul! I should be right glad to go further into the matter with you."

"And you, my Lord of Pommers," said Sir Nigel, pushing his way to the front, "it is in my mind that we might break a lance in gentle and honourable debate over the question."

For a moment a dozen challenges flashed backwards and forwards at this sudden bursting of the cloud which had lowered so long between the knights of the two nations. Furious and gesticulating the Gascons, white and cold and sneering the English, while the prince, with a half-smile, glanced from one party to the other, like a man who loved to dwell upon a fiery scene, and yet dreaded lest the mischief go so far that he might find it beyond his control.

"Friends, friends!" he cried at last, "this quarrel must go no further. The man shall answer to me, be he Gascon or English, who carries it beyond this room. I have overmuch need for your swords that you should turn them upon each other. Sir John Charnell, Lord Audley, you do not doubt the courage of our friends of Gascony?"

"Not I, sire," Lord Audley answered. "I have seen them fight too often not to know that they are very hardy and valiant gentlemen."

"And so say I," quoth the other Englishman, "but, certes, there is no fear of our forgetting it while they have a tongue in their heads."

"Nay, Sir John," said the prince, reprovingly, "all peoples have their own use and customs. There are some who might call us cold and dull and silent. But you hear, my lords of Gascony, that these gentlemen had no thought to throw a slur upon your honour or your valour, so let all anger fade from your mind. Clisson, Captal, De Pommers, I have your word?"

"We are your subjects, sire," said the Gascon barons, though with no very good grace. "Your words are our law."

"Then shall we bury all cause of unkindness in a flagon of malvoisie," said the prince, cheerily. "Ho, there! the doors of the banquet-hall! I have been overlong from my sweet spouse, but I shall be back with you anon. Let the sewers serve and the minstrels play, while we drain a cup to the brave days that are before us in the south!" He turned away, accompanied by the two monarchs, while the rest of the company, with many a compressed lip and menacing eye, filed slowly through the side-door to the great chamber in which the royal tables were set forth.

CHAPTER XX

HOW ALLEYNE WON HIS PLACE
IN AN HONOURABLE GUILD

WHILST the prince's council was sitting, Alleyne and Ford had remained in the outer hall, where they were soon surrounded by a noisy group of young Englishmen of their own rank, all eager to hear the latest news from England.

"How is it with the old man at Windsor?" asked one.

"And how with the good Queen Philippa?"

"And how with Dame Alice Perrers?" cried a third.

"The devil take your tongue, Wat!" shouted a tall young man, seizing the last speaker by the collar and giving him an admonitory shake. "The prince would take your head off for those words."

"By God's coif! Wat would miss it but little," said another. "It is as empty as a beggar's wallet."

"As empty as an English squire, coz," cried the first speaker. "What a devil has become of the maître-des-tables and his sewers? They have not put forth the trestles yet."

"Mon Dieu! if a man could eat himself into a knighthood, Humphrey, you had been a banneret at the least," observed another, amid a burst of laughter.

"And if you could drink yourself in, old leather-head, you had been first baron of the realm," cried the aggrieved Humphrey. "But how of England, my lads of Loring?"

"I take it," said Ford, "that it is much as it was when you were there last, save that perchance there is a little less noise there."

"And why less noise, young Solomon?"

"Ah, that is for your wit to discover."

"Pardieu! here is a paladin come over, with the Hampshire mud still sticking to his shoes. He means that the noise is less for our being out of the country."

"They are very quick in these parts," said Ford, turning to Alleyne.

"How are we to take this, sir?" asked the ruffling squire.

"You may take it as it comes," said Ford carelessly.

"Here is pertness!" cried the other.

"Sir, I honour your truthfulness," said Ford.

"Stint it, Humphrey," said the tall squire, with a burst of laughter. "You will have little credit from this gentleman, I perceive. Tongues are sharp in Hampshire, sir."

"And swords?"

"Hum! we may prove that. In two days' time is the vêpres du tournoi, when we may see if your lance is as quick as your wit."

"All very well, Roger Harcomb," cried a burly bull-necked young man, whose square shoulders and massive limbs told of exceptional personal strength. "You pass too lightly over the matter. We are not to be so easily overcrowed. The Lord Loring hath given his proofs: but we know nothing of his squires, save that one of them hath a railing tongue. And how of you, young sir?" bringing his heavy hand down on Alleyne's shoulder.

"And what of me, young sir?"

"Ma foi! this is my lady's page come over. Your cheek will be browner and your hand harder ere you see your mother again."

"If my hand is not hard, it is ready."

"Ready? Ready for what? For the hem of my lady's train?"

"Ready to chastise insolence, sir!" cried Alleyne with flashing eyes.

"Sweet little coz!" answered the burly squire. "Such a dainty colour! Such a mellow voice! Eyes of a bashful maid, and hair like a three years' babe! Voilà!" He passed his thick fingers roughly through the youth's crisp golden curls.

"You seek to force a quarrel, sir," said the young man, white with anger.

"And what then?"

"Why, you do it like a country boor, and not like a gentle squire. Hast been ill bred and as ill taught? I serve a master who could show you how such things should be done."

"And how would he do it, oh pink of squires?"

"He would neither be loud nor would he be unmannerly, but rather more gentle than is his wont. He would say, "Sir, I should take it as an honour to do some small deed of arms against you, not for mine own glory or advancement, but rather for the fame of my lady and for the upholding of chivalry." Then he would draw his glove, thus, and throw it on the ground: or, if he had cause to think that he had to deal with a churl, he might throw it in his face —as I do now!"

A buzz of excitement went up from the knot of squires as Alleyne, his gentle nature turned by this causeless attack into fiery resolution, dashed his glove with all his strength into the sneering face of his antagonist. From all parts of the hall squires and pages came running, until a dense swaying crowd surrounded the disputants.

"Your life for this!" said the bully, with a face which was distorted with rage.

"If you can take it," returned Alleyne.

"Good lad," whispered Ford. "Stick to it close as wax."

"I shall see justice," cried Norbury, Sir Oliver's silent attendant.

"You brought it upon yourself, John Tranter," said the tall squire, who had been addressed as Roger Harcomb. "You must ever plague the new-comers. But it were shame if this went further. The lad hath shown a proper spirit."

"But a blow! a blow! cried several of the older squires. There must be a finish to this."

"Nay; Tranter first laid hand upon his head," said Harcomb. "How say you, Tranter? The matter may rest where it stands?"

"My name is known in these parts," said Tranter, proudly, "I can let pass what might leave a stain upon another. Let him pick up his glove and say that he has done amiss."

"I would see him in the claws of the devil first," whispered Ford.

"You hear, young sir?" said the peacemaker. "Our friend will overlook the matter if you do but say that you have acted in heat and haste."

"I cannot say that," answered Alleyne.

"It is our custom, young sir, when new squires come amongst us from England, to test them in some such way. Bethink you that if a man have a destrier or a new lance he will ever try it in time of peace, lest in days of need it may fail him. How much more then is it proper to test those who are our comrades in arms?"

"I should draw out if it may honourably be done," murmured Norbury in Alleyne's ear. "The man is a noted swordsman and far above your strength."

Edricson came, however, of that sturdy Saxon blood which is very slowly heated, but once up not easily to be cooled. The hint of danger which Norbury threw out was the one thing needed to harden his resolution.

"I came here at the back of my master," he said, "and I looked on every man here as an Englishman and a friend. This gentleman hath shown me a rough welcome, and if I have answered him in the same spirit he has but himself to thank. I will pick the glove up; but, certes, I shall abide by what I have done unless he first crave my pardon for what he hath said and done."

Tranter shrugged his shoulders. "You have done what you could to save him, Harcomb," said he. "We had best settle at once."

"So say I," cried Alleyne.

"The council will not break up until the banquet," remarked a grey-headed squire. "You have a clear two hours."

"And the place?"

"The tilting-yard is empty at this hour."

"Nay; it must not be within the grounds of the court, or it may go hard with all concerned if it come to the ears of the prince."

"But there is a quiet spot near the river," said one youth. "We have but to pass through the abbey grounds, along the armoury wall, past the church of St Remi, and so down the Rue des Apôtres."

"En avant, then!" cried Tranter shortly, and the whole assembly flocked out into the open air, save only those whom the special orders of their masters held to their posts. These unfortunates crowded to the small casements, and craned their necks after the throng as far as they could catch a glimpse of them.

Close to the bank of the Garonne there lay a little tract of green sward, with the high wall of a prior's garden upon one side and an orchard with a thick bristle of leafless apple-trees upon the other. The river ran deep and swift up to the steep bank; but there were few boats upon it, and the ships were moored far out in the centre of the stream. Here the two combatants drew their swords and threw off their doublets, for neither had any defensive armour. The duello with its stately etiquette had not yet come into vogue, but rough and sudden encounters were as common as they must ever be when hotheaded youth goes abroad with a weapon strapped to its waist. In such combats, as well as in the more formal sports of the tilting-yard, Tranter had won a name for strength and dexterity which had caused Norbury to utter his well-meant warning. On the other hand, Alleyne had used his weapons in constant exercise and practice for every day for many months, and being by nature quick of eye and prompt of hand, he might pass now as no mean swordsman. A strangely opposed pair they appeared as they approached each other: Tranter dark and stout and stiff, with hairy chest and corded arms; Alleyne a model of comeliness and grace, with his golden hair and his skin as fair as a woman's. An unequal fight it seemed to most; but there were a few and they the most experienced who saw something in the youth's steady grey eye and wary step which left the issue open to doubt.

"Hold, sirs, hold!" cried Norbury, ere blow had been struck. "This gentleman hath a two-handed sword, a good foot longer than that of our friend."

"Take mine, Alleyne!" said Ford.

"Nay, friends," he answered, "I understand the weight and balance of mine own. To work, sir, for our lord may need us at the abbey!"

Tranter's great sword was indeed a mighty vantage in his favour. He stood with his feet close together, his knees bent outwards, ready for a dash inwards or a spring out. The weapon he held straight up in front of him with blade erect, so that he might either bring it down with a swinging blow, or by a turn of the heavy blade he might guard his own head and body. A further protection lay in the broad and powerful guard which crossed the hilt, and which was furnished with a deep and narrow notch, in which an expert swordsman might catch his foeman's blade, and by a quick turn of his wrist might snap it across. Alleyne, on the other hand, must trust for his defence to his quick eye and active foot— for his sword, though keen as a whetstone could make it, was of a light and graceful build, with a narrow sloping pommel and a tapering steel.

Tranter well knew his advantage and lost little time in putting it to use. As his opponent walked towards him he suddenly bounded forward and sent in a whistling cut which would have severed the other in twain had he not sprung lightly back from it. So close was it that the point ripped a gash in the jutting edge of his linen cyclas. Quick as a panther, Alleyne sprang in with a thrust, but Tranter, who was as active as he was strong, had already recovered himself and turned it aside with a movement of his heavy blade. Again he whizzed in a blow which made the spectators hold their breath, and again Alleyne very quickly and swiftly slipped from under it, and sent back two lightning thrusts which the other could scarce parry. So close were they to each other that Alleyne had no time to spring back from the next cut, which beat down his sword and grazed his forehead, sending the blood streaming into his eyes and down his cheeks. He sprang out beyond sword sweep, and the pair stood breathing heavily, while the crowd of young squires buzzed their applause.

"Bravely struck on both sides!" called Roger Harcomb. "You have both won honour from this meeting, and it would be sin and shame to let it go further."

"You have done enough, Edricson," said Norbury.

"You have carried yourself well," cried several of the older squires.

"For my part, I have no wish to slay this young man," said Tranter, wiping his heated brow.

"Does this gentleman crave my pardon for having used me despitefully?" asked Alleyne.

"Nay, not I."

"Then stand on your guard, sir!" With a clatter and clash the two blades met once more, Alleyne pressing in so as to keep within the full sweep of the heavy blade, while Tranter as continually sprang back to have space for one of his fatal cuts. A three-parts parried blow drew blood from Alleyne's left shoulder, but at the same moment he wounded Tranter slightly upon the thigh. Next instant, however, his blade had slipped into the fatal notch, there was a sharp cracking sound with a tinkling upon the ground, and he found a splintered piece of steel fifteen inches long was all that remained to him of his weapon.

"Your life is in my hands!" cried Tranter, with a bitter smile.

"Nay, nay, he makes submission!" broke in several squires.

"Another sword!" cried Ford.

"Nay, sir," said Harcomb, "that is not the custom."

"Throw down your hilt, Edricson," cried Norbury.

"Never!" said Alleyne. "Do you crave my pardon, sir?"

"You are mad to ask it."

"Then on guard again!" cried the young squire, and sprang in with a fire and a fury which more than made up for the shortness of his weapon. It had not escaped him that his opponent was breathing in short hoarse gasps, like a man who is dizzy with fatigue. Now was the time for the purer living and the more agile limb to show their value. Back and back gave Tranter, ever seeking time for a last cut. On and on came Alleyne, his jagged point now at his foeman's face, now at his throat, now at his chest, still stabbing and thrusting to pass the line of steel which covered him. Yet his experienced foeman knew well that such efforts could not be long sustained. Let him relax for one instant and his death-blow had come. Relax he must! Flesh and blood could not stand the strain. Already the thrusts were less fierce, the foot less ready, although there was no abatement of the spirit in the steady grey eyes. Tranter, cunning and wary from years of fighting, knew that his chance had come. He brushed aside the frail weapon which was opposed to him, whirled up his great blade, sprang back to get the fairer sweep—and vanished into the waters of the Garonne.

So intent had the squires, both combatants and spectators, been on the matter in hand, that all thought of the steep bank and swift still stream had gone from their minds. It was not until Tranter, giving back before the other's fiery rush, was upon the very brink, that a general cry warned him of his danger. That last spring, which he hoped would have brought the fight to a bloody end, carried him clear of the edge, and he found himself in an instant eight feet deep in the ice-cold stream. Once and twice his gasping face and clutching fingers broke up through the still green water, sweeping outwards in the swirl of the current. In vain were sword-sheaths, apple branches, and belts linked together, thrown out to him by his companions. Alleyne had dropped his shattered sword and was standing, trembling in every limb, with his rage all changed in an instant to pity. For the third time the drowning man came to the surface, his hands full of green slimy water-plants, his eyes turned in despair to the shore. Their glance fell upon Alleyne, and he could not withstand the mute appeal which he read in them. In an instant, he, too, was in the Garonne, striking out with powerful strokes for his late foeman.

Yet the current was swift and strong, and, good swimmer as he was, it was no easy task which Alleyne had set himself. To clutch at Tranter and to seize him by the hair was the work of a few seconds, but to hold his head above water and to make their way out of the current was another matter. For a hundred strokes he did not seem to gain an inch. Then at last, amid a shout of joy and praise from the bank, they slowly drew clear into more stagnant water, at the instant that a rope, made of a dozen sword-belts linked together by the buckles, was thrown by Ford into their very hands. Three pulls from eager arms, and the two combatants, dripping and pale, were dragged up the bank and lay panting upon the grass.

John Tranter was the first to come to himself, for, although he had been longer in the water, he had done nothing during that fierce battle with the current. He staggered to his feet and looked down upon his rescuer, who had raised himself upon his elbow, and was smiling faintly at the buzz of congratulation and of praise which broke from the squires around him.

"I am much beholden to you, sir," said Tranter, though in no very friendly voice. "Certes, I should have been in the river now but for you, for I was born in Warwickshire, which is but a dry county; and there are few who swim in those parts."

"I ask no thanks," Alleyne answered shortly. "Give me your hand to rise."

"The river has been my enemy," said Tranter, "but it hath been a good friend to you, for it hath saved your life this day."

"That is as it may be," replied Alleyne.

"But all is now well over," quoth Harcomb, "and no scath come of it, which is more than I had at one time hoped for. Our young friend here hath very fairly and honestly earned his right to be craftsman of the Honourable Guild of the Squires of Bordeaux. Here is your doublet, Tranter."

"Alas for my poor sword which lies at the bottom of the Garonne!" said the squire.

"Here is your pourpoint, Edricson," cried Norbury. "Throw it over your shoulders, that you may have at least one dry garment."

"And now away back to the abbey," said several.

"One moment, sirs," cried Alleyne, who was leaning on Ford's shoulder, with the broken sword, which he had picked up, still clutched in his right hand. "My ears may be somewhat dulled by the water, and perchance what has been said has escaped me, but I have not yet heard this gentleman crave pardon for the insult which he put upon me in the hall."

"What! do you still pursue the quarrel?" asked Tranter.

"And why not, sir? I am slow to take up such things, but once afoot I shall follow it while I have life or breath."

"Ma foi! you have not too much of either, for you are as white as marble," said Harcomb bluntly. "Take my rede, sir, and let it drop, for you have come very well out from it."

"Nay," said Alleyne, "this quarrel is none of my making, but, now that I am here, I swear to you that I shall never leave this spot until I have that which I have come for: so ask my pardon, sir, or choose another glaive and to it again."

The young squire was deadly white from his exertions, both on the land and in the water. Soaking and stained, with a smear of blood on his white shoulder, and another on his brow, there was still in his whole pose and set of face the trace of an inflexible resolution. His opponent's duller and more material mind quailed before the fire and intensity of a higher spiritual nature.

"I had not thought that you had taken it so amiss," said he awkwardly. "It was but such a jest as we play upon each other, and, if you must have it so, I am sorry for it."

"Then I am sorry too," quoth Alleyn warmly, "and here is my hand upon it."

"And the none-meat horn has blown three times," quoth Harcomb, as they all streamed in chattering groups from the ground. "I know not what the prince's maître-de-cuisine will say or think. By my troth! master Ford, your friend here is in need of a cup of wine, for he hath drunk deeply of Garonne water. I had not thought from his fair face that he had stood to this matter so shrewdly."

"Faith," said Ford, "this air of Bordeaux hath turned our turtle-dove into a game-cock. A milder or more courteous youth never came out of Hampshire."

"His master also, as I understand, is a very mild and courteous gentleman," remarked Harcomb, "yet I do not think that they are either of them men with whom it is very safe to trifle."

CHAPTER XXI

HOW AGOSTINO PISANO RISKED HIS HEAD

EVEN the squires' table at the Abbey of St Andrew's at Bordeaux was on a very sumptuous scale while the prince held his court there. Here first, after the meagre fare of Beaulieu and the stinted board of the Lady Loring, Alleyne learned the lengths to which luxury and refinement might be pushed. Roasted peacocks, with the feathers all carefully replaced so that the bird lay upon the dish even as it had strutted in life, boars' heads with the tusks gilded and the mouth lined with silver foil, jellies in the shape of the Twelve Apostles, and a great pasty which formed an exact model of the king's new castle at Windsor—these were a few of the strange dishes which faced him. An archer had brought him a change of clothes from the cog, and he had already, with the elasticity of youth, shaken off the troubles and fatigues of the morning. A page from the inner banqueting-hall had come with word that their master intended to drink wine at the lodgings of the Lord Chandos that night, and that he desired his squires to sleep at the hotel of the "Half Moon," on the Rue des Apôtres. Thither, then, they both set out in the twilight after the long course of juggling tricks and glee-singing with which the principal meal was concluded.

A thin rain was falling as the two youths, with their cloaks over their heads, made their way on foot through the streets of the old town, leaving their horses in the royal stables. An occasional oil-lamp at the corner of a street, or in the portico of some wealthy burgher, threw a faint glimmer over the shining cobblestones and the varied motley crowd who, in spite of the weather, ebbed and flowed along every highway. In those scattered circles of dim radiance might be seen the whole busy panorama of life in a wealthy and martial city. Here passed the round-faced burgher, swollen with prosperity, his sweeping dark-clothed gaberdine, flat velvet cap, broad leather belt and dangling pouch all speaking of comfort and wealth. Behind him his serving-wench, her blue wimple over her head, and one hand thrust forward to bear the lanthorn which threw a golden bar of light along her master's path. Behind them a group of swaggering half-drunken Yorkshire dalesmen, speaking a dialect which their own southland countrymen could scarce comprehend, their jerkins marked with the rampant lion, which showed that they had come over in the train of the north-country Stapletons. The burgher glanced back at their fierce faces and quickened his step, while the girl pulled her wimple closer round her; for there was a meaning in their wild eyes as they stared at the purse and the maiden, which men of all tongues could understand. Then came archers of the guard, shrill-voiced women of the camp, English pages with their fair skins and blue wondering eyes, dark-robed friars, lounging men-at-arms, swarthy loud-tongued Gascon serving men, seamen from the river, rude peasants of the Médoc, and becloaked and befeathered squires of the court, all jostling and pushing in an ever-changing many-coloured stream; while English, French, Welsh, Basque, and the varied dialects of Gascony and Guienne filled the air with their babel. From time to time the throng would be burst asunder and a lady's horse-litter would trot past towards the abbey, or there would come a knot of torch-bearing archers walking in front of Gascon baron or English knight, as he sought his lodgings after the palace revels. Clatter of hoofs, clinking of weapons, shouts from the drunken brawlers, and high laughter of women, they all rose up, like the mist from a marsh, out of the crowded streets of the dim-lit city.

One couple out of the moving throng especially engaged the attention of the two young squires, the more so as they were going in their own direction and immediately in front of them. They consisted of a man and a girl, the former very tall with rounded shoulders, a limp of one foot, and a large flat object covered with dark cloth under his arm. His companion was young and straight, with a quick elastic step and graceful bearing, though so swathed in a black mantle that little could be seen of her face save a flash of dark eyes and a curve of raven hair. The tall man leaned heavily upon her to take the weight off his tender foot, while he held his burden betwixt himself and the wall, cuddling it jealously to his side, and thrusting forward his young companion to act as a buttress whenever the pressure of the crowd threatened to bear him away. The evident anxiety of the man, the appearance of his attendant, and the joint care with which they defended their concealed possession, excited the interest of the two young Englishmen who walked within hand-touch of them.

"Courage, child!" they heard the tall man exclaim in strange hybrid French. "If we can win another sixty paces we are safe."

"Hold it safe, father," the other answered, in the same soft, mincing dialect. "We have no cause for fear."

"Verily, they are heathens and barbarians," cried the man, "mad, howling, drunken barbarians! Forty more paces, Tita mia, and I swear to the holy Eloi, patron of all learned craftsmen, that I will never set foot over my door again until the whole swarm are safely hived in their camp of Dax, or wherever else they curse with their presence. Twenty more paces, my treasure! Ah, my God! how they push and brawl! Get in their way, Tita mia! Put your little elbow bravely out! Set your shoulders squarely against them, girl! Why should you give way to these mad islanders? Ah, cospetto! we are ruined and destroyed!"

The crowd had thickened in front, so that the lame man and the girl had come to a stand. Several half-drunken English archers, attracted, as the squires had been, by their singular appearance, were facing towards them, and peering at them through the dim light.

"By the three kings!" cried one, "here is an old dotard shrew to have so goodly a crutch! Use the leg that God hath given you, man, and do not bear so heavily upon the wench."

"Twenty devils fly away with him!" shouted another. "What, how, man! are brave archers to go maidless while an old man uses one as a walking-staff?"

"Come with me, my honey-bird!" cried a third, plucking at the girl's mantle.

"Nay, with me, my heart's desire!" said the first. "By St George! our life is short, and we should be merry while we may. May I never see Chester Bridge again, if she is not a right winsome lass!"

"What hath the old toad under his arm?" cried one of the others. "He hugs it to him as the devil hugged the pardoner."

"Let us see, old bag of bones; let us see what it is that you have under your arm!" They crowded in upon him, while he, ignorant of their language, could but clutch the girl with one hand and the parcel with the other, looking wildly about in search of help.

"Nay, lads, nay!" cried Ford, pushing back the nearest archer. "This is but scurvy conduct. Keep your hands off, or it will be the worse for you."

"Keep your tongue still, or it will be the worse for you," shouted the most drunken of the archers. "Who are you to spoil sport?"

"A raw squire, new landed," said another. "By St Thomas of Kent! we are at the beck of our master, but we are not to be ordered by every babe whose mother hath sent him as far as Aquitaine."

"Oh, gentlemen," cried the girl in broken French, "for dear Christ's sake stand by us, and do not let these terrible men do us an injury."

"Have no fears, lady," Alleyne answered. "We shall see that all is well with you. Take your hand from the girl's wrist, you north-country rogue!"

"Hold to her, Wat!" said a great black-bearded man-at-arms, whose steel breast-plate glimmered in the dusk. "Keep your hands from your bodkins, you two, for that was my trade before you were born, and, by God's soul! I will drive a handful of steel through you if you move a finger."

"Thank God!" said Alleyne suddenly, as he spied in the lamp-light a shock of blazing red hair which fringed a steel cap high above the heads of the crowd. "Here is John, and Aylward, too! Help us, comrades, for there is wrong being done to this maid and to the old man."

"Holà, mon petit," said the old bowman, pushing his way through the crowd, with the huge forester at his heels. "What is all this, then? By the twang of string! I think that you will have some work upon your hands if you are to right all the wrongs that you may see upon this side of the water. It is not to be thought that a troop of bowmen, with the wine buzzing in their ears, will be as soft-spoken as so many young clerks in an orchard. When you have been a year with the Company you will think less of such matters. But what is amiss here? The provost-marshal with his archers is coming this way, and some of you may find yourselves in the stretchneck, if you take not heed."

"Why, it is old Sam Aylward of the White Company!" shouted the man-at-arms. "Why, Samkin, what hath come upon thee? I can call to mind the day when you were as roaring a blade as ever called himself a free companion. By my soul! from Limoges to Navarre, who was there who would kiss a wench or cut a throat as readily as bowman Aylward of Hawkwood's Company?"

"Like enough, Peter," said Aylward, "and by my hilt! I may not have changed so much. But it was ever a fair loose and a clear mark with me. The wench must be willing, or the man must be standing up against me, else, by these ten finger-bones! either were safe enough for me."

A glance at Aylward's resolute face, and at the huge shoulders of Hordle John, had convinced the archers that there was little to be got by violence. The girl and the old man began to shuffle on in the crowd without their tormentors venturing to stop them. Ford and Alleyne followed slowly behind them, but Aylward caught the latter by the shoulder.

"By my hilt! camarade," said he, "I hear that you have done great things at the Abbey today, but I pray you to have a care, for it was I who brought you into the Company, and it would be a black day for me if aught were to befall you."

"Nay, Aylward, I will have a care."

"Thrust not forward into danger too much, mon petit. In a little time your wrist will be stronger and your cut more shrewd. There will be some of us at the "Rose de Guienne" tonight, which is two doors from the hotel of the "Half Moon," so if you would drain a cup with a few simple archers you will be right welcome."

Alleyne promised to be there if his duties would allow, and then, slipping through the crowd, he rejoined Ford, who was standing in talk with the two strangers, who had now reached their own doorstep.

"Brave young signor," cried the tall man, throwing his arms round Alleyne, "how can we thank you enough for taking our parts against those horrible drunken barbarians? What should we have done without you? My Tita would have been dragged away, and my head would have been shivered into a thousand fragments."

"Nay, I scarce think that they would have mishandled you so," said Alleyne in surprise.

"Ho, ho!" cried he with a high crowing laugh, "it is not the head upon my shoulders that I think of. Cospetto! no. It is the head under my arm which you have preserved."

"Perhaps the signori would deign to come under our roof, father," said the maiden. "If we bide here, who knows that some fresh tumult may not break out?"

"Well said, Tita! Well said, my girl! I pray you, sirs, to honour my unworthy roof so far. A light, Giacomo! There are five steps up. Now two more. So! Here we are at last in safety. Corpo di Baccho! I would not have given ten maravedi for my head when those children of the devil were pushing us against the wall. Tita mia, you have been a brave girl, and it was better that you should be pulled and pushed than that my head should be broken."

"Yes, indeed, father," said she earnestly.

"But those English! Ach! Take a Goth, a Hun, and a Vandal; mix them together and add a Barbary rover; then take this creature and make him drunk—and you have an Englishman. My

God! were ever such people upon earth? What place is free from them? I hear that they swarm in Italy even as they swarm here. Everywhere you will find them, except in heaven."

"Dear father," cried Tita, still supporting the angry old man, as he limped up the curved oaken stair. "You must not forget that these good signori who have preserved us are also English."

"Ah yes. My pardon, sirs! Come into my room here. There are some who might find some pleasure in these paintings, but I learn that the art of war is the only art which is held in honour in your island."

The low-roofed, oak-panelled room into which he conducted them was brilliantly lighted by four scented oil-lamps. Against the walls, upon the table, on the floor, and in every part of the chamber, were great sheets of glass painted in the most brilliant colours. Ford and Edricson gazed around them in amazement, for never had they seen such magnificent works of art.

"You like them, then," the lame artist cried, in answer to the look of pleasure and of surprise in their faces. "There are, then, some of you who have a taste for such trifling."

"I could not have believed it," exclaimed Alleyne. "What colour! What outlines! See to this martyrdom of the holy Stephen, Ford. Could you not yourself pick up one of these stones which lie to the hand of the wicked murtherers?"

"And see this stag, Alleyne, with the cross betwixt its horns. By my faith! I have never seen a better one at the Forest of Bere,"

"And the green of this grass — how bright and clear! Why, all the painting that I have seen is but child's play beside this. This worthy gentleman must be one of those great painters of whom I have oft heard brother Bartholomew speak in the old days at Beaulieu."

The dark mobile face of the artist shone with pleasure at the unaffected delight of the two young Englishmen. His daughter had thrown off her mantle and disclosed a face of the finest and most delicate Italian beauty, which soon drew Ford's eyes from the pictures in front of him. Alleyne, however, continued with little cries of admiration and wonderment to turn from the walls to the table and yet again to the walls.

"What think you of this, young sir?" asked the painter, tearing off the cloth which concealed the flat object which he had borne beneath his arm. It was a leaf-shaped sheet of glass, bearing upon it a face with a halo round it, so delicately outlined, and of so perfect a tint, that it might have been indeed a human face which gazed with sad and thoughtful eyes upon the young squire. He clapped his hands, with that thrill of joy which true art will ever give to a true artist.

"It is great!" he cried. "It is wonderful! But I marvel, sir, that you should have risked a work of such beauty and value by bearing it at night through so unruly a crowd."

"I have indeed been rash," said the artist. "Some wine, Tita, from the Florence flask! Had it not been for you, I tremble to think of what might have come of it. See to the skin tint: it is not to be replaced; for, paint as you will, it is not once in a hundred times that it is not either burned too brown in the furnace or else the colour will not hold, and you get but a sickly white. There you can see the very veins and the throb of the blood. Yes, diavolo! if it had broken my heart would have broken too. It is for the choir window in the church of St Remi, and we had gone, my little helper and I, to see if it was indeed of the size for the stonework. Night had fallen ere we finished, and what could we do save carry it home as best we might? But you, young sir, you speak as if you knew something of the art."

"So little that I scarce dare speak of it in your presence," Alleyne answered. "I have been cloister bred, and it was no very great matter to handle the brush better than my brother novices."

"There are pigments, brush, and paper," said the old artist. "I do not give you glass, for that is another matter, and takes much skill in mixing of colours. Now I pray you to show me a touch of your art. I thank you, Tita! The Venetian glasses, cara mia, and fill them to the brim. A seat, signor!"

While Ford, in his English-French, was conversing with Tita in her, Italian-French, the old man was carefully examining his precious head to see that no scratch had been left upon its surface. When he glanced up again, Alleyne had, with a few bold strokes of the brush, tinted in a woman's face and neck upon the white sheet in front of him.

"Diavolo!" exclaimed the old artist, standing with his head on one side, "you have power; yes, cospetto! you have power. It is the face of an angel!"

"It is the face of the Lady Maude Loring!" cried Ford, even more astonished.

"Why, on my faith, it is not unlike her!" said Alleyne, in some confusion.

"Ah! a portrait! So much the better. Young man, I am Agostino Pisano, the son of Andrea Pisano, and I say again that you have power. Further, I say that, if you will stay with me I will teach you all the secrets of the glass-stainers' mystery: the pigments and their thickening, which will fuse into the glass and which will not, the furnace and the glazing—every trick, and method you shall know."

"I would be right glad to study under such a master," said Alleyne; "but I am sworn to follow my lord while this war lasts."

"War! war!" cried the old Italian. "Ever this talk of war. And the men that you hold to be great—what are they? Have I not heard their names? Soldiers, butchers, destroyers! Ah, per Baccho! we have men in Italy who are in very truth great. You pull down, you despoil; but they build up, they restore. Ah, if you could but see my own dear Pisa, the duomo, the cloisters of Campo Santo, the high campanile, with the mellow throb of her bells upon the warm Italian air! Those are the works of great men. And I have seen them with my own eyes, these very eyes which look upon you. I have seen Andrea Orcagna, Taddeo Gaddi, Giottino, Stefano, Simone Memmi—men whose very colours I am not worthy to mix. And I have seen the aged Giotto, and he in turn was pupil to Cimabue, before whom there was no art in Italy, for the Greeks were brought to paint the chapel of the Gondi at Florence. Ah, signori, these are the real great men whose names will be held in honour when your soldiers are shown to have been the enemies of human kind."

"Faith, sir," said Ford, "there is something to say for the soldiers, also; for, unless they be defended, how are all these gentlemen whom you have mentioned to preserve the pictures which they have painted?"

"And all these?" said Alleyne. "Have you indeed done them all? —and where are they to go?"

"Yes, signor, they are all from my hand. Some are, as you see, upon one sheet, and some are in many pieces which may fasten together. There are some who do but paint upon the glass, and then, by placing another sheet of glass upon the top and fastening it, they keep the air from their painting. Yet I hold that the true art of my craft lies as much in the furnace as in the brush. See this rose window, which is from the model of the Church of the Holy Trinity at Vendôme, and this other of the "Finding of the Grail," which is for the apse of the Abbey church. Time was when none but my countrymen could do these things; but there is Clement of Chartres and others in France who are very worthy workmen. But, ah! there is that ever-shrieking brazen tongue which will not let us forget for one short hour that it is the arm of the savage, and not the hand of the master, which rules over the world."

A stern clear bugle call had sounded close at hand to summon some following together for the night.

"It is a sign to us as well," said Ford. "I would fain stay here for ever amid all these beautiful things"—staring hard at the blushing Tita as he spoke—"but we must be back at our lord's hostel ere he reach it."

Amid renewed thanks and with promises to come again, the two squires bade their leave of the old Italian glass-stainer and his daughter. The streets were clearer now, and the rain had stopped, so they made their way quickly from the Rue du Roi, in which their new friends dwelt, to the Rue des Apôtres, where the hostel of the "Half Moon" was situated.

CHAPTER XXII

HOW THE BOWMEN HELD WASSAIL AT THE "ROSE DE GUIENNE"

"Mon Dieu! Alleyne, saw you ever so lively a face?" cried Ford as they hurried along together. "So pure, so peaceful, and so beautiful!"

"In sooth, yes. And the hue of the skin the most perfect that ever I saw. Marked you also how the hair curled round the brow? It was wonder fine."

"Those eyes too!" cried Ford. "How clear and how tender—simple, and yet so full of thought!"

"If there was a weakness, it was in the chin," said Alleyne.

"Nay, I saw none."

"It was well curved, it is true."

"Most daintily so."

"And yet—"

"What then, Alleyne? Wouldst find flaw in the sun?"

"Well, bethink you, Ford, would not more power and expression have been put into the face by a long and noble beard?"

"Holy Virgin!" cried Ford, "the man is mad. A beard on the face of little Tita!"

"Tita! Who spoke of Tita?"

"Who spoke of aught else?"

"It was the picture of St Remi, man, of which I have been discoursing."

"You are, indeed," cried Ford, laughing, "a Goth, Hun and Vandal, with all the other hard names which the old man called us. How could you think so much of a smear of pigments, when there was such a picture painted by the good God Himself in the very room with you? But who is this?"

"If it please you, sirs," said an archer, running across to them, "Aylward and others would be right glad to see you. They are within here. He bade me say to you that the Lord Loring will not need your service tonight, as he sleeps with the Lord Chandos."

"By my faith!" said Ford, "we do not need a guide to lead us to their presence." As he spoke there came a roar of singing from the tavern upon the right, with shouts of laughter and stamping of feet. Passing under a low door, and down a stone-flagged passage, they found themselves in a long narrow hall lighted up by a pair of blazing torches, one at either end. Trusses of straw had been thrown down along the walls, and reclining on them were some twenty or thirty archers, all of the Company, their steel caps and jacks thrown off, their tunics open, and their great limbs sprawling upon the clay floor. At every man's elbow stood his leather black-jack of beer, while at the further end a hogshead with its end knocked in promised an abundant supply for the future. Behind the hogshead, on a half-circle of kegs, boxes, and rude settles, sat Aylward, John, Black Simon and three or four other leading men of the archers, together with Goodwin Hawtayne, the master-shipman, who had left his yellow cog in the river to have a last rouse with his friends of the Company. Ford and Alleyne took their seats between Aylward and Black Simon without their entrance checking in any degree the hubbub which was going on.

"Ale, mes camarades?" cried the bowman, "or shall it be wine? Nay, but ye must have the one or the other. Here, Jacques, thou limb of the devil, bring a bottrine of the oldest vernage, and see that you do not shake it. Hast heard the news?"

"Nay," cried both the squires.

"That we are to have a brave tourney."

"A tourney?"

"Ay, lads. For the Captal de Buch hath sworn that he will find five knights from this side of the water who will ride over any five Englishmen who ever threw leg over saddle; and Chandos hath taken up the challenge, and the prince hath promised a golden vase for the man who carries himself best, and all the court is in a buzz over it."

"Why should the knights have all the sport?" growled Hordle John. "Could they not set up five archers for the honour of Aquitaine and of Gascony?"

"Or five men-at-arms," said Black Simon.

"But who are the English knights?" asked Hawtayne.

"There are three hundred and forty-one in the town," said Aylward, "and I hear that three hundred and forty cartels and defiances have already been sent in, the only one missing being Sir John Ravensholme, who is in his bed with the sweating sick-ness, and cannot set foot to ground."

"I have heard of it from one of the archers of the guard," cried a bowman from among the straw. "I hear that the prince wished to break a lance, but that Chandos would not hear of it, for the game is likely to be a rough one."

"Then there is Chandos."

"Nay, the prince would not permit it. He is to be marshal of the lists, with Sir William Felton and the Duc d'Armagnac. The English will be the Lord Audley, Sir Thomas Percy, Sir Thomas Wake, Sir William Beauchamp, and our own very good lord and leader."

"Hurrah for him, and God be with him!" cried several. "It is honour to draw string in his service."

"So you may well say," said Aylward. "By my ten finger-bones! If you march behind the pennon of the five roses you are like to see all that a good bowman would wish to see. Ha! yes, mes garçons, you laugh, but, by my hilt! you may not laugh when you find yourselves where he will take you, for you can never tell what strange vow he may not have sworn to. I see that he has a patch over his eye. There will come bloodshed of that patch, or I am the more mistaken."

"How chanced it at Poictiers, good Master Aylward?" asked one of the younger archers, leaning upon his elbows, with his eyes fixed respectfully upon the old bowman's rugged face.

"Ay, Aylward, tell us of it," cried Hordle John.

"Here is to old Samkin Aylward!" shouted several at the further end of the room, waving their black-jacks in the air.

"Ask him!" said Aylward, modestly, nodding towards Black Simon. "He saw more than I did. And yet, by the holy nails! there was not very much that I did not see either."

"Ah, yes," said Simon, shaking his head, "it was a great day. I never hope to see such another. There were some fine archers who drew their last shaft that day. We shall never see better men, Aylward."

"By my hilt! no. There was little Robby Withstaff, and Andrew Salblaster, and Wat Alspaye, who broke the neck of the German. Mon Dieu! what men they were! Take them how you would, at long butts or short, hoyles, rounds, or rovers, better bowmen never twirled a shaft over their thumb-nails."

"But the fight, Aylward, the fight!" cried several, impatiently.

"Let me fill my jack first, boys, for it is a thirsty tale. It was at the first fall of the leaf that the prince set forth, and he passed through Auvergne, and Berry, and Anjou, and Touraine. In Auvergne the maids are kind, but the wines are sour. In Berry it is the women that are sour, but the wines are rich. Anjou, however, is a very good land for bowmen, for wine and women are all that heart could wish. In Touraine I got nothing save a broken pate, but at Vierzon I had a great good fortune, for I had a golden pyx from the minster, for which I afterwards got nine Genoan janes from the goldsmith in the Rue Mont Olive. From thence we went to Bourges, where I had a tunic of flame-coloured silk and a very fine pair of shoes, with tassels of silk, and drops of silver."

"From a stall, Aylward?" asked one of the young archers.

"Nay, from a man's feet, lad. I had reason to think that he might not need them again, seeing that a thirty-inch shaft had feathered in his back."

"And what then, Aylward?"

"On we went, coz, some six thousand of us, until we came to Issodun, and there again a very great thing befell."

"A battle, Aylward?"

"Nay, hay; a greater thing than that. There is little to be gained out of a battle, unless one have the fortune to win a ransom. At Issodun I and three Welshmen came upon a house which all others had passed, and we had the profit of it to ourselves. For myself, I had a fine feather-bed—a thing which you will not see in a long day's journey in England. You have seen it, Alleyne, and you, John. You will bear me out that it is a noble bed. We put it on a sutler's mule, and bore it after the army. It was in my mind that I would lay it by until I came to start house of mine own, and I have it now in a very safe place near Lyndhurst."

"And what then, master-bowman?" asked Hawtayne. "By St Christopher! it is indeed a fair and goodly life which you have chosen, for you gather up the spoil as a Warsash man gathers lobsters, without grace or favour from any man."

"You are right, master-shipman," said another of the older archers. "It is an old bowyer's rede that the second feather of a fenny goose is better than the pinion of a tame one. Draw on, old lad, for I have come between you and the clout."

"On we went, then," said Aylward, after a long pull at his blackjack. "There were some six thousand of us, with the prince and his knights, and the feather-bed upon a sutler's mule in the centre. We made great havoc in Touraine, until we came into Romorantin, where I chanced upon a gold chain and two bracelets of jasper, which were stolen from me the same day by a black-eyed wench from the Ardennes. Mon Dieu! there are some folk who have no fear of Domesday in them, and no sign of grace in their souls, for ever clutching and clawing at another man's chattels."

"But the battle, Aylward, the battle!" cried several, amid a burst of laughter.

"I come to it, my young war-pups. Well, then, the King of France had followed us with fifty thousand men, and he made great haste to catch us; but when he had us he scarce knew what to do with us, for we were so drawn up among hedges and vineyards that they could not come nigh us, save by one lane. On both sides were archers, men-at-arms and knights behind, and in the centre the baggage, with my feather-bed upon a sutler's mule. Three hundred chosen knights came straight for it, and, indeed, they were brave men, but such a drift of arrows met them that few came back. Then came the Germans, and they also fought very bravely, so that one or two broke through the archers and came as far as the feather-bed, but all to no purpose. Then out rides our own little hot-head and my lord Audley with his four Cheshire squires, and a few others of like kidney, and after them went the prince and Chandos, and then the whole throng of us, with axe and sword, for we had shot away our arrows. Ma foi! it was a foolish thing, for we came forth from the hedges, and there was nought to guard the baggage had they ridden round behind us. But all went well with us, and the king was taken, and little Robby Withstaff and I fell in with a wain with twelve firkins of wine for the king's own table, and, by my hilt! if you asked me what happened after that, I cannot answer you, nor can little Robby Withstaff either."

"And next day?"

"By my faith! we did not tarry long, but we hied back to Bordeaux, where we came in safety with the King of France and also the feather-bed. I sold my spoil, mes garçons, for as many gold pieces as I could hold in my hufken, and for seven days I lit twelve wax candles upon the altar of Saint Andrew: for if you forget the blessed when things are well with you, they are very likely to forget you when you have need of them. I have a score of one hundred and nineteen pounds of wax against the holy Andrew, and, as he was a very just man, I doubt not that I shall have full weight and measure when I have most need of it."

"Tell me, Master Aylward," cried a young, fresh-faced archer at the further end of the room, "what was this great battle about?"

"Why, you jack-fool, what would it be about save who should wear the crown of France?"

"I thought that mayhap it might be as to who should have this feather-bed of thine."

"If I come down to you, Silas, I may lay my belt across your shoulders," Aylward answered, amid a general shout of laughter. "But it is time young chickens went to roost when they dare cackle against their elders. It is late, Simon."

"Nay, let us have another song."

"Here is Arnold of Sowley will troll as good a stave as any man in the Company."

"Nay, we have one here who is second to none," said Hawtayne, laying his hand upon big John's shoulder. "I have heard him on the cog with a voice like the wave upon the shore. I pray you, friend, to give us 'The Bells of Milton', or, if you will, 'The Franklin's Maid'."

Hordle John drew the back of his hand across his mouth, fixed his eyes upon the corner of the ceiling, and bellowed forth, in a voice which made the torches flicker, the southland ballad for which he had been asked:—

The franklin he hath gone to roam.
The franklin's maid she bides at home.
But she is cold and coy and staid,
And who may win the franklin's maid?

There came a knight of high renown
In bassinet and ciclatoun;
On bended knee full long he prayed:
He might not win the franklin's maid.

There came a squire so debonair,
His dress was rich, his words were fair,
He sweetly sang, he deftly played:
He could not win the franklin's maid.

There came a mercer wonder-fine
With velvet cap and gaberdine:
For all his ships, for all his trade,
He could not buy the franklin's maid.

There came an archer bold and true,
With bracer guard and stave of yew;
His purse was light, his jerkin frayed:
Haro, alas! the franklin's maid!

Oh, some have laughed and some have cried,
And some have scoured the country-side
But off they ride through wood and glade,
The bowman and the franklin's maid.

A roar of delight from his audience, with stamping of feet and beating of black-jacks against the ground, showed how thoroughly the song was to their taste, while John modestly retired into a quart pot, which he drained in four giant gulps. "I sang that ditty in Hordle ale-house ere I ever thought to be an archer myself," quoth he.

"Fill up your stoups!" cried Black Simon, thrusting his own goblet into the open hogshead in front of him. "Here is a last cup to the White Company, and every brave boy who walks behind the roses of Loring!"

"To the wood, the flax, and the gander's wing!" said an old grey-headed archer on the right.

"To a gentle loose, and the King of Spain for a mark at fourteen score!" cried another.

"To a bloody war!" shouted a fourth. "Many to go and few to come!"

"With the most gold to the best steel!" added a fifth.

"And a last cup to the maids of our heart!" cried Aylward. "A steady hand and a true eye, boys; so let two quarts be a bowman's portion." With shout and jest and snatch of song they streamed from the room, and all was peaceful once more in the "Rose de Guienne."

CHAPTER XXIII

HOW ENGLAND HELD THE LISTS
AT BORDEAUX

So used were the good burghers of Bordeaux to martial display and knightly sport, that an ordinary joust or tournament was an everyday matter with them. The fame and brilliancy of the prince's court had drawn the knights-errant and pursuivants-of-arms from every part of Europe. In the long lists by the Garonne on the landward side of the northern gate there had been many a strange combat, when the Teutonic knight, fresh from the conquest of the Prussian heathen, ran a course against the knight of Calatrava, hardened by continual struggle against the Moors, or cavaliers from Portugal broke a lance with Scandinavian warriors from the further shore of the great Northern Ocean. Here fluttered many an outland pennon, bearing symbol and blazonry from the banks of the Danube, the wilds of Lithuania, and the mountain strongholds of Hungary: for chivalry was of no clime and of no race, nor was any land so wild that the fame and name of the prince had not sounded through it from border to border.

Great, however, was the excitement through town and district when it was learned that on the third Wednesday in Advent there would be a passage-at-arms in which five knights of England would hold the lists against all comers. The great concourse of noblemen and famous soldiers, the national character of the contest, and the fact that this was a last trial of arms before what promised to be an arduous and bloody war, all united to make the event one of the most notable and brilliant that Bordeaux had ever seen. On the eve of the contest the peasants flocked in from the whole district of the Médoc, and the fields beyond the walls were whitened with the tents of those who could find no warmer lodging. From the distant camp of Dax, too, and from Blaye, Bourg, Libourne, St Emilion, Castillon, St Macaire, Cardillac, Ryons, and all the cluster of flourishing towns which looked upon Bordeaux as their mother, there thronged an unceasing stream of horsemen and of footmen, all converging upon the great city. By the morning of the day on which the courses were to be run, not less than eighty thousand people had assembled round the lists and along the low grassy ridge which looks down upon the scene of the encounter.

It was, as may well be imagined, no easy matter among so many noted cavaliers to choose out five on either side who should have precedence over their fellows. A score of secondary combats had nearly arisen from the rivalries and bad blood created by the selection, and it was only the influence of the prince and the efforts of the older barons which kept the peace among so many eager and fiery soldiers. Not till the day before the courses were the shields finally hung out for the inspection of the ladies and the heralds, so that all men might know the names of the champions and have the opportunity to prefer any charge against them should there be stain upon them which should disqualify them from taking part in so noble and honourable a ceremony.

Sir Hugh Calverley and Sir Robert Knolles had not yet returned from their raid into the marches of Navarre, so that the English party were deprived of two of their most famous lances. Yet there remained so many good names that Chandos and Felton, to whom the selection had been referred, had many an earnest consultation; in which every feat of arms and failure or success of each candidate was weighed and balanced against the rival claims of his companions. Lord Audley of Cheshire, the hero of Poictiers, and Loring of Hampshire, who was held to be the second lance in the army, were easily fixed upon. Then, of the younger men, Sir Thomas Percy of Northumberland, Sir Thomas Wake of Yorkshire, and Sir William Beauchamp of Gloucestershire, were finally selected to uphold the honour of England. On the other side were the veteran Captal de Buch and the brawny Olivier de Clisson, with the free companion Sir Perducas d'Albret, the valiant Lord of Mucident and Sigismond von Altenstadt, of the Teutonic order. The older soldiers among the English shook their heads as they looked upon the escutcheons of these famous warriors, for they were all men who had spent their lives upon the saddle, and bravery and strength can avail little against experience and wisdom of war.

"By my faith! Sir John," said the prince as he rode through the winding streets on his way to the lists, "I should have been glad to have splintered a lance today. You have seen me hold a spear since I had strength to lift one, and should know best whether I do not merit a place among this honourable company."

"There is no better seat and no truer lance, sire," said Chandos, "but, if I may say so without fear of offence, it were not fitting that you should join in this debate."

"And why, Sir John?"

"Because, sire, it is not for you take part with Gascons against English, or with English against Gascons, seeing that you are lord of both. We are not too well loved by the Gascons now, and it is but the golden link of your princely coronet which holds us together. If that be snapped I know not what would follow."

"Snapped, Sir John!" cried the prince, with an angry sparkle in his dark eyes. "What manner of talk is this? You speak as though the allegiance of our people were a thing which might be thrown off or on like a falcon's jessel."

"With a sorry hack one uses whip and spur, sire," said Chandos, "but with a horse of blood and spirit a good cavalier is gentle and soothing, coaxing rather than forcing. These folk are strange people, and you must hold their love, even as you have it now, for you will get from their kindness what all the pennons in your army could not wring from them."

"You are over-grave today, John," the prince answered. "We may keep such questions for our council-chamber. But how now, my brothers of Spain and of Majorca, what think you of this challenge?"

"I look to see some handsome jousting," said Don Pedro, who rode with the King of Majorca upon the right of the prince, while Chandos was on the left. "By St James of Compostella! but these burghers would bear some taxing. See to the broadcloth and velvet that the rogues bear upon their backs. By my troth! if they were my subjects they would be glad enough to wear falding and leather ere I had done with them. But mayhap it is best to let the wool grow long ere you clip it."

"It is our pride," the prince answered coldly, "that we rule over freemen and not slaves."

"Every man to his own humour," said Pedro carelessly. "Carajo! there is a sweet face at yonder window! Don Fernando, I pray you to mark the house, and to have the maid brought to us at the abbey."

"Nay, brother, nay!" cried the prince impatiently. "I have had occasion to tell you more than once that things are not ordered in this way in Aquitaine."

"A thousand pardons, dear friend," the Spaniard answered quickly, for a flush of anger had sprung to the dark cheek of the English prince. "You make my exile so like a home that I forget at times that I am not in very truth back in Castile. Every land hath indeed its own ways and manners; but I promise you, Edward, that when you are my guest in Toledo or Madrid you shall not yearn in vain for any commoner's daughter on whom you may deign to cast your eye."

"Your talk, sire," said the prince still more coldly, "is not such as I love to hear from your lips. I have no taste for such amours as you speak of, and I have sworn that my name shall be coupled with that of no woman save my ever dear wife."

"Ever the mirror of true chivalry!" exclaimed Pedro, while James of Majorca, frightened at the stern countenance of their all-powerful protector, plucked hard at the mantle of his brother-exile.

"Have a care, cousin," he whispered, "for the sake of the Virgin have a care, for you have angered him."

"Pshaw! fear not," the other answered, in the same low tone. "If I miss one stoop I will strike him on the next. Mark me else. Fair cousin," he continued, turning to the prince, "these be rare men-at-arms, and lusty bowmen. It would be hard indeed to match them."

"They have journeyed far, sire, but they have never yet found their match."

"Nor ever will, I doubt not. I feel myself to be back upon my throne when I look at them. But tell me, dear coz, what shall we do next, when we have driven this bastard Henry from the kingdom which he hath filched?"

"We shall then compel the King of Aragon to place our good friend and brother James of Majorca upon the throne."

"Noble and generous prince!" cried the little monarch.

"That done," said King Pedro, glancing out of the corners of his eyes at the young conqueror, "we shall unite the forces of England, of Aquitaine, of Spain, and of Majorca. It would be shame to us if we did not do some great deed with such forces ready to our hand."

"You say truly, brother," cried the prince, his eyes kindling at the thought. "Methinks that we could not do anything more pleasing to Our Lady than to drive the heathen Moors out of the country."

"I am with you, Edward, as true as hilt to blade. But, by St James! we shall not let these Moors make mock at us from over the sea. We must take ship and thrust them from Africa."

"By heaven, yes!" cried the prince. "And it is the dream of my heart that our English pennons shall wave upon the Mount of Olives, and the lions and lilies float over the holy city."

"And why not, dear coz? Your bowmen have cleared a path to Paris, and why not to Jerusalem? Once there, your arms might rest."

"Nay, there is more to be done," cried the prince, carried away by the ambitious dream. "There is still the city of Constantine to be taken, and war to be raged against the Soldan of Damascus. And beyond him again there is tribute to be levied

from the Cham of Tartary, and from the kingdom of Cathay. Ha!
John, what say you? Can we not go as far eastward as Richard of
the Lion Heart?"

"Old John will bide at home, sire," said the rugged soldier. "By
my soul! as long as I am seneschal of Aquitaine I will find enough
to do in guarding the marches which you have entrusted to me. It
would be a blithe day for the king of France when he heard that
the sea lay between him and us."

"By my soul! John," said the prince, "I have never known you
turn laggard before."

"The babbling hound, sire, is not always the first at the mort,"
the old knight answered.

"Nay, my true-heart! I have tried you too often not to know.
But, by my soul! I have not seen so dense a throng since the day
that we brought King John down Cheapside."

It was, indeed, an enormous crowd which covered the whole vast
plain from the line of vineyards to the river bank. From the northern gate the prince and his companions looked down at a dark sea
of heads, brightened here and there by the coloured hoods of the
women or by the sparkling head-pieces of archers and men-at-arms.
In the centre of this vast assemblage the lists seemed but a narrow
strip of green marked out with banners and streamers, while a
gleam of white with a flutter of pennons at either end showed where
the marquees were pitched, which served as the dressing-rooms of
the combatants. A path had been staked off from the city gate to the
stands, which had been erected for the court and the nobility. Down
this, amid the shouts of the enormous multitude, the prince cantered with his two attendant kings, his high officers of state, and his
long train of lords and ladies, courtiers, counsellors, and soldiers,
with toss of plume and flash of jewel, sheen of silk and glint of gold
—as rich and gallant a show as heart could wish. The head of the
cavalcade had reached the lists ere the rear had come clear of the
city gate, for the fairest and the bravest had assembled from all the
broad lands which are watered by the Dordogne and the Garonne.
Here rode dark-browed cavaliers from the sunny south, fiery sol-

diers from Gascony, graceful courtiers of Limousin or Saintonge, and gallant young Englishmen from beyond the seas. Here, too, were the beautiful brunettes of the Gironde, with eyes which out-flashed their jewels, while beside them rode their blonde sisters of England, clear cut and aquiline, swathed in swans'-down and in ermine, for the air was biting, though the sun was bright. Slowly the long and glittering train wound into the lists, until every horse had been tethered by the varlets in waiting, and every lord and lady seated in the long stands which stretched, rich in tapestry and velvet and blazoned arms, on either side of the centre of the arena.

The holders of the lists occupied the end which was nearest to the city gate. There, in front of their respective pavilions, flew the martlets of Audley, the roses of Loring, the scarlet bars of Wake, the lion of the Percys, and the silver wings of the Beauchamps, each supported by a squire clad in hanging green stuff to represent so many Tritons, and bearing a huge conch-shell in their left hands. Behind the tents the great war-horses, armed at all points, champed and reared, while their masters sat at the doors of their pavilions, with their helmets upon their knees, chatting as to the order of the day's doings. The English archers and men-at-arms had mustered at that end of the lists, but the vast majority of the spectators were in favour of the attacking party, for the English had declined in popularity ever since the bitter dispute as to the disposal of the royal captive after the battle of Poictiers. Hence the applause was by no means general when the herald-at-arms proclaimed, after a flourish of trumpets, the names and styles of the knights who were prepared, for the honour of their country and for the love of their ladies, to hold the field against all who might do them the favour to run a course with them. On the other hand, a deafening burst of cheering greeted the rival herald, who, advancing from the other end of the lists, rolled forth the well-known titles of the five famous warriors who had accepted the defiance.

"Faith, John," said the prince, "it sounds as though you were right. Ha! my grace D'Armagnac, it seems that our friends on this side will not grieve if our English champions lose the day."

"It may be so, sire," the Gascon nobleman answered. "I have little doubt that in Smithfield or at Windsor an English crowd would favour their own countrymen."

"By my faith! that's easily seen," said the prince, laughing, "for a few score English archers at yonder end are bellowing as though they would outshout the mighty multitude. I fear that they will have little to shout over this tourney, for my gold vase has small prospect of crossing the water. What are the conditions, John?"

"They are to tilt singly not less than three courses, sire, and the victory to rest with that party which shall have won the greater number of courses, each pair continuing till one or other have the vantage. He who carries himself best of the victors hath the prize, and he who is judged best of the other party hath a jewelled clasp. Shall I order that the nakirs sound, sire?"

The prince nodded, and the trumpets rang out, while the champions rode forth one after the other, each meeting his opponent in the centre of the lists. Sir William Beauchamp went down before the practised lance of the Captal de Buch, Sir Thomas Percy won the vantage over the Lord of Mucident, and the Lord Audley struck Sir Perducas d'Albret from the saddle. The burly De Clisson, however, restored the hopes of the attackers by beating to the ground Sir Thomas Wake of Yorkshire. So far, there was little to choose betwixt challengers and challenged.

"By Saint James of Santiago!" cried Don Pedro, with a tinge of colour upon his pale cheeks, "win who will, this has been a most noble contest."

"Who comes next for England, John?" asked the prince, in a voice which quivered with excitement.

"Sir Nigel Loring of Hampshire, sire."

"Ha! he is a man of good courage, and skilled in the use of all weapons."

"He is indeed, sire. But his eyes, like my own, are the worse for the wars. Yet he can tilt or play his part at handstrokes as merrily as ever. It was he, sire, who won the golden crown which Queen Philippa, your royal mother, gave to be jousted for by all the knights of England after the harrying of Calais. I have heard that at Twynham Castle there is a buffet which groans beneath the weight of his prizes."

"I pray that my vase may join them," said the prince. "But here is the cavalier of Germany, and, by my soul! he looks like a man of great valour and hardiness. Let them run their full three courses, for the issue is over-great to hang upon one."

As the prince spoke, amid a loud flourish of trumpets and the shouting of the Gascon party, the last of the assailants rode gallantly into the lists. He was a man of great size, clad in black armour without blazonry or ornament of any kind, for all worldly display was forbidden by the rules of the military brotherhood to which he belonged. No plume or nobloy fluttered from his plain tilting salade, and even his lance was devoid of the customary banderole. A white mantle fluttered behind him, upon the left side of which was marked the broad black cross picked out with silver which was the well-known badge of the Teutonic order. Mounted upon a horse as black and as forbidding as himself, he cantered slowly forward, with none of those prancings and gambades with which a cavalier was accustomed to show his command over his charger. Gravely and sternly he inclined his head to the prince, and took his place at the further end of the arena.

He had scarce done so before Sir Nigel rode out from the holders' enclosure, and galloping at full speed down the lists, drew his charger up before the prince's stand with a jerk which threw it back upon its haunches. With white armour, blazoned shield, and plume of ostrich-feathers from his helmet, he carried himself in so jaunty and joyous a fashion, with tossing pennon and curveting charger, that a shout of applause ran the full circle of the arena. With the air of a man who hastes to a joyous festival, he waved his lance in salute, and reining the pawing horse round without permitting its fore-feet to touch the ground, he hastened back to his station.

A great hush fell over the huge multitude as the last two champions faced each other. A double issue seemed to rest upon their contest, for their personal fame was at stake as well as their party's

honour. Both were famous warriors, but as their exploits had been
performed in widely sundered countries, they had never before
been able to cross lances. A course between such men would have
been enough in itself to cause the keenest interest, apart from its
being the crisis which would decide who should be the victors of
the day. For a moment they waited—the German sombre and col-
lected, Sir Nigel quivering in every fibre with eagerness and fiery
resolution. Then, amid a long-drawn breath from the spectators,
the glove fell from the marshal's hand, and the two steel-clad
horsemen met like a thunder-clap in front of the royal stand. The
German, though he reeled for an instant before the thrust of the
Englishman, struck his opponent so fairly upon the vizor that the
laces burst, the plumed helmet flew to pieces, and Sir Nigel galloped on down the list with his bald head shimmering in the sunshine. A thousand waving scarves and tossing caps announced that
the first bout had fallen to the popular party.

The Hampshire knight was not a man to be disheartened by a
reverse. He spurred back to his pavilion, and was out in a few
instants with another helmet. The second course was so equal that
the keenest judges could not discern any vantage. Each struck fire
from the other's shield, and each endured the jarring shock as
though welded to the horse beneath him. In the final bout, however, Sir Nigel struck his opponent with so true an aim that the
point of the lance caught between the bars of his vizor and tore the
front of his helmet out, while the German, aiming somewhat low,
and half stunned by the shock, had the misfortune to strike his
adversary upon the thigh, a breach of the rules of the tilting-yard, by
which he not only sacrificed his chances of success, but would also
have forfeited his horse and his armour, had the English knight
chosen to claim them. A roar of applause from the English soldiers,
with an ominous silence from the vast crowd who pressed round the
barriers, announced that the balance of victory lay with the holders.
Already the ten champions had assembled in front of the prince to
receive his award, when a harsh bugle call from the further end of
the lists drew all eyes to a new and unexpected arrival.

CHAPTER XXIV

HOW A CHAMPION CAME
FORTH FROM THE EAST

THE Bordeaux lists were, as has already been explained, situated upon the plain near the river upon those great occasions when the tilting-ground in front of the Abbey of St Andrew's was deemed to be too small to contain the crowd. On the eastern side of this plain the country-side sloped upwards, thick with vines in summer, but now ridged with the brown bare enclosures. Over the gently rising plain curved the white road which leads inland, usually flecked with travellers, but now with scarce a living form upon it, so completely had the lists drained all the district of its inhabitants. Strange it was to see so vast a concourse of people, and then to look upon that broad, white, empty highway which wound away, bleak and deserted, until it narrowed itself to a bare streak against the distant uplands.

Shortly after the contest had begun, anyone looking from the lists along this road might have remarked, far away in the extreme distance, two brilliant and sparkling points which glittered and twinkled in the bright shimmer of the winter sun. Within an hour these points had become clearer and nearer, until they might be seen to come from the reflection from the head-pieces of two horsemen who were riding at the top of their speed in the direction of Bordeaux. Another half-hour had brought them so close that every point of their bearing and equipment could be discerned. The first was a knight in full armour, mounted upon a brown horse with a white blaze upon breast and forehead. He was a short man of great breadth of shoulder, with vizor closed, and no blazonry upon his simple white surcoat or plain black shield. The other, who was evidently his squire and attendant, was unarmed save for the helmet upon his head, but bore in his right hand a very long and heavy oaken spear which belonged to his master. In his left hand the squire held not only the reins of his own horse but those of a great black war-horse fully harnessed, which trotted along at his side. Thus the three horses and their two riders rode swiftly to the lists, and it was the blare of the trumpet sounded by the squire as his lord rode into the arena which had broken in upon the prize-giving and drawn away the attention and interest of the spectators.

"Ha, John!" cried the prince, craning his neck, "who is this cavalier, and what is it that he desires?"

"On my word, sire," replied Chandos, with the utmost surprise upon his face, "it is my opinion that he is a Frenchman."

"A Frenchman!" repeated Don Pedro. "And how can you tell that, my Lord Chandos, when he has neither coat-armour, crest, nor blazonry?"

"By his armour, sire, which is rounder at elbow and at shoulder than any of Bordeaux or of England. Italian he might be were his bassinet more sloped, but I will swear that those plates were welded betwixt this and Rhine. Here comes his squire, however, and we shall hear what strange fortune hath brought him over the marches."

As he spoke the attendant cantered up the grassy enclosure, and pulling up his steed in front of the royal stand, blew a second fanfare upon his bugle. He was a raw-boned, swarthy-cheeked man, with black bristling beard and a swaggering bearing. Having sounded his call, he thrust the bugle into his belt, and pushing his way betwixt the groups of English and of Gascon knights, he reined up within a spear's length of the royal party.

"I come," he shouted in a hoarse thick voice, with a strong Breton accent, "as squire and herald from my master, who is a very valiant pursuivant-of-arms, and a liegeman to the great and powerful monarch, Charles, king of the French. My master has heard that there is jousting here, and prospect of honourable advancement, so he has come to ask that some English cavalier will vouchsafe for the love of his lady to run a course with sharpened lances with him, or to meet him with sword, mace, battle-axe, or dagger. He bade me say, however, that he would fight only with a true Englishman, and not with any mongrel who is neither English nor French, but speaks with the tongue of the one, and fights under the banner of the other."

"Sir!" cried De Clisson, with a voice of thunder, while his countrymen clapped their hands to their swords. The squire, however, took no notice of their angry faces, but continued with his master's message.

"He is now ready, sire," he said, "albeit his destrier has travelled many miles this day, and fast, for we were in fear lest we come too late for the jousting."

"Ye have indeed come too late," said the prince, "seeing that the prize is about to be awarded; yet I doubt not that one of these gentlemen will run a course for the sake of honour with this cavalier of France."

"And as to the prize, sir," quoth Sir Nigel, "I am sure that I speak for all when I say this French knight hath our leave to bear it away with him if he can fairly win it."

"Bear word of this to your master," said the prince, "and ask him which of these five Englishmen he would desire to meet. But stay; your master bears no coat-armour, and we have not yet heard his name."

"My master, sire, is under vow to the Virgin neither to reveal his name nor to open his vizor until he is back upon French ground once more."

"Yet what assurance have we," said the Prince, "that this is not some varlet masquerading in his master's harness, or some caitiff knight, the very touch of whose lance might bring infamy upon an honourable gentleman?"

"It is not so, sire," cried the squire earnestly. "There is no man upon earth who would demean himself by breaking a lance with my master."

"You speak out boldly, squire," the prince answered, "but unless I have some further assurance of your master's noble birth and gentle name I cannot match the choicest lances of my court against him."

"You refuse, sir?"

"I do refuse."

"Then, sir, I was bidden to ask you from my master whether you would consent if Sir John Chandos, upon hearing my master's name, should assure you that he was indeed a man with whom you might yourself cross swords without indignity."

"I ask no better," said the prince.

"Then I must ask, Lord Chandos, that you will step forth. I have your pledge that the name shall remain ever a secret, and that you will neither say nor write one word which might betray it. The name is—" He stooped down from his horse and whispered something into the old knight's ear which made him start with surprise, and stare with much curiosity at the distant knight, who was sitting his charger at the further end of the arena.

"Is this indeed sooth?" he exclaimed.

"It is, my lord, and I swear it by St Ives of Brittany."

"I might have known it," said Chandos, twisting his moustache, and still looking thoughtfully at the cavalier.

"What then, Sir John?" asked the prince.

"Sire, this is a knight whom it is indeed great honour to meet, and I would that your grace would grant me leave to send my squire for my harness, for I would dearly love to run a course with him."

"Nay, nay, Sir John, you have gained as much honour as one man can bear, and it were hard if you could not rest now. But I pray you, squire, to tell your master that he is very welcome to our court, and that wines and spices will be served him if he would refresh himself before jousting."

"My master will not drink," said the squire.

"Let him then name the gentleman with whom he would break a spear."

"He would contend with these five knights, each to choose such weapons as suit him best."

"I perceive," said the prince, "that your master is a man of great heart and high of enterprise. But the sun already is low in the west, and there will scarce be light for these courses. I pray you, gentlemen, to take your places, that we may see whether this stranger's deeds are as bold as his words."

The unknown knight had sat like a statue of steel looking neither to the right nor to the left during these preliminaries. He had changed from the horse upon which he had ridden, and bestrode the black charger which his squire had led beside him. His immense breadth, his stern composed appearance, and the mode in which he handled his shield and his lance, were enough in themselves to convince the thousands of critical spectators that he was a dangerous opponent. Aylward, who stood in the front row of the archers with Simon, big John, and others of the Company, had been criticizing the proceedings from the commencement with the ease and freedom of a man who had spent his life under arms and had learned in a hard school to know at a glance the points of a horse and his rider. He stared now at the stranger with a wrinkled brow and the air of a man who is striving to stir his memory.

"By my hilt! I have seen the thick body of him before today. Yet I cannot call to mind where it could have been. At Nogent belike, or was it at Auray? Mark me, lads, this man will prove to be one of the best lances of France, and there are no better in the world."

"It is but child's play, this poking game," said John. "I would fain try my hand at it, for, by the black rood! I think that it might be amended."

"What, then, would you do, John?" asked several.

"There are many things which might be done," said the forester thoughtfully. "Methinks that I would begin by breaking my spear."

"So they all strive to do."

"Nay, but not upon another man's shield. I would break it over my own knee."

"And what the better for that, old beef and bones?" asked Black Simon.

"So I would turn what is but a lady's bodkin of a weapon into a very handsome club."

"And then, John?"

"Then I would take the other's spear into my arm or my leg, or where it pleased him best to put it, and I would dash out his brains with my club."

"By my ten finger-bones! old John," said Aylward. "I would give my feather-bed to see you at a spear-running. This is a most courtly and gentle sport which you have devised."

"So it seems to me," said John seriously. "Or, again, one might seize the other round the middle, pluck him off his horse and bear him to the pavilion, there to hold him to ransom."

"Good!" cried Simon, amid a roar of laughter from all the archers round. "By Thomas of Kent! we shall make a camp-marshal of thee, and thou shalt draw up rules for our jousting. But, John, who is it that you would uphold in this knightly and pleasing fashion?"

"What mean you?"

"Why, John, so strong and strange a tilter must fight for the brightness of his lady's eyes or the curl of her eyelash, even as Sir Nigel does for the Lady Loring."

"I know not about that," said the big archer, scratching his head in perplexity. "Since Mary hath played me false, I can scarce fight for her."

"Yet any woman will serve."

"There is my mother, then," said John. "She was at much pains at my upbringing, and by my soul! I will uphold the curve of her eye-lashes, for it tickleth my very heartroot to think of her. But who is here?"

"It is Sir William Beauchamp. He is a valiant man, but I fear that he is scarce firm enough upon the saddle to bear the thrust of such a tilter as this stranger promises to be."

Aylward's words were speedily justified, for even as he spoke the two knights met in the centre of the lists. Beauchamp struck his opponent a shrewd blow upon the helmet, but was met with so frightful a thrust that he whirled out of his saddle and rolled over and over upon the ground. Sir Thomas Percy met with little better success, for his shield was split, his vambrace torn, and he himself wounded slightly in the side. Lord Audley and the unknown knight struck each other fairly upon the helmet; but while the stranger sat as firm and rigid as ever upon his charger, the Englishman was bent back to his horse's cropper by the weight of the blow and had galloped half-way down the lists ere he could recover himself. Sir Thomas Wake was beaten to the ground with a battle-axe—that being the weapon which he had selected—and had to be carried to the pavilion. These rapid successes, gained one after the other over four celebrated warriors, worked the crowd up to a pitch of wonder and admiration. Thunders of applause from the English soldiers, as well as from the citizens and peasants, showed how far the love of brave and knightly deeds could rise above the rivalries of race.

"By my soul! John," cried the prince, with his cheek flushed and his eyes shining, "this is a man of good courage and great hardiness. I could not have thought that there was any single arm upon earth which could have overthrown these four champions."

"He is indeed, as I have said, sire, a knight from whom much honour is to be gained. But the lower edge of the sun is wet, and it will be beneath the sea ere long."

"Here is Sir Nigel Loring, on foot and with his sword," said the prince. "I have heard that he is a fine swordsman."

"The finest in your army, sire," Chandos answered. "Yet I doubt not that he will need all his skill this day."

As he spoke, the two combatants advanced from either end in full armour with their two-handed swords sloping over their shoulders. The stranger walked heavily and with a measured stride, while the English knight advanced as briskly as though there was no iron shell to weigh down the freedom of his limbs. At four paces distance they stopped, eyed each other for a moment, and then in an instant fell to work with a clatter and clang as though two sturdy smiths were busy upon their anvils. Up and down went the long shining blades, round and round they circled in curves of glimmering light, crossing, meeting, disengaging, with flash of sparks at every parry. Here and there bounded Sir Nigel, his head erect, his jaunty plume fluttering in the air, while his dark opponent sent in crashing blow upon blow, following fiercely up with cut and with thrust, but never once getting past the practised blade of the skilled swordsman. The crowd roared with delight as Sir Nigel would stoop his head to avoid a blow, or by some slight movement of his body allow some terrible thrust to glance harmlessly past him. Suddenly, however, his time came. The Frenchman, whirling up his sword, showed for an instant a chink betwixt his shoulder-piece and the rerebrace which guarded his upper arm. In dashed Sir Nigel, and out again so swiftly that the eye could not follow the quick play of his blade, but a trickle of blood from the stranger's shoulder, and a rapidly widening red smudge upon his white surcoat, showed where the thrust had taken effect. The wound was, however, but a slight one, and the Frenchman was about to renew his onset, when, at a sign from the prince, Chandos threw down his bâton, and the marshals of the lists struck up the weapons and brought the contest to an end.

"It were time to check it," said the prince, smiling, "for Sir Nigel is too good a man for me to lose, and, by the five holy wounds! if one of those cuts came home I should have fears for our champion. What think you, Pedro?"

"I think, Edward, that the little man was very well able to take care of himself. For my part, I should wish to see so well matched a pair fight on while a drop of blood remained in their veins."

"We must have speech with him. Such a man must not go from my court without rest or sup. Bring him hither, Chandos, and certes, if the Lord Loring hath resigned his claim upon this goblet, it is right and proper that this cavalier should carry it to France with him as a sign of the prowess that he has shown this day."

As he spoke, the knight-errant, who had remounted his warhorse, galloped forward to the royal stand, with a silken kerchief bound round his wounded arm. The setting sun cast a ruddy glare upon his burnished armour, and sent his long black shadow streaming behind him up the level clearing. Pulling up his steed, he slightly inclined his head, and sat in the stern composed fashion with which he had borne himself throughout, heedless of the applauding shouts and the flutter of kerchiefs from the long lines of brave men and of fair women who were looking down upon him.

"Sir knight," said the prince, "we have all marvelled this day at the great skill and valour with which God has been pleased to endow you. I would fain that you should tarry at our court, for a time at least, until your hurt is healed and your horses rested."

"My hurt is nothing, sir, nor are my horses weary," returned the stranger in a deep stern voice.

"Will you not at least hie back to Bordeaux with us, that you may drain a cup of muscadine and sup at our table?"

"I will neither drink your wine nor sit at your table," returned the other. "I bear no love for you or for your race, and there is naught that I wish at your hands until the day when I see the last sail which bears you back to your island vanishing away against the western sky.'

"These are bitter words, sir knight," said Prince Edward, with an angry frown.

"And they come from a bitter heart," answered the unknown knight. "How long is it since there has been peace in my hapless country? Where are the steadings and orchards and vineyards which made France fair? Where are the cities which made her great? From Provence to Burgundy we are beset by all the prowling hirelings in Christendom, who rend and tear the country which you have left too weak to guard her own marches. Is it not a byword that a man may ride all day in that unhappy land without seeing thatch upon roof or hearing the crow of cock? Does not one fair kingdom content you, that you should strive so for this other one which has no love for you? Pardieu! a true Frenchman's words may well be bitter, for bitter is his lot, and bitter his thoughts as he rides through his thrice unhappy country."

"Sir knight," said the prince, "you speak like a brave man, and our cousin of France is happy in having a cavalier who is so fit to uphold his cause either with tongue or with sword. But if you think such evil of us, how comes it that you have trusted yourself to us without warranty or safe-conduct?"

"Because I knew that you would be here, sire. Had the man who sits upon your right been ruler of this land, I had indeed thought twice before I looked to him for aught that was knightly or generous." With a soldierly salute, he wheeled round his horse, and, galloping down the lists, disappeared amid the dense crowd of footmen and of horsemen who were streaming away from the scene of the tournament.

"The insolent villain!" cried Pedro, glaring furiously after him. "I have seen a man's tongue torn from his jaws for less. Would it not be well, even now, Edward, to send horsemen to hale him back? Bethink you that it may be one of the royal house of France, or at least some knight whose loss would be a heavy blow to his master. Sir William Felton, you are well mounted, gallop after the caitiff, I pray you."

"Do so, Sir William," said the prince, "and give him this purse of a hundred nobles as a sign of the respect which I bear for him; for by St George! he has served his master this day even as I would wish liegemen of mine to serve me." So saying, the prince turned his back upon the king of Spain, and, springing upon his horse, rode slowly homewards to the Abbey of St Andrew's.

CHAPTER XXV

HOW SIR NIGEL WROTE
TO TWYNHAM CASTLE

ON the morning after the jousting, when Alleyne Edricson went, as was his custom, into his master's chamber to wait upon him in his dressing, and to curl his hair, he found him already up and very busily at work. He sat at a table by the window, a deerhound on one side of him and a lurcher on the other, his feet tucked away under the trestle on which he sat, and his tongue in his cheek, with the air of a man who is much perplexed. A sheet of vellum lay upon the board in front of him, and he held a pen in his hand, with which he had been scribbling in a rude school-boy hand. So many were the blots, however, and so numerous the scratches and erasures, that he had at last given it up in despair, and sat with his single uncovered eye cocked upwards at the ceiling, as one who waits upon inspiration.

"By Saint Paul!" he cried, as Alleyne entered, "you are the man who will stand by me in this matter. I have been in sore need of you, Alleyne."

"God be with you, my fair lord!" the squire answered. "I trust that you have taken no hurt from all that you have gone through yesterday."

"Nay; I feel the fresher for it, Alleyne. It has eased my joints, which were somewhat stiff from these years of peace. I trust, Alleyne, that thou didst very carefully note and mark the bearing and carriage of this knight of France: for it is time, now when you are young, that you should see all that is best, and mould your own actions in accordance. This was a man from whom much honour might be gained, and I have seldom met anyone for whom I have conceived so much love and esteem. Could I but learn his name, I should send you to him with my cartel, that we might have further occasion to watch his goodly feats of arms."

"It is said, my fair lord, that none know his name, save only the Lord Chandos, and that he is under vow not to speak it. So ran the gossip at the squires' table."

"Be he who he might, he was a very hardy gentleman. But I have a task here, Alleyne, which is harder to me than aught that was set before me yesterday."

"Can I help you, my lord?"

"That indeed you can. I have been writing my greetings to my sweet wife; for I hear that a messenger goes from the prince to Southampton within the week, and he would gladly take a packet for me. I pray you, Alleyne, to cast your eyes upon what I have written, and see if they are such words as my lady will understand. My fingers, as you can see, are more used to iron and leather than to the drawing of strokes and turning of letters. What then? Is there aught amiss, that you should stare so?"

"It is this first word, my lord. In what tongue were you pleased to write?"

"In English; for my lady talks it more than she doth French."

"Yet this is no English word, my sweet lord. Here are four t's and never a letter betwixt them."

"By Saint Paul! it seemed strange to my eye when I wrote it," said Sir Nigel. "They bristle up together like a clump of lances. We must break their ranks and set them farther apart. The word is 'that.' Now I will read it to you, Alleyne, and you shall write it out fair; for we leave Bordeaux this day, and it would be great joy to me to think that the Lady Loring had word from me."

Alleyne sat down as ordered, with a pen in his hand and a fresh sheet of parchment before him, while Sir Nigel slowly spelled out his letter, running his forefinger on from word to word.

"That my heart is with thee, my dear sweeting, is what thine own heart will assure thee of. All is well with us here, save that Pepin hath the mange on his back, and Pommers hath scarce yet got clear of his stiffness from being four days on ship-board; and the more so because the sea was very high, and we were like to founder on account of a hole in her side, which was made by a stone cast at us by certain sea-rovers, who may the saints have in their keeping, for they have gone from amongst us, as has young Terlake and two score mariners and archers who would be the more welcome here, as there is like to be a very fine war, with much honour and all hopes of advancement; for which I go to gather my Company together, who are now at Montaubon, where they pillage and destroy; yet I hope that, by God's help, I may be able to show that I am their master, even as, my sweet lady, I am thy servant." "How of that, Alleyne?" continued Sir Nigel, blinking at his squire, with an expression of some pride upon his face. "Have I not told her all that hath befallen us?"

"You have said much, my fair lord; and yet, if I may say so, it is somewhat crowded together, so that my Lady Loring can, mayhap, scarce follow it. Were it in shorter periods—"

"Nay, it boots not how you marshal them, as long as they are all there at the muster. Let my lady have the words, and she will place them in such order as pleases her best. But I would have you add what it would please her to know."

"That will I," said Alleyne, blithely, and bent to the task.

"My fair lady and mistress," he wrote, "God hath had us in His keeping, and my lord is well and in good cheer. He hath won much honour at the jousting before the prince, when he alone was able to make it good against a very valiant man from France. Touching the monies, there is enough and to spare until we reach Montaubon. Herewith, my fair lady, I send my humble regards, entreating you that you will give the same to your daughter, the Lady Maude. May the holy saints have you both in their keeping is ever the prayer of thy servant," "ALLEYNE EDRICSON."

"That is very fairly set forth," said Sir Nigel, nodding his bald head as each sentence was read to him. "And for thyself, Alleyne, if there be any dear friend to whom you would fain give greeting, I can send it for thee within this packet."

"There is none," said Alleyne, sadly.

"Have you no kinsfolk, then?"

"None, save my brother."

"Ha! I had forgot that there was ill-blood betwixt you. But are there none in all England who love thee?"

"None that I dare say so."

"And none whom you love?"

"Nay, I will not say that," said Alleyne.

Sir Nigel shook his head and laughed softly to himself. "I see how it is with you," he said. "Have I not noted your frequent sighs, and vacant eye? Is she fair?"

"She is indeed," cried Alleyne from his heart, all tingling at this sudden turn of the talk.

"And good?"

"As an angel."

"And yet she loves you not?"

"Nay, I cannot say that she loves another."

"Then you have hopes?"

"I could not live else."

"Then must you strive to be worthy of her love. Be brave and pure, fearless to the strong and humble to the weak; and so, whether this love prosper or no, you will have fitted yourself to be honoured by a maiden's love, which is, in sooth, the highest guerdon which a true knight can hope for."

"Indeed, my lord, I do strive," said Alleyne, "but she is so sweet, so dainty, and of so noble a spirit, that I fear me that I shall never be worthy of her."

"By thinking so you become worthy. Is she then of noble birth?"

"She is, my lord," faltered Alleyne.

"Of a knightly house?"

"Yes."

"Have a care, Alleyne, have a care!" said Sir Nigel kindly. "The higher the steed the greater the fall. Hawk not at that which may be beyond thy flight."

"My lord, I know little of the ways and usages of the world," cried Alleyne, "but I would fain ask your rede upon the matter. You have known my father and my kin: is not my family one of good standing and repute?"

"Beyond all question."

"And yet you warn me that I must not place my love too high."

"Were Minstead yours, Alleyne, then, by Saint Paul! I cannot think that any family in the land would not be proud to take you among them, seeing that you come of so old a strain. But while the Socman lives—Ha, by my soul! if this is not Sir Oliver's step I am the more mistaken."

As he spoke, a heavy footfall was heard without, and the portly knight flung open the door and strode into the room.

"Why, my little coz," said he, "I have come across to tell you that I live above the barber's in the Rue de la Tour, and that there is a venison pasty in the oven and two flasks of the right vintage on the table. By St James! a blind man might find the place, for one has but to get in the wind from it, and follow the savoury smell. Put on your cloak, then, and come, for Sir Walter Hewett and Sir Robert Briquet, with one or two others, are awaiting us."

"Nay, Oliver, I cannot be with you, for I must to Montaubon this day."

"To Montaubon? But I have heard that your Company is to come with my forty Winchester rascals to Dax."

"If you will take charge of them, Oliver. For I will go to Montaubon with none save my two squires and two archers. Then, when I have found the rest of my Company, I shall lead them to Dax. We set forth this morning."

"Then I must go back to my pasty," said Sir Oliver. "You will find us at Dax, I doubt not, unless the prince throw me into prison, for he is very wroth against me."

"And why, Oliver?"

"Pardieu! because I have sent my cartel, gauntlet, and defiance to Sir John Chandos and to Sir William Felton."

"To Chandos? In God's name, Oliver, why have you done this?"

"Because he and the other have used me despitefully."

"And how?"

"Because they have passed me over in choosing those who should joust for England. Yourself and Audley I could pass, coz, for you are mature men; but who are Wake, and Percy, and Beauchamp? By my soul! I was prodding for my food into a camp-kettle when they were howling for their pap. Is a man of my weight and substance to be thrown aside for the first three half-grown lads who have learned the trick of the tiltyard? But hark ye, coz, I think of sending my cartel also to the prince."

"Oliver! Oliver! You are mad!"

"Not I, i' faith! I care not a denier whether he be prince or no. By Saint James! I see that your squire's eyes are starting from his head like a trussed crab. Well, friend, we are all three men of Hampshire, and not lightly to be jeered at."

"Has he jeered at you then?"

"Pardieu! yes. 'Old Sir Oliver's heart is still stout,' said one of his court. 'Else had it been out of keeping with the rest of him,' quoth the prince. 'And his arm is strong,' said another. 'So is the backbone of his horse,' quoth the prince. This very day I will send him my cartel and defiance."

"Nay, nay, my dear Oliver," said Sir Nigel, laying his hand upon his angry friend's arm. "There is naught in this, for it was but saying that you were a strong and robust man, who has need of a good destrier. And as to Chandos and Felton, bethink you that if when you yourself were young the older lances had ever been preferred, how would you then have had the chance to earn the good name and fame which you now bear? You do not ride as light as you did, Oliver, and I ride lighter by the weight of my hair, but it would be an ill thing if in the evening of our lives we showed that our hearts were less true and loyal than of old. If such a knight as

Sir Oliver Buttesthorn may turn against his own prince for the sake of a light word, then where are we to look for steadfast faith and constancy?"

"Ah! my dear little coz, it is easy to sit in the sunshine and preach to the man in the shadow. Yet you could ever win me over to your side with that soft voice of yours. Let us think no more of it then. But, Holy Mother! I had forgot the pasty, and it will be as scorched as Judas Iscariot! Come, Nigel, lest the foul fiend get the better of me again."

"For one hour, then; for we march at mid-day. Tell Aylward, Alleyne, that he is to come with me to Montaubon, and to choose one archer for his comrade. The rest will to Dax when the prince starts, which will be before the feast of the Epiphany. Have Pommers ready at mid-day with my sycamore lance, and place my harness on the sumpter mule."

With these brief directions, the two old soldiers strode off together, while Alleyne hastened to get all in order for their journey.

CHAPTER XXVI

HOW THE THREE COMRADES GAINED
A MIGHTY TREASURE

It was a bright crisp winter's day when the little party set off from
Bordeaux on their journey to Montaubon, where the missing half
of their Company had last been heard of. Sir Nigel and Ford had
ridden on in advance, the knight upon his hackney, while his great
war-horse trotted beside his squire. Two hours later Alleyne
Edricson followed; for he had the tavern reckoning to settle, and
many other duties which fell to him as squire of the body. With
him came Aylward and Hordle John, armed as of old, but
mounted for their journey upon a pair of clumsy Landes horses,
heavy-headed and shambling, but of great endurance, and capable of jogging along all day even when between the knees of the
huge archer, who turned the scale at two hundred and seventy
pounds. They took with them the sumpter mules which carried in
panniers the wardrobe and table furniture of Sir Nigel; for the
knight, though neither fop nor epicure, was very dainty in small
matters and loved, however bare the board or hard the life, that
his napery should still be white and his spoon of silver.

There had been frost during the night, and the white hard road
rang loud under their horses' irons as they spurred through the east
gate of the town, along the same broad highway which the unknown
French champion had traversed on the day of the jousts. The three
rode abreast, Alleyne Edricson with his eyes cast down and his mind
distrait, for his thoughts were busy with the conversation which he

had had with Sir Nigel in the morning. Had he done well to say so much, or had he not done better to have said more? What would the knight have said had he confessed to his love for the Lady Maude? Would he cast him off in disgrace, or might he chide him as having abused the shelter of his roof? It had been ready upon his tongue to tell him all when Sir Oliver had broken in upon them. Perchance Sir Nigel, with his love of all the dying usages of chivalry, might have contrived some strange ordeal or feat of arms by which his love should be put to the test. Alleyne smiled as he wondered what fantastic and wondrous deed would be exacted from him. Whatever it was, he was ready for it, whether it were to hold the lists in the court of the King of Tartary, to carry a cartel to the Sultan of Baghdad, or to serve a term against the wild heathen of Prussia. Sir Nigel had said that his birth was high enough for any lady, if his fortune could but be amended. Often had Alleyne curled his lip at the beggarly craving for land or for gold which blinded man to the higher and more lasting issues of life. Now it seemed as though it were only by this same land and gold that he might hope to reach his heart's desire. But then, again, the Socman of Minstead was no friend to the constable of Twynham Castle. It might happen that, should he amass riches by some happy fortune of war, this feud might hold the two families aloof. Even if Maude loved him, he knew her too well to think that she would wed him without the blessing of her father. Dark and murky was it all, but hope mounts high in youth, and it ever fluttered over all the turmoil of his thoughts like a white plume amid the shock of horsemen.

If Alleyne Edricson had enough to ponder over as he rode through the bare plains of Guienne, his two companions were more busy with the present and less thoughtful of the future. Aylward rode for half a mile with his chin upon his shoulder, looking back at a white kerchief which fluttered out of the gable window of a high house which peeped over the corner of the battlements. When at last a dip of the road hid it from his view, he cocked his steel cap, shrugged his broad shoulders, and rode on with laughter in his eyes, and his weather-beaten face all ashine with pleasant memories. John also rode in silence, but his eyes wandered slowly from one side of the road to the other, and he stared and pondered and nodded his head like a traveller who makes his notes and saves them up for the re-telling.

"By the rood!" he broke out suddenly, slapping his thigh with his great red hand, "I knew that there was something a-missing, but I could not bring to my mind what it was."

"What was it then?" asked Alleyne, coming with a start out of his reverie.

"Why, it is the hedgerows," roared John, with a shout of laughter. "The country is all scraped as clear as a friar's poll. But indeed I cannot think much of the folk in these parts. Why do they not get to work and dig up these long rows of black and crooked stumps which I see on every hand? A franklin of Hampshire would think shame to have such litter upon his soil."

"Thou foolish old John!" quoth Aylward. "You should know better, since I have heard that the monks of Beaulieu could squeeze a good cup of wine from their own grapes. Know then that if these rows were dug up the wealth of the country would be gone, and mayhap there would be dry throats and gaping mouths in England, for in three months' time these black roots will blossom and shoot and burgeon, and from them will come many a good ship-load of Médoc and Gascony which will cross the narrow seas. But see the little church in the hollow, and the folk who cluster in the churchyard! By my hilt! it is a burial, and there is a passing bell!" He pulled off his steel cap as he spoke and crossed himself, with a muttered prayer for the repose of the dead.

"There too," remarked Alleyne, as they rode on again, "that which seems to the eye to be dead is still full of the sap of life, even as the vines were. Thus God hath written Himself and His laws very broadly on all that is around us, if our poor dull eyes and duller souls could but read what He hath set before us."

"Ha! mon petit," cried the bowman, "you take me back to the days when you were new-fledged, as sweet a little chick as ever pecked his way out of a monkish egg. I had feared that in gaining our debonair young man-at-arms we had lost our soft-spoken clerk. In truth, I have noted much change in you since we came from Twynham Castle."

"Surely it would be strange else, seeing that I have lived in a world so new to me. Yet I must trust that there are many things in which I have not changed. If I have turned to serve an earthly master, and to carry arms for an earthly king, it would be an ill thing if I were to lose all thought of the great high King and Master of all, whose humble and unworthy servant I was ere ever I left Beaulieu. You, John, are also from the cloisters, but I trow that you do not feel that you have deserted the old service in taking on the new."

"I am a slow-witted man," said John, "and, in sooth, when I try to think about such matters it casts a gloom upon me. Yet I do not look upon myself as a worse man in an archer's jerkin than I was in a white cowl, if that be what you mean."

"You have but changed from one white company to the other," quoth Aylward. "But, by these ten finger-bones! it is a passing strange thing to me to think that it was but in the last fall of the leaf that we walked from Lyndhurst together, he so gentle and maidenly, and you, John, like a great red-limbed overgrown mooncalf; and now here you are as sprack a squire and as lusty an archer as ever passed down the highway from Bordeaux, while I am still the same old Samkin Aylward, with never a change, save that I have a few more sins on my soul and a few less crowns in my pouch. But I have never heard yet, John, what the reason was why you should come out of Beaulieu."

"There were seven reasons," said John, thoughtfully. "The first of them was that they threw me out."

"Ma foi! camarade, to the devil with the other six! That is enough for me and for thee also. I can see that they are very wise and discreet folk at Beaulieu. Ah! mon ange, what have you in the pipkin?"

"It is milk, worthy sire," answered the peasant-maid, who stood by the door of a cottage with a jug in her hand. "Would it please you, gentles, that I should bring you out three horns of it?"

"Nay, ma petite, but here is a two-sous piece for thy kindly tongue and for the sight of thy pretty face. Ma foi! but she has a bonne mien. I have a mind to bide and speak with her."

"Nay, nay, Aylward," cried Alleyne. "Sir Nigel will await us, and he in haste."

"True, true, camarade! Adieu, ma chérie! mon coeur est toujours à toi. Her mother is a well-grown woman also. See where she digs by the wayside. Ma foi! the riper fruit is ever the sweeter. Bon jour, ma belle dame! God have you in His keeping! Said Sir Nigel where he would await us?"

"At Marmande or Aiguillon. He said that we could not pass him, seeing that there is but the one road."

"Aye, and it is a road that I know as I know the Midhurst parish butts," quoth the bowman. "Thirty times have I journeyed it, forward and backward, and by the twang of string! I am wont to come back this way more laden than I went. I have carried all that I had into France in a wallet, and it hath taken four sumpter mules to carry it back again. God's benison on the man who first turned his hand to the making of war! But there, down in the dingle, is the church of Cardillac, and you may see the inn where three poplars grow beyond the village. Let us on, for a stoup of wine would hearten us upon our way."

The highway had lain through the swelling vineyard country, which stretched away to the north and east in gentle curves, with many a peeping spire and feudal tower, and cluster of village houses, all clear cut and hard in the bright wintry air. To their right stretched the blue Garonne running swiftly seawards, with boats and barges dotted over its broad bosom. On the other side lay a strip of vineyard, and beyond it the desolate and sandy region of the Landes, all tangled with faded gorse and heath and broom, stretching away in unbroken gloom to the blue hills which lay low upon the furthest sky-line. Behind them might still be seen the broad estuary of the Gironde, with the high towers of Saint André and Saint Remi shoooting up from the plain. In front, amid radiating lines of poplars, lay the riverside townlet of Cardillac—grey walls, white houses, and a feather of blue smoke.

"This is the 'Mouton d'Or'," said Aylward, as they pulled up their horses at a whitewashed straggling hostel. "What ho there!" he continued, beating upon the door with the hilt of his sword. "Tapster, ostler, varlet, hark hither, and a wannion on your lazy limbs! Ha! Michel, as red in the nose as ever! Three jacks of the wine of the country, Michel—for the air bites shrewdly. I pray you, Alleyne, to take note of this door, for I have a tale concerning it."

"Tell me, friend," said Alleyne to the portly, red-faced innkeeper, "have a knight and a squire passed this way within the hour?"

"Nay, sir, it would be two hours back. Was he a small man, weak in the eyes, with a want of hair, and speaks very quiet when he is most to be feared?"

"The same," the squire answered. "But I marvel how you should know how he speaks when he is in wrath, for he is very gentle-minded with those who are beneath him."

"Praise to the saints! it was not I who angered him," said the fat Michel.

"Who, then?"

"It was young Sieur de Brissac of Saintonge, who chanced to be here, and made game of the Englishman, seeing that he was but a small man and hath a face which is full of peace. But indeed this good knight was a very quiet and patient man, for he saw that the Sieur de Brissac was still young and spoke from an empty head, so he sat his horse and quaffed his wine, even as you are doing now, all heedless of his clacking tongue."

"And what then, Michel?"

"Well, messieurs, it chanced that the Sieur de Brissac, having said this and that, for the laughter of the varlets, cried out at last about the glove that the knight wore in his coif, asking if it was the custom in England for a man to wear a great archer's glove in his cap. Pardieu! I have never seen a man get off his horse as quick as did that stranger Englishman. Ere the words were past the other's lips he was beside him, his face nigh touching, and his breath hot upon his cheeks. 'I think, young sir,' quoth he softly, looking into the other's eyes, 'that how that I am nearer, you will very clearly see that the glove is not an archer's glove.' 'Perchance not,' said the Sieur de Brissac, with a twitching lip. 'Nor is it large, but very small,' quoth the Englishman. 'Less large than I had thought,' said the other, looking down, for the knight's gaze was heavy upon his eyelids. 'And in every way such a glove as might be worn by the fairest and sweetest lady in England,' quoth the Englishman. 'It may be so,' said the Sieur de Brissac, turning his face from him. 'I am myself weak in the eyes, and have often taken one thing for another,' quoth the knight, as he sprang back into his saddle and rode off, leaving the Sieur de Brissac biting his nails before my door. Ha! by the five wounds, many men of war have drunk my wine, but never one who was more to my fancy than this little Englishman."

"By my hilt! he is our master, Michel," quoth Aylward, "and such men as we do not serve under a laggart. But here are four deniers, Michel, and God be with you! En avant, camarades! for we have a long road before us."

At a brisk trot the three friends left Cardillac and its wine-house behind them, riding without a halt, past St Macaire, and on by ferry over the river Dorpt. At the further side the road winds through La Réolle, Bazaille, and Marmande, with the sunlit river still gleaming upon the right, and the bare poplars bristling up upon either side. John and Alleyne rode silent on either side, but every inn, farm-steading, or castle brought back to Aylward some remembrance of love, foray, or plunder, with which to beguile the way.

"There is the smoke from Bazas, on the further side of Garonne," quoth he. "There were three sisters yonder, the daughters of a far-rier, and, by these ten finger-bones! a man might ride for a long June day and never set eyes upon such maidens. There was Marie, tall and grave, and Blanche, petite and gay, and the dark Agnes, with eyes that went through you like a waxed arrow. I lingered there as long as four days, and was betrothed to them all; for it seemed shame to set one above her sisters, and might make ill blood in the family. Yet, for all my care, things were not merry in the house, and I thought it well to come away. There, too, is the mill of Le Souris.

Old Pierre Le Carron, who owned it, was a right good comrade, and had ever a seat and a crust for a weary archer. He was a man who wrought hard at all that he turned his hand to; but he cheated himself in grinding bones to mix with his flour, and so through over-diligence he brought a fever upon himself and died."

"Tell me, Aylward," said Alleyne, "what was amiss with the door of yonder inn that you should ask me to observe it?"

"Pardieu! yes, I had well-nigh forgot. What saw you on yonder door?"

"I saw a square hole, through which doubtless the host may peep when he is not too sure of those who knock."

"And you saw naught else?"

"I marked that beneath this hole there was a deep cut in the door, as though a great nail had been driven in."

"And naught else?"

"No."

"Had you looked more closely you might have seen that there was a stain upon the wood. The first time that I ever heard my comrade Black Simon laugh was in front of that door. I heard him once again when he slew a French squire with his teeth, he being unarmed and the Frenchman having a dagger."

"And why did Simon laugh in front of the inn-door?" asked John.

"Simon is a hard and perilous man when he hath the bitter drop in him; and, by my hilt! he was born for war, for there is little sweetness or rest in him. This inn, the 'Mouton d'Or,' was kept in the old days by one François Gourval, who had a hard fist and a harder heart. It was said that many and many an archer coming from the wars had been served with wine with simples in it, until he slept, and had then been stripped of all by this Gourval. Then on the morrow, if he made complaint, this wicked Gourval would throw him out upon the road or beat him, for he was a very lusty man, and had many stout varlets in his service. This chanced to come to Simon's ears when we were at Bordeaux together, and he would have it that we should ride to Cardillac with a good hempen cord and give this Gourval such a scourging as he merited. Forth we rode then, but when we came to the 'Mouton d'Or,' Gourval had had word of our coming and its purpose, so that the door was barred, nor was there any way into the house. 'Let us in, good Master Gourval!' cried Simon, and 'Let us in, Good Master Gourval!' cried I, but no word could we get through the hole in the door, save that he would draw an arrow upon us unless we went on our way. 'Well, Master Gourval,' quoth Simon at last, 'this is but a sorry welcome, seeing that we have ridden so far just to shake you by the hand.' 'Canst shake me by the hand without coming in,' said Gourval. 'And how that?' asked Simon. 'By passing in your hand through the hole,' said he. 'Nay, my hand is wounded,' quoth Simon, 'and of such a size that I cannot pass it in.' 'That need not hinder,' said Gourval, who was hot to be rid of us; 'pass in your left hand.' 'But I have something for thee, Gourval,' said Simon. 'What then?' he asked. 'There was an English archer who slept here last week of the name of Hugh of Nutbourne.' 'We have had many rogues here,' said Gourval. 'His conscience hath been heavy within him because he owes you a debt of fourteen deniers, having drunk wine for which he hath never paid. For the easing of his soul, he asked me to pay the money to you as I passed.' Now this Gourval was very greedy for money, so he thrust forth his hand for the fourteen deniers, but Simon had his dagger ready and he pinned his hand to the door. 'I have paid the Englishman's debt, Gourval!' quoth he, and so rode away, laughing so that he could scarce sit his horse, leaving mine host still nailed to his door. Such is the story of the hole which you have marked, and of the smudge upon the wood. I have heard that from that time English archers have been better treated in the auberge of Cardillac. But what have we here by the wayside?"

"It appears to be a very holy man," said Alleyne.

"And, by the rood! he hath some strange wares," cried John. "What are these bits of stone, and of wood, and rusted nails, which are set out in front of him?"

The man whom they had remarked sat with his back against a cherry-tree, and his legs shooting out in front of him, like one who is greatly at his ease. Across his thighs was a wooden board, and scattered all over it all manner of slips of wood and knobs of brick and stone, each laid separate from the other as a huckster places his wares. He was dressed in a long grey gown, and wore a broad hat of the same colour, much weather-stained, with three scallop-shells dangling from the brim. As they approached, the travellers observed that he was advanced in years, and that his eyes were upturned and yellow.

"Dear knights and gentlemen," he cried in a high crackling voice, "worthy Christian cavaliers, will ye ride past and leave an aged pilgrim to die of hunger? The sight hath been burned from mine eyes by the sands of the Holy Land, and I have had neither crust of bread nor cup of wine these two days past."

"By my hilt! father," said Aylward, looking keenly at him, "it is a marvel to me that thy girdle should have so goodly a span and clip thee so closely, if you have in sooth had so little to place within it."

"Kind stranger," answered the pilgrim, "you have unwittingly spoken words which are very grievous to me to listen to. Yet I should be loth to blame you, for I doubt not that what you said was not meant to sadden me, nor to bring my sore affliction back to my mind. It ill becomes me to prate too much of what I have endured for the faith, and yet, since you have observed it, I must tell you that this thickness and roundness of the waist is caused by a dropsy brought on by over-haste in journeying from the house of Pilate to the Mount of Olives."

"There, Aylward," said Alleyne, with a reddened cheek, "let that curb your blunt tongue. How could you bring a fresh pang to this holy man, who hath endured so much and hath journeyed as far as Christ's own blessed tomb?"

"May the foul fiend strike me dumb!" cried the bowman in hot repentance; but both the palmer and Alleyne threw up their hands to stop him.

"I forgive thee from my heart, dear brother," piped the blind man. "But, oh, these wild words of thine are worse to mine ears than aught which you could say of me."

"Not another word shall I speak," said Aylward, "but here is a florin for thee and I crave thy blessing."

"And here is another," said Alleyne.

"And another," cried Hordle John.

But the blind palmer would have none of their alms. "Foolish, foolish pride!" he cried, beating upon his chest with his large brown hand. "Foolish, foolish pride! How long then will it be ere I can scourge it forth? Am I then never to conquer it? Oh, strong, strong are the ties of flesh, and hard it is to subdue the spirit! I come, friends, of a noble house, and I cannot bring myself to touch this money, even though it be to save me from the grave."

"Alas! father," said Alleyne, "how then can we be of help to thee?"

"I had sat down here to die," quoth the palmer, "but for many years I have carried in my wallet these precious things which you see set forth now before me. It were sin, thought I, that my secret should perish with me. I shall therefore sell these things to the first worthy passers-by, and from them I shall have money enough to take me to the shrine of Our Lady at Rocamadour, where I hope to lay these old bones."

"What are these treasures, then, father?" asked Hordle John. "I can but see an old rusty nail, with bits of stone and slips of wood."

"My friend," answered the palmer, "not all the money that is in this country could pay a just price for these wares of mine. This nail," he continued, pulling off his hat and turning up his sightless orbs, "is one of those wherewith man's salvation was secured. I had it, together with this piece of the true rood, from the five-and-twentieth descendant of Joseph of Arimathea, who still lives in Jerusalem alive and well, though latterly much afflicted by boils. Aye, you may well cross yourselves, and I beg that you will not breathe upon it or touch it with your fingers."

"And the wood and stone, holy father?" asked Alleyne, with bated breath, as he stared awe-struck at his precious relics.

"This cantle of wood is from the true cross, this other from Noah his ark, and the third is from the door-post of the temple of the wise King Solomon. This stone was thrown at the sainted Stephen, and the other two are from the Tower of Babel. Here, too, is part of Aaron's rod and a lock of hair from Elisha the prophet."

"But, father," quoth Alleyne, "the holy Elisha was bald, which brought down upon him the revilements of the wicked children."

"It is very true that he had not much hair," said the palmer quickly, "and it is this which makes this relic so exceedingly precious. Take now your choice of these, my worthy gentlemen, and pay such a price as your consciences will suffer you to offer; for I am not a chapman nor a huckster, and I would never part with them, did I not know that I am very near to my reward."

"Aylward," said Alleyne excitedly, "this is such a chance as few folk have twice in one life. The nail I must have, and I will give it to the Abbey of Beaulieu, so that all the folk in England may go thither to wonder and to pray."

"And I will have the stone from the temple," cried Hordle John. "What would not my old mother give to have it hung over her bed?"

"And I will have Aaron's rod," quoth Aylward. "I have but five florins in the world, and here are four of them."

"Here are three more," said John.

"And here five more," added Alleyne. "Holy father, I hand you twelve florins, which is all that we can give, though we well know how poor a pay it is for the wondrous things which you sell us."

"Down, pride, down!" cried the pilgrim, still beating upon his chest. "Can I not bend myself then to take this sorry sum which is offered me for that which has cost me the labours of a life? Give me the dross! Here are the precious relics, and, oh, I pray you that you will handle them softly and with reverence, else had I rather left my unworthy bones here by the wayside."

With doffed caps and eager hands, the comrades took their new and precious possessions, and pressed onwards upon their journey, leaving the aged palmer still seated under the cherry-tree. They rode in silence, each with his treasure in his hand, glancing at it from time to time, and scarcely able to believe that chance had made them sole owners of relics of such holiness and worth that every abbey and church in Christendom would have bid eagerly for their possession. So they journeyed, full of this good fortune, until opposite the town of Le Mas, where John's horse cast a shoe, and they were glad to find a wayside smith who might set the matter to rights. To him Aylward narrated the good hap which had befallen them; but the smith, when his eyes lit upon the relics, leaned up against his anvil and laughed, with his hand to his side, until the tears hopped down his sooty cheeks.

"Why, masters," quoth he, "this man is a coquillart, or seller of false relics, and was here in this smithy not two hours ago. This nail that he hath sold you was taken from my nail-box, and as to the wood and the stones, you will see a heap of both outside from which he hath filled his scrip."

"Nay, nay," cried Alleyne, "this was a holy man who had journeyed to Jerusalem, and acquired a dropsy by running from the house of Pilate to the Mount of Olives."

"I know not about that," said the smith, "but I know that a man with a grey palmer's hat and gown was here no very long time ago, and that he sat on yonder stump and ate a cold pullet and drank a flask of wine. Then he begged from me one of my nails, and filling his scrip with stones, he went upon his way. Look at these nails, and see if they are not the same as that which he has sold you."

"Now may God save us!" cried Alleyne, all aghast. "Is there then no end to the wickedness of human kind? He so humble, so aged, so loth to take our money—and yet a villain and a cheat! Whom can we trust or believe in?"

"I will after him," said Aylward, flinging himself into the saddle. "Come, Alleyne, we may catch him ere John's horse be shod."

Away they galloped together, and ere long they saw the old grey palmer walking slowly along in front of them. He turned, however, at the sound of their hoofs, and it was clear that his blindness was a cheat like all the rest of him, for he ran swiftly through a field and so into a wood, where none could follow him. They hurled their relics after him, and so rode back to the blacksmith's the poorer both in pocket and in faith.

CHAPTER XXVII

HOW ROGER CLUB-FOOT WAS
PASSED INTO PARADISE

IT was evening before the three comrades came into Aiguillon. There they found Sir Nigel Loring and Ford safely lodged at the sign of the "Bâton Rouge," where they supped on good fare and slept between lavender-scented sheets. It chanced, however, that a knight of Poitou, Sir Gaston d'Estelle, was staying there on his way back from Lithuania, where he had served a term with the Teutonic knights under the land-master of the presbytery of Marienberg. He and Sir Nigel sat late in high converse as to bushments, outfalls, and the intaking of cities, with many tales of warlike men and valiant deeds. Then their talk turned to minstrelsy, and the stranger knight drew forth a cittern, upon which he played the minnelieder of the north, singing the while in a high cracked voice of Hildebrand and Brunhild and Siegfried, and all the strength and beauty of the land of Almain. To this Sir Nigel answered with the romances of Sir Eglamour, and of Sir Isumbras, and so through the long winter night they sat by the crackling wood-fire answering each other's songs until the crowing cocks joined in their concert. Yet, with scarce an hour of rest, Sir Nigel was as blithe and bright as ever as they set forth after breakfast upon their way.

"This Sir Gaston is a very worthy man," said he to his squires as they rode from the "Bâton Rouge." "He hath a very strong desire to advance himself, and would have entered upon some small knightly debate with me, had he not chanced to have his arm-bone broken by the kick of a horse. I have conceived a great love for him, and I have promised him that when his bone is mended I will exchange thrusts with him. But we must keep to this road upon the left."

"Nay, my fair lord," quoth Aylward. "The road to Montaubon is over the river, and so through Quercy and the Agenois."

"True, my good Aylward; but I have learned from this worthy knight, who hath come over the French marches, that there is a company of Englishmen who are burning and plundering in the country round Villefranche. I have little doubt, from what he says, that they are those whom we seek."

"By my hilt! it is like enough," said Aylward. "By all accounts they had been so long at Montaubon that there would be little there worth the taking. Then, as they have already been in the south, they would come north to the country of the Aveyron."

"We shall follow the Lot until we come to Cahors, and then cross the marches into Villefranche," said Sir Nigel. "By Saint Paul! as we are but a small band, it is very likely that we may have some very honourable and pleasing adventure, for I hear that there is little peace upon the French border."

All morning they rode down a broad and winding road, barred with the shadows of poplars. Sir Nigel rode in front with his squires, while the two archers followed behind with the sumpter mule between them. They had left Aiguillon and the Garonne far to the south, and rode now by the tranquil Lot, which curves blue and placid through a gently rolling country. Alleyne could not but mark that, whereas in Guienne there had been many townlets and few castles, there were now many castles and few houses. On either hand grey walls and square grim keeps peeped out at every few miles from amid the forests, while the few villages which they passed were all ringed round with rude walls, which spoke of the constant fear and sudden foray of a wild frontier land. Twice during the morning there came bands of horsemen swooping down upon them from the black gateways of wayside strongholds, with short stern questions as to whence they came and what their errand. Bands of armed men clanked along the highway and the few lines of laden mules which carried the merchandise of the trader were guarded by armed varlets, or by archers hired for the service.

"The peace of Bretigny hath not made much change in these parts," quoth Sir Nigel, "for the country is overrun with free companions and masterless men. Yonder towers, between the wood and the hill, mark the town of Cahors and beyond it is the land of France. But here is a man by the wayside, and as he hath two horses and a squire I make little doubt that he is a knight. I pray you, Alleyne, to give him greeting from me, and to ask him for his titles and coat-armour. It may be that I can relieve him of some vow, or perchance he hath a lady whom he would wish to advance."

"Nay, my fair lord," said Alleyne, "these are not horses and a squire, but mules and a varlet. The man is a mercer, for he hath a great bundle beside him."

"Now, God's blessing on your honest English voice!" cried the stranger, pricking up his ears at the sound of Alleyne's words. "Never have I heard music that was so sweet to mine ear. Come, Watkin lad, throw the bales over Laura's back! My heart was nigh broke, for it seemed that I had left all that was English behind me, and that I would never set eyes upon Norwich market square again." He was a tall, lusty, middle-aged man with a ruddy face, a brown forked beard shot with grey, and a broad Flanders hat set at the back of his head. His servant, as tall as himself, but gaunt and raw-boned, had swung the bales on the back of one mule, while the merchant mounted upon the other and rode to join the party. It was easy to see, as he approached, from the quality of his dress and the richness of his trappings, that he was a man of some wealth and position.

"Sir knight," said he, "my name is David Micheldene, and I am a burgher and alderman of the good town of Norwich, where I live five doors from the church of Our Lady, as all men know on the banks of Yare. I have here my bales of cloth which I carry to Cahors—woe worth the day that ever I started on such an errand!

I crave your gracious protection upon the way for me, my servant, and my mercery; for I have already had many perilous passages, and have now learned that Roger Club-foot, the robber-knight of Quercy, is out upon the road in front of me. I hereby agree to give you one rose-noble if you bring me safe to the inn of the 'Angel' in Cahors, the same to be repaid to me or my heirs if any harm come to me or my goods."

"By Saint Paul!" answered Sir Nigel, "I should be a sorry knight if I asked pay for standing by a countryman in a strange land. You may ride with me and welcome, Master Micheldene, and your varlet may follow with my archers."

"God's benison upon thy bounty!" cried the stranger. "Should you come to Norwich you may have cause to remember that you have been of service to Alderman Micheldene. It is not very far to Cahors, for surely I see the cathedral towers against the skyline; but I have heard much of this Roger Club-foot, and the more I hear the less do I wish to look upon his face. Oh, but I am sick and weary of it all, and I would give half that I am worth to see my good dame sitting in peace beside me, and to hear the bells of Norwich town."

"Your words are strange to me," quoth Sir Nigel, "for you have the appearance of a stout man, and I see that you wear a sword by your side."

"Yet it is not my trade," answered the merchant. "I doubt not that if I set you down in my shop at Norwich you might scarce tell fustian from falding, and know little difference between the velvet of Genoa and the threes-piled cloth of Bruges. There you might well turn to me for help. But here on a lone roadside, with thick woods and robber-knights, I turn to you, for it is the business to which you have been reared."

"There is sooth in what you say, Master Micheldene," said Sir Nigel, "and I trust that we may come upon this Roger Club-foot, for I have heard that he is a very stout and skilful soldier, and a man from whom much honour is to be gained."

"He is a bloody robber," said the trader, curtly, "and I wish I saw him kicking at the end of a halter."

"It is such men as he," Sir Nigel remarked, "who give the true knight honourable deeds to do, whereby he may advance himself."

"It is such men as he," retorted Micheldene, "who are like rats in a wheat-rick or moth in a woolfels, a harm and a hindrance to all peaceful and honest men."

"Yet, if the dangers of the road weigh so heavily upon you, master alderman, it is a great marvel to me that you should venture so far from home."

"And, sometimes, sir knight, it is a marvel to myself. But I am a man who may grutch and grumble, but when I have set my face to do a thing I will not turn my back upon it until it be done. There is one François Villet, at Cahors, who will send me wine-casks for my cloth-bales, so to Cahors I will go, though all the robber-knights of Christendom were to line the roads like yonder poplars."

"Stoutly spoken, master alderman! But how have you fared hitherto?"

"As a lamb fares in a land of wolves. Five times we have had to beg and pray ere we could pass. Twice I have paid toll to the wardens of the road. Three times we have had to draw, and once at La Réolle we stood over our wool-bales, Watkin and I, and we laid about us for as long as a man might chant a litany, slaying one rogue and wounding two others. By God's coif! we are men of peace, but we are free English burghers, not to be mishandled either in our country or abroad. Neither lord, baron, knight, nor commoner shall have as much as a strike of flax of mine whilst I have strength to wag this sword."

"And a passing strange sword it is," quoth Sir Nigel. "What make you, Alleyne, of these black lines which are drawn across the sheath?"

"I cannot tell you what they are, my fair lord."

"Nor can I," said Ford.

The merchant chuckled to himself. "It was a thought of mine own," said he; "for the sword was made by Thomas Wilson, the armourer, who is betrothed to my second daughter Margery.

Know then that the sheath is one cloth-yard in length, marked off according to feet and inches to serve me as a measuring wand. It is also of the exact weight of two pounds, so that I may use it in the balance."

"By Saint Paul!" quoth Sir Nigel, "it is very clear to me that the sword is like thyself, good alderman, apt either for war or for peace. But I doubt not that even in England you have had much to suffer from the hands of robbers and outlaws."

"It was only last Lammastide, sir knight, that I was left for dead near Reading as I journeyed to Winchester fair. Yet I had the rogues up at the court of pie-powder, and they will harm no more peaceful traders."

"You travel much, then?"

"To Winchester, Linn mart, Bristol fair, Stourbridge, and Bartholomew's in London Town. The rest of the year you may ever find me five doors from the church of Our Lady, where I would from my heart that I was at this moment, for there is no air like Norwich air, and no water like the Yare, nor can all the wines of France compare with the beer of old Sam Yelverton who keeps the 'Dun Cow.' But, out and alack, here is an evil fruit which hangs upon this chestnut-tree."

As he spoke they had ridden round a curve of the road and come upon a great tree which shot one strong brown branch across their path. From the centre of this branch there hung a man, with his head at a horrid slant to his body and his toes just touching the ground. He was naked save for a linen under-shirt and pair of woollen drawers. Beside him on a green bank there sat a small man with a solemn face, and a great bundle of papers of all colours thrusting forth from the scrip which lay beside him. He was very richly dressed, with furred robes, a scarlet hood, and wide hanging sleeves lined with flame-coloured silk. A great gold chain hung round his neck, and rings glittered from every finger of his hands. On his lap he had a little pile of gold and of silver, which he was dropping, coin by coin, into a plump pouch which hung from his girdle.

"May the saints be with you, good travellers!" he shouted, as the party rode up. "May the four Evangelists watch over you! May the twelve Apostles bear you up! May the blessed army of martyrs direct your feet and lead you to eternal bliss!"

"Gramercy for these good wishes!" said Sir Nigel. "But I perceive, master alderman, that this man who hangs here is, by mark of foot, the very robber-knight of whom we have spoken. But there is a cartel pinned upon his breast, and I pray you, Alleyne, to read it to me."

The dead robber swung slowly to and fro in the wintry wind, a fixed smile upon his swarthy face, and his bulging eyes still glaring down the highway of which he had so long been the terror; on a sheet of parchment upon his breast was printed in rude characters:

ROGER PIED-BOT
Par l'ordre du Sénéchal de
Castelnau, et de l'Échevin de
Cahors, servantes fidèles du
très vaillant et très puissant
Édouard, Prince des Galles et
d'Aquitaine.
Ne touchez pas,
Ne coupez pas,
Ne dépêchez pas.

"He took a sorry time in dying," said the man who sat beside him. "He could stretch one toe to the ground and bear himself up, so that I thought he would never have done. Now at last, however, he is safely in paradise, and so I may jog on upon my earthly way." He mounted, as he spoke, a white mule which had been grazing by the wayside, all gay with fustian of gold and silver bells, and rode onward with Sir Nigel's party.

"How know you then that he is in paradise?" asked Sir Nigel. "All things are possible to God, but, certes, without a miracle, I should scarce expect to find the soul of Roger Club-foot amongst the just."

"I know that he is there because I have just passed him in there," answered the stranger, rubbing his bejewelled hands together in placid satisfaction. "It is my holy mission to be a sompnour or pardoner. I am the unworthy servant and delegate of him who holds the keys. A contrite heart and ten nobles to holy Mother Church may stave off perdition; but he hath a pardon of the first degree, with a twenty-five livre benison, so that I doubt if he will so much as feel a twinge of purgatory. I came up even as the seneschal's archers were tying him up, and I gave him my foreword that I would bide with him until he had passed. There were two leaden crowns among the silver, but I would not for that stand in the way of his salvation."

"By Saint Paul!" said Sir Nigel, "if you have indeed this power to open and to shut the gates of hope, then indeed you stand high above mankind. But if you do but claim to have it, and yet have it not, then it seems to me, master clerk, that you may yourself find the gate barred when you shall ask admittance."

"Small of faith! Small of faith!" cried the sompnour. "Ah, Sir Didymus yet walks upon earth! And yet no words of doubt can bring anger to mine heart, or a bitter word to my lip, for am I not a poor unworthy worker in the cause of gentleness and peace? Of all these pardons which I bear every one is stamped and signed by our holy father, the prop and centre of Christendom."

"Which of them?" asked Sir Nigel.

"Ha, ha!" cried the pardoner, shaking a jewelled fore-finger. "Thou wouldst be deep in the secrets of Mother Church? Know then that I have both in my scrip. Those who hold with Urban shall have Urban's pardon, while I have Clement's for the Clementist—or he who is in doubt may have both, so that come what may he shall be secure. I pray you that you will buy one, for war is bloody work, and the end is sudden, with little time for thought or shrift. Or you, sir, for you seem to me to be a man who would do ill to trust to your own merits." This to the alderman of Norwich, who had listened to him with a frowning brow and a sneering lip.

"When I sell my cloth," quoth he, "he who buys may weigh and feel and handle. These goods which you sell are not to be seen, nor is there any proof that you hold them. Certes, if mortal man might control God's mercy, it would be one of a lofty and God-like life, and not one who is decked out with rings and chains and silks, like a pleasure-wench at a kermesse."

"Thou wicked and shameless man!" cried the clerk. "Dost thou dare to raise thy voice against the unworthy servant of Mother Church?"

"Unworthy enough!" quoth David Micheldene. "I would have you to know, clerk, that I am a free English burgher, and that I dare say my mind to our father the Pope himself, let alone such a lacquey's lacquey as you!"

"Base-born and foul-mouthed knave!" cried the sompnour. "You prate of holy things, to which your hog's mind can never rise. Keep silence, lest I call a curse upon you!"

"Silence yourself!" roared the other. "Foul bird! we found thee by the gallows like a carrion-crow. A fine life thou hast of it with thy silks and thy baubles, cozening the last few shillings from the pouches of dying men. A fig for thy curse! Bide here, if you will take my rede, for we will make England too hot for such as you when Master Wicliff has the ordering of it. Thou vile thief! it is you, and such as you, who bring an evil name upon the many churchmen who lead a pure and a holy life. Thou outside the door of heaven! Art more like to be inside the door of hell."

At this crowning insult the sompnour, with a face ashen with rage, raised up a quivering hand and began pouring Latin imprecations upon the angry alderman. The latter, however, was not a man to be quelled by words, for he caught up his ell-measure sword-sheath and belaboured the cursing clerk with it. The latter, unable to escape from the shower of blows, set spurs to his mule and rode for his life, with his enemy thundering behind him. At sight of his master's sudden departure, the varlet Watkin set off after him, with the pack-mule beside him, so that the four clattered away down the road together, until they swept round a curve, and their babble was but a drone in the distance. Sir Nigel and Alleyne gazed in astonishment at one another, while Ford burst out a-laughing.

"Pardieu!" said the knight, "this David Micheldene must be one of those Lollards about whom Father Christopher of the priory had so much to say. Yet he seemed to be no bad man from what I have seen of him."

"I have heard that Wicliff hath many followers in Norwich, answered Alleyne."

"By Saint Paul! I have no great love for them," quoth Sir Nigel. "I am a man who am slow to change; and, if you take away from me the faith that I have been taught, it would be long ere I could learn one to set in its place. It is but a chip here and a chip there, yet it may bring the tree down in time. Yet, on the other hand, I cannot but think it shame that a man should turn God's mercy on and off, as a cellarman doth wine with a spigot."

"Nor is it," said Alleyne, "part of the teachings of that Mother Church of which he had so much to say. There was sooth in what the alderman said of it."

"Then, by Saint Paul! they may settle it betwixt them," quoth Sir Nigel. "For me, I serve God, the king and my lady; and so long as I can keep the path of honour I am well content. My creed shall ever be that of Chandos:

'Fais ce que dois—adviegne que peut,
C'est commandé au chevalier'."

CHAPTER XXVIII

HOW THE COMRADES CAME OVER THE MARCHES OF FRANCE

AFTER passing Cahors, the party branched away from the main road, and leaving the river to the north of them, followed a smaller track which wound over a vast and desolate plain. This path led them amid marshes and woods, until it brought them out into a glade with a broad stream swirling swiftly down the centre of it. Through this the horses splashed their way, and on the farther shore Sir Nigel announced to them that they were now within the borders of the land of France. For some miles they still followed the same lonely track, which led them through a dense wood, and then widening out, curved down to an open rolling country, such as they had traversed between Aiguillon and Cahors.

If it were grim and desolate upon the English border, however, what can describe the hideous barrenness of this ten times harried tract of France? The whole face of the country was scarred and disfigured, mottled over with the black blotches of burned farm-steadings, and the grey gaunt gable-ends of what had been châteaux. Broken fences, crumbling walls, vineyards littered with stones, the shattered arches of bridges—look where you might, the signs of ruin and rapine met the eye. Here and there only, on the farthest sky-line, the gnarled turrets of a castle, or the graceful pinnacles of church or of monastery, showed where the forces of the sword or of the spirit had preserved some small islet of security in this universal flood of misery. Moodily and in silence the little party rode along the narrow and irregular track, their hearts weighed down by this far-stretching land of despair. It was indeed a stricken arid a blighted country, and a man might have ridden from Auvergne in the north to the marches of Foix, nor ever seen a smiling village or a thriving homestead.

From time to time as they advanced they saw strange lean figures scraping and scratching amid the weeds and thistles, who, on sight of the band of horsemen, threw up their arms and dived in among the brushwood as shy and as swift as wild animals. More than once, however, they came on families crouching by the wayside, who were too weak from hunger and disease to fly, so that they could but sit like hares on a tussock, with panting chests and terror in their eyes. So gaunt were these poor folk, so worn and spent—with bent and knotted frames, and sullen, hopeless, mutinous faces—that it made the young Englishmen heartsick to look upon them. Indeed, it seemed as though all hope and light had gone so far from them that it was not to be brought back; for when Sir Nigel threw down a handful of silver among them there came no softening of their lined faces, but they clutched greedily at the coins, peering questioningly at him, and champing with their animal jaws. Here and there amid the brushwood the travellers saw the rude bundle of sticks which served them as a home—more like a fowl's nest than the dwelling-place of man. Yet why should they build and strive, when the first adventurer who passed would set torch to their thatch, and when their own feudal lord would wring from them with blows and curses the last fruits of their toil? They sat at the lowest depth of human misery, and hugged a bitter comfort to their souls as they realised that they could go no lower. Yet they had still the human gift of speech, and would take counsel among themselves in their brushwood hovels, glaring with bleared eyes and pointing with thin fingers at the great widespread châteaux which ate like a cancer into the life of the country-side. When such men, who are beyond hope and fear, begin in their dim minds to see the source of their woes, it may be an evil time for those who have wronged them. The weak man becomes strong when he has nothing, for then only can he feel the wild, mad thrill of despair. High and strong the château, lowly and weak the brush-wood hut; but God help the seigneur and his lady when the men of the brushwood set their hands to the work of revenge!

Through such country did the party ride for eight or it might be nine miles, until the sun began to slope down in the west and their shadows to stream down the road in front of them. Wary and careful they must be, with watchful eyes to the right and the left, for this was no man's land, and their only passports were those which hung from their belts. Frenchmen and Englishmen, Gascon and Provençal, Brabanter, Tardvenu, Scorcher, Flayer, and Free Companion, wandered and struggled over the whole of this accursed district. So bare and cheerless was the outlook, and so few and poor the dwellings, that Sir Nigel began to have fears as to whether he might find food and quarters for his little troop. It was a relief to him, therefore, when their narrow track opened out upon a larger road, and they saw some little way down it a square white house with a great bunch of holly hung out at the end of a stick from one of the upper windows.

"By Saint Paul!" said he, "I am right glad; for I had feared that we might have neither provant nor herbergage. Ride on, Alleyne, and tell this innkeeper that an English knight with his party will lodge with him this night."

Alleyne set spurs to his horse and reached the inn door a long bow-shot before his companions. Neither varlet nor ostler could be seen, so he pushed open the door and called loudly for the land-lord. Three times he shouted, but, receiving no reply, he opened an inner door and advanced into the chief guest-room of the hostel.

A very cheerful wood-fire was sputtering and cracking in an open grate at the further end of the apartment. At one side of this fire, in a high-backed oak chair, sat a lady, her face turned towards the door. The firelight played over her features, and Alleyne thought that he had never seen such queenly power, such dignity and strength, upon a woman's face. She might have been five-and-thirty years of age, with aquiline nose, firm and yet sensitive mouth, dark curving brows, and deep-set eyes which shone and sparkled with a shifting brilliancy. Beautiful as she was, it was not her beauty which impressed itself upon the beholder; it was her strength, her power, the sense of wisdom which hung over the broad white brow, the decision which lay in the square jaw and delicately moulded chin. A chaplet of pearls sparkled amid her black hair, with a gauze of silver network flowing back from it over her shoulders; a black mantle was swathed round her, and she leaned back in her chair as one who is fresh from a journey.

In the opposite corner there sat a very burly and broad-shouldered man, clad in a black jerkin trimmed with sable, with a black velvet cap with curling white feather cocked upon the side of his head. A flask of red wine stood at his elbow, and he seemed to be very much at his ease, for his feet were stuck up on a stool, and between his thighs he held a dish full of nuts. These he cracked between his strong white teeth and chewed in a leisurely way, casting the shells into the blaze. As Alleyne gazed in at him he turned his face half round and cocked an eye at him over his shoulder; it seemed to the young Englishman that he had never seen so hideous a face, for the eyes were of the lightest green, the nose was broken and driven inwards, while the whole countenance was seared and puckered with wounds. The voice, too, when he spoke, was as deep and as fierce as the growl of a beast of prey.

"Young man," said he, "I know not who you may be, and I am not much inclined to bestir myself, but if it were not that I am bent upon taking my ease, I swear, by the sword of Joshua! that I would lay my dog-whip across your shoulders for daring to fill the air with these discordant bellowings."

Taken aback at this ungentle speech, and scarce knowing how to answer it fitly in the presence of the lady, Alleyne stood with his hand upon the handle of the door, while Sir Nigel and his companions dismounted. At the sound of these fresh voices, and of the tongue in which they spoke, the stranger crashed his dish of nuts down upon the floor, and began himself to call for the landlord until the whole house re-echoed with his roarings.

With an ashen face the white-aproned host came running at his call, his hands shaking and his very hair bristling with apprehension. "For the sake of God, sirs," he whispered as he passed, "speak him fair and do not rouse him! For the love of the Virgin, be mild with him!"

"Who is this, then?" asked Sir Nigel.

Alleyne was about to explain, when a fresh roar from the stranger interrupted him.

"Thou villain innkeeper," he shouted, "did I not ask you when I brought my lady here whether your inn was clean?"

"You did, sire."

"Did I not very particularly ask you whether there were any vermin in it?"

"You did, sire."

"And you answered me?"

"That there were not, sire."

"And yet ere I have been here an hour I find Englishmen crawling about within it. Where are we to be free from this pestilent race? Can a Frenchman upon French land not sit down in a French auberge without having his ears pained by the clack of their hideous talk? Send them packing, inn-keeper, or it may be the worse for them and for you."

"I will, sire, I will!" cried the frightened host, and bustled from the room, while the soft, soothing voice of the woman was heard remonstrating with her furious companion.

"Indeed, gentlemen, you had best go," said mine host. "It is but six miles to Villefranche, where there are very good quarters at the sign of the 'Lion Rouge'."

"Nay," answered Sir Nigel, "I cannot go until I have seen more of this person, for he appears to be a man from whom much is to be hoped. What is his name and title?"

"It is not for my lips to name it unless by his desire. But I beg and pray you, gentlemen, that you will go from my house, for I know not what may come of it if his rage should gain the mastery of him."

"By Saint Paul!" lisped Sir Nigel, "this is certainly a man whom it is worth journeying far to know. Go tell him that a humble knight of England would make his further honourable acquaintance, not from any presumption, pride, or ill-will, but for the advancement of chivalry and the glory of our ladies. Give him greeting from Sir Nigel Loring, and say that the glove which I bear in my cap belongs to the most peerless and lovely of her sex, whom I am now ready to uphold against any lady whose claim he might be desirous of advancing."

The landlord was hesitating whether to carry this message or no, when the door of the inner room was flung open, and the stranger bounded out like a panther from his den, his hair bristling and his deformed face convulsed with anger.

"Still here!" he snarled. "Dogs of England, must ye be lashed hence? Tiphaine, my sword!" He turned to seize his weapon, but as he did so his gaze fell upon the blazonry of Sir Nigel's shield, and he stood staring while the fire in his strange green eyes softened into a sly and humorous twinkle.

"Mort Dieu!" cried he, "it is my little swordsman of Bordeaux. I should remember that coat-armour, seeing that it is but three days since I looked upon it in the lists by Garonne. Ah! Sir Nigel, Sir Nigel! you owe me a return for this," and he touched his right arm, which was girt round just under the shoulder with a silken kerchief.

But the surprise of the stranger at the sight of Sir Nigel was as nothing compared with the astonishment and the delight which shone upon the face of the knight of Hampshire as he looked upon the strange face of the Frenchman. Twice he opened his mouth and twice he peered again, as though to assure himself that his eyes had not played him a trick.

"Bertrand!" he gasped at last. "Bertrand du Guesclin!"

"By Saint Ives!" shouted the French soldier with a hoarse roar of laughter, "it is well that I should ride with my visor down, for he that has once seen my face does not need to be told my name. It is indeed I, Sir Nigel, and here is my hand! I give you my word that there are but three Englishmen in this world whom I would touch save with the sharp edge of the sword: the prince is one, Chandos the second, and you the third; for I have heard much that is good of you."

"I am growing aged, and am somewhat spent in the wars," quoth Sir Nigel; "but I can lay by my sword now with an easy mind, for I can say that I have crossed swords with him who hath the bravest heart and the strongest arm of all this great kingdom of France. I have longed for it, I have dreamed of it, and now I can scarce bring my mind to understand that this great honour hath indeed been mine."

"By the Virgin of Rennes! you have given me cause to be very certain of it," said Du Guesclin, with a gleam of his broad white teeth.

"And perhaps, most honoured sir, it would please you to continue the debate. Perhaps you would condescend to go farther into the matter. God He knows that I am unworthy of such honour, yet I can show my four-and-sixty quarterings, and I have been present at some bickerings and scufflings during these twenty years."

"Your fame is very well known to me, and I shall ask my lady to enter your name upon my tablets," said Sir Bertrand. "There are many who wish to advance themselves, and who bide their turn, for I refuse no man who comes on such an errand. At present it may not be, for mine arm is stiff from this small touch, and I would fain do you full honour when we cross swords again. Come in with me, and let your squires come also, that my sweet spouse, the Lady Tiphaine, may say that she hath seen so famed and gentle a knight."

Into the chamber they went in all peace and concord, where the Lady Tiphaine sat like queen on throne for each in turn to be presented to her. Sooth to say, the stout heart of Sir Nigel, which cared little for the wrath of her lion-like spouse, was somewhat shaken by the calm, cold face of this stately dame, for twenty years of camp-life had left him more at ease in the lists than in a lady's boudoir. He bethought him, too, as he looked at her set lips and deep-set questioning eyes, that he had heard strange tales of this same Lady Tiphaine du Guesclin. Was it not she who was said to lay hands upon the sick and raise them from their couches when

the leeches had spent their last nostrums? Had she not forecast
the future, and were there not times when in the loneliness of her
chamber she was heard to hold converse with some being upon
whom mortal eye never rested—some dark familiar who passed
where doors were barred and windows high? Sir Nigel sunk his eye
and marked a cross on the side of his leg as he greeted this dangerous dame, and yet ere five minutes had passed he was hers, and
not he only but his two young squires as well. The mind had gone
out of them, and they could but look at this woman and listen to
the words which fell from her lips—words which thrilled through
their nerves and stirred their souls like the battle-call of a bugle.

Often in peaceful after-days was Alleyne to think of that scene of
the wayside inn of Auvergne. The shadows of evening had fallen,
and the corners of the long, low, wood-panelled room were draped
in darkness. The spluttering wood-fire threw out a circle of red flickering light which played over the little group of wayfarers, and
showed up every line and shadow upon their faces. Sir Nigel sat with
elbows upon knees, and chin upon hands, his patch still covering
one eye, but his other shining like a star, while the ruddy light
gleamed upon his smooth white head. Ford was seated at his left, his
lips parted, his eyes staring, and a fleck of deep colour on either
cheek, his limbs all rigid as one who fears to move. On the other
side the famous French captain leaned back in his chair, a litter of
nut-shells upon his lap, his huge head half buried in a cushion,
while his eyes wandered with an amused gleam from his dame to
the staring, enraptured Englishmen. Then, last of all, that pale
clear-cut face, that sweet clear voice, with its high thrilling talk of the
deathlessness of glory, of the worthlessness of life, of the pain of
ignoble joys, and of the joy which lies in all pains which lead to a
noble end. Still, as the shadows deepened, she spoke of valour and
virtue, of loyalty, honour and fame, and still they sat drinking in her
words while the fire burned down and the red ash turned to grey.

"By the sainted Ives!" cried Du Guesclin at last, "it is time that we
spoke of what we are to do this night, for I cannot think that in this
wayside auberge there are fit quarters for an honourable company."

Sir Nigel gave a long sigh as he came back from the dreams of chivalry and hardihood into which this strange woman's words had wafted him. "I care not where I sleep," said he; "but these are indeed somewhat rude lodgings for this fair lady."

"What contents my lord contents me," quoth she. "I perceive, Sir Nigel, that you are under vow," she added, glancing at his covered eye.

"It is my purpose to attempt some small deed," he answered.

"And the glove—is it your lady's?"

"It is indeed my sweet wife's."

"Who is doubtless proud of you."

"Say rather I of her," quoth he quickly. "God He knows that I am not worthy to be her humble servant. It is easy, lady, for a man to ride forth in the light of day, and do his devoir when all men have eyes for him. But in a woman's heart there is a strength and truth which asks no praise, and can but be known to him whose treasure it is."

The Lady Tiphaine smiled across at her husband. "You have often told me, Bertrand, that there were very gentle knights among the English," quoth she.

"Aye, aye," said he moodily. "But to horse, Sir Nigel, you and yours, and we shall seek the château of Sir Tristram de Rochefort, which is two miles on this side of Villefranche. He is Seneschal of Auvergne, and mine old war-companion."

"Certes, he would have a welcome for you," quoth Sir Nigel; "but indeed he might look askance at one who comes without permit over the marches."

"By the Virgin! when he learns that you have come to draw away these rascals he will be very blithe to look upon your face. Innkeeper, here are ten gold pieces. What is over and above your reckoning you may take off from your charges to the next needy knight who comes this way. Come then, for it grows late, and the horses are stamping in the roadway."

The Lady Tiphaine and her spouse sprang upon their steeds without setting feet to stirrup, and away they jingled down the white moonlit highway, with Sir Nigel at the lady's bridle-arm, and Ford a spear's length behind them. Alleyne had lingered for an instant in the passage, and as he did so there came a wild outcry from a chamber upon the left, and out there ran Aylward and John, laughing together like two schoolboys who are bent upon a prank. At sight of Alleyne they slunk past him with somewhat of a shamefaced air, and springing upon their horses galloped after their party. The hubbub within the chamber did not cease, however, but rather increased with yells of: "A moi, mes amis! A moi, camarades! A moi, l'honourable champion de l'Evêque de Montaubon! A la recousse de l'égliste sainte!" So shrill was the outcry that both the innkeeper and Alleyne, with every varlet within hearing, rushed wildly to the scene of the uproar.

It was indeed a singular scene which met their eyes. The room was a long and lofty one, stone-floored and bare, with a fire at the further end upon which a great pot was boiling. A deal table ran down the centre, with a wooden wine-pitcher upon it and two horn cups. Some way from it was a smaller table with a single beaker and a broken wine-bottle. From the heavy wooden rafters which formed the roof there hung rows of hooks which held up sides of bacon, joints of smoked beef, and strings of onions for winter use. In the very centre of all these, upon the largest hook of all, there hung a fat little red-faced man with enormous whiskers, kicking madly in the air and clawing at rafters, hams, and all else that was within hand-grasp. The huge steel hook had been passed through the collar of his leather jerkin, and there he hung like a fish on a line, writhing, twisting, and screaming, but utterly unable to free himself from his extraordinary position. It was not until Alleyne and the landlord had mounted on the table that they were able to lift him down, when he sank gasping with rage into a seat, and rolled his eyes round in every direction.

"Has he gone?" quoth he.

"Gone? Who?"

"He, the man with the red head, the giant man."

"Yes," said Alleyne, "he hath gone."

"And comes not back?"

"No."

"The better for him!" cried the little man, with a long sigh of relief. "Mon Dieu! What! am I not the champion of the Bishop of Montaubon? Ah, could I have descended, could I have come down, ere he fled! Then you would have seen. You would have beheld a spectacle then. There would have been one rascal the less upon earth. Ma foi, yes!"

"Good master Pelligny," said the landlord, "these gentlemen have not gone very fast, and I have a horse in the stable at your disposal, for I would rather have such bloody doings as you threaten outside the four walls of mine auberge."

"I hurt my leg and cannot ride," quoth the bishop's champion. "I strained a sinew on the day that I slew the three men at Castelnau."

"God save you, master Pelligny!" cried the landlord. "It must be an awesome thing to have so much blood upon one's soul. And yet I do not wish to see so valiant a man mis-handled, and so I will, for friendship's sake, ride after this Englishman and bring him back to you."

"You shall not stir," cried the champion, seizing the inn-keeper in a convulsive grasp. "I have a love for you, Gaston, and I would not bring your house into ill-repute, nor do such scath to these walls and chattels as must befall if two such men as this Englishman and I fall to work here."

"Nay, think not of me!" cried the innkeeper. "What are my walls when set against the honour of François Poursuivant d'Amour Pelligny, champion of the Bishop of Montaubon? My horse, André!"

"By the saints, no! Gaston, I will not have it! You have said truly that it is an awesome thing to have such rough work upon one's soul. I am but a rude soldier, yet I have a mind. Mon Dieu! I reflect, I weigh, I balance. Shall I not meet this man again? Shall I not bear him in mind? Shall I hot know him by his great paws and his red head? Ma foi, yes!"

"And may I ask, sir," said Alleyne, "why it is that you call yourself champion of the Bishop of Montaubon?"

"You may ask aught which it is becoming to me to answer. The bishop hath need of a champion, because, if any cause be set to test of combat, it would scarce become his office to go down into the lists with leathern shield and cudgel to exchange blows with any varlet. He looks around him then for some tried fighting man, some honest smiter who can give a blow or take one. It is not for me to say how far he hath succeeded, but it is sooth that he who thinks that he hath but to do with the Bishop of Montaubon finds himself face to face with François Poursuivant d'Amour Pelligny."

At this moment there was a clatter of hoofs upon the road, and a varlet by the door cried out that one of the Englishmen was coming back. The champion looked wildly about for some corner of safety, and was clambering up towards the window, when Ford's voice sounded from without, calling upon Alleyne to hasten, or he might scarce find his way. Bidding adieu to landlord and to champion, therefore, he set off at a gallop, and soon overtook the two archers.

"A pretty thing this, John," said he. "Thou wilt have holy Church upon you if you hang her champions upon iron hooks in an inn kitchen."

"It was done without thinking," he answered apologetically, while Aylward burst into a shout of laughter.

"By my hilt! mon petit," said he, "you would have laughed also could you have seen it. For this man was so swollen with pride that he would neither drink with us, nor sit at the same table with us, nor as much as answer a question, but must needs talk to the varlet all the time that it was well there was peace, and that he had slain more Englishmen than there were tags to his doublet. Our good old John could scarce lay his tongue to French enough to answer him, so he must needs reach out his great hand to him and place him very gently where you saw him. But we must on, for I can scarce hear their hoofs upon the road."

"I think that I can see them yet," said Ford, peering down the moonlit road.

"Pardieu! yes. Now they ride forth from the shadow. And yonder dark clump is the Castle of Villefranche. En avant, camarades! or Sir Nigel may reach the gates before us. But hark, mes amis, what sound is that?"

As he spoke the hoarse blast of a horn was heard from some woods upon the right. An answering call rung forth upon their left, and hard upon it two others from behind them.

"They are the horns of swineherds," quoth Aylward. "Though why they blow them so late I cannot tell."

"Let us on, then," said Ford, and the whole party, setting their spurs to their horses, soon found themselves at the Castle of Villefranche, where the drawbridge had already been lowered and the portcullis raised in response to the summons of Du Guesclin.

CHAPTER XXIX

HOW THE BLESSED HOUR OF SIGHT CAME TO THE LADY TIPHAINE

SIR Tristram de Rochefort, Seneschal of Auvergne and Lord of Villefranche, was a fierce and renowned soldier who had grown grey in the English wars. As lord of the marches and guardian of an exposed countryside there was little rest for him even in times of so-called peace, and his whole life was spent in raids and outfalls upon the Brabanters, late-comers, flayers, free companions, and roving archers who wandered over his province. At times he would come back in triumph, and a dozen corpses swinging from the summit of his keep would warn evil-doers that there was still a law in the land. At others his ventures were not so happy, and he and his troop would spur it over the drawbridge with clatter of hoofs hard at their heels and whistle of arrows about their ears. Hard he was of hand and harder of heart, hated by his foes, and yet not loved by those whom he protected, for twice he had been taken prisoner, and twice his ransom had been wrung by dint of blows and tortures out of the starving peasants and ruined farmers. Wolves or watch-dogs, it was hard to say from which the sheep had most to fear.

The Castle of Villefranche was harsh and stern as its master. A broad moat, a high outer wall turreted at the corners, with a great black keep towering above all—so it lay before them in the moonlight. By the light of two flambeaux, protruded through the narrow slit-shaped openings at either side of the ponderous gate, they caught a glimpse of the glitter of fierce eyes and of the gleam of the weapons of the guard. The sight of the two-headed eagle of Du Guesclin, however, was a passport into any fortalice in France, and ere they had passed the gate the old border knight came running forward with hands out-thrown to greet his famous countryman. Nor was he less glad to see Sir Nigel, when the Englishman's errand was explained to him, for these archers had been a sore thorn in his side, and had routed two expeditions which he had sent against them. A happy day it would be for the Seneschal of Auvergne when he should learn that the last yew bow was over the marches.

The material for a feast was ever at hand in days when, if there was grim want in the cottage, there was at least rude plenty in the castle. Within an hour the guests were seated around a board which creaked under the great pasties and joints of meat, varied by those more dainty dishes in which the French excelled, the spiced ortolan and the truffled beccaficoes. The Lady Rochefort, a bright and laughter-loving dame, sat upon the left of her warlike spouse, with the Lady Tiphaine upon the right. Beneath sat Du Guesclin and Sir Nigel, with Sir Amory Monticourt, of the order of the Hospitallers, and Sir Otto Harnit, a wandering knight from the kingdom of Bohemia. These, with Alleyne and Ford, four French squires, and the castle chaplain, made the company who sat together that night and made good cheer in the Castle of Villefranche. The great fire crackled in the grate, the hooded hawks slept upon their perches, the rough deer hounds with expectant eyes crouched upon the tiled floor; close at the elbows of the guests stood the dapper little lilac-coated pages; the laugh and jest circled round and all was harmony and comfort. Little they recked of the brushwood men who crouched in their rags along the fringe of the forest and looked up with wild and haggard eyes at the rich warm glow which shot a golden bar of light from the high arched windows of the castle.

Supper over, the tables dormant were cleared away as by magic, and trestles and bancals arranged round the blazing fire, for there was a bitter nip in the air. The Lady Tiphaine had sunk back in her cushioned chair, and her long dark lashes drooped low over her sparkling eyes. Alleyne, glancing at her, noted that her breath came quick and short, and that her cheeks had blanched to a lily white. Du Guesclin eyed her keenly from time to time, and passed his broad brown fingers through his crisp, curly black hair with the air of a man who is perplexed in his mind.

"These folk here," said the knight of Bohemia, "they do not seem too well fed."

"Ah, canaille!" cried the Lord of Villefranche. "You would scarce credit it, and yet it is sooth that when I was taken at Poictiers it was all that my wife and my foster-brother could do to raise the money from them for my ransom. The sulky dogs would rather have three twists of a rack, or the thumbikins for an hour, than pay out a denier for their own feudal father and liege lord. Yet there is not one of them but hath an old stocking full of gold pieces hid away in a snug corner."

"Why do they not buy food then?" asked Sir Nigel. "By Saint Paul! it seemed to me that their bones were breaking through their skin."

"It is their grutching and grumbling which makes them thin. We have a saying here, Sir Nigel, that if you pummel Jacques Bonhomme he will pat you, but if you pat him he will pummel you. Doubtless you find it so in England."

"Ma foi, no!" said Sir Nigel. "I have two Englishmen of this class in my train, who are at this instant, I make little doubt, as full of your wine as any cask in your cellar. He who pummelled them might come by such a pat as he would be likely to remember."

"I cannot understand it," quoth the Seneschal, "for the English knights and nobles whom I have met were not men to brook the insolence of the baseborn."

"Perchance, my fair lord, the poor folk are sweeter and of a better countenance in England," laughed the Lady Rochefort. "Mon Dieu! you cannot conceive to yourself how ugly they are! Without hair, without teeth, all twisted and bent; for me, I cannot think how the good God ever came to make such people. I cannot bear it, I, and so my trusty Raoul goes ever before me with a cudgel to drive them from my path."

"Yet they have souls, fair lady, they have souls!" murmured the chaplain, a white-haired man, with a weary, patient face.

"So I have heard you tell them," said the lord of the castle; "and for myself, father, though I am a true son of holy Church, yet I think that you were better employed in saying your mass, and in teaching the children of my men-at-arms, than in going over the countryside to put ideas in these folks' heads which would never have been there but for you. I have heard that you have said to them that their souls are as good as ours, and that it is likely that in another life they may stand as high as the oldest blood of Auvergne. For my part, I believe that there are so many worthy knights and gallant gentlemen in heaven, who know how such things should be arranged, that there is little fear that we shall find ourselves mixed up with base roturiers and swineherds. Tell your beads, father, and con your psalter, but do not come between me and those whom the king has given to me."

"God help them!" cried the old priest. "A higher King than yours has given them to me, and I tell you here in your own castle hall, Sir Tristram de Rochefort, that you have sinned deeply in your dealings with these poor folk, and that the hour will come, and may even now be at hand, when God's hand will be heavy upon you for what you have done." He rose as he spoke, and walked slowly from the room.

"Pest take him!" cried the French knight. "Now what is a man to do with a priest, Sir Bertrand?—for one can neither fight him like a man nor coax him like a woman."

"Ah, Sir Bertrand knows, the naughty one!" cried the Lady Rochefort. "Have we not all heard how he went to Avignon and squeezed fifty thousand crowns out of the Pope?"

"Ma foi!" said Sir Nigel, looking with a mixture of horror and admiration at Du Guesclin. "Did not your heart sink within you? Were you not smitten with fears? Have you not felt a curse hang over you?"

"I have not observed it," said the Frenchman carelessly. "But, by Saint Ives! Tristram, this chaplain of yours seems to me to be a worthy man, and you should give heed to his words, for though I care nothing for the curse of a bad Pope, it would be a grief to me to have aught but a blessing from a good priest."

"Hark to that, my fair lord," cried the Lady Rochefort. "Take heed, I pray thee, for I do not wish to have a blight cast over me, nor a palsy of the limbs. I remember that once before you angered Father Stephen, and my tire-woman said that I lost more hair in seven days than ever before in a month."

"If that be sign of sin, then, by Saint Paul! I have much upon my soul," said Sir Nigel, amid a general laugh. "But in very truth, Sir Tristram, if I may venture a word of counsel, I should advise that you make your peace with this good man."

"He shall have four silver candlesticks," said the Seneschal moodily. "And yet I would that he would leave the folk alone. You cannot conceive in your mind how stubborn and brainless they are. Mules and pigs are full of reason beside them. God He knows that I have had great patience with them. It was but last week that, having to raise some money, I called up to the castle Jean Goubert, who, as all men know, has a casketful of gold pieces hidden away in some hollow tree. I give you my word that I did not so much as lay a stripe upon his fool's back, but after speaking with him, and telling him how needful the money was to me, I left him for the night to think over the matter in my dungeon. What think you that the dog did? Why, in the morning we found that he had made a rope from strips of his leather jerkin, and had hung himself to the bar of the window."

"For me, I cannot conceive such wickedness!" cried the lady.

"And there was Gertrude Le Boeuf, as fair a maiden as eye could see, but as bad and bitter as the rest of them. When young Amory de Valance was here last Lammastide he looked kindly upon the girl, and even spoke of taking her into his service. What does she do, with her dog of a father? Why, they tie themselves together and leap into the Linden Pool, where the water is five spear's-length deep. I give you my word that it was a great grief to young Amory, and it was days ere he could cast it from his mind. But how can one serve people who are so foolish and so ungrateful?"

Whilst the Seneschal of Villefranche had been detailing the evil doings of his tenants, Alleyne had been unable to take his eyes from the face of the Lady Tiphaine. She had lain back in her chair, with drooping eye-lids and a bloodless face, so that he had feared at first that her journey had weighed heavily upon her, and that the strength was ebbing out of her. Of a sudden, however, there came a change, for a dash of bright colour flickered up on to either cheek, and her lids were slowly raised again upon eyes which sparkled with such a lustre as Alleyne had never seen in human eyes before, while their gaze was fixed intently, not upon the company, but on the dark tapestry which draped the wall. So transformed and so ethereal was her expression, that Alleyne, in his loftiest dream of archangel or of seraph, had never pictured so sweet, so womanly, and yet so wise a face. Glancing at Du Guesclin, Alleyne saw that he also was watching his wife closely, and from the twitching of his features, and the beads upon his brick-coloured brow, it was easy to see that he was deeply agitated by the change which he marked in her.

"How is it with you, lady?" he asked at last, in a tremulous voice.

Her eyes remained fixed intently upon the wall, and there was a long pause ere she answered him. Her voice, too, which had been so clear and ringing, was now low and muffled as that of one who speaks from a distance.

"All is very well with me, Bertrand," said she. "The blessed hour of sight has come round to me again."

"I could see it come! I could see it come!" he exclaimed, passing his fingers through his hair with the same perplexed expression as before.

"This is untoward, Sir Tristram," he said at last. "And I scarce know in what words to make it clear to you, and to your fair wife, and to Sir Nigel Loring, and to these other stranger knights. My tongue is a blunt one, and fitter to shout word of command than to clear up such a matter as this, of which I can myself understand little. This, however, I know, that my wife is come of a very sainted race, whom God hath in His wisdom endowed with wondrous powers, so that Tiphaine Raquenel was known throughout Brittany ere ever I first saw her at Dinan. Yet these powers are ever used for good, and they are the gift of God and not of the devil, which is the difference betwixt white magic and black."

"Perchance it would be as well that we should send for Father Stephen," said Sir Tristram.

"It would be best that he should come," cried the Hospitaller.

"And bring with him a flask of holy water," added the knight of Bohemia.

"Not so, gentlemen," answered Sir Bertrand. "It is not needful that this priest should be called, and it is in my mind that in asking for this ye cast some slight shadow or slur upon the good name of my wife, as though it were still doubtful whether her power came to her from above or below. If ye have indeed such a doubt I pray that you will say so, that we may discuss the matter in a fitting way."

"For myself," said Sir Nigel, "I have heard such words fall from the lips of this lady that I am of opinion that there is no woman, save only one, who can be in any way compared to her in beauty and in goodness. Should any gentleman think otherwise, I should deem it great honour to run a small course with him, or debate the matter in whatever way might be most pleasing to him."

"Nay, it would ill become me to cast a slur upon a lady who is both my guest and the wife of my comrade-in-arms," said the Seneschal of Villefranche. "I have perceived also that on her mantle there is marked a silver cross, which is surely sign enough that there is naught of evil in these strange powers which you say that she possesses."

This argument of the Seneschal's appealed so powerfully to the Bohemian and to the Hospitaller that they at once intimated that their objections had been entirely overcome, while even the Lady Rochefort, who had sat shivering and crossing herself, ceased to cast glances at the door, and allowed her fears to turn to curiosity.

"Among the gifts which have been vouchsafed to my wife," said Du Guesclin, "there is the wondrous one of seeing into the future; but it comes very seldom upon her, and goes as quickly, for none can command it. The blessed hour of sight, as she hath named it, has come but thrice since I have known her, and I can vouch for it that all that she hath told me was true, for on the evening of the Battle of Auray she said that the morrow would be an ill day for me and for Charles of Blois. Ere the sun had sunk again he was dead, and I the prisoner of Sir John Chandos. Yet it is not every question that she can answer, but only those—"

"Bertrand, Bertrand!" cried the lady in the same muttering faraway voice, "the blessed hour passes. Use it, Bertrand, while you may."

"I will, my sweet. Tell me, then, what fortune comes upon me?"

"Danger, Bertrand—deadly, pressing danger—which creeps upon you and you know it not."

The French soldier burst into a thunderous laugh, and his green eyes twinkled with amusement. "At what time during these twenty years would not that have been a true word?" he cried. "Danger is the air that I breathe. But is this so very close, Tiphaine?"

"Here—now—close upon you!" The words came out in broken strenuous speech, while the lady's fair face was writhed and drawn like that of one who looks upon a horror which strikes the words from her lips. Du Guesclin gazed round the tapestried room, at the screens, the tables, the abace, the credence, the buffet with its silver salver, and the half-circle of friendly wondering faces. There was an utter stillness, save for the sharp breathing of the Lady Tiphaine and for the gentle soughing of the wind outside, which wafted to their ears the distant call upon a swineherd's horn.

"The danger may bide," said he, shrugging his broad shoulders. "And now, Tiphaine, tell us what will come of this war in Spain."

"I can see little," she answered, straining her eyes and puckering her brow, as one who would fain clear her sight. "There are mountains, and dry plains, and flash of arms, and shouting of battle-cries. Yet it is whispered to me that by failure you will succeed."

"Ha! Sir Nigel, how like you that?" quoth Bertrand, shaking his head. "It is like mead and vinegar, half sweet, half sour. And is there no question which you would ask my lady?"

"Certes there is. I would fain know, fair lady, how all things are at Twynham Castle, and above all how my sweet lady employs herself."

"To answer this I would fain lay hand upon one whose thoughts turn strongly to this castle which you have named. Nay, my Lord Loring, it is whispered to me that there is another here who hath thought more deeply of it than you."

"Thought more of mine own home?" cried Sir Nigel. "Lady, I fear that in this matter at least you are mistaken."

"Not so, Sir Nigel. Come hither, young man, young English squire with the grey eyes! Now give me your hand, and place it here across my brow, that I may see that which you have seen. What is this that rises before me? Mist, mist, rolling mist with a square black tower above it. See it shreds out, it thins, it rises, and there lies a castle in a green plain, with the sea beneath it, and a great church within a bow-shot. There are two rivers which run through the meadows, and between them lie the tents of the besiegers."

"The besiegers!" cried Alleyne, Ford, and Sir Nigel all three in a breath.

"Yes, truly, and they press hard upon the castle, for they are an exceeding multitude and full of courage. See how they storm and rage against the gate, while some rear ladders, and others, line after line, sweep the walls with their arrows. There are many leaders who shout and beckon, and one, a tall man with a golden beard, who stands before the gate stamping his foot and hallooing them on, as a pricker doth the hounds. But those in the castle fight bravely. There is a woman, two women, who stand upon the walls, and give heart to the men-at-arms. They shower down arrows, darts, and great stones. Ah! they have struck down the tall leader, and the others give back. The mist thickens and I can see no more."

"By Saint Paul!" said Sir Nigel, "I do not think that there can be any such doings at Christchurch, and I am very easy of the fortalice so long as my sweet wife hangs the key of the outer bailey at the head of her bed. Yet I will not deny that you have pictured the castle as well as I could have done myself, and I am full of wonderment at all that I have heard and seen."

"I would, Lady Tiphaine," cried the Lady Rochefort, "that you would use your power to tell me what hath befallen my golden bracelet which I wore when hawking upon the second Sunday of Advent, and have never set eyes upon since."

"Nay, lady," said Du Guesclin, "it does not befit so great and wondrous a power to pry and search and play the varlet even to the beautiful châtelaine of Villefranche. Ask a worthy question, and, with the blessing of God, you shall have a worthy answer."

"Then I would fain ask," cried one of the French squires, "as to which may hope to conquer in these wars betwixt the English and ourselves."

"Both will conquer, and each will hold its own," answered the Lady Tiphaine.

"Then we shall still hold Gascony and Guienne?" cried Sir Nigel.

The lady shook her head. "French land, French blood, French speech," she answered. "They are French, and France shall have them."

"But not Bordeaux?" cried Sir Nigel excitedly.

"Bordeaux also is for France."

"But Calais?"

"Calais too."

"Woe worth me then, and ill hail to these evil words! If Bordeaux and Calais be gone, then what is left for England?"

"It seems indeed that there are evil times coming upon your country," said Du Guesclin. "In our fondest hopes we never thought to hold Bordeaux. By Saint Ives! this news hath warmed the heart within me. Our dear country will then be very great in the future, Tiphaine?"

"Great, and rich, and beautiful," she cried. "Far down the course of time I can see her still leading the nations, a wayward queen among the peoples, great in war, but greater in peace, quick in thought, deft in action, with her people's will for her sole monarch, from the sands of Calais to the blue seas of the south."

"Ha!" cried Du Guesclin, with his eyes flashing triumph, "you hear her, Sir Nigel?—and she never yet said word which was not sooth."

The English knight shook his head moodily. "What of my own poor country?" said he. "I fear, lady, that what you have said bodes but small good for her."

The lady sat with parted lips, and her breath came quick and fast. "My God!" she cried, "what is this that is shown me? Whence come they, these peoples, these lordly nations, these mighty countries which rise up before me? I look beyond, and others rise, and yet others, far and farther to the shores of the uttermost waters. They crowd! They swarm! the world is given to them, and it resounds with the clang of their hammers and the ringing of their church bells. They call them many names, and they rule them this way or that, but they are all English, for I can hear the voices of the people. On I go, and onwards over seas where man hath never yet sailed, and I see a great land under new stars and a stranger sky, and still the land is England. Where have her children not gone? What have they not done? Her banner is planted on ice. Her banner is scorched in the sun. She lies athwart the lands, and her shadow is over the seas. Bertrand, Bertrand! we are undone, for the buds of her bud are even as our choicest flower!" Her voice rose into a wild cry, and throwing up her arms she sank back white and nerveless into the deep oaken chair.

"It is over," said Du Guesclin moodily, as he raised her drooping head with his strong brown hand. "Wine for the lady, squire! The blessed hour of sight hath passed."

CHAPTER XXX

HOW THE BRUSHWOOD MEN CAME TO THE CHÂTEAU OF VILLEFRANCHE

IT was late ere Alleyne Edricson, having carried Sir Nigel the goblet of spiced wine which it was his custom to drink after the curling of his hair, was able at last to seek his chamber. It was a stone-flagged room upon the second floor, with a bed in a recess for him, and two smaller pallets on the other side, on which Aylward and Hordle John were already snoring. Alleyne had knelt down to his evening orisons, when there came a tap at his door, and Ford entered with a small lamp in his hand. His face was deadly pale, and his hand shook until the shadows flickered up and down the wall.

"What is it, Ford?" cried Alleyne, springing to his feet.

"I can scarce tell you," said he, sitting down on the side of the couch, and resting his chin upon his hand. "I know not what to say or what to think."

"Has aught befallen you, then?"

"Yes, or I have been slave to my own fancy. I tell you, lad, that I am all undone, like a fretted bow-string. Hark hither, Alleyne! it cannot be that you have forgotten little Tita, the daughter of the old glass-stainer at Bordeaux?"

"I remember her well."

"She and I, Alleyne, broke the lucky groat together ere we parted, and she wears my ring upon her finger. 'Caro mio,' quoth she when last we parted, 'I shall be near thee in the wars, and thy danger will be my danger.' Alleyne, as God is my help, as I came up the stairs this night I saw her stand before me, her face in tears, her hands out as though in warning—I saw it, Alleyne, even as I see those two archers upon their couches. Our very finger-tips seemed to meet, ere she thinned away like a mist in the sunshine."

"I would not give overmuch thought to it," answered Alleyne. "Our minds will play us strange pranks, and bethink you that these words of the Lady Tiphaine Du Guesclin have wrought upon us and shaken us."

Ford shook his head. "I saw little Tita as clearly as though I were back at the Rue des Apôtres at Bordeaux," said he. "But the hour is late, and I must go."

"Where do you sleep, then?"

"In the chamber above you. May the saints be with us all!" He rose from the couch and left the chamber, while Alleyne could hear his feet sounding upon the winding stair. The young squire walked across to the window and gazed out at the moon-lit landscape, his mind absorbed by the thought of the Lady Tiphaine, and of the strange words that she had spoken as to what was going forward at Castle Twynham. Leaning his elbows upon the stonework, he was deeply plunged in reverie, when in a moment his thoughts were brought back to Villefranche and to the scene before him.

The window at which he stood was in the second floor of that portion of the castle which was nearest to the keep. In front lay the broad moat with the moon lying upon its surface, now clear and round, now drawn lengthwise as the breeze stirred the waters. Beyond, the plain sloped down to a thick wood, while further to the left a second wood shut out the view. Between the two an open glade stretched, silvered in the moonshine, with the river curving across the lower end of it.

As he gazed, he saw of a sudden a man steal forth from the wood into the open clearing. He walked with his head sunk, his shoulders curved, and his knees bent, as one who strives hard to remain unseen. Ten paces from the fringe of trees he glanced around, and waving his hand he crouched down, and was lost to sight among a belt of furze-bushes. After him there came a second man, and after him a third, a fourth, and a fifth, stealing across the narrow open space and darting into the shelter of the brushwood. Nine-and-seventy Alleyne counted of these dark figures flitting across the line of the moonlight. Many bore huge burdens upon their backs, though what it was that they carried he could not tell at the distance. Out of the one wood and into the other they passed, all with the same crouching, furtive gait, until the black bristle of trees had swallowed up the last of them.

For a moment Alleyne stood in the window, still staring down at the silent forest, uncertain as to what he should think of these midnight walkers. Then he bethought him that there was one beside him who was fitter to judge on such a matter. His fingers had scarce rested upon Aylward's shoulder ere the bowman was on his feet, with his hand outstretched to his sword.

"Qui va?" he cried. "Holà! mon petit. By my hilt! I thought there had been a camisade. What then, mon gar?"

"Come hither by the window, Aylward," said Alleyne. "I have seen four-score men pass from yonder shaw across the glade, and nigh every man of them had a great burden on his back. What think you of it?"

"I think nothing of it, mon camarade! There are as many masterless folk in this country as there are rabbits on Cowdray Down, and there are many who show their faces by night, but would dance in a hempen collar if they stirred forth in the day. On all the French marches are droves of outcasts, rievers, spoilers, and drawlatches, of whom I judge that these are some, though I marvel that they should dare to come so nigh to the castle of the Seneschal. All seems very quiet now," he added, peering out of the window.

"They are in the further wood," said Alleyne.

"And there they may bide. Back to rest, mon petit; for, by my hilt! each day now will bring its own work. Yet it would be well to shoot the bolt in yonder door when one is in strange quarters. So!" He threw himself down upon his pallet and in an instant was fast asleep.

It might have been about three o'clock in the morning when Alleyne was aroused from a troubled sleep by a low cry or exclamation. He listened, but, as he heard no more, he set it down as the challenge of the guard upon the walls, and dropped off to sleep once more. A few minutes later he was disturbed by a gentle creaking of his own door, as though someone were pushing cautiously against it, and immediately afterwards he heard the soft thud of cautious footsteps upon the stair which led to the room above, followed by a confused noise and a muffled groan. Alleyne sat up on his couch with all his nerves in a tingle, uncertain whether these sounds might come from a simple cause—some sick archer and visiting leech perhaps—or whether they might have a more sinister meaning. But what danger could threaten them here in this strong castle, under the care of famous warriors, with high walls and a broad moat around them? Who was there that could injure them? He had well-nigh persuaded himself that his fears were a foolish fancy, when his eyes fell upon that which sent the blood cold to his heart and left him gasping, with hands clutching at the counterpane.

Right in front of him was the broad window of the chamber, with the moon shining brightly through it. For an instant something had obscured the light, and now a head was bobbing up and down outside, the face looking in at him, and swinging slowly from one side of the window to the other. Even in that dim light there could be no mistaking those features. Drawn, distorted and blood-stained, they were still those of the young fellow-squire who had sat so recently upon his own couch. With a cry of horror Alleyne sprang from his bed and rushed to the casement, while the two archers, aroused by the sound, seized their weapons and stared about them in bewilderment. One glance was enough to show Edricson that his fears were but too true. Foully murdered, with a score of wounds upon him and a rope round his neck, his poor friend had been cast from the upper window and swung slowly in the night wind, his body rasping against the wall and his disfigured face upon a level with the casement.

"My God!" cried Alleyne, shaking in every limb. "What has come upon us? What devil's deed is this?"

"Here is flint and steel," said John stolidly. "The lamp, Aylward! This moonshine softens a man's heart. Now we may use the eyes which God hath given us."

"By my hilt!" cried Aylward, as the yellow flame flickered up, "it is indeed young master Ford, and I think that this Seneschal is a black villain, who dare not face us in the day, but would murther us in our sleep. By the twang of string! if I do not soak a goose's feather with his heart's blood, it will be no fault of Samkin Aylward of the White Company."

"But, Aylward, think of the men whom I saw yesternight," said Alleyne. "It may not be the Seneschal. It may be that others have come into the castle. I must go to Sir Nigel ere it be too late. Let me go, Aylward, for my place is by his side."

"One moment, mon gar. Put that steel head-piece on the end of my yew-stave. So! I will put it first through the door; for it is ill to come out when you can neither see nor guard yourself. Now, camarades, out swords and stand ready! Holà, by my hilt! it is time that we were stirring!"

As he spoke, a sudden shouting broke forth in the castle, with the scream of a woman and the rush of many feet. Then came the sharp clink of clashing steel, and a roar like that of an angry lion — "Notre Dame Du Guesclin! Saint Ives! Saint Ives!" The bowman pulled back the bolt of the door, and thrust out the head-piece at the end of the bow. A crash, and the clatter of the steel-cap upon the ground, and, ere the man who struck could heave up for another blow, the archer had passed his sword through his body. "On, camarades, on!" he cried; and, breaking fiercely past two men who threw themselves in his way, he sped down the broad corridor in the direction of the shouting.

A sharp turning, and then a second one, brought them to the head of a short stair, from which they looked straight down upon the scene of the uproar. A square oak-floored hall lay beneath them, from which opened the doors of the principal guest-chambers. This hall was as light as day, for torches burned in numerous sconces upon the walls, throwing strange shadows from the tusked or antlered heads which ornamented them. At the very foot of the stair, close to the open door of their chamber, lay the Seneschal and his wife; she with her head shorn from her shoulders, he thrust through with a sharpened stake, which still protruded from either side of his body. Three servants of the castle lay dead beside them, all torn and draggled, as though a pack of wolves had been upon them. In front of the central guest-chamber stood Du Guesclin and Sir Nigel, half-clad and un-armoured, with the mad joy of battle gleaming in their eyes. Their heads were thrown back, their lips compressed, their blood-stained swords poised over their right shoulders, and their left feet thrown out. Three dead men lay huddled together in front of them; while a fourth, with the blood squirting from a severed vessel, lay back with updrawn knees, breathing in wheezy gasps. Further back—all panting together like the wind in a tree—there stood a group of fierce wild creatures, bare-armed and bare-legged, gaunt, unshaven, with deep-set murderous eyes and wild-beast faces. With their flashing teeth, their bristling hair, their mad leapings and screamings, they seemed to Alleyne more like fiends from the pit than men of flesh and blood. Even as he looked, they broke into a hoarse yell and dashed once more upon the two knights, hurling themselves madly upon their sword-points; clutching, scrambling, biting, tearing, careless of wounds if they could but drag the two soldiers to earth. Sir Nigel was thrown down by the sheer weight of them, and Sir Bertrand with his thunderous war-cry was swinging round his heavy sword to clear a space for him to rise, when the whistle of two long English arrows, and the rush of the squire and the two English archers down the stairs, turned the tide of the combat. The assailants gave back, the knights rushed forward, and in a very few moments the hall was cleared, and Hordle John had hurled the last of the wild men down the steep steps which led from the end of it.

"Do not follow them," cried Du Guesclin. "We are lost if we scatter. For myself I care not a denier, though it is a poor thing to meet one's end at the hands of such scum; but I have my dear lady here, who must by no means be risked. We have breathing-space now, and I would ask you, Sir Nigel, what it is that you counsel?"

"By Saint Paul!" answered Sir Nigel, "I can by no means under-stand what hath befallen us, save that I have been woken up by your battle-cry, and, rushing forth, found myself in the midst of this small bickering. Harrow and alas for the lady and the Seneschal! What dogs are they who have done this bloody deed?"

"They are the Jacks, the men of the brushwood. They have the castle, though I know not how it hath come to pass. Look from this window into the bailey."

"By heaven!" cried Sir Nigel, "it is as bright as day with the torches. The gates stand open, and there are three thousand of them within the walls. See how they rush and scream and wave! What is it that they thrust out through the postern door? My God, it is a man-at-arms, and they pluck him limb from limb, like hounds on a wolf. Now another, and yet another. They hold the whole castle, for I see their faces at the windows. See, there are some with great bundles on their backs."

"It is dried wood from the forest. They pile them against the walls and set them in a blaze. Who is this who tries to check them? By Saint Ives! it is the good priest who spake for them in the hall. He kneels, he prays, he implores! What! villains, would ye raise hands against those who have befriended you? Ah, the butcher has struck him! He is down! They stamp him under their feet! They tear off his gown and wave it in the air! See now, how the flames lick up the walls! Are there none left to rally round us? With a hundred men we might hold our own."

"Oh, for my Company!" cried Sir Nigel. "But where is Ford, Alleyne?"

"He is foully murdered, my fair lord."

"The saints receive him! May he rest in peace! But here come some at last who may give us counsel, for amid these passages it is ill to stir without a guide."

As he spoke, a French squire and the Bohemian knight came rushing down the steps, the latter bleeding from a slash across his forehead.

"All is lost!" he cried. "The castle is taken and on fire, the Seneschal is slain and there is naught left for us."

"On the contrary," quoth Sir Nigel, "there is much left to us, for there is a very honourable contention before us, and a fair lady for whom to give our lives. There are many ways in which a man might die, but none better than this."

"You can tell us, Godfrey," said Du Guesclin to the French squire: "how came these men into the castle, and what succours can we count upon? By Saint Ives! if we come not quickly to some counsel we shall be burned like young rooks in a nest."

The squire, a dark slender stripling, spoke firmly and quickly, as one who was trained to swift action. "There is a passage under the earth into the castle," said he, "and through it some of the Jacks made their way, casting open the gates for the others. They have had help from within the walls and the men-at-arms were heavy with wine: they must have been slain in their beds, for these devils crept from room to room with soft step and ready knife. Sir Amory the Hospitaller was struck down with an axe as he rushed before us from his sleeping chamber. Save only ourselves, I do not think there are any left alive."

"What, then, would you counsel?"

"That we make for the keep. It is unused, save in time of war, and the key hangs from my poor lord and master's belt."

"There are two keys there."

"It is the larger. Once there, we might hold the narrow stair; and at least, as the walls are of a greater thickness, it would be longer ere they could burn them. Could we but carry the lady across the bailey, all might be well with us."

"Nay; the lady hath seen something of the work of war," said Tiphaine, coming forth, as white, as grave, and as unmoved as ever. "I would not be a hamper to you, my dear spouse and gallant friends. Rest assured of this, that if all else fail I have always a safe-guard here"—drawing a small silver-hilted poniard from her bosom—"which sets me beyond the fear of these vile and blood-stained wretches."

"Tiphaine," cried Du Guesclin, "I have always loved you, and now, by Our Lady of Rennes! I love you more than ever. Did I not know that your hand will be as ready as your words, I would myself turn my last blow upon you, ere you should fall into their hands. Lead on, Godfrey! A new golden pyx shall shine in the Minster of Dinan if we come safely through with it."

The attention of the insurgents had been drawn away from murder to plunder, and all over the castle might be heard their cries and whoops of delight as they dragged forth the rich tapestries, the silver flagons, and the carved furniture. Down in the courtyard half-clad wretches, their bare limbs all mottled with blood-stains, strutted about with plumed helmets upon their heads, or with the Lady Rochefort's silken gowns girt round their loins and trailing on the ground behind them. Casks of choice wine had been rolled out from the cellars, and starving peasants squatted, goblet in hand, draining off vintages which De Rochefort had set aside for noble and royal guests. Others, with slabs of bacon and joints of dried meat upon the ends of their pikes, held them up to the blaze or tore at them ravenously with their teeth. Yet all order had not been lost amongst them, for some hundreds of the better armed stood together in a silent group, leaning upon their rude weapons and looking up at the fire, which had spread so rapidly as to involve one whole side of the castle. Already Alleyne could hear the crackling and roaring of the flames, while the air was heavy with heat and full of the pungent whiff of burning wood.

CHAPTER XXXI

HOW FIVE MEN HELD THE KEEP
OF VILLEFRANCHE

UNDER the guidance of the French squire the party passed down
two narrow corridors. The first was empty, but at the head of the
second stood a peasant sentry, who started off at the sight of them,
yelling loudly to his comrades. "Stop him or we are undone!" cried
Du Guesclin, and had started to run, when Aylward's great war-
bow twanged like a harp-string, and the man fell forward upon his
face, with twitching limbs and clutching fingers. Within five paces
of where he lay a narrow and little-used door led out into the bailey. From beyond it came such a babel of hooting and screaming,
horrible oaths and yet more horrible laughter, that the stoutest
heart might have shrunk from casting down the frail barrier
which faced them.

"Make straight for the keep!" said Du Guesclin, in a sharp stern
whisper. "The two archers in front, the lady in the centre, a squire
on either side, while we three knights shall bide behind and beat
back those who press upon us. So! Now open the door, and God
have us in His holy keeping!"

For a few minutes it seemed that their object would be attained
without danger, so swift and so silent had been their movements.
They were half-way across the bailey ere the frantic howling peasants made a movement to stop them. The few who threw themselves in their way were overpowered or brushed aside, while the
pursuers were beaten back by the ready weapons of the three cav-

aliers. Unscathed they fought their way to the door of the keep, and faced round upon the swarming mob, while the squire thrust the great key into the lock.

"My God!" he cried, "it is the wrong key!"

"The wrong key!"

"Dolt, fool that I am! This is the key of the castle gate; the other opens the keep. I must back for it!" He turned, with some wild intention of retracing his steps, but at the instant a great jagged rock, hurled by a brawny peasant, struck him full upon the ear, and he dropped senseless to the ground.

"This is key enough for me!" quoth Hordle John, picking up the huge stone, and hurling it against the door with all the strength of his enormous body. The lock shivered, the wood smashed, the stone flew into five pieces, but the iron clamps still held the door in its position. Bending down, he thrust his great fingers under it, and with a heave raised the whole mass of wood and iron from its hinges. For a moment it tottered and swayed, and then, falling outward, buried him in its ruin, while his comrades rushed into the dark archway which led to safety.

"Up the steps, Tiphaine!" cried Du Guesclin. "Now round, friends, and beat them back." The mob of peasants had surged in upon their heels, but the two trustiest blades in Europe gleamed upon that narrow stair, and four of their number dropped upon the threshold. The others gave back and gathered in a half-circle round the open door, gnashing their teeth and shaking their clenched hands at the defenders. The body of the French squire had been dragged out by them and hacked to pieces. Three or four others had pulled John from under the door, when he suddenly bounded to his feet, and clutching one in either hand dashed them together with such force that they fell senseless across each other upon the ground. With a kick and a blow he freed himself from two others who clung to him, and in a moment he was within the portal with his comrades.

Yet their position was a desperate one. The peasants from far and near had been assembled for this deed of vengeance, and not less than six thousand were within or around the walls of the

Château of Villefranche. Ill armed and half starved, they were still desperate men, to whom danger had lost all fears: for what was death that they should shun it to cling to such a life as theirs? The castle was theirs, and the roaring flames were spurting through the windows and flickering high above the turrets on two sides of the quadrangle. From either side they were sweeping down from room to room and from bastion to bastion in the direction of the keep. Faced by an army, and girt in by fire, were six men and one woman; but some of them were men so trained to danger and so wise in war that even now the combat was less unequal than it seemed. Courage and resource were penned in by desperation and numbers, while the great yellow sheets of flame threw their lurid glare over the scene of death.

"There is but space for two upon a step to give free play to our sword-arms," said Du Guesclin. "Do you stand with me, Nigel, upon the lowest. France and England will fight together this night. Sir Otto, I pray you to stand behind us with this young squire. The archers may go higher yet and shoot over our heads. I would that we had our harness, Nigel!"

"Often have I heard my dear Sir John Chandos say that a knight should never, even when a guest, be parted from it. Yet it will be more honour to us if we come well out of it. Ye have a vantage, since we see them against the light and they can scarce see us. It seems to me that they muster for an onslaught."

"If we can but keep them in play," said the Bohemian, "it is likely that these flames may bring us succour if there be any true men in the country."

"Bethink you, my fair lord," said Alleyne to Sir Nigel, "that we have never injured these men, nor have we cause of quarrel against them. Would it not be well, if but for the lady's sake, to speak them fair, and see if we may not come to honourable terms with them?"

"Not so, by Saint Paul!" cried Sir Nigel. "It does not accord with mine honour, nor shall it ever be said that I, a knight of England, was ready to hold parley with men who have slain a fair lady and a holy priest."

"As well hold parley with a pack of ravening wolves," said the French captain. "Ha! Notre Dame Du Guesclin! Saint Ives! Saint Ives!"

As he thundered forth his war-cry, the Jacks who had been gathering before the black arch of the gateway rushed in madly in a desperate effort to carry the staircase. Their leaders were a small man, dark in the face, with his beard done up in two plaits, and another larger man, very bowed in the shoulders, with a huge club studded with sharp nails in his hand. The first had not taken three steps ere an arrow from Aylward's bow struck him full in the chest, and he fell coughing and spluttering across the threshold. The other rushed onwards, and breaking between Du Guesclin and Sir Nigel, he dashed out the brains of the Bohemian with a single blow of his clumsy weapon. With three swords through him he still struggled on, and had almost won his way through them ere he fell dead upon the stair. Close at his heels came a hundred furious peasants, who flung themselves again and again against the five swords which confronted them. It was cut and parry and stab as quick as eye could see or hand act. The door was piled with bodies, and the stone floor was slippery with blood. The deep shout of Du Guesclin, the hard hissing breath of the pressing multitude, the clatter of steel, the thud of falling bodies, and the screams of the stricken, made up such a medley as came often in after years to break upon Alleyne's sleep. Slowly and suddenly at last the throng drew off, with many a fierce backward glance, while eleven of their number lay huddled in front of the stair which they had failed to win.

"The dogs have had enough," said Du Guesclin.

"By Saint Paul! there appear to be some very worthy and valiant persons among them," observed Sir Nigel. "They are men from whom, had they been of better birth, much honour and advancement might be gained. Even as it is, it is a great pleasure to have seen them. But what is this that they are bringing forward?"

"It is as I feared," growled Du Guesclin. "They will burn us out, since they cannot win their way past us. Shoot straight and hard, archers; for, by Saint Ives! our good swords are of little use to us."

As he spoke, a dozen men rushed forward, each screening himself behind a huge fardel of brushwood. Hurling their burdens in one vast heap within the portal, they threw burning torches upon the top of it. The wood had been soaked in oil, for in an instant it was ablaze, and a long hissing yellow flame licked over the heads of the defenders, and drove them further up to the first floor of the keep. They had scarce reached it, however, ere they found that the wooden joists and planks of the flooring were already on fire. Dry and worm-eaten, a spark upon them became a smoulder, and a smoulder a blaze. A choking smoke filled the air, and the five could scarce grope their way to the staircase which led up to the very summit of the square tower.

Strange was the scene which met their eyes from this eminence. Beneath them on every side stretched the long sweep of peaceful country, rolling plain, and tangled wood, all softened and mellowed in the silver moonshine. No light nor movement, nor any sign of human aid could be seen, but far away the hoarse clangour of a heavy bell rose and fell upon the wintry air. Beneath and around them blazed the huge fire, roaring and crackling on every side of the bailey, and even as they looked the two corner turrets fell in with a deafening crash, and the whole castle was but a shapeless mass, spouting flames and smoke from every window and embrasure. The great black tower upon which they stood rose like a last island of refuge amid this sea of fire; but the ominous crackling and roaring below showed that it would not be long ere it was engulfed also in the common ruin. At their very feet was the square courtyard, crowded with the howling and dancing peasants, their fierce faces upturned, their clenched hands waving, all drunk with bloodshed and with vengeance. A yell of execrations and a scream of hideous laughter burst from the vast throng, as they saw the faces of the last survivors of their enemies peering down at them from the height of the keep. They still piled the brushwood round the base of the tower, and gambolled hand in hand around the blaze, screaming out the doggerel lines which had long been the watchword of the Jacquerie:

Cessez, cessez, gens d'armes et piétons,
De piller et manger le bonhomme,
Qui de longtemps Jacques Bonhomme
     Se nomme.

Their thin shrill voices rose high above the roar of the flames and
the crash of the masonry, like the yelping of a pack of wolves who
see their quarry before them and know that they have well nigh
run him down.

"By my hilt!" said Aylward to John, "it is in my mind that we shall
not see Spain this journey. It is a great joy to me that I have placed
my feather-bed and other things of price with that worthy woman
at Lyndhurst, who will now have the use of them. I have thirteen
arrows yet, and if one of them fly unfleshed, then, by the twang of
string! I shall deserve my doom. First at him who flaunts with my
lady's silken frock. Clap in the clout, by God! though a hand's-
breath lower than I had meant. Now for the rogue with the head
upon his pike. Ha! to the inch, John. When my eye is true, I am
better at rovers than at long-butts or hoyles. A good shot for you
also, John! The villain hath fallen forward into the fire. But I pray
you, John, to loose gently, and not to pluck with the drawing-hand,
for it is a trick that hath marred many a fine bowman."

Whilst the two archers were keeping up a brisk fire upon the
mob beneath them, Du Guesclin and his lady were consulting with
Sir Nigel upon their desperate situation.

"'Tis a strange end for one who has seen so many stricken
fields," said the French chieftain. "For me one death is as another,
but it is the thought of my sweet lady which goes to my heart."

"Nay, Bertrand, I fear it as little as you," said she. "Had I my
dearest wish, it would be that we should go together."

"Well answered, fair lady!" cried Sir Nigel. "And very sure I am
that my own sweet wife would have said the same. If the end be now
come, I have had great good fortune in having lived in times when
so much glory was to be won, and in knowing so many valiant gentlemen and knights. But why do you pluck my sleeve, Alleyne?"

"If it please you, my fair lord, there are in this corner two great tubes of iron, with many heavy balls, which may perchance be those bombards and shot of which I have heard."

"By Saint Ives! it is true," cried Sir Bertrand, striding across to the recess where the ungainly, funnel-shaped, thick-ribbed engines were standing. "Bombards they are, and of good size. We may shoot down upon them."

"Shoot with them, quotha," cried Aylward in high disdain, for pressing danger is the great leveller of classes. "How is a man to take aim with these fool's toys, and how can he hope to do scath with them?"

"I will show you," answered Sir Nigel; "for here is the great box of powder, and if you will raise it for me, John, I will show you how it may be used. Come hither, where the folk are thickest round the fire. Now, Aylward, crane thy neck and see what would have been deemed an old wife's tale when we first turned our faces to the wars. Throw back the lid, John, and drop the box into the fire."

A deafening roar, a fluff of bluish light, and the great square tower rocked and trembled from its very foundations, swaying this way and that like a reed in the wind. Amazed and dizzy, the defenders, clutching at the cracking parapets for support, saw great stones, burning beams of wood, and mangled bodies hurtling past them through the air. When they staggered to their feet once more, the whole keep had settled down upon one side, so that they could scarce keep their footing upon the sloping platform. Gazing over the edge, they looked down upon the horrible destruction which had been caused by the explosion. For forty yards round the portal the ground was black with writhing, screaming figures, who struggled up and hurled themselves down again, tossing this way and that, sightless, scorched, with fire bursting from their tattered clothing. Beyond this circle of death, their comrades, bewildered and amazed, cowered away from this black tower and from these invincible men, who were most to be dreaded when hope was furthest from their hearts.

"A sally, Du Guesclin, a sally!" cried Sir Nigel. "By Saint Paul! they are in two minds, and a bold rush may turn them." He drew his sword as he spoke and darted down the winding stairs, closely followed by his four comrades. Ere he was at the first floor, however, he threw up his arms and stopped. "Mon Dieu!" he said, "we are lost men!"

"What then?" cried those behind him.

"The wall hath fallen in, the stair is blocked, and the fire still rages below. By Saint Paul! friends, we have fought a very honourable fight, and may say in all humbleness that we have done our devoir, but I think that we may now go back to the Lady Tiphaine and say our orisons, for we have played our parts in this world, and it is time that we made ready for another."

The narrow pass was blocked by huge stones littered in wild confusion over each other, with the blue choking smoke reeking up through the crevices. The explosion had blown in the wall and cut off the only path by which they could descend. Pent in, a hundred feet from earth, with a furnace raging under them and a ravening multitude all round who thirsted for their blood, it seemed indeed as though no men had ever come through such peril with their lives. Slowly they made their way back to the summit, but as they came out upon it, the Lady Tiphaine darted forward and caught her husband by the wrist.

"Bertrand," said she, "hush and listen! I have heard the voices of men all singing together in a strange tongue."

Breathless, they stood and silent, but no sound came up to them, save the roar of the flames and the clamour of their enemies.

"It cannot be, lady," said Du Guesclin. "This night hath overwrought you, and your senses play you false. What men are there in this country who would sing in a strange tongue?"

"Holà!" yelled Aylward, leaping suddenly into the air with waving hands and joyous face. "I thought I heard it ere we went down, and now I hear it again. We are saved, comrades! By these ten finger-bones, we are saved! It is the marching song of the White Company. Hush!"

With upraised forefinger and slanting head, he stood listening. Suddenly there came swelling up a deep-voiced rollicking chorus from somewhere out of the darkness. Never did choice or dainty ditty of Provence or Languedoc sound more sweetly in the ears than did the rough-tongued Saxon to the six who strained their ears from the blazing keep:

We'll drink all together
To the grey goose feather
   And the land where the grey goose flew.

"Ha, by my hilt!" shouted Aylward, "it is the dear old bow song of the Company. Here come two hundred as tight lads as ever twirled a shaft over their thumb-nails. Hark to the dogs, how lustily they sing!"

Nearer and clearer, swelling up out of the night, came the gay marching lilt:

What of the bow?
   The bow was made in England,
Of true wood, of yew wood,
   The wood of English bows;
For men who are free
Love the old yew-tree
   And the land where the yew-tree grows.

What of the men?
   The men were bred in England,
The bowmen, the yeomen,
   The lads of dale and fell.
Here's to you and to you,
To the hearts that are true,
   And the land where the true hearts dwell.

"They sing very joyfully," said Du Guesclin, "as though they were going to a festival."

"It is their wont when there is work to be done,"

"By Saint Paul!" quoth Sir Nigel, "it is in my mind that they come too late, for I cannot see how we are to come down from this tower."

"There they come, the hearts of gold!" cried Aylward. "See, they move out from the shadow. Now they cross the meadow. They are on the further side of the moat. Holà, camarades, holà! Johnston, Eccles, Cooke, Harward, Bligh! Would ye see a fair lady and two gallant knights done foully to death?"

"Who is there?" shouted a deep voice from below. "Who is this who speaks with an English tongue?"

"It is I, old lad. It is Sam Aylward of the Company; and here is your captain, Sir Nigel Loring, and four others, all laid out to be grilled like an Easterling's herrings."

"Curse me if I did not think that it was the style of speech of old Samkin Aylward," said the voice, amid a buzz from the ranks. "Wherever there are knocks going there is Sammy in the heart of it. But who are these ill-faced rogues who block the path? To your kennels, canaille! What! you dare look us in the eyes? Out swords, lads, and give them the flat of them! Waste not your shafts upon such runagate knaves."

There was little fight left in the peasants, however, still dazed by the explosion, amazed at their own losses, and disheartened by the arrival of the disciplined archers. In a very few minutes they were in full flight for their brushwood homes, leaving the morning sun to rise upon a blackened and blood-stained ruin, where it had left the night before the magnificent castle of the Seneschal of Auvergne. Already the white lines in the east were deepening into pink as the archers gathered round the keep and took counsel how to rescue the survivors.

"Had we a rope," said Alleyne, "there is one side which is not yet on fire, down which we might slip."

"But how to get a rope?"

"It is an old trick," quoth Aylward. "Holà! Johnston, cast me up a rope, even as you did at Maupertuis in the war time."

The grizzled archer thus addressed took several lengths of rope from his comrades, and knotting them firmly together, he stretched them out in the long shadow which the rising sun threw from the frowning keep. Then he fixed the yew-stave of his bow upon end and measured the long thin black line which it threw upon the surf.

"A six-foot stave throws a twelve-foot shadow," he muttered. "The keep throws a shadow of sixty paces. Thirty paces of rope will be enow and to spare. Another strand, Watkin! Now pull at the end that all may be safe. So! It is ready for them."

"But how are they to reach it?" asked the young archer beside him.

"Watch and see, young fool's-head," growled the old bowman. He took a long string from his pouch and fastened one end to an arrow.

"All ready, Samkin?"

"Ready, camarade."

"Close to your hand then." With an easy pull he sent the shaft flickering gently up, falling upon the stonework within a foot of where Aylward was standing. The other end was secured to the rope, so that in a minute a good strong cord was dangling from the only sound side of the blazing and shattered tower. The Lady Tiphaine was lowered with a noose drawn fast under the arms, and the other five slid swiftly down amid the cheers and joyous outcry of their rescuers.

CHAPTER XXXII

HOW THE COMPANY TOOK COUNSEL
ROUND THE FALLEN TREE

"Where is Sir Claude Latour?" asked Sir Nigel, as his feet touched ground.

"He is in camp, near Montpezat, two hours' march from here, my fair lord," said Johnston, the grizzled bowman who commanded the archers.

"Then we shall march thither, for I would fain have you all back at Dax in time to be in the prince's vanguard."

"My lord," cried Alleyne, joyfully, "here are our chargers in the field, and I see your harness amid the plunder which these rogues have left behind them."

"By Saint Ives! you speak sooth, young squire," said Du Guesclin. "There is my horse and my lady's jennet. The knaves led them from the stables, but fled without them. Now, Nigel, it is great joy to me to have seen one of whom I have often heard. Yet we must leave you now, for I must be with the King of Spain ere your army crosses the mountains."

"I had thought that you were in Spain with the valiant Henry of Trastamare."

"I have been there, but I came to France to raise succour for him. I shall ride back, Nigel, with four thousand of the best lances of France at my back, so that your prince may find he hath a task which is worthy of him. God be with you, friend, and may we meet again in better times."

"I do not think," said Sir Nigel, as he stood by Alleyne's side, looking after the French knight and his lady, "that in all Christendom you will meet with a more stout-hearted man or a fairer and sweeter dame. But your face is pale and sad, Alleyne. Have you perchance met with some hurt during the ruffle?"

"Nay, my fair lord, I was but thinking of my friend, Ford, and how he sat upon my couch no later than yesternight."

Sir Nigel shook his head sadly. "Two brave squires have I lost," said he. "I know not why the young shoots should be plucked and an old weed left standing, yet certes there must be some good reason, since God hath so planned it. Did you not note, Alleyne, that the Lady Tiphaine did give us warning last night that danger was coming upon us?"

"She did, my lord."

"By Saint Paul! my mind misgives me as to What she saw at Twynham Castle. And yet I cannot think that any Scottish or French rovers could land in such force as to beleaguer the fortalice. Call the company together, Aylward; and let us on, for it will be shame to us if we are not at Dax upon the trysting day."

The archers had spread themselves over the ruins, but a blast upon a bugle brought them all back to the muster with such booty as they could bear with them stuffed into their pouches or slung over their shoulders. As they formed into ranks, each man dropping silently into his place, Sir Nigel ran a questioning eye over them, and a smile of pleasure played over his face. Tall and sinewy, and brown, clear-eyed, hard-featured, with the stern and prompt bearing of experienced soldiers, it would be hard indeed for a leader to seek for a choicer following. Here and there in the ranks were old soldiers of the French wars, grizzled and lean, with fierce puckered features and shaggy bristling brows. The most, however, were young and dandy archers, with fresh English faces, their beards combed out, their hair curling from under their close steel hufkens, with gold or jewelled earrings gleaming in their ears, while their gold-spangled baldrics, their silken belts, and the chains which many of them wore round their thick brown necks, all spoke of the brave times which they had had as free companions. Each had a yew or hazel stave slung over his shoulder, plain and serviceable with the older men, but gaudily painted and carved at either end with the others. Steel caps, mail brigandines, white surcoats with the red lion of St George, and sword or battle-axe swinging from their belts, completed this equipment, while in some cases the murderous maule or five-foot mallet was hung across the bow-stave, being fastened to their leathern shoulder-belt by a hook in the centre of the handle. Sir Nigel's heart beat high as he looked upon their free bearing and fearless faces.

For two hours they marched through forest and marshland, along the left bank of the river Aveyron; Sir Nigel riding behind his Company, with Alleyne at his right hand, and Johnston, the old master bowman, walking by his left stirrup. Ere they had reached their journey's end the knight had learned all that he would know of his men, their doings and their intentions. Once as they marched they saw upon the further bank of the river a body of French men-at-arms, riding very swiftly in the direction of Villefranche.

"It is the Seneschal of Toulouse, with his following," said Johnston, shading his eyes with his hand. "Had he been on this side of the water he might have attempted something upon us."

"I think that it would be well that we should cross," said Sir Nigel. "It were pity to balk this worthy Seneschal, should he desire to try some small feat of arms."

"Nay, there is no ford nearer than Tourville," answered the old archer. "He is on his way to Villefranche, and short will be the shrift of any Jacks who come into his hands, for he is a man of short speech. It was he and the Seneschal of Beaucaire who hung Peter Wilkins, of the Company, last Lammastide; for which by the black rood of Waltham! they shall hang themselves if ever they come into our power. But here are our comrades, Sir Nigel, and here is our camp."

As he spoke, the forest pathway along which they marched opened out into a green glade, which sloped down towards the river. High leafless trees girt it in on three sides, with a thick undergrowth of holly between their trunks. At the farther end of this forest clearing there stood forty or fifty huts, built very neatly from wood and clay, with the blue smoke curling out from the roofs. A dozen tethered horses and mules grazed around the encampment, while a number of archers lounged about: some shooting at marks, while others built up great wooden fires in the open, and hung their cooking kettles above them. At the sight of their returning comrades there was a shout of welcome, and a horseman, who had been exercising his charger behind the camp, came cantering down to them. He was a dapper, brisk man, very richly clad, with a round clean-shaven face, and very bright black eyes, which danced and sparkled with excitement.

"Sir Nigel!" he cried. "Sir Nigel Loring, at last! By my soul! we have awaited you this month past. Right welcome, Sir Nigel! You have had my letter?"

"It was that which brought me here," said Sir Nigel, "But indeed, Sir Claude Latour, it is a great wonder to me that you did not yourself lead these bowmen, for surely they could have found no better leader."

"None, none, by the Virgin of L'Esparre!" he cried, speaking in the strange thick Gascon speech which turns every *v* into a *b*. "But you know what these islanders of yours are, Sir Nigel. They will not be led by any save their own blood and race. There is no persuading them. Not even I, Claude Latour, Seigneur of Montchâteau, master of the high justice, the middle and the low, could gain their favour. They must needs hold a council and put their two hundred thick heads together, and then there comes this fellow Aylward and another, as their spokesmen, to say that they will disband unless an Englishman of good name be set over them. There are many of them, as I understand, who come from some great forest which lies in Hampi, or Hampti—I cannot lay my tongue to the name. Your dwelling is in those parts, and so their thoughts turned to you as their leader. But we had hoped that you would bring a hundred men with you."

"They are already at Dax, where we shall join them," said Sir Nigel. "But let the men break their fast, and we shall then take counsel what to do."

"Come into my hut," said Sir Claude. "It is but poor fare that I can lay before you — milk, cheese, wine, and bacon — yet your squire and yourself will doubtless excuse it This is my house where the pennon flies before the door — a small residence to contain the Lord of Montchâteau."

Sir Nigel sat silent and distrait at his meal, while Alleyne hearkened to the chattering tongue of the Gascon, and to his talk of the glories of his own estate, his successes in love, and his triumphs in war.

"And now that you are here, Sir Nigel," he said at last, "I have many fine ventures all ready for us. I have heard that Montpezat is of no great strength, and that there are two hundred thousand crowns in the castle. At Castelnau also there is a cobbler who is in my pay, and who will throw us a rope any dark night from his house by the town wall. I promise you that you shall thrust your arms elbow deep among good silver pieces ere the nights are moonless again; for on every hand of us are fair women, rich wine, and good plunder, as much as heart could wish."

"I have other plans," answered Sir Nigel curtly; "for I have come hither to lead these bowmen to the help of the prince, our master, who may have sore need of them ere he set Pedro upon the throne of Spain. It is my purpose to start this very day for Dax upon the Adour, where he hath now pitched his camp."

The face of the Gascon darkened, and his eyes flashed with resentment. "For me," he said, "I care little for this war, and I find the life which I lead a very joyous and pleasant one. I will not go to Dax."

"Nay, think again, Sir Claude," said Sir Nigel gently; "for you have ever had the name of a true and loyal knight. Surely you will not hold back now when your master hath need of you."

"I will not go to Dax," the other shouted.

"But your devoir — your oath of fealty?"

"I say that I will not go."

"Then, Sir Claude, I must lead the Company without you."

"If they will follow," cried the Gascon, with a sneer. "These are not hired slaves, but free companions, who will do nothing save by their own good wills. In very sooth, my Lord Loring, they are ill men to trifle with, and it were easier to pluck a bone from a hungry bear than to lead a bowman out of a land of plenty and of pleasure."

"Then I pray you to gather them together," said Sir Nigel, "and I will tell them what is in my mind; for if I am their leader they must to Dax, and if I am not, then I know not what I am doing in Auvergne. Have my horse ready, Alleyne; for, by Saint Paul! come what may, I must be upon the homeward road ere midday."

A blast upon the bugle summoned the bowmen to counsel, and they gathered in little knots and groups around a great fallen tree which lay athwart the glade. Sir Nigel sprang lightly upon the trunk, and stood with blinking eye and firm lips looking down at the ring of upturned warlike faces.

"They tell me, bowmen," said he, "that ye have grown so fond of ease and plunder and high living that ye are not to be moved from this pleasant country. But, by Saint Paul! I will believe no such thing of you, for I can readily see that you are all very valiant men, who would scorn to live here in peace when your prince hath so great a venture before him. Ye have chosen me as a leader, and a leader I will be if ye come with me to Spain; and I vow to you that my pennon of the five roses shall, if God give me strength and life, be ever where there is most honour to be gained. But if it be your wish to loll and loiter in these glades, bartering glory and renown for vile gold and ill-gotten riches, then ye must find another leader; for I have lived in honour, and in honour I trust that I shall die. If there be forest men or Hampshire men amongst ye, I call upon them to say whether they will follow the banner of Loring."

"Here's a Romsey man for you!" cried a young bowman with a sprig of evergreen set in his helmet.

"And a lad from Alresford!" shouted another.

"And from Milton!"

"And from Burley!"

"And from Lymington!"

"And a little one from Brockenhurst!" shouted a huge-limbed fellow who sprawled beneath a tree.

"By my hilt! lads," cried Aylward, jumping upon the fallen trunk, "I think that we could not look the girls in the eyes if we let the prince cross the mountains and did not pull string to clear a path for him. It is very well in time of peace to lead such a life as we have had together, but now the war-banner is in the wind once more, and, by these ten finger-bones! if he go alone, old Samkin Aylward will walk beside it."

These words from a man so popular as Aylward decided many of the waverers, and a shout of approval burst from his audience.

"Far be it from me," said Sir Claude La tour suavely, "to persuade you against this worthy archer, or against Sir Nigel Loring; yet we have been together in many ventures, and perchance it may not be amiss if I say to you what I think upon the matter."

"Peace for the little Gascon!" cried the archers. "Let every man have his word. Shoot straight for the mark, lad, and fair play for all."

"Bethink you, then," said Sir Claude, "that you go under a hard rule, with neither freedom nor pleasure—and for what? For sixpence a day, at the most; while now you may walk across the country and stretch out either hand to gather in whatever you have a mind for. What do we not hear of our comrades who have gone with Sir John Hawkwood to Italy? In one night they have held to ransom six hundred of the richest noblemen of Mantua. They camp before a great city, and the base burghers come forth with the keys, and then they make great spoil; or, if it please them better, they take so many horse-loads of silver as a composition; and so they journey on from state to state, rich and free and feared by all. Now, is not that the proper life for a soldier?"

"The proper life for a robber!" roared Hordle John, in his thundering voice.

"And yet there is much in what the Gascon says," said a swarthy fellow in a weather-stained doublet; "and I for one would rather prosper in Italy than starve in Spain."

"You were always a cur and a traitor, Mark Shaw," cried Aylward. "By my hilt! if you will stand forth and draw your sword I will warrant you that you will see neither one nor the other."

"Nay, Aylward," said Sir Nigel, "we cannot mend the matter by broiling. Sir Claude, I think that what you have said does you little honour, and if my words aggrieve you, I am ever ready to go deeper into the matter with you. But you shall have such men as will follow you, and you may go where you will, so that you come not with us. Let all who love their prince and country stand fast, while those who think more of a well-lined purse step forth upon the other side."

Thirteen bowmen, with hung heads and sheepish faces, stepped forward with Mark Shaw and ranged themselves behind Sir Claude. Amid the hootings and hissings of their comrades, they marched off together to the Gascon's hut, while the main body broke up their meeting and set cheerily to work packing their possessions, furbishing their weapons, and preparing for the march which lay before them. Over the Tarn and the Garonne, through the vast quagmires of Armagnac, past the swift-flowing Losse, and so down the long valley of the Adour, there was many a long league to be crossed ere they could join themselves to that dark war-cloud which was drifting slowly southwards to the line of snowy peaks beyond which the banner of England had never yet been seen.

CHAPTER XXXIII

HOW THE ARMY MADE THE PASSAGE
OF RONCESVALLES

THE whole vast plain of Gascony and of Languedoc is an arid and profitless expanse in winter, save where the swift-flowing Adour and her snow-fed tributaries, the Louts, the Oloron and the Pau, run down to the sea of Biscay. South of the Adour the jagged line of mountains which fringe the sky-line send out long granite claws, running down into the lowlands and dividing them into "gaves" or stretches of valley. Hillocks grow into hills, and hills into mountains, each range over-lying its neighbour, until they soar up in the giant chain which raises its spotless and untrodden peaks, white and dazzling against the pale blue wintry sky.

A quiet land is this—a land where the slow-moving Basque, with his flat biretta-cap, his red sash and his hempen sandals, tills his scanty farm or drives his lean flock to their hill-side pastures. It is the country of the wolf and the isard, of the brown bear and the mountain-goat, a land of bare rock and of rushing water. Yet here it was that the will of a great prince had now assembled a gallant army; so that from the Adour to the passes of Navarre the barren valleys and wind-swept waters were populous with soldiers and loud with the shouting of orders and the neighing of horses. For the banners of war had been flung to the wind once more, and over those glistening peaks was the highway along which honour pointed in an age when men had chosen her as their guide.

And now all was ready for the enterprise. From Dax to St Jean Pied-du-Port the country was mottled with the white tents of Gascons, Aquitanians and English, all eager for the advance. From all sides the free companions had trooped in, until not less than twelve thousand of these veteran troops were cantoned along the frontiers of Navarre. From England had arrived the prince's brother, the Duke of Lancaster, with four hundred knights in his train and a strong company of archers. Above all, an heir to the throne had been born in Bordeaux, and the prince might leave his spouse with an easy mind, for all was well with mother and with child.

The keys of the mountain passes still lay in the hands of the shifty and ignoble Charles of Navarre, who had chaffered and bargained both with the English and with the Spanish, taking money from the one side to hold them open and from the other to keep them sealed. The mallet hand of Edward, however, had shattered all the schemes and wiles of the plotter. Neither entreaty nor courtly remonstrance came from the English prince; but Sir Hugh Calverley passed silently over the border with his company, and the blazing walls of the two cities of Miranda and Puenta de la Reyna warned the unfaithful monarch that there were other metals besides gold, and that he was dealing with a man to whom it was unsafe to lie. His price was paid, his objections silenced, and the mountain gorges lay open to the invaders. From the Feast of the Epiphany there was mustering and massing, until, in the first weeks of February—three days after the White Company joined the army—the word was given for a general advance through the defile of Roncesvalles. At five in the cold winter's morning the bugles were blowing in the hamlet of St Jean Pied-du-Port, and by six Sir Nigel's Company, three hundred strong, were on their way for the defile, pushing swiftly in the dim light up the steep curving road; for it was the prince's order that they should be the first to pass through, and that they should remain on guard at the further end until the whole army had emerged from the mountains. Day was already breaking in the east, and the summits of the great peaks had turned rosy red, while the valleys still lay in the shadow, when they found themselves with the cliffs on either hand and the long rugged pass stretching away before them.

Sir Nigel rode his great black war-horse at the head of his archers, dressed in full armour, with Black Simon bearing his banner behind him, while Alleyne at his bridle-arm carried his blazoned shield and his well-steeled ashen spear. A proud and happy man was the knight, and many a time he turned in his saddle to look at the long column of bowmen who swung swiftly along behind him.

"By Saint Paul! Alleyne," said he, "this pass is a very perilous place, and I would that the King of Navarre had held it against us, for it would have been a very honourable venture had it fallen to us to win a passage. I have heard the minstrels sing of one Sir Roland who was slain by the infidels in these very parts."

"If it please you, my fair lord," said Black Simon, "I know something of these parts, for I have twice served a term with the King of Navarre. There is a hospice of monks yonder, where you may see the roof among the trees, and there it was that Sir Roland was slain. The village upon the left is Orbaiceta, and I know a house therein where the right wine of Jurançon is to be bought, if it would please you to quaff a morning cup."

"There is smoke yonder upon the right."

"That is a village named Les Aldudes, and I know a hostel there also where the wine is of the best. It is said that the innkeeper hath a buried treasure, and I doubt not, my fair lord, that if you grant me leave I could prevail upon him to tell us where he hath hid it."

"Nay, nay, Simon," said Sir Nigel curtly, "I pray you to forget these free-companion tricks. Ha! Edricson, I see that you stare about you, and in good sooth these mountains must seem wondrous indeed to one who hath but seen Butser or the Portsdown Hill."

The broken and rugged road had wound along the crests of low hills, with wooded ridges on either side of it, over which peeped the loftier mountains, the distant Peak of the South and the vast Altabisca, which towered high above them and cast its black shadow from left to right across the valley. From where they now stood they could look forward down a long vista of beech woods and jagged rock-strewn wilderness, all white with snow, to where the pass opened out upon the uplands beyond. Behind them they could still catch a glimpse of the grey plains of Gascony and could see her rivers gleaming like coils of silver in the sunshine. As far as eye could see from among the rocky gorges and the bristles of the pine woods there came the quick twinkle and glitter of steel, while the wind brought with it sudden distant bursts of martial music from the great host which rolled by every road and by-path towards the narrow pass of Roncesvalles. On the cliffs on either side might also be seen the flash of arms and the waving of pennons where the force of Navarre looked down upon the army of strangers who passed through their territories.

"By Saint Paul!" said Sir Nigel, blinking up at them, "I think that we have much to hope for from these cavaliers, for they cluster very thickly upon our flanks. Pass word to the men, Aylward, that they unsling their bows, for I have no doubt that there are some very worthy gentlemen yonder who may give us some opportunity for honourable advancement."

"I hear that the prince hath the King of Navarre as hostage," said Alleyne, "and it is said that he hath sworn to put him to death if there be any attack upon us."

"It was not so that war was made when good King Edward first turned his hand to it," said Sir Nigel sadly. "Ah! Alleyne, I fear that you will never live to see such things, for the minds of men are more set upon money and gain than of old. By Saint Paul! it was a noble sight when two great armies would draw together upon a certain day, and all who had a vow would ride forth to discharge themselves of it. What noble spear-runnings have I not seen, and even in a humble way had a part in, when cavaliers would run a course for the easing of their souls and for the love of their ladies! Never a bad word have I for the French, for, though I have ridden twenty times up to their array, I have never yet failed to find some very gentle and worthy knight or squire who was willing to do what he might to enable me to attempt some small feat of arms. Then, when all cavaliers had been satisfied, the two armies would come to hand-strokes, and fight right merrily until one or other had the vantage. By Saint Paul! it was not our wont in those days to pay gold for the opening of passes, nor would we hold a king as hostage lest his people come to thrusts with us. In good sooth, if the war is to be carried out in such a fashion, then it is grief to me that I ever came away from Castle Twynham, for I would not have left my sweet lady had I not thought that there were deeds of arms to be done."

"But surely, my fair lord," said Alleyne, "you have done some great feats of arms since we left the Lady Loring."

"I cannot call any to mind," answered Sir Nigel.

"There was the taking of the sea-rovers and the holding of the keep against the Jacks."

"Nay, nay," said the knight, "these were not feats of arms, but mere wayside ventures and the chances of travel. By Saint Paul! if it were not that these hills are over steep for Pommers, I would ride to these cavaliers of Navarre and see if there were not some among them who would help me to take this patch from mine eye. It is a sad sight to me to see this very fine pass, which my own Company here could hold against an army, and yet to ride through it with as little profit as though it were the lane from my kennels to the Avon."

All morning Sir Nigel rode in a very ill-humour, with his Company tramping behind him. It was a toilsome march over broken ground and through snow, which came often as high as the knee, yet ere the sun had begun to sink they had reached the spot where the gorge opens out on to the uplands of Navarre, and could see the towers of Pampeluna jutting up against the Southern sky-line. Here the Company were quartered in a scattered mountain hamlet, and Alleyne spent the day looking down upon the swarming army which poured with gleam of spears and flaunt of standards through the narrow pass.

"Holà! mon gar," said Aylward, seating himself upon a boulder by his side. "This is indeed a sight upon which it is good to look, and a man might go far ere he would see so many brave men and

fine horses. By my hilt! our little lord is wroth because we have
come peacefully through the passes, but, I will warrant him that
we have fighting enow ere we turn our faces northward again. It is
said that there are fourscore thousand men behind the King of
Spain, with Du Guesclin and all the best knees of France, who
have sworn to shed their heart's blood ere this Pedro come again
to the throne."

"Yet our own army is a great one," said Alleyne.

"Nay, there are but seven-and-twenty thousand men. Chandos
hath persuaded the prince to leave many behind, and indeed I
think that he is right, for there is little food and less water in these
parts for which we are bound. A man without his meat or a horse
without his fodder is like a wet bow-string, fit for little. But voilà,
mon petit, here come Chandos and his company, and there is
many a pensil and banderole among yonder squadrons which
show that the best blood of England is riding under his banners."

Whilst Aylward had been speaking, a strong column of archers
had defiled through the pass beneath them. They were followed
by a banner-bearer who held high the scarlet wedge upon a silver
field which proclaimed the presence of the famous warrior. He
rode himself within a spear's-length of his standard, clad from
neck to foot in steel, but draped in the long linen gown or pare-
ment which was destined to be the cause of his death. His plumed
hat was carried behind him by his body-squire and his head was
covered by a small purple cap, from under which his snow-white
hair curled downwards to his shoulders. With his long beak-like
nose and his single gleaming eye, which shone brightly from
under a thick tuft of grizzled brow, he seemed to Alleyne to have
something of the look of some fierce old bird of prey. For a
moment he smiled, as his eye lit upon the banner of the five roses
waving from the hamlet; but his course lay for Pampeluna and he
rode after the archers.

Close at his heels came sixteen squires, all chosen from the
highest families, and behind them rode twelve hundred English
knights, with gleam of steel and tossing of plumes, their harness

jingling, their long straight swords clanking against their stirrup-irons, and the beat of their chargers' hoofs like the low deep roar of the sea upon the shore. Behind them marched six hundred Cheshire and Lancashire archers, bearing the badge of the Audleys, followed by the famous Lord Audley himself, with the four valiant squires, Dutton of Dutton, Delves of Doddington, Fowlehurst of Crewe, and Hawkestone of Wainehill, who had all won such glory at Poictiers. Two hundred heavily armed cavalry rode behind the Audley standard, while close at their heels came the Duke of Lancaster with a glittering train, heralds tabarded with the royal arms riding three deep upon cream-coloured chargers in front of him. On either side of the young prince rode the two Seneschals of Aquitaine, Sir Guiscard d'Angle and Sir Stephen Cossington, the one bearing the banner of the province and the other that of Saint George. Away behind him as far as eye could reach rolled the far-stretching, unbroken river of steel—rank after rank and column after column, with waving of plumes, glitter of arms, tossing of guidons, and flash and flutter of countless armorial devices. All day Alleyne looked down upon the changing scene, and all day the old bowman stood by his elbow, pointing out the crests of famous warriors and the arms of noble houses. Here were the gold mullets of the Pakingtons, the sable and ermine of the Mackworths, the scarlet bars of the Wakes, the gold and blue of the Grosvenors, the cinque-foils of the Cliftons, the annulets of the Musgraves, the silver pinions of the Beauchamps, the crosses of the Molineaux, the bloody chevron of the Woodhouses, the red and silver of the Worsleys, the swords of the Clarks, the boars'-heads of the Lucies, the crescents of the Boyntons, and the wolf and dagger of the Lips-combs. So through the sunny winter day the chivalry of England poured down through the dark pass of Roncesvalles to the plains of Spain.

It was on a Monday that the Duke of Lancaster's division passed safely through the Pyrenees. On the Tuesday there was a bitter frost, and the ground rung like iron beneath the feet of the horses; yet ere evening the prince himself, with the main battle of his army, had passed the gorge and united with his vanguard at Pampeluna. With him rode the King of Majorca, the hostage King of Navarre, and the fierce Bon Pedro of Spain, whose pale blue eyes gleamed with a sinister light as they rested once more upon the distant peaks of the land which had disowned him. Under the royal banners rode many a bold Gascon baron and many a hot-blooded islander. Here were the high stewards of Aquitaine, of Saintonge, of La Rochelle, of Quercy, of Limousin, of Agenois, of Poitou, and of Bigorre, with the banners and musters of their provinces. Here also were the valiant Earl of Angus, Sir Thomas Banaster with his garter over his greave, Sir Nele Loring, second son to Sir Nigel, and a long column of Welsh footmen who marched under the red banner of Merlin. From dawn to sundown the long train wound through the pass, their breath reeking up upon the frosty air like the steam from a caldron.

The weather was less keen upon the Wednesday, and the rear-guard made good their passage, with the bombards and the waggon-train. Free companions and Gascons made up this portion of the army to the number of ten thousand men. The fierce Sir Hugh Calverley with his yellow mane, and the rugged Sir Robert Knolles, with their war-hardened and veteran companies of English bow-men, headed the long column, while behind them came the turbu-lent band of the Bastard of Breteuil, Nandon de Bagerant, one-eyed Camus, Black Ortingo, La Nuit, and others whose very names seem to smack of hard hands and ruthless deeds. With them also were the pick of the Gascon chivalry—the old Duc d'Armagnac, his nephew Lord d'Albret, brooding and scowling over his wrongs, the giant Oliver de Clisson, the Captal de Buch, pink of knighthood, the sprightly Sir Perducas d'Albret, the red-bearded Lord d'Esparre, and a long train of needy and grasping border nobles, with long pedigrees and short purses, who had come down from their hill-side strongholds, all hungering for the spoils and the ransoms of Spain. By the Thursday morning the whole army was encamped in the Vale of Pampeluna, and the prince had called his council to meet him in the old palace of the ancient city of Navarre.

CHAPTER XXXIV

HOW THE COMPANY MADE SPORT IN THE VALE OF PAMPELUNA

WHILST the council was sitting in Pampeluna the White Company, having encamped in a neighbouring valley, close to the companies of La Nuit and of Black Ortingo, were amusing themselves at sword-play, wrestling, and shooting at the shields, which they had placed upon the hill-side to serve them as butts. The younger archers, with their coats of mail thrown aside, their brown or flaxen hair tossing in the wind, and their jerkins turned back to give free play to their brawny chests and arms, stood in lines, each loosing his shaft in turn, while Johnston, Aylward, Black Simon, and half a score of the elders lounged up and down with critical eyes, and a word of rough praise or of curt censure for the marksmen. Behind stood knots of Gascon and Brabant crossbowmen from the companies of Ortingo and of La Nuit, leaning upon their unsightly weapons and watching the practice of the Englishmen.

"A good shot, Hewett, a good shot!" said old Johnston to a young bowman who stood with his bow in his left hand, gazing with parted lips after his flying shaft. "You see, she finds the ring, as I knew she would from the moment that your string twanged."

"Loose it easy, steady, and yet sharp," said Aylward. "By my hilt! mon gar, it is very well when you do but shoot at a shield, but when there is a man behind the shield and he rides at you with wave of sword and glint of eyes from behind his vizor, you may find him a less easy mark."

"It is a mark that I have found before now," answered the young bowman.

"And shall again, camarade, I doubt not. But holà! Johnston, who is this who holds his bow like a crow-keeper?"

"It is Silas Peterson, of Horsham. Do not wink with one eye and look with the other, Silas, and do not hop and dance after you shoot, with your tongue out, for that will not speed it upon its way. Stand straight and firm, as God made you. Move not the bow-arm, and steady with the drawing-hand."

"I' faith," said Black Simon, "I am a spearman myself and am more fitted for hand-strokes than for such work as this. Yet I have spent my days among bowmen, and I have seen many a brave shaft sped. I will not say but that we have some good marksmen here, and that this Company would be accounted a fine body of archers at any time or place. Yet I do not see any men who bend so strong a bow or shoot as true a shaft as those whom I have known."

"You say sooth," said Johnston, turning his seamed and grizzled face upon the man-at-arms. "See yonder," he added, pointing to a bombard which lay within the camp: "there is what hath done scath to good bowmanship, with its filthy soot and foolish roaring mouth. I wonder that a true knight, like our prince, should carry such a scurvy thing in his train. Robin, thou redheaded lurden, how oft must I tell thee not to shoot straight with a quarter wind blowing across the mark?"

"By these ten finger-bones! there were some fine bowmen at the intaking of Calais," said Aylward. "I well remember that, on occasion of an outfall, a Genoan raised his arm over his mantlet and shook it at us, a hundred paces from our line. There were twenty who loosed shafts at him, and when the man was afterwards slain, it was found that he had taken eighteen through his forearm."

"And I can call to mind," remarked Johnston, "that when the great cog *Christopher*, which the French had taken from us, was moored two hundred paces from the shore, two archers, little Robin Withstaff and Elias Baddlesmere, in four shots each cut every strand of her hempen anchor-cord, so that she well-nigh came upon the rocks."

"Good shooting, i' faith, rare shooting," said Black Simon. "But I have seen you, Johnston, and you, Samkin Aylward, and one or two others who are still with us, shoot as well as the best. Was it not you, Johnston, who took the fat ox at Finsbury butts against the pick of London town?"

A sunburnt and black-eyed Brabanter had stood near the old archers, leaning upon a large crossbow and listening to their talk, which had been carried on in that hybrid camp dialect which both nations could understand. He was a squat, bull-necked man, clad in the iron helmet, mail tunic, and woollen gambesson of his class. A jacket with hanging sleeves, slashed with velvet at the neck and wrists, showed that he was a man of some consideration, an under-officer, or file-leader of his company.

"I cannot think," said he, "why you English should be so fond of your six-foot stick. If it amuse you to bend it, well and good; but why should I strain and pull, when my little moulinet will do all for me, and better than I can do it for myself?"

"I have seen good shooting with the prod and with the latch," said Aylward, "but, by my hilt! camarade, with all respect to you and to your bow, I think that is but a woman's weapon, which a woman can point and loose as easily as a man."

"I know not about that," answered the Brabanter, "but this I know, that though I have served for fourteen years, I have never yet seen an Englishman do aught with the long-bow which I could not do better with my arbalest. By the three kings! I would even go further, and say that I have done things with my arbalest which no Englishman could do with his long-bow."

"Well said, mon gar," cried Aylward. "A good cock has ever a brave call. Now, I have shot little of late, but there is Johnston here who will try a round with you for the honour of the Company."

"And I will lay a gallon of Jurançon wine upon the long-bow," said Black Simon, "though I had rather, for my own drinking, that it were a quart of Twynham ale."

"I take both your challenge and your wager," said the man of Brabant, throwing off his jacket, and glancing keenly about him with his black twinkling eyes. "I cannot see any fitting mark, for I care not to waste a bolt on these shields, which a drunken boor could not miss at a village kermesse."

"This is a perilous man," whispered an English man-at-arms, plucking at Aylward's sleeve. "He is the best marksman of all the crossbow companies, and it was he who brought down the Constable de Bourbon at Brignais. I fear that your man will come by little honour with him."

"Yet I have seen Johnston shoot this twenty years, and I will not flinch from it. How say you, old war-hound, will you not have a flight shot or two with this springald?"

"Tut, tut, Aylward," said the old bowman. "My day is past, and it is for the younger ones to hold what we have gained. I take it unkindly of thee, Samkin, that thou shouldst call all eyes thus upon a broken bowman who could once shoot a fair shaft. Let me feel that bow, Wilkins! It is a Scotch bow, I see, for the upper nock is without and the lower within. By the black rood! it is a good piece of yew well nocked, well strung, well waxed, and very joyful to the feel. I think even now that I might hit any large and goodly mark with a bow like this. Turn the quiver to me, Aylward. I love an ash arrow pierced with cornel-wood for a roving shaft."

"By my hilt! and so do I," cried Aylward. "These three gander-winged shafts are such."

"So I see, comrade. It has been my wont to choose a saddle-backed feather for a dead shaft, and a swine-backed for a smooth flier. I will take the two of them. Ah! Samkin, lad, the eye grows dim and the hand less firm as the years pass."

"Come then, are you not ready?" said the Brabanter, who had watched with ill-concealed impatience the slow and methodic movement of his antagonist.

"I will venture a rover with you, or try long-butts or hoyles," said old Johnston. "To my mind the long-bow is a better weapon than the arbalest, but it may be ill for me to prove it."

"So I think," quoth the other with a sneer. He drew his moulinet from his girdle, and, fixing it to the windlass, he drew back the powerful double cord until it had clicked into the catch. Then from his quiver he drew a short thick quarrel, which he placed with the utmost care upon the groove. Word had spread of what was going forward, and the rivals were already surrounded, not only by the English archers of the Company, but by hundreds of arbalestiers and men-at-arms from the bands of Ortingo and La Nuit, to the latter of which the Brabanter belonged.

"There is a mark yonder on the hill," said he; "mayhap you can discern it."

"I see something," answered Johnston, shading his eyes with his hand; "but it is a very long shoot."

"A fair shoot—a fair shoot! Stand aside, Arnaud, lest you find a bolt through your gizzard. Now, comrade, I take no flight shot, and I give you the vantage of watching my shaft."

As he spoke he raised his arbalest to his shoulder and was about to pull the trigger, when a large grey stork flapped heavily into view, skimming over the brow of the hill, and then soaring up into the air to pass the valley. Its shrill and piercing cries drew all eyes upon it, and, as it came nearer, a dark spot which circled above it resolved itself into a peregrine falcon, which hovered over its head, poising itself from time to time, and watching its chance of closing with its clumsy quarry. Nearer and nearer came the two birds, all absorbed in their own contest, the stork wheeling upwards, the hawk still fluttering above it, until they were not a hundred paces from the camp. The Bra-banter raised his weapon to the sky, and there came the short deep twang of his powerful string. His bolt struck the stork just where its wing meets the body, and the bird whirled aloft in a last convulsive flutter before falling wounded and flapping to the earth. A roar of applause burst from the cross-bowmen; but at the instant that the bolt struck its mark old Johnston who had stood listlessly with arrow on string, bent his bow and sped a shaft through the body of the falcon. Whipping the other from his belt, he set it skimming some few feet from the earth with so true an aim that it struck and transfixed the stork for the second time ere it could reach the ground. A deep-chested shout of delight burst from the archers at the sight of this double feat, and Aylward, dancing with joy, threw his arms round the old marksman and embraced him with such vigour that their mail tunics clanged again.

"Ah! camarade," he cried, "you shall have a stoup with me for this! What then, old dog, would not the hawk please thee, but thou must have the stork as well? Oh, to my heart again!"

"It is a pretty piece of yew, and well strung," said Johnston with a twinkle in his deep-set grey eyes. "Even an old broken bowman might find the clout with a bow like this."

"You have done very well," remarked the Brabanter in a surly voice. "But it seems to me that you have not yet shown yourself to be a better marksman than I, for I have struck that at which I aimed, and, by the three kings! no man can do more."

"It would ill beseem me to claim to be a better marksman," answered Johnston, "for I have heard great things of your skill. I did but wish to show that the long-bow could do that which an arbalest could not do, for you could not with your moulinet have your string ready to speed another shaft ere the bird drop to the earth."

"In that you have vantage," said the crossbowman. "By Saint James! it is now my turn to show you where my weapon has the better of you. I pray you to draw a flight shaft with all your strength down the valley, that we may see the length of your shoot."

"That is a very strong prod of yours," said Johnston, shaking his grizzled head as he glanced at the thick arch and powerful strings of his rival's arbalest. "I have little doubt that you can overshoot me, and yet I have seen bowmen who could send a cloth-yard arrow further than you could speed a quarrel."

"So I have heard," remarked the Brabanter: "and yet it is a strange thing that these wondrous bowmen are never where I chance to be. Pace out the distances with a wand, at every five-score, and do you, Arnaud, stand at the fifty wand to carry back my bolts to me."

A line was measured down the valley, and Johnston, drawing an arrow to the very head, sent it whistling over the row of wands.

"Bravely drawn! A rare shoot," shouted the bystanders. "It is well up to the fourth mark."

"By my hilt! it is over it," cried Aylward. "I can see where they have stooped to gather up the shaft."

"We shall hear anon," said Johnston quietly, and presently a young archer came running to say that the arrow had fallen twenty paces beyond the fourth wand.

"Four hundred paces and a score," cried Black Simon. "I' faith it is a very long flight. Yet wood and steel may do more than flesh and blood."

The Brabanter stepped forward with a smile of conscious triumph, and loosed the cord of his weapon. A shout burst from his comrades as they watched the swift and lofty flight of the heavy bolt.

"Over the fourth!" groaned Aylward. "By my hilt! I think that it is well up to the fifth."

"It is over the fifth!" cried a Gascon loudly, and a comrade came running with waving arms to say that the bolt had pitched eight paces beyond the mark of the five hundred.

"Which weapon hath the vantage now?" cried the Brabanter, strutting proudly about with shouldered arbalest, amid the applause of his companions.

"You can overshoot me," said Johnston, gently.

"Or any other man who ever bent a long-bow," cried his victorious adversary.

"Nay, not so fast," said a huge archer, whose mighty shoulders and red head towered high above the throng of his comrades. "I must have a word with you ere you crow so loudly. Where is my little popper? By sainted Dick of Hampole! it will be a strange thing if I cannot outshoot that thing of thine, which to my eyes is more like a rat-trap than a bow. Will you try another flight, or do you stand by your last?,"

"Five hundred and eight paces will serve my turn," answered the Brabanter, looking askance at this new opponent.

"Tut, John," whispered Aylward, "you never were a marksman. Why must you thrust your spoon into this dish?"

"Easy and slow, Aylward. There are very many things which I cannot do, but there are also one or two which I have the trick of. It is in my mind that I can beat this shoot, if my bow will but hold together."

"Go on, old babe of the woods! Have at it, Hampshire!" cried the archers, laughing.

"By my soul! you may grin," cried John. "But I learned how to make the long shoot from old Hob Miller of Milford."

He took up a great black bow as he spoke, and sitting down upon the ground he placed his two feet on either end of the stave. With an arrow fitted, he then pulled the string towards him with both hands until the head of the shaft was level with the wood. The great bow creaked and groaned and the cord vibrated with the tension.

"Who is this fool's-head who stands in the way of my shoot?" said he, craning up his neck from the ground.

"He stands on the further side of my mark," answered the Brabanter, "so he has little to fear from you."

"Well, the saints assoil him!" cried John. "Though I think he is over near to be scathed." As he spoke he raised his two feet, with the bow-stave upon their soles, and his cord twanged with a deep rich hum which might be heard across the valley. The measurer in the distance fell flat upon his face, and then, jumping up again, began to run in the opposite direction.

"Well shot, old lad! It is indeed over his head," cried the bowmen.

"Mon Dieu!" exclaimed the Brabanter, "who ever saw such a shoot!"

"It is but a trick," quoth John. "Many a time have I won a gallon of ale by covering a mile in three flights down Wilverley Chase."

"It fell a hundred and thirty paces beyond the fifth mark," shouted an archer in the distance.

"Six hundred and thirty paces! Mon Dieu! but that is a shoot! And yet it says nothing for your weapon, mon gros camarade, for it was by turning yourself into a crossbow that you did it."

"By my hilt! there is truth in that," cried Aylward. "And now, friend, I will myself show you a vantage of the long-bow. I pray you to speed a bolt against yonder shield with all your force. It is an inch of elm with bull's hide over it."

"I scarce shot as many shafts at Brignais," growled the man of Brabant; "though I found a better mark there than a cantle of bull's hide. But what is this, Englishman? The shield hangs not one hundred paces from me, and a blind man could strike it." He screwed up his string to the furthest pitch, and shot his quarrel at the dangling shield. Aylward, who had drawn an arrow from his quiver, carefully greased the head of it, and sped it at the same mark.

"Run, Wilkins," quoth he, "and fetch me the shield."

Long were the faces of the Englishmen and broad the laugh of the crossbowmen as the heavy mantlet was carried towards them, for there in the centre was the thick Brabant bolt driven deeply into the wood, while there was neither sign nor trace of the cloth-yard shaft.

"By the three kings!" cried the Brabanter, "this time at least there is no gainsaying which is the better weapon, or which the truer hand that held it. You have missed the shield, Englishman."

"Tarry a bit! Tarry a bit, mon gar!" quoth Aylward, and turning round the shield he showed a round clear hole in the wood at the back of it. "My shaft has passed through it, camarade, and I trow the one which goes through is more to be feared than that which bides on the way."

The Brabanter stamped his foot with mortification, and was about to make some angry reply, when Alleyne Edricson came riding up to the crowds of archers.

"Sir Nigel will be here anon," said he, "and it is his wish to speak with the Company."

In an instant order and method took the place of general confusion. Bows, steel caps, and jacks were caught up from the grass. A long cordon cleared the camp of all strangers, while the main body fell into four lines with under-officers and file-leaders in front and on either flank. So they stood, silent and motionless, when their leader came riding towards them, his face shining and his whole small figure swelling with the news which he bore.

"Great honour has been done to us, men," cried he: "for of all the army, the prince has chosen us out that we should ride onwards into the lands of Spain to spy upon our enemies. Yet, as there are many of us, and as the service may not be to the liking of all, I pray that those will step forward from the ranks who have the will to follow me."

There was a rustle among the bowmen, but when Sir Nigel looked up at them no man stood forward from his fellows, but the four lines of men stretched unbroken as before. Sir Nigel blinked at them in amazement, and a look of the deepest sorrow shadowed his face.

"That I should have lived to see the day!" he cried "What! not one—"

"My fair lord," whispered Alleyne, "they have all stepped forward."

"Ah, by Saint Paul! I see how it is with them. I could not think that they would desert me. We start at dawn tomorrow, and ye are to have the horses of Sir Robert Chesney's company. Be ready, I pray ye, at early cock-crow."

A buzz of delight burst from the archers, as they broke their ranks and ran hither and thither, whooping and cheering like boys who have news of a holiday. Sir Nigel gazed after them with a smiling face, when a heavy hand fell upon his shoulder.

"What ho! my knight-errant of Twynham!" said a voice. "You are off to Ebro, I hear; and, by the holy fish of Tobias! you must take me under your banner."

"What! Sir Oliver Buttesthorn!" cried Sir Nigel. "I had heard that you were come into camp, and had hoped to see you. Glad and proud shall I be to have you with me."

"I have a most particular and weighty reason for wishing to go," said the sturdy knight.

"I can well believe it," returned Sir Nigel; "I have met no man who is quicker to follow where honour leads."

"Nay, it is not for honour that I go, Nigel."

"For what then?"

"For pullets."

"Pullets?"

"Yes, for the rascal vanguard have cleared every hen from the country-side. It was this very morning that Norbury, my squire, lamed his horse in riding round in quest of one, for we have a bag of truffles, and nought to eat with them. Never have I seen such locusts as this vanguard of ours. Not a pullet shall we see until we are in front of them; so I shall leave my Winchester runagates to the care of the provost-marshal, and I shall hie south with you, Nigel, with my truffles at my saddle-bow."

"Oliver, Oliver, I know you over well," said Sir Nigel, shaking his head, and the two old soldiers rode off together to their pavilion.

CHAPTER XXXV

HOW SIR NIGEL HAWKED AT AN EAGLE

To the south of Pampeluna in the kingdom of Navarre there stretched a high table-land, rising into bare, sterile hills, brown or grey in colour, and strewn with huge boulders of granite. On the Gascon side of the great mountains there had been running streams, meadows, forests, and little nestling villages. Here, on the contrary, were nothing but naked rocks, poor pasture, and savage stone-strewn wastes. Gloomy defiles or barrancas intersected this wild country with mountain torrents dashing and foaming between their rugged sides. The clatter of waters, the scream of the eagle, and the howling of wolves, were the only sounds which broke upon the silence in that dreary and inhospitable region.

Through this wild country it was that Sir Nigel and his Company pushed their way, riding at times through vast defiles where the brown gnarled cliffs shot up on either side of them, and the sky was but a long winding blue slit between the clustering lines of box which fringed the lips of the precipices; or again leading their horses along the narrow and rocky paths worn by the muleteers upon the edges of the chasm, where under their very elbows they could see the white streak which marked the *gave* which foamed a thousand feet below them. So for two days they pushed their way through the wild places of Navarre, past Fuente, over the rapid Ega, through Estella, until upon a winter's evening the mountains fell away from in front of them, and they saw the broad blue Ebro curving betwixt its double line of homesteads and of villages. The fishers of Viana were aroused that night by rough voices speaking in a strange tongue, and ere morning Sir Nigel and his men had ferried the river and were safe upon the land of Spain.

All the next day they lay in a pine wood near to the town of Logrono, resting their horses and taking counsel as to what they should do. Sir Nigel had with him Sir William Felton, Sir Oliver Buttesthorn, stout old Sir Simon Burley, the Scotch knight-errant, the Earl of Angus, and Sir Richard Causton, all accounted among the bravest knights in the army, together with sixty veteran men-at-arms, and three hundred and twenty archers. Spies had been sent out in the morning, and returned after nightfall to say that the King of Spain was encamped some fourteen miles off in the direction of Burgos, having with him twenty thousand horse and forty-five thousand foot.

A dry-wood fire had been lit, and round this the leaders crouched, the glare beating upon their rugged faces, while the hardy archers lounged and chattered amid the tethered horses, while they munched their scanty provisions.

"For my part," said Sir Simon Burley, "I am of opinion that we have already done that which we have come for. For do we not now know where the king is, and how great a following he hath, which was the end of our journey?"

"True," answered Sir William Felton, "but I have come on this venture because it is a long time since I have broken a spear in war, and, certes, I shall not go back until I have run a course with some cavalier of Spain. Let those go back who will, but I must see more of these Spaniards ere I turn."

"I will not leave you, Sir William," returned Sir Simon Burley; "and yet, as an old soldier and one who hath seen much of war, I cannot but think that it is an ill thing for four hundred men to find themselves between an army of sixty thousand on the one side and a broad river on the other."

"Yet," said Sir Richard Causton, "we cannot for the honour of England go back without a blow struck."

"Nor for the honour of Scotland either," cried the Earl of Angus. "By Saint Andrew! I wish that I may never set eyes upon the water of Leith again, if I pluck my horse's bridle ere I have seen this camp of theirs."

"By Saint Paul! you have spoken very well," said Sir Nigel, "and I have always heard that there were very worthy gentlemen among the Scots, and fine skirmishing to be had upon their border. Bethink you, Sir Simon, that we have this news from the lips of common spies, who can scarce tell us as much of the enemy and of his forces as the prince would wish to hear."

"You are the leader in this venture, Sir Nigel," the other answered, "and I do but ride under your banner."

"Yet I would fain have your rede and counsel, Sir Simon. But, touching what you say of the river, we can take heed that we shall not have it at the back of us, for the prince hath now advanced to Salvatierra, and thence to Vittoria, so that if we come upon their camp from the further side we can make good our retreat."

"What then would you propose?" asked Sir Simon, shaking his grizzled head as one who is but half convinced.

"That we ride forward ere the news reach them that we have crossed the river. In this way we may have sight of their army, and perchance even find occasion for some small deed against them."

"So be it, then," said Sir Simon Burley; and the rest of the council having approved, a scanty meal was hurriedly snatched, and the advance resumed under the cover of the darkness. All night they led their horses, stumbling and groping through wild defiles and rugged valleys, following the guidance of a frightened peasant who was strapped by the wrist to Black Simon's stirrup-leather. With the early dawn they found themselves in a black ravine, with others sloping away from it on either side, and the bare brown crags rising in long bleak terraces all round them.

"If it please you, fair lord," said Black Simon, "this man hath misled us, and since there is no tree upon which we may hang him, it might be well to hurl him over yonder cliff."

The peasant, reading the soldier's meaning in his fierce eyes and harsh accents, dropped upon his knees, screaming loudly for mercy.

'How comes it, dog?" asked Sir William Felton in Spanish. "Where is this camp to which you swore that you would lead us?"

"By the sweet Virgin! By the blessed Mother of God!" cried the trembling peasant, "I swear to you that in the darkness I have myself lost the path."

"Over the cliff with him!" shouted half a dozen voices; but ere the archers could drag him from the rocks to which he clung Sir Nigel had ridden up and called upon them to stop.

"How is this, sirs?" said he. "As long as the prince doth me the honour to entrust this venture to me, it is for me only to give orders; and, by Saint Paul! I shall be right blithe to go very deeply into the matter with anyone to whom my words may give offence. How say you, Sir William? Or you, my Lord of Angus? Or you, Sir Richard?"

"Nay, nay, Nigel!" cried Sir William. "This base peasant is too small a matter for old comrades to quarrel over. But he hath betrayed us, and certes he hath merited a dog's death."

"Hark ye, fellow," said Sir Nigel. "We give you one more chance to find the path. We are about to gain much honour, Sir William, in this enterprise, and it would be a sorry thing if the first blood shed were that of an unworthy boor. Let us say our morning orisons, and it may chance that ere we finish he may strike upon the track."

With bowed heads and steel caps in hand the archers stood at their horses' heads, while Sir Simon Burley repeated the Pater, the Ave, and the Credo. Long did Alleyne bear the scene in mind — the knot of knights in their dull leaden-hued armour, the ruddy visage of Sir Oliver, the craggy features of the Scottish earl, the shining scalp of Sir Nigel, with the dense ring of hard bearded faces and the long brown heads of the horses, all topped and circled by the beetling cliffs. Scarce had the last deep "Amen" broken from the Company, when, in an instant, there rose the scream of a hundred bugles, with the deep rolling of drums and the clashing of cymbals, all sounding together in one deafening uproar.

Knights and archers sprang to arms, convinced that some great host was upon them; but the guide dropped upon his knees and thanked heaven for its mercies.

"We have found them, caballeros!" he cried. "This is their morning call. If ye will but deign to follow me, I will set them before you ere a man might tell his beads."

As he spoke he scrambled down one of the narrow ravines, and, climbing over a low ridge at the further end, he led them into a short valley with a stream purling down the centre of it and a very thick growth of elder and of box upon either side. Pushing their way through the dense brushwood, they looked out upon a scene which made their hearts beat harder and their breath come faster.

In front of them there lay a broad plain watered by two winding streams and covered with grass, stretching away to where, in the furthest distance, the towers of Burgos bristled up against the light blue morning sky. Over all this vast meadow there lay a great city of tents—thousands upon thousands of them laid out in streets and in squares like a well-ordered town. High silken pavilions or coloured marquees, shooting up from among the crowd of meaner dwellings, marked where the great lords and barons of Leon and Castile displayed their standards, while over the white roofs, as far as eye could reach, the waving of ancients, pavons, pensils, and banderoles, with flash of gold and glow of colours, proclaimed that all the chivalry of Iberia were mustered in the plain beneath them. Far off, in the centre of the camp, a huge palace of red and white silk with the royal arms of Castile waving from the summit, announced that the gallant Henry lay there in the midst of his warriors.

As the English adventurers, peeping out from behind their brushwood screen, looked down upon this wondrous sight, they could see that the vast army in front of them was already afoot. The first pink light of the rising sun glittered upon the steel caps and breastplates of dense masses of slingers and crossbow-men, who drilled and marched in the spaces which had been left for their exercise. A thousand columns of smoke reeked up into the pure morning air where the faggots were piled and the camp-kettles already simmering. In the open plain clouds of light horse galloped and swooped with swaying bodies and waving javelins, after the fashion which the Spanish had adopted from their Moorish enemies. All along by the sedgy banks of the rivers long lines of pages led their masters' chargers down to water, while the knights themselves lounged in gaily dressed groups about the doors of their pavilions, or rode out, with their falcons upon their wrists and their greyhounds behind them, in quest of quail or of leveret.

"By my hilt! mon gar!" whispered Aylward to Alleyne, as the young squire stood with parted lips and wondering eyes gazing down at the novel scene before him, "we have been seeking them all night, but now that we have found them I know not what we are to do with them."

"You say sooth, Samkin," quoth old Johnston. "I would that we were upon the far side of Ebro again, for there is neither honour nor profit to be gained here. What say you, Simon?"

"By the rood!" cried the fierce man-at-arms, "I will see the colour of their blood ere I turn my mare's head for the mountains. Am I a child, that I should ride for three days and nought but words at the end of it?"

"Well said, my sweet honeysuckle!" cried Hordle John. "I am with you, like hilt to blade. Could I but lay hands upon one of those gay prancers yonder, I doubt not that I should have ransom enough from him to buy my mother a new cow."

"A cow!" said Aylward. "Say rather ten acres and a homestead on the banks of Avon."

"Say you so? Then, by Our Lady! here is for yonder one in the red jerkin."

He was about to push recklessly forward into the open, when Sir Nigel himself darted in front of him, with his hand upon his breast.

"Back!" said he. "Our time is not yet come, and we must lie here until evening. Throw off your jackets and headpieces, lest their eyes catch the shine, and tether the horses among the rocks."

The order was swiftly obeyed, and in ten minutes the archers were stretched along by the side of the brook, munching the bread and bacon which they had brought in their bags, and craning their necks to watch the ever-changing scene beneath them. Very quiet and still they lay, save for a muttered jest or whispered order, for twice during the long morning they heard bugle-calls from amid the hills on either side of them, which showed that they had thrust themselves in between the outposts of the enemy. The leaders sat amongst the box-wood, and took counsel together as to what they should do; while from below there surged up the buzz of voices, the shouting, the neighing of horses, and all the uproar of a great camp.

"What boots it to wait?" said Sir William Felton. "Let us ride down upon their camp ere they discover us."

"And so say I," cried the Scottish earl; "for they do not know that there is any enemy within thirty long leagues of them."

"For my part," said Sir Simon Burley, "I think that it is madness, for you cannot hope to rout this great army; and where are you to go and what are you to do when they have turned upon you? How say you, Sir Oliver Buttesthorn?"

"By the apple of Eve!" cried the fat knight, "it appears to me that this wind brings a very savoury smell of garlic and of onions from their cooking-kettles. I am in favour of riding down upon them at once, if my old friend and comrade here is of the same mind."

"Nay," said Sir Nigel, "I have a plan by which we may attempt some small deed upon them, and yet, by the help of God, may be able to draw off again; which, as Sir Simon Burley hath said, would be scarce possible in any other way."

"How then, Sir Nigel?" asked several voices.

"We shall lie here all day; for amid this brushwood it is ill for them to see us. Then, when evening comes, we shall sally out upon them and see if we may not gain some honourable advancement from them."

"But why then rather than now?"

"Because we shall have nightfall to cover us when we draw off, so that we may make our way back through the mountains. I would station a score of archers here in the pass, with all our pennons jutting forth from the rocks, and as many nakirs and drums and bugles as we have with us, so that those who follow us in the fading light may think that the whole army of the prince is upon them, and fear to go further. What think you of my plan, Sir Simon?"

"By my troth! I think very well of it," cried the prudent old commander. "If four hundred men must needs run a tilt against sixty thousand, I cannot see how they can do it better or more safely."

"And so say I," cried Felton, heartily. "But I wish the day were over, for it will be an ill thing for us if they chance to light upon us."

The words were scarce out of his mouth when there came a clatter of loose stones, the sharp clink of trotting hoofs, and a dark-faced cavalier, mounted upon a white horse, burst through the bushes and rode swiftly down the valley from the end which was farthest from the Spanish camp. Lightly armed, with his vizor open and a hawk perched upon his left wrist, he looked about him with the careless air of a man who is bent wholly upon pleasure, and unconscious of the possibility of danger. Suddenly, however, his eyes lit upon the fierce faces which glared out at him from the brushwood. With a cry of terror, he thrust his spurs into his horse's sides and dashed for the narrow opening of the gorge. For a moment it seemed as though he would have reached it, for he had trampled over or dashed aside the archers who threw themselves in his way, but Hordle John seized him by the foot in his grasp of iron and dragged him from the saddle, while two others caught the frightened horse.

"Ho, ho!" roared the great archer. "How many cows wilt buy my mother, if I set thee free?"

"Hush that bull's bellowing!" cried Sir Nigel, impatiently. "Bring the man here. By Saint Paul it is not the first time that we have met; for, if I mistake not, it is Don Diego Alvarez, who was once at the prince's court."

"It is indeed I," said the Spanish knight, speaking in the French tongue, "and I pray you to pass your sword through my heart; for how can I live — I, a caballero of Castile — after being dragged from my horse by the base hands of a common archer?"

"Fret not for that," answered Sir Nigel. "For, in sooth, had he not pulled you down, a dozen cloth-yard shafts had crossed each other in your body."

"By Saint James! it were better so than to be polluted by his touch," answered the Spaniard, with his black eyes sparkling with rage and hatred. "I trust that I am now the prisoner of some honourable knight or gentleman."

"You are the prisoner of the man who took you, Sir Diego," answered Sir Nigel. "And I may tell you that better men than either you or I have found themselves before now prisoners in the hands of the archers of England."

"What ransom, then, does he demand?" asked the Spaniard

Big John scratched his red head and grinned in high delight when the question was propounded to him. "Tell him," said he, "that I shall have ten cows and a bull too, if it be but a little one. Also a dress of blue sendall for mother and a red one for Joan; with five acres of pasture-land, two scythes, and a fine new grindstone. Likewise a small house, with stalls for the cows, and thirty-six gallons of beer for the thirsty weather."

"Tut, tut!" cried Sir Nigel, laughing. "All these things may be had for money; and I think, Don Diego, that five thousand crowns is not too much for so renowned a knight"

"It shall be duly paid him."

"For some days we must keep you with us; and I must crave leave also to use your shield, your armour, and your horse."

"My harness is yours by the law of arms," said the Spaniard gloomily.

"I do but ask the loan of it. I have need of it this day, but it shall be duly returned to you. Set guards, Aylward, with arrow on string, at either end of the pass; for it may happen that some other cavaliers may visit us ere the time be come." All day the little band of

Englishmen lay in the sheltered gorge, looking down upon the vast host of their unconscious enemies. Shortly after mid-day, a great uproar of shouting and cheering broke out in the camp, with mustering of men and calling of bugles. Clambering up among the rocks, the companions saw a long rolling cloud of dust along the whole eastern sky-line, with the glint of spears and the flutter of pennons, which announced the approach of a large body of cavalry. For a moment a wild hope came upon them that perhaps the prince had moved more swiftly than had been planned, that he had crossed the Ebro, and that this was his vanguard sweeping to the attack.

"Surely I see the red pile of Chandos at the head of yonder squadron!" cried Sir Richard Causton, shading his eyes with his hand.

"Not so," answered Sir Simon Burley, who had watched the approaching host with a darkening face. "It is even as I feared. That is the double eagle of Du Guesclin."

"You say very truly," cried the Earl of Angus. "These are the levies of France, for I can see the ensigns of the Marshal d'Andreghen, with that of the Lord of Antoing and of Briseuil, and of many another from Brittany and Anjou."

"By Saint Paul! I am very glad of it," said Sir Nigel. "Of these Spaniards I know nothing; but the French are very worthy gentlemen, and will do what they can for our advancement."

"There are at least four thousand of them, and all men-at-arms," cried Sir William Felton. "See, there is Bertrand himself, beside his banner, and there is King Henry, who rides to welcome him. Now they all turn and come into the camp together."

As he spoke, the vast throng of Spaniards and of Frenchmen trooped across the plain, with brandished arms and tossing banners. All day long the sound of revelry and of rejoicing from the crowded camp swelled up to the ears of the Englishmen, and they could see the soldiers of the two nations throwing themselves into each other's arms and dancing hand-in-hand round the blazing fires. The sun had sunk behind a cloud-bank in the west before Sir Nigel at last gave word that the men should resume their arms and have their horses ready. He had himself thrown off his armour, and had dressed himself from head to foot in the harness of the captured Spaniard.

"Sir William," said he, "it is my intention to attempt a small deed, and I ask you therefore that you will lead this outfall upon the camp. For me, I will ride into their camp with my squire and two archers. I pray you to watch me, and to ride forth when I am come among the tents. You will leave twenty men behind here, as we planned this morning, and you will ride back here after you have ventured as far as seems good to you."

"I will do as you order, Nigel; but what is it that you propose to do?"

"You will see anon, and indeed it is but a trifling matter. Alleyne, you will come with me, and lead a spare horse by the bridle. I will have the two archers who rode with us through France, for they are trusty men and of stout heart. Let them ride behind us, and let them leave their bows here among the bushes, for it is not my wish that they should know that we are Englishmen. Say no word to any whom we may meet, and, if any speak to you, pass on as though you heard them not. Are you ready?"

"I am ready, my fair lord," said Alleyne.

"And I," "And I," cried Aylward and John.

"Then the rest I leave to your wisdom, Sir William; and if God sends us fortune we shall meet you again in this gorge ere it be dark."

So saying, Sir Nigel mounted the white horse of the Spanish cavalier, and rode quietly forth from his concealment with his three companions behind him, Alleyne leading his master's own steed by the bridle. So many small parties of French and Spanish horse were sweeping hither and thither that the small band attracted little notice, and making its way at a gentle trot across the plain, they came as far as the camp without challenge or hindrance. On and on they pushed past the endless lines of tents, amid the dense swarms of horsemen and of footmen, until the huge royal pavilion stretched in front of them. They were close upon it when of a sudden there broke out a wild hubbub from a distant portion of the camp, with screams and war-cries and all the wild tumult of battle. At the sound the soldiers came rushing from their tents, knights shouted loudly for their squires, and there was mad turmoil on every hand of bewildered men and plunging horses. At the royal tent a crowd of gorgeously dressed servants ran hither and thither in helpless panic, for the guard of soldiers who were stationed there had already ridden off in the direction of the alarm. A man-at-arms on either side of the doorway were the sole protectors of the royal dwelling.

"I have come for the king," whispered Sir Nigel; "and, by Saint Paul! he must back with us or I must bide here."

Alleyne and Aylward sprang from their horses and flew at the two sentries, who were disarmed and beaten down in an instant by so furious and unexpected an attack. Sir Nigel dashed into the royal tent, and was followed by Hordle John as soon as the horses had been secured. From within came wild screamings and the clash of steel, and then the two emerged once more, their swords and forearms reddened with blood, while John bore over his shoulder the senseless body of a man whose gay surcoat, adorned with the lions and towers of Castile, proclaimed him to belong to the royal house. A crowd of white-faced sewers and pages swarmed at their heels, those behind pushing forwards, while the foremost shrank back from the fierce faces and reeking weapons of the adventurers. The senseless body was thrown across the spare horse, the four sprang to their saddles, and away they thundered with loose reins and busy spurs through the swarming camp.

But confusion and disorder still reigned among the Spaniards, for Sir William Felton and his men had swept through half their camp, leaving a long litter of the dead and the dying to mark their course. Uncertain who were their attackers, and unable to tell their English armies from their newly arrived Breton allies, the Spanish knights rode wildly hither and thither in aimless fury. The mad turmoil, the mixture of races, and the fading light, were all in favour of the four who alone knew their own purpose among the vast uncertain multitude. Twice ere they reached open ground they had to break their way through small bodies of horse, and once there came a whistle of arrows and singing of stones about their ears; but, still dashing onwards, they shot out from among the tents and found their own comrades retreating for the mountains at no very great distance from them. Another five minutes of wild galloping over the plain, and they were all back in their gorge, while their pursuers fell back before the rolling of drums and blare of trumpets, which seemed to proclaim that the whole army of the prince was about to emerge from the mountain passes.

"By my soul! Nigel," cried Sir Oliver, waving a great boiled ham over his head, "I have come by something which I may eat with my truffles! I had a hard fight for it, for there were three of them with their mouths open and the knives in their hands, all sitting agape round the table when I rushed in upon them. How say you, Sir William, will you not try the smack of the famed Spanish swine, though we have but the brook water to wash it down?"

"Later, Sir Oliver," answered the old soldier, wiping his grimed face. "We must further into the mountains ere we be in safety. But what have we here, Nigel?"

"It is a prisoner whom I have taken, and in sooth, as he came from the royal tent and wears the royal arms upon his jupon, I trust that he is the King of Spain."

"The King of Spain!" cried the companions, crowding round in amazement.

"Nay, Sir Nigel," said Felton, peering at the prisoner through the uncertain light. "I have twice seen Henry of Trastamare, and certes this man in no way resembles him."

"Then, by the light of heaven! I will ride back for him," cried Sir Nigel.

"Nay, nay, the camp is in arms, and it would be rank madness. Who are you, fellow?" he added in Spanish, "and how is it that you dare to wear the arms of Castile?"

The prisoner was but recovering the consciousness which had been squeezed from him by the grip of Hordle John. "If it please you," he answered, "I and nine others are the body-squires of the

King, and must ever wear his arms, so as to shield him from even such perils as have threatened him this night. The king is at the tent of the brave Du Guesclin, where he will sup tonight. But I am a caballero of Aragon, Don Sancho Penelosa, and, though I be no king, I am yet ready to pay a fitting price for my ransom."

"By Saint Paul! I will not touch your gold," cried Sir Nigel. "Go back to your master and give him greeting from Sir Nigel Loring of Twynham Castle, telling him that I had hoped to make his better acquaintance this night, and that, if I have disordered his tent, it was but in my eagerness to know so famed and courteous a knight. Spur on, comrades! for we must cover many a league ere we can venture to light fire or to loosen girth. I had hoped to ride without this patch tonight, but it seems that I must carry it yet a little longer."

CHAPTER XXXVI

HOW SIR NIGEL TOOK THE PATCH
FROM HIS EYE

IT was a cold bleak morning in the beginning of March, and the mist was drifting in dense rolling clouds through the passes of the Cantabrian mountains. The Company, who had passed the night in a sheltered gully, were already astir, some crowding round the blazing fires and others romping or leaping over each other's backs, for their limbs were chilled and the air biting. Here and there, through the dense haze which surrounded them, there loomed out huge pinnacles and jutting boulders of rock; while high above the sea of vapour there towered up one gigantic peak, with the pink glow of the early sunshine upon its snow-capped head. The ground was wet, the rocks dripping, the grass and ever-greens sparkling with beads of moisture; yet the camp was loud with laughter and merriment, for a messenger had ridden in from the prince with words of heart-stirring praise for what they had done, and with orders that they should still bide in the fore-front of the enemy.

Round one of the fires were clustered four or five of the lead-ing men of the archers, cleaning the rust from their weapons and glancing impatiently from time to time at a great pot which smoked over the blaze. There was Aylward squatting cross-legged in his shirt, while he scrubbed away at his chain-mail brigandine, whistling loudly the while. On one side of him sat old Johnston, who was busy in trimming the feathers of some arrows to his liking; and on the other Hordle John, who lay with his great limbs all asprawl, and his headpiece balanced upon his uplifted foot. Black Simon of Norwich crouched amid the rocks, crooning an Eastland ballad to himself, while he whetted his sword upon a flat stone which lay across his knee; while beside him sat Alleyne Edricson, and Norbury, the silent squire of Sir Oliver, holding out their chilled hands towards the crackling faggots.

"Cast on another culpon, John, and stir the broth with thy sword-sheath," growled Johnston, looking anxiously for the twentieth time at the reeking pot.

"By my hilt!" cried Aylward, "now that John hath come by this great ransom, he will scarce abide the fare of poor archer lads. How say you, camarade? When you see Hordle once more, there will be no penny ale and fat bacon, but Gascon wines and baked meats every day of the seven."

"I know not about that," said John, kicking his helmet up into the air and catching it in his hand. "I do but know that whether the broth be ready or no, I am about to dip this into it."

"It simmers and it boils," cried Johnston, pushing his hard-lined face through the smoke. In an instant the pot had been plucked from the blaze, and its contents had been scooped up in half a dozen steel headpieces which were balanced betwixt their owners' knees, while, with spoon and with gobbet of bread, they devoured their morning meal.

"It is ill weather for bows," remarked John at last, when, with a long sigh, he had drained the last drop from his helmet. "My strings are as limp as a cow's tail this morning."

"You should rub them with water glue," quoth Johnston. "You remember, Samkin, that it was wetter than this on the morning of Crécy, and yet I cannot call to mind that there was aught amiss with our strings."

"It is in my thoughts," said Black Simon, still pensively grinding his sword, "that we may have need of your strings ere sundown. I dreamed of the red cow last night."

"And what is this red cow, Simon?" asked Alleyne.

"I know not, young sir; but I can only say that on the eve of Cadsand, and on the eve of Crécy, and on the eve of Nogent, I dreamed of a red cow; and now the dream has come upon me again, so I am now setting a very keen edge to my blade."

"Well said, old war-dog!" cried Aylward. "By my hilt I pray that your dream may come true, for the prince hath not set us out here to drink broth or to gather whortle-berries. One more fight, and I am ready to hang up my bow, marry a wife, and take to the fire corner. But how now, Robin? Whom is it that you seek?"

"The Lord Loring craves your attendance in his tent," said a young archer to Alleyne.

The squire rose and proceeded to the pavilion, where he found the knight seated upon a cushion, with his legs crossed in front of him and a broad ribbon of parchment laid across his knees, over which he was poring with frowning brows and pursed lips.

"It came this morning by the prince's messenger," said he, "and was brought from England by Sir John Fallislee, who is new come from Sussex. What make you of this upon the outer side?"

"It is fairly and clearly written," Alleyne answered, "and it signifies 'To Sir Nigel Loring, Knight, Constable of Twynham Castle, by the hand of Christopher, the servant of God at the priory of Christchurch'."

"So I read it," said Sir Nigel. "Now I pray you to read what is set forth within."

Alleyne turned to the letter, and, as his eyes rested upon it, his face turned pale, and a cry of surprise and grief burst from his lips.

"What then?" asked the knight, peering at him anxiously. "There is nought amiss with the Lady Mary or with the Lady Maude?"

"It is my brother—my poor unhappy brother!" cried Alleyne, with his hand to his brow. "He is dead."

"By Saint Paul! I have never heard that he had shown so much love for you that you should mourn him so."

"Yet he was my brother—the only kith and kin that I had upon earth. Maybe he had cause to be bitter against me, for his land was given to the Abbey for my upbringing. Alas! alas! and I raised my staff against him when last we met! he has been slain—and slain, I fear, amidst crime and violence."

"Ha!" said Sir Nigel. "Read on, I pray you."

"God be with thee, my honoured lord, and have thee in His holy keeping. The Lady Loring hath asked me to set down in writing what hath befallen at Twynham, and all that concerns the death of thy ill neighbour, the Socman of Minstead. For when ye had left us, this evil man gathered around him all outlaws, villeins, and masterless men, until they were come to such a force that they slew and scattered the king's men who went against them. Then, coming forth from the woods, they laid seige to thy castle, and for two days they girt us in and shot hard against us, with such numbers as were a marvel to see. Yet the Lady Loring held the place stoutly, and on the second day the Socman was slain—by his own men, as some think—so that we were delivered from their hands; for which praise be to all the saints, and more especially to the holy Anselm, upon whose feast it came to pass. The Lady Loring, and the Lady Maude, thy fair daughter, are in good health; and so also am I, save for an imposthume of the toe-joint, which hath been sent me for my sins. May all the saints preserve thee!"

"It was the vision of the Lady Tiphaine," said Sir Nigel after a pause. "Marked you not how she said that the leader was one with a yellow beard, and how he fell before the gate? But how came it, Alleyne, that this woman, to whom all things are as crystal, and who hath not said one word which has not come to pass, was yet so led astray as to say that your thoughts turned to Twynham Castle even more than mine own?"

"My fair lord," said Alleyne, with a flush on his weather-stained cheeks, "the Lady Tiphaine may have spoken sooth when she said it; for Twynham Castle is in my heart by day and in my dreams by night."

"Ha!" cried Sir Nigel, with a sidelong glance.

"Yes, my fair lord; for, indeed, I love your daughter, the Lady Maude; and, unworthy as I am, I would yet give my heart's blood to serve her."

"By Saint Paul! Edricson," said the knight coldly, arching his eyebrows, "you aim high in this matter. Our blood is very old."

"And mine also is very old," answered the squire.

"And the Lady Maude is our single child. All our name and lands centre upon her."

"Alas! that I should say it, but I also am now the only Edricson."

"And why have I not heard this from you before, Alleyne? In sooth, I think that you have used me ill."

"Nay, my fair lord, say not so; for I know not whether your daughter loves me, and there is no pledge between us."

Sir Nigel pondered for a few moments, and then burst out a-laughing. "By Saint Paul!" said he, "I know not why I should mix in the matter, for I have ever found that the Lady Maude was very well able to look after her own affairs. Since first she could stamp her little foot, she hath ever been able to get that for which she craved; and if she set her heart on thee, Alleyne, and thou on her, I do not think that this Spanish king, with his threescore thousand men, could hold you apart. Yet this I will say, that I would see you a full knight ere you go to my daughter with words of love, I have ever said that a brave lance should wed her; and, by my soul! Edricson, if God spare you, I think that you will acquit yourself well. But enough of such trifles, for we have our work before us, and it will be time to speak of this matter when we see the white cliffs of England once more. Go to Sir William Felton, I pray you, and ask him to come hither, for it is time that we were marching. There is no pass at the further end of the valley, and it is a perilous place should an enemy come upon us."

Alleyn delivered his message, and then wandered forth from the camp, for his mind was in a whirl with this unexpected news, and with his talk with Sir Nigel. Sitting upon a rock, with his burning brow resting upon his hands, he thought of his brother, of their quarrel, of the Lady Maude in her bedraggled riding-dress, of the grey old castle, of the proud pale face in the armoury, and of the last fiery words with which she had sped him on his way.

Then he was but a penniless monk-bred lad, unknown and unfriended. Now he was himself Socman of Minstead, the head of an old stock, and the lord of an estate which, if reduced from its former size, was still ample to preserve the dignity of his family. Further, he had become a man of experience, was counted brave among brave men, had won the esteem and confidence of her father, and above all, had been listened to by him when he told him the secret of his love. As to the gaining of knighthood, in such stirring times it was no great matter for a brave squire of gentle birth to aspire to that honour. He would leave his bones among these Spanish ravines, or he would do some deed which would call the eyes of men upon him.

Alleyne was still seated on the rock, his griefs and his joys drifting swiftly over his mind like the shadow of clouds upon a sunlit meadow, when of a sudden he became conscious of a low, deep sound which came booming up to him through the fog. Close behind him he could hear the murmur of the bowmen, the occasional burst of hoarse laughter, and the champing and stamping of their horses. Behind it all, however, came that low-pitched deep-toned hum, which seemed to come from every quarter and to fill the whole air. In the old monastic days he remembered to have heard such a sound when he walked out one windy night at Bucklershard, and had listened to the long waves breaking upon the shingly shore. Here, however, was neither wind nor sea, and yet the dull murmur rose ever louder and stronger out of the heart of the rolling sea of vapour. He turned and ran to the camp, shouting an alarm at the top of his voice.

It was but a hundred paces, and yet ere he had crossed it every bowman was ready at his horse's head, and the group of knights were out and listening intently to the ominous sound.

"It is a great body of horse," said Sir William Felton, "and they are riding very swiftly hitherwards."

"Yet they must be from the prince's army," remarked Sir Richard Causton, "for they come from the north."

"Nay," said the Earl of Angus, "it is not so certain; for the peasant with whom we spoke last night said that it was rumoured that Don Tello, the Spanish king's brother, had ridden with six thousand chosen men to beat up the prince's camp. It may be that on their backward road they have come this way."

"By Saint Paul!" cried Sir Nigel, "I think that it is even as you say, for that same peasant had a sour face and a shifting eye, as one who bore us little goodwill. I doubt not that he has brought these cavaliers upon us."

"But the mist covers us," said Sir Simon Burley. "We have yet time to ride through the further end of the pass."

"Were we a troop of mountain goats we might do so," answered Sir William Felton, "but it is not to be passed by a company of horsemen. If these be indeed Don Tello and his men, then we must bide where we are, and do what we may to make them rue the day that they found us in their path."

"Well spoken, William!" cried Sir Nigel, in high delight. "If there be so many as has been said, then there will be much honour to be gained from them and every hope of advancement. But the sound has ceased, and I fear that they have gone some other way."

"Or mayhap they have come to the mouth of the gorge, and are marshalling their ranks. Hush and hearken! for they are no great way from us."

The Company stood peering into the dense fog-wreath amidst a silence so profound that the dripping of the water from the rocks and the breathing of the horses grew loud upon the ear. Suddenly from out of the sea of mist came the shrill sound of a neigh, followed by a long blast upon a bugle.

"It is a Spanish call, my fair lord," said Black Simon. "It is used by their prickers and huntsmen when the beast hath not fled, but is still in its lair."

"By my faith," said Sir Nigel, smiling, "if they are in a humour for venerie we may promise them some sport ere they sound the mort over us. But there is a hill in the centre of the gorge on which we might make our stand."

"I marked it yester-night," said Felton, "and no better spot could be found for our purpose, for it is very steep at the back. It is but a bowshot to the left, and, indeed, I can see the shadow of it."

The whole Company, leading their horses, passed across to the small hill which loomed in front of them out of the mist. It was, indeed, admirably designed for defence, for it sloped down in front, all jagged and boulder-strewn, while it fell away behind in a sheer cliff of a hundred feet or more. On the summit was a small, uneven plateau, with a stretch across of a hundred paces, and a depth of half as much again.

"Unloose the horses!" said Sir Nigel. "We, have no space for them, and if we hold our own we shall have horses and to spare when this day's work is done. Nay, keep yours, my fair sirs, for we may have work for them. Aylward, Johnston, let your men form a harrow on either side of the ridge. Sir Oliver and you, my Lord Angus, I give you the right wing, and the left to you, Sir Simon, and to you Sir Richard Causton. I and Sir William Felton will hold the centre with our men-at-arms. Now order the ranks, and fling wide the banners, for our souls are God's and our bodies the king's and our swords for Saint George and for England!"

Sir Nigel had scarcely spoken when the mist seemed to thin in the valley, and to shred away into long ragged clouds which trailed from the edges of the cliffs. The gorge in which they had camped was a mere wedge-shaped cleft among the hills, three-quarters of a mile deep, with a small rugged rising upon which they stood at the further end, and the brown crags walling it in on three sides. As the mist parted and the sun broke through, it gleamed and shimmered with dazzling brightness upon the armour and head-pieces of a vast body of horsemen who stretched across the barranca from one cliff to the other, and extended backwards until their rearguard were far out upon the plain beyond. Line after line, and rank after rank, they choked the neck of the valley with a long vista of tossing pennons, twinkling lances, waving plumes and streaming banderoles, while the curvets and gambades of the chargers lent a constant motion and shimmer to the glittering many-coloured mass. A yell of exultation, and a forest of waving steel through the length and breadth of their column, announced that they could at last see their entrapped enemies, while the swelling notes of a hundred bugles and drums, mixed with the clash of Moorish cymbals, broke forth into a proud peal of martial triumph. Strange it was to these gallant and sparkling cavaliers of Spain to look upon this handful of men upon the hill, the thin lines of bowmen, the knot of knights and men-at-arms with armour rusted and discoloured from long service, and to learn that these were indeed the soldiers whose fame and prowess had been the camp-fire talk of every army in Christendom. Very still and silent they stood, leaning upon their bows, while their leaders took counsel together in front of them. No clang of bugle rose from their stern ranks, but in the centre waved the leopards of England, on the right the ensign of the Company with the roses of Loring, and on the left, over three-score of Welsh bowmen, there floated the red banner of Merlin with the boars'-heads of the Buttesthorns. Gravely and sedately they stood beneath the morning sun waiting for the onslaught of their foemen.

"By Saint Paul!" said Sir Nigel, gazing with puckered eye down the valley, "there appear to be some worthy people among them. What is this golden banner which waves upon the left?"

"It is the ensign of the Knights of Calatrava," answered Felton.

"And the other upon the right?"

"It marks the Knights of Santiago, and I see by his flag that their grand-master rides at their head. There, too, is the banner of Castile amid yonder sparkling squadron which heads the main battle. There are six thousand men-at-arms with ten squadrons of slingers, as far as I may judge their numbers."

"There are Frenchmen among them, my fair lord," remarked Black Simon. "I can see the pennons of De Couvette, De Brieux, Saint Pol, and many others who struck in against us for Charles of Blois."

"You are right," said Sir William, "for I can also see them. There is much Spanish blazonry also, if I could but read it. Don Diego, you know the arms of your own land. Who are they who have done us this honour?"

The Spanish prisoner looked with exultant eyes upon the deep and serried ranks of his countrymen.

"By Saint James!" said he, "if ye fall this day ye fall by no mean hands, for the flower of the knighthood of Castile ride under the banner of Don Tello, with the chivalry of Asturias, Toledo, Leon, Cordova, Galicia, and Seville. I see the guidons of Albornez, Caçorla, Rodriguez, Tavora, with the two great orders, and the knights of France and of Aragon. If you will take my rede you will come to a composition with them, for they will give you such terms as you have given me."

"Nay, by Saint Paul! it were pity if so many brave men were drawn together, and no little deed of arms to come of it. Ha! William, they advance upon us; and, by my soul! it is a sight that is worth coming over the seas to see."

As he spoke, the two wings of the Spanish host, consisting of the Knights of Calatrava on the one side and of Santiago upon the other, came swooping swiftly down the valley, while the main body followed more slowly behind. Five hundred paces from the English the two great bodies of horse crossed each other, and sweeping round in a curve, retired in feigned confusion towards their centre. Often in bygone wars had the Moors tempted the hot-blooded Spaniards from their places of strength by such pretended flights, but there were men upon the hill to whom every ruse and trick of war were as their daily trade and practice. Again and ever nearer came the rallying Spaniards, and again with cry of fear and stooping bodies they swerved off to right and left, but the English still stood stolid and observant among their rocks. The vanguard halted a long bow-shot from the hill, and with waving spears and vaunting shouts challenged their enemies to come forth, while two cavaliers, pricking forward from the glittering ranks, walked their horses slowly between the two arrays with targets braced and lances in rest like the challengers in a tourney.

"By Saint Paul!" cried Sir Nigel, with his one eye glowing like an ember, "these appear to be two very worthy and debonair gentlemen. I do not call to mind when I have seen any people who seemed of so great a heart and so high of enterprise. We have our horses, Sir William: shall we not relieve them of any vow which they might have upon their souls?"

Felton's reply was to bound upon his charger, and to urge it down the slope, while Sir Nigel followed not three spears' lengths behind him. It was a rugged course, rocky and uneven; yet the two knights, choosing their men, dashed onwards at the top of their speed, while the gallant Spaniards flew as swiftly to meet them. The one to whom Felton found himself opposed was a tall stripling with a stag's head upon his shield, while Sir Nigel's man was broad and squat, with plain steel harness, and a pink and white torse bound round his helmet. The first struck Felton on the target with such force as to split it from side to side, but Sir William's lance Crashed through the camail which shielded the Spaniard's throat, and he fell, screaming hoarsely, to the ground. Carried away by the heat and madness of fight, the English knight never drew rein, but charged straight on into the array of the Knights of Calatrava. Long time the silent ranks upon the hill could see a swirl and eddy deep down in the heart of the Spanish column, with a circle of rearing chargers and flashing blades. Here and there tossed the white plume of the English helmet, rising and falling like the foam upon a wave, with the fierce gleam and sparkle ever circling round it, until at last it had sunk from view, and another brave man had turned from war to peace.

Sir Nigel, meanwhile, had found a foeman worthy of his steel, for his opponent was none other than Sebastian Gomez, the picked lance of the monkish Knights of Santiago, who had won fame in a hundred bloody combats with the Moors of Andalusia. So fierce was their meeting that their spears shivered up to the very grasp, and the horses reared backwards until it seemed that they must crash down upon their riders. Yet with consummate horsemanship they both swung round in a long curvet, and then, plucking out their swords, they lashed at each other like two lusty smiths hammering upon an anvil. The chargers spun round each other, biting and striking, while the two blades wheeled and whizzled and circled in gleams of dazzling light. Cut, parry, and thrust followed so quickly upon each other that the eye could not follow them, until at last, coming thigh to thigh, they cast their arms round each other and rolled off their saddles to the ground. The heavier Spaniard threw himself upon his enemy, and pinning him down beneath him raised his sword to slay him, while a shout of triumph rose from the ranks of his countrymen. But the fatal blow never fell, for even as his arm quivered before descending, the Spaniard gave a shudder, and stiffening himself rolled heavily over upon his side, with the blood gushing from his armpit and from the slit of his vizor. Sir Nigel sprang to his feet with his bloody dagger in his left hand and gazed down upon his adversary, but that fatal and sudden stab in the vital spot, which the Spaniard had exposed by raising his arm, had proved instantly mortal. The Englishman leaped upon his horse and made for the hill, at the very instant that a yell of rage from a thousand voices and the clang of a score of bugles announced the Spanish onset.

But the islanders were ready and eager for the encounter. With feet firmly planted, their sleeves rolled back to give free play to their muscles, their long yellow bow-staves in their left hands, and their quivers slung to the front, they had waited in the four-deep harrow formation which gave strength to their array; and yet permitted every man to draw his arrow freely without harm to those in front. Aylward and Johnston had been engaged in throwing light tufts of grass into the air to gauge the wind force, and a hoarse whisper passed down the ranks from the file-leaders to the men, with scraps of advice and admonition.

"Do not shoot outside the fifteen-score paces," cried Johnston. "We may need all our shafts ere we have done with them."

"Better to overshoot than to undershoot," added Aylward. "Better to strike the rearguard than to feather a shaft in the earth."

"Loose quick and sharp when they come," added another. "Let it be the eye to the string, the string to the shaft, and the shaft to the mark. By Our Lady! their banners advance, and we must hold our ground now if ever we are to see Southampton Water again."

Alleyne, standing with his sword drawn amidst the archers, saw a long toss and heave of the glittering squadrons. Then the front ranks began to surge slowly forward, to trot, to canter, to gallop, and in an instant the whole vast array was hurtling onward, line after line, the air full of the thunder of their cries, the ground shaking with the beat of their hoofs, the valley choked with the rushing torrent of steel, topped by the waving plumes, the slanting spears and the fluttering banderoles. On they swept over the level and up to the slope, ere they met the blinding storm of the English arrows. Down went whole ranks in a whirl of mad confusion, horses plunging and kicking, bewildered men falling, rising, staggering on or back, while ever new lines of horsemen came spurring through the gaps and urged their chargers up the fatal slope. All around him Alleyne could hear the stern short orders of the master-bowmen, while the air was filled with the keen twanging of the strings and the swish and patter of the shafts. Right across the foot of the hill there had sprung up a long wall of struggling horses and stricken men, which ever grew and heightened as fresh squadrons poured on the attack. One young knight on a grey jennet leaped over his fallen comrades and galloped swiftly up the hill, shrieking loudly upon Saint James, ere he fell within a spear-length of the English line, with the feathers of arrows thrusting out from every crevice and joint of his armour. So for five long minutes the gallant horsemen of Spain and France strove ever and again to force a passage until the wailing note of a bugle called them back, and they rode slowly out of bow-shot, leaving their best and their bravest in the ghastly blood-mottled heap behind them.

But there was little rest for the victors. Whilst the knights had charged them in front the slingers had crept round upon either flank and had gained a footing upon the cliffs and behind the outlying rocks. A storm of stones broke suddenly upon the defenders, who, drawn up in lines upon the exposed summit, offered a fair mark to their hidden foes. Johnston, the old archer, was struck upon the temple and fell dead without a groan, while fifteen of his bowmen and six of the men-at-arms were struck down at the same moment. The others lay on their faces to avoid the deadly hail, while at each side of the plateau a fringe of bowmen exchanged shots with the slingers and cross-bowmen among the rocks, aiming mainly at those who had swarmed up the cliffs, and bursting into laughter and cheers when a well-aimed shaft brought one of their opponents toppling down from his lofty perch.

"I think, Nigel," said Sir Oliver, striding across to the little knight, "that we should all acquit ourselves better had we our none-meat, for the sun is high in the heaven."

"By Saint Paul!" quoth Sir Nigel, plucking the patch from his eye, "I think that I am now clear of my vow, for this Spanish knight was a person from whom much honour might be won. Indeed he was a very worthy gentleman, of good courage, and great hardiness, and it grieves me that he should have come by such a hurt. As to what you say of food, Oliver, it is not to be thought of, for we have nothing with us upon the hill."

"Nigel!" cried Sir Simon Burley, hurrying up with consternation upon his face. "Aylward tells me that there are not ten-score arrows left in all their sheaves. See they are springing from their horses, and cutting their sollerets that they may rush upon us. Might we not even now make a retreat?"

"My soul will retreat from my body first!" cried the little knight. "Here I am, and here I abide, while God gives me strength to lift a sword."

"And so say I!" shouted Sir Oliver, throwing his mace high into the air and catching it again by the handle.

"To your arms, men!" roared Sir Nigel. "Shoot while you may, and then out sword, and let us live or die together!"

CHAPTER XXXVII

HOW THE WHITE COMPANY
CAME TO BE DISBANDED

THEN up rose from the hill in the rugged Cantabrian valley a sound such as had not been heard in those parts before, nor was again, until the streams which rippled amid the rocks had been frozen over four hundred winters and thawed by as many returning springs. Deep and full and strong it thundered down the ravine, the fierce battle-call of a warrior race, the last stern welcome to who so should join with them in that world-old game where the stake is death. Thrice it swelled forth and thrice it sank away, echoing and reverberating amidst the crags. Then, with set faces, the Company rose up among the storm of stones, and looked down upon the thousands who sped swiftly up the slope against them. Horse and spear had been set aside, but on foot, with sword and battle-axe, their broad shields slung in front of them, the chivalry of Spain rushed to the attack.

And now arose a struggle so fell, so long, so evenly sustained, that even now the memory of it is handed down amongst the Cantabrian mountaineers, and the ill-omened knoll is still pointed out by fathers to their children as the "Altura de los Ingleses," where the men from across the sea fought the great fight with the knights of the south. The last arrow was quickly shot, nor could the slingers hurl their stones, so close were friend and foe. From side to side stretched the thin line of the English, lightly armed and quick-footed, while against it stormed and raged the pressing throng of fiery Spaniards and of gallant Bretons. The clink of crossing sword-blades, the dull thudding of heavy blows, the panting and gasping of weary and wounded men, all rose together in a wild long-drawn note, which swelled upwards to the ears of the wondering peasants who looked down from the edges of the cliffs upon the swaying turmoil of the battle beneath them. Back and forward reeled the leopard banner, now borne up the slope by the rush and weight of the onslaught, now pushing downwards again as Nigel, Burley, and Black Simon, with their veteran men-at-arms flung themselves madly into the fray. Alleyne, at his lord's right hand, found himself swept hither and thither in the desperate struggle, exchanging savage thrusts one instant with a Spanish cavalier, and the next torn away by the whirl of men and dashed up against some new antagonist. To the right Sir Oliver, Aylward, Hordle John, and the bowmen of the Company fought furiously against the monkish Knights of Santiago, who were led up the hill by their prior—a great deep-chested man, who wore a brown monastic habit over his suit of mail. Three archers he slew in three giant strokes, but Sir Oliver flung his arms round him, and the two staggering and straining, reeled backwards and fell, locked in each other's grasp, over the edge of the steep cliff which flanked the hill. In vain his knights stormed and raved against the thin line which barred their path; the sword of Aylward and the great axe of John gleamed in the forefront of the battle, and the huge jagged pieces of rock hurled by the strong arms of the bowmen, crashed and hurtled amid their ranks. Slowly they gave back down the hill, the archers still hanging upon their skirts, with a long litter of writhing and twisted figures to mark the course which they had taken. At the same instant the Welshmen upon the left, led on by the Scotch earl, had charged out from among the rocks which sheltered them, and by the fury of their outfall had driven the Spaniards in front of them in headlong flight down the hill. In the centre only things seemed to be going ill with the defenders. Black Simon was down—dying, as he would wish to have died, like a grim old wolf in its lair—with a ring of his slain around him. Twice

Sir Nigel had been overborne, and twice Alleyne had fought over him until he had staggered to his feet once more. Burley lay senseless, stunned by a blow from a mace, and half of the men-at-arms lay littered upon the ground around him. Sir Nigel's shield was broken, his crest shorn, his armour cut and smashed, and the vizor torn from his helmet; yet he sprang hither and thither with light foot and ready hand, engaging two Bretons and a Spaniard at the same instant—thrusting, stooping, dashing in, springing out —while Alleyne still fought by his side, stemming with a handful of men the fierce tide which surged up against them. Yet it would have fared ill with them had not the archers from either side closed in upon the flanks of the attackers, and pressed them very slowly and foot by foot down the long slope, until they were on the plain once more, where their fellows were already rallying for a fresh assault.

But terrible indeed was the cost at which the last had been repelled. Of the three hundred and seventy men who had held the crest, one hundred and seventy-two were left standing, many of whom were sorely wounded and weak from loss of blood. Sir Oliver Buttesthorn, Sir Richard Causton, Sir Simon Burley, Black Simon, Johnston, a hundred and fifty archers and forty-seven men-at-arms had fallen, while the pitiless hail of stones was already whizzing and piping once more about their ears, threatening every instant to further reduce their numbers.

Sir Nigel looked about him at his shattered ranks, and his face flushed with a soldier's pride.

"By Saint Paul!" he cried, "I have fought in many a little bickering, but never one that I would be more loth to have missed than this. But you are wounded, Alleyne?"

"It is naught," answered his squire, staunching the blood which dripped from a sword-cut across his forehead.

"These gentlemen of Spain seem to be most courteous and worthy people. I see that they are already forming to continue this debate with us. Form up the bowmen two deep instead of four. By my faith! some very brave men have gone from among us.

Aylward, you are a trusty soldier, for all that your shoulder has never felt accolade, nor your heels worn the gold spurs. Do you take charge of the right; I will hold the centre, and you, my Lord of Angus, the left."

"Ho! for Sir Samkin Aylward," cried a rough voice among the archers, and a roar of laughter greeted their new leader.

"By my hilt!" said the old bowman, "I never thought to lead a wing in a stricken field. Stand close, camarades, for, by these finger-bones! we must play the man this day."

"Come hither, Alleyne," said Sir Nigel, walking back to the edge of the cliff which formed the rear of their position. "And you, Norbury," he continued, beckoning to the squire of Sir Oliver, "do you also come here."

The two squires hurried across to him, and the three stood looking down into the rocky ravine which lay a hundred and fifty feet beneath them.

"The prince must hear of how things are with us," said the knight. "Another onfall we may withstand, but they are many and we are few, so that the time must come when we can no longer form line across the hill. Yet if help were brought us we might hold the crest until it comes. See yonder horses which stray among the rocks beneath us?"

"I see them, my fair lord."

"And see yonder path which winds along the hill upon the further end of the valley?"

"I see it."

"Were you on those horses, and riding up yonder track, steep and rough as it is, I think that you might gain the valley beyond. Then on to the prince, and tell him how we fare."

"But, my fair lord, how can we hope to reach the horses?" asked Norbury.

"Ye cannot go round to them, for they would be upon ye ere ye could come to them. Think ye that ye have heart enough to clamber down this cliff?"

"Had we but a rope."

"There is one here. It is but one hundred feet long, and for the rest ye must trust to God and to your fingers. Can you try it, Alleyne?"

"With all my heart, my dear lord, but how can I leave you in such a strait?"

"Nay, it is to serve me that ye go. And you, Norbury?"

The silent squire said nothing, but he took up the rope, and, having examined it, he tied one end firmly round a projecting rock. Then he cast off his breastplate, thighpieces, and greaves, while Alleyne followed his example.

"Tell Chandos, or Calverley, or Knolles, should the prince have gone forward," cried Sir Nigel. "Now may God speed ye, for ye are brave and worthy men."

It was, indeed, a task which might make the heart of the bravest sink within him. The thin cord, dangling down the face of the brown cliff, seemed from above to reach little more than halfway down it. Beyond stretched the rugged rock, wet and shiny with a green tuft here and there thrusting out from it, but little sign of ridge or foothold. Far below the jagged points of the boulders bristled up, dark and menacing. Norbury tugged thrice with all his strength upon the cord, and then lowered himself over the edge, while a hundred anxious faces peered over at him as he slowly clambered downwards to the end of the rope. Twice he stretched out his foot, and twice he failed to reach the point at which he aimed, but even as he swung himself for a third effort a stone from a sling buzzed like a wasp from amid the rocks and struck him full upon the side of his head. His grasp relaxed, his feet slipped, and in an instant he was a crushed and mangled corpse upon the sharp ridges beneath him.

"If I have no better fortune," said Alleyne, leading Sir Nigel aside, "I pray you, my dear lord, that you will give my humble service to the Lady Maude, and say to her that I was ever her true servant and most unworthy cavalier."

The old knight said no word, but he put a hand on either shoulder and kissed his squire, with the tears shining in his eyes. Alleyne sprang to the rope, and sliding swiftly down, soon found himself at its extremity. From above it seemed as though rope and cliff were well-nigh touching, but now, when swinging a hundred feet down, the squire found that he could scarce reach the face of the rock with his foot, and that it was as smooth as glass, with no resting place where a mouse could stand. Some three feet lower, however, his eye lit on a long jagged crack which slanted downwards, and this he must reach if he would save not only his own poor life but that of the eight score men above him. Yet it were madness to spring for that narrow slit with nought but the wet smooth rock to cling to. He swung for a moment, full of thought, and even as he hung there another of the hellish stones sang through his curls, and struck a chip from the face of the cliff. Up he clambered a few feet, drew up the loose end after him, unslung his belt, held on with knee and with elbow while he spliced the long tough leathern belt to the end of the cord; then lowering himself as far as he could go, he swung backwards and forwards until his hand reached the crack, when he left the rope and clung to the face of the cliff. Another stone struck him on the side, and he heard a sound like a breaking stick, with a keen stabbing pain which shot through his chest. Yet it was no time now to think of pain or ache. There was his lord and his eight score comrades, and they must be plucked from the jaws of death. On he clambered, with his hands shuffling down the long sloping crack, sometimes bearing all his weight upon his arms, at others finding some small shelf or tuft on which to rest his foot. Would he never pass over that fifty feet? He dared not look down, and could but grope slowly onwards, his face to the cliff, his fingers clutching, his feet scraping and feeling for a support. Every vein and crack and mottling of that face of rock remained for ever stamped upon his memory. At last, however, his foot came upon a broad resting-place, and he ventured to cast a glance downwards. Thank God! he had reached the highest of those fatal pinnacles upon which his comrade had fallen. Quickly now he sprang from rock to rock until his feet were on the ground, and he had his hand stretched out for the horse's rein, when a sling-stone struck him on the head, and he dropped senseless upon the ground.

An evil blow it was for Alleyne, but a worse one still for him who struck it. The Spanish slinger, seeing the youth lie slain, and judging from his dress that he was no common man, rushed forward to plunder him, knowing well that the bowmen above him had expended their last shaft. He was still three paces, however, from his victim's side when John upon the cliff above plucked up a huge boulder, and, poising it for an instant, dropped it with fatal aim upon the slinger beneath him. It struck upon his shoulder, and hurled him crushed and screaming, to the ground, while Alleyne, recalled to his senses by these shrill cries in his very ear, staggered on to his feet, and gazed wildly about him. His eyes fell upon the horses grazing upon the scanty pasture, and in an instant all had come back to him—his mission, his comrades, the need for haste. He was dizzy, sick, faint, but he must not die, and he must not tarry, for his life meant many lives that day. In an instant he was in his saddle and spurring down the valley.

Loud rang the swift charger's hoofs over rock and reef, while the fire flew from the stroke of iron, and the loose stones showered up behind him. But his head was whirling round, the blood was gushing from his brow, his temple, his mouth. Ever keener and sharper was the deadly pain which shot like a red-hot arrow through his side. He felt that his eye was glazing, his senses slipping from him, his grasp upon the reins relaxing. Then, with one mighty effort, he called up all his strength for a single minute. Stooping down he loosened the stirrup-straps, bound his knees tightly to his saddle flaps, twisted his hands in the bridle, and then, putting the gallant horse's head for the mountain path, he dashed the spurs in and fell forward fainting, with his face buried in the coarse black mane.

Little could he ever remember of that wild ride. Half conscious, but ever with one thought beating in his mind, he goaded the horse onwards, rushing swiftly down steep ravines, over huge boulders, along the edges of black abysses. Dim memories he had of beetling cliffs, of a group of huts with wondering faces at the doors, of foaming, clattering water, and of a bristle of mountain beeches. Once, ere he had ridden far, he heard behind him three deep sullen shouts, which told him that his comrades had set their faces to the foe once more. Then all was blank, until he woke to find kindly blue English eyes peering down upon him and to hear the blessed sound of his country's speech.

They were but a foraging party—a hundred archers and as many men-at-arms—but their leader was Sir Hugh Calverley, and he was not a man to bide idle when good blows were to be had not three leagues from him. A scout was sent flying with a message to the camp, and Sir Hugh, with his two hundred men, thundered off to the rescue. With them went Alleyne, still bound to his saddle, still dripping with blood, and swooning and recovering, and swooning once again. On they rode, and on, until, at last, topping a ridge, they looked down upon the fateful-valley. Alas! and alas for the sight that met their eyes.

There, beneath them, was the blood-bathed hill, and from the highest pinnacle there flaunted the yellow and white banner with the lions and the towers of the royal house of Castile. Up the long slope rushed ranks and ranks of men—exultant, shouting, with waving pennons and brandished arms. Over the whole summit were dense throngs of knights, with no enemy that could be seen to face them, save only that at one corner of the plateau an eddy and swirl amid the crowded mass seemed to show that all resistance was not yet at an end. At the sight a deep groan of rage and of despair went up from the baffled rescuers, and, spurring on their horses, they clattered down the long and winding path which led to the valley beneath.

But they were too late to avenge, as they had been too late to save. Long ere they could gain the level ground, the Spaniards, seeing them riding swiftly amid the rocks, and being ignorant of their numbers, drew off from the captured hill, and, having secured their few prisoners, rode slowly in a long column, with drum-beating and cymbal-clashing, out of the valley. Their rear ranks were already passing out of sight ere the new-comers were urging their panting, foaming horses up the slope which had been the scene of that long-drawn and bloody fight.

And a fearsome sight it was that met their eyes! Across the lower end lay the dense heap of men and horses where the first arrow-storm had burst. Above, the bodies of the dead and the dying—French, Spanish, and Aragonese—lay thick and thicker, until they covered the whole ground two and three deep in one dreadful tangle of slaughter. Above them lay the Englishmen in their lines, even as they had stood, and higher yet upon the plateau, a wild medley of the dead of all nations, where the last deadly grapple had left them. In the further corner, under the shadow of a great rock, there crouched seven bowmen, with great John in the centre of them—all wounded, weary, and in sorry case, but still unconquered, with their bloodstained weapons waving and their voices ringing a welcome to their countrymen. Alleyne rode across to John, while Sir Hugh Calverley followed close behind him.

"By Saint George!" cried Sir Hugh, "I have never seen signs of so stern a fight, and I am right glad that we have been in time to save you."

"You have saved more than us," said John, pointing to the banner which leaned against the rock behind him.

"You have done nobly," cried the old Free Companion, gazing with a soldier's admiration at the huge frame and bold face of the archer. "But why is it, my good fellow, that you sit upon this man?"

"By the rood! I had forgot him," John answered, rising and dragging from under him no less a person than the Spanish caballero, Don Diego Alverez. "This man, my fair lord, means to me a new house, ten cows, one bull—if it be but a little one—a grindstone, and I know not what beside; so that I thought it well to sit upon him, lest he should take a fancy to leave me."

"Tell me, John," cried Alleyne, faintly, "where is my dear lord, Sir Nigel Loring?"

"He is dead, I fear. I saw them throw his body across a horse and ride away with it, but I fear the life had gone from him."

"Now woe worth me! And where is Aylward?"

"He sprang upon a riderless horse and rode after Sir Nigel to save him. I saw them throng around him, and he is either taken or slain."

"Blow the bugles!" cried Sir Hugh, with a scowling brow. "We must back to camp, and ere three days I trust that we may see these Spaniards again. I would fain have ye all in my company."

"We are of the White Company, my fair lord," said John.

"Nay, the White Company is here disbanded," answered Sir Hugh solemnly, looking round him at the lines of silent figures. "Look to the brave squire, for I fear that he will never see the sun rise again."

CHAPTER XXXVIII

OF THE HOME-COMING TO HAMPSHIRE

IT was a bright July morning four months after that fatal fight in
the Spanish barranca. A blue heaven stretched above, a green
rolling plain undulated below, intersected with hedgerows and
flecked with grazing sheep. The sun was yet low in the heaven, and
the red cows stood in the long shadow of the elms, chewing the
cud and gazing with great vacant eyes at two horsemen who were
spurring it down the long white road which dipped and curved
away back to where the towers and pinnacles beneath the flat-
topped hill marked the old town of Winchester.

Of the riders, one was young, graceful, and fair, clad in plain
doublet and hosen of blue Brussels cloth, which served to show
his active and well-knit figure. A flat velvet cap was drawn forward to keep the glare from his eyes, and he rode with lips compressed and anxious face, as one who has much care upon his
mind. Young as he was, and peaceful as was his dress, the dainty
golden spurs which twinkled upon his heels proclaimed his
knighthood, while a long seam upon his brow and a scar upon
his temple gave a manly grace to his refined and delicate countenance. His comrade was a large red-headed man upon a great
black horse, with a huge canvas bag slung from his saddle-bow,
which jingled and clinked with every movement of his steed. His
broad brown face was lighted up by a continual smile, and he
looked slowly from side to side with eyes which twinkled and

shone with delight. Well might John rejoice, for was he not back in his native Hampshire, had he not Don Diego's five thousand crowns rasping against his knee, and above all was he not himself squire now to Sir Alleyne Edricson, the young Socman of Minstead, lately knighted by the sword of the Black Prince himself, and esteemed by the whole army as one of the most rising of the soldiers of England?

For the last stand of the Company had been told throughout Christendom wherever a brave deed of arms was loved, and honours had flowed in upon the few who had survived it. For two months Alleyne had wavered betwixt death and life, with a broken rib and a shattered head, yet youth and strength and a cleanly life were all upon his side, and he awoke from his long delirium to find that the war was over, that the Spaniards and their allies had been crushed at Navaretta, and that the prince had himself heard the tale of his ride for succour, and had come in person to his bedside to touch his shoulder with his sword, and to ensure that so brave and true a man should die, if he could not live, within the order of chivalry. The instant that he could set foot to ground, Alleyne had started in search of his lord, but no word could he hear of him, dead or alive, and he had come home now sad-hearted in the hope of raising money upon his estates and so starting upon his quest once more. Landing at London he had hurried on with a mind full of care, for he had heard no word from Hampshire since the short note which had announced his brother's death.

"By the rood!" cried John, looking around him exultantly, "where have we seen since we left such noble cows, such fleecy sheep, grass so green, or a man so drunk as yonder rogue who lies in the gap of the hedge?"

"Ah, John," Alleyne answered wearily, "it is well for you, but I never thought that my home-coming would be so sad a one. My heart is heavy for my dear lord and for Aylward, and I know not how I may break the news to the Lady Mary and to the Lady Maude, if they have not yet had tidings of it."

John gave a groan which made the horses shy. "It is indeed a black business," said he. "But be not sad, for I shall give half these crowns to my old mother, and half I will add to the money which you may have, and so we shall buy that yellow cog wherein we sailed to Bordeaux, and in it we shall go forth and seek Sir Nigel."

Alleyne smiled, but shook his head. "Were he alive we should have had word of him ere now," said he. "But what is this town before us?"

"Why, it is Romsey!" cried John. "See the tower of the old grey church, and the long stretch of the nunnery. But here sits a very holy man, and I shall give him a crown for his prayers."

Three large stones formed a rough cot by the roadside and beside it, basking in the sun, sat the hermit, with clay-coloured face, dull eyes, and long withered hands. With crossed ankles and sunken head, he sat as though all his life had passed out of him, with the beads slipping slowly through his thin yellow fingers. Behind him lay the narrow cell, clay floored and damp, comfortless, profitless, and sordid. Beyond it there lay amid the trees the wattle-and-daub hut of a labourer, the door open, and the single room exposed to view. The man, ruddy and yellow-haired, stood leaning upon the spade wherewith he had been at work upon the garden patch. From behind him came the ripple of a happy woman's laughter, and two young urchins darted forth from the hut, bare-legged and towsy, while the mother, stepping out, laid her hand upon her husband's arm and watched the gambols of the children. The hermit frowned at the untoward noise which broke upon his prayers, but his brow relaxed as he looked upon the broad silver-piece which John held out to him.

"There lies the image of our past and of our future," cried Alleyne, as they rode on upon their way. "Now, which is better, to till God's earth, to have happy faces round one's knee, and to love and be loved, or to sit for ever moaning over one's soul, like a mother over a sick babe?"

"I know not about that," said John, "for it casts a great cloud over me when I think of such matters. But I know that my crown was well spent, for the man had the look of a very holy person. As to the other, there was naught holy about him that I could see, and it would be cheaper for me to pray for myself than to give a crown to one who spent his days in digging for lettuces."

Ere Alleyne could answer there swung round the curve of the road a lady's carriage drawn by three horses abreast with a postilion upon the outer one. Very fine and rich it was, with beams painted and gilt, wheels and spokes carved in strange figures, and over all an arched cover of red and white tapestry. Beneath its shade there sat a stout and elderly lady in a pink *côte-hardie,* leaning back among a pile of cushions, and plucking out her eyebrows with a small pair of silver tweezers. None could seem more safe and secure and at her ease than this lady, yet here also was a symbol of human life, for in an instant, even as Alleyne reined aside to let the carriage pass, a wheel flew out from among its fellows, and over it all toppled — carving, tapestry and gilt — in one wild heap, with the horses plunging, the postilion shouting, and the lady screaming from within. In an instant Alleyne and John were on foot, and had lifted her forth all in a shake with fear, but little the worse for her mischance.

"Now woe worth me!" she cried, "and ill fall on Michael Easover of Romsey! for I told him that the pin was loose, and yet he must needs gainsay me, like the foolish daffe that he is."

"I trust that you have taken no hurt, my fair lady," said Alleyne, conducting her to the bank, upon which John had already placed a cushion.

"Nay, I have had no scath, though I have lost my silver tweezers. Now, lack-a-day! did God ever put breath into such a fool as Michael Easover of Romsey? But I am much beholden to you, gentle sirs. Soldiers ye are, as one may readily see. I am myself a soldier's daughter," she added, casting a somewhat languishing glance at John, "and my heart ever goes out to a brave man."

"We are indeed fresh from Spain," quoth Alleyne.

"From Spain, says you? Ah! it was an ill and sorry thing that so many should throw away the lives that Heaven gave them. In sooth, it is bad for those who fall, but worse for those who bide behind. I have but now bid farewell to one who hath lost all in this cruel war."

"And how that, lady?"

"She is a young damsel of these parts, and she goes now into a nunnery. Alack! it is not a year since she was the fairest maid from Avon to Itchen, and now it was more than I could abide to wait at Romsey Nunnery to see her put the white veil upon her face, for she was made for a wife and not for the cloister. Did you ever, gentle sir, hear of a body of men called 'The White Company' over yonder?"

"Surely so," cried both comrades.

"Her father was the leader of it, and her lover served under him as squire. News hath come that not one of the Company was left alive, and so, poor lamb, she hath—"

"Lady!" cried Alleyne, with catching breath, "is it the Lady Maude Loring of whom you speak?"

"It is, in sooth."

"Maude! And in a nunnery! Did, then, the thought of her father's death so move her?"

"Her father!" cried the lady, smiling. "Nay; Maude is a good daughter, but I think it was this young golden-haired squire of whom I have heard who has made her turn her back upon the world."

"And I stand talking here!" cried Alleyne wildly. "Come, John, come!"

Rushing to his horse, he swung himself into the saddle, and was off down the road in a rolling cloud of dust as fast as his good steed could bear him.

Great had been the rejoicing amid the Romsey nuns when the Lady Maude Loring had craved admission into their order—for was she not sole child and heiress of the old knight, with farms and fiefs which she could bring to the great nunnery? Long and earnest had been the talks of the gaunt lady abbess, in which she had conjured the young novice to turn for ever from the world, and to rest her bruised heart under the broad and peaceful shelter of the Church. And now, when all was settled, and when abbess and lady superior had had their will, it was but fitting that some pomp and show should mark the glad occasion. Hence it was that the good burghers of Romsey were all in the streets, that gay flags and flowers brightened the path from the nunnery to the church, and that a long procession wound up to the old arch door, leading up the bride to these spiritual nuptials. There was lay-sister Agatha with the high gold crucifix, and the three incense-bearers, and the two-and-twenty garbed in white, who cast flowers upon either side of them and sang sweetly the while. Then, with four attendants, came the novice, her drooping head wreathed with white blossoms, and, behind, the abbess and her council of older nuns, who were already counting in their minds whether their own bailiff could manage the farms of Twynham, or whether a reeve would be needed beneath him to draw the utmost from these new possessions which this young novice was about to bring them.

But alas! for plots and plans when love and youth and nature, and, above all, fortune are arrayed against them. Who is this travel-stained youth who dares to ride so madly through the lines of staring burghers? Why does he fling himself from his horse and stare so strangely about him? See how he has rushed through the incense-bearers, thrust aside lay-sister Agatha, scattered the two-and-twenty damosels who sang so sweetly—and he stands before the novice with his hands outstretched, and his face shining, and the light of love in his grey eyes. Her foot is on the very threshold of the church, and yet he bars the way—and she, she thinks no more of the wise words and holy rede of the lady abbess, but she hath given a sobbing cry and hath fallen forward with his arms around her drooping body and her wet cheek upon his breast. A sorry sight this for the gaunt abbess, an ill lesson, too, for the stainless two-and-twenty who have ever been taught that the way of nature is the way of sin. But Maude and Alleyne care little for this. A dank cold air conies out from the black arch before them. Without, the sun shines bright and the birds are singing amid the ivy on the drooping beeches. Their choice is made, and they turn away hand-in-hand, with their backs to the darkness and their faces to the light.

Very quiet was the wedding in the old priory church at Christchurch, where Father Christopher read the service, and there were few to see save the Lady Loring and John, and a dozen bowmen from the castle. The Lady of Twynham had drooped and pined for weary months, so that her face was harsher and less comely than before, yet she still hoped on, for her lord had come through so many dangers that she could scarce believe that he might be stricken down at last. It had been her wish to start for Spain and to search for him, but Alleyne had persuaded her to let him go in her place. There was much to look after, now that the lands of Minstead were joined to those of Twynham, and Alleyne had promised her that if she would but bide with his wife he would never come back to Hampshire again until he had gained some news, good or ill, of her lord and lover.

The yellow cog had been engaged, with Goodwin Hawtayne in command, and a month after the wedding Alleyne rode down to Bucklershard to see if she had come round yet from Southampton. On the way he passed the fishing village of Pitt's Deep, and marked that a little creyer or brig was tacking off the land, as though about to anchor there. On his way back, as he rode towards the village, he saw that she had indeed anchored and that many boats were round her, bearing cargo to the shore.

A bow-shot from Pitt's Deep there was an inn a little back from the road, very large and widespread, with a great green bush hung upon a pole from one of the upper windows. At this window he marked, as he rode up, that a man was seated who appeared to be craning his neck in his direction. Alleyne was still looking up at him, when a woman came rushing from the open door of the inn, and made as though she would climb a tree, looking back the while with a laughing face. Wondering what these doings might mean, Alleyne tied his horse to a tree, and was walking amid the trunks towards the inn, when there shot from the entrance a second woman who made also for the trees. Close at her heels came a burly, brown-faced man, who leaned against the door-post and laughed loudly with his hand to his side.

"Ah, mes belles!" he cried, "and is it thus you treat me? Ah, mes petites! I swear by these finger-bones that I would not hurt a hair of your pretty heads; but I have been among the black paynim, and, by my hilt! it does me good to look at your English cheeks. Come, drink a stoup of muscadine with me, mes anges, for my heart is warm to be among ye again."

At the sight of the man Alleyne had stood staring, but at the sound of his voice such a thrill of joy bubbled up in his heart that he had to bite his lip to keep himself from shouting outright. But a deeper pleasure yet was in store. Even as he looked, the window above was pushed outwards, and the voice of the man whom he had seen there came out from it.

"Aylward," cried the voice, "I have seen just now a very worthy person come down the road, though my eyes could scarce discern whether he carried coat-armour. I pray you to wait upon him and tell him that a very humble knight of England abides here, so that if he be in need of advancement, or have any small vow upon his soul, or desire to exalt his lady, I may help him to accomplish it."

Aylward at this order came shuffling forward amid the trees, and in an instant the two men were clinging in each other's arms, laughing and shouting and patting each other in their delight; while old Sir Nigel came running with his sword, under the impression that some small bickering had broken out, only to embrace and be embraced himself, until all three were hoarse with their questions and outcries and congratulations.

On their journey home through the woods Alleyne learnt their wondrous story, how when Sir Nigel came to his senses, he with his fellow-captive had been hurried to the coast, and conveyed by sea to their captor's castle; how upon the way they had been taken by a Barbary rover, and how they exchanged their light captivity for a seat on a galley bench and hard labour at the pirate's oars; how, in the port of Barbary, Sir Nigel had slain the Moorish captain, and had swum, with Aylward, to a small coaster which they had taken and so made their way to England with a rich cargo to reward them for their toils. All this Alleyne listened to, until the dark keep of Twynham towered above them in the gloaming, and they saw the red sun lying athwart the rippling Avon. No need to speak of the glad hearts at Twynham Castle that night, nor of the rich offerings from out of that Moorish cargo which found their way to the chapel of Father Christopher.

Sir Nigel Loring lived for many years, full of honour and laden with every blessing. He rode no more to the wars, but he found his way to every jousting within thirty miles; and the Hampshire youth treasured it as the highest honour when a word of praise fell from him as to their management of their horses, or their breaking of their lances. So he lived and so he died, the most revered and the happiest man in all his native shire.

For Sir Alleyne Edricson and for his beautiful bride the future had also naught but what was good. Twice he fought in France, and came back each time laden with honours. A high place at court was given to him, and he spent many years at Windsor under the second Richard and the fourth Henry—where he received the honour of the Garter, and won the name of being a brave soldier, a true-hearted gentleman, and a great lover and patron of every art and science which refines or ennobles life.

As to John, he took unto himself a village maid, and settled in Lyndhurst, where his five thousand crowns made him the richest franklin for many miles around. For many years he drank his ale every night at the "Pied Merlin," which was now kept by his friend Aylward, who had wedded the good widow to whom he had committed his plunder. The strong men and the bowmen of the country round used to drop in there of an evening to wrestle a fall with John or to shoot a round with Aylward; but though a silver shilling was to be the prize of the victor, it has never been reported that any man earned much money in that fashion. So they lived, these men in their own lusty, cheery fashion—rude and rough, but honest, kindly, and true. Let us thank God if we have outgrown their vices. Let us pray to God that we may ever hold their virtues. The sky may darken, and the clouds may gather, and again the day may come when Britain may have sore need of her children, on whatever shore of the sea they be found. Shall they not muster at her call?

SIR NIGEL

INTRODUCTION

DAME History is so austere a lady that if one, has been so ill-advised as to take a liberty with her, one should hasten to make amends by repentance and confession. Events have been transposed to the extent of some few months in this narrative in order to preserve the continuity and evenness of the story. I hope so small a divergence may seem a venial error after so many centuries. For the rest, it is as accurate as a good deal of research and hard work could make it.

The matter of diction is always a question of taste and discretion in a historical reproduction. In the year 1350 the upper classes still spoke Norman-French, though they were just beginning to condescend to English. The lower classes spoke the English of the original Piers Plowman text, which would be considerably more obscure than their superiors' French if the two were now reproduced or imitated. The most which the chronicles can do is to catch the cadence and style of their talk, and to infuse here and there such a dash of the archaic as may indicate their fashion of speech.

I am aware that there are incidents which may strike the modern reader as brutal and repellent. It is useless, however, to draw the Twentieth Century and label it the Fourteenth. It was a sterner age, and men's code of morality, especially in matters of cruelty, was very different. There is no incident in the text for which very good warrant may not be given. The fantastic graces of Chivalry lay upon the surface of life, but beneath it was a half-savage population, fierce and animal, with little ruth or mercy. It was a raw, rude England, full of elemental passions, and redeemed only by elemental virtues. Such I have tried to draw it.

For good or bad, many books have gone to the building of this one. I look round my study table and I survey those which lie with me at the moment, before I happily disperse them forever. I see La Croix's "Middle Ages," Oman's "Art of War," Rietstap's "Armorial General," De la Borderie's "Histoire de Bretagne," Dame Berner's "Boke of St. Albans," "The Chronicle of Jocelyn of Brokeland," "The Old Road," Hewitt's "Ancient Armour," Coussan's "Heraldry," Boutell's "Arms," Browne's "Chaucer's England," Cust's "Scenes of the Middle Ages," Husserand's "Wayfaring Life," Ward's "Canterbury Pilgrims;" Cornish's "Chivalry," Hastings' "British Archer," Strutt's "Sports," Johnes Froissart, Hargrove's "Archery," Longman's "Edward III," Wright's "Domestic Manners." With these and many others I have lived for months. If I have been unable to combine and transfer their effect, the fault is mine.

ARTHUR CONAN DOYLE.

"UNDERSHAW," November 30, 1905.

CHAPTER I

THE HOUSE OF LORING

In the month of July of the year 1348, between the feasts of St. Benedict and of St. Swithin, a strange thing came upon England, for out of the east there drifted a monstrous cloud, purple and piled, heavy with evil, climbing slowly up the hushed heaven. In the shadow of that strange cloud the leaves drooped in the trees, the birds ceased their calling, and the cattle and the sheep gathered cowering under the hedges. A gloom fell upon all the land, and men stood with their eyes upon the strange cloud and a heaviness upon their hearts. They crept into the churches where the trembling people were blessed and shriven by the trembling priests. Outside no bird flew, and there came no rustling from the woods, nor any of the homely sounds of Nature. All was still, and nothing moved, save only the great cloud which rolled up and onward, with fold on fold from the black horizon. To the west was the light summer sky, to the east this brooding cloud-bank, creeping ever slowly across, until the last thin blue gleam faded away and the whole vast sweep of the heavens was one great leaden arch.

Then the rain began to fall. All day it rained, and all the night and all the week and all the month, until folk had forgotten the blue heavens and the gleam of the sunshine. It was not heavy, but it was steady and cold and unceasing, so that the people were weary of its hissing and its splashing, with the slow drip from the eaves. Always the same thick evil cloud flowed from east to west with the rain beneath it. None could see for more than a bow-shot from their dwellings for the drifting veil of the rain-storms. Every morning the folk looked upward for a break, but their eyes rested always upon the same endless cloud, until at last they ceased to look up, and their hearts despaired of ever seeing the change. It was raining at Lammas-tide and raining at the Feast of the Assumption and still raining at Michaelmas. The crops and the hay, sodden and black, had rotted in the fields, for they were not worth the garnering. The sheep had died, and the calves also, so there was little to kill when Martinmas came and it was time to salt the meat for the winter. They feared a famine, but it was worse than famine which was in store for them.

For the rain had ceased at last, and a sickly autumn sun shone upon a land which was soaked and sodden with water. Wet and rotten leaves reeked and festered under the foul haze which rose from the woods. The fields were spotted with monstrous fungi of a size and color never matched before — scarlet and mauve and liver and black. It was as though the sick earth had burst into foul pustules; mildew and lichen mottled the walls, and with that filthy crop Death sprang also from the water-soaked earth. Men died, and women and children, the baron of the castle, the franklin on the farm, the monk in the abbey and the villein in his wattle-and-daub cottage. All breathed the same polluted reek and all died the same death of corruption. Of those who were stricken none recovered, and the illness was ever the same — gross boils, raving, and the black blotches which gave its name to the disease. All through the winter the dead rotted by the wayside for want of some one to bury them. In many a village no single man was left alive. Then at last the spring came with sunshine and health and lightness and laughter — the greenest, sweetest, tenderest spring that England had ever known — but only half of England could know it. The other half had passed away with the great purple cloud.

Yet it was there in that stream of death, in that reek of corruption, that the brighter and freer England was born. There in that dark hour the first streak of the new dawn was seen. For in no way save by a great upheaval and change could the nation break away from that iron feudal system which held her limbs. But now it was a new country which came out from that year of death. The barons were dead in swaths. No high turret nor cunning moat could keep out that black commoner who struck them down. Oppressive laws slackened for want of those who could enforce them, and once slackened could never be enforced again. The laborer would be a slave no longer. The bondsman snapped his shackles. There was much to do and few left to do it. Therefore the few should be free men, name their own price, and work where and for whom they would. It was the black death which cleared the way for that great rising thirty years later which left the English peasant the freest of his class in Europe.

But there were few so far-sighted that they could see that here, as ever, good was coming out of evil. At the moment misery and ruin were brought into every family. The dead cattle, the ungarnered crops, the untilled lands—every spring of wealth had dried up at the same moment. Those who were rich became poor; but those who were poor already, and especially those who were poor with the burden of gentility upon their shoulders, found themselves in a perilous state. All through England the smaller gentry were ruined, for they had no trade save war, and they drew their living from the work of others. On many a manor-house there came evil times, and on none more than on the Manor of Tilford, where for many generations the noble family of the Lorings had held their home.

There was a time when the Lorings had held the country from the North Downs to the Lakes of Frensham, and when their grim castle-keep rising above the green meadows which border the River Wey had been the strongest fortalice betwixt Guildford Castle in the east and Winchester in the west. But there came that Barons' War, in which the King used his Saxon subjects as a whip with which to scourge his Norman barons, and Castle Loring, like so many other great strongholds, was swept from the face of the land. From that time the Lorings, with estates sadly curtailed, lived in what had been the dower-house, with enough for splendor.

And then came their lawsuit with Waverley Abbey, and the Cistercians laid claim to their richest land, with peccary, turbary and feudal rights over the remainder. It lingered on for years, this great lawsuit, and when it was finished the men of the Church and the men of the Law had divided all that was richest of the estate between them. There was still left the old manor-house from which with each generation there came a soldier to uphold the credit of the name and to show the five scarlet roses on the silver shield where it had always been shown — in the van. There were twelve bronzes in the little chapel where Matthew the priest said mass every morning, all of men of the house of Loring. Two lay with their legs crossed, as being from the Crusades. Six others rested their feet upon lions, as having died in war. Four only lay with the effigy of their hounds to show that they had passed in peace.

Of this famous but impoverished family, doubly impoverished by law and by pestilence, two members were living in the year of grace 1349 — Lady Ermyntrude Loring and her grandson Nigel. Lady Ermyntrude's husband had fallen before the Scottish spears-men at Stirling, and her son Eustace, Nigel's father, had found a glorious death nine years before this chronicle opens upon the poop of a Norman galley at the sea-fight of Sluys. The lonely old woman, fierce and brooding like the falcon mewed in her cham-ber, was soft only toward the lad whom she had brought up. All the tenderness and love of her nature, so hidden from others that they could not imagine their existence, were lavished upon him. She could not bear him away from her, and he, with that respect for authority which the age demanded, would not go without her blessing and consent.

So it came about that Nigel, with his lion heart and with the blood of a hundred soldiers thrilling in his veins, still at the age of two and twenty, wasted the weary days reclaiming his hawks with leash and lure or training the alans and spaniels who shared with the family the big earthen-floored hall of the manor-house.

Day by day the aged Lady Ermyntrude had seen him wax in strength and in manhood, small of stature, it is true, but with muscles of steel and a soul of fire. From all parts, from the warden of Guildford Castle, from the tilt-yard of Farnham, tales of his prowess were brought back to her, of his daring as a rider, of his debonair courage, of his skill with all weapons; but still she, who had both husband and son torn from her by a bloody death, could not bear that this, the last of the Lorings, the final bud of so famous an old tree, should share the same fate. With a weary heart, but with a smiling face, he bore with his uneventful days, while she would ever put off the evil time until the harvest was better, until the monks of Waverley should give up what they had taken, until his uncle should die and leave money for his outfit, or any other excuse with which she could hold him to her side.

And indeed, there was need for a man at Tilford, for the strife betwixt the Abbey and the manor-house had never been appeased, and still on one pretext or another the monks would clip off yet one more slice of their neighbor's land. Over the winding river, across the green meadows, rose the short square tower and the high gray walls of the grim Abbey, with its bell tolling by day and night, a voice of menace and of dread to the little household.

It is in the heart of the great Cistercian monastery that this chronicle of old days must take its start, as we trace the feud betwixt the monks and the house of Loring, with those events to which it gave birth, ending with the coming of Chandos, the strange spear-running of Tilford Bridge and the deeds with which Nigel won fame in the wars. Elsewhere, in the chronicle of the White Company, it has been set forth what manner of man was Nigel Loring. Those who love him may read herein those things which went to his making. Let us go back together and gaze upon this green stage of England, the scenery, hill, plain and river even as now, the actors in much our very selves, in much also so changed in thought and act that they might be dwellers in another world to ours.

CHAPTER II

HOW THE DEVIL CAME TO WAVERLEY

THE day was the first of May, which was the Festival of the Blessed Apostles Philip and James. The year was the 1,349th from man's salvation. From tierce to sext, and then again from sext to nones, Abbot John of the House of Waverley had been seated in his study while he conducted the many high duties of his office. All around for many a mile on every side stretched the fertile and flourishing estate of which he was the master. In the center lay the broad Abbey buildings, with church and cloisters, hospitium, chapter-house and frater-house, all buzzing with a busy life. Through the open window came the low hum of the voices of the brethren as they walked in pious converse in the ambulatory below. From across the cloister there rolled the distant rise and fall of a Gregorian chant, where the precentor was hard at work upon the choir, while down in the chapter-house sounded the strident voice of Brother Peter, expounding the rule of Saint Bernard to the novices.

Abbot John rose to stretch his cramped limbs. He looked out at the greensward of the cloister, and at the graceful line of open Gothic arches which skirted a covered walk for the brethren within. Two and two in their black-and-white garb with slow step and heads inclined, they paced round and round. Several of the more studious had brought their illuminating work from the scriptorium, and sat in the warm sunshine with their little platters of pigments and packets of gold-leaf before them, their shoulders rounded and their faces sunk low over the white sheets of vellum. There too was the copper-worker with his burin and graver. Learning and art were not traditions with the Cistercians as with the parent Order of the Benedictines, and yet the library of Waverley was well filled both with precious books and with pious students.

But the true glory of the Cistercian lay in his outdoor work, and so ever and anon there passed through the cloister some sun-burned monk, soiled mattock or shovel in hand, with his gown looped to his knee, fresh from the fields or the garden. The lush green water-meadows speckled with the heavy-fleeced sheep, the acres of corn-land reclaimed from heather and bracken, the vine-yards on the southern slope of Crooksbury Hill, the rows of Hankley fish-ponds, the Frensham marshes drained and sown with vegetables, the spacious pigeon-cotes, all circled the great Abbey round with the visible labors of the Order.

The Abbot's full and florid face shone with a quiet content as he looked out at his huge but well-ordered household. Like every head of a prosperous Abbey, Abbot John, the fourth of the name, was a man of various accomplishments. Through his own chosen instruments he had to minister a great estate and to keep order and decorum among a large body of men living a celibate life. He was a rigid disciplinarian toward all beneath him, a sup-ple diplomatist to all above. He held high debate with neighbor-ing abbots and lords, with bishops, with papal legates, and even on occasion with the King's majesty himself. Many were the sub-jects with which he must be conversant. Questions of doctrine, questions of building, points of forestry, of agriculture, of drainage, of feudal law, all came to the Abbot for settlement. He held the scales of justice in all the Abbey banlieue which stretched over many a mile of Hampshire and of Surrey. To the monks his displeasure might mean fasting, exile to some sterner community, or even imprisonment in chains. Over the layman also he could hold any punishment save only corporeal death, instead of which he had in hand the far more dreadful weapon of spiritual excommunication.

SIR ARTHUR CONAN DOYLE

Such were the powers of the Abbot, and it is no wonder that there were masterful lines in the ruddy features of Abbot John, or that the brethren, glancing up, should put on an even meeker carriage and more demure expression as they saw the watchful face in the window above them.

A knock at the door of his studio recalled the Abbot to his immediate duties, and he returned to his desk. Already he had spoken with his cellarer and prior, almoner, chaplain and lector, but now in the tall and gaunt monk who obeyed his summons to enter he recognized the most important and also the most importunate of his agents, Brother Samuel the sacrist, whose office, corresponding to that of the layman's bailiff, placed the material interests of the monastery and its dealings with the outer world entirely under his control, subject only to the check of the Abbot. Brother Samuel was a gnarled and stringy old monk whose stern and sharp-featured face reflected no light from above but only that sordid workaday world toward which it was forever turned. A huge book of accounts was tucked under one of his arms, while a great bunch of keys hung from the other hand, a badge of his office, and also on occasion of impatience a weapon of offense, as many a scarred head among rustics and lay brothers could testify.

The Abbot sighed wearily, for he suffered much at the hands of his strenuous agent. "Well, Brother Samuel, what is your will?" he asked.

"Holy father, I have to report that I have sold the wool to Master Baldwin of Winchester at two shillings a bale more than it fetched last year, for the murrain among the sheep has raised the price."

"You have done well, brother."

"I have also to tell you that I have distrained Wat the warrener from his cottage, for his Christmas rent is still unpaid, nor the hen-rents of last year."

"He has a wife and four children, brother." He was a good, easy man, the Abbot, though liable to be overborne by his sterner subordinate.

"It is true, holy father; but if I should pass him, then how am I to ask the rent of the foresters of Puttenham, or the hinds in the village? Such a thing spreads from house to house, and where then is the wealth of Waverley?"

"What else, Brother Samuel?"

"There is the matter of the fish-ponds."

The Abbot's face brightened. It was a subject upon which he was an authority. If the rule of his Order had robbed him of the softer joys of life, he had the keener, zest for those which remained.

"How have the char prospered, brother?"

"They have done well, holy father, but the carp have died in the Abbot's pond."

"Carp prosper only upon a gravel bottom. They must be put in also in their due proportion, three milters to one spawner, brother sacrist, and the spot must be free from wind, stony and sandy, an ell deep, with willows and grass upon the banks. Mud for tench, brother, gravel for carp."

The sacrist leaned forward with the face of one who bears tidings of woe. "There are pike in the Abbot's pond," said he.

"Pike!" cried the Abbot in horror. "As well shut up a wolf in our sheepfold. How came a pike in the pond? There were no pike last year, and a pike does not fall with the rain nor rise in the springs. The pond must be drained, or we shall spend next Lent upon stockfish, and have the brethren down with the great sickness ere Easter Sunday has come to absolve us from our abstinence."

"The pond shall be drained, holy father; I have already ordered it. Then we shall plant pot-herbs on the mud bottom, and after we have gathered them in, return the fish and water once more from the lower pond, so that they may fatten among the rich stubble."

"Good!" cried the Abbot. "I would have three fish-stews in every well-ordered house—one dry for herbs, one shallow for the fry and the yearlings, and one deep for the breeders and the table-fish. But still, I have not heard you say how the pike came in the Abbot's pond."

A spasm of anger passed over the fierce face of the sacrist, and his keys rattled as his bony hand clasped them more tightly. "Young Nigel Loring!" said he. "He swore that he would do us scathe, and in this way he has done it."

"How know you this?"

"Six weeks ago he was seen day by day fishing for pike at the great Lake of Frensham. Twice at night he has been met with a bundle of straw under his arm on the Hankley Down. Well, I wot that the straw was wet and that a live pike lay within it."

The Abbot shook his head. "I have heard much of this youth's wild ways; but now indeed he has passed all bounds if what you say be truth. It was bad enough when it was said that he slew the King's deer in Woolmer Chase, or broke the head of Hobbs the chapman, so that he lay for seven days betwixt life and death in our infirmary, saved only by Brother Peter's skill in the pharmacies of herbs; but to put pike in the Abbot's pond—why should he play such a devil's prank?"

"Because he hates the House of Waverley, holy father; because he swears that we hold his father's land."

"In which there is surely some truth."

"But, holy father, we hold no more than the law has allowed."

"True, brother, and yet between ourselves, we may admit that the heavier purse may weigh down the scales of Justice. When I have passed the old house and have seen that aged woman with her ruddled cheeks and her baleful eyes look the curses she dare not speak, I have many a time wished that we had other neighbors."

"That we can soon bring about, holy father. Indeed, it is of it that I wished to speak to you. Surely it is not hard for us to drive them from the country-side. There are thirty years' claims of escuage unsettled, and there is Sergeant Wilkins, the lawyer of Guildford, whom I will warrant to draw up such arrears of dues and rents and issues of hidage and fodder-corn that these folk, who are as beggarly as they are proud, will have to sell the roof-tree over them ere they can meet them. Within three days I will have them at our mercy."

"They are an ancient family and of good repute. I would not treat them too harshly, brother."

"Bethink you of the pike in the carp pond!"

The Abbot hardened his heart at the thought. "It was indeed a devil's deed—when we had but newly stocked it with char and with carp. Well, well, the law is the law, and if you can use it to hurt, it is still lawful to do so. Have these claims been advanced?"

"Deacon the bailiff with his two varlets went down to the Hall yesternight on the matter of the escuage, and came screaming back with this young hothead raging at their heels. He is small and slight, yet he has the strength of many men in the hour of his wrath. The bailiff swears that he will go no more, save with half a score of archers to uphold him."

The Abbot was red with anger at this new offense. "I will teach him that the servants of Holy Church, even though we of the rule of Saint Bernard be the lowliest and humblest of her children, can still defend their own against the froward and the violent! Go, cite this man before the Abbey court. Let him appear in the chapter-house after tierce to-morrow."

But the wary sacrist shook his head: "Nay, holy father, the times are not yet ripe. Give me three days, I pray you, that my case against him may be complete. Bear in mind that the father and the grandfather of this unruly squire were both famous men of their day and the foremost knights in the King's own service, living in high honor and dying in their knightly duty. The Lady Ermyntrude Loring was first lady to the King's mother. Roger FitzAlan of Farnham and Sir Hugh Walcott of Guildford Castle were each old comrades-in-arms of Nigel's father, and sib to him on the distaff side. Already there has been talk that we have dealt harshly with them. Therefore, my rede is that we be wise and wary and wait until his cup be indeed full."

The Abbot had opened his mouth to reply, when the consultation was interrupted by a most unwonted buzz of, excitement from among the monks in the cloister below. Questions and answers in excited voices sounded from one side of the ambulatory to the other. Sacrist and Abbot were gazing at each other in amazement at such a breach of the discipline and decorum of their well-trained flock, when there came a swift step upon the stair, and a white-faced brother flung open the door and rushed into the room.

"Father Abbot!" he cried. "Alas, alas! Brother John is dead, and the holy subprior is dead, and the Devil is loose in the five- virgate field!"

CHAPTER III

THE YELLOW HORSE OF CROOKSBURY

IN those simple times there was a great wonder and mystery in life. Man walked in fear and solemnity, with Heaven very close above his head, and Hell below his very feet. God's visible hand was everywhere, in the rainbow and the comet, in the thunder and the wind. The Devil too raged openly upon the earth; he skulked behind the hedge-rows in the gloaming; he laughed loudly in the night-time; he clawed the dying sinner, pounced on the unbaptized babe, and twisted the limbs of the epileptic. A foul fiend slunk ever by a man's side and whispered villainies in his ear, while above him there hovered an angel of grace who pointed to the steep and narrow track. How could one doubt these things, when Pope and priest and scholar and King were all united in believing them, with no single voice of question in the whole wide world?

Every book read, every picture seen, every tale heard from nurse or mother, all taught the same lesson. And as a man traveled through the world his faith would grow the firmer, for go where he would there were the endless shrines of the saints, each with its holy relic in the center, and around it the tradition of incessant miracles, with stacks of deserted crutches and silver votive hearts to prove them. At every turn he was made to feel how thin was the veil, and how easily rent, which screened him from the awful denizens of the unseen world.

Hence the wild announcement of the frightened monk seemed terrible rather than incredible to those whom he addressed. The Abbot's ruddy face paled for a moment, it is true, but he plucked the crucifix from his desk and rose valiantly to his feet.

"Lead me to him!" said he. "Show me the foul fiend who dares to lay his grip upon brethren of the holy house of Saint Bernard! Run down to my chaplain, brother! Bid him bring the exorcist with him, and also the blessed box of relics, and the bones of Saint James from under the altar! With these and a contrite and humble heart we may show front to all the powers of darkness."

But the sacrist was of a more critical turn of mind. He clutched the monk's arm with a grip which left its five purple spots for many a day to come.

"Is this the way to enter the Abbot's own chamber, without knock or reverence, or so much as a '*Pax vobiscum*'?" said he sternly. "You were wont to be our gentlest novice, of lowly carriage in chapter, devout in psalmody and strict in the cloister. Pull your wits together and answer me straightly. In what form has the foul fiend appeared, and how has he done this grievous scathe to our brethren? Have you seen him with your own eyes, or do you repeat from hearsay? Speak, man, or you stand on the penance-stool in the chapter-house this very hour!"

Thus adjured, the frightened monk grew calmer in his bearing, though his white lips and his startled eyes, with the gasping of his breath, told of his inward tremors.

"If it please you, holy father, and you, reverend sacrist, it came about in this way. James the subprior, and Brother John and I had spent our day from sext onward on Hankley, cutting bracken for the cow-houses. We were coming back over the five-virgate field, and the holy subprior was telling us a saintly tale from the life of Saint Gregory, when there came a sudden sound like a rushing torrent, and the foul fiend sprang over the high wall which skirts the water-meadow and rushed upon us with the speed of the wind. The lay brother he struck to the ground and trampled into the mire. Then, seizing the good subprior in his teeth, he rushed round the field, swinging him as though he were a fardel of old clothes.

"Amazed at such a sight, I stood without movement and had said a credo and three aves, when the Devil dropped the subprior and sprang upon me. With the help of Saint Bernard I clambered over the wall, but not before his teeth had found my leg, and he had torn away the whole back skirt of my gown." As he spoke he turned and gave corroboration to his story by the hanging ruins of his long trailing garment

"In what shape then did Satan appear?" the Abbot demanded.

"As a great yellow horse, holy father—a monster horse, with eyes of fire and the teeth of a griffin."

"A yellow horse!" The sacrist glared at the scared monk. "You foolish brother! How will you behave when you have indeed to face the King of Terrors himself if you can be so frightened by the sight of a yellow horse? It is the horse of Franklin Aylward, my father, which has been distrained by us because he owes the Abbey fifty good shillings and can never hope to pay it. Such a horse, they say, is not to be found betwixt this and the King's stables at Windsor, for his sire was a Spanish destrer, and his dam an Arab mare of the very breed which Saladin, whose soul now reeks in Hell, kept for his own use, and even it has been said under the shelter of his own tent. I took him in discharge of the debt, and I ordered the varlets who had haltered him to leave him alone in the water-meadow, for I have heard that the beast has indeed a most evil spirit, and has killed more men than one."

"It was an ill day for Waverley that you brought such a monster within its bounds," said the Abbot. "If the subprior and Brother John be indeed dead, then it would seem that if the horse be not the Devil he is at least the Devil's instrument."

"Horse or Devil, holy father, I heard him shout with joy as he trampled upon Brother John, and had you seen him tossing the subprior as a dog shakes a rat you would perchance have felt even as I did."

"Come then," cried the Abbot, "let us see with our own eyes what evil has been done."

And the three monks hurried down the stair which led to the cloisters.

They had no sooner descended than their more pressing fears were set at rest, for at that very moment, limping, disheveled and mud-stained, the two sufferers were being led in amid a crowd of sympathizing brethren. Shouts and cries from outside showed, however, that some further drama was in progress, and both Abbot and sacrist hastened onward as fast as the dignity of their office would permit, until they had passed the gates and gained the wall of the meadow. Looking over it, a remarkable sight presented itself to their eyes.

Fetlock deep in the lush grass there stood a magnificent horse, such a horse as a sculptor or a soldier might thrill to see. His color was a light chestnut, with mane and tail of a more tawny tint. Seventeen hands high, with a barrel and haunches which bespoke tremendous strength, he fined down to the most delicate lines of dainty breed in neck and crest and shoulder. He was indeed a glorious sight as he stood there, his beautiful body leaning back from his wide-spread and propped fore legs, his head craned high, his ears erect, his mane bristling, his red nostrils opening and shutting with wrath, and his flashing eyes turning from side to side in haughty menace and defiance.

Scattered round in a respectful circle, six of the Abbey lay servants and foresters, each holding a halter, were creeping toward him. Every now and then, with a beautiful toss and swerve and plunge, the great creature would turn upon one of his would-be captors, and with outstretched head, flying mane and flashing teeth, would chase him screaming to the safety of the wall, while the others would close swiftly in behind and cast their ropes in the hope of catching neck or leg, but only in their, turn to be chased to the nearest refuge.

Had two of these ropes settled upon the horse, and had their throwers found some purchase of stump or boulder by which they could hold them, then the man's brain might have won its wonted victory over swiftness and strength. But the brains were themselves at fault which imagined that one such rope would serve any purpose save to endanger the thrower.

Yet so it was, and what might have been foreseen occurred at the very moment of the arrival of the monks. The horse, having chased one of his enemies to the wall, remained so long snorting his contempt over the coping that the others were able to creep upon him from behind. Several ropes were flung, and one noose settled over the proud crest and lost itself in the waving mane. In an instant the creature had turned and the men were flying for their lives; but he who had cast the rope lingered, uncertain what use to make of his own success. That moment of doubt was fatal. With a yell of dismay, the man saw the great creature rear above him. Then with a crash the fore feet fell upon him and dashed him to the ground. He rose screaming, was hurled over once more, and lay a quivering, bleeding heap, while the savage horse, the most cruel and terrible in its anger of all creatures on earth, bit and shook and trampled the writhing body.

A loud wail of horror rose from the lines of tonsured heads which skirted the high wall—a wail which suddenly died away into a long hushed silence, broken at last by a rapturous cry of thanksgiving and of joy.

On the road which led to the old dark manor-house upon the side of the hill a youth had been riding. His mount was a sorry one, a weedy, shambling, long-haired colt, and his patched tunic of faded purple with stained leather belt presented no very smart appearance; yet in the bearing of the man, in the poise of his head, in his easy graceful carriage, and in the bold glance of his large blue eyes, there was that stamp of distinction and of breed which would have given him a place of his own in any assembly. He was of small stature, but his frame was singularly elegant and graceful. His face, though tanned with the weather, was delicate in features and most eager and alert in expression. A thick fringe of crisp yellow curls broke from under the dark flat cap which he was wearing, and a short golden beard hid the outline of his strong square chin. One white osprey feather thrust through a gold brooch in the front of his cap gave a touch of grace to his somber garb. This and other points of his attire, the short hanging mantle, the leather-sheathed hunting-knife, the cross belt which sustained a brazen horn, the soft doe-skin boots and the prick spurs, would all disclose themselves to an observer; but at the first glance the brown face set in gold and the dancing light of the quick, reckless, laughing eyes, were the one strong memory left behind.

Such was the youth who, cracking his whip joyously, and followed by half a score of dogs, cantered on his rude pony down the Tilford Lane, and thence it was that with a smile of amused contempt upon his face he observed the comedy in the field and the impotent efforts of the servants of Waverley.

Suddenly, however, as the comedy turned swiftly to black tragedy, this passive spectator leaped into quick strenuous life. With a spring he was off his pony, and with another he was over the stone wall and flying swiftly across the field. Looking up from his victim, the great yellow horse saw this other enemy approach, and spurning the prostrate, but still writhing body with its heels, dashed at the newcomer.

But this time there was no hasty flight, no rapturous pursuit to the wall. The little man braced himself straight, flung up his metal-headed whip, and met the horse with a crashing blow upon the head, repeated again and again with every attack. In vain the horse reared and tried to overthrow its enemy with swooping shoulders and pawing hoofs. Cool, swift and alert, the man sprang swiftly aside from under the very shadow of death, and then again came the swish and thud of the unerring blow from the heavy handle.

The horse drew off, glared with wonder and fury at this masterful man, and then trotted round in a circle, with mane bristling, tail streaming and ears on end, snorting in its rage and pain. The man, hardly deigning to glance at his fell neighbor, passed on to the wounded forester, raised him in his arms with a strength which could not have been expected in so slight a body, and carried him, groaning, to the wall, where a dozen hands were outstretched to help him over. Then, at his leisure, the young man also climbed the wall, smiling back with cool contempt at the yellow horse, which had come raging after him once more.

As he sprang down, a dozen monks surrounded him to thank him or to praise him; but he would have turned sullenly away without a word had he not been stopped by Abbot John in person.

"Nay, Squire Loring," said he, "if you be a bad friend to our Abbey, yet we must needs own that you have played the part of a good Christian this day, for if there is breath left in our servant's body it is to you next to our blessed patron Saint Bernard that we owe it."

"By Saint Paul! I owe you no good-will, Abbot John," said the young man. "The shadow of your Abbey has ever fallen across the house of Loring. As to any small deed that I may have done this day, I ask no thanks for it. It is not for you nor for your house that I have done it, but only because it was my pleasure so to do."

The Abbot flushed at the bold words, and bit his lip with vexation.

It was the sacrist, however, who answered: "It would be more fitting and more gracious," said he, "if you were to speak to the holy Father Abbot in a manner suited to his high rank and to the respect which is due to a Prince of the Church."

The youth turned his bold blue eyes upon the monk, and his sunburned face darkened with anger. "Were it not for the gown upon your back, and for your silvering hair, I would answer you in another fashion," said he. "You are the lean wolf which growls ever at our door, greedy for the little which hath been left to us. Say and do what you will with me, but by Saint Paul! if I find that Dame Ermyntrude is baited by your ravenous pack I will beat them off with this whip from the little patch which still remains of all the acres of my fathers."

"Have a care, Nigel Loring, have a care!" cried the Abbot, with finger upraised. "Have you no fears of the law of England?"

"A just law I fear and obey."

"Have you no respect for Holy Church?"

"I respect all that is holy in her. I do not respect those who grind the poor or steal their neighbor's land."

"Rash man, many a one has been blighted by her ban for less than you have now said! And yet it is not for us to judge you harshly this day. You are young and hot words come easily to your lips. How fares the forester?"

"His hurt is grievous, Father Abbot, but he will live," said a brother, looking up from the prostrate form. "With a blood-letting and an electuary, I will warrant him sound within a month."

"Then bear him to the hospital. And now, brother, about this terrible beast who still gazes and snorts at us over the top of the wall as though his thoughts of Holy Church were as uncouth as those of Squire Nigel himself, what are we to do with him?"

"Here is Franklin Aylward," said one of the brethren. "The horse was his, and doubtless he will take it back to his farm."

But the stout red-faced farmer shook his head at the proposal. "Not I, in faith!" said he. "The beast hath chased me twice round the paddock; it has nigh slain my boy Samkin. He would never be happy till he had ridden it, nor has he ever been happy since. There is not a hind in my employ who will enter his stall. Ill fare the day that ever I took the beast from the Castle stud at Guildford, where they could do nothing with it and no rider could be found bold enough to mount it! When the sacrist here took it for a fifty-shilling debt he made his own bargain and must abide by it. He comes no more to the Crooksbury farm."

"And he stays no more here," said the Abbot. "Brother sacrist, you have raised the Devil, and it is for you to lay it again."

"That I will most readily," cried the sacrist. "The pittance-master can stop the fifty shillings from my very own weekly dole, and so the Abbey be none the poorer. In the meantime here is Wat with his arbalist and a bolt in his girdle. Let him drive it to the head through this cursed creature, for his hide and his hoofs are of more value than his wicked self."

A hard brown old woodman who had been shooting vermin in the Abbey groves stepped forward with a grin of pleasure. After a lifetime of stoats and foxes, this was indeed a noble quarry which was to fall before him. Fitting a bolt on the nut of his taut crossbow, he had raised it to his shoulder and leveled it at the fierce, proud, disheveled head which tossed in savage freedom at the other side of the wall. His finger was crooked on the spring, when a blow from a whip struck the bow upward and the bolt flew harmless over the Abbey orchard, while the woodman shrank abashed from Nigel Loring's angry eyes.

"Keep your bolts for your weasels!" said he. "Would you take life from a creature whose only fault is that its spirit is so high that it has met none yet who dare control it? You would slay such a horse as a king might be proud to mount, and all because a country franklin, or a monk, or a monk's varlet, has not the wit nor the hands to master him?"

The sacrist turned swiftly on the Squire. "The Abbey owes you an offering for this day's work, however rude your words may be," said he. "If you think so much of the horse, you may desire to own it. If I am to pay for it, then with the holy Abbot's permission it is in my gift and I bestow it freely upon you."

The Abbot plucked at his subordinate's sleeve. "Bethink you, brother sacrist," he whispered, "shall we not have this man's blood upon our heads?"

"His pride is as stubborn as the horse's, holy father," the sacrist answered, his gaunt face breaking into a malicious smile. "Man or beast, one will break the other and the world will be the better for it. If you forbid me——"

"Nay, brother, you have bought the horse, and you may have the bestowal of it."

"Then I give it—hide and hoofs, tail and temper—to Nigel Loring, and may it be as sweet and as gentle to him as he hath been to the Abbot of Waverley!"

The sacrist spoke aloud amid the tittering of the monks, for the man concerned was out of earshot. At the first words which had shown him the turn which affairs had taken he had run swiftly to the spot where he had left his pony. From its mouth he removed the bit and the stout bridle which held it. Then leaving the creature to nibble the grass by the wayside he sped back whence he came.

"I take your gift, monk," said he, "though I know well why it is that you give it. Yet I thank you, for there are two things upon earth for which I have ever yearned, and which my thin purse could never buy. The one is a noble horse, such a horse as my father's son should have betwixt his thighs, and here is the one of all others which I would have chosen, since some small deed is to be done in the winning of him, and some honorable advancement to be gained. How is the horse called?"

"Its name," said the franklin, "is Pommers. I warn you, young sir, that none may ride him, for many have tried, and the luckiest is he who has only a staved rib to show for it."

"I thank you for your rede," said Nigel, "and now I see that this is indeed a horse which I would journey far to meet. I am your man, Pommers, and you are my horse, and this night you shall own it or I will never need horse again. My spirit against thine, and God hold thy spirit high, Pommers, so that the greater be the adventure, and the more hope of honor gained!"

While he spoke the young Squire had climbed on to the top of the wall and stood there balanced, the very image of grace and spirit and gallantry, his bridle hanging from one hand and his whip grasped in the other. With a fierce snort, the horse made for him instantly, and his white teeth flashed as he snapped; but again a heavy blow from the loaded whip caused him to swerve, and even at the instant of the swerve, measuring the distance with steady eyes, and bending his supple body for the spring, Nigel bounded into the air and fell with his legs astride the broad back of the yellow horse. For a minute, with neither saddle nor stirrups to help him, and the beast ramping and rearing like a mad thing beneath him, he was hard pressed to hold his own. His legs were like two bands of steel welded on to the swelling arches of the great horse's ribs, and his left hand was buried deep in the tawny mane.

Never had the dull round of the lives of the gentle brethren of Waverley been broken by so fiery a scene. Springing to right and swooping to left, now with its tangled wicked head betwixt its forefeet, and now pawing eight feet high in the air, with scarlet, furious nostrils and maddened eyes, the yellow horse was a thing of terror and of beauty. But the lithe figure on his back, bending like a reed in the wind to every movement, firm below, pliant above, with calm inexorable face, and eyes which danced and gleamed with the joy of contest, still held its masterful place for all that the fiery heart and the iron muscles of the great beast could do.

Once a long drone of dismay rose from the monks, as rearing higher and higher yet a last mad effort sent the creature toppling over backward upon its rider. But, swift and cool, he had writhed from under it ere it fell, spurned it with his foot as it rolled upon the earth, and then seizing its mane as it rose swung himself lightly on to its back once more. Even the grim sacrist could not but join the cheer, as Pommers, amazed to find the rider still upon his back, plunged and curveted down the field.

But the wild horse only swelled into a greater fury. In the sullen gloom of its untamed heart there rose the furious resolve to dash the life from this clinging rider, even if it meant destruction to beast and man. With red, blazing eyes it looked round for death. On three sides the five-virgate field was bounded by a high wall, broken only at one spot by a heavy four-foot wooden gate. But on the fourth side was a low gray building, one of the granges of the Abbey, presenting a long flank unbroken by door or window. The horse stretched itself into a gallop, and headed straight for that craggy thirty-foot wall. He would break in red ruin at the base of it if he could but dash forever the life of this man, who claimed mastery over that which had never found its master yet.

The great haunches gathered under it, the eager hoofs drummed the grass, as faster and still more fast the frantic horse bore himself and his rider toward the wall. Would Nigel spring off? To do so would be to bend his will to that of the beast beneath him. There was a better way than that. Cool, quick and decided, the man swiftly passed both whip and bridle into the left hand which still held the mane. Then with the right he slipped his short mantle from his shoulders and lying forward along the creature's strenuous, rippling back he cast the flapping cloth over the horse's eyes.

The result was but too successful, for it nearly brought about the downfall of the rider. When those red eyes straining for death were suddenly shrouded in unexpected darkness the amazed horse propped on its forefeet and came to so dead a stop that Nigel was shot forward on to its neck and hardly held himself by his hair-entwined hand. Ere he had slid back into position the moment of danger had passed, for the horse, its purpose all blurred in its mind by this strange thing which had befallen, wheeled round once more, trembling in every fiber, and tossing its petulant head until at last the mantle had been slipped from its eyes and the chilling darkness had melted into the homely circle of sunlit grass once more.

But what was this new outrage which had been inflicted upon it? What was this defiling bar of iron which was locked hard against its mouth? What were these straps which galled the tossing neck, this band which spanned its chest? In those instants of stillness ere the mantle had been plucked away Nigel had lain forward, had slipped the snaffle between the champing teeth, and had deftly secured it.

Blind, frantic fury surged in the yellow horse's heart once more at this new degradation, this badge of serfdom and infamy. His spirit rose high and menacing at the touch. He loathed this place, these people, all and everything which threatened his freedom. He would have done with them forever; he would see them no more. Let him away to the uttermost parts of the earth, to the great plains where freedom is. Anywhere over the far horizon where he could get away from the defiling bit and the insufferable mastery of man.

He turned with a rush, and one magnificent deer-like bound carried him over the four-foot gate. Nigel's hat had flown off, and his yellow curls streamed behind him as he rose and fell in the leap. They were in the water-meadow now, and the rippling stream twenty feet wide gleamed in front of them running down to the main current of the Wey. The yellow horse gathered his haunches under him and flew over like an arrow. He took off from behind a bowlder and cleared a furze-bush on the farther side. Two stones still mark the leap from hoof-mark to hoof-mark, and they are eleven good paces apart. Under the hanging branch of the great oak-tree on the farther side (that *Quercus Tilfordiensis* is still shown as the bound of the Abby's immediate precincts) the great horse passed. He had hoped to sweep off his rider, but Nigel sank low on the heaving back with his face buried in the flying mane. The rough bough rasped him rudely, but never shook his spirit nor his grip. Rearing, plunging and struggling, Pommers broke through the sapling grove and was out on the broad stretch of Hankley Down.

And now came such a ride as still lingers in the gossip of the lowly country folk and forms the rude jingle of that old Surrey ballad, now nearly forgotten, save for the refrain:

> The Doe that sped on Hinde Head,
> The Kestril on the winde,
> And Nigel on the Yellow Horse
> Can leave the world behinde.

Before them lay a rolling ocean of dark heather, knee-deep, swelling in billow on billow up to the clear-cut hill before them. Above stretched one unbroken arch of peaceful blue, with a sun which was sinking down toward the Hampshire hills. Through the deep heather, down the gullies, over the water-courses, up the broken slopes, Pommers flew, his great heart bursting with rage, and every fiber quivering at the indignities which he had endured.

And still, do what he would, the man clung fast to his heaving sides and to his flying mane, silent, motionless, inexorable, letting him do what he would, but fixed as Fate upon his purpose. Over Hankley Down, through Thursley Marsh, with the reeds up to his mud-splashed withers, onward up the long slope of the Headland of the Hinds, down by the Nutcombe Gorge, slipping, blundering, bounding, but never slackening his fearful speed, on went the great yellow horse. The villagers of Shottermill heard the wild clatter of hoofs, but ere they could swing the ox-hide curtains of their cottage doors horse and rider were lost amid the high bracken of the Haslemere Valley. On he went, and on, tossing the miles behind his flying hoofs. No marsh-land could clog him, no hill could hold him back. Up the slope of Linchmere and the long ascent of Fernhurst he thundered as on the level, and it was not until he had flown down the incline of Henley Hill, and the gray castle tower of Midhurst rose over the coppice in front, that at last the eager outstretched neck sank a little on the breast, and the breath came quick and fast. Look where he would in woodland and on down, his straining eyes could catch no sign of those plains of freedom which he sought.

And yet another outrage! It was bad that this creature should still cling so tight upon his back, but now he would even go to the intolerable length of checking him and guiding him on the way that he would have him go. There was a sharp pluck at his mouth, and his head was turned north once more. As well go that way as another, but the man was mad indeed if he thought that such a horse as Pommers was at the end of his spirit or his strength. He would soon show him that he was unconquered, if it strained his sinews or broke his heart to do so. Back then he flew up the long, long ascent. Would he ever get to the end of it? Yet he would not own that he could go no farther while the man still kept his grip. He was white with foam and caked with mud. His eyes were gorged with blood, his mouth open and gasping, his nostrils expanded, his coat stark and reeking. On he flew down the long Sunday Hill until he reached the deep Kingsley Marsh at the bottom. No, it was too much! Flesh and blood could go no farther. As he struggled out from the reedy slime with the heavy black mud still clinging to his fetlocks, he at last eased down with sobbing breath and slowed the tumultuous gallop to a canter.

Oh, crowning infamy! Was there no limit to these degradations? He was no longer even to choose his own pace. Since he had chosen to gallop so far at his own will he must now gallop farther still at the will of another. A spur struck home on either flank. A stinging whip-lash fell across his shoulder. He bounded his own height in the air at the pain and the shame of it. Then, forgetting his weary limbs, forgetting his panting, reeking sides, forgetting everything save this intolerable insult and the burning spirit within, he plunged off once more upon his furious gallop. He was out on the heather slopes again and heading for Weydown Common. On he flew and on. But again his brain failed him and again his limbs trembled beneath him, and yet again he strove to ease his pace, only to be driven onward by the cruel spur and the falling lash. He was blind and giddy with fatigue.

He saw no longer where he placed his feet, he cared no longer whither he went, but his one mad longing was to get away from this dreadful thing, this torture which clung to him and would not let him go. Through Thursley village he passed, his eyes straining in his agony, his heart bursting within him, and he had won his way to the crest of Thursley Down, still stung forward by stab and blow, when his spirit weakened, his giant strength ebbed out of him, and with one deep sob of agony the yellow horse sank among the heather. So sudden was the fall that Nigel flew forward over his shoulder, and beast and man lay prostrate and gasping while the last red rim of the sun sank behind Butser and the first stars gleamed in a violet sky.

The young Squire was the first to recover, and kneeling by the panting, overwrought horse he passed his hand gently over the tangled mane and down the foam-flecked face. The red eye rolled up at him; but it was wonder not hatred, a prayer and not a threat, which he could read in it. As he stroked the reeking muzzle, the horse whinnied gently and thrust his nose into the hollow of his hand. It was enough. It was the end of the contest, the acceptance of new conditions by a chivalrous foe from a chivalrous victor.

"You are my horse, Pommers," Nigel whispered, and he laid his cheek against the craning head. "I know you, Pommers, and you know me, and with the help of Saint Paul we shall teach some other folk to know us both. Now let us walk together as far as this moorland pond, for indeed I wot not whether it is you or I who need the water most."

And so it was that some belated monks of Waverley passing homeward from the outer farms saw a strange sight which they carried on with them so that it reached that very night the ears both of sacrist and of Abbot. For, as they passed through Tilford they had seen horse and man walking side by side and head by head up the manor-house lane. And when they had raised their lanterns on the pair it was none other than the young Squire himself who was leading home, as a shepherd leads a lamb, the fearsome yellow horse of Crooksbury.

CHAPTER IV

HOW THE SUMMONER CAME
TO THE MANOR-HOUSE OF TILFORD

By the date of this chronicle the ascetic sternness of the old
Norman castles had been humanized and refined so that the new
dwellings of the nobility, if less imposing in appearance, were
much more comfortable as places of residence. A gentle race had
built their houses rather for peace than for war. He who compares
the savage bareness of Pevensey or Guildford with the piled
grandeur of Bodmin or Windsor cannot fail to understand the
change in manners which they represent.

The earlier castles had a set purpose, for they were built that
the invaders might hold down the country; but when the
Conquest was once firmly established a castle had lost its meaning save as a refuge from justice or as a center for civil strife. On
the marches of Wales and of Scotland the castle might continue
to be a bulwark to the kingdom, and there still grew and flourished; but in all other places they were rather a menace to the
King's majesty, and as such were discouraged and destroyed. By
the reign of the third Edward the greater part of the old fighting castles had been converted into dwelling-houses or had
been ruined in the civil wars, and left where their grim gray
bones are still littered upon the brows of our hills. The new
buildings were either great country-houses, capable of defense,
but mainly residential, or they were manor-houses with no military significance at all.

Such was the Tilford Manor-house where the last survivors of the old and magnificent house of Loring still struggled hard to keep a footing and to hold off the monks and the lawyers from the few acres which were left to them. The mansion was a two-storied one, framed in heavy beams of wood, the interstices filled with rude blocks of stone. An outside staircase led up to several sleeping-rooms above. Below there were only two apartments, the smaller of which was the bower of the aged Lady Ermyntrude. The other was the hall, a very large room, which served as the living-room of the family and as the common dining-room of themselves and of their little group of servants and retainers. The dwellings of these servants, the kitchens, the offices and the stables were all represented by a row of pent-houses and sheds behind the main building. Here lived Charles the page, Peter the old falconer, Red Swire who had followed Nigel's grandfather to the Scottish wars, Weathercote the broken minstrel, John the cook, and other survivors of more prosperous days, who still clung to the old house as the barnacles to some wrecked and stranded vessel.

One evening about a week after the breaking of the yellow horse, Nigel and his grandmother sat on either side of the large empty fireplace in this spacious apartment. The supper had been removed, and so had the trestle tables upon which it had been served, so that the room seemed bare and empty. The stone floor was strewed with a thick layer of green rushes, which was swept out every Saturday and carried with it all the dirt and dèbris of the week. Several dogs were now crouched among these rushes, gnawing and cracking the bones which had been thrown from the table. A long wooden buffet loaded with plates and dishes filled one end of the room, but there was little other furniture save some benches against the walls, two dorseret chairs, one small table littered with chessmen, and a great iron coffer. In one corner was a high wickerwork stand, and on it two stately falcons were perched, silent and motionless, save for an occasional twinkle of their fierce yellow eyes.

But if the actual fittings of the room would have appeared scanty to one who had lived in a more luxurious age, he would have been surprised on looking up to see the multitude of objects which were suspended above his head. Over the fireplace were the coats-of-arms of a number of houses allied by blood or by marriage to the Lorings. The two cresset-lights which flared upon each side gleamed upon the blue lion of the Percies, the red birds of de Valence, the black engrailed cross of de Mohun, the silver star of de Vere, and the ruddy bars of FitzAlan, all grouped round the famous red roses on the silver shield which the Lorings had borne to glory upon many a bloody field. Then from side to side the room was spanned by heavy oaken beams from which a great number of objects were hanging. There were mail-shirts of obsolete pattern, several shields, one or two rusted and battered helmets, bow-staves, lances, otter-spears, harness, fishing-rods, and other implements of war or of the chase, while higher still amid the black shadows of the peaked roof could be seen rows of hams, flitches of bacon, salted geese, and those other forms of preserved meat which played so great a part in the housekeeping of the Middle Ages.

Dame Ermyntrude Loring, daughter, wife, and mother of warriors, was herself a formidable figure. Tall and gaunt, with hard craggy features and intolerant dark eyes, even her snow-white hair and stooping back could not entirely remove the sense of fear which she inspired in those around her. Her thoughts and memories went back to harsher times, and she looked upon the England around her as a degenerate and effeminate land which had fallen away from the old standard of knightly courtesy and valor.

The rising power of the people, the growing wealth of the Church, the increasing luxury in life and manners, and the gentler tone of the age were all equally abhorrent to her, so that the dread of her fierce face, and even of the heavy oak staff with which she supported her failing limbs, was widespread through all the country round.

Yet if she was feared she was also respected, for in days when books were few and readers scarce, a long memory and a ready tongue were of the more value; and where, save from Dame Ermyntrude, could the young unlettered Squires of Surrey and Hampshire hear of their grandfathers and their battles, or learn that lore of heraldry and chivalry which she handed down from a ruder but a more martial age? Poor as she was, there was no one in Surrey whose guidance would be more readily sought upon a question of precedence or of conduct than the Dame Ermyntrude Loring.

She sat now with bowed back by the empty fireplace, and looked across at Nigel with all the harsh lines of her old ruddled face softening into love and pride. The young Squire was busy cutting bird-bolts for his crossbow, and whistling softly as he worked. Suddenly he looked up and caught the dark eyes which were fixed upon him. He leaned forward and patted the bony hand.

"What hath pleased you, dear dame? I read pleasure in your eyes."

"I have heard to-day, Nigel, how you came to win that great war-horse which stamps in our stable."

"Nay, dame; I had told you that the monks had given it to me."

"You said so, fair son, but never a word more. Yet the horse which you brought home was a very different horse I wot, to that which was given you. Why did you not tell me?"

"I should think it shame to talk of such a thing."

"So would your father before you, and his father no less. They would sit silent among the knights when the wine went round and listen to every man's deeds; but if perchance there was anyone who spoke louder than the rest and seemed to be eager for honor, then afterwards your father would pluck him softly by the sleeve and whisper in his ear to learn if there was any small vow of which he could relieve him, or if he would deign to perform some noble deed of arms upon his person. And if the man were a braggart and would go no further, your father would be silent and none would know it. But if he bore himself well, your father would spread his fame far and wide, but never make mention of himself."

Nigel looked at the old woman with shining eyes. "I love to hear you speak of him," said he. "I pray you to tell me once more of the manner of his death."

"He died as he had lived, a very courtly gentleman. It was at the great sea-battle upon the Norman coast, and your father was in command of the after-guard in the King's own ship. Now the French had taken a great English ship the year before when they came over and held the narrow seas and burned the town of Southampton. This ship was the Christopher, and they placed it in the front of their battle; but the English closed upon it and stormed over its side, and slew all who were upon it.

"But your father and Sir Lorredan of Genoa, who commanded the Christopher, fought upon the high poop, so that all the fleet stopped to watch it, and the King himself cried aloud at the sight, for Sir Lorredan was a famous man-at-arms and bore himself very stoutly that day, and many a knight envied your father that he should have chanced upon so excellent a person. But your father bore him back and struck him such a blow with a mace that he turned the helmet half round on his head, so that he could no longer see through the eyeholes, and Sir Lorredan threw down his sword and gave himself to ransom. But your father took him by the helmet and twisted it until he had it straight upon his head. Then, when he could see once again, he handed him his sword, and prayed him that he would rest himself and then continue, for it was great profit and joy to see any gentleman carry himself so well. So they sat together and rested by the rail of the poop; but even as they raised their hands again your father was struck by a stone from a mangonel and so died."

"And this Sir Lorredan," cried Nigel, "he died also, as I understand?"

"I fear that he was slain by the archers, for they loved your father, and they do not see these things with our eyes."

"It was a pity," said Nigel; "for it is clear that he was a good knight and bore himself very bravely."

"Time was, when I was young, when commoners dared not have laid their grimy hands upon such a man. Men of gentle blood and coat-armor made war upon each other, and the others, spearmen or archers, could scramble amongst themselves. But now all are of a level, and only here and there one like yourself, fair son, who reminds me of the men who are gone."

Nigel leaned forward and took her hands in his. "What I am you have made me," said he.

"It is true, Nigel. I have indeed watched over you as the gardener watches his most precious blossom, for in you alone are all the hopes of our ancient house, and soon—very soon—you will be alone."

"Nay, dear lady, say not that."

"I am very old, Nigel, and I feel the shadow closing in upon me. My heart yearns to go, for all whom I have known and loved have gone before me. And you—it will be a blessed day for you, since I have held you back from that world into which your brave spirit longs to plunge."

"Nay, nay, I have been happy here with you at Tilford."

"We are very poor, Nigel. I do not know where we may find the money to fit you for the wars. Yet we have good friends. There is Sir John Chandos, who has won such credit in the French wars and who rides ever by the King's bridle-arm. He was your father's friend and they were Squires together. If I sent you to court with a message to him he would do what he could."

Nigel's fair face flushed. "Nay, Dame Ermyntrude, I must find my own gear, even as I have found my own horse, for I had rather ride into battle in this tunic than owe my suit to another."

"I feared that you would say so, Nigel; but indeed I know not how else we may get the money," said the old woman sadly. "It was different in the days of my father. I can remember that a suit of mail was but a small matter in those days, for in every English town such things could be made. But year by year since men have come to take more care of their bodies, there have been added a plate of proof here and a cunning joint there, and all must be from Toledo or Milan, so that a knight must have much metal in his purse ere he puts any on his limbs."

Nigel looked up wistfully at the old armor which was slung on the beams above him. "The ash spear is good," said he, "and so is the oaken shield with facings of steel. Sir Roger FitzAlan handled them and said that he had never seen better. But the armor—"

Lady Ermyntrude shook her old head and laughed.

"You have your father's great soul, Nigel, but you have not his mighty breadth of shoulder and length of limb. There was not in all the King's great host a taller or a stronger man. His harness would be little use to you. No, fair son, I rede you that when the time comes you sell this crumbling house and the few acres which are still left, and so go forth to the wars in the hope that with your own right hand you will plant the fortunes of a new house of Loring."

A shadow of anger passed over Nigel's fresh young face.

"I know not if we may hold off these monks and their lawyers much longer. This very day there came a man from Guildford with claims from the Abbey extending back before my father's death."

"Where are they, fair son?"

"They are flapping on the furze-bushes of Hankley, for I sent his papers and parchments down wind as fast as ever falcon flew."

"Nay! you were mad to do that, Nigel. And the man, where is he?"

"Red Swire and old George the archer threw him into the Thursley bog."

"Alas! I fear me such things cannot be done in these days, though my father or my husband would have sent the rascal back to Guildford without his ears. But the Church and the Law are too strong now for us who are of gentler blood. Trouble will come of it, Nigel, for the Abbot of Waverley is not one who will hold back the shield of the Church from those who are her servants."

"The Abbot would not hurt us. It is that gray lean wolf of a sacrist who hungers for our land. Let him do his worst. I fear him not."

"He has such an engine at his back, Nigel, that even the bravest must fear him. The ban which blasts a man's soul is in the keeping of his church, and what have we to place against it? I pray you to speak him fair, Nigel."

"Nay, dear lady, it is both my duty and my pleasure to do what you bid me; but I would die ere I ask as a favor that which we can claim as a right. Never can I cast my eyes from yonder window that I do not see the swelling down-lands and the rich meadows, glade and dingle, copse and wood, which have been ours since Norman-William gave them to that Loring who bore his shield at Senlac. Now, by trick and fraud, they have passed away from us, and many a franklin is a richer man than I; but never shall it be said that I saved the rest by bending my neck to their yoke. Let them do their worst, and let me endure it or fight it as best I may."

The old lady sighed and shook her head. "You speak as a Loring should, and yet I fear that some great trouble will befall us. But let us talk no more of such matters, since we cannot mend them. Where is your citole, Nigel? Will you not play and sing to me?"

The gentleman of those days could scarce read and write; but he spoke in two languages, played at least one musical instrument as a matter of course, and possessed a number of other accomplishments, from the imping of hawk's feathers, to the mystery of venery, with knowledge of every beast and bird, its time of grace and when it was seasonable. As far as physical feats went, to vault barebacked upon a horse, to hit a running hare with a crossbow-bolt, or to climb the angle of a castle courtyard, were feats which had come by nature to the young Squire; but it was very different with music, which had called for many a weary hour of irksome work. Now at last he could master the strings, but both his ear and his voice were not of the best, so that it was well perhaps that there was so small and so unprejudiced an audience to the Norman-French chanson, which he sang in a high reedy voice with great earnestness of feeling, but with many a slip and quaver, waving his yellow head in cadence to the music:

> A sword! A sword! Ah, give me a sword!
>> For the world is all to win.
> Though the way be hard and the door be barred,
>> The strong man enters in.

If Chance and Fate still hold the gate,
    Give me the iron key,
And turret high my plume shall fly,
    Or you may weep for me!

A horse! A horse! Ah, give me a horse!
    To bear me out afar,
Where blackest need and grimmest deed
    And sweetest perils are.
Hold thou my ways from glutted days
    Where poisoned leisure lies,
And point the path of tears and wrath
    Which mounts to high emprise!

A heart! A heart! Ah, give me a heart
    To rise to circumstance!
Serene and high and bold to try
    The hazard of the chance,
With strength to wait, but fixed as fate
    To plan and dare and do,
The peer of all, and only thrall,
    Sweet lady mine, to you!

It may have been that the sentiment went for more than the music, or it may have been the nicety of her own ears had been dulled by age, but old Dame Ermyntrude clapped her lean hands together and cried out in shrill applause.

"Weathercote has indeed had an apt pupil!" she said. "I pray you that you will sing again."

"Nay, dear dame, it is turn and turn betwixt you and me. I beg that you will recite a romance, you who know them all. For all the years that I have listened I have never yet come to the end of them, and I dare swear that there are more in your head than in all the great books which they showed me at Guildford Castle. I would fain hear 'Doon of Mayence,' or 'The Song of Roland,' or 'Sir Isumbras.'"

So the old dame broke into a long poem, slow and dull in the inception, but quickening as the interest grew, until with darting hands and glowing face she poured forth the verses which told of the emptiness of sordid life, the beauty of heroic death, the high sacredness of love and the bondage of honor. Nigel, with set, still features and brooding eyes, drank in the fiery words, until at last they died upon the old woman's lips and she sank back weary in her chair. Nigel stooped over her and kissed her brow.

"Your words will ever be as a star upon my path," said he. Then, carrying over the small table and the chessmen, he proposed that they should play their usual game before they sought their rooms for the night.

But a sudden and rude interruption broke in upon their gentle contest. A dog pricked its ears and barked. The others ran growling to the door. And then there came a sharp clash of arms, a dull heavy blow as from a club or sword-pommel, and a deep voice from without summoned them to open in the King's name. The old dame and Nigel had both sprung to their feet, their table overturned and their chessmen scattered among the rushes. Nigel's hand had sought his crossbow, but the Lady Ermyntrude grasped his arm.

"Nay, fair son! Have you not heard that it is in the King's name?" said she. "Down, Talbot! Down, Bayard! Open the door and let his messenger in!"

Nigel undid the bolt, and the heavy wooden door swung outward upon its hinges. The light from the flaring cressets beat upon steel caps and fierce bearded faces, with the glimmer of drawn swords and the yellow gleam of bow-staves. A dozen armed archers forced their way into the room. At their head were the gaunt sacrist of Waverley and a stout elderly man clad in a red-velvet doublet and breeches much stained and mottled with mud and clay. He bore a great sheet of parchment with a fringe of dangling seals, which he held aloft as he entered.

"I call on Nigel Loring!" he cried. "I, the officer of the King's law and the lay summoner of Waverley, call upon the man named Nigel Loring!"

"I am he."

"Yes, it is he!" cried the sacrist. "Archers, do as you were ordered!"

In an instant the band threw themselves upon him like the hounds on a stag. Desperately Nigel strove to gain his sword which lay upon the iron coffer. With the convulsive strength which comes from the spirit rather than from the body, he bore them all in that direction, but the sacrist snatched the weapon from its place, and the rest dragged the writhing Squire to the ground and swathed him in a cord.

"Hold him fast, good archers! Keep a stout grip on him!" cried the summoner. "I pray you, one of you, prick off these great dogs which snarl at my heels. Stand off, I say, in the name of the King! Watkin, come betwixt me and these creatures who have as little regard for the law as their master."

One of the archers kicked off the faithful dogs. But there were others of the household who were equally ready to show their teeth in defense of the old house of Loring. From the door which led to their quarters there emerged the pitiful muster of Nigel's threadbare retainers. There was a time when ten knights, forty men-at-arms and two hundred archers would march behind the scarlet roses. Now at this last rally when the young head of the house lay bound in his own hall, there mustered at his call the page Charles with a cudgel, John the cook with his longest spit, Red Swire the aged man-at-arms with a formidable ax swung over his snowy head, and Weathercote the minstrel with a boar-spear. Yet this motley array was fired with the spirit of the house, and under the lead of the fierce old soldier they would certainly have flung themselves upon the ready swords of the archers, had the Lady Ermyntrude not swept between them.

"Stand back, Swire!" she cried. "Back, Weathercote! Charles, put a leash on Talbot, and hold Bayard back!" Her black eyes blazed upon the invaders until they shrank from that baleful gaze. "Who are you, you rascal robbers, who dare to misuse the King's name and to lay hands upon one whose smallest drop of blood has more worth than all your thrall and caitiff bodies?"

"Nay, not so fast, dame, not so fast, I pray you!" cried the stout summoner, whose face had resumed its natural color, now that he had a woman to deal with. "There is a law of England, mark you, and there are those who serve and uphold it, who are the true men and the King's own lieges. Such a one am I. Then again, there are those who take such as me and transfer, carry or convey us into a bog or morass. Such a one is this graceless old man with the ax, whom I have seen already this day. There are also those who tear, destroy or scatter the papers of the law, of which this young man is the chief. Therefore, I would rede you, dame, not to rail against us, but to understand that we are the King's men on the King's own service."

"What then is your errand in this house at this hour of the night?"

The summoner cleared his throat pompously, and turning his parchment to the light of the cressets he read out a long document in Norman-French, couched in such a style and such a language that the most involved and foolish of our forms were simplicity itself compared to those by which the men of the long gown made a mystery of that which of all things on earth should be the plainest and the most simple. Despair fell cold upon Nigel's heart and blanched the face of the old dame as they listened to the dread catalogue of claims and suits and issues, questions of peccary and turbary, of house-bote and fire-bote, which ended by a demand for all the lands, hereditaments, tenements, messuages and curtilages, which made up their worldly all.

Nigel, still bound, had been placed with his back against the iron coffer, whence he heard with dry lips and moist brow this doom of his house. Now he broke in on the recital with a vehemence which made the summoner jump:

"You shall rue what you have done this night!" he cried. "Poor as we are, we have our friends who will not see us wronged, and I will plead my cause before the King's own majesty at Windsor, that he, who saw the father die, may know what things are done in his royal name against the son. But these matters are to be settled in course of law in the King's courts, and how will you excuse yourself for this assault upon my house and person?"

"Nay, that is another matter," said the sacrist. "The question of debt may indeed be an affair of a civil court. But it is a crime against the law and an act of the Devil, which comes within the jurisdiction of the Abbey Court of Waverley when you dare to lay hands upon the summoner or his papers."

"Indeed, he speaks truth," cried the official. "I know no blacker sin."

"Therefore," said the stern monk, "it is the order of the holy father Abbot that you sleep this night in the Abbey cell, and that to-morrow you be brought before him at the court held in the chapter-house so that you receive the fit punishment for this and the many other violent and froward deeds which you have wrought upon the servants of Holy Church. Enough is now said, worthy master summoner. Archers, remove your prisoner!"

As Nigel was lifted up by four stout archers, the Dame Ermyntrude would have rushed to his aid, but the sacrist thrust her back.

"Stand off, proud woman! Let the law take its course, and learn to humble your heart before the power of Holy Church. Has your life not taught its lesson, you, whose horn was exalted among the highest and will soon not have a roof above your gray hairs? Stand back, I say, lest I lay a curse upon you!"

The old dame flamed suddenly into white wrath as she stood before the angry monk: "Listen to me while I lay a curse upon you and yours!" she cried as she raised her shriveled arms and blighted him with her flashing eyes "As you have done to the house of Loring, so may God do to you, until your power is swept from the land of England, and of your great Abbey of Waverley there is nothing left but a pile of gray stones in a green meadow! I see it! I see it! With my old eyes I see it! From scullion to Abbot and from cellar to tower, may Waverley and all within it droop and wither from this night on!"

The monk, hard as he was, quailed before the frantic figure and the bitter, burning words. Already the summoner and the archers with their prisoner were clear of the house. He turned and with a clang he shut the heavy door behind him.

CHAPTER V

HOW NIGEL WAS TRIED
BY THE ABBOT OF WAVERLEY

THE law of the Middle Ages, shrouded as it was in old Norman-French dialect, and abounding in uncouth and incomprehensible terms, in deodands and heriots, in infang and outfang, was a fearsome weapon in the hands of those who knew how to use it. It was not for nothing that the first act of the rebel commoners was to hew off the head of the Lord Chancellor. In an age when few knew how to read or to write, these mystic phrases and intricate forms, with the parchments and seals which were their outward expression, struck cold terror into hearts which were steeled against mere physical danger.

Even young Nigel Loring's blithe and elastic spirit was chilled as he lay that night in the penal cell of Waverley and pondered over the absolute ruin which threatened his house from a source against which all his courage was of no avail. As well take up sword and shield to defend himself against the black death, as against this blight of Holy Church. He was powerless in the grip of the Abbey. Already they had shorn off a field here and a grove there, and now in one sweep they would take in the rest, and where then was the home of the Lorings, and where should Lady Ermyntrude lay her aged head, or his old retainers, broken and spent, eke out the balance of their days? He shivered as he thought of it.

It was very well for him to threaten to carry the matter before the King, but it was years since royal Edward had heard the name of Loring, and Nigel knew that the memory of princes was a short one. Besides, the Church was the ruling power in the palace as well as in the cottage, and it was only for very good cause that a King could be expected to cross the purposes of so high a prelate as the Abbot of Waverley, as long as they came within the scope of the law. Where then was he to look for help? With the simple and practical piety of the age, he prayed for the aid of his own particular saints: of Saint Paul, whose adventures by land and sea; had always endeared him; of Saint George, who had gained much honorable advancement from the Dragon; and of Saint Thomas, who was a gentleman of coat-armor, who would understand and help a person of gentle blood. Then, much comforted by his naïve orisons he enjoyed the sleep of youth and health until the entrance of the lay brother with the bread and small beer, which served as breakfast, in the morning.

The Abbey court sat in the chapter-house at the canonical hour of tierce, which was nine in the forenoon. At all times the function was a solemn one, even when the culprit might be a villain who was taken poaching on the Abbey estate, or a chapman who had given false measure from his biased scales. But now, when a man of noble birth was to be tried, the whole legal and ecclesiastical ceremony was carried out with every detail, grotesque or impressive, which the full ritual prescribed. The distant roll of church music and the slow tolling of the Abbey bell; the white-robed brethren, two and two, walked thrice round the hall singing the "*Benedicite*" and the "*Veni, Creator*" before they settled in their places at the desks on either side. Then in turn each high officer of the Abbey from below upward, the almoner, the lector, the chaplain, the subprior and the prior, swept to their wonted places.

Finally there came the grim sacrist, with demure triumph upon his downcast features, and at his heels Abbot John himself, slow and dignified, with pompous walk and solemn, composed face, his iron-beaded rosary swinging from his waist, his breviary in his hand, and his lips muttering as he hurried through his office for the day. He knelt at his high pre-dieu; the brethren, at a signal from the prior, prostrated themselves upon the floor, and the low deep voices rolled in prayer, echoed back from the arched and vaulted roof like the wash of waves from an ocean cavern. Finally the monks resumed their seats; there entered clerks in seemly black with pens and parchment; the red-velveted summoner appeared to tell his tale; Nigel was led in with archers pressing close around him; and then, with much calling of old French and much legal incantation and mystery, the court of the Abbey was open for business.

It was the sacrist who first advanced to the oaken desk reserved for the witnesses and expounded in hard, dry, mechanical fashion the many claims which the House of Waverley had against the family of Loring. Some generations back in return for money advanced or for spiritual favor received the Loring of the day had admitted that his estate had certain feudal duties toward the Abbey. The sacrist held up the crackling yellow parchment with swinging leaden seals on which the claim was based. Amid the obligations was that of escuage, by which the price of a knight's fee should be paid every year. No such price had been paid, nor had any service been done. The accumulated years came now to a greater sum than the fee simple of the estate. There were other claims also. The sacrist called for his books, and with thin, eager forefinger he tracked them down: dues for this, and tailage for that, so many shillings this year, and so many marks that one. Some of it occurred before Nigel was born; some of it when he was but a child. The accounts had been checked and certified by the sergeant of the law.

Nigel listened to the dread recital, and felt like some young stag who stands at bay with brave pose and heart of fire, but who sees himself compassed round and knows clearly that there is no escape. With his bold young face, his steady blue eyes, and the proud poise of his head, he was a worthy scion of the old house, and the sun, shining through the high oriel window, and showing up the stained and threadbare condition of his once rich doublet, seemed to illuminate the fallen fortunes of his family.

The sacrist had finished his exposition, and the sergeant-at-law was about to conclude a case which Nigel could in no way controvert, when help came to him from an unexpected quarter. It may have been a certain malignity with which the sacrist urged his suit, it may have been a diplomatic dislike to driving matters to extremes, or it may have been some genuine impulse of kindliness, for Abbot John was choleric but easily appeased. Whatever the cause, the result was that a white plump hand, raised in the air with a gesture of authority, showed that the case was at an end.

"Our brother sacrist hath done his duty in urging this suit," said he, "for the worldly wealth of this Abbey is placed in his pious keeping, and it is to him that we should look if we suffered in such ways, for we are but the trustees of those who come after us. But to my keeping has been consigned that which is more precious still, the inner spirit and high repute of those who follow the rule of Saint Bernard. Now it has ever been our endeavor, since first our saintly founder went down into the valley of Clairvaux and built himself a cell there, that we should set an example to all men in gentleness and humility. For this reason it is that we built our houses in lowly places, that we have no tower to our Abbey churches, and that no finery and no metal, save only iron or lead, come within our walls. A brother shall eat from a wooden platter, drink from an iron cup, and light himself from a leaden sconce. Surely it is not for such an order who await the exaltation which is promised to the humble, to judge their own case and so acquire the lands of their neighbor! If our cause be just, as indeed I believe that it is, then it were better that it be judged at the King's assizes at Guildford, and so I decree that the case be now dismissed from the Abbey court so that it can be heard elsewhere."

Nigel breathed a prayer to the three sturdy saints who had stood by him so manfully and well in the hour of his need. "Abbot John," said he, "I never thought that any man of my

name would utter thanks to a Cistercian of Waverley; but by
Saint Paul! you have spoken like a man this day, for it would
indeed be to play with cogged dice if the Abbey's case is to be
tried in the Abbey court."

The eighty white-clad brethren looked with half resentful,
half amused eyes as they listened to this frank address to one
who, in their small lives, seemed to be the direct vice-regent of
Heaven. The archers had stood back from Nigel, as though he
was at liberty to go, when the loud voice of the summoner broke
in upon the silence:

"If it please you, holy father Abbot," cried the voice, "this decision of yours is indeed *secundum legem* and *intra vires* so far as the
civil suit is concerned which lies between this person and the
Abbey. That is your affair; but it is I, Joseph the summoner, who
have been grievously and criminally mishandled, my writs, papers
and indentures destroyed, my authority flouted, and my person
dragged through a bog, quagmire or morass, so that my velvet
gabardine and silver badge of office were lost and are, as I verily
believe, in the morass, quagmire or bog aforementioned, which is
the same bog, morass——"

"Enough!" cried the Abbot sternly. "Lay aside this foolish fashion of speech and say straitly what you desire."

"Holy father, I have been the officer of the King's law no less
than the servant of Holy Church, and I have been let, hindered
and assaulted in the performance of my lawful and proper duties,
whilst my papers, drawn in the King's name, have been shended
and rended and cast to the wind. Therefore, I demand justice
upon this man in the Abbey court, the said assault having been
committed within the banlieue of the Abbey's jurisdiction."

"What have you to say to this, brother sacrist?" asked the Abbot
in some perplexity.

"I would say, father, that it is within our power to deal gently
and charitably with all that concerns ourselves, but that where a
the King's officer is concerned we are wanting in our duty if we
give him less than the protection that he demands. I would

remind you also, holy father, that this is not the first of this man's violence, but that he has before now beaten our servants, defied our authority, and put pike in the Abbot's own fish-pond."

The prelate's heavy cheeks flushed with anger as this old grievance came fresh into his mind. His eyes hardened as he looked at the prisoner. "Tell me, Squire Nigel, did you indeed put pike in the pond?"

The young man drew himself proudly up. "Ere I answer such a question, father Abbot, do you answer one from me, and tell me what the monks of Waverley have ever done for me that I should hold my hand when I could injure them?"

A low murmur ran round the room, partly wonder at his frankness, and partly anger at his boldness.

The Abbot settled down in his seat as one who has made up his mind. "Let the case of the summoner be laid before me," said he. "Justice shall be done, and the offender shall be punished, be he noble or simple. Let the plaint be brought before the court."

The tale of the summoner, though rambling and filled with endless legal reiteration, was only too clear in its essence. Red Swire, with his angry face framed in white bristles, was led in, and confessed to his ill treatment of the official. A second culprit, a little wiry nut-brown archer from Churt, had aided and abetted in the deed. Both of them were ready to declare that young Squire Nigel Loring knew nothing of the matter. But then there was the awkward incident of the tearing of the writs. Nigel, to whom a lie was an impossibility, had to admit that with his own hands he had shredded those august documents. As to an excuse or an explanation, he was too proud to advance any. A cloud gathered over the brow of the Abbot, and the sacrist gazed with an ironical smile at the prisoner, while a solemn hush fell over the chapter-house as the case ended and only judgment remained.

"Squire Nigel," said the Abbot, "it was for you, who are, as all men know, of ancient lineage in this land, to give a fair example by which others should set their conduct. Instead of this, your manor-house has ever been a center for the stirring up of strife, and now not content with your harsh showing toward us, the Cistercian monks of Waverley, you have even marked your contempt for the King's law, and through your servants have mishandled the person of his messenger. For such offenses it is in my power to call the spiritual terrors of the Church upon your head, and yet I would not be harsh with you, seeing that you are young, and that even last week you saved the life of a servant of the Abbey when in peril. Therefore, it is by temporal and carnal means that I will use my power to tame your overbold spirit, and to chasten that headstrong and violent humor which has caused such scandal in your dealings with our Abbey. Bread and water for six weeks from now to the Feast of Saint Benedict, with a daily exhortation from our chaplain, the pious Father Ambrose, may still avail to bend the stiff neck and to soften the hard heart."

At this ignominious sentence by which the proud heir of the house of Loring would share the fate of the meanest village poacher, the hot blood of Nigel rushed to his face, and his eye glanced round him with a gleam which said more plainly than words that there could be no tame acceptance of such a doom. Twice he tried to speak, and twice his anger and his shame held the words in his throat.

"I am no subject of yours, proud Abbot!" he cried at last. "My house has ever been vavasor to the King. I deny the power of you and your court to lay sentence upon me. Punish these your own monks, who whimper at your frown, but do not dare to lay your hand upon him who fears you not, for he is a free man, and the peer of any save only the King himself."

The Abbot seemed for an instant taken aback by these bold words, and by the high and strenuous voice in which they were uttered. But the sterner sacrist came as ever to stiffen his will. He held up the old parchment in his hand.

"The Lorings were indeed vavasors to the King," said he; "but here is the very seal of Eustace Loring which shows that he made himself vassal to the Abbey and held his land from it."

"Because he was gentle," cried Nigel, "because he had no thought of trick or guile."

"Nay!" said the summoner. "If my voice may be heard, father Abbot, upon a point of the law, it is of no weight what the causes may have been why a deed is subscribed, signed or confirmed, but a court is concerned only with the terms, articles, covenants and contracts of the said deed."

"Besides," said the sacrist, "sentence is passed by the Abbey court, and there is an end of its honor and good name if it be not upheld."

"Brother sacrist," said the Abbot angrily, "methinks you show overmuch zeal in this case, and certes, we are well able to uphold the dignity and honor of the Abbey court without any rede of thine. As to you, worthy summoner, you will give your opinion when we crave for it, and not before, or you may yourself get some touch of the power of our tribunal. But your case hath been tried, Squire Loring, and judgment given. I have no more to say."

He motioned with his hand, and an archer laid his grip upon the shoulder of the prisoner. But that rough plebeian touch woke every passion of revolt in Nigel's spirit. Of all his high line of ancestors, was there one who had been subjected to such ignominy as this? Would they not have preferred death? And should he be the first to lower their spirit or their traditions? With a quick, lithe movement, he slipped under the arm of the archer, and plucked the short, straight sword from the soldier's side as he did so. The next instant he had wedged himself into the recess of one of the narrow windows, and there were his pale set face, his burning eyes, and his ready blade turned upon the assembly.

"By Saint Paul!" said he, "I never thought to find honorable advancement under the roof of an abbey, but perchance there may, be some room for it ere you hale me to your prison."

The chapter-house was in an uproar. Never in the long and decorous history of the Abbey had such a scene been witnessed within its walls. The monks themselves seemed for an instant to be infected by this spirit of daring revolt. Their own lifelong fetters hung more loosely as they viewed this unheard-of defiance of authority. They broke from their seats on either side and huddled half-scared, half-fascinated, in a large half-circle round the defiant captive, chattering, pointing, grimacing, a scandal for all time. Scourges should fall and penance be done for many a long week before the shadow of that day should pass from Waverley. But meanwhile there was no effort to bring them back to their rule. Everything was chaos and disorder. The Abbot had left his seat of justice and hurried angrily forward, to be engulfed and hustled in the crowd of his own monks like a sheep-dog who finds himself entangled amid a flock.

Only the sacrist stood clear. He had taken shelter behind the half-dozen archers, who looked with some approval and a good deal of indecision at this bold fugitive from justice.

"On him!" cried the sacrist. "Shall he defy the authority of the court, or shall one man hold six of you at bay? Close in upon him and seize him. You, Baddlesmere, why do you hold back?"

The man in question, a tall bushy-bearded fellow, clad like the others in green jerkin and breeches with high brown boots, advanced slowly, sword in hand, against Nigel. His heart was not in the business, for these clerical courts were not popular, and everyone had a tender heart for the fallen fortunes of the house of Loring and wished well to its young heir.

"Come, young sir, you have caused scathe enough," said he. "Stand forth and give yourself up!"

"Come and fetch me, good fellow," said Nigel, with a dangerous smile.

The archer ran in. There was a rasp of steel, a blade flickered like a swift dart of flame, and the man staggered back, with blood running down his forearm and dripping from his fingers. He wrung them and growled a Saxon oath.

"By the black rood of Bromeholm!" he cried, "I had as soon put my hand down a fox's earth to drag up a vixen from her cubs."

"Standoff!" said Nigel curtly. "I would not hurt you; but by Saint Paul! I will not be handled, or some one will be hurt in the handling."

So fierce was his eye and so menacing his blade as he crouched in the narrow bay of the window that the little knot of archers were at a loss what to do. The Abbot had forced his way through the crowd and stood, purple with outraged dignity, at their side.

"He is outside the law," said he. "He hath shed blood in a court of justice, and for such a sin there is no forgiveness. I will not have my court so flouted and set at naught. He who draws the sword, by the sword also let him perish. Forester Hugh lay a shaft to your bow!"

The man, who was one of the Abbey's lay servants, put his weight upon his long bow and slipped the loose end of the string into the upper notch. Then, drawing one of the terrible three-foot arrows, steel-tipped and gaudily winged, from his waist, he laid it to the string.

"Now draw your bow and hold it ready!" cried the furious Abbot. "Squire Nigel, it is not for Holy Church to shed blood, but there is naught but violence which will prevail against the violent, and on your head be the sin. Cast down the sword which you hold in your hand!"

"Will you give me freedom to leave your Abbey?"

"When you have abided your sentence and purged your sin."

"Then I had rather die where I stand than give up my sword."

A dangerous flame lit in the Abbot's eyes. He came of a fighting Norman stock, like so many of those fierce prelates who, bearing a mace lest they should be guilty of effusion of blood, led their troops into battle, ever remembering that it was one of their own cloth and dignity who, crosier in hand, had turned the long-drawn bloody day of Hastings. The soft accent of the churchman was gone and it was the hard voice of a soldier which said:

"One minute I give you, and no more. Then when I cry 'Loose!' drive me an arrow through his body."

The shaft was fitted, the bow was bent, and the stern eyes of the woodman were fixed on his mark. Slowly the minute passed, while Nigel breathed a prayer to his three soldier saints, not that they should save his body in this life, but that they should have a kindly care for his soul in the next. Some thought of a fierce wildcat sally crossed his mind, but once out of his corner he was lost indeed. Yet at the last he would have rushed among his enemies, and his body was bent for the spring, when with a deep sonorous hum, like a breaking harp-string, the cord of the bow was cloven in twain, and the arrow tinkled upon the tiled floor. At the same moment a young curly-headed bowman, whose broad shoulders and deep chest told of immense strength, as clearly as his frank, laughing face and honest hazel eyes did of good humor and courage, sprang forward sword in hand and took his place by Nigel's side.

"Nay, comrades!" said he. "Samkin Aylward cannot stand by and see a gallant man shot down like a bull at the end of a baiting. Five against one is long odds; but two against four is better, and by my finger-bones! Squire Nigel and I leave this room together, be it on our feet or no."

The formidable appearance of this ally and his high reputation among his fellows gave a further chill to the lukewarm ardor of the attack. Aylward's left arm was passed through his strung bow, and he was known from Woolmer Forest to the Weald as the quickest, surest archer that ever dropped a running deer at ten-score paces.

"Nay, Baddlesmere, hold your fingers from your string-case, or I may chance to give your drawing hand a two months' rest," said Aylward. "Swords, if you will, comrades, but no man strings his bow till I have loosed mine."

Yet the angry hearts of both Abbot and sacrist rose higher with a fresh obstacle.

"This is an ill day for your father, Franklin Aylward, who holds the tenancy of Crooksbury," said the sacrist. "He will rue it that ever he begot a son who will lose him his acres and his steading."

"My father is a bold yeoman, and would rue it evermore that ever his son should stand by while foul work was afoot," said Aylward stoutly. "Fall on, comrades! We are waiting."

Encouraged by promises of reward if they should fall in the service of the Abbey, and by threats of penalties if they should hold back, the four archers were about to close, when a singular interruption gave an entirely new turn to the proceedings.

At the door of the chapter-house, while these fiery doings had been afoot, there had assembled a mixed crowd of lay brothers, servants and varlets who had watched the development of the drama with the interest and delight with which men hail a sudden break in a dull routine. Suddenly there was an agitation at the back of this group, then a swirl in the center, and finally the front rank was violently thrust aside, and through the gap there emerged a strange and whimsical figure, who from the instant of his appearance dominated both chapter-house and Abbey, monks, prelates and archers, as if he were their owner and their master.

He was a man somewhat above middle age, with thin lemon-colored hair, a curling mustache, a tufted chin of the same hue, and a high craggy face, all running to a great hook of the nose, like the beak of an eagle. His skin was tanned a brown-red by much exposure to the wind and sun. In height he was tall, and his figure was thin and loose-jointed, but stringy and hard-bitten. One eye was entirely covered by its lid, which lay flat over an empty socket, but the other danced and sparkled with a most roguish light, darting here and there with a twinkle of humor and criticism and intelligence, the whole fire of his soul bursting through that one narrow cranny.

His dress was as noteworthy as his person. A rich purple doublet and cloak was marked on the lapels with a strange scarlet device shaped like a wedge. Costly lace hung round his shoulders, and amid its soft folds there smoldered the dull red of a heavy golden chain. A knight's belt at his waist and a knight's golden spurs twinkling from his doeskin riding-boots proclaimed his rank, and on the wrist of his left gauntlet there sat a demure little hooded falcon of a breed which in itself was a mark of the dignity of the owner. Of weapons he had none, but a mandolin was slung by a black silken band over his back, and the high brown end projected above his shoulder. Such was the man, quaint, critical, masterful, with a touch of what is formidable behind it, who now surveyed the opposing groups of armed men and angry monks with an eye which commanded their attention.

"*Excusez!*" said he, in a lisping French. "*Excusez, mes amis!* I had thought to arouse from prayer or meditation, but never have I seen such a holy exercise as this under an abbey's roof, with swords for breviaries and archers for acolytes. I fear that I have come amiss, and yet I ride on an errand from one who permits no delay."

The Abbot, and possibly the sacrist also, had begun to realize that events had gone a great deal farther than they had intended, and that without an extreme scandal it was no easy matter for them to save their dignity and the good name of Waverley. Therefore, in spite of the debonair, not to say disrespectful, bearing of the newcomer, they rejoiced at his appearance and intervention.

"I am the Abbot of Waverley, fair son," said the prelate. "If your message deal with a public matter it may be fitly repeated in the chapter-house; if not I will give you audience in my own chamber; for it is clear to me that you are a gentle man of blood and coat-armor who would not lightly break in upon the business of our court—a business which, as you have remarked, is little welcome to men of peace like myself and the brethren of the rule of Saint Bernard."

"*Pardieu!* Father Abbot," said the stranger. "One had but to glance at you and your men to see that the business was indeed little to your taste, and it may be even less so when I say that rather than see this young person in the window, who hath a noble bearing, further molested by these archers, I will myself adventure my person on his behalf."

The Abbot's smile turned to a frown at these frank words. "It would become you better, sir, to deliver the message of which you say that you are the bearer, than to uphold a prisoner against the rightful judgment of a court."

The stranger swept the court with his questioning eye. "The message is not for you, good father Abbot. It is for one whom I know not. I have been to his house, and they have sent me hither. The name is Nigel Loring."

"It is for me, fair sir."

"I had thought as much. I knew your father, Eustace Loring, and though he would have made two of you, yet he has left his stamp plain enough upon your face."

"You know not the truth of this matter," said the Abbot. "If you are a loyal man, you will stand aside, for this young man hath grievously offended against the law, and it is for the King's lieges to give us their support."

"And you have haled him up for judgment," cried the stranger with much amusement. "It is as though a rookery sat in judgment upon a falcon. I warrant that you have found it easier to judge than to punish. Let me tell you, father Abbot, that this standeth not aright. When powers such as these were given to the like of you, they were given that you might check a brawling underling or correct a drunken woodman, and not that you might drag the best blood in England to your bar and set your archers on him if he questioned your findings."

The Abbot was little used to hear such words of reproof uttered in so stern a voice under his own abbey roof and before his listening monks. "You may perchance find that an Abbey court has more powers than you wot of, Sir Knight," said he, "if knight indeed you be who are so uncourteous and short in your speech. Ere we go further, I would ask your name and style?"

The stranger laughed. "It is easy to see that you are indeed men of peace," said he proudly. "Had I shown this sign," and he touched the token upon his lapels, "whether on shield or pennon, in the marches of France or Scotland, there is not a cavalier but would have known the red pile of Chandos."

Chandos, John Chandos, the flower of English chivalry, the pink of knight-errantry, the hero already of fifty desperate enterprises, a man known and honored from end to end of Europe! Nigel gazed at him as one who sees a vision. The archers stood back abashed, while the monks crowded closer to stare at the famous soldier of the French wars. The Abbot abated his tone, and a smile came to his angry face.

"We are indeed men of peace, Sir John, and little skilled in warlike blazonry," said he; " yet stout as are our Abbey walls, they are not so thick that the fame of your exploits has not passed through them and reached our ears. If it be your pleasure to take an interest in this young and misguided Squire, it is not for us to thwart your kind intention or to withhold such grace as you request. I am glad indeed that he hath one who can set him so fair an example for a friend."

"I thank you for your courtesy, good father Abbot," said Chandos carelessly. "This young Squire has, however, a better friend than myself, one who is kinder to those he loves and more terrible to those he hates. It is from him I bear a message."

"I pray you, fair and honored sir," said Nigel, "that you will tell me what is the message that you bear."

"The message, *mon ami,* is that your friend comes into these parts and would have a night's lodging at the manor-house of Tilford for the love and respect that he bears your family."

"Nay, he is most welcome," said Nigel, "and yet I hope that he is one who can relish a soldier's fare and sleep under a humble roof, for indeed we can but give our best, poor as it is."

"He is indeed a soldier and a good one," Chandos answered, laughing, "and I warrant he has slept in rougher quarters than Tilford Manor-house."

"I have few friends, fair sir," said Nigel, with a puzzled face. "I pray you give me this gentleman's name."

"His name is Edward."

"Sir Edward Mortimer of Kent, perchance, or is it Sir Edward Brocas of whom the Lady Ermyntrude talks?"

"Nay, he is known as Edward only, and if you ask a second name it is Plantagenet, for he who comes to seek the shelter of your roof is your liege lord and mine, the King's high majesty, Edward of England."

CHAPTER VI

IN WHICH LADY ERMYNTRUDE OPENS
THE IRON COFFER

As in a dream Nigel heard these stupendous and incredible words. As in a dream also he had a vision of a smiling and conciliatory Abbot, of an obsequious sacrist, and of a band of archers who cleared a path for him and for the King's messenger through the motley crowd who had choked the entrance of the Abbey court. A minute later he was walking by the side of Chandos through the peaceful cloister, and in front in the open archway of the great gate was the broad yellow road between its borders of green meadow-land. The spring air was the sweeter and the more fragrant for that chill dread of dishonor and captivity which had so recently frozen his ardent heart. He had already passed the portal when a hand plucked at his sleeve and he turned to find himself confronted by the brown honest face and hazel eyes of the archer who had interfered in his behalf. "

Well," said Aylward, "what have you to say to me, young sir?"

"What can I say, my good fellow, save that I thank you with all my heart? By Saint Paul! if you had been my blood brother you could not have stood by me more stoutly."

"Nay! but this is not enough."

Nigel colored with vexation, and the more so as Chandos was listening with his critical smile to their conversation. "If you had heard what was said in the court," said he, "you would understand that I am not blessed at this moment with much of this world's gear. The black death and the monks have between them been heavy upon our estate. Willingly would I give you a handful of gold for your assistance, since that is what you seem to crave; but indeed I have it not, and so once more I say that you must be satisfied with my thanks."

"Your gold is nothing to me," said Aylward shortly, "nor would you buy my loyalty if you filled my wallet with rose nobles, so long as you were not a man after my own heart. But I have seen you back the yellow horse, and I have seen you face the Abbot of Waverley, and you are such a master as I would very gladly serve if you have by chance a place for such a man. I have seen your following, and I doubt not that they were stout fellows in your grandfather's time; but which of them now would draw a bow-string to his ear? Through you I have left the service of the Abbey of Waverley, and where can I look now for a post? If I stay here I am all undone like a fretted bowstring."

"Nay, there can be no difficulty there," said Chandos. *"Pardieu!* a roistering, swaggering dare-devil archer is worth his price on the French border. There are two hundred such who march behind my own person, and I would ask nothing better than to see you among them."

"I thank you, noble sir, for your offer," said Aylward, "and I had rather follow your banner than many another one, for it is well known that it goes ever forward, and I have heard enough of the wars to know that there are small pickings for the man who lags behind. Yet, if the Squire will have me, I would choose to fight under the five roses of Loring, for though I was born in the hundred of Easebourne and the rape of Chichester, yet I have grown up and learned to use the longbow in these parts, and as the free son of a free franklin I had rather serve my own neighbor than a stranger."

"My good fellow," said Nigel, "I have told you that I could in no wise reward you for such service."

"If you will but take me to the wars I will see to my own reward," said Aylward. "Till then I ask for none, save a corner of your table and six feet of your floor, for it is certain that the only reward I would get from the Abbey for this day's work would be the scourge for my back and the stocks for my ankles. Samkin Aylward is your man, Squire Nigel, from this hour on, and by these ten finger-bones he trusts the Devil will fly away with him if ever he gives you cause to regret it!" So saying he raised his hand to his steel cap in salute, slung his great yellow bow over his back, and followed on some paces in the rear of his new master.

"*Pardieu!* I have arrived *à la bonne heure,*" said Chandos. "I rode from Windsor and came to your manor-house, to find it empty save for a fine old dame, who old me of your troubles. From her I walked across to the Abbey, and none too soon, for what with cloth-yard shafts for your body, and bell, book and candle for your soul, it was no very cheerful outlook. But here is the very dame herself, if I mistake not."

It was indeed the formidable figure of the Lady Ermyntrude, gaunt, bowed and leaning on her staff, which had emerged from the door of the manor-house and advanced to greet them. She croaked with laughter, and shook her stick at the great building as she heard of the discomfiture of the Abbey court. Then she led the way into the hall where the best which she could provide had been laid out for their illustrious guest. There was Chandos blood in her own veins, traceable back through the de Greys, de Multons, de Valences, de Montagues and other high and noble strains, so that the meal had been eaten and cleared before she had done tracing the network of intermarriages and connections, with quarterings, impalements, lozenges and augmentations by which the blazonry of the two families might be made to show a common origin. Back to the Conquest and before it there was not a noble family-tree every twig and bud of which was not familiar to the Dame Ermyntrude.

And now when the trestles were cleared and the three were left alone in the hall, Chandos broke his message to the lady. "King Edward hath ever borne in mind that noble knight your son Sir Eustace," said he. "He will journey to Southampton next week, and I am his harbinger. He bade me say, noble and honored lady, that he would come from Guildford in any easy stage so that he might spend one night under your roof."

The old dame flushed with pleasure, and then turned white with vexation at the words. "It is in truth great honor to the house of Loring," said she, "yet our roof is now humble and, as you have seen, our fare is plain. The King knows not that we are so poor. I fear lest we seem churlish and niggard in his eyes."

But Chandos reasoned away her fears. The King's retinue would journey on to Farnham Castle. There were no ladies in his party. Though he was King, still he was a hardy soldier, and cared little for his ease. In any case, since he had declared his coming, they must make the best of it. Finally, with all delicacy, Chandos offered his own purse if it would help in the matter. But already the Lady Ermyntrude had recovered her composure.

"Nay, fair kinsman, that may not be," said she. "I will make such preparation as I may for the King. He will bear in mind that if the house of Loring can give nothing else, they have always held their blood and their lives at his disposal."

Chandos was to ride on to Farnham Castle and beyond, but he expressed his desire to have a warm bath ere he left Tilford, for like most of his fellow-knights, he was much addicted to simmering in the hottest water that he could possibly endure. The bath therefore, a high hooped arrangement like a broader but shorter churn, was carried into the privacy of the guest-chamber, and thither it was that Nigel was summoned to hold him company while he stewed and sweltered in his tub.

Nigel perched himself upon the side of the high bed, swinging his legs over the edge and gazing with wonder and amusement at the quaint face, the ruffled yellow hair, and the sinewy shoulders of the famous warrior, dimly seen amid a pillar of steam. He was in a mood for talk; so Nigel with eager lips plied him with a thousand questions about the wars, hanging upon every word which came back to him, like those of the ancient oracles, out of the mist and the cloud. To Chandos himself, the old soldier for whom war had lost its freshness, it was a renewal of his own ardent youth to listen to Nigel's rapid questions and to mark the rapt attention with which he listened.

"Tell me of the Welsh, honored sir," asked the Squire. "What manner of soldiers are the Welsh?"

"They are very valiant men of war," said Chandos, splashing about in his tub. "There is good skirmishing to be had in their valleys if you ride with a small following. They flare up like a furze-bush in the flames, but if for a short space you may abide the heat of it, then there is a chance that it may be cooler."

"And the Scotch?" asked Nigel. "You have made war upon them also, as I understand."

"The Scotch knights have no masters in the world, and he who can hold his own with the best of them, be it a Douglas, a Murray or a Seaton, has nothing more to learn. Though you be a hard man, you will always meet as hard a one if you ride northward. If the Welsh be like the furze fire, then, *"Pardieu!* the Scotch are the peat, for they will smolder and you will never come to the end of them. I have had many happy hours on the marches of Scotland, for even if there be no war the Percies of Alnwick or the Governor of Carlisle can still raise a little bickering with the border clans."

"I bear in mind that my father was wont to say that they were very stout spearmen."

"No better in the world, for the spears are twelve foot long and they hold them in very thick array; but their archers are weak, save only the men of Ettrick and Selkirk who come from the forest. I pray you to open the lattice, Nigel, for the steam is overthick. Now in Wales it is the spearmen who are weak, and there are no archers in these islands like the men of Gwent with their bows of elm, which shoot with such power that I have known a cavalier to have his horse killed when the shaft had passed through his mail breeches, his thigh and his saddle. And yet, what is the most strongly shot arrow to these new balls of iron driven by the fire-powder which will crush a man's armor as an egg is crushed by a stone? Our fathers knew them not."

"Then the better for us," cried Nigel, "since there is at least one honorable venture which is all our own."

Chandos chuckled and turned upon the flushed youth a twinkling and sympathetic eye. "You have a fashion of speech which carries me back to the old men whom I met in my boyhood," said he. "There were some of the real old knight-errants left in those days, and they spoke as you do. Young as you are, you belong to another age. Where got you that trick of thought and word?"

"I have had only one to teach me, the Lady Ermyntrude."

"*Pardieu!* she has trained a proper young hawk ready to stoop at a lordly quarry," said Chandos. "I would that I had the first unhooding of you. Will you not ride with me to the wars?"

The tears brimmed over from Nigel's eyes, and he wrung the gaunt hand extended from the bath. "By Saint Paul! what could I ask better in the world? I fear to leave her, for she has none other to care for her. But if it can in any way be arranged—"

"The King's hand may smooth it out. Say no more until he is here. But if you wish to ride with me—"

"What could man wish for more? Is there a Squire in England who would not serve under the banner of Chandos! Whither do you go, fair sir? And when do you go? Is it to Scotland? Is it to Ireland? Is it to France? But alas, alas!"

The eager face had clouded. For the instant he had forgotten that a suit of armor was as much beyond his means as a service of gold plate. Down in a twinkling came all his high hopes to the ground. Oh, these sordid material things, which come between our dreams and their fulfilment! The Squire of such a knight must dress with the best. Yet all the fee simple of Tilford would scarce suffice for one suit of plate.

Chandos, with his quick wit and knowledge of the world, had guessed the cause of this sudden change. "If you fight under my banner it is for me to find the weapons," said he. "Nay, I will not be denied."

But Nigel shook his head sadly. "It may not be. The Lady Ermyntrude would sell this old house and every acre round it, ere she would permit me to accept this gracious bounty which you offer. Yet I do not despair, for only last week I won for myself a noble war-horse for which I paid not a penny, so perchance a suit of armor may also come my way."

"And how won you the horse?"

"It was given me by the monks of Waverley."

"This is wonderful. *Pardieu!* I should have expected, from what I had seen, that they would have given you little save their malediction."

"They had no use for the horse, and they gave it to me."

"Then we have only to find some one who has no use for a suit of armor and will give it to you. Yet I trust that you will think better of it and let me, since that good lady proves that I am your kinsman, fit you for the wars."

"I thank you, noble sir, and if I should turn to anyone it would indeed be to you; but there are other ways which I would try first. But I pray you, goon Sir John, to tell me of some of your noble spear-runnings against the French, for the whole land rings with the tale of your deeds and I have heard that in one morning three champions have fallen before your lance. Was it not so?"

"That it was indeed so these scars upon my body will prove; but these were the follies of my youth."

"How can you call them follies? Are they not the means by which honorable advancement may be gained and one's lady exalted?"

"It is right that you should think so, Nigel. At your age a man should have a hot head and a high heart. I also had both and fought for my lady's glove or for my vow or for the love of fighting. But as one grows older and commands men one has other things to think of. One thinks less of one's own honor and more of the safety of the army. It is not your own spear, your own sword, your own arm, which will turn the tide of fight; but a cool head may save a stricken field. He who knows when his horsemen should charge and when they should fight on foot, he who can mix his archers with his men-at-arms in such a fashion that each can support the other, he who can hold up his reserve and pour it into the battle when it may turn the tide, he who has a quick eye for boggy land and broken ground—that is the man who is of more worth to an army than Roland, Oliver and all the paladins."

"Yet if his knights fail him, honored sir, all his head-work will not prevail."

"True enough, Nigel; so may every Squire ride to the wars with his soul on fire, as yours is now. But I must linger no longer, for the King's service must be done. I will dress, and when I have bid farewell to the noble Dame Ermyntrude I will on to Farnham; but you will see me here again on the day that the King comes."

So Chandos went his way that evening, walking his horse through the peaceful lanes and twanging his citole as he went, for he loved music and was famous for his merry songs. The cottagers came from their huts and laughed and clapped as the rich full voice swelled and sank to the cheery tinkling of the strings. There were few who saw him pass that would have guessed that the quaint one-eyed man with the yellow hair was the toughest fighter and craftiest man of war in Europe. Once only, as he entered Farnham, an old broken man-at-arms ran out in his rags and clutched at his horse as a dog gambols round his master. Chandos threw him a kind word and a gold coin as he passed on to the castle.

In the meanwhile young Nigel and the Lady Ermyntrude, left alone with their difficulties, looked blankly in each other's faces.

"The cellar is well nigh empty," said Nigel. "There are two firkins of small beer and a tun of canary. How can we set such drink before the King and his court?"

"We must have some wine of Bordeaux. With that and the mottled cow's calf and the fowls and a goose, we can set forth a sufficient repast if he stays only for the one night. How many will be with him?"

"A dozen, at the least."

The old dame wrung her hands in despair. "Nay, take it not to heart, dear lady!" said Nigel. "We have but to say the word and the King would stop at Waverley, where he and his court would find all that they could wish."

"Never!" cried the Lady Ermyntrude. "It would be shame and disgrace to us forever if the King were to pass our door when he has graciously said that he was fain to enter in. Nay, I will do it. Never did I think that I would be forced to this, but I know that he would wish it, and I will do it."

She went to the old iron coffer, and taking a small key from her girdle she unlocked it. The rusty hinges, screaming shrilly as she threw back the lid, proclaimed how seldom it was that she had penetrated into the sacred recesses of her treasure-chest. At the top were some relics of old finery: a silken cloak spangled with golden stars, a coif of silver filigree, a roll of Venetian lace. Beneath were little packets tied in silk which the old lady handled with tender care: a man's hunting-glove, a child's shoe, a love-knot done in faded green ribbon, some letters in rude rough script, and a vernicle of Saint Thomas. Then from the very bottom of the box she drew three objects, swathed in silken cloth, which she uncovered and laid upon the table. The one was a bracelet of rough gold studded with uncut rubies, the second was a gold salver, and the third was a high goblet of the same metal.

"You have heard me speak of these, Nigel, but never before have you seen them, for indeed I have not opened the hutch for fear that we might be tempted in our great need to turn them into money. I have kept them out of my sight and even out of my thoughts. But now it is the honor of the house which calls, and even these must go. This goblet was that which my husband, Sir Nele Loring, won after the intaking of Belgrade when he and his comrades held the lists from matins to vespers against the flower of the French chivalry. The salver was given him by the Earl of Pembroke in memory of his valor upon the field of Falkirk."

"And the bracelet, dear lady?"

"You will not laugh, Nigel?"

"Nay, why should I laugh?"

"The bracelet was the prize for the Queen of Beauty which was given to me before all the high-born ladies of England by Sir Nele Loring a month before our marriage — the Queen of Beauty,

Nigel—I, old and twisted, as you see me. Five strong men went down before his lance ere he won that trinket for me. And now in my last years—"

"Nay, dear and honored lady, we will not part with it."

"Yes, Nigel, he would have it so. I can hear his whisper in my ear. Honor to him was everything—the rest nothing. Take it from me, Nigel, ere my heart weakens. Tomorrow you will ride with it to Guildford; you will see Thorold the goldsmith; and you will raise enough money to pay for all that we shall need for the King's coming." She turned her face away to hide the quivering of her wrinkled features, and the crash of the iron lid covered the sob which burst from her overwrought soul.

CHAPTER VII

HOW NIGEL WENT MARKETING
TO GUILDFORD

IT was on a bright June morning that young Nigel, with youth and springtime to make his heart light, rode upon his errand from Tilford to Guildford town. Beneath him was his great yellow war-horse, caracoling and curveting as he went, as blithe and free of spirit as his master. In all England one would scarce have found upon that morning so high-mettled and so debonair a pair. The sandy road wound through groves of fir, where the breeze came soft and fragrant with resinous gums, or over heathery downs, which rolled away to north and to south, vast and untenanted, for on the uplands the soil was poor and water scarce. Over Crooksbury Common he passed, and then across the great Heath of Puttenham, following a sandy path which wound amid the bracken and the heather, for he meant to strike the Pilgrims' Way where it turned eastward from Farnham and from Seale. As he rode he continually felt his saddle-bag with his hand, for in it, securely strapped, he had placed the precious treasures of the Lady Ermyntrude. As he saw the grand tawny neck tossing before him, and felt the easy heave of the great horse and heard the muffled drumming of his hoofs, he could have sung and shouted with the joy of living.

Behind him, upon the little brown pony which had been Nigel's former mount, rode Samkin Aylward the bowman, who had taken upon himself the duties of personal attendant and body-guard. His great shoulders and breadth of frame seemed dangerously top-heavy upon the tiny steed, but he ambled along, whistling a merry lilt and as light-hearted as his master. There was no countryman who had not a nod and no woman who had not a smile for the jovial bowman, who rode for the most part with his face over his shoulder, staring at the last petticoat which had passed him. Once only he met with a harsher greeting. It was from a tall, white-headed, red-faced man whom they met upon the moor.

"Good-morrow, dear father!" cried Aylward. "How is it with you at Crooksbury? And how are the new black cow and the ewes from Alton and Mary the dairymaid and all your gear?"

"It ill becomes you to ask, you ne'er-do-weel," said the old man. "You have angered the monks of Waverley, whose tenant I am, and they would drive me out of my farm. Yet there are three more years to run, and do what they may I will bide till then. But little did I think that I should lose my homestead through you, Samkin, and big as you are I would knock the dust out of that green jerkin with a good hazel switch if I had you at Crooksbury."

"Then you shall do it to-morrow morning, good father, for I will come and see you then. But indeed I did not do more at Waverley than you would have done yourself. Look me in the eye, old hot-head, and tell me if you would have stood by while the last Loring—look at him as he rides with his head in the air and his soul in the clouds—was shot down before your very eyes at the bidding of that fat monk! If you would, then I disown you as my father."

"Nay, Samkin, if it was like that, then perhaps what you did was not so far amiss. But it is hard to lose the old farm when my heart is buried deep in the good brown soil."

"Tut, man! there are three years to run, and what may not happen in three years? Before that time I shall have gone to the wars, and when I have opened a French strong box or two you can buy the good brown soil and snap your fingers at Abbot John and his bailiffs. Am I not as proper a man as Tom Withstaff of Churt? And yet he came back after six months with his pockets full of rose nobles and a French wench on either arm."

"God preserve us from the wenches, Samkin! But indeed I think that if there is money to be gathered you are as likely to get your fist full as any man who goes to the war. But hasten, lad, hasten! Already your young master is over the brow."

Thus admonished, the archer waved his gauntleted hand to his father, and digging his heels into the sides of his little pony soon drew up with the Squire. Nigel glanced over his shoulder and slackened speed until the pony's head was up to his saddle.

"Have I not heard, archer," said he, "that an outlaw has been loose in these parts?"

"It is true, fair sir. He was villain to Sir Peter Mandeville, but he broke his bonds and fled into the forests. Men call him the 'Wild Man of Puttenham.'"

"How comes it that he has not been hunted down? If the man be a draw-latch and a robber it would be an honorable deed to clear the country of such an evil."

"Twice the sergeants-at-arms from Guildford have come out against him, but the fox has many earths, and it would puzzle you to get him out of them."

"By Saint Paul! were my errand not a pressing one I would be tempted to turn aside and seek him. Where lives he, then?"

"There is a great morass beyond Puttenham, and across it there are caves in which he and his people lurk."

"His people? He hath a band?"

"There are several with him."

"It sounds a most honorable enterprise," said Nigel. "When the King hath come and gone we will spare a day for the outlaws of Puttenham. I fear there is little chance for us to see them on this journey."

"They prey upon the pilgrims who pass along the Winchester Road, and they are well loved by the folk in these parts, for they rob none of them and have an open hand for all who will help them."

"It is right easy to have an open hand with the money that you have stolen," said Nigel; "but I fear that they will not try to rob two men with swords at their girdles like you and me, so we shall have no profit from them."

They had passed over the wild moors and had come down now into the main road by which the pilgrims from the west of England made their way to the national shrine at Canterbury. It passed from Winchester, and up the beautiful valley of the Itchen until it reached Farnham, where it forked into two branches, one of which ran along the Hog's Back, while the second wound to the south and came out at Saint Catherine's Hill where stands the Pilgrim shrine, a gray old ruin now, but once so august, so crowded and so affluent. It was this second branch upon which Nigel and Aylward found themselves as they rode to Guildford.

No one, as it chanced, was going the same way as themselves, but they met one large drove of pilgrims returning from their journey with pictures of Saint Thomas and snails' shells or little leaden ampullæ in their hats and bundles of purchases over their shoulders. They were a grimy, ragged, travel-stained crew, the men walking, the women borne on asses. Man and beast, they limped along as if it would be a glad day when they saw their homes once more. These and a few beggars or minstrels, who crouched among the heather on either side of the track in the hope of receiving an occasional farthing from the passer-by, were the only folk they met until they had reached the village of Puttenham. Already there was a hot sun and just breeze enough to send the dust flying down the road, so they were glad to clear their throats with a glass of beer at the ale-stake in the village, where the fair alewife gave Nigel a cold farewell because he had no attentions for her, and Aylward a box on the ear because he had too many.

On the farther side of Puttenham the road runs through thick woods of oak and beech, with a tangled undergrowth of fern and bramble. Here they met a patrol of sergeants-at-arms, tall fellows, well-mounted, clad in studded-leather caps and tunics, with lances and swords. They walked their horses slowly on the shady side of the road, and stopped as the travelers came up, to ask if they had been molested on the way.

"Have a care," they added, "for the 'Wild Man' and his wife are out. Only yesterday they slew a merchant from the west and took a hundred crowns."

"His wife, you say?"

"Yes, she is ever at his side, and has saved him many a time, for if he has the strength it is she who has the wit. I hope to see their heads together upon the green grass one of these mornings."

The patrol passed downward toward Farnham, and so, as it proved, away from the robbers, who had doubtless watched them closely from the dense brushwood which skirted the road. Coming round a curve, Nigel and Aylward were aware of a tall and graceful woman who sat, wringing her hands and weeping bitterly, upon the bank by the side of the track. At such a sight of beauty in distress Nigel pricked Pommers with the spur and in three bounds was at the side of the unhappy lady.

"What ails you, fair dame?" he asked. "Is there any small matter in which I may stand your friend, or is it possible that anyone hath so hard a heart as to do you an injury."

She rose and turned upon him a face full of hope and entreaty. "Oh, save my poor, poor father!" she cried. "Have you perchance seen the way-wardens? They passed us, and I fear they are beyond reach."

"Yes, they have ridden onward, but we may serve as well."

"Then hasten, hasten, I pray you! Even now they may be doing him to death. They have dragged him into yonder grove and I have heard his voice growing ever weaker in the distance. Hasten, I implore you!"

Nigel sprang from his horse and tossed the rein to Aylward.

"Nay, let us go together. How many robbers were there, lady?"

"Two stout fellows."

"Then I come also."

"Nay, it is not possible," said Nigel. "The wood is too thick for horses, and we cannot leave them in the road."

"I will guard them," cried the lady.

"Pommers is not so easily held. Do you bide here, Aylward, until you hear from me. Stir not, I command you!" So saying, Nigel, with the light of adventure gleaming in his joyous eyes, drew his sword and plunged swiftly into the forest.

Far and fast he ran, from glade to glade, breaking through the bushes, springing over the brambles, light as a young deer, peering this way and that, straining his ears for a sound, and catching only the cry of the wood-pigeons. Still on he went, with the constant thought of the weeping woman behind and of the captured man in front. It was not until he was footsore and out of breath that he stopped with his hand to his side, and considered that his own business had still to be done, and that it was time once more that he should seek the road to Guildford.

Meantime Aylward had found his own rough means of consoling the woman in the road, who stood sobbing with her face against the side of Pommers' saddle.

"Nay, weep not, my pretty one," said he. "It brings the tears to my own eyes to see them stream from thine."

"Alas! good archer, he was the best of fathers, so gentle and so kind! Had you but known him, you must have loved him."

"Tut, tut! he will suffer no scathe. Squire Nigel will bring him back to you anon."

"No, no, I shall never see him more. Hold me, archer, or I fall!"

Aylward pressed his ready arm round the supple waist. The fainting woman leaned with her hand upon his shoulder. Her pale face looked past him, and it was some new light in her eyes, a flash of expectancy, of triumph, of wicked joy, which gave him sudden warning of his danger.

He shook her off and sprang to one side, but only just in time to avoid a crashing blow from a great club in the hands of a man even taller and stronger than himself. He had one quick vision of great white teeth clenched in grim ferocity, a wild flying beard and blazing wild-beast eyes. The next instant he had closed, ducking his head beneath another swing of that murderous cudgel.

With his arms round the robber's burly body and his face buried in his bushy beard, Aylward gasped and strained and heaved. Back and forward in the dusty road the two men stamped and staggered, a grim wrestling-match, with life for the prize. Twice the great strength of the outlaw had Aylward nearly down, and twice with his greater youth and skill the archer restored his grip and his balance. Then at last his turn came. He slipped his leg behind the other's knee, and, giving a mighty wrench, tore him across it. With a hoarse shout the outlaw toppled backward and had hardly reached the ground before Aylward had his knee upon his chest and his short sword deep in his beard and pointed to his throat.

"By these ten finger-bones!" he gasped, "one more struggle and it is your last!"

The man lay still enough, for he was half-stunned by the crashing fall. Aylward looked round him, but the woman had disappeared. At the first blow struck she had vanished into the forest. He began to have fears for his master, thinking that he perhaps had been lured into some deathtrap; but his forebodings were soon at rest, for Nigel himself came hastening down the road, which he had struck some distance from the spot where he left it.

"By Saint Paul!" he cried, "who is this man on whom you are perched, and where is the lady who has honored us so far as to crave our help? Alas, that I have been unable to find her father!"

"As well for you, fair sir," said Aylward, "for I am of opinion that her father was the Devil. This woman is, as I believe, the wife of the 'Wild Man of Puttenham,' and this is the 'Wild Man' himself who set upon me and tried to brain me with his club."

The outlaw, who had opened his eyes, looked with a scowl from his captor to the new-comer. "You are in luck, archer," said he, "for I have come to grips with many a man, but I cannot call to mind any who have had the better of me."

"You have indeed the grip of a bear," said Aylward; "but it was a coward deed that your wife should hold me while you dashed out my brains with a stick. It is also a most villainous thing to lay a snare for wayfarers by asking for their pity and assistance, so that it was our own soft hearts which brought us into such danger. The next who hath real need of our help may suffer for your sins."

"When the hand of the whole world is against you," said the outlaw in a surly voice, "you must fight as best you can."

"You well deserve to be hanged, if only because you have brought this woman, who is fair and gentle-spoken, to such a life," said Nigel. "Let us tie him by the wrist to my stirrup leather, Aylward, and we will lead him into Guildford."

The archer drew a spare bowstring from his case and had bound the prisoner as directed, when Nigel gave a sudden start and cry of alarm.

"Holy Mary!" he cried. "Where is the saddle-bag?"

It had been cut away by a sharp knife. Only the two ends of strap remained. Aylward and Nigel stared at each other in blank dismay. Then the young Squire shook his clenched hands and pulled at his yellow curls in his despair.

"The Lady Ermyntrude's bracelet! My grandfather's cup!" he cried. "I would have died ere I lost them! What can I say to her? I dare not return until I have found them. Oh, Aylward, Aylward! how came you to let them be taken?"

The honest archer had pushed back his steel cap and was scratching his tangled head. "Nay, I know nothing of it. You never said that there was aught of price in the bag, else had I kept a better eye upon it. Certes! it was not this fellow who took it, since I have never had my hands from him. It can only be the woman who fled with it while we fought."

Nigel stamped about the road in his perplexity. "I would follow her to the world's end if I knew where I could find her, but to search these woods for her is to look for a mouse in a wheat-field. Good Saint George, thou who didst overcome the Dragon, I pray you by that most honorable and knightly achievement that you will be with me now! And you also, great Saint Julian, patron of all wayfarers in distress! Two candles shall burn before your shrine at Godalming, if you will but bring me back my saddle-bag. What would I not give to have it back?"

"Will you give me my life?" asked the outlaw. "Promise that I go free, and you shall have it back, if it be indeed true that my wife has taken it."

"Nay, I cannot do that," said Nigel. "My honor would surely be concerned, since my loss is a private one; but it would be to the public scathe that you should go free. By Saint Paul! it would be an ungentle deed if in order to save my own I let you loose upon the gear of a hundred others."

"I will not ask you to let me loose," said the "Wild Man." "If you will promise that my life be spared I will restore your bag."

"I cannot give such a promise, for it will lie with the Sheriff and reeves of Guildford."

"Shall I have your word in my favor?"

"That I could promise you, if you will give back the bag, though I know not how far my word may avail. But your words are vain, for you cannot think that we will be so fond as to let you go in the hope that you return?"

"I would not ask it," said the "Wild Man," "for I can get your bag and yet never stir from the spot where I stand. Have I your promise upon your honor and all that you hold dear that you will ask for grace?"

"You have."

"And that my wife shall be unharmed?"

"I promise it."

The outlaw laid back his head and uttered a long shrill cry like the howl of a wolf. There was a silent pause, and then, clear and shrill, there rose the same cry no great distance away in the forest. Again the "Wild Man" called, and again his mate replied. A third time he summoned, as the deer bells to the doe in the greenwood. Then with a rustle of brushwood and snapping of twigs the woman was before them once more, tall, pale, graceful, wonderful. She glanced neither at Aylward nor Nigel, but ran to the side of her husband.

"Dear and sweet lord," she cried, "I trust they have done you no hurt. I waited by the old ash, and my heart sank when you came not."

"I have been taken at last, wife."

"Oh, cursed, cursed day! Let him go, kind, gentle sirs, do not take him from me!"

"They will speak for me at Guildford," said the "Wild Man." "They have sworn it. But hand them first the bag that you have taken."

She drew it out from under her loose cloak. "Here it is, gentle sir. Indeed it went to my heart to take it, for you had mercy upon me in my trouble. But now I am, as you see, in real and very sore distress. Will you not have mercy now? Take ruth on us, fair sir! On my knees I beg it of you, most gentle and kindly Squire!"

Nigel had clutched his bag, and right glad he was to feel that the treasures were all safe within it. "My proffer is given," said he. "I will say what I can; but the issue rests with others. I pray you to stand up, for indeed I cannot promise more."

"Then I must be content," said she, rising, with a composed face. "I have prayed you to take ruth, and indeed I can do no more; but ere I go back to the forest I would rede you to be on your guard lest you lose your bag once more. Wot you how I took it, archer? Nay, it was simple enough, and may happen again, so I make it clear to you. I had this knife in my sleeve, and though it is small it is very sharp. I slipped it down like this. Then when I seemed to weep with my face against the saddle, I cut down like this——"

In an instant she had shorn through the stirrup leather which bound her man, and he, diving under the belly of the horse, had slipped like a snake into the brushwood. In passing he had struck Pommers from beneath, and the great horse, enraged and insulted, was rearing high, with two men hanging to his bridle. When at last he had calmed there was no sign left of the "Wild Man or of his wife. In vain did Aylward, an arrow on his string, run here and there among the great trees and peer down the shadowy glades. When he returned he and his master cast a shamefaced glance at each other.

"I trust that we are better soldiers than jailers," said Aylward, as he climbed on his pony.

But Nigel's frown relaxed into a smile. "At least we have gained back what we lost," said he. "Here I place it on the pommel of my saddle, and I shall not take my eyes from it until we are safe in Guildford town."

So they jogged on together until passing Saint Catherine's shrine they crossed the winding Wey once more, and so found themselves in the steep high street with its heavy-eaved gabled houses, its monkish hospitium upon the left, where good ale may still be quaffed, and its great square-keeped castle upon the right, no gray and grim skeleton of ruin, but very quick and alert, with blazoned banner flying free, and steel caps twinkling from the battlement. A row of booths extended from the castle gate to the high street, and two doors from the Church of the Trinity was that of Thorold the goldsmith, a rich burgess and Mayor of the town.

He looked long and lovingly at the rich rubies and at the fine work upon the goblet. Then he stroked his flowing gray beard as he pondered whether he should offer fifty nobles or sixty, for he knew well that he could sell them again for two hundred. If he offered too much his profit would be reduced. If he offered too little the youth might go as far as London with them, for they were rare and of great worth. The young man was ill-clad, and his eyes were anxious. Perchance he was hard pressed and was ignorant of the value of what he bore. He would sound him.

"These things are old and out of fashion, fair sir," said he. "Of the stones I can scarce say if they are of good quality or not, but they are dull and rough. Yet, if your price be low I may add them to my stock, though indeed this booth was made to sell and not to buy. What do you ask?"

Nigel bent his brows in perplexity. Here was a game in which neither his bold heart nor his active limbs could help him. It was the new force mastering the old: the man of commerce conquering the man of war — wearing him down and weakening him through the centuries until he had him as his bond-servant and his thrall."

I know not what to ask, good sir," said Nigel. "It is not for me, nor for any man who bears my name, to chaffer and to haggle. You know the worth of these things, for it is your trade to do so. The Lady Ermyntrude lacks money, and we must have it against the King's coming, so give me that which is right and just, and we will say no more."

The goldsmith smiled. The business was growing more simple and more profitable. He had intended to offer fifty, but surely it would be sinful waste to give more than twenty-five.

"I shall scarce know what to do with them when I have them," said he. "Yet I should not grudge twenty nobles if it is a matter in which the King is concerned."

Nigel's heart turned to lead. This sum would not buy one-half what was needful. It was clear that the Lady Ermyntrude had overvalued her treasures. Yet he could not return empty-handed, so if twenty nobles was the real worth, as this good old man assured him, then he must be thankful and take it.

"I am concerned by what you say," said he. "You know more of these things than I can do. However, I will take—"

"A hundred and fifty," whispered Aylward's voice in his ear.

"A hundred and fifty," said Nigel, only too relieved to have found the humblest guide upon these unwonted paths.

The goldsmith started. This youth was not the simple soldier that he had seemed. That frank face, those blue eyes, were traps for the unwary. Never had he been more taken aback in a bargain.

"This is fond talk and can lead to nothing, fair sir," said he, turning away and fiddling with the keys of his strong boxes. "Yet I have no wish to be hard on you. Take my outside price, which is fifty nobles."

"And a hundred," whispered Aylward.

"And a hundred," said Nigel, blushing at his own greed.

"Well, well, take a hundred!" cried the merchant. "Fleece me, skin me, leave me a loser, and take for your wares the full hundred!"

"I should be shamed forever if I were to treat you so badly," said Nigel. "You have spoken me fair, and I would not grind you down. Therefore, I will gladly take one hundred——"

"And fifty," whispered Aylward.

"And fifty," said Nigel.

"By Saint John of Beverley!" cried the merchant. "I came hither from the North Country, and they are said to be shrewd at a deal in those parts; but I had rather bargain with a synagogue full of Jews than with you, for all your gentle ways. Will you indeed take no less than a hundred and fifty? Alas! you pluck from me my profits of a month. It is a fell morning's work for me. I would I had never seen you!" With groans and lamentations he paid the gold pieces across the counter, and Nigel, hardly able to credit his own good fortune, gathered them into the leather saddle-bag.

A moment later with flushed face he was in the street and pouring out his thanks to Aylward.

"Alas, my fair lord! the man has robbed us now," said the archer." We could have had another twenty had we stood fast."

"How know you that, good Aylward?"

"By his eyes, Squire Loring. I wot I have little store of reading where the parchment of a book or the pinching of a blazon is concerned, but I can read men's eyes, and I never doubted that he would give what he has given."

The two travelers had dinner at the monk's hospitium, Nigel at the high table and Aylward among the commonalty. Then again they roamed the high street on business intent. Nigel bought taffeta for hangings, wine, preserves, fruit, damask table linen and many other articles of need. At last he halted before the armorer's shop at the castle-yard, staring at the fine suits of plate, the engraved pectorals, the plumed helmets, the cunningly jointed gorgets, as a child at a sweet-shop.

"Well, Squire Loring," said Wat the armorer, looking sidewise from the furnace where he was tempering a sword-blade, "what can I sell you this morning? I swear to you by Tubal Cain, the father of all workers in metal, that you might go from end to end of Cheapside and never see a better suit than that which hangs from yonder hook!"

"And the price, armorer?"

"To anyone else, two hundred and fifty rose nobles. To you two hundred."

"And why cheaper to me, good fellow?"

"Because I fitted your father also for the wars, and a finer suit never went out of my shop. I warrant that it turned many an edge before he laid it aside. We worked in mail in those days, and I had as soon have a well-made thick-meshed mail as any plates; but a young knight will be in the fashion like any dame of the court, and so it must be plate now, even though the price be trebled."

"Your rede is that the mail is as good?"

"I am well sure of it."

"Hearken then, armorer! I cannot at this moment buy a suit of plate, and yet I sorely need steel harness on account of a small deed which it is in my mind to do. Now I have at my home at Tilford that very suit of mail of which you speak, with which my father first rode to the wars. Could you not so alter it that it should guard my limbs also?"

The armorer looked at Nigel's small upright figure and burst out laughing. "You jest, Squire Loring! The suit was made for one who was far above the common stature of man."

"Nay, I jest not. If it will but carry me through one spear-running it will have served its purpose."

The armorer leaned back on his anvil and pondered while Nigel stared anxiously at his sooty face.

"Right gladly would I lend you a suit of plate for this one venture, Squire Loring, but I know well that if you should be overthrown your harness becomes prize to the victor. I am a poor man with many children, and I dare not risk the loss of it. But as to what you say of the old suit of mail, is it indeed in good condition?"

"Most excellent, save only at the neck, which is much frayed."

"To shorten the limbs is easy. It is but to cut out a length of the mail and then loop up the links. But to shorten the body—nay, that is beyond the armorer's art."

"It was my last hope. Nay, good armorer, if you have indeed served and loved my gallant father, then I beg you by his memory that you will help me now."

The armorer threw down his heavy hammer with a crash upon the floor. "It is not only that I loved your father, Squire Loring, but it is that I have seen you, half armed as you were, ride against the best of them at the Castle tiltyard. Last Martinmas my heart bled for you when I saw how sorry was your harness, and yet you held your own against the stout Sir Oliver with his Milan suit. When go you to Tilford?"

"Even now."

"Heh, Jenkin, fetch out the cob!" cried the worthy Wat. "May my right hand lose its cunning if I do not send you into battle in your father's suit! To-morrow I must be back in my booth, but to-day I give to you without fee and for the sake of the good-will which I bear to your house. I will ride with you to Tilford, and before night you shall see what Wat can do."

So it came about that there was a busy evening at the old Tilford Manor-house, where the Lady Ermyntrude planned and cut and hung the curtains for the hall, and stocked her cupboards with the good things which Nigel had brought from Guildford.

Meanwhile the Squire and the armorer sat with their heads touching and the old suit of mail with its gorget of overlapping plates laid out across their knees. Again and again old Wat shrugged his shoulders, as one who has been asked to do more than can be demanded from mortal man. At last, at a suggestion from the Squire, he leaned back in his chair and laughed long and loudly in his bushy beard, while the Lady Ermyntrude glared her black displeasure at such plebeian merriment. Then taking his fine chisel and his hammer from his pouch of tools, the armorer, still chuckling at his own thoughts, began to drive a hole through the center of the steel tunic.

CHAPTER VIII

HOW THE KING HAWKED
ON CROOKSBURY HEATH

The King and his attendants had shaken off the crowd who had followed them from Guildford along the Pilgrims' Way and now, the mounted archers having beaten off the more persistent of the spectators, they rode at their ease in a long, straggling, glittering train over the dark undulating plain of heather.

In the van was the King himself, for his hawks were with him and he had some hope of sport. Edward at that time was a well-grown, vigorous man in the very prime of his years, a keen sportsman, an ardent gallant and a chivalrous soldier. He was a scholar too, speaking Latin, French, German, Spanish, and even a little English.

So much had long been patent to the world, but only of recent years had he shown other and more formidable characteristics: a restless ambition which coveted his neighbor's throne, and a wise foresight in matters of commerce, which engaged him now in transplanting Flemish weavers and sowing the seeds of what for many years was the staple trade of England. Each of these varied qualities might have been read upon his face. The brow, shaded by a crimson cap of maintenance, was broad and lofty. The large brown eyes were ardent and bold. His chin was clean-shaven, and the close-cropped dark mustache did not conceal the strong mouth, firm, proud and kindly, but capable of setting tight in merciless ferocity. His complexion was tanned to copper by a life spent in field sports or in war, and he rode his magnificent black horse carelessly and easily, as one who has grown up in the saddle. His own color was black also, for his active; sinewy figure was set off by close-fitting velvet of that hue, broken only by a belt of gold, and by a golden border of open pods of the broom-plant.

With his high and noble bearing, his simple yet rich attire and his splendid mount, he looked every inch a King. The picture of gallant man on gallant horse was completed by the noble Falcon of the Isles which fluttered along some twelve feet above his head, "waiting on," as it was termed, for any quarry which might arise. The second bird of the cast was borne upon the gauntleted wrist of Raoul the chief falconer in the rear.

At the right side of the monarch and a little behind him rode a youth some twenty years of age, tall, slim and dark, with noble aquiline features and keen penetrating eyes which sparkled with vivacity and affection as he answered the remarks of the King. He was clad in deep crimson diapered with gold, and the trappings of his white palfrey were of a magnificence which proclaimed the rank of its rider. On his face, still free from mustache or beard, there sat a certain gravity and majesty of expression which showed that young as he was great affairs had been in his keeping and that his thoughts and interests were those of the statesman and the warrior. That great day when, little more than a school-boy, he had led the van of the victorious army which had crushed the power of France and Crécy, had left this stamp upon his features; but stern as they were they had not assumed that tinge of fierceness which in after years was to make "The Black Prince" a name of terror on the marches of France. Not yet had the first shadow of fell disease come to poison his nature ere it struck at his life, as he rode that spring day, light and debonair, upon the heath of Crooksbury.

On the left of the King, and so near to him that great intimacy was implied, rode a man about his own age, with the broad face, the projecting jaw and the flattish nose which are often the outward indications of a pugnacious nature. His complexion was crimson, his large blue eyes somewhat prominent, and his whole appearance full-blooded and choleric. He was short, but massively built, and evidently possessed of immense strength. His voice, however, when he spoke was gentle and lisping, while his manner was quiet and courteous. Unlike the King or the Prince, he was clad in light armor and carried a sword by his side and a mace at his saddle-bow, for he was acting as Captain of the King's Guard, and a dozen other knights in steel followed in the escort. No hardier soldier could Edward have at his side, if, as was always possible in those lawless times, sudden danger was to threaten, for this was the famous knight of Hainault, now naturalized as an Englishman, Sir Walter Manny, who bore as high a reputation for chivalrous valor and for gallant temerity as Chandos himself.

Behind the knights, who were forbidden to scatter and must always follow the King's person, there was a body of twenty or thirty hobblers or mounted bowmen, together with several squires, unarmed themselves but leading spare horses upon which the heavier part of their knights' equipment was carried. A straggling tail of falconers, harbingers, varlets, body-servants and huntsmen holding hounds in leash completed the long and many-colored train which rose and dipped on the low undulations of the moor.

Many weighty things were on the mind of Edward the King. There was truce for the moment with France, but it was a truce broken by many small deeds of arms, raids, surprises and ambushes upon either side, and it was certain that it would soon dissolve again into open war. Money must be raised, and it was no light matter to raise it, now that the Commons had once already voted the tenth lamb and the tenth sheaf. Besides, the Black Death had ruined the country, the arable land was all turned to pasture, the laborer, laughing at statutes, would not work under fourpence a day, and all society was chaos. In addition, the Scotch were growling over the border, there was the perennial trouble in half-conquered Ireland, and his allies abroad in Flanders and in Brabant were clamoring for the arrears of their subsidies.

All this was enough to make even a victorious monarch full of care; but now Edward had thrown it all to the winds and was as light-hearted as a boy upon a holiday. No thought had he for the dunning of Florentine bankers or the vexatious conditions of those busybodies at Westminster. He was out with his hawks, and his thoughts and his talk should be of nothing else. The varlets beat the heather and bushes as they passed, and whooped loudly as the birds flew out.

"A magpie! A magpie!" cried the falconer.

"Nay, nay, it is not worthy of your talons, my brown-eyed queen," said the King, looking up at the great bird which flapped from side to side above his head, waiting for the whistle which should give her the signal. "The tercels, falconer—a cast of tercels! Quick, man, quick! Ha! the rascal makes for wood! He puts in! Well flown, brave peregrine! He makes his point. Drive him out to thy comrade. Serve him, varlets! Beat the bushes! He breaks! He breaks! Nay, come away then! You will see Master Magpie no more."

The bird had indeed, with the cunning of its race, flapped its way through brushwood and bushes to the thicker woods beyond, so that neither the hawk amid the cover nor its partner above nor the clamorous beaters could harm it. The King laughed at the mischance and rode on. Continually birds of various sorts were flushed, and each was pursued by the appropriate hawk, the snipe by the tercel, the partridge by the goshawk, even the lark by the little merlin. But the King soon tired of this petty sport and went slowly on his way, still with the magnificent silent attendant flapping above his head.

"Is she not a noble bird, fair son?" he asked, glancing up as her shadow fell upon him.

"She is indeed, sire. Surely no finer ever came from the isles of the north."

"Perhaps not, and yet I have had a hawk from Barbary as good a footer and a swifter flyer. An Eastern bird in yarak has no peer."

"I had one once from the Holy Land," said de Manny. "It was fierce and keen and swift as the Saracens themselves. They say of old Saladin that in his day his breed of birds, of hounds and of horses had no equal on earth."

"I trust, dear father, that the day may come when we shall lay our hands on all three," said the Prince, looking with shining eyes upon the King. "Is the Holy Land to lie forever in the grasp of these unbelieving savages, or the Holy Temple to be defiled by their foul presence? Ah! my dear and most sweet lord, give to me a thousand lances with ten thousand bowmen like those I led at Crécy, and I swear to you by God's soul that within a year I will have done homage to you for the Kingdom of Jerusalem!"

The King laughed as he turned to Walter Manny. "Boys will still be boys," said he.

"The French do not count me such!" cried the young Prince, flushing with anger.

"Nay, fair son, there is no one sets you at a higher rate than your father. But you have the nimble mind and quick fancy of youth, turning over from the thing that is half done to a further task beyond. How would we fare in Brittany and Normandy while my young paladin with his lances and his bowmen was besieging Ascalon or battering at Jerusalem?"

"Heaven would help in Heaven's work."

"From what I have heard of the past," said the King dryly, "I cannot see that Heaven has counted for much as an ally in these wars of the East. I speak with reverence, and yet it is but sooth to say that Richard of the Lion Heart or Louis of France might have found the smallest earthly principality of greater service to him than all the celestial hosts. How say you to that, my Lord Bishop?"

A stout churchman who had ridden behind the King on a solid bay cob, well-suited to his weight and dignity, jogged up to the monarch's elbow. "How say you, sire? I was watching the goshawk on the partridge and heard you not."

"Had I said that I would add two manors to the See of Chichester, I warrant that you would have heard me, my Lord Bishop."

"Nay, fair lord, test the matter by saying so," cried the jovial Bishop.

The King laughed aloud. "A fair counter, your reverence. By the rood! you broke your lance that passage. But the question I debated was this: How is it that since the Crusades have manifestly been fought in God's quarrel, we Christians have had so little comfort or support in fighting them. After all our efforts and the loss of more men than could be counted, we are at last driven from the country, and even the military orders which were formed only for that one purpose can scarce hold a footing in the islands of the Greek sea. There is not one seaport nor one fortress in Palestine over which the flag of the Cross still waves. Where then was our ally?"

"Nay, sire, you open a great debate which extends far beyond this question of the Holy Land, though that may indeed be chosen as a fair example. It is the question of all sin, of all suffering, of all injustice—why it should pass without the rain of fire and the lightnings of Sinai. The wisdom of God is beyond our understanding."

The King shrugged his shoulders. "This is an easy answer, my Lord Bishop. You are a prince of the Church. It would fare ill with an earthly prince who could give no better answer to the affairs which concerned his realm."

"There are other considerations which might be urged, most gracious sire. It is true that the Crusades were a holy enterprise which might well expect the immediate blessing of God; but the Crusaders—is it certain that they deserved such a blessing? Have I not heard that their camp was the most dissolute ever seen?"

"Camps are camps all the world over, and you cannot in a moment change a bowman into a saint. But the holy Louis was a crusader after your own heart. Yet his men perished at Mansurah and he himself at Tunis."

"Bethink you also that this world is but the antechamber of the next," said the prelate. "By suffering and tribulation the soul is cleansed, and the true victor may be he who by the patient endurance of misfortune merits the happiness to come."

"If that be the true meaning of the Church's blessing, then I hope that it will be long before it rests upon our banners in France," said the King. "But methinks that when one is out with a brave horse and a good hawk one might find some other subject than theology. Back to the birds, Bishop, or Raoul the falconer will come to interrupt thee in thy cathedral."

Straightway the conversation came back to the mystery of the woods and the mystery of the rivers, to the dark-eyed hawks and the yellow-eyed, to hawks of the lure and hawks of the fist. The Bishop was as steeped in the lore of falconry as the King, and the others smiled as the two wrangled hard over disputed and technical questions: if an eyas trained in the mews can ever emulate the passage hawk taken wild, or how long the young hawks should be placed at hack, and how long weathered before they are fully reclaimed.

Monarch and prelate were still deep in this learned discussion, the Bishop speaking with a freedom and assurance which he would never have dared to use in affairs of Church and State, for in all ages there is no such leveler as sport. Suddenly, however, the Prince, whose keen eyes had swept from time to time over the great blue heaven, uttered a peculiar call and reined up his palfrey, pointing at the same time into the air.

"A heron!" he cried. "A heron on passage!"

To gain the full sport of hawking a heron must not be put up from its feeding-ground, where it is heavy with its meal, and has no time to get its pace on before it is pounced upon by the more active hawk, but it must be aloft, traveling from point to point, probably from the fish-stream to the heronry. Thus to catch the bird on passage was the prelude of all good sport. The object to which the Prince had pointed was but a black dot in the southern sky, but his strained eyes had not deceived him, and both Bishop and King agreed that it was indeed a heron, which grew larger every instant as it flew in their direction.

"Whistle him off, sire! Whistle off the gerfalcon!" cried the Bishop.

"Nay, nay, he is overfar. She would fly at check."

"Now, sire, now!" cried the Prince, as the great bird with the breeze behind him came sweeping down the sky.

The King gave the shrill whistle, and the well-trained hawk raked out to the right and to the left to make sure which quarry she was to follow. Then, spying the heron, she shot up in a swift ascending curve to meet him.

"Well flown, Margot! Good bird!" cried the King, clapping his hands to encourage the hawk, while the falconers broke into the shrill whoop peculiar to the sport.

Going on her curve, the hawk would soon have crossed the path of the heron; but the latter, seeing the danger in his front and confident in his own great strength of wing and lightness of body, proceeded to mount higher in the air, flying in such small rings that to the spectators it almost seemed as if the bird was going perpendicularly upward.

"He takes the air!" cried the King. "But strong as he flies, he cannot out fly Margot. Bishop, I lay you ten gold pieces to one that the heron is mine."

"I cover your wager, sire," said the Bishop. "I may not take gold so won, and yet I warrant that there is an altar-cloth somewhere in need of repairs."

"You have good store of altar-cloths, Bishop, if all the gold I have seen you win at tables goes to the mending of them," said the King. "Ah! by the rood, rascal, rascal! See how she flies at check!"

The quick eyes of the Bishop had perceived a drift of rooks when on their evening flight to the rookery were passing along the very line which divided the hawk from the heron. A rook is a hard temptation for a hawk to resist. In an instant the inconstant bird had forgotten all about the great heron above her and was circling over the rooks, flying westward with them as she singled out the plumpest for her stoop.

"There is yet time, sire! Shall I cast off her mate?" cried the falconer.

"Or shall I show you, sire, how a peregrine may win where a gerfalcon fails?" said the Bishop. "Ten golden pieces to one upon my bird."

"Done with you, Bishop!" cried the King, his brow dark with vexation. "By the rood! if you were as learned in the fathers as you are in hawks you would win to the throne of Saint Peter! Cast off your peregrine and make your boasting good."

Smaller than the royal gerfalcon, the Bishop's bird was none the less a swift and beautiful creature. From her perch upon his wrist she had watched with fierce, keen eyes the birds in the heaven, mantling herself from time to time in her eagerness. Now when the button was undone and the leash uncast the peregrine dashed off with a whir of her sharp-pointed wings, whizzing round in a great ascending circle which mounted swiftly upward, growing ever smaller as she approached that lofty point where, a mere speck in the sky, the heron sought escape from its enemies. Still higher and higher the two birds mounted, while the horsemen, their faces upturned, strained their eyes in their efforts to follow them.

"She rings! She still rings!" cried the Bishop. "She is above him! She has gained her pitch."

"Nay, nay, she is far below," said the King.

"By my soul, my Lord Bishop is right!" cried the Prince. "I believe she is above. See! See! She swoops!"

"She binds! She binds!" cried a dozen voices as the two dots blended suddenly into one.

There could be no doubt that they were falling rapidly. Already they grew larger to the eye. Presently the heron disengaged himself and flapped heavily away, the worse for that deadly embrace, while the peregrine, shaking her plumage, ringed once more so as to get high above the quarry and deal it a second and more fatal blow. The Bishop smiled, for nothing, as it seemed, could hinder his victory.

"Thy gold pieces shall be well spent, sire," said he. "What is lost to the Church is gained by the loser."

But a most unlooked-for chance deprived the Bishop's altar-cloth of its costly mending. The King's gerfalcon having struck down a rook, and finding the sport but tame, bethought herself suddenly of that noble heron, which she still perceived fluttering over Crooksbury Heath. How could she have been so weak as to allow these silly, chattering rooks to entice her away from that lordly bird? Even now it was not too late to atone for her mistake. In a great spiral she shot upward until she was over the heron. But what was this? Every fiber of her, from her crest to her deck feathers, quivered with jealousy and rage at the sight of this creature, a

mere peregrine, who had dared to come between a royal gerfalcon and her quarry. With one sweep of her great wings she shot up
until she was above her rival. The next instant—

"They crab! They crab!" cried the King, with a roar of laughter,
following them with his eyes as they bustled down through the air.
"Mend thy own altar-cloths, Bishop. Not a groat shall you have
from me this journey. Pull them apart, falconer, lest they do each
other an injury. And now, masters, let us on, for the sun sinks
toward the west."

The two hawks, which had come to the ground interlocked
with clutching talons and ruffled plumes, were torn apart and
brought back bleeding and panting to their perches, while the
heron after its perilous adventure flapped its way heavily onward
to settle safely in the heronry of Waverley. The cortège, who had
scattered in the excitement of the chase, came together again, and
the journey was once more resumed.

A horseman who had been riding toward them across the moor
now quickened his pace and closed swiftly upon them. As he came
nearer, the King and the Prince cried out joyously and waved their
hands in greeting.

"It is good John Chandos!" cried the King. "By the rood,
John, I have missed your merry songs this week or more! Glad I
am to see that you have your citole slung to your back. Whence
come you then?"

"I come from Tilford, sire, in the hope that I should
meet your majesty."

"It was well thought of. Come, ride here between the Prince and
me, and we will believe that we are back in France with our war harness on our backs once more. What is your news, Master John?"

Chandos' quaint face quivered with suppressed amusement and
his one eye twinkled like a star. "Have you had sport, my liege?"

"Poor sport, John. We flew two hawks on the same heron. They
crabbed, and the bird got free. But why do you smile so?"

"Because I hope to show you better sport ere you come to Tilford."

"For the hawk? For the hound?"

"A nobler sport than either."

"Is this a riddle, John? What mean you?"

"Nay, to tell all would be to spoil all. I say again that there is rare sport betwixt here and Tilford, and I beg you, dear lord, to mend your pace that we make the most of the daylight."

Thus adjured, the King set spurs to his horse, and the whole cavalcade cantered over the heath in the direction which Chandos showed. Presently as they came over a slope they saw beneath them a winding river with an old high-backed bridge across it. On the farther side was a village green with a fringe of cottages and one dark manor-house upon the side of the hill.

"This is Tilford," said Chandos. "Yonder is the house of the Lorings."

The King's expectations had been aroused and his face showed his disappointment.

"Is this the sport that you have promised us, Sir John? How can you make good your words?"

"I will make them good, my liege."

"Where then is the sport?"

"On the high crown of the bridge a rider in armor was seated, lance in hand, upon a great yellow steed. Chandos touched the King's arm and pointed."

"That is the sport," said he.

CHAPTER IX

HOW NIGEL HELD THE BRIDGE AT TILFORD

THE King looked at the motionless figure, at the little crowd of hushed expectant rustics beyond the bridge, and finally at the face of Chandos, which shone with amusement.

"What is this, John?" he asked.

"You remember Sir Eustace Loring, sire?"

"Indeed I could never forget him nor the manner of his death."

"He was a knight errant in his day."

"That indeed he was—none better have I known."

"So is his son Nigel, as fierce a young war-hawk as ever yearned to use beak and claws; but held fast in the mews up to now. This is his trial fight. There he stands at the bridge-head, as was the wont in our fathers' time, ready to measure himself against all comers."

Of all Englishmen there was no greater knight errant than the King himself, and none so steeped in every quaint usage of chivalry; so that the situation was after his own heart.

"He is not yet a knight?"

"No, sire, only a Squire."

"Then he must bear himself bravely this day if he is to make good what he has done. Is it fitting that a young untried Squire should venture to couch his lance against the best in England?"

"He bath given me his cartel and challenge," said Chandos, drawing a paper from his tunic. "Have I your permission, sire, to issue it?"

"Surely, John, we have no cavalier more versed in the laws of chivalry than yourself. You know this young man, and you are aware how far he is worthy of the high honor which he asks. Let us hear his defiance,"

The knights and squires of the escort, most of whom were veterans of the French war, had been gazing with interest and some surprise at the steel-clad figure in front of them. Now at a call from Sir Walter Manny they assembled round the spot where the King and Chandos had halted. Chandos cleared his throat and read from his paper:

"'A tous seigneurs, chevaliers et escuyers,' so it is headed, gentlemen. It is a message from the good Squire Nigel Loring of Tilford, son of Sir Eustace Loring, of honorable memory. Squire Loring awaits you in arms, gentlemen, yonder upon the crown of the old bridge. Thus says he: 'For the great desire that I, a most humble and unworthy Squire, entertain, that I may come to the knowledge of the noble gentlemen who ride with my royal master, I now wait on the Bridge of the Way in the hope that some of them may condescend to do some small deed of arms upon me, or that I may deliver them from any vow which they may have taken. This I say out of no esteem for myself, but solely that I may witness the noble bearing of these famous cavaliers and admire their skill in the handling of arms. Therefore, with the help of Saint George, I will hold the bridge with sharpened lances against any or all who may deign to present themselves while daylight lasts."

"What say you to this, gentlemen?" asked the King, looking round with laughing eyes.

"Truly it is issued in very good form," said the Prince. "Neither Claricieux nor Red Dragon nor any herald that ever wore tabard could better it. Did he draw it of his own hand?"

"He hath a grim old grandmother who is one of the ancient breed," said Chandos. "I doubt not that the Dame Ermyntrude hath drawn a challenge or two before now. But hark ye, sire, I would have a word in your ear—and yours too, most noble Prince."

Leading them aside, Chandos whispered some explanations, which ended by them all three bursting into a shout of laughter.

"By the rood! no honorable gentleman should be reduced to such straits," said the King. "It behooves me to look to it. But how now, gentlemen? This worthy cavalier still waits his answer."

The soldiers had all been buzzing together; but now Walter Manny turned to the King with the result of their counsel.

"If it please your majesty," said he, "we are of opinion that this Squire hath exceeded all bounds in desiring to break a spear with a belted knight ere he has given his proofs. We do him sufficient honor if a Squire ride against him, and with your consent I have chosen my own body-squire, John Widdicombe, to clear the path for us across the bridge."

"What you say, Walter, is right and fair," said the King. "Master Chandos, you will tell our champion yonder what hath been arranged. You will advise him also that it is our royal will that this contest be not fought upon the bridge, since it is very clear that it must end in one or both going over into the river, but that he advance to the end of the bridge and fight upon the plain. You will tell him also that a blunted lance is sufficient for such an encounter, but that a hand-stroke or two with sword or mace may well be exchanged, if both riders should keep their saddles. A blast upon Raoul's horn shall be the signal to close."

Such ventures as these where an aspirant for fame would wait for days at a cross-road, a ford, or a bridge, until some worthy antagonist should ride that way, were very common in the old days of adventurous knight erranty, and were still familiar to the minds of all men because the stories of the romancers and the songs of the trouvères were full of such incidents. Their actual occurrence however had become rare. There was the more curiosity, not unmixed with amusement, in the thoughts of the courtiers as they watched Chandos ride down to the bridge and commented upon the somewhat singular figure of the challenger. His build was strange, and so also was his figure, for the limbs were short for so tall a man. His head also was sunk forward as if he were lost in thought or overcome with deep dejection.

"This is surely the Cavalier of the Heavy Heart," said Manny. "What trouble has he, that he should hang his head?"

"Perchance he hath a weak neck," said the King.

"At least he hath no weak voice," the Prince remarked, as Nigel's answer to Chandos came to their ears. "By our lady, he booms like a bittern."

As Chandos rode back again to the King, Nigel exchanged the old ash spear which had been his father's for one of the blunted tournament lances which he took from the hands of a stout archer in attendance. He then rode down to the end of the bridge where a hundred-yard stretch of greensward lay in front of him. At the same moment the Squire of Sir Walter Manny, who had been hastily armed by his comrades, spurred forward and took up his position.

The King raised his hand; there was a clang from the falconer's horn, and the two riders, with a thrust of their heels and a shake of their bridles, dashed furiously at each other. In the center the green strip of marshy meadowland, with the water squirting from the galloping hoofs, and the two crouching men, gleaming bright in the evening sun, on one side the half circle of motionless horsemen, some in steel, some in velvet, silent and attentive, dogs, hawks, and horses all turned to stone; on the other the old peaked bridge, the blue lazy river, the group of open-mouthed rustics, and the dark old manor-house with one grim face which peered from the upper window.

A good man was John Widdicombe, but he had met a better that day. Before that yellow whirlwind of a horse and that rider who was welded and riveted to his saddle his knees could not hold their grip. Nigel and Pommers were one flying missile, with all their weight and strength and energy centered on the steady end of the lance. Had Widdicombe been struck by a thunderbolt he could not have flown faster or farther from his saddle. Two full somersaults did he make, his plates clanging like cymbals, ere he lay prone upon his back.

For a moment the King looked grave at that prodigious fall. Then smiling once more as Widdicombe staggered to his feet, he clapped his hands loudly in applause. "A fair course and fairly run!" he cried. "The five scarlet roses bear themselves in peace even as I have seen them in war. How now, my good Walter? Have you another Squire or will you clear a path for us yourself?"

Manny's choleric face had turned darker as he observed the mischance of his representative. He beckoned now to a tall knight, whose gaunt and savage face looked out from his open bassinet as an eagle might from a cage of steel.

"Sir Hubert," said he, "I bear in mind the day when you overbore the Frenchman at Caen. Will you not be our champion now?"

"When I fought the Frenchman, Walter, it was with naked weapons," said the knight sternly. "I am a soldier and I love a soldier's work, but I care not for these tiltyard tricks which were invented for nothing but to tickle the fancies of foolish women."

"Oh, most ungallant speech!" cried the King. "Had my good consort heard you she would have arraigned you to appear at a Court of Love with a jury of virgins to answer for your sins. But I pray you to take a tilting spear, good Sir Hubert!"

"I had as soon take a peacock's feather, my fair lord; but I will do it, if you ask me. Here, page, hand me one of those sticks, and let me see what I can do."

But Sir Hubert de Burgh was not destined to test either his skill or his luck. The great bay horse which he rode was as unused to this warlike play as was its master, and had none of its master's stoutness of heart; so that when it saw the leveled lance, the gleaming figure and the frenzied yellow horse rushing down upon it, it swerved, turned and galloped furiously down the riverbank. Amid roars of laughter from the rustics on the one side and from the courtiers on the other, Sir Hubert was seen, tugging vainly at his bridle, and bounding onward, clearing gorse-bushes and heather-clumps, until he was but a shimmering, quivering gleam upon the dark hillside. Nigel, who had pulled Pommers on to his very haunches at the instant that his opponent turned, saluted with his lance and trotted back to the bridge-head, where he awaited his next assailant.

"The ladies would say that a judgment hath fallen upon our good Sir Hubert for his impious words," said the King.

"Let us hope that his charger may be broken in ere they venture to ride out between two armies," remarked the Prince. "They might mistake the hardness of his horse's mouth for a softness of the rider's heart. See where he rides, still clearing every bush upon his path."

"By the rood!" said the King, "if the bold Hubert has not increased his repute as a jouster he has gained great honor as a horseman. But the bridge is still closed, Walter. How say you now? Is this young Squire never to be unhorsed, or is your King himself to lay lance in rest ere his way can be cleared? By the head of Saint Thomas! I am in the very mood to run a course with this gentle youth."

"Nay, nay, sire, too much honor hath already been done him!" said Manny, looking angrily at the motionless horseman. "That this untried boy should be able to say that in one evening he has unhorsed my Squire, and seen the back of one of the bravest knights in England is surely enough to turn his foolish head. Fetch me a spear, Robert! I will see what I can make of him."

The famous knight took the spear when it was brought to him as a master-workman takes a tool. He balanced it, shook it once or twice in the air, ran his eyes down it for a flaw in the wood, and then finally having made sure of its poise and weight laid it carefully in rest under his arm. Then gathering up his bridle so as to have his horse under perfect command, and covering himself with the shield, which was slung round his neck, he rode out to do battle.

Now, Nigel, young and inexperienced, all Nature's aid will not help you against the mixed craft and strength of such a warrior. The day will come when neither Manny nor even Chandos could sweep you from your saddle; but now, even had you some less cumbrous armor, your chance were small. Your downfall is near; but as you see the famous black chevrons on a golden ground your gallant heart which never knew fear is only filled with joy and amazement at the honor done you. Your downfall is near, and yet in your wildest dreams you would never guess how strange your downfall is to be.

Again with a dull thunder of hoofs the horses gallop over the soft water-meadow. Again with a clash of metal the two riders meet. It is Nigel now, taken clean in the face of his helmet with the blunted spear, who flies backward off his horse and falls clanging on the grass.

But good heavens! what is this? Manny has thrown up his hands in horror and the lance has dropped from his nerveless fingers. From all sides, with cries of dismay, with oaths and shouts and ejaculations to the saints, the horsemen ride wildly in. Was ever so dreadful, so sudden, so complete, an end to a gentle passage at arms? Surely their eyes must be at fault? Some wizard's trick has been played upon them to deceive their senses. But no, it was only too clear. There on the greensward lay the trunk of the stricken cavalier, and there, a good dozen yards beyond, lay his helmeted head.

"By the Virgin!" cried Manny wildly, as he jumped from his horse, "I would give my last gold piece that the work of this evening should be undone! How came it? What does it mean? Hither, my Lord Bishop, for surely it smacks of witchcraft and the Devil."

With a white face the Bishop had sprung down beside the prostrate body, pushing through the knot of horrified knights and squires.

"I fear that the last offices of the Holy Church come too late," said he in a quivering voice. "Most unfortunate young man! How sudden an end! In medio vitæ, as the Holy Book has it—one moment in the pride of his youth, the next his head torn from his body. Now God and his saints have mercy upon me and guard me from evil!"

The last prayer was shot out of the Bishop with an energy and earnestness unusual in his orisons. It was caused by the sudden outcry of one of the Squires who, having lifted the helmet from the ground, cast it down again with a scream of horror.

"It is empty!" he cried. "It weighs as light as a feather."

"'Fore God, it is true!" cried Manny, laying his hand on it. "There is no one in it. With what have I fought, father Bishop? Is it of this world or of the next?"

The Bishop had clambered on his horse the better to consider the point. "If the foul fiend is abroad," said he, "my place is over yonder by the King's side. Certes that sulphur-colored horse hath a very devilish look. I could have sworn that I saw both smoke and flame from its nostrils. The beast is fit to bear a suit of armor which rides and fights and yet hath no man within it."

"Nay, not too fast, father Bishop," said one of the knights. "It may be all that you say and yet come from a human workshop. When I made a campaign in South Germany I have seen at Nuremberg a cunning figure, devised by an armorer, which could both ride and wield a sword. If this be such a one —"

"I thank you all for your very gentle courtesy," said a booming voice from the figure upon the ground.

At the words even the valiant Manny sprang into his saddle. Some rode madly away from the horrid trunk. A few of the boldest lingered.

"Most of all," said the voice, "would I thank the most noble knight, Sir Walter Manny, that he should deign to lay aside his greatness and condescend to do a deed of arms upon so humble a Squire."

"'Fore God!" said Manny," if this be the Devil, then the Devil hath a very courtly tongue. I will have him out of his armor, if he blast me!"

So saying he sprang once more from his horse and plunging his hand down the slit in the collapsed gorget he closed it tightly upon a fistful of Nigel's yellow curls. The groan that came forth was enough to convince him that it was indeed a man who lurked within. At the same time his eyes fell upon the hole in the mail corselet which had served the Squire as a vizor, and he burst into deep-chested mirth. The King, the Prince and Chandos, who had watched the scene from a distance, too much amused by it to explain or interfere, rode up weary with laughter, now that all was discovered.

"Let him out!" said the King, with his hand to his side. "I pray you to unlace him and let him out! I have shared in many a spear-running, but never have I been nearer falling from my horse than as I watched this one. I feared the fall had struck him senseless, since he lay so still."

Nigel had indeed lain with all the breath shaken from his body, and as he was unaware that his helmet had been carried off, he had not understood either the alarm or the amusement that he had caused. Now freed from the great hauberk in which he had been shut like a pea in a pod, he stood blinking in the light, blushing deeply with shame that the shifts to which his poverty had reduced him should be exposed to all these laughing courtiers. It was the King who brought him comfort.

"You have shown that you can use your father's weapons," said he, "and you have proved also that you are the worthy bearer of his name and his arms, for you have within you that spirit for which he was famous. But I wot that neither he nor you would suffer a train of hungry men to starve before your door; so lead on, I pray you, and if the meat be as good as this grace before it, then it will be a feast indeed."

CHAPTER X

HOW THE KING GREETED
HIS SENESCHAL OF CALAIS

It would have fared ill with the good name of Tilford Manor-house and with the housekeeping of the aged Dame Ermyntrude had the King's whole retinue, with his outer and inner marshal, his justiciar, his chamberlain and his guard, all gathered under the one roof. But by the foresight and the gentle management of Chandos this calamity was avoided, so that some were quartered at the great Abbey and others passed on to enjoy the hospitality of Sir Roger FitzAlan at Farnham Castle. Only the King himself, the Prince, Manny, Chandos, Sir Hubert de Burgh, the Bishop and two or three more remained behind as the guests of the Lorings.

But small as was the party and humble the surroundings, the King in no way relaxed that love of ceremony, of elaborate form and of brilliant coloring which was one of his characteristics. The sumpter-mules were unpacked, squires ran hither and thither, baths smoked in the bed-chambers, silks and satins were unfolded, gold chains gleamed and clinked, so that when at last, to the long blast of two court trumpeters, the company took their seats at the board, it was the brightest, fairest scene which those old black rafters had ever spanned.

The great influx of foreign knights who had come in their splendor from all parts of Christendom to take part in the opening of the Round Tower of Windsor six years before, and to try their luck and their skill at the tournament connected with it, had deeply modified the English fashions of dress. The old tunic, over-tunic and cyclas were too sad and simple for the new fashions, so now strange and brilliant cote-hardies, pourpoints, courtepies, paltocks, hanselines and many other wondrous garments, party-colored or diapered, with looped, embroidered or escalloped edges, flamed and glittered round the King. He himself, in black velvet and gold, formed a dark rich center to the finery around him. On his right sat the Prince, on his left the Bishop, while Dame Ermyntrude marshaled the forces of the household outside, alert and watchful, pouring in her dishes and her flagons at the right moment, rallying her tired servants, encouraging the van, hurrying the rear, hastening up her reserves, the tapping of her oak stick heard everywhere the pressure was the greatest.

Behind the King, clad in his best, but looking drab and sorry amid the brilliant costumes round him, Nigel himself, regardless of an aching body and a twisted knee, waited upon his royal guests, who threw many a merry jest at him over their shoulders as they still chuckled at the adventure of the bridge.

"By the rood!" said King Edward, leaning back, with a chicken-bone held daintily between the courtesy fingers of his left hand, "the play is too good for this country stage. You must to Windsor with me, Nigel, and bring with you this great suit of harness in which you lurk. There you shall hold the lists with your eyes in your midriff, and unless some one cleave you to the waist I see not how any harm can befall you. Never have I seen so small a nut in so great a shell."

The Prince, looking back with laughing eyes, saw by Nigel's flushed and embarrassed face that his poverty hung heavily upon him. "Nay," said he kindly, "such a workman is surely worthy of better tools."

"And it is for his master to see that he has them," added the King. "The court armorer will look to it that the next time your helmet is carried away, Nigel, your head shall be inside it."

Nigel, red to the roots of his flaxen hair, stammered out some words of thanks.

John Chandos, however, had a fresh suggestion, and he cocked a roguish eye as he made it: "Surely, my liege, your bounty is little needed in this case. It is the ancient law of arms that if two cavaliers start to joust, and one either by maladdress or misadventure fail to meet the shock, then his arms become the property of him who still holds the lists. This being so, methinks, Sir Hubert de Burgh, that the fine hauberk of Milan and the helmet of Bordeaux steel in which you rode to Tilford should remain with our young host as some small remembrance of your visit."

The suggestion raised a general chorus of approval and laughter, in which all joined, save only Sir Hubert himself, who, flushed with anger, fixed his baleful eyes upon Chandos' mischievous and smiling face.

"I said that I did not play that foolish game, and I know nothing of its laws," said he; "but you know well, John, that if you would have a bout with sharpened spear or sword, where two ride to the ground, and only one away from it, you have not far to go to find it."

"Nay, nay, would you ride to the ground? Surely you had best walk, Hubert," said Chandos. "On your feet I know well that I should not see your back as we have seen it to-day. Say what you will, your horse has played you false, and I claim your suit of harness for Nigel Loring."

"Your tongue is overlong, John, and I am weary of its endless clack!" said Sir Hubert, his yellow mustache bristling from a scarlet face. "If you claim my harness, do you yourself come and take it. If there is a moon in the sky you may try this very night when the board is cleared."

"Nay, fair sirs," cried the King, smiling from one to the other, "this matter must be followed no further. Do you fill a bumper of Gascony, John, and you also, Hubert. Now pledge each other, I pray you, as good and loyal comrades who would scorn to fight save in your King's quarrel. We can spare neither of you while there is so much work for brave hearts over the sea. As to this matter of the harness, John Chandos speaks truly where it concerns a joust in the lists, but we hold that such a law is scarce binding in this, which was but a wayside passage and a gentle trial of arms. On the other hand, in the case of your Squire, Master Manny, there can be no doubt that his suit is forfeit."

"It is a grievous hearing for him, my liege," said Walter Manny; "for he is a poor man and hath been at sore pains to fit himself for the wars. Yet what you say shall be done, fair sire. So, if you will come to me in the morning, Squire Loring, John Widdicombe's suit will be handed over to you."

"Then with the King's leave, I will hand it back to him," said Nigel, troubled and stammering; "for indeed I had rather never ride to the wars than take from a brave man his only suit of plate."

"There spoke your father's spirit!" cried the King. "By the rood! Nigel, I like you full well. Let the matter bide in my hands. But I marvel much that Sir Aymery the Lombard hath not come to us yet from Windsor."

From the moment of his arrival at Tilford, again and again King Edward had asked most eagerly whether Sir Aymery had come, and whether there was any news of him, so that the courtiers glanced at each other in wonder. For Aymery was known to all of them as a famous mercenary of Italy, lately appointed Governor of Calais, and this sudden and urgent summons from the King might well mean some renewal of the war with France, which was the dearest wish of every soldier. Twice the King had stopped his meal and sat with sidelong head; his wine-cup in his hand, listening attentively when some sound like the clatter of hoofs was heard from outside; but the third time there could be no mistake. The tramp and jingle of the horses broke loud upon the ear, and ended in hoarse voices calling out of the darkness, which were answered by the archers posted as sentries without the door.

"Some traveler has indeed arrived, my liege," said Nigel. "What is your royal will?"

"It can be but Aymery," the King answered, "for it was only to him that I left the message that he should follow me hither. Bid him come in, I pray you, and make him very welcome at your board."

Nigel cast open the door, plucking a torch from its bracket as he did so. Half a dozen men-at-arms sat on their horses outside, but one had dismounted, a short, squat, swarthy man with a rat face and quick, restless brown eyes which peered eagerly past Nigel into the red glare of the well-lit hall.

"I am Sir Aymery of Pavia," he whispered. "For God's sake, tell me! is the King within?"

"He is at table, fair sir, and he bids you to enter."

"One moment, young man, one moment, and a secret word in your ear. Wot you why it is that the King has sent for me?"

Nigel read terror in the dark cunning eyes which glanced in sidelong fashion into his. "Nay, I know not."

"I would I knew—I would I was sure ere I sought his presence."

"You have but to cross the threshold, fair sir, and doubtless you will learn from the King's own lips."

Sir Aymery seemed to gather himself as one who braces for a spring into ice-cold water. Then he crossed with a quick stride from the darkness into the light. The King stood up and held out his hand with a smile upon his long handsome face, and yet it seemed to the Italian that it was the lips which smiled but not the eyes.

"Welcome!" cried Edward. "Welcome to our worthy and faithful Seneschal of Calais! Come, sit here before me at the board, for I have sent for you that I may hear your news from over the sea, and thank you for the care that you have taken of that which is as dear to me as wife or child. Set a place for Sir Aymery there, and give him food and drink, for he has ridden fast and far in our service to-day."

Throughout the long feast which the skill of the Lady Ermyntrude had arranged, Edward chatted lightly with the Italian as well as with the barons near him. Finally, when the last dish was removed and the gravy-soaked rounds of coarse bread which served as plates had been cast to the dogs, the wine-flagons were passed round; and old Weathercote the minstrel entered timidly with his harp in the hope that he might be allowed to play before the King's majesty. But Edward had other, sport afoot.

"I pray you, Nigel, to send out the servants, so that we may be alone. I would have two men-at-arms at every door lest we be disturbed in our debate, for it is a matter of privacy. And now, Sir Aymery, these noble lords as well as I, your master, would fain hear from your own lips how all goes forward in France."

The Italian's face was calm; but he looked restlessly from one to another along the line of his listeners.

"So far as I know, my liege, all is quiet on the French marches," said he.

"You have not heard then that they have mustered or gathered to a head with the intention of breaking the truce and making some attempt upon our dominions?"

"Nay, sire, I have heard nothing of it."

"You set my mind much at ease, Aymery," said the King; "for if nothing has come to your ears, then surely it cannot be. It was said that the wild Knight de Chargny had come down to St. Omer with his eyes upon my precious jewel and his mailed hands ready to grasp it."

"Nay, sire, let him come. He will find the jewel safe in its strong box, with a goodly guard over it."

"You are the guard over my jewel, Aymery."

"Yes, sire, I am the guard."

"And you are a faithful guard and one whom I can trust, are you not? You would not barter away that which is so dear to me when I have chosen you out of all my army to hold it for me?"

"Nay, sire, what reasons can there be for such questions? They touch my honor very nearly. You know that I would part with Calais only when I parted with my soul."

"Then you know nothing of de Chargny's attempt?"

"Nothing sire."

"Liar and villain!" yelled the King, springing to his feet and dashing his fist upon the table until the glasses rattled again. "Seize him, archers! Seize him this instant! Stand close by either elbow, lest he do himself a mischief! Now do you dare to tell me to my face, you perjured Lombard, that you know nothing of de Chargny and his plans?"

"As God is my witness I know nothing of him!" The man's lips were white, and he spoke in a thin, sighing, reedy voice, his eyes wincing away from the fell gaze of the angry King.

Edward laughed bitterly, and drew a paper from his breast. "You are the judges in this case, you, my fair son, and you, Chandos, and you, Manny, and you, Sir Hubert, and you also, my Lord Bishop. By my sovereign power I make you a court that you may deal justice upon this man, for by God's eyes I will not stir from this room until I have sifted the matter to the bottom. And first I would read you this letter. It is superscribed to Sir Aymery of Pavia, *nomme* Le Lombard, Château de Calais. Is not that your name and style, you rogue?"

"It is my name, sire; but no such letter has come to me."

"Else had your villainy never been disclosed. It is signed 'Isidore de Chargny'. What says my enemy de Chargny to my trusted servant? Listen! 'We could not come with the last moon, for we have not gathered sufficient strength, nor have we been able to collect the twenty thousand crowns which are your price. But with the next turn of the moon in the darkest hour we will come and you will be paid your money at the small postern gate with the rowan-bush beside it.' Well, rogue, what say you now?"

"It is a forgery!" gasped the Italian.

"I pray you that you will let me see it, sire," said Chandos. "De Chargny was my prisoner, and so many letters passed ere his ransom was paid that his script is well-known to me. Yes, yes, I will swear that this is indeed his. If my salvation were at stake I could swear it."

"If it were indeed written by de Chargny it was to dishonor me," cried Sir Aymery.

"Nay, nay!" said the young Prince. "We all know de Chargny and have fought against him. Many faults he has, a boaster and a brawler, but a braver man and one of greater heart and higher of enterprise does not ride beneath the lilies of France. Such a man would never stoop to write a letter for the sake of putting dishonor upon one of knightly rank. I, for one, will never believe it."

A gruff murmur from the others showed that they were of one mind with the Prince. The light of the torches from the walls beat upon the line of stern faces at the high table. They had sat like flint, and the Italian shrank from their inexorable eyes. He looked swiftly round, but armed men choked every entrance. The shadow of death had fallen athwart his soul.

"This letter," said the King, "was given by de Chargny to one Dom Beauvais, a priest of St. Omer, to carry into Calais. The said priest, smelling a reward, brought it to one who is my faithful servant, and so it came to me. Straightway I sent for this man that he should come to me. Meanwhile the priest has returned so that de Chargny may think that his message is indeed delivered."

"I know nothing of it," said the Italian doggedly, licking his dry lips.

A dark flush mounted to the King's forehead, and his eyes were gorged with his wrath. "No more of this, for God's dignity!" he cried. "Had we this fellow at the Tower, a few turns of the rack would tear a confession from his craven soul. But why should we need his word for his own guilt? You have seen, my lords, you have heard! How say you, fair son? Is the man guilty?"

"Sire, he is guilty."

"And you, John? And you, Walter? And you, Hubert? And you, my Lord Bishop? You are all of one mind, then. He is guilty of the betrayal of his trust. And the punishment?"

"It can only be death," said the Prince, and each in turn the others nodded their agreement.

"Aymery of Pavia, you have heard your doom," said Edward, leaning his chin upon his hand and glooming at the cowering Italian. "Step forward, you archer at the door, you with the black beard. Draw your sword! Nay, you white-faced rogue, I would not dishonor this roof-tree by your blood. It is your heels, not your head, that we want. Hack off these golden spurs of knighthood with your sword, archer! 'Twas I who gave them, and I who take them back. Ha! they fly across the hall, and with them every bond betwixt you and the worshipful order whose sign and badge they are! Now lead him out on the heath afar from the house where his carrion can best lie, and hew his scheming head from his body as a warning to all such traitors!"

The Italian, who had slipped from his chair to his knees, uttered a cry of despair, as an archer seized him by either shoulder. Writhing out of their grip, he threw himself upon the floor and clutched at the King's feet.

"Spare me, my most dread lord, spare me, I beseech you! In the name of Christ's passion, I implore your grace and pardon! Bethink you, my good and dear lord, how many years I have served under your banners and how many services I have rendered. Was it not I who found the ford upon the Seine two days before the great battle? Was it not I also who marshaled the attack at the intaking of Calais? I have a wife and four children in Italy, great King; and it was the thought of them which led me to fall from my duty, for this money would have allowed me to leave the wars and to see them once again. Mercy, my liege, mercy, I implore!"

The English are a rough race, but not a cruel one. The King sat with a face of doom; but the others looked askance and fidgeted in their seats.

"Indeed, my fair liege," said Chandos, "I pray you that you will abate somewhat of your anger."

Edward shook his head curtly. "Be silent, John. It shall be as I have said."

"I pray you, my dear and honored liege, not to act with overmuch haste in the matter," said Manny. "Bind him and hold him until the morning, for other counsels may prevail."

"Nay, I have spoken. Lead him out!"

But the trembling man clung to the King's knees in such a fashion that the archers could not disengage his convulsive grip. "Listen to me a moment, I implore you! Give me but one minute to plead with you, and then do what you will."

The King leaned back in his chair. "Speak and have done," said he.

"You must spare me, my noble liege. For your own sake I say that you must spare me, for I can set you in the way of such a knightly adventure as will gladden your heart. Bethink you, sire, that this de Chargny and his comrades know nothing of their plans having gone awry. If I do but send them a message they will surely come to the postern gate. Then, if we have placed our bushment with skill we shall have such a capture and such a ransom as will fill your coffers. He and his comrades should be worth a good hundred thousand crowns."

Edward spurned the Italian away from him with his foot until he sprawled among the rushes, but even as he lay there like a wounded snake his dark eyes never left the King's face.

"You double traitor! You would sell Calais to de Chargny, and then in turn you would sell de Chargny to me. How dare you suppose that I or any noble knight had such a huckster's soul as to think only of ransoms where honor is to be won? Could I or any true man be so caitiff and so thrall? You have sealed your own doom. Lead him out!"

"One instant, I pray you, my fair and most sweet lord," cried the Prince. "Assuage your wrath yet a little while, for this man's rede deserves perhaps more thought than we have given it. He has turned your noble soul sick with his talk of ransoms; but look at it, I pray you, from the side of honor, and where could we find such hope of worshipfully winning worship? I pray you to let me put my body in this adventure, for it is one from which, if rightly handled, much advancement is to be gained."

Edward looked with sparkling eyes at the noble youth at his side. "Never was hound more keen on the track of a stricken hart than you on the hope of honor, fair son," said he. "How do you conceive the matter in your mind?"

"De Chargny and his men will be such as are worth going far to meet, for he will have the pick of France under his banner that night. If we did as this man says and awaited him with the same number of lances, then I cannot think that there is any spot in Christendom where one would rather be than in Calais that night."

"By the rood, fair son, you are right!" cried the King, his face shining with the thought. "Now which of you, John Chandos or Walter Manny, will take the thing in charge?" He looked mischievously from one to the other like a master who dangles a bone betwixt two fierce old hounds. All they had to say was in their burning, longing eyes. "Nay, John, you must not take it amiss; but it is Walter's turn, and he shall have it."

"Shall we not all go under your banner, sire, or that of the Prince?"

"Nay, it is not fitting that the royal banners of England should be advanced in so small an adventure. And yet, if you have space in your ranks for two more cavaliers, both the Prince and I would ride with you that night."

The young man stooped and kissed his father's hand.

"Take this man in your charge, Walter, and do with him as you will. Guard well lest he betray us once again. Take him from my sight, for his breath poisons the room. And now, Nigel, if that worthy graybeard of thine would fain twang his harp or sing to us— but what in God's name would you have?"

He had turned, to find his young host upon his knee and his flaxen head bent in entreaty.

"What is it, man? What do you crave?"

"A boon, fair liege!"

"Well, well, am I to have no peace to-night, with a traitor kneeling to me in front, and a true man on his knees behind? Out with it, Nigel. What would you have?"

"To come with you to Calais."

"By the rood! your request is fair enough, seeing that our plot is hatched beneath your very roof. How say you, Walter? Will you take him, armor and all?" asked King Edward.

"Say rather will you take me?" said Chandos. "We two are rivals in honor, Walter, but I am very sure that you would not hold me back."

"Nay, John, I will be proud to have the best lance in Christendom beneath my banner."

"And I to follow so knightly a leader. But Nigel Loring is my Squire, and so he comes with us also."

"Then that is settled," said the King, "and now there is no need for hurry, since there can be no move until the moon has changed. So I pray you to pass the flagon once again, and to drink with me to the good knights of France. May they be of great heart and high of enterprise when we all meet once more within the castle wall of Calais!"

CHAPTER XI

IN THE HALL OF THE KNIGHT OF DUPLIN

THE King had come and had gone. Tilford Manor-house stood once more dark and silent, but joy and contentment reigned within its walls. In one night every trouble had fallen away like some dark curtain which had shut out the sun. A princely sum of money had come from the King's treasurer, given in such fashion that there could be no refusal. With a bag of gold pieces at his saddle-bow Nigel rode once more into Guildford, and not a beggar on the way who had not cause to bless his name.

There he had gone first to the goldsmith and had bought back cup and salver and bracelet, mourning with the merchant over the evil chance that gold and gold-work had for certain reasons which only those in the trade could fully understand gone up in value during the last week, so that already fifty gold pieces had to be paid more than the price which Nigel had received. In vain the faithful Aylward fretted and fumed and muttered a prayer that the day would come when he might feather a shaft in the merchant's portly paunch. The money had to be paid.

Thence Nigel hurried to Wat the armorer's and there he bought that very suit for which he had yearned so short a time before. Then and there he tried it on in the booth, Wat and his boy walking round him with spanner and wrench, fixing bolts and twisting rivets.

"How is that, my fair sir?" cried the armorer as he drew the bassinet over the head and fastened it to the camail which extended to the shoulders. "I swear by Tubal Cain that it fits you as the shell fits the crab! A finer suit never came from Italy or Spain."

Nigel stood in front of a burnished shield which served as a mirror, and he turned this way and that, preening himself like a little shining bird. His smooth breastplate, his wondrous joints with their deft protection by the disks at knee and elbow and shoulder, the beautifully flexible gauntlets and sollerets, the shirt of mail and the close-fitting greave-plates were all things of joy and of beauty in his eyes. He sprang about the shop to show his lightness, and then running out he placed his hand on the pommel and vaulted into Pommers' saddle, while Wat and his boy applauded in the doorway.

Then springing off and running into the shop again he clanked down upon his knees before the image of the Virgin upon the smithy wall. There from his heart he prayed that no shadow or stain should come upon his soul or his honor whilst these arms incased his body, and that he might be strengthened to use them for noble and godly ends. A strange turn this to a religion of peace, and yet for many a century the sword and the faith had upheld each other and in a darkened world the best ideal of the soldier had turned in some dim groping fashion toward the light. "Benedictus dominus deus meus qui docet manus meas ad Prælium et digitos meos ad bellum!" There spoke the soul of the knightly soldier.

So the armor was trussed upon the armorer's mule and went back with them to Tilford, where Nigel put it on once more for the pleasure of the Lady Ermyntrude, who clapped her skinny hands and shed tears of mingled pain and joy—pain that she should lose him, joy that he should go so bravely to the wars. As to her own future, it had been made easy for her, since it was arranged that a steward should look to the Tilford estate whilst she had at her disposal a suite of rooms in royal Windsor, where with other venerable dames of her own age and standing she could spend the twilight of her days discussing long-forgotten scandals and whispering sad things about the grandfathers and the grandmothers of the young courtiers all around them. There Nigel might leave her with an easy mind when he turned his face to France.

But there was one more visit to be paid and one more farewell to be spoken ere Nigel could leave the moorlands where he had dwelled so long. That evening he donned his brightest tunic, dark purple velvet of Genoa, with trimming of miniver, his hat with the snow-white feather curling round the front, and his belt of embossed silver round his loins. Mounted on lordly Pommers, with his hawk upon wrist and his sword by his side, never did fairer young gallant or one more modest in mind set forth upon such an errand. It was but the old Knight of Duplin to whom he would say farewell; but the Knight of Duplin had two daughters, Edith and Mary, and Edith was the fairest maid in all the heather-country.

Sir John Buttesthorn, the Knight of Duplin, was so called because he had been present at that strange battle, some eighteen years before, when the full power of Scotland had been for a moment beaten to the ground by a handful of adventurers and mercenaries, marching under the banner of no nation, but fighting in their own private quarrel. Their exploit fills no pages of history, for it is to the interest of no nation to record it, and yet the rumor and fame of the great fight bulked large in those times, for it was on that day when the flower of Scotland was left dead upon the field, that the world first understood that a new force had arisen in war, and that the English archer, with his robust courage and his skill with the weapon which he had wielded from his boyhood, was a power with which even the mailed chivalry of Europe had seriously to reckon.

Sir John after his return from Scotland had become the King's own head huntsman, famous through all England for his knowledge of venery, until at last, getting overheavy for his horses, he had settled in modest comfort into the old house of Cosford upon the eastern slope of the Hindhead hill. Here, as his face grew redder and his beard more white, he spent the evening of his days, amid hawks and hounds, a flagon of spiced wine ever at his elbow, and his swollen foot perched upon a stool before him. There it was that many an old comrade broke his journey as he passed down the rude road which led from London to Portsmouth, and thither also came the young gallants of the country to hear the stout knight's tales of old wars, or to learn from him that lore of the forest and the chase which none could teach so well as he.

But sooth to say, whatever the old knight might think, it was not merely his old tales and older wine which drew the young men to Cosford, but rather the fair face of his younger daughter, or the strong soul and wise counsel of the elder. Never had two more different branches sprung from the same trunk. Both were tall and of a queenly graceful figure. But there all resemblance began and ended.

Edith was yellow as the ripe corn, blue-eyed, winning, mischievous, with a chattering tongue, a merry laugh, and a smile which a dozen of young gallants, Nigel of Tilford at their head, could share equally amongst them. Like a young kitten she played with all things that she found in life, and some there were who thought that already the claws could be felt amid the patting of her velvet touch.

Mary was dark as night, grave-featured, plain-visaged, with steady brown eyes looking bravely at the world from under a strong black arch of brows. None could call her beautiful, and when her fair sister cast her arm round her and placed her cheek against hers, as was her habit when company was there, the fairness of the one and the plainness of the other leaped visibly to the eyes of all, each the clearer for that hard contrast. And yet, here and there, there was one who, looking at her strange, strong face, and at the passing gleams far down in her dark eyes, felt that this silent woman with her proud bearing and her queenly grace had in her something of strength, of reserve and of mystery which was more to them than all the dainty glitter of her sister.

Such were the ladies of Cosford toward whom Nigel Loring rode that night with doublet of Genoan velvet and the new white feather in his cap.

He had ridden over Thursley Ridge past that old stone where in days gone by at the place of Thor the wild Saxons worshiped their war-god. Nigel looked at it with a wary eye and spurred Pommers onward as he passed it, for still it was said that wild fires danced round it on the moonless nights, and they who had ears for such things could hear the scream and sob of those whose lives had been ripped from them that the fiend might be honored. Thor's stone, Thor's jumps, Thor's punch-bowl—the whole country-side was one grim monument to the God of Battles, though the pious monks had changed his uncouth name for that of the Devil his father, so that it was the Devil's jumps and the Devil's punch-bowl of which they spoke. Nigel glanced back at the old gray boulder, and he felt for an instant a shudder pass through his stout heart. Was it the chill of the evening air, or was it that some inner voice had whispered to him of the day when he also might lie bound on such a rock and have such a blood-stained pagan crew howling around him.

An instant later the rock and his vague fear and all things else had passed from his mind, for there, down the yellow sandy path, the setting sun gleaming on her golden hair, her lithe figure bending and swaying with every heave of the cantering horse, was none other than the same fair Edith, whose face had come so often betwixt him and his sleep. His blood rushed hot to his face at the sight, for fearless of all else, his spirit was attracted and yet daunted by the delicate mystery of woman. To his pure and knightly soul not Edith alone, but every woman, sat high and aloof, enthroned and exalted, with a thousand mystic excellencies and virtues which raised her far above the rude world of man. There was joy in contact with them; and yet there was fear, fear lest his own unworthiness, his untrained tongue or rougher ways should in some way break rudely upon this delicate and tender thing. Such was his thought as the white horse cantered toward him; but a moment later his vague doubts were set at rest by the frank voice of the young girl, who waved her whip in merry greeting.

"Hail and well met, Nigel!" she cried. "Whither away this evening? Sure I am that it is not to see your friends of Cosford, for when did you ever don so brave a doublet for us? Come, Nigel, her name, that I may hate her for ever."

"Nay, Edith," said the young Squire, laughing back at the laughing girl. "I was indeed coming to Cosford."

"Then we shall ride back together, for I will go no farther. How think you that I am looking?"

Nigel's answer was in his eyes as he glanced at the fair flushed face, the golden hair, the sparkling eyes and the daintily graceful figure set off in a scarlet-and-black riding-dress. "You are as fair as ever, Edith."

"Oh, cold of speech! Surely you were bred for the cloisters and not for a lady's bower, Nigel. Had I asked such a question from young Sir George Brocas or the Squire of Fernhurst, he would have raved from here to Cosford. They are both more to my taste than you are, Nigel."

"It is the worse for me, Edith," said Nigel ruefully.

"Nay, but you must not lose heart."

"Have I not already lost it?" said he.

"That is better," she cried, laughing. "You can be quick enough when you choose, Master Malapert. But you are more fit to speak of high and weary matters with my sister Mary. She will have none of the prattle and courtesy of Sir George, and yet I love them well. But tell me, Nigel, why do you come to Cosford to-night?"

"To bid you farewell."

"Me alone?"

"Nay, Edith, you and your sister Mary and the good knight your father."

"Sir George would have said that he had come for me alone. Indeed you are but a poor courtier beside him. But is it true, Nigel, that you go to France?"

"Yes, Edith."

"It was so rumored after the King had been to Tilford. The story goes that the King goes to France and you in his train. Is that true?"

"Yes, Edith, it is true."

"Tell me, then, to what part you go, and when?"

"That, alas! I may not say."

"Oh, in sooth!" She tossed her fair head and rode onward in silence, with compressed lips and angry eyes.

Nigel glanced at her in surprise and dismay. "Surely, Edith," said he at last, "you have overmuch regard for my honor that you should wish me to break the word that I have given?"

"Your honor belongs to you, and my likings belong to me," said she. "You hold fast to the one, and I will do the same by the other."

They rode in silence through Thursley village. Then a thought came to her mind and in an instant her anger was forgotten and she was hot on a new scent.

"What would you do if I were injured, Nigel? I have heard my father say that small as you are there is no man in these parts could stand against you. Would you be my champion if I suffered wrong?"

"Surely I or any man of gentle blood would be the champion of any woman who had suffered wrong."

"You or any and I or any—what sort of speech is that? Is it a compliment, think you, to be mixed with a drove in that fashion? My question was of you and me. If I were wronged would you be my man?"

"Try me and see, Edith!"

"Then I will do so, Nigel. Either Sir George Brocas or the Squire of Fernhurst would gladly do what I ask, and yet I am of a mind, Nigel, to turn to you."

"I pray you to tell me what it is."

" You know Paul de la Fosse of Shalford?"

"You mean the small man with the twisted back?"

"He is no smaller than yourself, Nigel, and as to his back there are many folk that I know who would be glad to have his face."

"Nay, I am no judge of that, and I spoke out of no discourtesy. What of the man?"

"He has flouted me, Nigel, and I would have revenge."

"What—on that poor twisted creature?"

"I tell you that he has flouted me!"

"But how?"

"I should have thought that a true cavalier would have flown to my aid, withouten all these questions. But I will tell you, since I needs must. Know then that he was one of those who came around me and professed to be my own. Then, merely because he thought that there were others who were as dear to me as himself he left me, and now he pays court to Maude Twynham, the little freckle-faced hussy in his village."

"But how has this hurt you, since he was no man of thine?"

"He was one of my men, was he not? And he has made game of me to his wench. He has told her things about me. He has made me foolish in her eyes. Yes, yes, I can read it in her saffron face and in her watery eyes when we meet at the church door on Sundays. She smiles—yes, smiles at me! Nigel, go to him! Do not slay him, nor even wound him, but lay his face open with thy riding- whip, and then come back to me and tell me how I can serve you."

Nigel's face was haggard with the strife within, for desire ran hot in every vein, and yet reason shrank with horror. "By Saint Paul! Edith," he cried, "I see no honor nor advancement of any sort in this thing which you have asked me to do. Is it for me to strike one who is no better than a cripple? For my manhood I could not do such a deed, and I pray you, dear lady, that you will set me some other task."

Her eyes flashed at him in contempt. "And you are a man-at-arms!" she cried, laughing in bitter scorn. "You are afraid of a little man who can scarce walk. Yes, yes, say what you will, I shall ever believe that you have heard of his skill at fence and of his great spirit, and that your heart has failed you! You are right, Nigel. He is indeed a perilous man. Had you done what I asked he would have slain you, and so you have shown your wisdom."

Nigel flushed and winced under the words, but he said no more, for his mind was fighting hard within him, striving to keep that high image of woman which seemed for a moment to totter on the edge of a fall. Together in silence, side by side, the little man and the stately woman, the yellow charger and the white jennet, passed up the sandy winding track with the gorse and the bracken head-high on either side. Soon a path branched off through a gateway marked with the boar-heads of the Buttesthorns, and there was the low widespread house heavily timbered, loud with the barking of dogs. The ruddy Knight limped forth with outstretched hand and roaring voice:

"What how, Nigel! Good welcome and all hail! I had thought that you had given over poor friends like us, now that the King had made so much of you. The horses, varlets, or my crutch will be across you! Hush, Lydiard! Down, Pelamon! I can scarce hear my voice for your yelping. Mary, a cup of wine for young Squire Loring!"

She stood framed in the doorway, tall, mystic, silent, with strange, wistful face and deep soul shining in her dark, questioning eyes. Nigel kissed the hand that she held out, and all his faith in woman and his reverence came back to him as he looked at her. Her sister had slipped behind her and her fair elfish face smiled her forgiveness of Nigel over Mary's shoulder.

The Knight of Duplin leaned his weight upon the young man's arm and limped his way across the great high-roofed hall to his capacious oaken chair. "Come, come, the stool, Edith!" he cried. "As God is my help, that girl's mind swarms with gallants as a granary with rats. Well, Nigel, I hear strange tales of your spear-running at Tilford and of the visit of the King. How seemed he? And my old friend Chandos—many happy hours in the woodlands have we had together—and Manny too, he was ever a bold and a hard rider—what news of them all?"

Nigel told to the old Knight all that had occurred, saying little of his own success and much of his own failure, yet the eyes of the dark woman burned the brighter as she sat at her tapestry and listened.

Sir John followed the story with a running fire of oaths, prayers, thumps with his great fist and flourishes of his crutch. "Well, well, lad, you could scarce expect to hold your saddle against Manny, and you have carried yourself well. We are proud of you, Nigel, for you are our own man, reared in the heather country. But indeed I take shame that you are not more skilled in the mystery of the woods, seeing that I have had the teaching of you, and that no one in broad England is my master at the craft. I pray you to fill your cup again whilst I make use of the little time that is left to us."

And straightway the old Knight began a long and weary lecture upon the times of grace and when each beast and bird was seasonable, with many anecdotes, illustrations, warnings and exceptions, drawn from his own great experience. He spoke also of the several ranks and grades of the chase: how the hare, hart and boar must ever take precedence over the buck, the doe, the fox, the marten and the roe, even as a knight banneret does over a knight, while these in turn are of a higher class to the badger, the wildcat or the otter, who are but the common populace of the world of beasts. Of blood-stains also he spoke—how the skilled hunter may see at a glance if blood be dark and frothy, which means a mortal hurt, or thin and clear, which means that the arrow has struck a bone.

"By such signs," said he, "you will surely know whether to lay on the hounds and cast down the blinks which hinder the stricken deer in its flight. But above all I pray you, Nigel, to have a care in the use of the terms of the craft, lest you should make some blunder at table, so that those who are wiser may have the laugh of you, and we who love you may be shamed."

"Nay, Sir John," said Nigel. "I think that after your teaching I can hold my place with the others."

The old Knight shook his white head doubtfully. "There is so much to be learned that there is no one who can be said to know all," said he. "For example, Nigel, it is sooth that for every collection of beasts of the forest, and for every gathering of birds of the air, there is their own private name so that none may be confused with another."

"I know it, fair sir."

"You know it, Nigel, but you do not know each separate name, else are you a wiser man than I had thought you. In truth none can say that they know all, though I have myself picked off eighty and six for a wager at court, and it is said that the chief huntsman of the Duke of Burgundy has counted over a hundred—but it is in my mind that he may have found them as he went, for there was none to say him nay. Answer me now, lad, how would you say if you saw ten badgers together in the forest?"

"A cete of badgers, fair sir."

"Good, Nigel—good, by my faith! And if you walk in Woolmer Forest and see a swarm of foxes, how would you call it?"

"A skulk of foxes."

"And if they be lions?"

"Nay, fair sir, I am not like to meet several lions in Woolmer Forest."

"Aye, lad, but there are other forests besides Woolmer, and other lands besides England, and who can tell how far afield such a knight errant as Nigel of Tilford may go, when he sees worship to be won? We will say that you were in the deserts of Nubia, and that afterward at the court of the great Sultan you wished to say that you had seen several lions, which is the first beast of the chase, being the king of all animals. How then would you say it?"

Nigel scratched his head. "Surely, fair sir, I would be content to say that I had seen a number of lions, if indeed I could say aught after so wondrous an adventure."

"Nay, Nigel, a huntsman would have said that he had seen a pride of lions, and so proved that he knew the language of the chase. Now had it been boars instead of lions?"

"One says a singular of boars."

"And if they be swine?"

"Surely it is a herd of swine."

"Nay, nay, lad, it is indeed sad to see how little you know. Your hands, Nigel, were always better than your head. No man of gentle birth would speak of a herd of swine; that is the peasant speech. If you drive them it is a herd. If you hunt them it is other. What call you them, then, Edith?"

"Nay, I know not," said the girl listlessly. A crumpled note brought in by a varlet was clinched in her right hand and her blue eyes looked afar into the deep shadows of the roof.

"But you can tell us, Mary?"

"Surely, sweet sir, one talks of a sounder of swine."

The old Knight laughed exultantly. "Here is a pupil who never brings me shame!" he cried. "Be it lore of chivalry or heraldry or woodcraft or what you will, I can always turn to Mary. Many a man can she put to the blush."

"Myself among them," said Nigel.

"Ah, lad, you are a Solomon to some of them. Hark ye! only last week that jack-fool, the young Lord of Brocas, was here talking of having seen a covey of pheasants in the wood. One such speech would have been the ruin of a young Squire at the court. How would you have said it, Nigel?"

"Surely, fair sir, it should be a nye of pheasants."

"Good, Nigel—a nye of pheasants, even as it is a gaggle of geese or a badling of ducks, a fall of woodcock or a wisp of snipe. But a covey of pheasants! What sort of talk is that? I made him sit even where you are sitting, Nigel, and I saw the bottom of two pots of Rhenish ere I let him up. Even then I fear that he had no great profit from his lesson, for he was casting his foolish eyes at Edith when he should have been turning his ears to her father. But where is the wench?"

"She hath gone forth, father."

"She ever doth go forth when there is a chance of learning aught that is useful indoors. But supper will soon be ready, and there is a boar's ham fresh from the forest with which I would ask your help, Nigel, and a side of venison from the King's own chase. The tinemen and verderers have not forgotten me yet, and my larder is ever full. Blow three moots on the horn, Mary, that the varlets may set the table, for the growing shadow and my loosening belt warn me that it is time."

CHAPTER XII

HOW NIGEL FOUGHT THE TWISTED MAN OF SHALFORD

In the days of which you read all classes, save perhaps the very poor, fared better in meat and in drink than they have ever done since. The country was covered with woodlands — there were seventy separate forests in England alone, some of them covering half a shire. Within these forests the great beasts of the chase were strictly preserved, but the smaller game, the hares, the rabbits, the birds, which swarmed round the coverts, found their way readily into the poor man's pot. Ale was very cheap, and cheaper still was the mead which every peasant could make for himself out of the wild honey in the tree-trunks. There were many tea-like drinks also, which were brewed by the poor at no expense: mallow tea, tansy tea, and others the secret of which has passed.

Amid the richer classes there was rude profusion, great joints ever on the sideboard, huge pies, beasts of the field and beasts of the chase, with ale and rough French or Rhenish wines to wash them down. But the very rich had attained to a high pitch of luxury in their food, and cookery was a science in which the ornamentation of the dish was almost as important as the dressing of the food. It was gilded, it was silvered, it was painted, it was surrounded with flame. From the boar and the peacock down to such strange food as the porpoise and the hedgehog, every dish had its own setting and its own sauce, very strange

544

and very complex, with flavorings of dates, currants, cloves, vinegar, sugar and honey, of cinnamon, ground ginger, sandal-wood, saffron, brawn and pines. It was the Norman tradition to eat in moderation, but to have a great profusion of the best and of the most delicate from which to choose. From them came this complex cookery, so unlike the rude and often gluttonous simplicity of the old Teutonic stock.

Sir John Buttesthorn was of that middle class who fared in the old fashion, and his great oak supper-table groaned beneath the generous pasties, the mighty joints and the great flagons. Below were the household, above on a raised dais the family table, with places ever ready for those frequent guests who dropped in from the high road outside. Such a one had just come, an old priest, journeying from the Abbey of Chertsey to the Priory of Saint John at Midhurst. He passed often that way, and never without breaking his journey at the hospitable board of Cosford.

"Welcome again, good Father Athanasius!" cried the burly Knight. "Come sit here on my right and give me the news of the country-side, for there is never a scandal but the priests are the first to know it."

The priest, a kindly, quiet man, glanced at an empty place upon the farther side of his host. "Mistress Edith?" said he.

"Aye, aye, where is the hussy?" cried her father impatiently. "Mary, I beg you to have the horn blown again, that she may know that the supper is on the table. What can the little owlet do abroad at this hour of the night?"

There was trouble in the priest's gentle eyes as he touched the Knight upon the sleeve. "I have seen Mistress Edith within this hour," said he. "I fear that she will hear no horn that you may blow, for she must be at Milford ere now."

"At Milford? What does she there?"

"I pray you, good Sir John, to abate your voice somewhat, for indeed this matter is for our private discourse, since it touches the honor of a lady."

"Her honor?" Sir John's ruddy face had turned redder still, as he stared at the troubled features of the priest. "Her honor, say you—the honor of my daughter? Make good those words, or never set your foot over the threshold of Cosford again!"

"I trust that I have done no wrong, Sir John, but indeed I must say what I have seen, else would I be a false friend and an unworthy priest."

"Haste man, haste! What in the Devil's name have you seen?"

"Know you a little man, partly misshapen, named Paul de la Fosse?"

"I know him well. He is a man of noble family and coat-armor, being the younger brother of Sir Eustace de la Fosse of Shalford. Time was when I had thought that I might call him son, for there was never a day that he did not pass with my girls, but I fear that his crooked back sped him ill in his wooing."

"Alas, Sir John! It is his mind that is more crooked than his back. He is a perilous man with women, for the Devil hath given him such a tongue and such an eye that he charms them even as the basilisk. Marriage may be in their mind, but never in his, so that I could count a dozen and more whom he has led to their undoing. It is his pride and his boast over the whole countryside."

"Well, well, and what is this to me or mine?"

"Even now, Sir John, as I rode my mule up the road I met this man speeding toward his home. A woman rode by his side, and though her face was hooded I heard her laugh as she passed me. That laugh I have heard before, and it was under this very roof, from the lips of Mistress Edith."

The Knight's knife dropped from his hand. But the debate had been such that neither Mary nor Nigel could fail to have heard it. Mid the rough laughter and clatter of voices from below the little group at the high table had a privacy of their own.

"Fear not, father," said the girl—"indeed, the good Father Athanasius hath fallen into error, and Edith will be with us anon. I have heard her speak of this man many times of late, and always with bitter words."

"It is true, sir," cried Nigel eagerly. "It was only this very evening as we rode over Thursley Moor that Mistress Edith told me that she counted him not a fly, and that she would be glad if he were beaten for his evil deeds."

But the wise priest shook his silvery locks. "Nay, there is ever danger when a woman speaks like that. Hot hate is twin brother to hot love. Why should she speak so if there were not some bond between them?"

"And yet," said Nigel, "what can have changed her thoughts in three short hours? She was here in the hall with us since I came. By Saint Paul, I will not believe it!"

Mary's face darkened. "I call to mind," said she, "that a note was brought her by Hannekin the stable varlet when you were talking to us, fair sir, of the terms of the chase. She read it and went forth."

Sir John sprang to his feet, but sank into his chair again with a groan. "Would that I were dead," he cried, "ere I saw dishonor come upon my house, and am so tied with this accursed foot that I can neither examine if it be true, nor yet avenge it! If my son Oliver were here, then all would be well. Send me this stable varlet that I may question him."

"I pray you, fair and honored sir," said Nigel, "that you will take me for your son this night, that I may handle this matter in the way which seems best. On jeopardy of my honor I will do all that a man may."

"Nigel, I thank you. There is no man in Christendom to whom I would sooner turn."

"But I would learn your mind in one matter, fair sir. This man, Paul de la Fosse, owns broad acres, as I understand, and comes of noble blood. There is no reason if things be as we fear that he should not marry your daughter?"

"Nay, she could not wish for better."

"It is well. And first I would question this Hannekin; but it shall be done in such a fashion that none shall know, for indeed it is not a matter for the gossip of servants. But if you will show me the man, Mistress Mary, I will take him out to tend my own horse, and so I shall learn all that he has to tell."

Nigel was absent for some time, and when he returned the shadow upon his face brought little hope to the anxious hearts at the high table. "I have locked him in the stable-loft, lest he talk too much," said he, "for my questions must have shown him whence the wind blew. It was indeed from this man that the note came, and he had brought with him a spare horse for the lady."

The old Knight groaned, and his face sank upon his hands.

"Nay, father they watch you!" whispered Mary. "For the honor of our house let us keep a bold face to all." Then, raising her young clear voice, so that it sounded through the room: "If you ride eastward, Nigel, I would fain go with you, that my sister may not come back alone."

"We will ride together, Mary," said Nigel, rising; then in a lower voice: "But we cannot go alone, and if we take a servant all is known. I pray you to stay at home and leave the matter with me."

"Nay, Nigel, she may sorely need a woman's aid, and what woman should it be save her own sister? I can take my tire-woman with us."

"Nay, I shall ride with you myself if your impatience can keep within the powers of my mule," said the old priest.

"But it is not your road, father?"

"The only road of a true priest is that which leads to the good of others. Come, my children, and we will go together."

And so it was that stout Sir John Buttesthorn, the aged Knight of Duplin, was left alone at his own high table, pretending to eat, pretending to drink, fidgeting in his seat, trying hard to seem unconcerned with his mind and body in a fever, while below him his varlets and handmaids laughed and jested, clattering their cups and clearing their trenchers, all unconscious of the dark shadow which threw its gloom over the lonely man upon the dais above.

Meantime the Lady Mary upon the white jennet which her sister had ridden on the same evening, Nigel on his war-horse, and the priest on the mule, clattered down the rude winding road which led to London. The country on either side was a wilderness of heather moors and of morasses from which came the strange crying of night-fowl. A half-moon shone in the sky between the rifts of hurrying clouds. The lady rode in silence, absorbed in the thought of the task before them, the danger and the shame.

Nigel chatted in a low tone with the priest. From him he learned more of the evil name of this man whom they followed. His house at Shalford was a den of profligacy and vice. No woman could cross that threshold and depart unstained. In some strange fashion, inexplicable and yet common, the man, with all his evil soul and his twisted body, had yet some strange fascination for women, some mastery over them which compelled them to his will. Again and again he had brought ruin to a household, again and again his adroit tongue and his cunning wit had in some fashion saved him from the punishment of his deeds. His family was great in the county, and his kinsmen held favor with the King, so that his neighbors feared to push things too far against him. Such was the man, malignant and ravenous, who had stooped like some foul night-hawk and borne away to his evil nest the golden beauty of Cosford. Nigel said little as he listened, but he raised his hunting-dagger to his tightened lips, and thrice he kissed the cross of its handle.

They had passed over the moors and through the village of Milford and the little township of Godalming, until their path turned southward over the Pease marsh and crossed the meadows of Shalford. There on the dark hillside glowed the red points of light which marked the windows of the house which they sought. A somber arched avenue of oak-trees led up to it, and then they were in the moon-silvered clearing in front.

From the shadow of the arched door there sprang two rough serving-men, bearded and gruff, great cudgels in their hands, to ask them who they were and what their errand. The Lady Mary had slipped from her horse and was advancing to the door, but they rudely barred her way.

"Nay, nay, our master needs no more!" cried one, with a hoarse laugh. "Stand back, mistress, whoever you be! The house is shut, and our lord sees no guests to-night."

"Fellow," said Nigel, speaking low and clear, "stand back from us! Our errand is with your master."

"Bethink you, my children," cried the old priest, "would it not be best perchance, that I go in to him and see whether the voice of the Church may not soften this hard heart? I fear bloodshed if you enter."

"Nay, father, I pray you to stay here for the nonce," said Nigel. "And you, Mary, do you bide with the good priest, for we know not what may be within."

Again he turned to the door, and again the two men barred his passage.

"Stand back, I say, back for your lives!" said Nigel. "By Saint Paul! I should think it shame to soil my sword with such as you, but my soul is set, and no man shall bar my path this night."

The men shrank from the deadly menace of that gentle voice.

"Hold!" said one of them, peering through the darkness, "is it not Squire Loring of Tilford? "

"That is indeed my name."

"Had you spoken it I for one would not have stopped your way. Put down your staff, Wat, for this is no stranger, but the Squire of Tilford."

"As well for him," grumbled the other, lowering his cudgel with an inward prayer of thanksgiving. "Had it been otherwise I should have had blood upon my soul to-night. But our master said nothing of neighbors when he ordered us to hold the door. I will enter and ask him what is his will."

But already Nigel was past them and had pushed open the outer door. Swift as he was, the Lady Mary was at his very heels, and the two passed together into the hall beyond.

It was a great room, draped and curtained with black shadows, with one vivid circle of light in the center, where two oil lamps shone upon a small table. A meal was laid upon the table, but only two were seated at it, and there were no servants in the room. At the near end was Edith, her golden hair loose and streaming down over the scarlet and black of her riding-dress.

At the farther end the light beat strongly upon the harsh face and the high-drawn misshapen shoulders of the lord of the house. A tangle of black hair surmounted a high rounded forehead, the forehead of a thinker, with two deep-set cold gray eyes twinkling sharply from under tufted brows. His nose was curved and sharp, like the beak of some cruel bird, but below the whole of his clean-shaven powerful face was marred by the loose slabbing mouth and the round folds of the heavy chin. His knife in one hand and a half-gnawed bone in the other, he looked fiercely up, like some beast disturbed in his den, as the two intruders broke in upon his hall.

Nigel stopped midway between the door and the table. His eyes and those of Paul de la Fosse were riveted upon each other. But Mary, with her woman's soul flooded over with love and pity, had rushed forward and cast her arms round her younger sister. Edith had sprung up from her chair, and with averted face tried to push the other away from her.

"Edith, Edith! By the Virgin, I implore you to come back with us, and to leave this wicked man!" cried Mary. "Dear sister, you would not break our father's heart, nor bring his gray head in dishonor to the grave! Come back! Edith, come back and all is well."

But Edith pushed her away, and her fair cheeks were flushed with her anger. "What right have you over me, Mary, you who are but two years older, that you should follow me over the countryside as though I were a runagate villain and you my mistress? Do you yourself go back, and leave me to do that which seems best in my own eyes."

But Mary still held her in her arms, and still strove to soften the hard and angry heart. "Our mother is dead, Edith. I thank God that she died ere she saw you under this roof! But I stand for her, as I have done all my life, since I am indeed your elder. It is with her voice that I beg and pray you that you will not trust this man further, and that you will come back ere it be too late!"

Edith writhed from her grasp, and stood flushed and defiant, with gleaming, angry eyes fixed upon her sister. "You may speak evil of him now," said she, "but there was a time when Paul de la Fosse came to Cosford, and who so gentle and soft-spoken to him then as wise, grave, sister Mary? But he has learned to love another; so now he is the wicked man, and it is shame to be seen under his roof! From what I see of my good pious sister and her cavalier it is sin for another to ride at night with a man at your side, but it comes easy enough to you. Look at your own eye, good sister, ere you would take the speck from that of another."

Mary stood irresolute and greatly troubled, holding down her pride and her anger, but uncertain how best to deal with this strong wayward spirit.

"It is not a time for bitter words, dear sister," said she, and again she laid her hand upon her sister's sleeve. "All that you say may be true. There was indeed a time when this man was friend to us both, and I know even as you do the power which he may have to win a woman's heart. But I know him now, and you do not. I know the evil that he has wrought, the dishonor that he has brought, the perjury that lies upon his soul, the confidence betrayed, the promise unfulfilled—all this I know. Am I to see my own sister caught in the same well-used trap? Has it shut upon you, child? Am I indeed already too late? For God's sake, tell me, Edith, that it is not so?"

Edith plucked her sleeve from her sister and made two swift steps to the head of the table. Paul de la Fosse still sat silent with his eyes upon Nigel. Edith laid her hand upon his shoulder. "This is the man I love, and the only man that I have ever loved. This is my husband," said she.

At the word Mary gave a cry of joy.

"And is it so?" she cried. "Nay, then all is in honor, and God will see to the rest. If you are man and wife before the altar, then indeed why should I, or any other, stand between you? Tell me that it is indeed so, and I return this moment to make your father a happy man."

Edith pouted like a naughty child. "We are man and wife in the eyes of God. Soon also we shall be wedded before all the world. We do but wait until next Monday when Paul's brother, who is a priest at St. Albans, will come to wed us. Already a messenger has sped for him, and he will come, will he not, dear love?"

"He will come," said the master of Shalford, still with his eyes fixed upon the silent Nigel.

"It is a lie; he will not come," said a voice from the door.

It was the old priest, who had followed the others as far as the threshold.

"He will not come," he repeated as he advanced into the room. "Daughter, my daughter, hearken to the words of one who is indeed old enough to be your earthly father. This lie has served before. He has ruined others before you with it. The man has no brother at Saint Albans. I know his brothers well, and there is no priest among them. Before Monday, when it is all too late, you will have found the truth as others have done before you. Trust him not, but come with us!"

Paul de la Fosse looked up at her with a quick smile and patted the hand upon his shoulder.

"Do you speak to them, Edith," said he.

Her eyes flashed with scorn as she surveyed them each in turn, the woman, the youth and the priest.

"I have but one word to say to them," said she. "It is that they go hence and trouble us no more. Am I not a free woman? Have I not said that this is the only man I ever loved? I have loved him long. He did not know it, and in despair he turned to another. Now he knows all and never again can doubt come between us. Therefore I will stay here at Shalford and come to Cosford no more save upon the arm of my husband. Am I so weak that I would believe the tales you tell against him? Is it hard for a jealous woman and a wandering priest to agree upon a lie? No, no, Mary, you can go hence and take your cavalier and your priest with you, for here I stay, true to my love and safe in my trust upon his honor!"

"Well spoken, on my faith, my golden bird!" said the little master of Shalford. "Let me add my own word to that which has been said. You would not grant me any virtue in your unkindly speech, good Lady Mary, and yet you must needs confess that at least I have good store of patience, since I have not set my dogs upon your friends who have come between me and my ease. But even to the most virtuous there comes at last a time when poor human frailty may prevail, and so I pray you to remove both yourself, your priest and your valiant knight errant, lest perhaps there be more haste and less dignity when at last you do take your leave. Sit down, my fair love, and let us turn once more to our supper." He motioned her to her chair, and he filled her wine-cup as well as his own.

Nigel had said no word since he had entered the room, but his look had never lost its set purpose, nor had his brooding eyes ever wandered from the sneering face of the deformed master of Shalford. Now he turned with swift decision to Mary and to the priest.

"That is over," said he in a low voice. "You have done all that you could, and now it is for me to play my part as well as I am able. I pray you, Mary, and you, good father, that you will await me outside."

"Nay, Nigel, if there is danger——"

"It is easier for me, Mary, if you are not there. I pray you to go. I can speak to this man more at my ease."

She looked at him with questioning eyes and then obeyed.

Nigel plucked at the priest's gown.

"I pray you, father, have you your book of offices with you?"

"Surely, Nigel, it is ever in my breast."

"Have it ready, father!"

"For what, my son?"

"There are two places you may mark; there is the service of marriage and there is the prayer for the dying. Go with her, father, and be ready at my call."

He closed the door behind them and was alone with this ill-matched couple. They both turned in their chairs to look at him, Edith with a defiant face, the man with a bitter smile upon his lips and malignant hatred in his eyes.

"What," said he, "the knight errant still lingers? Have we not heard of his thirst for glory? What new venture does he see that he should tarry here?"

Nigel walked to the table.

"There is no glory and little venture," said he; "but I have come for a purpose and I must do it. I learn from your own lips, Edith, that you will not leave this man."

"If you have ears you have heard it."

"You are, as you have said, a free woman, and who can gainsay you? But I have known you, Edith, since we played as boy and girl on the heather-hills together. I will save you from this man's cunning and from your own foolish weakness."

"What would you do?"

"There is a priest without. He will marry you now. I will see you married ere I leave this hall."

"Or else?" sneered the man.

"Or else you never leave this hall alive. Nay, call not for your servants or your dogs! By Saint Paul! I swear to you that this matter lies between us three, and that if any fourth comes at your call you, at least, shall never live to see what comes of it! Speak then, Paul of Shalford! Will you wed this woman now, or will you not?"

Edith was on her feet with outstretched arms between them. "Stand back, Nigel! He is small and weak. You would not do him a hurt! Did you not say so this very day? For God's sake, Nigel, do not look at him so! There is death in your eyes."

"A snake may be small and weak, Edith, yet every honest man would place his heel upon it. Do you stand back yourself, for my purpose is set."

"Paul!" she turned her eyes to the pale sneering face. "Bethink you, Paul! Why should you not do what he asks? What matter to you whether it be now or on Monday? I pray you, dear

Paul, for my sake let him have his way! Your brother can read the service again if it so please him. Let us wed now, Paul, and then all is well."

He had risen from his chair, and he dashed aside her appealing hands. "You foolish woman," he snarled, "and you, my savior of fair damsels, who are so bold against a cripple, you have both to learn that if my body be weak there is the soul of my breed within it! To marry because a boasting, ranting, country Squire would have me do so — no, by the soul of God, I will die first! On Monday I will marry, and no day sooner, so let that be your answer."

"It is the answer that I wished," said Nigel, "for indeed I see no happiness in this marriage, and the other may well be the better way. Stand aside, Edith!" He gently forced her to one side and drew his sword.

De la Fosse cried aloud at the sight. "I have no sword. You would not murder me?" said he, leaning back with haggard face and burning eyes against his chair. The bright steel shone in the lamp-light. Edith shrank back, her hand over her face.

"Take this sword!" said Nigel, and he turned the hilt to the cripple. "Now!" he added, as he drew his hunting-knife. "Kill me if you can, Paul de la Fosse, for as God is my help I will do as much for you!"

The woman, half swooning and yet spellbound and fascinated, looked on at that strange combat. For a moment the cripple stood with an air of doubt, the sword grasped in his nerveless fingers. Then as he saw the tiny blade in Nigel's hand the greatness of the advantage came home to him, and a cruel smile tightened his loose lips. Slowly, step by step he advanced, his chin sunk upon his chest, his eyes glaring from under the thick tangle of his brows like fires through the brushwood. Nigel waited for him, his left hand forward, his knife down by his hip, his face grave, still and watchful.

Nearer and nearer yet, with stealthy step, and then with a bound and a cry of hatred and rage Paul de la Fosse had sped his blow. It was well judged and well swung, but point would have been wiser than edge against that supple body and those active feet. Quick as a flash, Nigel had sprung inside the sweep of the blade, taking a flesh wound on his left forearm, as he pressed it under the hilt. The next instant the cripple was on the ground and Nigel's dagger was at his throat.

"You dog!" he whispered. "I have you at my mercy! Quick ere I strike, and for the last time! Will you marry or no?"

The crash of the fall and the sharp point upon his throat had cowed the man's spirit. He looked up with a white face and the sweat gleamed upon his forehead. There was terror in his eyes.

"Nay, take your knife from me!" he cried. "I cannot die like a calf in the shambles."

"Will you marry?"

"Yes, yes, I will wed her! After all she is a good wench and I might do worse. Let me up! I tell you I will marry her! What more would you have?"

Nigel stood above him with his foot upon his misshapen body. He had picked up his sword, and the point rested upon the cripple's breast.

"Nay, you will bide where you are! If you are to live—and my conscience cries loud against it—at least your wedding will be such as your sins have deserved. Lie there, like the crushed worm that you are!" Then he raised his voice. "Father Athanasius!" he cried. "What ho! Father Athanasius!"

The old priest ran to the cry, and so did the Lady Mary. A strange sight it was that met them now in the circle of light, the frightened girl, half-unconscious against the table, the prostrate cripple, and Nigel with foot and sword upon his body.

"Your book, father!" cried Nigel. "I know not if what we do is good or ill; but we must wed them, for there is no way out."

But the girl by the table had given a great cry, and she was clinging and sobbing with her arms round her sister's neck.

"Oh, Mary, I thank the Virgin that you have come! I thank the Virgin that it is not too late! What did he say? He said that he was a de la Fosse and that he would not be married at the sword-point. My heart went out to him when he said it. But I, am I not a Buttesthorn, and shall it be said that I would marry a man who could be led to the altar with a knife at his throat? No, no, I see him as he is! I know him now, the mean spirit, the lying tongue! Can I not read in his eyes that he has indeed deceived me, that he would have left me as you say that he has left others? Take me home, Mary, my sister, for you have plucked me back this night from the very mouth of Hell!"

And so it was that the master of Shalford, livid and brooding, was left with his wine at his lonely table, while the golden beauty of Cosford, hot with shame and anger, her fair face wet with tears, passed out safe from the house of infamy into the great calm and peace of the starry night.

CHAPTER XIII

HOW THE COMRADES JOURNEYED DOWN THE OLD, OLD ROAD

AND now the season of the moonless nights was drawing nigh and the King's design was ripe. Very secretly his preparations were made. Already the garrison of Calais, which consisted of five hundred archers and two hundred men-at-arms, could, if forewarned, resist any attack made upon it. But it was the King's design not merely to resist the attack, but to capture the attackers. Above all it was his wish to find the occasion for one of those adventurous passages of arms which had made his name famous throughout Christendom as the very pattern and leader of knight-errant chivalry.

But the affair wanted careful handling. The arrival of any, reinforcements, or even the crossing of any famous soldier, would have alarmed the French and warned them that their plot had been discovered. Therefore it was in twos and threes in the creyers and provision ships which were continually passing from shore to shore that the chosen warriors and their squires were brought to Calais. There they were passed at night through the water-gate into the castle where they could lie hidden, unknown to the townsfolk, until the hour for action had come.

Nigel had received word from Chandos to join him at "The Sign of the Broom-Pod" in Winchelsea. Three days beforehand he and Aylward rode from Tilford all armed and ready for the wars. Nigel was in hunting-costume, blithe and gay, with his precious armor and his small baggage trussed upon the back of a spare horse which Aylward led by the bridle. The archer had himself a good black mare, heavy and slow, but strong enough to be fit to carry his powerful frame. In his brigandine of chain mail and his steel cap, with straight strong sword by his side, his yellow longbow jutting over his shoulder, and his quiver of arrows supported by a scarlet baldric, he was such a warrior as any knight might well be proud to have in his train. All Tilford trailed behind them, as they rode slowly over the long slope of heath land which skirts the flank of Crooksbury Hill.

At the summit of the rise Nigel reined in Pommers and looked back at the little village behind him. There was the old dark manor-house, with one bent figure leaning upon a stick and gazing dimly after him from beside the door. He looked at the high-pitched roof, the timbered walls, the long trail of swirling blue smoke which rose from the single chimney, and the group of downcast old servants who lingered at the gate, John the cook, Weathercote the minstrel, and Red Swire the broken soldier. Over the river amid the trees he could see the grim, gray tower of Waverley, and even as he looked, the iron bell, which had so often seemed to be the hoarse threatening cry of an enemy, clanged out its call to prayer. Nigel doffed his velvet cap and prayed also — prayed that peace might remain at home, and good warfare, in which honor and fame should await him, might still be found abroad. Then, waving his hand to the people, he turned his horse's head and rode slowly eastward. A moment later Aylward broke from the group of archers and laughing girls who clung to his bridle and his stirrup straps, and rode on, blowing kisses over his shoulder. So at last the two comrades, gentle and simple, were fairly started on their venture.

There are two seasons of color in those parts: the yellow, when the country-side is flaming with the gorse-blossoms, and the crimson, when all the long slopes are smoldering with the heather. So it was now. Nigel looked back from time to time, as he rode along the narrow track where the ferns and the ling brushed his feet on either side, and as he looked it seemed to him that wander where he might he would never see a fairer scene than that of his own home. Far to the westward, glowing in the morning light, rolled billow after billow of ruddy heather land, until they merged into the dark shadows of Woolmer Forest and the pale clear green of the Butser chalk downs. Never in his life had Nigel wandered far beyond these limits, and the woodlands, the down and the heather were dear to his soul. It gave him a pang in his heart now as he turned his face away from them; but if home lay to the westward, out there to the eastward was the great world of adventure, the noble stage where each of his kinsmen in turn had played his manly part and left a proud name behind.

How often he had longed for this day! And now it had come with no shadow cast behind it. Dame Ermyntrude was under the King's protection. The old servants had their future assured. The strife with the monks of Waverley had been assuaged. He had a noble horse under him, the best of weapons, and a stout follower at his back. Above all he was bound on a gallant errand with the bravest knight in England as his leader. All these thoughts surged together in his mind, and he whistled and sang, as he rode, out of the joy of his heart, while Pommers sidled and curveted in sympathy with the mood of his master. Presently, glancing back, he saw from Aylward's downcast eyes and puckered brow that the archer was clouded with trouble. He reined his horse to let him come abreast of him.

"How now, Aylward?" said he. "Surely of all men in England you and I should be the most blithe this morning, since we ride forward with all hopes of honorable advancement. By Saint Paul! ere we see these heather hills once more we shall either worshipfully win worship, or we shall venture our persons in the attempt. These be glad thoughts, and why should you be downcast?"

Aylward shrugged his broad shoulders, and a wry smile dawned upon his rugged face. "I am indeed as limp as a wetted bowstring," said he. "It is the nature of a man that he should be sad when he leaves the woman he loves."

"In truth, yes!" cried Nigel, and in a flash the dark eyes of Mary Buttesthorn rose before him, and he heard her low, sweet, earnest voice as he had heard it that night when they brought her frailer sister back from Shalford Manor, a voice which made all that was best and noblest in a man thrill within his soul. "Yet, bethink you, archer, that what a woman loves in man is not his gross body, but rather his soul, his honor, his fame, the deeds with which he has made his life beautiful. Therefore you are winning love as well as glory when you turn to the wars."

"It may be so," said Aylward; "but indeed it goes to my heart to see the pretty dears weep, and I would fain weep as well to keep them company. When Mary—or was it Dolly?—nay, it was Martha, the red-headed girl from the mill—when she held tight to my baldric it was like snapping my heart-string to pluck myself loose."

"You speak of one name and then of another," said Nigel. "How is she called then, this maid whom you love?"

Aylward pushed back his steel cap and scratched his bristling head with some embarrassment. "Her name," said he, "is Mary Dolly Martha Susan Jane Cicely Theodosia Agnes Johanna Kate."

Nigel laughed as Aylward rolled out this prodigious title. "I had no right to take you to the wars," said he; "for by Saint Paul! it is very clear that I have widowed half the parish. But I saw your aged father the franklin. Bethink you of the joy that will fill his heart when he hears that you have done some small deed in France, and so won honor in the eyes of all."

"I fear that honor will not help him to pay his arrears of rent to the sacrist of Waverley," said Aylward. "Out he will go on the road-side, honor and all, if he does not find ten nobles by next Epiphany. But if I could win a ransom or be at the storming of a rich city, then indeed the old man would be proud of me. 'Thy sword must help my spade, Samkin,' said he as he kissed me good-by. Ah! it would indeed be a happy day for him and for all if I could ride back with a saddle-bag full of gold pieces, and please God, I shall dip my hand in somebody's pocket before I see Crooksbury Hill once more!"

Nigel shook his head, for indeed it seemed hopeless to try to bridge the gulf between them. Already they had made such good progress along the bridle-path through the heather that the little hill of Saint Catharine and the ancient shrine upon its summit loomed up before them. Here they crossed the road from the south to London, and at the crossing two wayfarers were waiting who waved their hands in greeting, the one a tall, slender, dark woman upon a white jennet, the other a very thick and red-faced old man, whose weight seemed to curve the back of the stout gray cob which he bestrode.

"What how, Nigel!" he cried. "Mary has told me that you make a start this morning, and we have waited here this hour and more on the chance of seeing you pass. Come, lad, and have a last stoup of English ale, for many a time amid the sour French wines you will long for the white foam under your nose, and the good homely twang of it."

Nigel had to decline the draft, for it meant riding into Guildford town, a mile out of his course, but very gladly he agreed with Mary that they should climb the path to the old shrine and offer a last orison together. The knight and Aylward waited below with the horses; and so it came about that Nigel and Mary found themselves alone under the solemn old Gothic arches, in front of the dark shadowed recess in which gleamed the golden reliquary of the saint. In silence they knelt side by side in prayer, and then came forth once more out of the gloom and the shadow into the fresh sunlit summer morning. They stopped ere they descended the path, and looked to right and left at the fair meadows and the blue Wey curling down the valley.

"What have you prayed for, Nigel?" said she.

"I have prayed that God and His saints will hold my spirit high and will send me back from France in such a fashion that I may dare to come to you and to claim you for my own."

"Bethink you well what it is that you say, Nigel," said she. "What you are to me only my own heart can tell; but I would never set eyes upon your face again rather than abate by one inch that height of honor and worshipful achievement to which you may attain."

"Nay, my dear and most sweet lady, how should you abate it, since it is the thought of you which will nerve my arm and uphold my heart?"

"Think once more, my fair lord, and hold yourself bound by no word which you have said. Let it be as the breeze which blows past our faces and is heard of no more. Your soul yearns for honor. To that has it ever turned. Is there room in it for love also? or is it possible that both shall live at their highest in one mind? Do you not call to mind that Galahad and other great knights of old have put women out of their lives that they might ever give their whole soul and strength to the winning of honor? May it not be that I shall be a drag upon you, that your heart may shrink from some honorable task, lest it should bring risk and pain to me? Think well before you answer, my fair lord, for indeed my very heart would break if it should ever happen that through love of me your high hopes and great promise should miss fulfilment."

Nigel looked at her with sparkling eyes. The soul which shone through her dark face had transformed it for the moment into a beauty more lofty and more rare than that of her shallow sister. He bowed before the majesty of the woman, and pressed his lips to her hand. "You are like a star upon my path which guides me on the upward way," said he. "Our souls are set together upon the finding of honor, and how shall we hold each other back when our purpose is the same?"

She shook her proud head. "So it seems to you now, fair lord, but it may be otherwise as the years pass. How shall you prove that I am indeed a help and not a hindrance?"

"I will prove it by my deeds, fair and dear lady," said Nigel. "Here at the shrine of the holy Catharine, on this, the Feast of Saint Margaret, I take my oath that I will do three deeds in your honor as a proof of my high love before I set eyes upon your face again, and these three deeds shall stand as a proof to you that if I love you dearly, still I will not let the thought of you stand betwixt me and honorable achievement!"

Her face shone with her love and her pride. "I also make my oath," said she, "and I do it in the name of the holy Catharine whose shrine is hard by. I swear that I will hold myself for you until these three deeds be done and we meet once more; also that if— which may dear Christ forfend!—you fall in doing them then I shall take the veil in Shalford nunnery and look upon no man's face again! Give me your hand, Nigel."

She had taken a little bangle of gold filigree work from her arm and fastened it upon his sunburnt wrist, reading aloud to him the engraved motto in old French: "*Fais ce que dois, adviegne que pourra —c'est commandé au chevalier.*" Then for one moment they fell into each other's arms and with kiss upon kiss, a loving man and a tender woman, they swore their troth to each other. But the old knight was calling impatiently from below and together they hurried down the winding path to where the horses waited under the sandy bluff.

As far as the Shalford crossing Sir John rode by Nigel's arm, and many were the last injunctions which he gave him concerning woodcraft, and great his anxiety lest he confuse a spay with a brocket, or either with a hind. At last when they came to the reedy edge of the Wey the old knight and his daughter reined up their horses. Nigel looked back at them ere he entered the dark Chantry woods, and saw them still gazing after him and waving their hands. Then the path wound amongst the trees and they were lost to sight; but long afterwards when a clearing exposed once more the Shalford meadows Nigel saw that the old man upon the gray cob was riding slowly toward Saint Catharine's Hill, but that the girl was still where he had seen her last, leaning forward in her saddle and straining her eyes to pierce the dark forest which screened her lover from her view. It was but a fleeting glance through a break in the foliage, and yet in after days of stress and toil in far distant lands it was that one little picture—the green meadow, the reeds, the slow blue-winding river, and the eager bending graceful figure upon the white horse—which was the clearest and the dearest image of that England which he had left behind him.

But if Nigel's friends had learned that this was the morning of his leaving, his enemies too were on the alert. The two comrades had just emerged from the Chantry woods and were beginning the ascent of that curving path which leads upward to the old Chapel of the Martyr when with a hiss like an angry snake a long white arrow streaked under Pommers and struck quivering in the grassy turf. A second whizzed past Nigel's ear, as he tried to turn; but Aylward struck the great war-horse a sharp blow over the haunches, and it had galloped some hundreds of yards before its rider could pull it up. Aylward followed as hard as he could ride, bending low over his horse's neck, while arrows whizzed all around him.

"By Saint Paul!" said Nigel, tugging at his bridle and white with anger, "they shall not chase me across the country as though I was a frighted doe. Archer, how dare you to lash my horse when I would have turned and ridden in upon them?"

"It is well that I did so," said Aylward, "or by these ten finger-bones! our journey would have begun and ended on the same day. As I glanced round I saw a dozen of them at the least amongst the brushwood. See now how the light glimmers upon their steel caps yonder in the bracken under the great beech-tree. Nay, I pray you, my fair lord, do not ride forward. What chance has a man in the open against all these who lie at their ease in the underwood? If you will not think of yourself, then consider your horse, which would have a cloth-yard shaft feathered in its hide ere it could reach the wood."

Nigel chafed in impotent anger. "Am I to be shot at like a popinjay at a fair, by any reaver or outlaw that seeks a mark for his bow?" he cried. "By Saint Paul! Aylward, I will put on my harness and go further into the matter. Help me to untruss, I pray you!"

"Nay, my fair lord, I will not help you to your own downfall. It is a match with cogged dice betwixt a horseman on the moor and archers amid the forest. But these men are no outlaws, or they would not dare to draw their bows within a league of the sheriff of Guildford."

"Indeed, Aylward, I think that you speak truth," said Nigel. "It may be that these are the men of Paul de la Fosse of Shalford, whom I have given, little cause to love me. Ah! there is indeed the very man himself."

They sat their horses with their backs to the long slope which leads up to the old chapel on the hill. In front of them was the dark ragged edge of the wood, with a sharp twinkle of steel here and there in its shadows which spoke of these lurking foes. But now there was a long moot upon a horn, and at once a score of russet-clad bowmen ran forward from amid the trees, spreading out into a scattered line and closing swiftly in upon the travelers. In the midst of them, upon a great gray horse, sat a small mis-shapen man, waving and cheering as one sets hounds on a badger, turning his head this way and that as he whooped and pointed, urging his bowmen onward up the slope.

"Draw them on, my fair lord! Draw them on until we have them out on the down!" cried Aylward, his eyes shining with joy. "Five hundred paces more, and then we may be on terms with them. Nay, linger not, but keep them always just clear of arrow-shot until our turn has come."

Nigel shook and trembled with eagerness, as with his hand on his sword-hilt he looked at the line of eager hurrying men. But it flashed through his mind what Chandos had said of the cool head which is better for the warrior than the hot heart. Aylward's words were true and wise. He turned Pommers' head therefore, and amid a cry of derision from behind them the comrades trotted over the down. The bowmen broke into a run, while their leader screamed and waved more madly than before. Aylward cast many a glance at them over his shoulder.

"Yet a little farther! Yet a little farther still!" he muttered. "The wind is towards them and the fools have forgot that I can over-shoot them by fifty paces. Now, my good lord, I pray you for one instant to hold the horses, for my weapon is of more avail this day than thine can be. They may make sorry cheer ere they gain the shelter of the wood once more."

He had sprung from his horse, and with a downward wrench of his arm and a push with his knee he slipped the string into the upper nock of his mighty war-bow. Then in a flash he notched his shaft and drew it to the pile, his keen blue eyes glowing fiercely behind it from under his knotted brows. With thick legs planted sturdily apart, his body laid to the bow, his left arm motionless as wood, his right bunched into a double curve of swelling muscles as he stretched the white well-waxed string, he looked so keen and fierce a fighter that the advancing line stopped for an instant at the sight of him. Two or three loosed off their arrows, but the shafts flew heavily against the head wind, and snaked along the hard turf some score of paces short of the mark. One only, a short bandy-legged man, whose squat figure spoke of enormous muscular strength, ran swiftly in and then drew so strong a bow that the arrow quivered in the ground at Aylward's very feet.

"It is Black Will of Lynchmere," said the bowman. "Many a match have I shot with him, and I know well that no other man on the Surrey marches could have sped such a shaft. I trust that you are houseled and shriven, Will, for I have known you so long that I would not have your damnation upon my soul."

He raised his bow as he spoke, and the string twanged with a rich deep musical note. Aylward leaned upon his bow-stave as he keenly watched the long swift flight of his shaft, skimming smoothly down the wind.

"On him, on him! No, over him, by my hilt!" he cried. "There is more wind than I had thought. Nay, nay, friend, now that I have the length of you, you can scarce hope to loose again."

Black Will had notched an arrow and was raising his bow when Aylward's second shaft passed through the shoulder of his drawing arm. With a shout of anger and pain he dropped his weapon, and dancing in his fury he shook his fist and roared curses at his rival.

"I could slay him; but I will not, for good bowmen are not so common," said Aylward. "And now, fair sir, we must on, for they are spreading round on either side, and if once they get behind us, then indeed our journey has come to a sudden end. But ere we go I would send a shaft through yonder horseman who leads them on."

"Nay, Aylward, I pray you to leave him," said Nigel. "Villain as he is, he is none the less a gentleman of coat-armor, and should die by some other weapon than thine."

"As you will," said Aylward, with a clouded brow. "I have been told that in the late wars many a French prince and baron has not been too proud to take his death wound from an English yeoman's shaft, and that nobles of England have been glad enough to stand by and see it done."

Nigel shook his head sadly. "It is sooth you say, archer, and indeed it is no new thing, for that good knight Richard of the Lion Heart met his end in such a lowly fashion, and so also did Harold the Saxon. But this is a private matter, and I would not have you draw your bow against him. Neither can I ride at him myself, for he is weak in body, though dangerous in spirit. Therefore, we will go upon our way, since there is neither profit nor honor to be gained, nor any hope of advancement."

Aylward, having unstrung his bow, had remounted his horse during this conversation, and the two rode swiftly past the little squat Chapel of the Martyr and over the brow of the hill. From the summit they looked back. The injured archer lay upon the ground, with several of his comrades gathered in a knot around him. Others ran aimlessly up the hill, but were already far behind. The leader sat motionless upon his horse, and as he saw them look back he raised his hand and shrieked his curses at them. An instant later the curve of the ground had hid them from view. So, amid love and hate, Nigel bade adieu to the home of his youth.

And now the comrades were journeying upon that old, old road which runs across the south of England and yet never turns toward London, for the good reason that the place was a poor hamlet when first the road was laid. From Winchester, the Saxon capital, to Canterbury, the holy city of Kent, ran that ancient highway, and on from Canterbury to the narrow straits where, on a clear day, the farther shore can be seen. Along this track as far back as history can trace the metals of the west have been carried and passed the pack-horses which bore the goods which Gaul sent in exchange. Older than the Christian faith and older than the Romans, is the old road. North and south are the woods and the marshes, so that only on the high dry turf of the chalk land could a clear track be found. The Pilgrim's Way, it still is called; but the pilgrims were the last who ever trod it, for it was already of immemorial age before the death of Thomas a Becket gave a new reason why folk should journey to the scene of his murder.

From the hill of Weston Wood the travelers could see the long white band which dipped and curved and rose over the green downland, its course marked even in the hollows by the line of the old yew-trees which flanked it. Neither Nigel nor Aylward had wandered far from their own country, and now they rode with light hearts and eager eyes taking note of all the varied pictures of nature and of man which passed before them. To their left was a hilly country, a land of rolling heaths and woods, broken here and there into open spaces round the occasional farm-house of a franklin. Hackhurst Down, Dunley Hill, and Ranmore Common swelled and sank, each merging into the other. But on the right, after passing the village of Shere and the old church of Gomshall, the whole south country lay like a map at their feet. There was the huge wood of the Weald, one unbroken forest of oak-trees stretching away to the South Downs, which rose olive-green against the deep blue sky. Under this great canopy of trees strange folk lived and evil deeds were done. In its recesses were wild tribes, little changed from their heathen ancestors, who danced round the altar of Thor, and well was it for the peaceful traveler that he could tread the high open road of the chalk land with no need to wander into so dangerous a tract, where soft clay, tangled forest and wild men all barred his progress.

But apart from the rolling country upon the left and the great forest-hidden plain upon the right, there was much upon the road itself to engage the attention of the wayfarers. It was crowded with people. As far as their eyes could carry they could see the black dots scattered thickly upon the thin white band, sometimes single, sometimes several abreast, sometimes in moving crowds, where a drove of pilgrims held together for mutual protection, or a nobleman showed his greatness by the number of retainers who trailed at his heels. At that time the main roads were very crowded, for there were many wandering people in the land. Of all sorts and kinds, they passed in an unbroken stream before the eyes of Nigel and of Aylward, alike only in the fact that one and all were powdered from their hair to their shoes with the gray dust of the chalk.

There were monks journeying from one cell to another, Benedictines with their black gowns looped up to show their white skirts, Carthusians in white, and pied Cistercians. Friars also of the three wandering orders—Dominicans in black, Carmelites in white and Franciscans in gray. There was no love lost between the cloistered monks and the free friars, each looking on the other as a rival who took from him the oblations of the faithful; so they passed on the high road as cat passes dog, with eyes askance and angry faces.

Then besides the men of the church there were the men of trade, the merchant in dusty broadcloth and Flanders hat riding at the head of his line of pack-horses. He carried Cornish tin, West-country wool, or Sussex iron if he traded eastward, or if his head should be turned westward then he bore with him the velvets of Genoa, the ware of Venice, the wine of France, or the armor of Italy and Spain. Pilgrims were everywhere, poor people for the most part, plodding wearily along with trailing feet and bowed heads, thick staves in their hands and bundles over their shoulders. Here and there on a gaily caparisoned palfrey, or in the greater luxury of a horse-litter, some West-country lady might be seen making her easy way to the shrine of Saint Thomas.

Besides all these a constant stream of strange vagabonds drifted along the road: minstrels who wandered from fair to fair, a foul and pestilent crew; jugglers and acrobats, quack doctors and tooth-drawers, students and beggars, free workmen in search of better wages, and escaped bondsmen who would welcome any wages at all. Such was the throng which set the old road smoking in a haze of white dust from Winchester to the narrow sea.

But of all the wayfarers those which interested Nigel most were the soldiers. Several times they passed little knots of archers or men-at-arms, veterans from France, who had received their discharge and were now making their way to their southland homes. They were half drunk all of them, for the wayfarers treated them to beer at the frequent inns and ale-stakes which lined the road, so that they cheered and sang lustily as they passed. They roared rude pleasantries at Aylward, who turned in his saddle and shouted his opinion of them until they were out of hearing.

Once, late in the afternoon, they overtook a body of a hundred archers all marching together with two knights riding at their head. They were passing from Guildford Castle to Reigate Castle, where they were in garrison. Nigel rode with the knights for some distance, and hinted that if either was in search of honorable advancement, or wished to do some small deed, or to relieve himself of any vow, it might be possible to find some means of achieving it. They were both, however, grave and elderly men, intent upon their business and with no mind for fond wayside adventures, so Nigel quickened his pace and left them behind.

They had left Boxhill and Headley Heath upon the left, and the towers of Reigate were rising amid the trees in front of them, when they overtook a large, cheery, red-faced man, with a forked beard, riding upon a good horse and exchanging a nod or a merry word with all who passed him. With him they rode nearly as far as Bletchingley, and Nigel laughed much to hear him talk; but always under the raillery there was much earnestness and much wisdom in all his words. He rode at his ease about the country, he said, having sufficient money to keep him from want and to furnish him for the road. He could speak all the three languages of England, the north, the middle and the south, so that he was at home with the people of every shire and could hear their troubles and their joys. In all parts in town and in country there was unrest, he said; for the poor folk were weary of their masters both of the Church and State, and soon there would be such doings in England as had never been seen before.

But above all this man was earnest against the Church: its enormous wealth, its possession of nearly one-third of the whole land of the country, its insatiable greed for more at the very time when it claimed to be poor and lowly. The monks and friars, too, he lashed with his tongue: their roguish ways, their laziness and their cunning. He showed how their wealth and that of the haughty lord must always be founded upon the toil of poor humble Peter the Plowman, who worked and strove in rain and cold out in the fields, the butt and laughing-stock of everyone, and still bearing up the whole world upon his weary shoulders. He had set it all out in a fair parable; so now as he rode he repeated some of the verses, chanting them and marking time with his forefinger, while Nigel and Aylward on either side of him with their heads inclined inward listened with the same attention, but with very different feelings—Nigel shocked at such an attack upon authority, and Aylward chuckling as he heard the sentiments of his class so shrewdly expressed. At last the stranger halted his horse outside the "Five Angels" at Gatton.

"It is a good inn, and I know the ale of old," said he. "When I had finished that 'Dream of Piers the Plowman' from which I have recited to you, the last verses were thus:

"'Now have I brought my little booke to an ende
  God's blessing be on him who a drinke will me sende'—

I pray you come in with me and share it."

"Nay," said Nigel, "we must on our way, for we have far to go. But give me your name, my friend, for indeed we have passed a merry hour listening to your words."

"Have a care!" the stranger answered, shaking his head. "You and your class will not spend a merry hour when these words are turned into deeds and Peter the Plowman grows weary of swinking in the fields and takes up his bow and his staff in order to set this land in order."

"By Saint Paul! I expect that we shall bring Peter to reason and also those who have put such evil thoughts into his head," said Nigel. "So once more I ask your name, that I may know it if ever I chance to hear that you have been hanged?"

The stranger laughed good-humoredly. "You can call me Thomas Lackland," said he. "I should be Thomas Lack-brain if I were indeed to give my true name, since a good many robbers, some in black gowns and some in steel, would be glad to help me upwards in the way you speak of. So good-day to you, Squire, and to you also, archer, and may you find your way back with whole bones from the wars!"

That night the comrades slept in Godstone Priory, and early next morning they were well upon their road down the Pilgrim's Way. At Titsey it was said that a band of villeins were out in Westerham Wood and had murdered three men the day before; so that Nigel had high hopes of an encounter; but the brigands showed no sign, though the travelers went out of their way to ride their horses along the edges of the forest. Farther on they found traces of their work, for the path ran along the hillside at the base of a chalk quarry, and there in the cutting a man was lying dead. From his twisted limbs and shattered frame it was easy to see that he had been thrown over from above, while his pockets turned outward showed the reason for his murder. The comrades rode past without too close a survey, for dead men were no very uncommon objects on the King's highway, and if sheriff or bailiff should chance upon you near the body you might find yourself caught in the meshes of the law.

Near Sevenoaks their road turned out of the old Canterbury way and pointed south toward the coast, leaving the chalk lands and coming down into the clay of the Weald. It was a wretched, rutted mule-track running through thick forests with occasional clearings in which lay the small Kentish villages, where rude shock-headed peasants with smocks and galligaskins stared with bold, greedy eyes at the travelers. Once on the right they caught a distant view of the Towers of Penshurst, and once they heard the deep tolling of the bells of Bayham Abbey, but for the rest of their day's journey savage peasants and squalid cottages were all that met their eyes, with endless droves of pigs who fed upon the litter of acorns. The throng of travelers who crowded the old road were all gone, and only here and there did they meet or overtake some occasional merchant or messenger bound for Battle Abbey, Pevensey Castle or the towns of the south.

That night they slept in a sordid inn, overrun with rats and with fleas, one mile south of the hamlet of Mayfield. Aylward scratched vigorously and cursed with fervor. Nigel lay without movement or sound. To the man who had learned the old rule of chivalry there were no small ills in life. It was beneath the dignity of his soul to stoop to observe them. Cold and heat, hunger and thirst, such things did not exist for the gentleman. The armor of his soul was so complete that it was proof not only against the great ills of life but even against the small ones; so the flea-bitten Nigel lay grimly still while Aylward writhed upon his couch.

They were now but a short distance from their destination; but they had hardly started on their journey through the forest next morning, when an adventure befell them which filled Nigel with the wildest hopes.

Along the narrow winding path between the great oak-trees there rode a dark sallow man in a scarlet tabard who blew so loudly upon a silver trumpet that they heard the clanging call long before they set eyes on him. Slowly he advanced, pulling up every fifty paces to make the forest ring with another warlike blast. The comrades rode forward to meet him.

"I pray you," said Nigel, "to tell me who you are and why you blow upon this trumpet."

The fellow shook his head, so Nigel repeated the question in French, the common language of chivalry, spoken at that age by every gentleman in Western Europe.

The man put his lips to the trumpet and blew another long note before he answered. "I am Gaston de Castrier," said he, "the humble Squire of the most worthy and valiant knight Raoul de

Tubiers, de Pestels, de Grimsard, de Mersac, de Leoy, de Bastanac, who also writes himself Lord of Pons. It is his order that I ride always a mile in front of him to prepare all to receive him, and he desires me to blow upon a trumpet not out of vainglory, but out of greatness of spirit, so that none may be ignorant of his coming should they desire to encounter him."

Nigel sprang from his horse with a cry of joy, and began to unbutton his doublet. "Quick, Aylward, quick!" he said. "He comes, a knight errant comes! Was there ever such a chance of worshipfully winning worship? Untruss the harness whilst I loose my clothes! Good sir, I beg you to warn your noble and valiant master that a poor Squire of England would implore him to take notice of him and to do some small deed upon him as he passes."

But already the Lord of Pons had come in sight. He was a huge man upon an enormous horse, so that together they seemed to fill up the whole long dark archway under the oaks. He was clad in full armor of a brazen hue with only his face exposed, and of this face there was little visible save a pair of arrogant eyes and a great black beard, which flowed through the open vizor and down over his breastplate. To the crest of his helmet was tied a small brown glove, nodding and swinging above him. He bore a long lance with a red square banner at the end, charged with a black boar's head, and the same symbol was engraved upon his shield. Slowly he rode through the forest, ponderous, menacing, with dull thudding of his charger's hoofs and constant clank of metal, while always in front of him came the distant peal of the silver trumpet calling all men to admit his majesty and to clear his path ere they be cleared from it.

Never in his dreams had so perfect a vision come to cheer Nigel's heart, and as he struggled with his clothes, glancing up continually at this wondrous traveler, he pattered forth prayers of thanksgiving to the good Saint Paul who had shown such loving-kindness to his unworthy servant and thrown him in the path of so excellent and debonair a gentleman.

But alas! how often at the last instant the cup is dashed from the lips! This joyful chance was destined to change suddenly to unexpected and grotesque disaster — disaster so strange and so complete that through all his life Nigel flushed crimson when he thought of it. He was busily stripping his hunting-costume, and with feverish haste he had doffed boots, hat, hose, doublet and cloak, so that nothing remained save a pink jupon and pair of silken drawers. At the same time Aylward was hastily unbuckling the load with the intention of handing his master his armor piece by piece, when the Squire gave one last challenging peal from his silver trumpet into the very ear of the spare horse.

In an instant it had taken to its heels, the precious armor upon its back, and thundered away down the road which they had traversed. Aylward jumped upon his mare, drove his prick spurs into her sides and galloped after the runaway as hard as he could ride. Thus it came about that in an instant Nigel was shorn of all his little dignity, had lost his two horses, his attendant and his outfit, and found himself a lonely and unarmed man standing in his shirt and drawers upon the pathway down which the burly figure of the Lord of Pons was slowly advancing.

The knight errant, whose mind had been filled by the thought of the maiden whom he had left behind at St. Jean — the same whose glove dangled from his helmet — had observed nothing that had occurred. Hence, all that met his eyes was a noble yellow horse, which was tethered by the track, and a small young man, who appeared to be a lunatic since he had undressed hastily in the heart of the forest, and stood now with an eager anxious face clad in his underlinen amid the scattered débris of his garments. Of such a person the high Lord of Pons could take no notice, and so he pursued his inexorable way, his arrogant eyes looking out into the distance and his thoughts set intently upon the maiden of St. Jean. He was dimly aware that the little crazy man in the undershirt ran a long way beside him in his stockings, begging, imploring and arguing.

"Just one hour, most fair sir, just one hour at the longest, and a poor Squire of England shall ever hold himself your debtor! Do but condescend to rein your horse until my harness comes back to me! Will you not stoop to show me some small deed of arms? I implore you, fair sir, to spare me a little of your time and a hand-stroke or two ere you go upon your way!"

Lord de Pons motioned impatiently with his gauntleted hand, as one might brush away an importunate fly, but when at last Nigel became desperate in his clamor he thrust his spurs into his great war-horse, and clashing like a pair of cymbals he thundered off through the forest. So he rode upon his majestic way, until two days later he was slain by Lord Reginald Cobham in a field near Weybridge.

When after a long chase Aylward secured the spare horse and brought it back, he found his master seated upon a fallen tree, his face buried in his hands and his mind clouded with humiliation and grief. Nothing was said, for the matter was beyond words, and so in moody silence they rode upon their way.

But soon they came upon a scene which drew Nigel's thoughts away from his bitter trouble, for in front of them there rose the towers of a great building with a small gray sloping village around it, and they learned from a passing hind that this was the hamlet and Abbey of Battle. Together they drew rein upon the low ridge and looked down into that valley of death from which even now the reek of blood seems to rise. Down beside that sinister lake and amid those scattered bushes sprinkled over the naked flank of the long ridge was fought that long-drawn struggle betwixt two most noble foes with broad England as the prize of victory. Here, up and down the low hill, hour by hour the grim struggle had waxed and waned, until the Saxon army had died where it stood, King, court, house-carl and fyrdsman, each in their ranks even as they had fought. And now, after all the stress and toil, the tyranny, the savage revolt, the fierce suppression, God had made His purpose complete, for here were Nigel the Norman and Aylward the Saxon with good-fellowship in their hearts and a common respect in their minds, with the same banner and the same cause, riding forth to do battle for their old mother England.

And now the long ride drew to an end. In front of them was the blue sea, flecked with the white sails of ships. Once more the road passed upward from the heavy-wooded plain to the springy turf of the chalk downs. Far to the right rose the grim fortalice of Pevensey, squat and powerful, like one great block of rugged stone, the parapet twinkling with steel caps and crowned by the royal banner of England. A flat expanse of reeded marshland lay before them, out of which rose a single wooded hill, crowned with towers, with a bristle of masts rising out of the green plain some distance to the south of it. Nigel looked at it with his hand shading his eyes, and then urged Pommers to a trot. The town was Winchelsea, and there amid that cluster of houses on the hill the gallant Chandos must be awaiting him.

CHAPTER XIV

HOW NIGEL CHASED THE RED FERRET

THEY passed a ferry, wound upward by a curving path, and then, having satisfied a guard of men-at-arms, were admitted through the frowning arch of the Pipewell Gate. There waiting for them, in the middle of the east street, the sun gleaming upon his lemon-colored beard, and puckering his single eye, stood Chandos himself, his legs apart, his hands behind his back, and a welcoming smile upon hiss quaint high-nosed face. Behind him a crowd of little boys were gazing with reverent eyes at the famous soldier.

"Welcome, Nigel!" said he, "and you also, good archer! I chanced to be walking on the city wall, and I thought from the color of your horse that it was indeed you upon the Udimore Road. How have you fared, young squire errant? Have you held bridges or rescued damsels or slain oppressors on your way from Tilford?"

"Nay, my fair lord, I have accomplished nothing; but I once had hopes—" Nigel flushed at the remembrance.

"I will give you more than hopes, Nigel. I will put you where you can dip both arms to the elbow into danger and honor, where peril will sleep with you at night and rise with you in the morning and the very air you breathe be laden with it. Are you ready for that, young sir?"

"I can but pray, fair lord, that my spirit will rise to it."

Chandos smiled his approval and laid his thin brown hand on the youth's shoulder. "Good!" said he. "It is the mute hound which bites the hardest. The babbler is ever the hang-back. Bide with me here, Nigel, and walk upon the ramparts. Archer, do you lead the horses to the 'Sign of the Broom Pod' in the high street, and tell my varlets to see them aboard the cog Thomas before nightfall. We sail at the second hour after curfew. Come hither, Nigel, to the crest of the corner turret, for from it I will show you what you have never seen."

It was but a dim and distant white cloud upon the blue water seen far off over the Dungeness Point, and yet the sight of it flushed the young Squire's cheeks and sent the blood hot through his veins. It was the fringe of France, that land of chivalry and glory, the stage where name and fame were to be won. With burning eyes he gazed across at it, his heart rejoicing to think that the hour was at hand when he might tread that sacred soil. Then his gaze crossed the immense stretch of the blue sea, dotted over with the sails of fishing-boats, until it rested upon the double harbor beneath packed with vessels of every size and shape, from the pessoners and creyers which plied up and down the coast to the great cogs and galleys which were used either as war-ships or merchantmen as the occasion served. One of them was at that instant passing out to sea, a huge galleass, with trumpets blowing and nakers banging, the flag of Saint George flaunting over the broad purple sail, and the decks sparkling from end to end with steel. Nigel gave a cry of pleasure at the splendor of the sight.

"Aye, lad," said Chandos, "it is the Trinity of Rye, the very ship on which I fought at Sluys. Her deck ran blood from stem to stern that day. But turn your eyes this way, I beg you, and tell me if you see aught strange about this town."

Nigel looked down at the noble straight street, at the Roundel Tower, at the fine church of Saint Thomas, and the other fair buildings of Winchelsea. "It is all new," said he—"church, castle, houses, all are new."

"You are right, fair son. My grandfather can call to mind the time when only the conies lived upon this rock. The town was down yonder by the sea, until one night the waves rose upon it and not a house was left. See, yonder is Rye, huddling also on a hill, the two towns like poor sheep when the waters are out. But down there under the blue water and below the Camber Sand lies the true Winchelsea — tower, cathedral, walls and all, even as my grandfather knew it, when the first Edward was young upon the throne."

For an hour or more Chandos paced upon the ramparts with his young Squire at his elbow and talked to him of his duties and of the secrets and craft of warfare, Nigel drinking in and storing in his memory every word from so revered a teacher. Many a time in after life, in stress and in danger, he strengthened himself by the memory of that slow walk with the blue sea on one side and the fair town on the other, when the wise soldier and noble-hearted knight poured forth his precept and advice as the master-workman to the apprentice.

"Perhaps, fair son," said he, "you are like so many other lads who ride to the wars, and know so much already that it is waste of breath to advise them?"

"Nay, my fair lord, I know nothing save that I would fain do my duty and either win honorable advancement or die worshipful on the field."

"You are wise to be humble," said Chandos; "for indeed he who knows most of war knows best that there is much to learn. As there is a mystery of the rivers and a mystery of woodcraft, even so there is a mystery of warfare by which battles may be lost and gained; for all nations are brave, and where the brave meets the brave it is he who is crafty and war-wise who will win the day. The best hound will run at fault if he be ill laid on, and the best hawk will fly at check if he be badly loosed, and even so the bravest army may go awry if it be ill handled. There are not in Christendom better knights and squires than those of the French, and yet we have had the better of them, for in our Scottish Wars and elsewhere we have learned more of this same mystery of which I speak."

"And wherein lies our wisdom, honored sir?" asked Nigel. "I also would fain be war-wise and learn to fight with my wits as well as with my sword."

Chandos shook his head and smiled. "It is in the forest and on the down that you learn to fly the hawk and loose the hound," said he. "So also it is in camp and on the field that the mystery of war can be learned. There only has every great captain come to be its master. To start he must have a cool head, quick to think, soft as wax before his purpose is formed, hard as steel when once he sees it before him. Ever alert he must be, and cautious also, but with judgment to turn his caution into rashness where a large gain may be put against a small stake. An eye for country also, for the trend of the rivers, the slope of the hills, the cover of the woods, and the light green of the bog-land."

Poor Nigel, who had trusted to his lance and to Pommers to break his path to glory, stood aghast at this list of needs.

"Alas!" he cried. "How am I to gain all this? — I, who could scarce learn to read or write though the good Father Matthew broke a hazel stick a day across my shoulders?"

"You will gain it, fair son, where others have gained it before you. You have that which is the first thing of all, a heart of fire from which other colder hearts may catch a spark. But you must have knowledge also of that which warfare has taught us in olden times. We know, par exemple, that horse-men alone cannot hope to win against good foot-soldiers. Has it not been tried at Courtrai, at Stirling, and again under my own eyes at Crécy, where the chivalry of France went down before our bowmen?"

Nigel stared at him, with a perplexed brow. "Fair sir, my heart grows heavy as I hear you. Do you then say that our chivalry can make no head against archers, billmen and the like?"

"Nay, Nigel, for it has also been very clearly shown that the best foot-soldiers unsupported cannot hold their own against the mailed horsemen."

"To whom then is the victory?" asked Nigel.

"To him who can mix his horse and foot, using each to strengthen the other. Apart they are weak. Together they are strong. The archer who can weaken the enemy's line, the horseman who can break it when it is weakened, as was done at Falkirk and Duplin, there is the secret of our strength. Now touching this same battle of Falkirk, I pray you for one instant to give it your attention."

With his whip he began to trace a plan of the Scottish battle upon the dust, and Nigel with knitted brows was trying hard to muster his small stock of brains and to profit by the lecture, when their conversation was interrupted by a strange new arrival.

It was a very stout little man, wheezy and purple with haste, who scudded down the rampart as if he were blown by the wind, his grizzled hair flying and his long black gown floating behind him. He was clad in the dress of a respectable citizen, a black jerkin trimmed with sable, a black-velvet beaver hat and a white feather. At the sight of Chandos he gave a cry of joy and quickened his pace so that when he did at last reach him he could only stand gasping and waving his hands.

"Give yourself time, good Master Wintersole, give yourself time!" said Chandos in a soothing voice.

"The papers!" gasped the little man. "Oh, my Lord Chandos, the papers!"

"What of the papers, my worthy sir?"

"I swear by our good patron Saint Leonard, it is no fault of mine! I had locked them in my coffer. But the lock was forced and the coffer rifled."

A shadow of anger passed over the soldier's keen face.

"How now, Master Mayor? Pull your wits together and do not stand there babbling like a three-year child. Do you say that some one hath taken the papers?"

"It is sooth, fair sir! Thrice I have been Mayor of the town, and fifteen years burgess and jurat, but never once has any public matter gone awry through me. Only last month there came an order from Windsor on a Tuesday for a Friday banquet, a thousand soles, four thousand plaice, two thousand mackerel, five hundred crabs, a thousand lobsters, five thousand whiting—"

"I doubt not, Master Mayor, that you are an excellent fishmonger; but the matter concerns the papers I gave into your keeping. Where are they?"

"Taken, fair sir—gone!"

"And who hath dared to take them?"

"Alas! I know not. It was but for as long as you would say an angelus that I left the chamber, and when I came back there was the coffer, broken and empty, upon my table."

"Do you suspect no one?"

"There was a varlet who hath come with the last few days into my employ. He is not to be found, and I have sent horsemen along both the Udimore road and that to Rye, that they may seize him. By the help of Saint Leonard they can scarce miss him, for one can tell him a bow-shot off by his hair."

"Is it red?" asked Chandos eagerly. "Is it fox-red, and the man a small man pocked with sun-spots, and very quick in his movements?"

"It is the man himself."

Chandos shook his clenched hand with annoyance, and then set off swiftly down the street.

"It is Peter the Red Ferret once more!" said he. "I knew him of old in France, where he has done us more harm than a company of men-at-arms. He speaks English as he speaks French, and he is of such daring and cunning that nothing is secret from him. In all France there is no more dangerous man, for though he is a gentleman of blood and coat-armor he takes the part of a spy, because it hath the more danger and therefore the more honor."

"But, my fair lord," cried the Mayor, as he hurried along, keeping pace with the long strides of the soldier, "I knew that you warned me to take all care of the papers; but surely there was no matter of great import in it? It was but to say what stores were to be sent after you to Calais?"

"Is that not everything?" cried Chandos impatiently. "Can you not see, oh foolish Master Wintersole, that the French suspect we are about to make some attempt and that they have sent Peter the Red Ferret, as they have sent him many times before, to get tidings of whither we are bound? Now that he knows that the stores are for Calais, then the French near Calais will take his warning, and so the King's whole plan come to nothing."

"Then he will fly by water. We can stop him yet. He has not an hour's start."

"It may be that a boat awaits him at Rye or Hythe; but it is more like that he has all ready to depart from here. Ah, see yonder! I'll warrant that the Red Ferret is on board!"

Chandos had halted in front of his inn, and now he pointed down to the outer harbor, which lay two miles off across the green plain. It was connected by a long winding canal with the inner dock at the base of the hill, upon which the town was built. Between the two horns formed by the short curving piers a small schooner was running out to sea, dipping and rising before a sharp southerly breeze.

"It is no Winchelsea boat," said the Mayor. "She is longer and broader in the beam than ours."

"Horses! bring horses!" cried Chandos. "Come, Nigel, let us go further into the matter."

A busy crowd of varlets, archers, and men-at-arms swarmed round the gateway of the "Sign of the Broom Pod," singing, shouting, and jostling in rough good-fellowship. The sight of the tall thin figure of Chandos brought order amongst them, and a few minutes later the horses were ready and saddled. A breakneck ride down a steep declivity, and then a gallop of two miles over the sedgy plain carried them to the outer harbor. A dozen vessels were lying there, ready to start for Bordeaux or Rochelle, and the quay was thick with sailors, laborers and townsmen and heaped with wine-barrels and wool-packs.

"Who is warden here?" asked Chandos, springing from his horse.

"Badding! Where is Cock Badding? Badding is warden!" shouted the crowd.

A moment later a short swarthy man, bull-necked and deep-chested, pushed through the people. He was clad in rough russet wool with a scarlet cloth tied round his black curly head. His sleeves were rolled up to his shoulders, and his brown arms, all stained with grease and tar, were like two thick gnarled branches from an oaken stump. His savage brown face was fierce and frowning, and was split from chin to temple with the long white wale of an ill-healed wound.

"How now, gentles, will you never wait your turn?" he rumbled in a deep angry voice. "Can you not see that we are warping the Rose of Guienne into midstream for the ebb-tide? Is this a time to break in upon us? Your goods will go aboard in due season, I promise you; so ride back into the town and find such pleasure as you may, while I and my mates do our work without let or hindrance."

"It is the gentle Chandos!" cried some one in the crowd. "It is the good Sir John."

The rough harbor-master changed his gruffness to smiles in an instant. "Nay, Sir John, what would you? I pray you to hold me excused if I was short of speech, but we port-wardens are sore plagued with foolish young lordlings, who get betwixt us and our work and blame us because we do not turn an ebb-tide into a flood, or a south wind into a north. I pray you to tell me how I can serve you."

"That boat!" said Chandos, pointing to the already distant sail rising and falling on the waves. "What is it?"

Cock Badding shaded his keen eyes with his strong brows hand. "She has but just gone out," said he. "She is La Pucelle, a small wine-sloop from Gascony, home-bound and laden with barrel-staves."

"I pray you did any man join her at the very last?"

"Nay, I know not. I saw no one."

"But I know," cried a seaman in the crowd. "I was standing at the wharf-side and was nigh knocked into the water by a little red-headed fellow, who breathed as though he had run from the town. Ere I had time to give him a cuff he had jumped aboard, the ropes were cast off, and her nose was seaward."

In a few words Chandos made all clear to Badding, the crowd pressing eagerly round.

"Aye, aye!" cried a seaman, "the good Sir John is right. See how she points. It is Picardy and not Gascony that she will fetch this journey in spite of her wine-staves."

"Then we must lay her aboard!" cried Cock Badding. "Come, lads, here is my own Marie Rose ready to cast off. Who's for a trip with a fight at the end of it?"

There was a rush for the boat; but the stout little seaman picked his men. "Go back, Jerry! Your heart is good, but you are overfat for the work. You, Luke, and you, Thomas, and the two Deedes, and William of Sandgate. You will work the boat. And now we need a few men of their hands. Do you come, little sir?"

"I pray you, my dear lord, to let me go!" cried Nigel.

"Yes, Nigel, you can go, and I will bring your gear over to Calais this night."

"I will join you there, fair sir, and with the help of Saint Paul I will bring this Red Ferret with me."

"Aboard, aboard! Time passes!" cried Badding impatiently, while already his seamen were hauling on the line and raising the mainsail. "Now then, sirrah! who are you?"

It was Aylward, who had followed Nigel and was pushing his way aboard.

"Where my master goes I go also," cried Aylward, "so stand clear, master-shipman, or you may come by a hurt."

"By Saint Leonard! archer," said Cock Badding, "had I more time I would give you a lesson ere I leave land. Stand back and give place to others!"

"Nay, stand back and give place to me!" cried Aylward, and seizing Badding round the waist he slung him into the dock.

There was a cry of anger from the crowd, for Badding was the hero of all the Cinque Ports and had never yet met his match in manhood. The epitaph still lingers in which it was said that he "could never rest until he had foughten his fill." When, therefore, swimming like a duck, he reached a rope and pulled himself hand over hand up to the quay, all stood aghast to see what fell fate would befall this bold stranger. But Badding laughed loudly, dashing the saltwater from his eyes and hair.

"You have fairly won your place, archer," said he. "You are the very man for our work. Where is Black Simon of Norwich?"

A tall dark young man with a long, stern, lean face came forward. "I am with you, Cock," said he, "and I thank you for my place."

"You can come, Hugh Baddlesmere, and you, Hal Masters, and you, Dicon of Rye. That is enough. Now off, in God's name, or it will be night ere we can come up with them!"

Already the head-sails and the mainsail had been raised, while a hundred willing hands poled her off from the wharf. Now the wind caught her; heeling over, and quivering with eagerness like an unleashed hound she flew through the opening and out into the Channel. She was a famous little schooner, the Marie Rose of Winchelsea, and under her daring owner Cock Badding, half trader and half pirate, had brought back into port many a rich cargo taken in mid-Channel, and paid for in blood rather than money. Small as she was, her great speed and the fierce character of her master had made her a name of terror along the French coast, and many a bulky Eastlander or Fleming as he passed the narrow seas had scanned the distant Kentish shore, fearing lest that ill-omened purple sail with a gold Christopher upon it should shoot out suddenly from the dim gray cliffs. Now she was clear of the land, with the wind on her larboard quarter, every inch of canvas set, and her high sharp bows smothered in foam, as she dug through the waves.

Cock Badding trod the deck with head erect and jaunty bearing, glancing up at the swelling sails and then ahead at the little tilted white triangle, which stood out clear and hard against the bright blue sky. Behind was the lowland of the Camber marshes, with the bluffs of Rye and Winchelsea, and the line of cliffs behind them. On the larboard bow rose the great white walls of Folkestone and of Dover, and far on the distant sky-line the gray shimmer of those French cliffs for which the fugitives were making.

"By Saint Paul!" cried Nigel, looking with eager eyes over the tossing waters, "it seems to me, Master Badding, that already we draw in upon them."

The master measured the distance with his keen steady gaze, and then looked up at the sinking sun. "We have still four hours of day-light," said he; "but if we do not lay her aboard ere darkness falls she will save herself, for the nights are as black as a wolf's mouth, and if she alter her course I know not how we may follow her."

"Unless, indeed, you might guess to which port she was bound and reach it before her."

"Well thought of, little master!" cried Badding. "If the news be for the French outside Calais, then Ambleteuse would be nearest to Saint Omer. But my sweeting sails three paces to that lubber's two, and if the wind holds we shall have time and to spare. How now, archer? You do not seem so eager as when you made your way aboard this boat by slinging me into the sea."

Aylward sat on the upturned keel of a skiff which lay upon the deck. He groaned sadly and held his green face between his two hands. "I would gladly sling you into the sea once more, master-shipman," said he, "if by so doing I could get off this most accursed vessel of thine. Or if you would wish to have your turn, then I would thank you if you would lend me a hand over the side, for indeed I am but a useless weight upon your deck. Little did I think that Samkin Aylward could be turned into a weakling by an hour of salt water. Alas the day that ever my foot wandered from the good red heather of Crooksbury!"

Cock Badding laughed loud and long. "Nay, take it not to heart, archer," he cried; "for better men than you or I have groaned upon this deck. The Prince himself with ten of his cho-sen knights crossed with me once, and eleven sadder faces I never saw. Yet within a month they had shown at Crécy that they were no weaklings, as you will do also, I dare swear, when the time comes. Keep that thick head of thine down upon the planks, and all will be well anon. But we raise her, we raise her with every blast of the wind!"

It was indeed evident, even to the inexperienced eyes of Nigel, that the Marie Rose was closing in swiftly upon the stranger. She was a heavy, bluff-bowed, broad-sterned vessel which labored clumsily through the seas. The swift, fierce little Winchelsea boat swooping and hissing through the waters behind her was like some keen hawk whizzing down wind at the back of a flapping heavy-bodied duck. Half an hour before La Pucelle had been a distant patch of canvas. Now they could see the black hull, and soon the cut of her sails and the lines of her bulwarks. There were at least a dozen men upon her deck, and the twinkle of weapons from amongst them showed that they were preparing to resist. Cock Badding began to muster his own forces.

He had a crew of seven rough, hardy mariners, who had been at his back in many a skirmish. They were armed with short swords, but Cock Badding carried a weapon peculiar to himself, a twenty-pound blacksmith's hammer, the memory of which, as "Badding's cracker," still lingers in the Cinque Ports. Then there were the eager Nigel, the melancholy Aylward, Black Simon who was a tried swordsman, and three archers, Baddlesmere, Masters and Dicon of Rye, all veterans of the French War. The numbers in the two vessels might be about equal; but Badding as he glanced at the bold harsh faces which looked to him for orders had little fear for the result.

Glancing round, however, he saw something which was more dangerous to his plans than the resistance of the enemy. The wind, which had become more fitful and feebler, now fell suddenly away, until the sails hung limp and straight above them. A belt of calm lay along the horizon, and the waves around had smoothed down into a long oily swell on which the two little vessels rose and fell. The great boom of the Marie Rose rattled and jarred with every lurch, and the high thin prow pointed skyward one instant and seaward the next in a way that drew fresh groans from the unhappy Aylward. In vain Cock Badding pulled on his sheets and tried hard to husband every little wandering gust which ruffled for an instant the sleek rollers. The French master was as adroit a sailor, and his boom swung round also as each breath of wind came up from astern.

At last even these fitful puffs died finally away, and a cloudless sky overhung a glassy sea. The sun was almost upon the horizon behind Dungeness Point, and the whole western heaven was bright with the glory of the sunset, which blended sea and sky in one blaze of ruddy light. Like rollers of molten gold, the long swell heaved up Channel from the great ocean beyond. In the midst of the immense beauty and peace of nature the two little dark specks with the white sail and the purple rose and fell, so small upon the vast shining bosom of the waters, and yet so charged with all the unrest and the passion of life.

The experienced eye of the seaman told him that it was hopeless to expect a breeze before nightfall. He looked across at the Frenchman, which lay less than a quarter of a mile ahead, and shook his gnarled fist at the line of heads which could be seen looking back over her stern. One of them waved a white kerchief in derision, and Cock Badding swore a bitter oath at the sight.

"By Saint Leonard of Winchelsea," he cried, "I will rub my side up against her yet! Out with the skiff, lads, and two of you to the oars. Make fast the line to the mast, Will. Do you go in the boat, Hugh, and I'll make the second. Now if we bend our backs to it we may have them yet ere night cover them."

The little skiff was swiftly lowered over the side and the slack end of the cable fastened to the after thwart. Cock Badding and his comrades pulled as if they would snap their oars, and the little vessel began slowly to lurch forward over the rollers. But the next moment a larger skiff had splashed over the side of the Frenchman, and no less than four seamen were hard at work under her bows. If the Marie Rose advanced a yard the Frenchman was going two. Again Cock Badding raved and shook his fist. He clambered aboard, his face wet with sweat and dark with anger.

"Curse them! they have had the best of us!" he cried. "I can do no more. Sir John has lost his papers, for indeed now that night is at hand I can see no way in which we can gain them."

Nigel had leaned against the bulwark during these events, watching with keen attention the doings of the sailors, and praying alternately to Saint Paul, Saint George, and Saint Thomas for a slant of wind which would put them alongside their enemy. He was silent; but his hot heart was simmering within him. His spirit had risen even above the discomfort of the sea, and his mind was too absorbed in his mission to have a thought for that which had laid Aylward flat upon the deck. He had never doubted that Cock Badding in one way or another would accomplish his end, but when he heard his speech of despair he bounded off the bulwark and stood before the seaman with his face flushed and all his soul afire.

"By Saint Paul! master-shipman," he cried, "we should never hold up our heads in honor if we did not go further into the matter! Let us do some small deed this night upon the water, or let us never see land again, for indeed we could not wish fairer prospect of winning honorable advancement."

"With your leave, little master, you speak like a fool," said the gruff seaman. "You and all your kind are as children when once the blue water is beneath you. Can you not see that there is no wind, and that the Frenchman can warp her as swiftly as we? What then would you do?"

Nigel pointed to the boat which towed astern. "Let us venture forth in her," said he, "and let us take this ship or die worshipful in the attempt."

His bold and fiery words found their echo in the brave rough hearts around him. There was a deep-chested shout from both archers and seamen. Even Aylward sat up, with a wan smile upon his green face.

But Cock Badding shook his head. "I have never met the man who could lead where I would not follow," said he; "but by Saint Leonard! this is a mad business, and I should be a fool if I were to risk my men and my ship. Bethink you, little master, that the skiff can hold only five, though you load her to the water's edge. If there is a man yonder, there are fourteen, and you have to climb their side from the boat. What chance would you have? Your boat stove and you in the water—there is the end of it. No man of mine goes on such a fool's errand, and so I swear!"

"Then, Master Badding, I must crave the loan of your skiff, for by Saint Paul! the good Lord Chandos' papers are not to be so lightly lost. If no one else will come, then I will go alone."

The shipman smiled at the words; but the smile died away from his lips when Nigel, with features set like ivory and eyes as hard as steel, pulled on the rope so as to bring the skiff under the counter. It was very clear that he would do even as he said. At the same time Aylward raised his bulky form from the deck, leaned for a moment against the bulwarks, and then tottered aft to his master's side.

"Here is one that will go with you," said he, "or he would never dare show his face to the girls of Tilford again. Come, archers, let us leave these salt herrings in their pickle tub and try our luck out on the water."

The three archers at once ranged themselves on the same side as their comrade. They were bronzed, bearded men, short in stature, as were most Englishmen of that day, but hardy, strong and skilled with their weapons. Each drew his string from its waterproof case and bent the huge arc of his war-bow as he fitted it into the nocks.

"Now, master, we are at your back," said they as they pulled and tightened their sword-belts.

But already Cock Badding had been carried away by the hot lust of battle and had thrown aside every fear and doubt which had clouded him. To see a fight and not to be in it was more than he could bear.

"Nay, have it your own way!" he cried, "and may Saint Leonard help us, for a madder venture I have never seen! And yet it may be worth the trial. But if it be done let me have the handling of it, little master, for you know no more of a boat than I do of a war-horse. The skiff can bear five and not a man more. Now, who will come?"

They had all caught fire, and there was not one who would be left out.

Badding picked up his hammer. "I will come myself," said he, "and you also, little master, since it is your hot head that has planned it. Then there is Black Simon, the best sword of the Cinque Ports. Two archers can pull on the oars, and it may be that they can pick off two or three of these Frenchmen before we close with them. Hugh Baddlesmere, and you, Dicon of Rye—into the boat with you!"

"What?" cried Aylward. "Am I to be left behind? I, who am the Squire's own man? Ill fare the bowman who comes betwixt me and yonder boat!"

"Nay, Aylward," said his master, "I order that you stay, for indeed you are a sick man."

"But now that the waves have sunk I am myself again. Nay, fair sir, I pray that you will not leave me behind."

"You must needs take the space of a better man; for what do you know of the handling of a boat?" said Badding shortly. "No more fool's talk, I pray you, for the night will soon fall. Stand aside!"

Aylward looked hard at the French boat. "I could swim ten times up and down Frensham pond," said he, "and it will be strange if I cannot go as far as that. By these finger-bones, Samkin Aylward may be there as soon as you!"

The little boat with its five occupants pushed off from the side of the schooner, and dipping and rising, made its slow way toward the Frenchman. Badding and one archer had single oars, the second archer was in the prow, while Black Simon and Nigel huddled into the stern with the water lapping and hissing at their very elbows. A shout of defiance rose from the Frenchmen, and they stood in a line along the side of their vessel shaking their fists and waving their weapons. Already the sun was level with Dungeness, and the gray of evening was blurring sky and water into one dim haze. A great silence hung over the broad expanse of nature, and no sound broke it save the dip and splash of the oars and the slow deep surge of the boat upon the swell. Behind them their comrades of the Marie Rose stood motionless and silent, watching their progress with eager eyes.

They were near enough now to have a good look at the Frenchmen. One was a big swarthy man with a long black beard. He had a red cap and an ax over his shoulder. There were ten other hardy-looking fellows, all of them well armed, and there were three who seemed to be boys.

"Shall we try a shaft upon them?" asked Hugh Baddlesmere. "They are well within our bowshot."

"Only one of you can shoot at a time, for you have no footing," said Badding. "With one foot in the prow and one over the thwart you will get your stance. Do what you may, and then we will close in upon them."

The archer balanced himself in the rolling boat with the deftness of a man who has been trained upon the sea, for he was born and bred in the Cinque Ports. Carefully he nocked his arrow, strongly he drew it, steadily he loosed it, but the boat swooped at the instant, and it buried itself in the waves. The second passed over the little ship, and the third struck in her black side. Then in quick succession—so quick that two shafts were often in the air at the same instant—he discharged a dozen arrows, most of which just cleared the bulwarks and dropped upon the deck. There was a cry on the Frenchman, and the heads vanished from the side.

"Enough!" cried Badding. "One is down, and it may be two. Close in, close in, in God's name, before they rally!"

He and the other bent to their oars; but at the same instant there was a sharp zip in the air and a hard clear sound like a stone striking a wall. Baddlesmere clapped his hand to his head, groaned and fell forward out of the boat, leaving a swirl of blood upon the surface. A moment later the same fierce hiss ended in a loud wooden crash, and a short, thick crossbow-bolt was buried deep in the side of their boat.

"Close in, close in!" roared Badding, tugging at his oar. "Saint George for England! Saint Leonard for Winchelsea! Close in!"

But again that fatal crossbow twanged. Dicon of Rye fell back with a shaft through his shoulder. "God help me, I can no more!" said he.

Badding seized the oar from his hand; but it was only to sweep the boat's head round and pull her back to the Marie Rose. The attack had failed.

"What now, master-shipman?" cried Nigel. "What has befallen to stop us? Surely the matter does not end here?"

"Two down out of five," said Badding, "and twelve at the least against us. The odds are too long, little master. Let us at least go back, fill up once more, and raise a mantelet against the bolts, for they have an arbalist which shoots both straight and hard. But what we do we must do quickly, for the darkness falls apace."

Their repulse had been hailed by wild yells of delight from the Frenchmen, who danced with joy and waved their weapons madly over their heads. But before their rejoicings had finished they saw the little boat creeping out once more from the shadow of the Marie Rose, a great wooden screen in her bows to protect her from the arrows. Without a pause she came straight and fast for her enemy. The wounded archer had been put on board, and Aylward would have had his place had Nigel been able to see him upon the deck. The third archer, Hal Masters, had sprung in, and one of the seamen, Wat Finnis of Hythe. With their hearts hardened to conquer or to die, the five ran alongside the Frenchman and sprang upon her deck. At the same instant a great iron weight crashed through the bottom of their skiff, and their feet had hardly left her before she was gone. There was no hope and no escape save victory.

The crossbowman stood under the mast, his terrible weapon at his shoulder, the steel string stretched taut, the heavy bolt shining upon the nut. One life at least he would claim out of this little band. Just for one instant too long did he dwell upon his aim, shifting from the seaman to Cock Badding, whose formidable appearance showed him to be the better prize. In that second of time Hal Masters' string twanged and his long arrow sped through the arbalister's throat. He dropped on the deck, with blood and curses pouring from his mouth.

A moment later Nigel's sword and Badding's hammer had each claimed a victim and driven back the rush of assailants. The five were safe upon the deck, but it was hard for them to keep a footing there. The French seamen, Bretons and Normans, were stout, powerful fellows, armed with axes and swords, fierce fighters and brave men. They swarmed round the little band, attacking them from all sides. Black Simon felled the black-bearded French Captain, and at the same instant was cut over the head and lay with his scalp open upon the deck. The seaman Wat of Hythe was killed by a crashing blow from an ax. Nigel was struck down, but was up again like a flash, and drove his sword through the man who had felled him.

But Badding, Masters the archer and he had been hustled back to the bulwark and were barely holding their own from minute to minute against the fierce crowd who assailed them, when an arrow coming apparently from the sea struck the foremost Frenchman to the heart. A moment later a boat dashed up alongside and four more men from the Marie Rose scrambled on to the blood-stained deck. With one fierce rush the remaining Frenchmen were struck down or were seized by their assailants. Nine prostrate men upon the deck showed how fierce had been the attack, how desperate the resistance.

Badding leaned panting upon his blood-clotted hammer.
"By Saint Leonard!" he cried, "I thought that this little master had been the death of us all. God wot you were but just in time, and how you came I know not. This archer has had a hand in it, by the look of him."

Aylward, still pale from his seasickness and dripping from head to foot with water, had been the first man in the rescue party.

Nigel looked at him in amazement. "I sought you aboard the ship, Aylward, but I could not lay eyes on you," said he.

"It was because I was in the water, fair sir, and by my hilt! it suits my stomach better than being on it," he answered. "When you first set forth I swam behind you, for I saw that the Frenchman's boat hung by a rope, and I thought that while you kept him in play I might gain it. I had reached it when you were driven back, so I hid behind it in the water and said my prayers as I have not said them for many a day. Then you came again, and no one had an eye for me, so I clambered into it, cut the rope, took the oars which I found there and brought her back for more men."

"By Saint Paul! you have acted very wisely and well," said Nigel, "and I think that of all of us it is you who have won most honor this day. But of all these men dead and alive I see none who resembles that Red Ferret whom my Lord Chandos has described and who has worked such despite upon us in the past. It would indeed be an evil chance if he has in spite of all our pains made his way to France in some other boat."

"That we shall soon find out," said Badding. "Come with me and we will search the ship from truck to keel ere he escapes us."

There was a scuttle at the base of the mast which led down into the body of the vessel, and the Englishmen were approaching this when a strange sight brought them to a stand. A round brazen head had appeared in the square dark opening. An instant afterward a pair of shining shoulders followed. Then slowly the whole figure of a man in complete plate-armor emerged on the deck. In his gauntleted hand he carried a heavy steel mace. With this uplifted he moved toward his enemies, silent save for the ponderous clank of his footfall. It was an inhuman, machine-like figure, menacing and terrible, devoid of all expression, slow-moving, inexorable and awesome.

A sudden wave of terror passed over the English seamen. One of them tried to pass and get behind the brazen man, but he was pinned against the side by a quick movement and his brains dashed out by a smashing blow from the heavy mace. Wild panic seized the others, and they rushed back to the boat. Aylward strung an arrow, but his bowstring was damp and the shaft rang loudly upon the shining breast-plate and glanced off into the sea. Masters struck the brazen head with a sword, but the blade snapped without injuring the helmet, and an instant later the bowman was stretched senseless on the deck. The seamen shrank from this terrible silent creature and huddled in the stern, all the fight gone out of them.

Again he raised his mace and was advancing on the helpless crowd where the brave were encumbered and hampered by the weaklings, when Nigel shook himself clear and bounded forward into the open, his sword in his hand and a smile of welcome upon his lips.

The sun had set, and one long mauve gash across the western Channel was closing swiftly into the dull grays of early night. Above, a few stars began to faintly twinkle; yet the twilight was still bright enough for an observer to see every detail of the scene: the Marie Rose, dipping and rising on the long rollers astern; the broad French boat with its white deck blotched with blood and littered with bodies; the group of men in the stern, some trying to advance and some seeking to escape—all a confused, disorderly, struggling rabble.

Then betwixt them and the mast the two figures: the armed shining man of metal, with hand upraised, watchful, silent, motionless, and Nigel, bareheaded and crouching, with quick foot, eager eyes and fearless happy face, moving this way and that, in and out, his sword flashing like a gleam of light as he sought at all points for some opening in the brazen shell before him.

It was clear to the man in armor that if he could but pen his antagonist in a corner he would beat him down without fail. But it was not to be done. The unhampered man had the advantage of speed. With a few quick steps he could always glide to either side and escape the clumsy rush. Aylward and Badding had sprung out to Nigel's assistance; but he shouted to them to stand back, with such authority and anger in his voice that their weapons dropped to their sides. With staring eyes and set features they stood watching that unequal fight.

Once it seemed that all was over with the Squire, for in springing back from his enemy he tripped over one of the bodies which strewed the deck and fell flat upon his back, but with a swift wriggle he escaped the heavy blow which thundered down upon him, and springing to his feet he bit deeply into the Frenchman's helmet with a sweeping cut in return. Again the mace fell, and this time Nigel had not quite cleared himself. His sword was beaten down and the blow fell partly upon his left shoulder. He staggered, and once more the iron club whirled upward to dash him to the ground.

Quick as a flash it passed through his mind that he could not leap beyond its reach. But he might get within it. In an instant he had dropped his sword, and springing in he had seized the brazen man round the waist. The mace was shortened and the handle jobbed down once upon the bare flaxen head. Then, with a sonorous clang, and a yell of delight from the spectators, Nigel with one mighty wrench tore his enemy from the deck and hurled him down upon his back. His own head was whirling and he felt that his senses were slipping away, but already his hunting-knife was out and pointing through the slit in the brazen helmet.

"Give yourself up, fair sir!" said he.

"Never to fishermen and to archers! I am a gentleman of coat-armor. Kill me!"

"I also am a gentleman of coat-armor. I promise you quarter."

"Then, sir, I surrender myself to you."

The dagger tinkled down upon the deck. Seamen and archers ran forward, to find Nigel half senseless upon his face. They drew him off, and a few deft blows struck off the helmet of his enemy. A head, sharp-featured, freckled and foxy-red, disclosed itself beneath it. Nigel raised himself on his elbow for an instant.

"You are the Red Ferret?" said he.

"So my enemies call me," said the Frenchman, with a smile. "I rejoice, sir, that I have fallen to so valiant and honorable a gentleman."

"I thank you, fair sir," said Nigel feebly. "I also rejoice that I have encountered so debonair a person, and I shall ever bear in mind the pleasure which I have had from our meeting."

So saying, he laid his bleeding head upon his enemy's brazen front and sank into a dead faint.

CHAPTER XV

HOW THE RED FERRET CAME TO COSFORD

THE old chronicler in his *"Gestes du Sieur Nigel"* has bewailed his broken narrative, which rose from the fact that out of thirty-one years of warfare no less than seven were spent by his hero at one time or another in the recovery from his wounds or from those illnesses which arose from privation and fatigue. Here at the very threshold of his career, on the eve of a great enterprise, this very fate befell him.

Stretched upon a couch in a low-roofed and ill-furnished chamber, which looks down from under the machicolated corner turret upon the inner court of the Castle of Calais, he lay half-unconscious and impotent, while great deeds were doing under his window. Wounded in three places, and with his head splintered by the sharp pommel of the Ferret's mace, he hovered betwixt life and death, his shattered body drawing him downward, his youthful spirit plucking him up.

As in some strange dream he was aware of that deed of arms within the courtyard below. Dimly it came back to his memory afterwards the sudden startled shout, the crash of metal, the slamming of great gates, the roar of many voices, the clang, clang, clang, as of fifty lusty smiths upon their anvils, and then at last the dwindling of the hubbub, the low groans and sudden shrill cries to the saints, the measured murmur of many voices, the heavy clanking of armored feet.

Sometime in that fell struggle he must have drawn his weakened body as far as the narrow window, and hanging to the iron bars have looked down on the wild scene beneath him. In the red glare of torches held from windows and from roof he saw the rush and swirl of men below, the ruddy light shining back from glowing brass and gleaming steel. As a wild vision it came to him afterward, the beauty and the splendor, the flying lambrequins, the jeweled crests, the blazonry and richness of surcoat and of shield, where sable and gules, argent and vair, in every pattern of saltire, bend or chevron, glowed beneath him like a drift of many-colored blossoms, tossing, sinking, stooping into shadow, springing into light. There glared the blood-red gules of Chandos, and he saw the tall figure of his master, a thunderbolt of war, raging in the van. There too were the three black chevrons on the golden shield which marked the noble Manny. That strong swordsman must surely be the royal Edward himself, since only he and the black-armored swift-footed youth at his side were marked by no symbol of heraldry. "Manny! Manny! George for England!" rose the deep-throated bay, and ever the gallant counter-cry: "A Chargny! A Chargny! Saint Denis for France!" thundered amid the clash and thudding of the battle.

Such was the vague whirling memory still lingering in Nigel's mind when at last the mists cleared away from it and he found himself weak but clear on the low couch in the corner turret. Beside him, crushing lavender betwixt his rough fingers and strewing it over floor and sheets, was Aylward the archer. His longbow leaned at the foot of the bed, and his steel cap was balanced on the top of it, while he himself, sitting in his shirt-sleeves, fanned off the flies and scattered the fragrant herbs over his helpless master.

"By my hilt!" he cried with a sudden shout, every tooth in his head gleaming with joy, "I thank the Virgin and all the saints for this blessed sight! I had not dared to go back to Tilford had I lost you. Three weeks have you lain there and babbled like a babe, but now I see in your eyes that you are your own man again."

"I have indeed had some small hurt," said Nigel feebly; "but it is shame and sorrow that I should lie here if there is work for my hands. Whither go you, archer?"

"To tell the good Sir John that you are mending."

"Nay, bide with me a little longer, Aylward. I can call to mind all that has passed. There was a bickering of small boats, was there not, and I chanced upon a most worthy person and exchanged handstrokes with him? He was my prisoner, was he not?"

"He was, fair sir."

"And where is he now?"

"Below in the castle."

A smile stole over Nigel's pale face. "I know what I will do with him," said he.

"I pray you to rest, fair sir," said Aylward anxiously. "The King's own leech saw you this morning, and he said that if the bandage was torn from your head you would surely die."

"Nay, good archer, I will not move. But tell me what befell upon the boat?"

"There is little to tell, fair sir. Had this Ferret not been his own squire and taken so long a time to don his harness it is likely that they would have had the better of us. He did not reach the battle till his comrades were on their backs. Him we took to the Marie Rose, because he was your man. The others were of no worth, so we threw them into the sea."

"The quick and the dead?"

"Every man of them."

"It was an evil deed."

Aylward shrugged his shoulders. "I tried to save one boy," said he; "but Cock Badding would not have it, and he had Black Simon and the others at his back. 'It is the custom of the Narrow Seas,' said they: 'To-day for them; to-morrow for us.' Then they tore him from his hold and cast him screaming over the side. By my hilt! I have no love for the sea and its customs, so I care not if I never set foot on it again when it has once borne me back to England."

"Nay, there are great happenings upon the sea, and many worthy people to be found upon ships," said Nigel. "In all parts, if one goes far enough upon the water, one would find those whom it would be joy to meet. If one crosses over the Narrow Sea, as we have done, we come on the French who are so needful to us; for how else would we win worship? Or if you go south, then in time one may hope to come to the land of the unbelievers, where there is fine skirmishing and much honor for him who will venture his person. Bethink you, archer, how fair a life it must be when one can ride forth in search of advancement with some hope of finding many debonair cavaliers upon the same quest, and then if one be overborne one has died for the faith, and the gates of Heaven are open before you. So also the sea to the north is a help to him who seeks honor, for it leads to the country of the Eastlanders and to those parts where the heathen still dwell who turn their faces from the blessed Gospel. There also a man might find some small deeds to do, and by Saint Paul! Aylward, if the French hold the truce and the good Sir John permits us, I would fain go down into those parts. The sea is a good friend to the cavalier, for it takes him where he may fulfil his vows."

Aylward shook his head, for his memories were too recent; but he said nothing, because at this instant the door opened and Chandos entered. With joy in his face he stepped forward to the couch and took Nigel's hand in his. Then he whispered a word in Aylward's ear, who hurried from the room.

"*Pardieu!* this is a good sight," said the knight. "I trust that you will soon be on your feet again."

"I crave your pardon, my honored lord, that I have been absent from your side," said Nigel.

"In truth my heart was sore for you, Nigel; for you have missed such a night as comes seldom in any man's life. All went even as we had planned. The postern gate was opened, and a party made their way in; but we awaited them, and all were taken or slain. But the greater part of the French had remained without upon the plain of Nieullet, so we took horse and went out against them. When we drew near them they were surprised, but they made good cheer among themselves, calling out to each other: 'If we fly we lose all. It is better to fight on, in the hopes that the day may be ours.' This was heard by our people in the van, who cried out to them: 'By Saint George! you speak truth. Evil befall him who thinks of flying!' So they held their ground like worthy people for the space of an hour, and there were many there whom it is always good to meet: Sir Geoffrey himself, and Sir Pepin de Werre, with Sir John de Landas, old Ballieul of the Yellow Tooth, and his brother Hector the Leopard. But above all Sir Eustace de Ribeaumont was at great pains to meet us worthily, and he was at handstrokes with the King for a long time. Then, when we had slain or taken them, all the prisoners were brought to a feast which was ready for them, and the knights of England waited upon them at the table and made good cheer with them. And all this, Nigel, we owe to you."

The Squire flushed with pleasure at the words. "Nay, most honored lord, it was but a small thing which I have been able to do. But I thank God and our Lady that I have done some service, since it has pleased you to take me with you to the wars. Should it chance——"

But the words were cut short upon Nigel's lips, and he lay back with amazed eyes staring from his pallid face. The door of his little chamber had opened, and who was this, the tall stately man with the noble presence, the high forehead, the long handsome face, the dark, brooding eyes—who but the noble Edward of England?"

"Ha, my little cock of Tilford Bridge, I still bear you in mind," said he. "Right glad I was to hear that you had found your wits again, and I trust that I have not helped to make you take leave of them once more."

Nigel's stare of astonishment had brought a smile to the King's lips. Now the Squire stammered forth some halting words of gratitude at the honor done to him.

"Nay, not a word," said the King. "But in sooth it is a joy to my heart to see the son of my old comrade Eustace Loring carry himself so bravely. Had this boat got before us with news of our coming, then all our labor had been in vain, and no Frenchman ventured to

Calais that night. But above all I thank you for that you have delivered into my hands one whom I had vowed to punish in that he has caused us more scathe by fouler means than any living man. Twice have I sworn that Peter the Red Ferret shall hang, for all his noble blood and coat-armor, if ever he should fall into my hands. Now at last his time has come; but I would not put him to death until you, who had taken him, could be there to see it done. Nay, thank me not, for I could do no less, seeing that it is to you that I owe him."

But it was not thanks which Nigel was trying to utter. It was hard to frame his words, and yet they must be said. "Sire," he murmured, "it ill becomes me to cross your royal will——"

The dark Plantagenet wrath gathered upon the King's high brow and gloomed in his fierce deep-set eyes. "By God's dignity! no man has ever crossed it yet and lived unscathed. How now, young sir, what mean such words, to which we are little wont? Have a care, for this is no light thing which you venture."

"Sire," said Nigel, "in all matters in which I am a free man I am ever your faithful liege, but some things there are which may not be done."

"How?" cried the King. "In spite of my will?"

"In spite of your will, sire," said Nigel, sitting up on his couch, with white face and blazing eyes.

"By the Virgin!" the angry King thundered, "we are come to a pretty pass! You have been held too long at home, young man. The overstabled horse will kick. The unweathered hawk will fly at check. See to it, Master Chandos! He is thine to break, and I hold you to it that you break him. And what is it that Edward of England may not do, Master Loring?"

Nigel faced the King with a face as grim as his own. "You may not put to death the Red Ferret."

"*Pardieu!* And why?"

"Because he is not thine to slay, sire. Because he is mine. Because I promised him his life, and it is not for you, King though you be, to constrain a man of gentle blood to break his plighted word and lose his honor."

Chandos laid his soothing hand upon his Squire's shoulder. "Excuse him, sire; he is weak from his wounds," said he. "Perhaps we have stayed overlong, for the leech has ordered repose."

But the angry King was not easily to be appeased. "I am not wont to be so browbeat," said he hotly. "This is your Squire, Master John. How comes it that you can stand there and listen to his pert talk, and say no word to chide him? Is this how you guide your household? Have you not taught him that every promise given is subject to the King's consent, and that with him only lie the springs of life and death? If he is sick, you at least are hale. Why stand you there in silence?"

"My liege," said Chandos gravely, "I have served you for over a score of years, and have shed my blood through as many wounds in your cause, so that you should not take my words amiss. But indeed I should feel myself to be no true man if I did not tell you that my Squire Nigel, though perchance he has spoken more bluntly than becomes him, is none the less right in this matter, and that you are wrong. For bethink you, sire——"

"Enough!" cried the King, more furious than ever. "Like master, like man, and I might have known why it is that this saucy Squire dares to bandy words with his sovereign lord. He does but give out what he hath taken in. John, John, you grow over-bold. But this I tell you, and you also, young man, that as God is my help, ere the sun has set this night the Red Ferret will hang as a warning to all spies and traitors from the highest tower of Calais, that every ship upon the Narrow Seas, and every man for ten miles round may see him as he swings and know how heavy is the hand of the English King. Do you bear it in mind, lest you also may feel its weight!" With a glare like an angry lion he walked from the room, and the iron-clamped door clanged loudly behind him.

Chandos and Nigel looked ruefully at each other. Then the knight patted his Squire upon his bandaged head.

"You have carried yourself right well, Nigel. I could not wish for better. Fear not. All will be well."

"My fair and honored lord," cried Nigel, "I am heavy at heart, for indeed I could do no other, and yet I have brought trouble upon you."

"Nay, the clouds will soon pass. If he does indeed slay this Frenchman, you have done all that lay within your power, and your mind may rest easy."

"I pray that it will rest easy in Paradise," said Nigel; "for at the hour that I hear that I am dishonored and my prisoner slain I tear this bandage from my head and so end all things. I will not live when once my word is broken."

"Nay, fair son, you take this thing too heavily," said Chandos, with a grave face. "When a man has done all he may there remains no dishonor; but the King hath a kind heart for all his hot head, and it may be that if I see him I will prevail upon him. Bethink you how he swore to hang the six burghers of this very town, and yet he pardoned them. So keep a high heart, fair son, and I will come with good news ere evening."

For three hours, as the sinking sun traced the shadow higher and ever higher upon the chamber wall, Nigel tossed feverishly upon his couch, his ears straining for the footfall of Aylward or of Chandos, bringing news of the fate of the prisoner. At last the door flew open, and there before him stood the one man whom he least expected, and yet would most gladly have seen. It was the Red Ferret himself, free and joyous.

With swift furtive steps he was across the room and on his knees beside the couch, kissing the pendent hand. "You have saved me, most noble sir!" he cried. "The gallows was fixed and the rope slung, when the good Lord Chandos told the King that you would die by your own hand if I were slain. 'Curse this mule-headed Squire!' he cried. 'In God's name let him have his prisoner, and let him do what he will with him so long as he troubles me no more!' So here I have come, fair sir, to ask you what I shall do."

"I pray you to sit beside me and be at your ease," said Nigel. "In a few words I will tell you what I would have you do. Your armor I will keep, that I may have some remembrance of my good fortune in meeting so valiant a gentleman. We are of a size, and I make little doubt that I can wear it. Of ransom I would ask a thousand crowns."

"Nay, nay!" cried the Ferret. "It would be a sad thing if a man of my position was worth less than five thousand."

"A thousand will suffice, fair sir, to pay my charges for the war. You will not again play the spy, nor do us harm until the truce is broken."

"That I will swear."

"And lastly there is a journey that you shall make."

The Frenchman's face lengthened. "Where you order I must go," said he; "but I pray you that it is not to the Holy Land."

"Nay," said Nigel; "but it is to a land which is holy to me. You will make your way back to Southampton."

"I know it well. I helped to burn it down some years ago."

"I rede you to say nothing of that matter when you get there. You will then journey as though to London until you come to a fair town named Guildford."

"I have heard of it. The King hath a hunt there."

"The same. You will then ask for a house named Cosford, two leagues from the town on the side of a long hill."

"I will bear it in mind."

"At Cosford you will see a good knight named Sir John Buttesthorn, and you will ask to have speech with his daughter, the Lady Mary."

"I will do so; and what shall I say to the Lady Mary, who lives at Cosford on the slope of a long hill two leagues from the fair town of Guildford?"

"Say only that I sent my greeting, and that Saint Catharine has been my friend—only that and nothing more. And now leave me, I pray you, for my head is weary and I would fain have sleep."

Thus it came about that a month later on the eve of the Feast of Saint Matthew, the Lady Mary, as she walked front Cosford gates, met with a strange horseman, richly clad, a serving-man behind him, looking shrewdly about him with quick blue eyes, which twinkled from a red and freckled face. At sight of her he doffed his hat and reined his horse.

"This house should be Cosford," said he. "Are you by chance the Lady Mary who dwells there?"

The lady bowed her proud dark head.

"Then," said he, "Squire Nigel Loring sends you greeting and tells you that Saint Catharine has been his friend." Then turning to his servant he cried: "Heh, Raoul, our task is done! Your master is a free man once more. Come, lad, come, the nearest port to France! Hola! Hola! Hola!" And so without a word more the two, master and man, set spurs to their horses and galloped like madmen down the long slope of Hindhead, until as she looked after them they were but two dark dots in the distance, waist-high in the ling and the bracken.

She turned back to the house, a smile upon her face. Nigel had sent her greeting. A Frenchman had brought it. His bringing it had made him a freeman. And Saint Catharine had been Nigel's friend. It was at her shrine that he had sworn that three deeds should be done ere he should set eyes upon her again. In the privacy of her room the Lady Mary sank upon her prie-dieu and poured forth the thanks of her heart to the Virgin that one deed was accomplished; but even as she did so her joy was overcast by the thought of those two others which lay before him.

CHAPTER XVI

HOW THE KING'S COURT FEASTED
IN CALAIS CASTLE

IT was a bright sunshiny morning when Nigel found himself at last able to leave his turret chamber and to walk upon the rampart of the castle. There was a brisk northern wind, heavy and wet with the salt of the sea, and he felt, as he turned his face to it, fresh life and strength surging in his blood and bracing his limbs. He took his hand from Aylward's supporting arm and stood with his cap off, leaning on the rampart and breathing in the cool strong air. Far off upon the distant sky-line, half hidden by the heave of the waves, was the low white fringe of cliffs which skirted England. Between him and them lay the broad blue Channel, seamed and flecked with flashing foam, for a sharp sea was running and the few ships in sight were laboring heavily. Nigel's eyes traversed the wide-spread view, rejoicing in the change from the gray wall of his cramped chamber. Finally they settled upon a strange object at his very feet.

It was a long trumpet-shaped engine of leather and iron bolted into a rude wooden stand and fitted with wheels. Beside it lay a heap of metal slugs and lumps of stone. The end of the machine was raised and pointed over the battlement. Behind it stood an iron box which Nigel opened. It was filled with a black coarse powder, like gritty charcoal.

"By Saint Paul!" said he, passing his hands over the engine, "I have heard men talk of these things, but never before have I seen one. It is none other than one of those wondrous new-made bombards."

"In sooth, it is even as you say," Aylward answered, looking at it with contempt and dislike in his face. "I have seen them here upon the ramparts, and have also exchanged a buffet or two with him who had charge of them. He was jack-fool enough to think that with this leather pipe he could outshoot the best archer in Christendom. I lent him a cuff on the ear that laid him across his foolish engine."

"It is a fearsome thing," said Nigel, who had stooped to examine it. "We live in strange times when such things can be made. It is loosed by fire, is it not, which springs from the black dust?"

"By my hilt! fair sir, I know not. And yet I call to mind that ere we fell out this foolish bombardman did say something of the matter. The fire-dust is within and so also is the ball. Then you take more dust from this iron box and place it in the hole at the farther end—so. It is now ready. I have never seen one fired, but I wot that this one could be fired now."

"It makes a strange sound, archer, does it not?" said Nigel wistfully.

"So I have heard, fair sir—even as the bow twangs, so it also has a sound when you loose it."

"There is no one to hear, since we are alone upon the rampart, nor can it do scathe, since it points to sea. I pray you to loose it and I will listen to the sound." He bent over the bombard with an attentive ear, while Aylward, stooping his earnest brown face over the touch-hole, scraped away diligently with a flint and steel. A moment later both he and Nigel were seated some distance off upon the ground while amid the roar of the discharge and the thick cloud of smoke they had a vision of the long black snake-like engine shooting back upon the recoil. For a minute or more they were struck motionless with astonishment while the reverberations died away and the smoke wreaths curled slowly up to the blue heavens.

"Good lack!" cried Nigel at last, picking himself up and looking round him. "Good lack, and Heaven be my aid! I thank the Virgin that all stands as it did before. I thought that the castle had fallen."

"Such a bull's bellow I have never heard," cried Aylward, rubbing his injured limbs. "One could hear it from Frensham Pond to Guildford Castle. I would not touch one again—not for a hide of the best land in Puttenham!"

"It may fare ill with your own hide, archer, if you do," said an angry voice behind them. Chandos had stepped from the open door of the corner turret and stood looking at them with a harsh gaze. Presently, as the matter was made clear to him his face relaxed into a smile.

"Hasten to the warden, archer, and tell him how it befell. You will have the castle and the town in arms. I know not what the King may think of so sudden an alarm. And you, Nigel, how in the name of the saints came you to play the child like this?"

"I knew not its power, fair lord."

"By my soul, Nigel, I think that none of us know its power. I can see the day when all that we delight in, the splendor and glory of war, may all go down before that which beats through the plate of steel as easily as the leathern jacket. I have bestrode my war-horse in my armor and have looked down at the sooty, smoky bombardman beside me, and I have thought that perhaps I was the last of the old and he the first of the new; that there would come a time when he and his engines would sweep you and me and the rest of us from the field."

"But not yet, I trust, honored sir?"

"No, not yet, Nigel. You are still in time to win your spurs even as your fathers did. How is your strength?"

"I am ready for any task, my good and honored lord."

"It is well, for work awaits us—good work, pressing work, work of peril and of honor. Your eyes shine and your face flushes, Nigel. I live my own youth over again as I look at you. Know then that though there is truce with the French here, there is not truce in Brittany where the houses of Blois and of Montfort still struggle for the dukedom. Half Brittany fights for one, and half for the other. The French have taken up the cause of Blois, and we of Montfort, and it is such a war that many a great leader, such as Sir

Walter Manny, has first earned his name there. Of late the war has gone against us, and the bloody hands of the Rohans, of Gaptooth Beaumanoir, of Oliver the Flesher and others have been heavy upon our people. The last tidings have been of disaster, and the King's soul is dark with wrath for that his friend and comrade Gilles de St. Pol has been done to death in the Castle of La Brohinière. He will send succors to the country, and we go at their head. How like you that, Nigel?"

"My honored lord, what could I ask for better?"

"Then have your harness ready, for we start within the week. Our path by land is blocked by the French, and we go by sea. This night the King gives a banquet ere he returns to England, and your place is behind my chair. Be in my chamber that you may help me to dress, and so we will to the hall together."

With satin and with samite, with velvet and with fur, the noble Chandos was dressed for the King's feast, and Nigel too had donned his best silk jupon, faced with the five scarlet roses, that he might wait upon him. In the great hall of Calais Castle the tables were set, a high table for the lords, a second one for the less distinguished knights, and a third at which the squires might feast when their masters were seated.

Never had Nigel in his simple life at Tilford pictured a scene of such pomp and wondrous luxury. The grim gray walls were covered from ceiling to floor with priceless tapestry of Arras, where hart, hounds and huntsmen circled the great hall with one long living image of the chase. Over the principal table drooped a line of banners, and beneath them rows of emblazoned shields upon the wall carried the arms of the high noblemen who sat beneath. The red light of cressets and of torches burned upon the badges of the great captains of England. The lions and lilies shone over the high dorseret chair in the center, and the same august device marked with the cadency label indicated the seat of the Prince, while glowing to right and to left were the long lines of noble insignia, honored in peace and terrible in war. There shone the gold and sable of Manny, the engrailed cross of Suffolk, the red chevron of

Stafford, the scarlet and gold of Audley, the blue lion rampant of the Percies, the silver swallows of Arundel, the red roebuck of the Montacutes, the star of the de Veres, the silver scallops of Russell, the purple lion of de Lacy, and the black crosses of Clinton.

A friendly Squire at Nigel's elbow whispered the names of the famous warriors beneath. "You are young Loring of Tilford, the Squire of Chandos, are you not?" said he. "My name is Delves, and I come from Doddington in Cheshire. I am the Squire of Sir James Audley, yonder round-backed man with the dark face and close-cropped beard, who hath the Saracen head as a crest above him."

"I have heard of him as a man of great valor," said Nigel, gazing at him with interest.

"Indeed, you may well say so, Master Loring. He is the bravest knight in England, and in Christendom also, as I believe. No man hath done such deeds of valor."

Nigel looked at his new acquaintance with hope in his eyes. "You speak as it becomes you to speak when you uphold your own master," said he. "For the same reason, Master Delves, and in no spirit of ill-will to you, it behooves me to tell you that he is not to be compared in name or fame with the noble knight on whom I wait. Should you hold otherwise, then surely we can debate the matter in whatever way or time may please you best."

Delves smiled good-humoredly. "Nay, be not so hot," said he. "Had you upheld any other knight, save perhaps Sir Walter Manny, I had taken you at your word, and your master or mine would have had place for a new Squire. But indeed it is only truth that no knight is second to Chandos, nor would I draw my sword to lower his pride of place. Ha, Sir James' cup is low! I must see to it!" He darted off, a flagon of Gascony in his hand. "The King hath had good news to-night," he continued when he returned. "I have not seen him in so merry a mind since the night when we took the Frenchmen and he laid his pearl chaplet upon the head of de Ribeaumont. See how he laughs, and the Prince also. That laugh bodes some one little good, or I am the more mistaken. Have a care! Sir John's plate is empty."

It was Nigel's turn to dart away; but ever in the intervals he returned to the corner whence he could look down the hall and listen to the words of the older Squire. Delves was a short, thick-set man past middle age, weather-beaten and scarred, with a rough manner and bearing which showed that he was more at his ease in a tent than a hall. But ten years of service had taught him much, and Nigel listened eagerly to his talk.

"Indeed the King hath some good tidings," he continued. "See now, he has whispered it to Chandos and to Manny. Manny spreads it on to Sir Reginald Cobham, and he to Robert Knolles, each smiling like the Devil over a friar."

"Which is Sir Robert Knolles?" asked Nigel with interest. "I have heard much of him and his deeds."

"He is the tall hard-faced man in yellow silk, he with the hairless cheeks and the split lip. He is little older than yourself, and his father was a cobbler in Chester, yet he has already won the golden spurs. See how he dabs his great hand in the dish and hands forth the gobbets. He is more used to a camp-kettle than a silver plate. The big man with the black beard is Sir Bartholomew Berghersh, whose brother is the Abbot of Beaulieu. Haste, haste! for the boar's head is come and the plate's to be cleaned."

The table manners of our ancestors at this period would have furnished to the modern eye the strangest mixture of luxury and of barbarism. Forks were still unknown, and the courtesy fingers, the index and the middle of the left hand, took their place. To use any others was accounted the worst of manners. A crowd of dogs lay among the rushes growling at each other and quarreling over the gnawed bones which were thrown to them by the feasters. A slice of coarse bread served usually as a plate, but the King's own high table was provided with silver platters, which were wiped by the Squire or page after each course. On the other hand the table-linen was costly, and the courses, served with a pomp and dignity now unknown, comprised such a variety of dishes and such complex marvels of cookery as no modern banquet could show. Besides all our domestic animals and every kind of game, such strange delicacies as hedgehogs, bustards, porpoises, squirrels, bitterns and cranes lent variety to the feast.

Each new course, heralded by a flourish of silver trumpets, was borne in by liveried servants walking two and two, with rubicund marshals strutting in front and behind, bearing white wands in their hands, not only as badges of their office, but also as weapons with which to repel any impertinent inroad upon the dishes in the journey from the kitchen to the hall. Boar's heads, enarmed and endored with gilt tusks and flaming mouths, were followed by wondrous pasties molded to the shape of ships, castles and other devices with sugar seamen or soldiers who lost their own bodies in their fruitless defense against the hungry attack. Finally came the great nef, a silver vessel upon wheels laden with fruit and sweetmeats which rolled with its luscious cargo down the line of guests. Flagons of Gascony, of Rhine wine, of Canary and of Rochelle were held in readiness by the attendants; but the age, though luxurious, was not drunken, and the sober habits of the Norman had happily prevailed over the license of those Saxon banquets where no guest might walk from the table without a slur upon his host. Honor and hardihood go ill with a shaking hand or a blurred eye.

Whilst wine, fruit and spices were handed round the high tables the squires had been served in turn at the farther end of the hall. Meanwhile round the King there had gathered a group of statesmen and soldiers, talking eagerly among themselves. The Earl of Stafford, the Earl of Warwick, the Earl of Arundel, Lord Beauchamp and Lord Neville were assembled at the back of his chair, with Lord Percy and Lord Mowbray at either side. The little group blazed with golden chains and jeweled chaplets, flame-colored paltocks and purple tunics.

Of a sudden the King said something over his shoulder to Sir William de Pakyngton the herald, who advanced and stood by the royal chair. He was a tall and noble-featured man, with long grizzled beard which rippled down to the gold-linked belt girdling his many-colored tabard. On his head he had placed the heraldic barret-cap which bespoke his dignity, and he slowly raised his white wand high in the air, while a great hush fell upon the hall.

"My lords of England," said he, "knight bannerets, knights, squires, and all others here present of gentle birth and coat-armor, know that your dread and sovereign lord, Edward, King of England and of France, bids me give you greeting and commands you to come hither that he may have speech with you."

In an instant the tables were deserted and the whole company had clustered in front of the King's chair. Those who had sat on either side of him crowded inward so that his tall dark figure upreared itself amid the dense circle of his guests.

With a flush upon his olive cheeks and with pride smoldering in his dark eyes, he looked round him at the eager faces of the men who had been his comrades from Sluys and Cadsand to Crécy and Calais. They caught fire from that warlike gleam in his masterful gaze, and a sudden wild, fierce shout pealed up to the vaulted ceiling, a soldierly thanks for what was passed and a promise for what was to come. The King's teeth gleamed in a quick smile, and his large white hand played with the jeweled dagger in his belt.

"By the splendor of God!" said he in a loud clear voice, "I have little doubt that you will rejoice with me this night, for such tidings have come to my ears as may well bring joy to everyone of you. You know well that our ships have suffered great scathe from the Spaniards, who for many years have slain without grace or ruth all of my people who have fallen into their cruel hands. Of late they have sent their ships into Flanders, and thirty great cogs and galleys lie now at Sluys well-filled with archers and men-at-arms and ready in all ways for battle. I have it to-day from a sure hand that, having taken their merchandise aboard, these ships will sail upon the next Sunday and will make their way through our Narrow Sea. We have for a great time been long-suffering to these people, for which they have done us many contraries and despites, growing ever more arrogant as we grow more patient. It is in my mind therefore that we hie us to-morrow to Winchelsea, where we have twenty ships, and make ready to sally out upon them as they pass. May God and Saint George defend the right!"

A second shout, far louder and fiercer than the first, came like a thunderclap after the King's words. It was the bay of a fierce pack to their trusted huntsman.

Edward laughed again as he looked round at the gleaming eyes, the waving arms and the flushed joyful faces of his liegemen. "Who hath fought against these Spaniards?" he asked. "Is there anyone here who can tell us what manner of men they be?"

A dozen hands went up into the air; but the King turned to the Earl of Suffolk at his elbow.

"You have fought them, Thomas?" said he.

"Yes, sire, I was in the great sea-fight eight years ago at the Island of Guernsey, when Lord Lewis of Spain held the sea against the Earl of Pembroke."

"How found you them, Thomas?"

"Very excellent people, sire, and no man could ask for better. On every ship they have a hundred crossbowmen of Genoa, the best in the world, and their spearmen also are very hardy men. They would throw great cantles of iron from the tops of the masts, and many of our people met their death through it. If we can bar their way in the Narrow Sea, then there will be much hope of honor for all of us."

"Your words are very welcome, Thomas," said the King, "and I make no doubt that they will show themselves to be very worthy of what we prepare for them. To you I give a ship, that you may have the handling of it. You also, my dear son, shall have a ship, that evermore honor may be thine."

"I thank you, my fair and sweet father," said the Prince, with joy flushing his handsome boyish face.

"The leading ship shall be mine. But you shall have one, Walter Manny, and you, Stafford, and you, Arundel, and you, Audley, and you, Sir Thomas Holland, and you, Brocas, and you,

Berkeley, and you, Reginald. The rest shall be awarded at Winchelsea, whither we sail to-morrow. Nay, John, why do you pluck so at my sleeve?"

Chandos was leaning forward, with an anxious face. "Surely, my honored lord, I have not served you so long and so faithfully that you should forget me now. Is there then no ship for me?"

The King smiled, but shook his head. "Nay, John, have I not given you two hundred archers and a hundred men-at-arms to take with you into Brittany? I trust that your ships will be lying in Saint Malo-Bay ere the Spaniards are abreast of Winchelsea. What more would you have, old war-dog? Wouldst be in two battles at once?"

"I would be at your side, my liege, when the lion banner is in the wind once more. I have ever been there. Why should you cast me now? I ask little, dear lord—a galley, a balinger, even a pinnace, so that I may only be there."

"Nay, John, you shall come. I cannot find it in my heart to say you nay. I will find you place in my own ship, that you may indeed be by my side."

Chandos stooped and kissed the King's hand. "My Squire?" he asked.

The King's brows knotted into a frown. "Nay, let him go to Brittany with the others," said he harshly. "I wonder, John, that you should bring back to my memory this youth whose pertness is too fresh that I should forget it. But some one must go to Brittany in your stead, for the matter presses and our people are hard put to it to hold their own." He cast his eyes over the assembly, and they rested upon the stern features of Sir Robert Knolles.

"Sir Robert," he said, "though you are young in years you are already old in war, and I have heard that you are as prudent in council as you are valiant in the field. To you I commit the charge of this venture to Brittany in place of Sir John Chandos, who will follow thither when our work has been done upon the waters. Three ships lie in Calais port and three hundred men are ready to your hand. Sir John will tell you what our mind is in the matter. And now, my friends and good comrades, you will haste you each to his own quarters, and you will make swiftly such preparations as are needful, for, as God is my aid, I will sail with you to Winchelsea to-morrow!"

Beckoning to Chandos, Manny and a few of his chosen leaders, the King led them away to an inner chamber, where they might discuss the plans for the future. At the same time the assembly broke up, the knights in silence and dignity, the squires in mirth and noise, but all joyful at heart for the thought of the great days which lay before them.

CHAPTER XVII

THE SPANIARDS ON THE SEA

DAY had not yet dawned when Nigel was in the chamber of Chandos preparing him for his departure and listening to the last cheery words of advice and direction from his noble master. That same morning, before the sun was half-way up the heaven, the King's great nef Philippa, bearing within it the most of those present at his banquet the night before, set its huge sail, adorned with the lions and the lilies, and turned its brazen beak for England. Behind it went five smaller cogs crammed with squires, archers and men-at-arms.

Nigel and his companions lined the ramparts of the castle and waved their caps as the bluff, burly vessels, with drums beating and trumpets clanging, a hundred knightly pennons streaming from their decks and the red cross of England over all, rolled slowly out to the open sea. Then when they had watched them until they were hull down they turned, with hearts heavy at being left behind, to make ready for their own more distant venture.

It took them four days of hard work ere their preparations were complete, for many were the needs of a small force sailing to a strange country. Three ships had been left to them, the cog Thomas of Romney, the Grace Dieu of Hythe, and the Basilisk of Southampton, into each of which one hundred men were stowed, besides the thirty seamen who formed the crew. In the hold were forty horses, amongst them Pommers, much wearied by his long idleness, and homesick for the slopes of Surrey where his great limbs might find the work he craved. Then the food and the water, the bow-staves and the sheaves of arrows, the horseshoes, the nails, the hammers, the knives, the axes, the ropes, the vats of hay, the green fodder and a score of other things were packed aboard. Always by the side of the ships stood the stern young knight Sir Robert, checking, testing, watching and controlling, saying little, for he was a man of few words, but with his eyes, his hands, and if need be his heavy, dog-whip, wherever they were wanted.

The seamen of the Basilisk, being from a free port, had the old feud against the men of the Cinque Ports, who were looked upon by the other mariners of England as being unduly favored by the King. A ship of the West Country could scarce meet with one from the Narrow Seas without blood flowing. Hence sprang sudden broils on the quay side, when with yell and blow the Thomases and Grace Dieus, Saint Leonard on their lips and murder in their hearts, would fall upon the Basilisks. Then amid the whirl of cudgels and the clash of knives would spring the tiger figure of the young leader, lashing mercilessly to right and left like a tamer among his wolves, until he had beaten them howling back to their work. Upon the morning of the fourth day all was ready, and the ropes being cast off the three little ships were warped down the harbor by their own pinnaces until they were swallowed up in the swirling folds of a Channel mist.

Though small in numbers, it was no mean force which Edward had dispatched to succor the hard-pressed English garrisons in Brittany. There was scarce a man among them who was not an old soldier, and their leaders were men of note in council and in war. Knolles flew his flag of the black raven aboard the Basilisk. With him were Nigel and his own Squire John Hawthorn. Of his hundred men, forty were Yorkshire Dalesmen and forty were men of Lincoln, all noted archers, with old Wat of Carlisle, a grizzled veteran of border warfare, to lead them.

Already Aylward by his skill and strength had won his way to an under-officership amongst them, and shared with Long Ned Widdington, a huge North Countryman, the reputation of coming next to famous Wat Carlisle in all that makes an archer. The men-at-arms too were war-hardened soldiers, with Black Simon of Norwich, the same who had sailed from Winchelsea, to lead them. With his heart filled with hatred for the French who had slain all who were dear to him, he followed like a bloodhound over land and sea to any spot where he might glut his vengeance. Such also were the men who sailed in the other ships, Cheshire men from the Welsh borders in the cog Thomas, and Cumberland men, used to Scottish warfare, in the Grace Dieu.

Sir James Astley hung his shield of cinquefoil ermine over the quarter of the Thomas. Lord Thomas Percy, a cadet of Alnwick, famous already for the high spirit of that house which for ages was the bar upon the landward gate of England, showed his blue lion rampant as leader of the Grace Dieu. Such was the goodly company Saint-Malo bound, who warped from Calais Harbor to plunge into the thick reek of a Channel mist.

A slight breeze blew from the eastward, and the high-ended, round-bodied craft rolled slowly down the Channel. The mist rose a little at times, so that they had sight of each other dipping and rising upon a sleek, oily sea, but again it would sink down, settling over the top, shrouding the great yard, and finally frothing over the deck until even the water alongside had vanished from their view and they were afloat on a little raft in an ocean of vapor. A thin cold rain was falling, and the archers were crowded under the shelter of the overhanging poop and forecastle, where some spent the hours at dice, some in sleep, and many in trimming their arrows or polishing their weapons.

At the farther end, seated on a barrel as a throne of honor, with trays and boxes of feathers around him, was Bartholomew the bowyer and Fletcher, a fat, bald-headed man, whose task it was to see that every man's tackle was as it should be, and who had the privilege of selling such extras as they might need. A group of archers with their staves and quivers filed before him with complaints or requests, while half a dozen of the seniors gathered at his back and listened with grinning faces to his comments and rebukes.

"Canst not string it?" he was saying to a young bowman. "Then surely the string is overshort or the stave overlong. It could not by chance be the fault of thy own baby arms more fit to draw on thy hosen than to dress a warbow. Thou lazy lurdan, thus is it strung!" He seized the stave by the center in his right hand, leaned the end on the inside of his right foot, and then, pulling the upper nock down with the left hand, slid the eye of the string easily into place. "Now I pray thee to unstring it again," handing it to the bowman.

The youth with an effort did so, but he was too slow in disengaging his fingers, and the string sliding down with a snap from the upper nock caught and pinched them sorely against the stave. A roar of laughter, like the clap of a wave, swept down the deck as the luckless bowman danced and wrung his hand.

"Serve thee well right, thou redeless fool!" growled the old bowyer. "So fine a bow is wasted in such hands. How now, Samkin? I can teach you little of your trade, I trow. Here is a bow dressed as it should be; but it would, as you say, be the better for a white band to mark the true nocking point in the center of this red wrapping of silk. Leave it and I will tend to it anon. And you, Wat? A fresh head on yonder stele? Lord, that a man should carry four trades under one hat, and be bowyer, fletcher, stringer and headmaker! Four men's work for old Bartholomew and one man's pay!"

"Nay, say no more about that," growled an old wizened bowman, with a brown-parchment skin and little beady eyes. "It is better in these days to mend a bow than to bend one. You who never looked a Frenchman in the face are pricked off for ninepence a day, and I, who have fought five stricken fields, can earn but fourpence."

"It is in my mind, John of Tuxford, that you have looked in the face more pots of mead than Frenchmen," said the old bowyer. "I am swinking from dawn to night, while you are guzzling in an alestake. How now, youngster? Overbowed? Put your bow in the tiller.

It draws at sixty pounds—not a pennyweight too much for a man of your inches. Lay more body to it, lad, and it will come to you. If your bow be not stiff, how can you hope for a twenty-score flight. Feathers? Aye, plenty and of the best. Here, peacock at a groat each. Surely a dandy archer like you, Tom Beverley, with gold earrings in your ears, would have no feathering but peacocks?"

"So the shaft fly straight, I care not of the feather," said the bowman, a tall young Yorkshireman, counting out pennies on the palm of his horny hand.

"Gray goose-feathers are but a farthing. These on the left are a halfpenny, for they are of the wild goose, and the second feather of a fenny goose is worth more than the pinion of a tame one. These in the brass tray are dropped feathers, and a dropped feather is better than a plucked one. Buy a score of these, lad, and cut them saddle-backed or swine-backed, the one for a dead shaft and the other for a smooth flyer, and no man in the company will swing a better-fletched quiver over his shoulder."

It chanced that the opinion of the bowyer on this and other points differed from that of Long Ned of Widdington, a surly straw-bearded Yorkshireman, who had listened with a sneering face to his counsel. Now he broke in suddenly upon the bowyer's talk. "You would do better to sell bows than to try to teach others how to use them," said he; "for indeed, Bartholomew, that head of thine has no more sense within it than it has hairs without. If you had drawn string for as many months as I have years you would know that a straight-cut feather flies smoother than a swine-backed, and pity it is that these young bowmen have none to teach them better!"

This attack upon his professional knowledge touched the old bowyer on the raw. His fat face became suffused with blood and his eyes glared with fury as he turned upon the archer. "You seven-foot barrel of lies!" he cried. " All-hallows be my aid, and I will teach you to open your slabbing mouth against me! Pluck forth your sword and stand out on yonder deck, that we may see who is the man of us twain. May I never twirl a shaft over my thumb nail if I do not put Bartholomew's mark upon your thick head!"

A score of rough voices joined at once in the quarrel, some upholding the bowyer and others taking the part of the North Countryman. A red-headed Dalesman snatched up a sword, but was felled by a blow from the fist of his neighbor. Instantly, with a buzz like a swarm of angry hornets, the bowmen were out on the deck; but ere a blow was struck Knolles was amongst them with granite face and eyes of fire.

"Stand apart, I say! I will warrant you enough fighting to cool your blood ere you see England once more. Loring, Hawthorn, cut any man down who raises his hand. Have you aught to say, you fox-haired rascal?" He thrust his face within two inches of that of the red man who had first seized his sword. The fellow shrank back, cowed, from his fierce eyes. "Now stint your noise, all of you, and stretch your long ears. Trumpeter, blow once more!"

A bugle call had been sounded every quarter of an hour so as to keep in touch with the other two vessels who were invisible in the fog. Now the high clear note rang out once more, the call of a fierce sea-creature to its mates, but no answer came back from the thick wall which pent them in. Again and again they called, and again and again with bated breath they waited for an answer.

"Where is the Shipman?" asked Knolles. "What is your name, fellow? Do you dare call yourself master-mariner?"

"My name is Nat Dennis, fair sir," said the gray-bearded old seaman. "It is thirty years since first I showed my cartel and blew trumpet for a crew at the water-gate of Southampton. If any man may call himself master-mariner, it is surely I."

"Where are our two ships?"

"Nay, sir, who can say in this fog?"

"Fellow, it was your place to hold them together."

"I have but the eyes God gave me, fair sir, and they cannot see through a cloud."

"Had it been fair, I, who am a soldier, could have kept them in company. Since it was foul, we looked to you, who are called a mariner, to do so. You have not done it. You have lost two of my ships ere the venture is begun."

THE WHITE COMPANY AND SIR NIGEL

"Nay, fair sir, I pray you to consider—"

"Enough words!" said Knolles sternly. "Words will not give me back my two hundred men. Unless I find them before I come to Saint-Malo, I swear by Saint Wilfrid of Ripon that it will be an evil day for you! Enough! Go forth and do what you may!"

For five hours with a light breeze behind them they lurched through the heavy fog, the cold rain still matting their beards and shining on their faces. Sometimes they could see a circle of tossing water for a bowshot or so in each direction, and then the wreaths would crawl in upon them once more and bank them thickly round. They had long ceased to blow the trumpet for their missing comrades, but had hopes when clear weather came to find them still in sight. By the shipman's reckoning they were now about midway between the two shores.

Nigel was leaning against the bulwarks, his thoughts away in the dingle at Cosford and out on the heather-clad slopes of Hindhead, when something struck his ear. It was a thin clear clang of metal, pealing out high above the dull murmur of the sea, the creak of the boom and the flap of the sail. He listened, and again it was borne to his ear.

"Hark, my lord!" said he to Sir Robert. "Is there not a sound in the fog?"

They both listened together with sidelong heads. Then it rang clearly forth once more, but this time in another direction. It had been on the bow; now it was on the quarter. Again it sounded, and again. Now it had moved to the other bow; now back to the quarter again; now it was near; and now so far that it was but a faint tinkle on the ear. By this time every man on board, seamen, archers and men-at-arms, were crowding the sides of the vessel. All round them there were noises in the darkness, and yet the wall of fog lay wet against their very faces. And the noises were such as were strange to their ears, always the same high musical clashing.

The old shipman shook his head and crossed himself.

"In thirty years upon the waters I have never heard the like," said he. "The Devil is ever loose in a fog. Well is he named the Prince of Darkness."

A wave of panic passed over the vessel, and these rough and hardy men who feared no mortal foe shook with terror at the shadows of their own minds. They stared into the cloud with blanched faces and fixed eyes, as though each instant some fearsome shape might break in upon them. And as they stared there came a gust of wind. For a moment the fog-bank rose and a circle of ocean lay before them.

It was covered with vessels. On all sides they lay thick upon its surface. They were huge caracks, high-ended and portly, with red sides and bulwarks carved and crusted with gold. Each had one great sail set and was driving down channel on the same course at the Basilisk. Their decks were thick with men, and from their high poops came the weird clashing which filled the air. For one moment they lay there, this wondrous fleet, surging slowly forward, framed in gray vapor. The next the clouds closed in and they had vanished from view. There was a long hush, and then a buzz of excited voices.

"The Spaniards!" cried a dozen bowmen and sailors.

"I should have known it," said the shipman. "I call to mind on the Biscay Coast how they would clash their cymbals after the fashion of the heathen Moor with whom they fight; but what would you have me do, fair sir? If the fog rises we are all dead men."

"There were thirty ships at the least," said Knolles, with a moody brow. "If we have seen them I trow that they have also seen us. They will lay us aboard."

"Nay, fair sir, it is in my mind that our ship is lighter and faster than theirs. If the fog hold another hour we should be through them."

"Stand to your arms!" yelled Knolles. "Stand to your arms! They are on us!"

The Basilisk had indeed been spied from the Spanish Admiral's ship before the fog closed down. With so light a breeze, and such a fog, he could not hope to find her under sail. But by an evil chance not a bowshot from the great Spanish carack was a low galley, thin and swift, with oars which could speed her against wind or tide. She also had seen the Basilisk and it was to her that the Spanish leader shouted his orders. For a few minutes she hunted through the fog, and then sprang out of it like a lean and stealthy beast upon its prey. It was the sight of the long dark shadow gliding after them which had brought that wild shout of alarm from the lips of the English knight. In another instant the starboard oars of the galley had been shipped, the sides of the two vessels grated together, and a stream of swarthy, red-capped Spaniards were swarming up the sides of the Basilisk and dropped with yells of triumph upon her deck.

For a moment it seemed as if the vessel was captured without a blow being struck, for the men of the English ship had run wildly in all directions to look for their arms. Scores of archers might be seen under the shadow of the forecastle and the poop bending their bowstaves to string them with the cords from their waterproof cases. Others were scrambling over saddles, barrels and cases in wild search of their quivers. Each as he came upon his arrows pulled out a few to lend to his less fortunate comrades. In mad haste the men-at-arms also were feeling and grasping in the dark corners, picking up steel caps which would not fit them, hurling them down on the deck, and snatching eagerly at any swords or spears that came their way.

The center of the ship was held by the Spaniards, and having slain all who stood before them, they were pressing up to either end before they were made to understand that it was no fat sheep but a most fierce old wolf which they had taken by the ears.

If the lesson was late, it was the more thorough. Attacked on both sides and hopelessly outnumbered, the Spaniards, who had never doubted that this little craft was a merchant-ship, were cut off to the last man. It was no fight, but a butchery. In vain the survivors ran screaming prayers to the saints and threw themselves down into the galley alongside. It also had been riddled with arrows from the poop of the Basilisk, and both the crew on the deck and the galley-slaves in the outriggers at either side lay dead in rows under the overwhelming shower from above. From stem to rudder every foot of her was furred with arrows. It was but a floating coffin piled with dead and dying men, which wallowed in the waves behind them as the Basilisk lurched onward and left her in the fog.

In their first rush on to the Basilisk, the Spaniards had seized six of the crew and four unarmed archers. Their throats had been cut and their bodies tossed overboard. Now the Spaniards who littered the deck, wounded and dead, were thrust over the side in the same fashion. One ran down into the hold and had to be hunted and killed squealing under the blows like a rat in the darkness. Within half an hour no sign was left of this grim meeting in the fog save for the crimson splashes upon bulwarks and deck. The archers, flushed and merry, were unstringing their bows once more, for in spite of the water glue the damp air took the strength from the cords. Some were hunting about for arrows which might have stuck inboard, and some tying up small injuries received in the scuffle. But an anxious shadow still lingered upon the face of Sir Robert, and he peered fixedly about him through the fog.

"Go among the archers, Hawthorne," said he to his Squire. "Charge them on their lives to make no sound! You also, Loring. Go to the afterguard and say the same to them. We are lost if one of these great ships should spy us."

For an hour with bated breath they stole through the fleet, still hearing the cymbals clashing all round them, for in this way the Spaniards held themselves together. Once the wild music came from above their very prow, and so warned them to change their course. Once also a huge vessel loomed for an instant upon their quarter, but they turned two points away from her, and she blurred and vanished. Soon the cymbals were but a distant tinkling, and at last they died gradually away.

"It is none too soon," said the old shipman, pointing to a yellowish tint in the haze above them. "See yonder! It is the sun which wins through. It will be here anon. Ah! said I not so?"

A sickly sun, no larger and far dimmer than the moon, had indeed shown its face, with cloud-wreaths smoking across it. As they looked up it waxed larger and brighter before their eyes—a yellow halo spread round it, one ray broke through, and then a funnel of golden light poured down upon them, widening swiftly at the base. A minute later they were sailing on a clear blue sea with an azure cloud-flecked sky above their heads, and such a scene beneath it as each of them would carry in his memory while memory remained.

They were in mid-channel. The white and green coasts of Picardy and of Kent lay clear upon either side of them. The wide channel stretched in front, deepening from the light blue beneath their prow to purple on the far sky-line. Behind them was that thick bank of cloud from which they had just burst. It lay like a gray wall from east to west, and through it were breaking the high shadowy forms of the ships of Spain. Four of them had already emerged, their red bodies, gilded sides and painted sails shining gloriously in the evening sun. Every instant a fresh golden spot grew out of the fog, which blazed like a star for an instant, and then surged forward to show itself as the brazen beak of the great red vessel which bore it. Looking back, the whole bank of cloud was broken by the widespread line of noble ships which were bursting through it. The Basilisk lay a mile or more in front of them and two miles clear of their wing. Five miles farther off, in the direction of the French coast, two other small ships were running down Channel. A cry of joy from Robert Knolles and a hearty prayer of gratitude to the saints from the old shipman hailed them as their missing comrades, the cog Thomas and the Grace Dieu.

But fair as was the view of their lost friends, and wondrous the appearance of the Spanish ships, it was not on those that the eyes of the men of the Basilisk were chiefly bent. A greater sight lay before them—a sight which brought them clustering to the forecastle with eager eyes and pointing fingers. The English fleet was coming forth from the Winchelsea Coast. Already before the fog lifted a fast galleass had brought the news down Channel that the Spanish were on the sea, and the King's fleet was under way. Now their long array of sails, gay with the coats and colors of the towns which had furnished them, lay bright against the Kentish coast from Dungeness Point to Rye. Nine and twenty ships were there from Southampton, Shoreham, Winchelsea, Hastings, Rye, Hythe, Romney, Folkestone, Deal, Dover and Sandwich. With their great sails slued round to catch the wind they ran out, whilst the Spanish, like the gallant foes that they have ever been, turned their heads landward to meet them. With flaunting banners and painted sails, blaring trumpets and clashing cymbals, the two glittering fleets, dipping and rising on the long Channel swell, drew slowly together.

King Edward had been lying all day in his great ship the Philippa, a mile out from the Camber Sands, waiting for the coming of the Spaniards. Above the huge sail which bore the royal arms flew the red cross of England. Along the bulwarks were shown the shields of forty knights, the flower of English chivalry, and as many pennons floated from the deck. The high ends of the ship glittered with the weapons of the men-at-arms, and the waist was crammed with the archers. From time to time a crash of nakers and blare of trumpets burst from the royal ship, and was answered by her great neighbors, the Lion on which the Black Prince flew his flag, the Christopher with the Earl of Suffolk, the Salle du Roi of Robert of Namur, and the Grace Marie of Sir Thomas Holland. Farther off lay the White Swan, bearing the arms of Mowbray, the Palmer of Deal, flying the Black Head of Audley, and the Kentish man under the Lord Beauchamp. The rest lay, anchored but ready, at the mouth of Winchelsea Creek.

The King sat upon a keg in the fore part of his ship, with little John of Richmond, who was no more than a schoolboy, perched upon his knee. Edward was clad in the black velvet jacket which was his favorite garb, and wore a small brown-beaver hat with a white plume at the side. A rich cloak of fur turned up with miniver drooped from his shoulders. Behind him were a score of his knights, brilliant in silks and sarcenets, some seated on an upturned boat and some swinging their legs from the bulwark.

In front stood John Chandos in a party-colored jupon, one foot raised upon the anchor-stock, picking at the strings of his guitar and singing a song which he had learned at Marienburg when last he helped the Teutonic knights against the heathen. The King, his knights, and even the archers in the waist below them, laughed at the merry lilt and joined lustily in the chorus, while the men of the neighboring ships leaned over the side to hearken to the deep chant rolling over the waters.

But there came a sudden interruption to the song. A sharp, harsh shout came down from the lookout stationed in the circular top at the end of the mast. "I spy a sail—two sails!" he cried.

John Bunce the King's shipman shaded his eyes and stared at the long fog-bank which shrouded the northern channel. Chandos, with his fingers over the strings of his guitar, the King, the knights, all gazed in the same direction. Two small dark shapes had burst forth, and then after some minutes a third.

"Surely they are the Spaniards?" said the King.

"Nay, sire," the seaman answered, "the Spaniards are greater ships and are painted red. I know not what these may be."

"But I could hazard a guess!" cried Chandos. "Surely they are the three ships with my own men on their way to Brittany."

"You have hit it, John," said the King. "But look, I pray you! What in the name of the Virgin is that?"

Four brilliant stars of flashing light had shone out from different points of the cloud-bank. The neat instant as many tall ships had swooped forth into the sunshine. A fierce shout rang from the King's ship, and was taken up all down the line, until the whole coast from Dungeness to Winchelsea echoed the warlike greeting. The King sprang up with a joyous face.

"The game is afoot, my friends!" said he. "Dress, John! Dress, Walter! Quick all of you! Squires, bring the harness! Let each tend to himself, for the time is short."

A strange sight it was to see these forty nobles tearing off their clothes and littering the deck with velvets and satins, whilst the squire of each, as busy as an ostler before a race, stooped and pulled and strained and riveted, fastening the bassinets, the leg-pieces, the front and the back plates, until the silken courtier had become the man of steel. When their work was finished, there stood a stern group of warriors where the light dandies had sung and jested round Sir John's guitar. Below in orderly silence the archers were mustering under their officers and taking their allotted stations. A dozen had swarmed up to their hazardous post in the little tower in the tops.

"Bring wine, Nicholas!" cried the King. "Gentlemen, ere you close your visors I pray you to take a last rouse with me. You will be dry enough, I promise you, before your lips are free once more. To what shall we drink, John?"

"To the men of Spain," said Chandos, his sharp face peering like a gaunt bird through the gap in his helmet. "May their hearts be stout and their spirits high this day!"

"Well said, John!" cried the King, and the knights laughed joyously as they drank. "Now, fair sirs, let each to his post! I am warden here on the forecastle. Do you, John, take charge of the afterguard. Walter, James, William, Fitzallan, Goldesborough, Reginald—you will stay with me! John, you may pick whom you will and the others will bide with the archers. Now bear straight at the center, mastershipman. Ere yonder sun sets we will bring a red ship back as a gift to our ladies, or never look upon a lady's face again."

The art of sailing into a wind had not yet been invented, nor was there any fore-and-aft canvas, save for small headsails with which a vessel could be turned. Hence the English fleet had to take a long slant down channel to meet their enemies; but as the Spaniards coming before the wind were equally anxious to engage there was the less delay. With stately pomp and dignity, the two great fleets approached.

It chanced that one fine carack had outstripped its consorts and came sweeping along, all red and gold, with a fringe of twinkling steel, a good half-mile before the fleet. Edward looked at her with a kindling eye, for indeed she was a noble sight with the blue water creaming under her gilded prow.

"This is a most worthy and debonair vessel, Master Bunce," said he to the shipman beside him. "I would fain have a tilt with her. I pray you to hold us straight that we may bear her down."

"If I hold her straight, then one or other must sink, and it may be both," the seaman answered.

"I doubt not that with the help of our Lady we shall do our part," said the King. "Hold her straight, master-shipman, as I have told you."

Now the two vessels were within arrow flight, and the bolts from the crossbowmen pattered upon the English ship. These short thick devil's darts were everywhere humming like great wasps through the air, crashing against the bulwarks, beating upon the deck, ringing loudly on the armor of the knights, or with a soft muffled thud sinking to the socket in a victim.

The bowmen along either side of the Philippa had stood motionless waiting for their orders, but now there was a sharp shout from their leader, and every string twanged together. The air was full of their harping, together with the swish of the arrows, the long-drawn keening of the bowmen and the short deep bark of the under-officers. "Steady, steady! Loose steady! Shoot wholly together! Twelve score paces! Ten score! Now eight! Shoot wholly together!" Their gruff shouts broke through the high shrill cry like the deep roar of a wave through the howl of the wind.

As the two great ships hurtled together the Spaniard turned away a few points so that the blow should be a glancing one. None the less it was terrific. A dozen men in the tops of the carack were balancing a huge stone with the intention of dropping it over on the English deck. With a scream of horror they saw the mast cracking beneath them. Over it went, slowly at first, then faster, until with a crash it came down on its side, sending them flying like stones from a sling far out into the sea. A swath of crushed bodies lay across the deck where the mast had fallen. But the English ship had not escaped unscathed. Her mast held, it is true, but the mighty shock not only stretched every man flat upon the deck, but had shaken a score of those who lined her sides into the sea. One bowman was hurled from the top, and his body fell with a dreadful crash at the very side of the prostrate King upon the forecastle. Many were thrown down with broken arms and legs from the high castles at either end into the waist of the ship. Worst of all, the seams had been opened by the crash and the water was gushing in at a dozen places.

But these were men of experience and of discipline, men who had already fought together by sea and by land, so that each knew his place and his duty. Those who could staggered to their feet and helped up a score or more of knights who were rolling and clashing in the scuppers unable to rise for the weight of their armor. The bowmen formed up as before. The seamen ran to the gaping seams with oakum and with tar. In ten minutes order had been restored and the Philippa, though shaken and weakened, was ready for battle once more. The King was glaring round him like a wounded boar.

"Grapple my ship with that," he cried, pointing to the crippled Spaniard, "for I would have possession of her!"

But already the breeze had carried them past it, and a dozen Spanish ships were bearing down full upon them.

"We cannot win back to her, lest we show our flank to these others," said the shipman.

"Let her go, her way!" cried the knights. "You shall have better than her."

"By Saint George! you speak the truth," said the King, "for she is ours when we have time to take her. These also seem very worthy ships which are drawing up to us, and I pray you, master-shipman, that you will have a tilt with the nearest."

A great carack was within a bowshot of them and crossing their bows. Bunce looked up at his mast, and he saw that already it was shaken and drooping. Another blow and it would be over the side and his ship a helpless log upon the water. He jammed his helm round therefore, and ran his ship alongside the Spaniard, throwing out his hooks and iron chains as he did so.

They, no less eager, grappled the Philippa both fore and aft, and the two vessels, linked tightly together, surged slowly over the long blue rollers. Over their bulwarks hung a cloud of men locked together in a desperate struggle, sometimes surging forward on to the deck of the Spaniard, sometimes recoiling back on to the King's ship, reeling this way and that, with the swords flickering like silver flames above them, while the long-drawn cry of rage and agony swelled up like a wolf's howl to the calm blue heaven above them.

But now ship after ship of the English had come up, each throwing its iron over the nearest Spaniard and striving to board her high red sides. Twenty ships were drifting in furious single combat after the manner of the Philippa, until the whole surface of the sea was covered with a succession of these desperate duels. The dismasted carack, which the King's ship had left behind it, had been carried by the Earl of Suffolk's Christopher, and the water was dotted with the heads of her crew. An English ship had been sunk by a huge stone discharged from an engine, and her men also were struggling in the waves, none having leisure to lend them a hand. A second English ship was caught between two of the Spanish vessels and overwhelmed by a rush of boarders so that not a man of her was left alive. On the other hand, Mowbray and Audley had each taken the caracks which were opposed to them, and the battle in the center, after swaying this way and that, was turning now in favor of the Islanders.

The Black Prince, with the Lion, the Grace Marie and four other ships had swept round to turn the Spanish flank; but the movement was seen, and the Spaniards had ten ships with which to meet it, one of them their great carack the St. Iago di Compostella. To this ship the Prince had attached his little cog and strove desperately to board her, but her side was so high and the defense so desperate that his men could never get beyond her bulwarks but were hurled down again and again with a clang and clash to the deck beneath. Her side bristled with crossbowmen, who shot straight down on to the packed waist of the Lion, so that the dead lay there in heaps. But the most dangerous of all was a swarthy black-bearded giant in the tops, who crouched so that none could see him, but rising every now and then with a huge lump of iron between his hands, hurled it down with such force that nothing would stop it. Again and again these ponderous bolts crashed through the deck and hurtled down into the bottom of the ship, starting the planks and shattering all that came in their way.

The Prince, clad in that dark armor which gave him his name, was directing the attack from the poop when the shipman rushed wildly up to him with fear on his face.

"Sire!" he cried. "The ship may not stand against these blows. A few more will sink her! Already the water floods inboard."

The Prince looked up, and as he did so the shaggy beard showed once more and two brawny arms swept downward. A great slug, whizzing down, beat a gaping hole in the deck, and fell rending and riving into the hold below. The master-mariner tore his grizzled hair.

"Another leak!" he cried. "I pray to Saint Leonard to bear us up this day! Twenty of my shipmen are bailing with buckets, but the water rises on them fast. The vessel may not float another hour."

The Prince had snatched a crossbow from one of his attendants and leveled it at the Spaniard's tops. At the very instant when the seaman stood erect with a fresh bar in his hands, the bolt took him full in the face, and his body fell forward over the parapet, hanging there head downward. A howl of exultation burst from the English at the sight, answered by a wild roar of anger from the Spaniards. A seaman had run from the Lion's hold and whispered in the ear of the shipman. He turned an ashen face upon the Prince.

"It is even as I say, sire. The ship is sinking beneath our feet!" he cried.

"The more need that we should gain another," said he. "Sir Henry Stokes, Sir Thomas Stourton, William, John of Clifton, here lies our road! Advance my banner, Thomas de Mohun! On, and the day is ours!"

By a desperate scramble a dozen men, the Prince at their bead, gained a footing on the edge of the Spaniard's deck. Some slashed furiously to clear a space, others hung over, clutching the rail with one hand and pulling up their comrades from below. Every instant that they could hold their own their strength increased, till twenty had become thirty and thirty forty, when of a sudden the new-comers, still reaching forth to their comrades below, saw the deck beneath them reel and vanish in a swirling sheet of foam. The Prince's ship had foundered.

A yell went up from the Spaniards as they turned furiously upon the small band who had reached their deck. Already the Prince and his men had carried the poop, and from that high station they beat back their swarming enemies. But crossbow darts pelted and thudded among their ranks till a third of their number were stretched upon the planks. Lined across the deck they could hardly keep an unbroken front to the leaping, surging crowd who pressed upon them. Another rush, or another after that, must assuredly break them, for these dark men of Spain, hardened by an endless struggle with the Moors, were fierce and stubborn fighters. But hark to this sudden roar upon the farther side of them!

"Saint George! Saint George! A Knolles to the rescue!" A small craft had run alongside and sixty men had swarmed on the deck of the St. Iago. Caught between two fires, the Spaniards wavered and broke. The fight became a massacre. Down from the poop sprang the Prince's men. Up from the waist rushed the new-comers. There were five dreadful minutes of blows and screams and prayers with struggling figures clinging to the bulwarks and sullen splashes into the water below. Then it was over, and a crowd of weary, over-strained men leaned panting upon their weapons, or lay breathless and exhausted upon the deck of the captured carack.

The Prince had pulled up his visor and lowered his beaver. He smiled proudly as he gazed around him and wiped his streaming face. "Where is the shipman?" he asked. "Let him lead us against another ship."

"Nay, sire, the shipman and all his men have stink in the Lion," said Thomas de Mohun, a young knight of the West Country, who carried the standard. "We have lost our ship and the half of our following. I fear that we can fight no more."

"It matters the less since the day is already ours," said the Prince, looking over the sea. "My noble father's royal banner flies upon yonder Spaniard. Mowbray, Audley, Suffolk, Beauchamp, Namur, Tracey, Stafford, Arundel, each has his flag over a scarlet carack, even as mine floats over this. See, yonder squadron is already far beyond our reach. But surely we owe thanks to you who came at so perilous a moment to our aid. Your face I have seen, and your coat-armor also, young sir, though I cannot lay my tongue to your name. Let me know that I may thank you."

He had turned to Nigel, who stood flushed and joyous at the head of the boarders from the Basilisk.

"I am but a Squire, sire, and can claim no thanks, for there is nothing that I have done. Here is our leader."

The Prince's eyes fell upon the shield charged with the Black Raven and the stern young face of him who bore it.

"Sir Robert Knolles," said he, "I had thought you were on your way to Brittany."

"I was so, sire, when I had the fortune to see this battle as I passed."

The Prince laughed. "It would indeed be to ask too much, Robert, that you should keep on your course when much honor was to be gathered so close to you. But now I pray you that you will come back with us to Winchelsea, for well I know that my father would fain thank you for what you have done this day."

But Robert Knolles shook his head. "I have your father's command, sire, and without his order I may not go against it. Our people are hard-pressed in Brittany, and it is not for me to linger on the way. I pray you, sire, if you must needs mention me to the King, to crave his pardon that I should have broken my journey thus."

"You are right, Robert. God-speed you on your way! And I would that I were sailing under your banner, for I see clearly that you will take your people where they may worshipfully win worship. Perchance I also maybe in Brittany before the year is past."

The Prince turned to the task of gathering his weary people together, and the Basilisks passed over the side once more and dropped down on to their own little ship. They poled her off from the captured Spaniard and set their sail with their prow for the south. Far ahead of them were their two consorts, beating towards them in the hope of giving help, while down Channel were a score of Spanish ships with a few of the English vessels hanging upon their skirts. The sun lay low on the water, and its level beams glowed upon the scarlet and gold of fourteen great caracks, each flying the cross of Saint George, and towering high above the cluster of English ships which, with brave waving of flags and blaring of music, were moving slowly towards the Kentish coast.

CHAPTER XVIII

HOW BLACK SIMON CLAIMED FORFEIT FROM THE KING OF SARK

FOR a day and a half the small fleet made good progress, but on the second morning, after sighting Cape de la Hague, there came a brisk land wind which blew them out to sea. It grew into a squall with rain and fog so that they were two more days beating back. Next morning they found themselves in a dangerous rock-studded sea with a small island upon their starboard quarter. It was girdled with high granite cliffs of a reddish hue, and slopes of bright-green grassland lay above them. A second smaller island lay beside it. Dennis the shipman shook his head as he looked.

"That is Brechou," said he, "and the larger one is the Island of Sark. If ever I be cast away, I pray the saints that I may not be upon yonder coast!"

Knolles gazed across at it. "You say well, master-shipman," said he. "It does appear to be a rocky and perilous spot."

"Nay, it is the rocky hearts of those who dwell upon it that I had in my mind," the old sailor answered. "We are well safe in three goodly vessels, but had we been here in a small craft I make no doubt that they would have already had their boats out against us."

"Who then are these people, and how do they live upon so small and windswept an island?" asked the soldier.

"They do not live from the island, fair sir, but from what they can gather upon the sea around it. They are broken folk from all countries, justice-fliers, prison-breakers, reavers, escaped bondsmen, murderers and staff-strikers who have made their way to this out-land place and hold it against all comers. There is one here who could tell you of them and of their ways, for he was long time pris-oner amongst them." The seaman pointed to Black Simon, the dark man from Norwich, who was leaning against the side lost in moody thought and staring with a brooding eye at the distant shore.

"How now, fellow?" asked Knolles. "What is this I hear? Is it indeed sooth that you have been a captive upon this island?"

"It is true, fair sir. For eight months I have been servant to the man whom they call their King. His name is La Muette, and he comes from Jersey nor is there under God's sky a man whom I have more desire to see."

"Has he then mishandled you?"

Black Simon gave a wry smile and pulled off his jerkin. His lean sinewy back was waled and puckered with white scars. "He has left his sign of hand upon me," said he. "He swore that he would break me to his will, and thus he tried to do it. But most I desire to see him because he hath lost a wager to me and I would fain be paid."

"This is a strange saying," said Knolles. "What is this wager, and why should he pay you?"

"It is but a small matter," Simon answered; "but I am a poor man and the payment would be welcome. Should it have chanced that we stopped at this island I should have craved your leave that I go ashore and ask for that which I have fairly won."

Sir Robert Knolles laughed. "This business tickleth my fancy," said he. "As to stopping at the island, this shipman tells me that we must needs wait a day and a night, for that we have strained our planks. But if you should go ashore, how will you be sure that you will be free to depart, or that you will see this King of whom you speak?"

Black Simon's dark face was shining with a fierce joy. "Fair sir, I will ever be your debtor if you will let me go. Concerning what you ask, I know this island even as I know the streets of Norwich, as you may well believe seeing that it is but a small place and I upon it for near a year. Should I land after dark, I could win my way to the

King's house, and if he be not dead or distraught with drink I could have speech with him alone, for I know his ways and his hours and how he may be found. I would ask only that Aylward the archer may go with me, that I may have one friend at my side if things should chance to go awry."

Knolles thought awhile. "It is much that you ask," said he, "for by God's truth I reckon that you and this friend of yours are two of my men whom I would be least ready to lose. I have seen you both at grips with the Spaniards and I know you. But I trust you, and if we must indeed stop at this accursed place, then you may do as you will. If you have deceived me, or if this is a trick by which you design to leave me, then God be your friend when next we meet, for man will be of small avail!"

It proved that not only the seams had to be calked but that the cog Thomas was out of fresh water. The ships moored therefore near the Isle of Brechou, where springs were to be found. There were no people upon this little patch, but over on the farther island many figures could be seen watching them, and the twinkle of steel from among them showed that they were armed men. One boat had ventured forth and taken a good look at them, but had hurried back with the warning that they were too strong to be touched.

Black Simon found Aylward seated under the poop with his back against Bartholomew the bowyer. He was whistling merrily as he carved a girl's face upon the horn of his bow.

"My friend," said Simon, "will you come ashore to-night—for I have need of your help?"

Aylward crowed lustily. "Will I come, Simon? By my hilt, I shall be right glad to put my foot on the good brown earth once more. All my life I have trod it, and yet I would never have learned its worth had I not journeyed in these cursed ships. We will go on shore together, Simon, and we will seek out the women, if there be any there, for it seems a long year since I heard their gentle voices, and my eyes are weary of such faces as Bartholomew's or thine."

Simon's grim features relaxed into a smile. "The only face that you will see ashore, Samkin, will bring you small comfort," said he, "and I warn you that this is no easy errand, but one which may be neither sweet nor fair, for if these people take us our end will be a cruel one."

"By my hilt," said Aylward, "I am with you, gossip, wherever you may go! Say no more, therefore, for I am weary of living like a cony in a hole, and I shall be right glad to stand by you in your venture."

That night, two hours after dark, a small boat put forth from the Basilisk. It contained Simon, Aylward and two seamen. The soldiers carried their swords, and Black Simon bore a brown biscuit-bag over his shoulder. Under his direction the rowers skirted the dangerous surf which beat against the cliffs until they came to a spot where an outlying reef formed a breakwater. Within was a belt of calm water and a shallow cover with a sloping beach. Here the boat was dragged up and the seamen were ordered to wait, while Simon and Aylward started on their errand.

With the assured air of a man who knows exactly where he is and whither he is going, the man-at-arms began to clamber up a narrow fern-lined cleft among the rocks. It was no easy ascent in the darkness, but Simon climbed on like an old dog hot upon a scent, and the panting Aylward struggled after as best he might. At last they were at the summit and the archer threw himself down upon the grass.

"Nay, Simon, I have not enough breath to blow out a candle," said he. "Stint your haste for a minute, since we have a long night before us. Surely this man is a friend indeed, if you hasten so to see him."

"Such a friend," Simon answered, "that I have often dreamed of our next meeting. Now before that moon has set it will have come."

"Had it been a wench I could have understood it," said Aylward. "By these ten finger-bones, if Mary of the mill or little Kate of Compton had waited me on the brow of this cliff, I should have come up it and never known it was there. But surely I see houses and hear voices over yonder in the shadow?"

"It is their town," whispered Simon. "There are a hundred as bloody-minded cutthroats as are to be found in Christendom beneath those roofs. Hark to that!"

A fierce burst of laughter came out of the darkness, followed by a long cry of pain.

"All-hallows be with us!" cried Aylward. "What is that?"

"As like as not some poor devil has fallen into their clutches, even as I did. Come this way, Samkin, for there is a peat-cutting where we may hide. Aye, here it is, but deeper and broader than of old. Now follow me close, for if we keep within it we shall find ourselves a stone cast off the King's house."

Together they crept along the dark cutting. Suddenly Simon seized Aylward by the shoulder and pushed him into the shadow of the bank. Crouching in the darkness, they heard footsteps and voices upon the farther side of the trench. Two men sauntered along it and stopped almost at the very spot where the comrades were lying. Aylward could see their dark figures outlined against the starry sky.

"Why should you scold, Jacques," said one of them, speaking a strange half-French, half-English lingo. "*Le diable t'emporte* for a grumbling rascal. You won a woman and I got nothing. What more would you have?"

"You will have your chance off the next ship, *mon garçon*, but mine is passed. A woman, it is true—an old peasant out of the fields, with a face as yellow as a kite's claw. But Gaston, who threw a nine against my eight, got as fair a little Normandy lass as ever your eyes have seen. Curse the dice, I say! And as to my woman, I will sell her to you for a firkin of Gascony."

"I have no wine to spare, but I will give you a keg of apples," said the other. "I had it out of the Peter and Paul, the Falmouth boat that struck in Creux Bay."

"Well, well your apples may be the worse for keeping, but so is old Marie, and we can cry quits on that. Come round and drink a cup over the bargain."

They shuffled onward in the darkness.

"Heard you ever such villainy?" cried Aylward, breathing fierce and hard. "Did you hear them, Simon? A woman for a keg of apples! And my heart's root is sad for the other one, the girl of Normandy. Surely we can land to-morrow and burn all these water- rats out of their nest."

"Nay, Sir Robert will not waste time or strength ere he reach Brittany."

"Sure I am that if my little master Squire Loring had the handling of it, every woman on this island would be free ere another day had passed."

"I doubt it not," said Simon. "He is one who makes an idol of woman, after the manner of those crazy knight errants. But Sir Robert is a true soldier and hath only his purpose in view."

"Simon," said Aylward, "the light is not overgood and the place is cramped for sword-play, but if you will step out into the open I will teach you whether my master is a true soldier or not."

"Tut, man! you are as foolish yourself," said Simon. "Here we are with our work in hand, and yet you must needs fall out with me on our way to it. I say nothing against your master save that he hath the way of his fellows who follow dreams and fancies. But Knolles looks neither to right nor left and walks forward to his mark. Now, let us on, for the time passes."

"Simon, your words are neither good nor fair. When we are back on shipboard we will speak further of this matter. Now lead on, I pray you, and let us see some more of this ten-devil island."

For half a mile Simon led the way until they came to a large house which stood by itself. Peering at it from the edge of the cutting, Aylward could see that it was made from the wreckage of many vessels, for at each corner a prow was thrust out. Lights blazed within, and there came the sound of a strong voice singing a gay song which was taken up by a dozen others in the chorus.

"All is well, lad!" whispered Simon in great delight. "That is the voice of the King. It is the very song he used to sing. '*Les deux filles de Pierre.*' 'Fore God, my back tingles at the very sound of it. Here we will wait until his company take their leave."

Hour after hour they crouched in the peat-cutting, listening to the noisy songs of the revelers within, some French, some English, and all growing fouler and less articulate as the night wore on. Once a quarrel broke out and the clamor was like a cageful of wild beasts at feeding-time. Then a health was drunk and there was much stamping and cheering.

Only once was the long vigil broken. A woman came forth from the house and walked up and down, with her face sunk upon her breast. She was tall and slender, but her features could not be seen for a wimple over her head. Weary sadness could be read in her bowed back and dragging steps. Once only they saw her throw her two hands up to Heaven as one who is beyond human aid. Then she passed slowly into the house again. A moment later the door of the hall was flung open, and a shouting stumbling throng came crowding forth, with whoop and yell, into the silent night. Linking arms and striking up a chorus, they marched past the peat-cutting, their voices dwindling slowly away as they made for their homes.

"Now, Samkin, now!" cried Simon, and jumping out from the hiding-place he made for the door. It had not yet been fastened. The two comrades sprang inside. Then Simon drew the bolts so that none might interrupt them.

A long table littered with flagons and beakers lay before them. It was lit up by a line of torches, which flickered and smoked in their iron sconces. At the farther end a solitary man was seated. His head rested upon his two hands, as if he were befuddled with wine, but at the harsh sound of the snapping bolts he raised his face and looked angrily around him. It was a strange powerful head, tawny and shaggy like a lion's, with a tangled beard and a large harsh face, bloated and blotched with vice. He laughed as the new-comers entered, thinking that two of his boon companions had returned to finish a flagon. Then he stared hard and he passed his hand over his eyes like one who thinks he may be dreaming.

"*Mon Dieu!*" he cried. "Who are you and whence come you at this hour of the night? Is this the way to break into our royal presence?"

Simon approached up one side of the table and Aylward up the other. When they were close to the King, the man-at-arms plucked a torch from its socket and held it to his own face. The King staggered back with a cry, as he gazed at that grim visage.

"*Le diable noir!*" he cried. "Simon, the Englishman! What make you here?"

Simon put his hand upon his shoulder. "Sit here!" said he, and he forced the King into his seat. "Do you sit on the farther side of him, Aylward. We make a merry group, do we not? Often have I served at this table, but never did I hope to drink at it. Fill your cup, Samkin, and pass the flagon."

The King looked from one to the other with terror in his bloodshot eyes. "What would you do?" he asked. "Are you mad, that you should come here. One shout and you are at my mercy."

"Nay, my friend, I have lived too long in your house not to know the ways of it. No man-servant ever slept beneath your roof, for you feared lest your throat would be cut in the night-time. You may shout and shout, if it so please you. It chanced that I was passing on my way from England in those ships which lie off La Brechou, and I thought I would come in and have speech with you."

"Indeed, Simon, I am right glad to see you," said the King, cringing away from the fierce eyes of the soldier. "We were good friends in the past, were we not, and I cannot call to mind that I have ever done you injury. When you made your way to England by swimming to the Levantine there was none more glad in heart than I."

"If I cared to doff my doublet I could show you the marks of what your friendship has done for me in the past," said Simon. "It is printed on my back as clearly as on my memory. Why, you foul dog, there are the very rings upon the wall to which my hands were fastened, and there the stains upon the boards on which my blood has dripped! Is it not so, you king of butchers?"

The pirate chief turned whiter still. "It may be that life here was somewhat rough, Simon, but if I have wronged you in anyway, I will surely make amends. What do you ask?"

"I ask only one thing, and I have come hither that I may get it. It is that you pay me forfeit for that you have lost your wager."

"My wager, Simon! I call to mind no wager."

"But I will call it to your mind, and then I will take my payment. Often have you sworn that you would break my courage. 'By my head!' you have cried to me. 'You will crawl at my feet!' and again: 'I will wager my head that I will tame you!' Yes, yes, a score of times you have said so. In my heart, as I listened, I have taken up your gage. And now, dog, you have lost and I am here to claim the forfeit."

His long heavy sword flew from its sheath. The King, with a howl of despair, flung his arms round him, and they rolled together under the table. Aylward sat with a ghastly face, and his toes curled with horror at the sight, for he was still new to scenes of strife and his blood was too cold for such a deed. When Simon rose he tossed something into his bag and sheathed his bloody sword.

"Come, Samkin, our work is well done," said he.

"By my hilt, if I had known what it was I would have been less ready to come with you," said the archer. "Could you not have clapped a sword in his fist and let him take his chance in the hall?"

"Nay, Samkin, if you had such memories as I, you would have wished that he should die like a sheep and not like a man. What chance did he give me when he had the power? And why should I treat him better? But, Holy Virgin, what have we here?"

At the farther end of the table a woman was standing. An open door behind her showed that she had come from the inner room of the house. By her tall figure the comrades knew that she was the same that they had already seen. Her face had once been fair, but now was white and haggard with wild dark eyes full of a hopeless terror and despair. Slowly she paced up the room, her gaze fixed not upon the comrades, but upon the dreadful thing beneath the table. Then as she stooped and was sure she burst into loud laughter and clapped her hands.

"Who shall say there is no God?" she cried. "Who shall say that prayer is unavailing? Great sir, brave sir, let me kiss that conquering hand!"

"Nay, nay, dame, stand back! Well, if you must needs have one of them, take this which is the clean one."

"It is the other I crave — that which is red with his blood! Oh! joyful night when my lips have been wet with it! Now I can die in peace!"

"We must go, Aylward," said Simon. "In another hour the dawn will have broken. In daytime a rat could not cross this island and pass unseen. Come, man, and at once!"

But Aylward was at the woman's side. "Come with us, fair dame," said he. "Surely we can, at least, take you from this island, and no such change can be for the worse."

"Nay," said she, "the saints in Heaven cannot help me now until they take me to my rest. There is no place for me in the world beyond, and all my friends were slain on the day I was taken. Leave me, brave men, and let me care for myself. Already it lightens in the east, and black will be your fate if you are taken. Go, and may the blessing of one who was once a holy nun go with you and guard you from danger!"

Sir Robert Knolles was pacing the deck in the early morning, when he heard the sound of oars, and there were his two night-birds climbing up the side.

"So, fellow," said he, "have you had speech with the King of Sark?"

"Fair sir, I have seen him."

"And he has paid his forfeit?"

"He has paid it, sir!"

Knolles looked with curiosity at the bag which Simon bore. "What carry you there?" he asked.

"The stake that he has lost."

"What was it then? A goblet? A silver plate?"

For answer Simon opened his bag and shook it on the deck.

Sir Robert turned away with a whistle. "'Fore God!" said he, "it is in my mind that I carry some hard men with me to Brittany."

CHAPTER XIX

HOW A SQUIRE OF ENGLAND
MET A SQUIRE OF FRANCE

S I R Robert Knolles with his little fleet had sighted the Breton coast
near Cancale; they had rounded the Point du Grouin, and finally
had sailed past the port of St. Malo and down the long narrow estuary of the Rance until they were close to the old walled city of
Dinan, which was held by that Montfort faction whose cause the
English had espoused. Here the horses had been disembarked,
the stores were unloaded, and the whole force encamped outside
the city, whilst the leaders waited for news as to the present state of
affairs, and where there was most hope of honor and profit.

The whole of France was feeling the effects of that war with
England which had already lasted some ten years, but no Province
was in so dreadful a condition as this unhappy land of Brittany.
In Normandy or Picardy the inroads of the English were periodi-
cal with intervals of rest between; but Brittany was torn asunder
by constant civil war apart from the grapple of the two great combatants, so that there was no surcease of her sufferings. The
struggle had begun in 1341 through the rival claims of Montfort
and of Blois to the vacant dukedom. England had taken the part
of Montfort, France that of Blois. Neither faction was strong
enough to destroy the other, and so after ten years of continual
fighting, history recorded a long ineffectual list of surprises and
ambushes, of raids and skirmishes, of towns taken and retaken,
of alternate victory and defeat, in which neither party could claim

a supremacy. It mattered nothing that Montfort and Blois had both disappeared from the scene, the one dead and the other taken by the English. Their wives caught up the swords which had dropped from the hands of their lords, and the long struggle went on even more savagely than before.

In the south and east the Blois faction held the country, and Nantes the capital was garrisoned and occupied by a strong French army. In the north and west the Montfort party prevailed, for the island kingdom was at their back and always fresh sails broke the northern sky-line bearing adventurers from over the channel.

Between these two there lay a broad zone comprising all the center of the country which was a land of blood and violence, where no law prevailed save that of the sword. From end to end it was dotted with castles, some held for one side, some for the other, and many mere robber strongholds, the scenes of gross and monstrous deeds, whose brute owners, knowing that they could never be called to account, made war upon all mankind, and wrung with rack and with flame the last shilling from all who fell into their savage hands. The fields had long been untilled. Commerce was dead. From Rennes in the east to Hennebon in the west, and from Dinan in the north to Nantes in the south, there was no spot where a man's life or a woman's honor was safe. Such was the land, full of darkness and blood, the saddest, blackest spot in Christendom, into which Knolles and his men were now advancing.

But there was no sadness in the young heart of Nigel, as he rode by the side of Knolles at the head of a clump of spears, nor did it seem to him that Fate had led him into an unduly arduous path. On the contrary, he blessed the good fortune which had sent him into so delightful a country, and it seemed to him as he listened to dreadful stories of robber barons, and looked round at the black scars of war which lay branded upon the fair faces of the hills, that no hero of romances or trouveur had ever journeyed through such a land of promise, with so fair a chance of knightly venture and honorable advancement.

The Red Ferret was one deed toward his vow. Surely a second, and perhaps a better, was to be found somewhere upon this glorious country-side. He had borne himself as the others had in the sea-fight, and could not count it to his credit where he had done no more than mere duty. Something beyond this was needed for such a deed as could be laid at the feet of the Lady Mary. But surely it was to be found here in fermenting war-distracted Brittany. Then with two done it would be strange if he could not find occasion for that third one, which would complete his service and set him free to look her in the face once more. With the great yellow horse curveting beneath him, his Guildford armor gleaming in the sun, his sword clanking against his stirrup-iron, and his father's tough ash-spear in his hand, he rode with a light heart and a smiling face, looking eagerly to right and to left for any chance which his good Fate might send.

The road from Dinan to Caulnes, along which the small army was moving, rose and dipped over undulating ground, with a bare marshy plain upon the left where the river Rance ran down to the sea, while upon the right lay a wooded country with a few wretched villages, so poor and sordid that they had nothing with which to tempt the spoiler. The peasants had left them at the first twinkle of a steel cap, and lurked at the edges of the woods, ready in an instant to dive into those secret recesses known only to themselves. These creatures suffered sorely at the hands of both parties, but when the chance came they revenged their wrongs on either in a savage way which brought fresh brutalities upon their heads.

The new-comers soon had a chance of seeing to what lengths they would go, for in the roadway near to Caulnes they came upon an English man-at-arms who had been waylaid and slain by them. How they had overcome him could not be told, but how they had slain him within his armor was horribly apparent, for they had carried such a rock as eight men could lift, and had dropped it upon him as he lay, so that he was spread out in his shattered case like a crab beneath a stone. Many a fist was shaken at the distant woods and many a curse hurled at those who haunted them, as the column of scowling soldiers passed the murdered man, whose badge of the Molene cross showed him to have been a follower of that House of Bentley, whose head, Sir Walter, was at that time leader of the British forces in the country.

Sir Robert Knolles had served in Brittany before, and he marshaled his men on the march with the skill and caution of the veteran soldier, the man who leaves as little as possible to chance, having too steadfast a mind to heed the fool who may think him overcautious. He had recruited a number of bowmen and men-at-arms at Dinan; so that his following was now close upon five hundred men. In front under his own leadership were fifty mounted lancers, fully armed and ready for any sudden attack. Behind them on foot came the archers, and a second body of mounted men closed up the rear. Out upon either flank moved small bodies of cavalry, and a dozen scouts, spread fanwise, probed every gorge and dingle in front of the column. So for three days he moved slowly down the Southern Road.

Sir Thomas Percy and Sir James Astley had ridden to the head of the column, and Knolles conferred with them as they marched concerning the plan of their campaign. Percy and Astley were young and hot-headed with wild visions of dashing deeds and knight errantry, but Knolles with cold, clear brain and purpose of iron held ever his object in view.

"By the holy Dunstan and all the saints of Lindisfarne!" cried the fiery Borderer, "it goes to my heart to ride forward when there are such honorable chances on either side of us. Have I not heard that the French are at Evran beyond the river, and is it not sooth that yonder castle, the towers of which I see above the woods, is in the hands of a traitor, who is false to his liege lord of Montford? There is little profit to be gained upon this road, for the folk seem to have no heart for war. Had we ventured as far over the marches of Scotland as we now are in Brittany, we should not have lacked some honorable venture or chance of winning worship."

"You say truth, Thomas," cried Astley, a red-faced and choleric young man. "It is well certain that the French will not come to us, and surely it is the more needful that we go to them. In sooth, any soldier who sees us would smile that we should creep for three days along this road as though a thousand dangers lay before us, when we have but poor broken peasants to deal with."

But Robert Knolles shook his head. "We know not what are in these woods, or behind these hills," said he, "and when I know nothing it is my wont to prepare for the worst which may befall. It is but prudence so to do."

"Your enemies might find some harsher name for it," said Astley with a sneer. "Nay, you need not think to scare me by glaring at me, Sir Robert, nor will your ill-pleasure change my thoughts. I have faced fiercer eyes than thine, and I have not feared."

"Your speech, Sir James, is neither courteous nor good," said Knolles, "and if I were a free man I would cram your words down your throat with the point of my dagger. But I am here to lead these men in profit and honor, not to quarrel with every fool who has not the wit to understand how soldiers should be led. Can you not see that if I make attempts here and there, as you would have me do, I shall have weakened my strength before I come to that part where it can best be spent?"

"And where is that?" asked Percy. "'Fore God, Astley, it is in my mind that we ride with one who knows more of war than you or I, and that we would be wise to be guided by his rede. Tell us then what is in your mind."

"Thirty miles from here," said Knolles, "there is, as I am told, a fortalice named Ploermel, and within it is one Bambro, an Englishman, with a good garrison. No great distance from him is the Castle of Josselin where dwells Robert of Beaumanoir with a great following of Bretons. It is my intention that we should join Bambro, and so be in such strength that we may throw ourselves upon Josselin, and by taking it become the masters of all mid-Brittany, and able to make head against the Frenchmen in the south."

"Indeed I think that you can do no better," said Percy heartily, "and I swear to you on jeopardy of my soul that I will stand by you in the matter! I doubt not that when we come deep into their land they will draw together and do what they may to make head against us; but up to now I swear by all the saints of Lindisfarne that I should have seen more war in a summer's day in Liddesdale or at the Forest of Jedburgh than any that Brittany has shown us. But see, yonder horsemen are riding in. They are our own hobblers, are they not? And who are these who are lashed to their stirrups?"

A small troop of mounted bowmen had ridden out of an oak grove upon the left of the road. They trotted up to where the three knights had halted. Two wretched peasants whose wrists had been tied to their leathers came leaping and straining beside the horses in their effort not to be dragged off their feet. One was a tall, gaunt, yellow-haired man, the other short and swarthy, but both so crusted with dirt, so matted and tangled and ragged, that they were more like beasts of the wood than human beings.

"What is this?" asked Knolles. "Have I not ordered you to leave the countryfolk at peace?"

The leader of the archers, old Wat of Carlisle, held up a sword, a girdle and a dagger. "If it please you, fair sir," said he, "I saw the glint of these, and I thought them no fit tools for hands which were made for the spade and the plow. But when we had ridden them down and taken them, there was the Bentley cross upon each, and we knew that they had belonged to yonder dead Englishman upon the road. Surely then, these are two of the villains who have slain him, and it is right that we do justice upon them."

Sure enough, upon sword, girdle and dagger shone the silver Molene cross which had gleamed on the dead man's armor. Knolles looked at them and then at the prisoners with a face of stone. At the sight of those fell eyes they had dropped with inarticulate howls upon their knees, screaming out their protests in a tongue which none could understand.

"We must have the roads safe for wandering Englishmen," said Knolles. "These men must surely die. Hang them to yonder tree."

He pointed to a live-oak by the roadside, and rode onward upon his way in converse with his fellow-knights. But the old bowman had ridden after him.

"If it please you, Sir Robert, the bowmen would fain put these men to death in their own fashion," said he.

"So that they die, I care not how," Knolles answered carelessly, and looked back no more.

Human life was cheap in those stern days when the footmen of a stricken army or the crew of a captured ship were slain without any question or thought of mercy by the victors. War was a rude game with death for the stake, and the forfeit was always claimed on the one side and paid on the other without doubt or hesitation. Only the knight might be spared, since his ransom made him worth more alive than dead. To men trained in such a school, with death forever hanging over their own heads, it may be well believed that the slaying of two peasant murderers was a small matter.

And yet there was special reason why upon this occasion the bowmen wished to keep the deed in their own hands. Ever since their dispute aboard the Basilisk, there had been ill-feeling betwixt Bartholomew the old bald-headed bowyer, and long Ned Widdington the Dalesman, which had ended in a conflict at Dinan, in which not only they, but a dozen of their friends had been laid upon the cobble-stones. The dispute raged round their respective knowledge and skill with the bow, and now some quick wit amongst the soldiers had suggested a grim fashion in which it should be put to the proof, once for all, which could draw the surer shaft.

A thick wood lay two hundred paces from the road upon which the archers stood. A stretch of smooth grassy sward lay between. The two peasants were led out fifty yards from the road, with their faces toward the wood. There they stood, held on a leash, and casting many a wondering frightened glance over their shoulders at the preparations which were being made behind them.

Old Bartholomew and the big Yorkshireman had stepped out of the ranks and stood side by side each with his strung bow in his left hand and a single arrow in his right. With care they had drawn on and greased their shooting-gloves and fastened their bracers. They plucked and cast up a few blades of grass to measure the wind, examined every small point of their tackle, turned their sides to the mark, and widened their feet in a firmer stance. From all sides came chaff and counsel from their comrades.

"A three-quarter wind, bowyer!" cried one. "Aim a body's breadth to the right!"

"But not thy body's breadth, bowyer," laughed another. "Else may you be overwide."

"Nay, this wind will scarce turn a well-drawn shaft," said a third. "Shoot dead upon him and you will be clap in the clout."

"Steady, Ned, for the good name of the Dales," cried a Yorkshireman. "Loose easy and pluck not, or I am five crowns the poorer man."

"A week's pay on Bartholomew!" shouted another. "Now, old fat-pate, fail me not!"

"Enough, enough! Stint your talk!" cried the old bowman, Wat of Carlisle. "Were your shafts as quick as your tongues there would be no facing you. Do you shoot upon the little one, Bartholomew, and you, Ned, upon the other. Give them law until I cry the word, then loose in your own fashion and at your own time. Are you ready! Hola, there, Hayward, Beddington, let them run!"

The leashes were torn away, and the two men, stooping their heads, ran madly for the shelter of the wood amid such a howl from the archers as beaters may give when the hare starts from its form. The two bowmen, each with his arrow drawn to the pile, stood like russet statues, menacing, motionless, their eager eyes fixed upon the fugitives, their bow-staves rising slowly as the distance between them lengthened. The Bretons were half-way to the wood, and still Old Wat was silent. It may have been mercy or it may have been mischief, but at least the chase should have a fair chance of life. At six score paces he turned his grizzled head at last.

"Loose!" he cried.

At the word the Yorkshireman's bow-string twanged. It was not for nothing that he had earned the name of being one of the deadliest archers of the North and had twice borne away the silver arrow of Selby. Swift and true flew the fatal shaft and buried itself to the feather in the curved back of the long yellow-haired peasant. Without a sound he fell upon his face and lay stone-dead upon the grass, the one short white plume between his dark shoulders to mark where Death had smote him.

The Yorkshireman threw his bowstave into the air and danced in triumph, whilst his comrades roared their fierce delight in a shout of applause, which changed suddenly into a tempest of hooting and of laughter.

The smaller peasant, more cunning than his comrade, had run more slowly, but with many a backward glance. He had marked his companion's fate and had waited with keen eyes until he saw the bowyer loose his string. At the moment he had thrown himself flat upon the grass and had heard the arrow scream above him, and seen it quiver in the turf beyond. Instantly he had sprung to his feet again and amid wild whoops and halloos from the bowmen had made for the shelter of the wood. Now he had reached it, and ten score good paces separated him from the nearest of his persecutors. Surely they could not reach him here. With the tangled brushwood behind him he was as safe as a rabbit at the mouth of his burrow. In the joy of his heart he must needs dance in derision and snap his fingers at the foolish men who had let him slip. He threw back his head, howling at them like a dog, and at the instant an arrow struck him full in the throat and laid him dead among the bracken. There was a hush of surprised silence and then a loud cheer burst from the archers.

"By the rood of Beverley!" cried old Wat, "I have not seen a finer roving shaft this many a year. In my own best day I could not have bettered it. Which of you loosed it?"

"It was Aylward of Tilford—Samkin Aylward," cried a score of voices, and the bowman, flushed at his own fame, was pushed to the front.

"Indeed I would that it had been at a nobler mark," said he. "He might have gone free for me, but I could not keep my fingers from the string when he turned to jeer at us."

"I see well that you are indeed a master-bowman," said old Wat, "and it is comfort to my soul to think that if I fall I leave such a man behind me to hold high the credit of our craft. Now gather your shafts and on, for Sir Robert awaits us on the brow of the hill."

All day Knolles and his men marched through the same wild and deserted country, inhabited only by these furtive creatures, hares to the strong and wolves to the weak, who hovered in the shadows of the wood. Ever and anon upon the tops of the hills they caught a glimpse of horsemen who watched them from a distance and vanished when approached. Sometimes bells rang an alarm from villages amongst the hills, and twice they passed castles which drew up their drawbridges at their approach and lined their walls with hooting soldiers as they passed. The Englishmen gathered a few oxen and sheep from the pastures of each, but Knolles had no mind to break his strength upon stone walls, and so he went upon his way.

Once at St. Meen they passed a great nunnery, girt with a high gray lichened wall, an oasis of peace in this desert of war, the black-robed nuns basking in the sun or working in the gardens, with the strong gentle hand of Holy Church shielding them ever from evil. The archers doffed caps to them as they passed, for the boldest and roughest dared not cross that line guarded by the dire ban and blight which was the one only force in the whole steel-ridden earth which could stand betwixt the weakling and the spoiler.

The little army halted at St. Meen and cooked its midday meal. It had gathered into its ranks again and was about to start, when Knolles drew Nigel to one side.

"Nigel," said he, "it seems to me that I have seldom set eyes upon a horse which hath more power and promise of speed than this great beast of thine."

"It is indeed a noble steed, fair sir," said Nigel. Betwixt him and his young leader there had sprung up great affection and respect since the day that they set foot in the Basilisk.

"It will be the better if you stretch his limbs, for he grows over-heavy," said the knight. "Now mark me, Nigel! Yonder betwixt the ash-tree and the red rock what do you see on the side of the far hill?"

"There is a white dot upon it. Surely it is a horse."

"I have marked it all morning, Nigel. This horseman has kept ever upon our flank, spying upon us or waiting to make some attempt upon us. Now I should be right glad to have a prisoner, for it is my wish to know something of this country-side, and these peasants can speak neither French nor English. I would have you linger here in hiding when we go forward. This man will still follow us. When he does so, yonder wood will lie betwixt you and him. Do you ride round it and come upon him from behind. There is broad plain upon his left, and we will cut him off upon the right. If your horse be indeed the swifter, then you cannot fail to take him."

Nigel had already sprung down and was tightening Pommers' girth.

"Nay, there is no need of haste, for you cannot start until we are two miles upon our way. And above all I pray you, Nigel, none of your knight-errant ways. It is this man that I want, him and the news that he can bring me. Think little of your own advancement and much of the needs of the army. When you get him, ride westwards upon the sun, and you cannot fail to find the road."

Nigel waited with Pommers under the shadow of the nunnery wall, horse and man chafing with impatience, whilst above them six round-eyed innocent nun-faces looked down on this strange and disturbing vision from the outer world. At last the long column wound itself out of sight round a curve of the road, and the white dot was gone from the bare green flank of the hill. Nigel bowed his steel head to the nuns, gave his bridle a shake, and bounded off upon his welcome mission. The round-eyed sisters saw yellow horse and twinkling man sweep round the skirt of the wood, caught a last glimmer of him through the tree-trunks, and paced slowly back to their pruning and their planting, their minds filled with the beauty and the terror of that outer world beyond the high gray lichen-mottled wall.

Everything fell out even as Knolles had planned. As Nigel rounded the oak forest, there upon the farther side of it, with only good greensward between, was the rider upon the white horse. Already he was so near that Nigel could see him clearly, a young cavalier, proud in his bearing, clad in purple silk tunic with a red curling feather in his low black cap. He wore no armor, but his sword gleamed at his side. He rode easily and carelessly, as one who cares for no man, and his eyes were forever fixed upon the English soldiers on the road. So intent was he upon them that he gave no thought to his own safety, and it was only when the low thunder of the great horse's hoofs broke upon his ears that he turned in his saddle, looked very coolly and steadily at Nigel, then gave his own bridle a shake and darted off, swift as a hawk, toward the hills upon the left.

Pommers had met his match that day. The white horse, two parts Arab, bore the lighter weight, since Nigel was clad in full armor. For five miles over the open neither gained a hundred yards upon the other. They had topped the hill and flew down the farther side, the stranger continually turning in his saddle to have a look at his pursuer. There was no panic in his flight, but rather the amused rivalry with which a good horseman who is proud of his mount contends with one who has challenged him. Below the hill was a marshy plain, studded with great Druidic stones, some prostrate, some erect, some bearing others across their tops like the huge doors of some vanished building. A path ran through the marsh with green rushes as a danger signal on either side of it. Across this path many of the huge stones were lying, but the white horse cleared them in its stride and Pommers followed close upon his heels. Then came a mile of soft ground where the lighter weight again drew to the front, but it ended in a dry upland and once again Nigel gained. A sunken road crossed it, but the white cleared it with a mighty spring, and again the yellow followed. Two small hills lay before them with a narrow gorge of deep bushes between. Nigel saw the white horse bounding chest-deep amid the underwood.

Next instant its hind legs were high in the air, and the rider had been shot from its back. A howl of triumph rose from amidst the bushes, and a dozen wild figures armed with club and with spear, rushed upon the prostrate man.

"*À moi, Anglais, à moi!*" cried a voice, and Nigel saw the young rider stagger to his feet, strike round him with his sword, and then fall once more before the rush of his assailants.

There was a comradeship among men of gentle blood and bearing which banded them together against all ruffianly or unchivalrous attack. These rude fellows were no soldiers. Their dress and arms, their uncouth cries and wild assault, marked them as banditti — such men as had slain the Englishman upon the road. Waiting in narrow gorges with a hidden rope across the path, they watched for the lonely horseman as a fowler waits by his bird-trap, trusting that they could overthrow the steed and then slay the rider ere he had recovered from his fall.

Such would have been the fate of the stranger, as of so many cavaliers before him, had Nigel not chanced to be close upon his heels. In an instant Pommers had burst through the group who struck at the prostrate man, and in another two of the robbers had fallen before Nigel's sword. A spear rang on his breastplate, but one blow shore off its head, and a second that of him who held it. In vain they thrust at the steel-girt man. His sword played round them like lightning, and the fierce horse ramped and swooped above them with pawing iron-shod hoofs and eyes of fire. With cries and shrieks they flew off to right and left amidst the bushes, springing over boulders and darting under branches where no horseman could follow them. The foul crew had gone as swiftly and suddenly as it had come, and save for four ragged figures littered amongst the trampled bushes, no sign remaining of their passing.

Nigel tethered Pommers to a thorn-bush and then turned his attention to the injured man. The white horse had regained his feet and stood whinnying gently as he looked down on his prostrate master. A heavy blow, half broken by his sword, had beaten him down and left a great raw bruise upon his forehead. But a stream gurgled through the gorge, and a capful of water dashed over his face brought the senses back to the injured man. He was a mere stripling, with the delicate features of a woman, and a pair of great violet-blue eyes which looked up presently with a puzzled stare into Nigel's face.

"Who are you?" he asked. "Ah yes! I call you to mind. You are the young Englishman who chased me on the great yellow horse. By our Lady of Rocamadour whose vernicle is round my neck! I could not have believed that any horse could have kept at the heels of Charlemagne so long. But I will wager you a hundred crowns, Englishman, that I lead you over a five-mile course."

"Nay," said Nigel, "we will wait till you can back a horse ere we talk of racing it. I am Nigel of Tilford, of the family of Loring, a squire by rank and the son of a knight. How are you called, young sir?"

"I also am a squire by rank and the son of a knight. I am Raoul de la Roche Pierre de Bras, whose father writes himself Lord of Grosbois, a free vavasor of the noble Count of Toulouse, with the right of fossa and of furca, the high justice, the middle and the low." He sat up and rubbed his eyes. "Englishman, you have saved my life as I would have saved yours, had I seen such yelping dogs set upon a man of blood and of coat-armor. But now I am yours, and what is your sweet will?"

"When you are fit to ride, you will come back with me to my people."

"Alas! I feared that you would say so. Had I taken you, Nigel— that is your name, is it not?—had I taken you, I would not have acted thus."

"How then would you have ordered things?" asked Nigel, much taken with the frank and debonair manner of his captive.

"I would not have taken advantage of such a mischance as has befallen me which has put me in your power. I would give you a sword and beat you in fair fight, so that I might send you to give greeting to my dear lady and show her the deeds which I do for her fair sake."

"Indeed, your words are both good and fair," said Nigel. "By Saint Paul! I cannot call to mind that I have ever met a man who bore himself better. But since I am in my armor and you without, I see not how we can debate the matter."

"Surely, gentle Nigel, you could doff your armor."

"Then have I only my underclothes."

"Nay, there shall be no unfairness there, for I also will very gladly strip to my underclothes."

Nigel looked wistfully at the Frenchman; but he shook his head. "Alas! it may not be," said he. "The last words that Sir Robert said to me were that I was to bring you to his side, for he would have speech with you. Would that I could do what you ask, for I also have a fair lady to whom I would fain send you. What use are you to me, Raoul, since I have gained no honor in the taking of you? How is it with you now?"

The young Frenchman had risen to his feet. "Do not take my sword," he said. "I am yours, rescue or no rescue. I think now that I could mount my horse, though indeed my head still rings like a cracked bell."

Nigel had lost all traces of his comrades; but he remembered Sir Robert's words that he should ride upon the sun with the certainty that sooner or later he would strike upon the road. As they jogged slowly along over undulating hills, the Frenchman shook off his hurt and the two chatted merrily together.

"I had but just come from France," said he, "and I had hoped to win honor in this country, for I have ever heard that the English are very hardy men and excellent people to fight with. My mules and my baggage are at Evran; but I rode forth to see what I could see, and I chanced upon your army moving down the road, so I coasted it in the hopes of some profit or adventure. Then you came after me and I would have given all the gold goblets upon my father's table if I had my harness so that I could have turned upon you. I have promised the Countess Beatrice that I will send her an Englishman or two to kiss her hands."

"One might perchance have a worse fate," said Nigel. "Is this fair dame your betrothed?"

"She is my love," answered the Frenchman. "We are but waiting for the Count to be slain in the wars, and then we mean to marry. And this lady of thine, Nigel? I would that I could see her."

"Perchance you shall, fair sir," said Nigel, "for all that I have seen of you fills me with desire to go further with you. It is in my mind that we might turn this thing to profit and to honor, for when Sir Robert has spoken with you, I am free to do with you as I will."

"And what will you do, Nigel?"

"We shall surely try some small deed upon each other, so that either I shall see the Lady Beatrice, or you the Lady Mary. Nay, thank me not, for like yourself, I have come to this country in search of honor, and I know not where I may better find it than at the end of your sword-point. My good lord and master, Sir John Chandos, has told me many times that never yet did he meet French knight nor squire that he did not find great pleasure and profit from their company, and now I very clearly see that he has spoken the truth."

For an hour these two friends rode together, the Frenchman pouring forth the praises of his lady, whose glove he produced from one pocket, her garter from his vest, and her shoe from his saddle-bag. She was blond, and when he heard that Mary was dark, he would fain stop then and there to fight the question of color. He talked too of his great château at Lauta, by the head waters of the pleasant Garonne; of the hundred horses in the stables, the seventy hounds in the kennels, the fifty hawks in the mews. His English friend should come there when the wars were over, and what golden days would be theirs! Nigel too, with his English coldness thawing before this young sunbeam of the South, found himself talking of the heather slopes of Surrey, of the forest of Woolmer, even of the sacred chambers of Cosford.

But as they rode onward towards the sinking sun, their thoughts far away in their distant homes, their horses striding together, there came that which brought their minds back in an instant to the perilous hillsides of Brittany.

It was the long blast of a trumpet blown from somewhere on the farther side of a ridge toward which they were riding. A second long-drawn note from a distance answered it.

"It is your camp," said the Frenchman.

"Nay," said Nigel; "we have pipes with us and a naker or two, but I have heard no trumpet-call from our ranks. It behooves us to take heed, for we know not what may be before us. Ride this way, I pray you, that we may look over and yet be ourselves unseen."

Some scattered boulders crowned the height, and from behind them the two young Squires could see the long rocky valley beyond. Upon a knoll was a small square building with a battlement round it. Some distance from it towered a great dark castle, as massive as the rocks on which it stood, with one strong keep at the corner, and four long lines of machicolated walls. Above, a great banner flew proudly in the wind, with some device which glowed red in the setting sun. Nigel shaded his eyes and stared with wrinkled brow.

"It is not the arms of England, nor yet the lilies of France, nor is it the ermine of Brittany," said he. "He who holds this castle fights for his own hand, since his own device flies above it. Surely it is a head gules on an argent field."

"The bloody head on a silver tray!" cried the Frenchman. "Was I not warned against him? This is not a man, friend Nigel. It is a monster who wars upon English, French and all Christendom. Have you not heard of the Butcher of La Brohinière?"

"Nay, I have not heard of him."

" His name is accursed in France. Have I not been told also that he put to death this very year Gilles de St. Pol, a friend of the English King?"

"Yes, in very truth it comes back to my mind now that I heard something of this matter in Calais before we started."

"Then there he dwells, and God guard you if ever you pass under yonder portal, for no prisoner has ever come forth alive! Since these wars began he hath been a king to himself, and the plunder of eleven years lies in yonder cellars. How can justice come to him, when no man knows who owns the land? But when we have packed you all back to your island, by the Blessed Mother of God, we have a heavy debt to pay to the man who dwells in yonder pile!"

But even as they watched, the trumpet-call burst forth once more. It came not from the castle but from the farther end of the valley. It was answered by a second call from the walls. Then in a long, straggling line there came a wild troop of marauders streaming homeward from some foray. In the van, at the head of a body of spearmen, rode a tall and burly man, clad in brazen armor, so that he shone like a golden image in the slanting rays of the sun. His helmet had been loosened from his gorget and was held before him on his horse's neck. A great tangled beard flowed over his breastplate, and his hair hung down as far behind. A squire at his elbow bore high the banner of the bleeding head. Behind the spearmen were a line of heavily laden mules, and on either side of them a drove of poor country folk, who were being herded into the castle. Lastly came a second strong troop of mounted spearmen, who conducted a score or more of prisoners who marched together in a solid body.

Nigel stared at them and then, springing on his horse, he urged it along the shelter of the ridge so as to reach unseen a spot which was close to the castle gate. He had scarce taken up his new position when the cavalcade reached the drawbridge, and amid yells of welcome from those upon the wall, filed in a thin line across it. Nigel stared hard once more at the prisoners in the rear, and so absorbed was he by the sight that he had passed the rocks and was standing sheer upon the summit.

"By Saint Paul!" he cried, "it must indeed be so. I see their russet jackets. They are English archers!"

As he spoke, the hindmost one, a strongly built, broad-shouldered man, looked round and saw the gleaming figure above him upon the hill, with open helmet, and the five roses glowing upon his breast. With a sweep of his hands he had thrust his guardians aside and for a moment was clear of the throng.

"Squire Loring! Squire Loring!" he cried. "It is I, Aylward the archer! It is I, Samkin Aylward!" The next minute a dozen hands had seized him, his cries were muffled with a gag, and he was hurled, the last of the band, through the black and threatening archway of the gate. Then with a clang the two iron wings came together, the portcullis swung upward, and captives and captors, robbers and booty, were all swallowed up within the grim and silent fortress.

CHAPTER XX

HOW THE ENGLISH ATTEMPTED
THE CASTLE OF LA BROHINIÈRE

FOR some minutes Nigel remained motionless upon the crest of the hill, his heart, like lead within him, and his eyes fixed upon the huge gray walls which contained his unhappy henchman. He was roused by a sympathetic hand upon his shoulder and the voice of his young prisoner in his ear.

"*Peste!*" said he. "They have some of your birds in their cage, have they not? What then, my friend? Keep your heart high! Is it not the chance of war, to-day to them, to-morrow to thee, and death at last for us all? And yet I had rather they were in any hands than those of Oliver the Butcher."

"By Saint Paul, we cannot suffer it!" cried Nigel distractedly. "This man has come with me from my own home. He has stood between me and death before now. It goes to my very heart that he should call upon me in vain. I pray you, Raoul, to use your wits, for mine are all curdled in my head. Tell me what I should do and how I may bring him help."

The Frenchman shrugged his shoulders. "As easy to get a lamb unscathed out of a wolves' lair as a prisoner safe from La Brohinière. Nay, Nigel, whither do you go? Have you indeed taken leave of your wits?"

The Squire had spurred his horse down the hillside and never halted until he was within a bowshot of the gate. The French prisoner followed hard behind him, with a buzz of reproaches and expostulations.

"You are mad, Nigel!" he. cried. "What do you hope to do then? Would you carry the castle with your own hands? Halt, man, halt, in the name of the Virgin!"

But Nigel had no plan in his head and only obeyed the fevered impulse to do something to ease his thoughts. He paced his horse up and down, waving his spear, and shouting insults and challenges to the garrison. Over the high wall a hundred jeering faces looked down upon him. So rash and wild was his action that it seemed to those within to mean some trap, so the drawbridge was still held high and none ventured forth to seize him. A few long-range arrows pattered on the rocks, and then with a deep booming sound a huge stone, hurled from a mangonel, sang over the head of the two Squires and crushed into splinters amongst the bowlders behind them. The Frenchman seized Nigel's bridle and forced him farther from the gateway.

"By the dear Virgin!" he cried, "I care not to have those pebbles about my ears, yet I cannot go back alone, so it is very clear, my crazy comrade, that you must come also. Now we are beyond their reach! But see, my friend Nigel, who are those who crown the height?"

The sun had sunk behind the western ridge, but the glowing sky was fringed at its lower edge by a score of ruddy twinkling points. A body of horsemen showed hard and black upon the bare hill. Then they dipped down the slope into the valley, whilst a band of footmen followed behind.

"They are my people," cried Nigel joyously. "Come, my friend, hasten, that we may take counsel what we shall do."

Sir Robert Knolles rode a bowshot in front of his men, and his brow was as black as night. Beside him, with crestfallen face, his horse bleeding, his armor dinted and soiled, was the hot-headed knight, Sir James Astley. A fierce discussion raged between them.

"I have done my devoir as best I might," said Astley. "Alone I had ten of them at my sword-point. I know not how I have lived to tell it."

"What is your devoir to me? Where are my thirty bowmen?" cried Knolles in bitter wrath. "Ten lie dead upon the ground and twenty are worse than dead in yonder castle. And all because you must needs show all men how bold you are, and ride into a bush-ment such as a child could see. Alas for my own folly that ever I should have trusted such a one as you with the handling of men!"

"By God, Sir Robert, you shall answer to me for those words!" cried Astley with a choking voice. "Never has a man dared to speak to me as you have done this day."

"As long as I hold the King's order I shall be master, and by the Lord I will hang you, James, on a near tree if I have further cause of offense! How now, Nigel? I see by yonder white horse that you at least have not failed me. I will speak with you anon. Percy, bring up your men, and let us gather round this castle, for, as I hope for my soul's salvation, I win not leave it until I have my archers, or the head of him who holds them."

That night the English lay thick round the fortress of La Brohinière so that none might come forth from it. But if none could come forth it was hard to see how any could win their way in, for it was full of men, the walls were high and strong, and a deep dry ditch girt it round. But the hatred and fear which its master had raised over the whole country-side could now be plainly seen, for during the night the brushwood men and the villagers came in from all parts with offers of such help as they could give for the intaking of the castle. Knolles set them cutting bushes and tying them into fagots. When morning came he rode out before the wall and he held counsel with his knights and squires as to how he should enter in.

"By noon," said he, "we shall have so many fagots that we may make our way over the ditch. Then we will beat in the gates and so win a footing."

The young Frenchman had come with Nigel to the conference, and now, amid the silence which followed the leader's proposal, he asked if he might be heard. He was clad in the brazen armor which Nigel had taken from the Red Ferret.

"It may be that it is not for me to join in your counsel," said he, "seeing that I am a prisoner and a Frenchman. But this man is the enemy of all, and we of France owe him a debt even as you do, since many a good Frenchman has died in his cellars. For this reason I crave to be heard."

"We will hear you," said Knolles.

"I have come from Evran yesterday," said he. "Sir Henry Spinnefort, Sir Peter La Roye and many other brave knights and squires lie there, with a good company of men, all of whom would very gladly join with you to destroy this butcher and his castle, for it is well known amongst us that his deeds are neither good nor fair. There are also bombards which we could drag over the hills, and so beat down this iron gate. If you so order it I will ride to Evran and bring my companions back with me."

"Indeed, Robert," said Percy, "it is in my mind that this Frenchman speaks very wisely and well."

"And when we have taken the castle—what then?" asked Knolles.

"Then you could go upon your way, fair sir, and we upon ours. Or if it please you better you could draw together on yonder hill and we on this one, so that the valley lies between us. Then if any cavalier wished to advance himself or to shed a vow and exalt his lady, an opening might be found for him. Surely it would be shame if so many brave men drew together and no small deed were to come of it."

Nigel clasped his captive's hand to show his admiration and esteem, but Knolles shook his head.

"Things are not ordered thus, save in the tales of the minstrels," said he. "I have no wish that your people at Evran should know our numbers or our plans. I am not in this land for knight errantry, but I am here to make head against the King's enemies. Has no one aught else to say?"

Percy pointed to the small outlying fortalice upon the knoll, on which also flew the flag of the bloody head. "This smaller castle, Robert, is of no great strength and cannot hold more than fifty men. It is built, as I conceive it, that no one should seize the high ground and shoot down into the other. Why should we not turn all our strength upon it, since it is the weaker of the twain?"

But again the young leader shook his head. "If I should take it," said he, "I am still no nearer to my desire, nor will it avail me in getting back my bowmen. It may cost a score of men, and what profit shall I have from it? Had I bombards, I might place them on yonder hill, but having none it is of little use to me."

"It may be," said Nigel, "that they have scant food or water, and so must come forth to fight us."

"I have made inquiry of the peasants," Knolles answered, "and they are of one mind that there is a well within the castle, and good store of food. Nay, gentlemen, there is no way before us save to take it by arms, and no spot where we can attempt it save through the great gate. Soon we will have so many fagots that we can cast them down into the ditch, and so win our way across. I have ordered them to cut a pine-tree on the hill and shear the branches so that we may beat down the gate with it. But what is now amiss, and why do they run forward to the castle?"

A buzz had risen from the soldiers in the camp, and they all crowded in one direction, rushing toward the castle wall. The knights and squires rode after them, and when in view of the main gate, the cause of the disturbance lay before them. On the tower above the portal three men were standing in the garb of English archers, ropes round their necks and their hands bound behind them. Their comrades surged below them with cries of recognition and of pity.

"It is Ambrose!" cried one. "Surely it is Ambrose of Ingleton."

"Yes, in truth, I see his yellow hair. And the other, him with the beard, it is Lockwood of Skipton. Alas for his wife who keeps the booth by the bridge-head of Ribble! I wot not who the third may be."

"It is little Johnny Alspaye, the youngest man in the company," cried old Wat, with the tears running down his cheeks, "'Twas I who brought him from his home. Alas! Alas! Foul fare the day that ever I coaxed him from his mother's side that he might perish in a far land."

There was a sudden flourish of a trumpet and the drawbridge fell. Across it strode a portly man with a faded herald's coat. He halted warily upon the farther side and his voice boomed like a drum. "I would speak with your leader." he cried.

Knolles rode forward.

"Have I your knightly word that I may advance unscathed with all courteous entreaty as befits a herald?"

Knolles nodded his head.

The man came slowly and pompously forward. "I am the messenger and liege servant," said he, "of the high baron, Oliver de St. Yvon, Lord of La Brohinière. He bids me to say that if you continue your journey and molest him no further he will engage upon his part to make no further attack upon you. As to the men whom he holds, he will enroll them in his own honorable service, for he has need of longbowmen, and has heard much of their skill. But if you constrain him or cause him further displeasure by remaining before his castle he hereby gives you warning that he will hang these three men over his gateway and every morning another three until all have been slain. This he has sworn upon the rood of Calvery, and as he has said so he will do upon jeopardy of his soul."

Robert Knolles looked grimly at the messenger. "You may thank the saints that you have had my promise," said he, "else would I have stripped that lying tabard from thy back and the skin beneath it from thy bones, that thy master might have a fitting answer to his message. Tell him that I hold him and all that are within his castle as hostage for the lives of my men, and that should he dare to do them scathe he and every man that is with him shall hang upon his battlements. Go, and go quickly, less my patience fail."

There was that in Knolles' cold gray eyes and in his manner of speaking those last words which sent the portly envoy back at a quicker gait than he had come. As he vanished into the gloomy arch of the gateway the drawbridge swung up with creak and rattle behind him.

A few minutes later a rough-bearded fellow stepped out over the portal where the condemned archers stood and seizing the first by the shoulders he thrust him over the wall. A cry burst from the man's lips and a deep groan from those of his comrades below as he fell with a jerk which sent him half-way up to the parapet again, and then after dancing like a child's toy swung slowly backward and forward with limp limbs and twisted neck.

The hangman turned and bowed in mock reverence to the spectators beneath him. He had not yet learned in a land of puny archers how sure and how strong is the English bow. Half a dozen men, old Wat amongst them, had run forward toward the wall. They were too late to save their comrades, but at least their deaths were speedily avenged. The man was in the act of pushing off the second prisoner when an arrow crashed through his head, and he fell stone dead upon the parapet. But even in falling he had given the fatal thrust and a second russet figure swung beside the first against the dark background of the castle wall.

There only remained the young lad, Johnny Alspaye, who stood shaking with fear, an abyss below him, and the voices of those who would hurl him over it behind. There was a long pause before anyone would come forth to dare those deadly arrows. Then a fellow, crouching double, ran forward from the shelter, keeping the young archer's body as a shield between him and danger.

"Aside, John! Aside!" cried his comrades from below.

The youth sprang as far as the rope would allow him, and slipped it half over his face in the effort. Three arrows flashed past his side, and two of them buried themselves in the body of the man behind. A howl of delight burst from the spectators as he dropped first upon his knees and then upon his face. A life for a life was no bad bargain.

But it was only a short respite which the skill of his comrades had given to the young archer. Over the parapet there appeared a ball of brass, then a pair of great brazen shoulders, and lastly the full figure of an armored man. He walked to the edge and they heard his hoarse guffaw of laughter as the arrows clanged and clattered against his impenetrable mail. He slapped his breast-plate, as he jeered at them. Well he knew that at the distance no dart ever sped by mortal hands could cleave through his plates of metal. So he stood, the great burly Butcher of La Brohinière, with head uptossed, laughing insolently at his foes. Then with slow and ponderous tread he walked toward his boy victim, seized him by the ear, and dragged him across so that the rope might be straight. Seeing that the noose had slipped across the face, he tried to push it down, but the mail glove hampering him he pulled it off, and grasped the rope above the lad's head with his naked hand.

Quick as a flash old Wat's arrow had sped, and the Butcher sprang back with a howl of pain, his hand skewered by a cloth-yard shaft. As he shook it furiously at his enemies a second grazed his knuckles. With a brutal kick of his metal-shod feet he hurled young Alspaye over the edge, looked down for a few moments at his death agonies, and then walked slowly from the parapet, nursing his dripping hand, the arrows still ringing loudly upon his back-piece as he went.

The archers below, enraged at the death of their comrades, leaped and howled like a pack of ravening wolves.

"By Saint Dunstan," said Percy, looking round at their flushed faces, "if ever we are to carry it now is the moment, for these men will not be stopped if hate can take them forward."

"You are right, Thomas!" cried Knolles. "Gather together twenty men-at-arms each with his shield to cover him. Astley, do you place the bowmen so that no head may show at window or parapet. Nigel, I pray you to order the countryfolk forward with their fardels of fagots. Let the others bring up the lopped pine-tree which lies yonder behind the horse lines. Ten men-at-arms can bear it on the right, and ten on the left, having shields over their heads. The gate once down, let every man rush in. And God help the better cause!"

Swiftly and yet quietly the dispositions were made, for these were old soldiers whose daily trade was war. In little groups the archers formed in front of each slit or crevice in the walls, whilst others scanned the battlements with wary eyes, and sped an arrow at every face which gleamed for an instant above them. The garrison shot forth a shower of crossbow bolts and an occasional stone from their engine, but so deadly was the hail which rained upon them that they had no time to dwell upon their aim, and their discharges were wild and harmless. Under cover of the shafts of the bowmen a line of peasants ran unscathed to the edge of the ditch, each hurling in the bundle which he bore in his arms, and then hurrying back for another one. In twenty minutes a broad pathway of fagots lay level with the ground upon one side and the gate upon the other. With the loss of two peasants slain by bolts and one archer crushed by a stone, the ditch had been filled up. All was ready for the battering-ram.

With a shout, twenty picked men rushed forward with the pine-tree under their arms, the heavy end turned toward the gate. The arbalesters on the tower leaned over and shot into the midst of them, but could not stop their advance. Two dropped, but the others raising their shields ran onward still shouting, crossed the bridge of fagots, and came with a thundering crash against the door. It splintered from base to arch, but kept its place.

Swinging their mighty weapon, the storming party thudded and crashed upon the gate, every blow loosening and widening the cracks which rent it from end to end. The three knights, with Nigel, the Frenchman Raoul and the other squires, stood beside the ram, cheering on the men, and chanting to the rhythm of the swing with a loud "Ha!" at every blow. A great stone loosened from the parapet roared through the air and struck Sir James Astley and another of the attackers, but Nigel and the Frenchman had taken their places in an instant, and the ram thudded and smashed with greater energy than ever. Another blow and another! the lower part was staving inward, but the great central bar still held firm. Surely another minute would beat it from its sockets.

But suddenly from above there came a great deluge of liquid. A hogshead of it had been tilted from the battlement until soldiers, bridge, and ram were equally drenched in yellow slime. Knolles rubbed his gauntlet in it, held it to his visor, and smelled it.

"Back, back!" he cried. " Back before it is too late!"

There was a small barred window above their heads at the side of the gate. A ruddy glare shone through it, and then a blazing torch was tossed down upon them. In a moment the oil had caught and the whole place was a sheet of flame. The fir-tree that they carried, the fagots beneath them, their very weapons, were all in a blaze.

To right and left the men sprang down into the dry ditch, rolling with screams upon the ground in their endeavor to extinguish the flames. The knights and squires protected by their armor strove hard, stamping and slapping, to help those who had but leather jacks to shield their bodies. From above a ceaseless shower of darts and of stones were poured down upon them, while on the other hand the archers, seeing the greatness of the danger, ran up to the edge of the ditch, and shot fast and true at every face which showed above the wall.

Scorched, wearied and bedraggled, the remains of the storming party clambered out of the ditch as best they could, clutching at the friendly hands held down to them, and so limped their way back amid the taunts and howls of their enemies. A long pile of smoldering cinders was all that remained of their bridge, and on it lay Astley and six other red-hot men glowing in their armor.

Knolles clinched his hands as he looked back at the ruin that was wrought, and then surveyed the group of men who stood or lay around him nursing their burned limbs and scowling up at the exultant figures who waved on the castle wall. Badly scorched himself, the young leader had no thought for his own injuries in the rage and grief which racked his soul. "We will build another bridge," he cried. "Set the peasants binding fagots once more."

But a thought had flashed through Nigel's mind. "See, fair sir," said he. "The nails of yonder door are red-hot and the wood as white as ashes. Surely we can break our way through it."

"By the Virgin, you speak truly!" cried the French Squire. "If we can cross the ditch the gate will not stop us. Come, Nigel, for our fair ladies' sakes, I will race you who will reach it first, England or France."

Alas for all the wise words of the good Chandos! Alas for all the lessons in order and discipline learned from the wary Knolles. In an instant, forgetful of all things but this noble challenge, Nigel was running at the top of his speed for the burning gate. Close at his heels was the Frenchman, blowing and gasping, as he rushed along in his brazen armor. Behind came a stream of howling archers and men-at-arms, like a flood which has broken its dam. Down they slipped into the ditch, rushed across it, and clambered on each other's backs up the opposite side. Nigel, Raoul and two archers gained a foothold in front of the burning gate at the same moment. With blows and kicks they burst it to pieces, and dashed with a yell of triumph through the dark archway beyond. For a moment they thought with mad rapture that the castle was carried. A dark tunnel lay before them, down which they rushed. But alas! at the farther end it was blocked by a second gateway as strong as that which had been burned. In vain they beat upon it with their swords and axes. On each side the tunnel was pierced with slits, and the crossbow bolts discharged at only a few yards' distance crashed through armor as if it were cloth and laid man after man upon the stones. They raged and leaped before the great iron-clamped barrier, but the wall itself was as easy to tear down.

It was bitter to draw back; but it was madness to remain. Nigel looked round and saw that half his men were down. At the same moment Raoul sank with a gasp at his feet, a bolt driven to its socket through the links of the camail which guarded his neck. Some of the archers, seeing that certain death awaited them, were already running back to escape from the fatal passage.

"By Saint Paul!" cried Nigel hotly. "Would you leave our wounded where this butcher may lay his hands upon them? Let the archers shoot inwards and hold them back from the slits. Now let each man raise one of our comrades, lest we leave our honor in the gate of this castle."

With a mighty effort he had raised Raoul upon his shoulders and staggered with him to the edge of the ditch. Several men were waiting below where the steep bank shield them from the arrows, and to them Nigel handed down his wounded friend, and each archer in turn did the same. Again and again Nigel went back until no one lay in the tunnel save seven who had died there. Thirteen wounded were laid in the shelter of the ditch, and there they must remain until night came to cover them. Meanwhile the bowmen on the farther side protected them from attack, and also prevented the enemy from all attempts to build up the outer gate. The gaping smoke-blackened arch was all that they could show for a loss of thirty men, but that at least Knolles was determined to keep.

Burned and bruised, but unconscious of either pain or fatigue for the turmoil of his spirit within him, Nigel knelt by the Frenchman and loosened his helmet. The girlish face of the young Squire was white as chalk, and the haze of death was gathering over his violet eyes, but a faint smile played round his lips as he looked up at his English comrade.

"I shall never see Beatrice again," he whispered. "I pray you, Nigel, that when there is a truce you will journey as far as my father's château and tell him how his son died. Young Gaston will rejoice, for to him come the land and the coat, the war-cry and the profit. See them, Nigel, and tell them that I was as forward as the others."

"Indeed Raoul, no man could have carried himself with more honor or won more worship than you have done this day. I will do your behest when the time comes."

"Surely you are happy, Nigel," the dying Squire murmured, "for this day has given you one more deed which you may lay at the feet of your lady-love."

"It might have been so had we carried the gate," Nigel answered sadly; "but by Saint Paul! I cannot count it a deed where I have come back with my purpose unfulfilled. But this is no time, Raoul, to talk of my small affairs. If we take the castle and I bear a good part in it, then perchance all this may indeed avail."

The Frenchman sat up with that strange energy which comes often as the harbinger of death. "You will win your Lady Mary, Nigel, and your great deeds will be not three but a score, so that in all Christendom there shall be no man of blood and coat-armor who has not heard your name and your fame. This I tell you—I, Raoul de la Roche Pierre de Bras, dying upon the field of honor. And now kiss me, sweet friend, and lay me back, for the mists close round me and I am gone!"

With tender hands the Squire lowered his comrade's head, but even as he did so there came a choking rush of blood, and the soul had passed. So died a gallant cavalier of France, and Nigel as he knelt in the ditch beside him prayed that his own end might be as noble and as debonair.

CHAPTER XXI

HOW THE SECOND MESSENGER
WENT TO COSFORD

UNDER cover of night the wounded men were lifted from the ditch and carried back, whilst pickets of archers were advanced to the very gate so that none should rebuild it. Nigel, sick at heart over his own failure, the death of his prisoner and his fears for Aylward, crept back into the camp, but his cup was not yet full, for Knolles was waiting for him with a tongue which cut like a whip-lash. Who was he, a raw squire, that he should lead an attack without orders? See what his crazy knight errantry had brought about. Twenty men had been destroyed by it and nothing gained. Their blood was on his head. Chandos should hear of his conduct. He should be sent back to England when the castle had fallen.

Such were the bitter words of Knolles, the more bitter because Nigel felt in his heart that he had indeed done wrong, and that Chandos would have said the same though, perchance, in kinder words. He listened in silent respect, as his duty was, and then having saluted his leader he withdrew apart, threw himself down amongst the bushes, and wept the hottest tears of his life, sobbing bitterly with his face between his hands. He had striven hard, and yet everything had gone wrong with him. He was bruised, burned and aching from head to foot. Yet so high is the spirit above the body that all was nothing compared to the sorrow and shame which racked his soul.

But a little thing changed the current of his thoughts and brought some peace to his mind. He had slipped off his mail gauntlets, and as he did so his fingers lighted upon the tiny bangle which Mary had fastened there when they stood together upon St. Catharine's Hill on the Guildford Road. He remembered the motto curiously worked in filigree of gold. It ran: *"Fais ce que dois, adviegne que pourra—c'est commandé au chevalier."*

The words rang in his weary brain. He had done what seemed right, come what might. It had gone awry, it is true; but all things human may do that. If he had carried the castle, he felt that Knolles would have forgiven and forgotten all else. If he had not carried it, it was no fault of his. No man could have done more. If Mary could see she would surely have approved. Dropping into sleep, he saw her dark face, shining with pride and with pity, stooping over him as he lay. She stretched out her hand in his dream and touched him on the shoulder. He sprang up and rubbed his eyes, for fact had woven itself into dream in the strange way that it does, and some one was indeed leaning over him in the gloom, and shaking him from his slumbers. But the gentle voice and soft touch of the Lady Mary had changed suddenly to the harsh accents and rough grip of Black Simon, the fierce Norfolk man-at-arms.

"Surely you are the Squire Loring," he said, peering close to his face in the darkness.

"I am he. What then?"

"I have searched through the camp for you, but when I saw the great horse tethered near these bushes, I thought you would be found hard by. I would have a word with you."

"Speak on."

"This man Aylward the bowman was my friend, and it is the nature that God has given me to love my friends even as I hate my foes. He is also thy servant, and it has seemed to me that you love him also."

"I have good cause so to do."

"Then you and I, Squire Loring, have more reason to strive on his behalf than any of these others, who think more of taking the castle than of saving those who are captives within. Do you not see that such a man as this robber lord would, when all else had failed him, most surely cut the throats of his prisoners at the last instant before the castle fell, knowing well that come what might he would have short shrift himself? Is that not certain?"

"By Saint Paul! I had not thought of it."

"I was with you, hammering at the inner gate," said Simon, "and yet once when I thought that it was giving way I said in my heart: 'Good-by, Samkin! I shall never see you more.' This Baron has gall in his soul, even as I have myself, and do you think that I would give up my prisoners alive, if I were constrained so to do? No, no; had we won our way this day it would have been the death-stroke for them all."

"It may be that you are right, Simon," said Nigel, "and the thought of it should assuage our grief. But if we cannot save them by taking the castle, then surely they are lost indeed."

"It may be so, or it may not," Simon answered slowly. "It is in my mind that if the castle were taken very suddenly, and in such a fashion that they could not foresee it, then perchance we might get the prisoners before they could do them scathe."

Nigel bent forward eagerly, his hand on the soldier's arm.

"You have some plan in your mind, Simon. Tell me what it is."

"I had wished to tell Sir Robert, but he is preparing the assault for to-morrow and will not be turned from his purpose. I have indeed a plan, but whether it be good or not I cannot say until I have tried it. But first I will tell you what put it into my thoughts. Know then that this morning when I was in yonder ditch I marked one of their men upon the wall. He was a big man with a white face, red hair and a touch of Saint Anthony's fire upon the cheek."

"But what has this to do with Aylward?"

"I will show you. This evening after the assault I chanced to walk with some of my fellows, round yonder small fort upon the knoll to see if we could spy a weak spot in it. Some of them came to the wall to curse us, and among them whom should I see but a big man with a white face, red hair and a touch of Anthony's fire upon his cheek? What make you of that, Squire Nigel?"

"That this man had crossed from the castle to the fort."

"In good sooth, it must indeed be so. There are not two such ken-speckled men in the world. But if he crossed from the castle to the fort, it was not above the ground, for our own people were between."

"By Saint Paul! I see your meaning!" cried Nigel. "It is in your mind that there is a passage under the earth from one to the other."

"I am well sure of it."

"Then if we should take the small fort we may pass down this tunnel, and so carry the great castle also."

"Such a thing might happen," said Simon, "and yet it is dangerous also, for surely those in the castle would hear our assault upon the fort and so be warned to bar the passage against us, and to slay the prisoners before we could come."

"What then is your rede?"

"Could we find where the tunnel lay, Squire Nigel, I know not what is to prevent us from digging down upon it and breaking into it so that both fort and castle are at our mercy before either knows that we are there."

Nigel clapped his hands with joy. "'Fore God!" he cried. "It is a most noble plan! But alas! Simon, I see not how we can tell the course of this passage or where we should dig."

"I have peasants yonder with spades," said Simon. "There are two of my friends, Harding of Barnstable and West-country John who are waiting for us with their gear. If you will come to lead us, Squire Nigel, we are ready to venture our bodies in the attempt."

What would Knolles say in case they failed? The thought flashed through Nigel's mind, but another came swiftly behind it. He would not venture further unless he found hopes of success. And if he did venture further he would put his life upon it. Giving that, he made amends for all errors. And if on the other hand success crowned their efforts, then Knolles would forgive his failure at the gateway. A minute later, every doubt banished from his mind, he was making his way through the darkness under the guidance of Black Simon.

Outside the camp the two other men-at-arms were waiting for them, and the four advanced together. Presently a little group of figures loomed up in the darkness. It was a cloudy night, and a thin rain was falling which obscured both the castle and the fort; but a stone had been placed by Simon in the daytime which assured that they were between the two.

"Is blind Andreas there?" asked Simon.

"Yes, kind sir, I am here," said a voice.

"This man," said Simon, "was once rich and of good repute, but he was beggared by this robber lord, who afterwards put out his eyes so that he has lived for many years in darkness at the charity of others."

"How can he help us in our enterprise if he be indeed blind?" asked Nigel.

"It is for that very reason, fair lord, that he can be of greater service than any other man," Simon answered; "for it often happens that when a man has lost a sense the good God will strengthen those that remain. Hence it is that Andreas has such ears that he can hear the sap in the trees or the cheep of the mouse in its burrow. He has come to help us to find the tunnel."

"And I have found it," said the blind man proudly. "Here I have placed my staff upon the line of it. Twice as I lay there with my ear to the ground I have heard footsteps pass beneath me."

"I trust you make no mistake, old man," said Nigel.

For answer the blind man raised his staff and smote twice upon the ground, once to the right and once to the left. The one gave a dull thud, the other a hollow boom.

"Can you not hear that?" he asked. "Will you ask me now if I make a mistake?"

"Indeed, we are much beholden to you!" cried Nigel. "Let the peasants dig then, and as silently as they may. Do you keep your ear upon the ground, Andreas, so that if anyone pass beneath us we shall be warned."

So, amid the driving rain, the little group toiled in the darkness. The blind man lay silent, flat upon his face, and twice they heard his warning hiss and stopped their work, whilst some one passed beneath. In an hour they had dug down to a stone arch which was clearly the outer side of the tunnel roof. Here was a sad obstacle, for it might take long to loosen a stone, and if their work was not done by the break of day then their enterprise was indeed hopeless. They loosened the mortar with a dagger, and at last dislodged one small stone which enabled them to get at the others. Presently a dark hole blacker than the night around them yawned at their feet, and their swords could touch no bottom to it. They had opened the tunnel.

"I would fain enter it first," said Nigel. "I pray you to lower me down." They held him to the full length of their arms and then letting him drop they heard him land safely beneath them. An instant later the blind man started up with a low cry of alarm.

"I hear steps coming," said he. "They are far off, but they draw nearer."

Simon thrust his head and neck down the hole. "Squire Nigel," he whispered, "can you hear me?"

"I can hear you, Simon."

"Andreas says that some one comes."

"Then cover over the hole," came the answer. "Quick, I pray you, cover it over!"

A mantle was stretched across it, so that no glimmer of light should warn the new-comer. The fear was that he might have heard the sound of Nigel's descent. But soon it was clear that he had not done so, for Andreas announced that he was still advancing. Presently Nigel could hear the distant thud of his feet. If he bore a lantern all was lost. But no gleam of light appeared in the black tunnel, and still the footsteps drew nearer.

Nigel breathed a prayer of thanks to all his guardian saints as he crouched close to the slimy wall and waited breathless, his dagger in his hand. Nearer yet and nearer came the steps. He could hear the stranger's coarse breathing in the darkness. Then as he brushed past Nigel bounded upon him with a tiger spring. There was one gasp of astonishment, and not a sound more, for the Squire's grip was on the man's throat and his body was pinned motionless against the wall.

"Simon! Simon!" cried Nigel loudly.

The mantle was moved from the hole.

"Have you a cord? Or your belts linked together may serve."

One of the peasants had a rope, and Nigel soon felt it dangling against his hand. He listened and there was no sound in the passage. For an instant he released his captive's throat. A torrent of prayers and entreaties came forth. The man was shaking like a leaf in the wind. Nigel pressed the point of his dagger against his face and dared him to open his lips. Then he slipped the rope beneath his arms and tied it.

"Pull him up!" he whispered, and for an instant the gray glimmer above him was obscured.

"We have him, fair sir," said Simon.

"Then drop me the rope and hold it fast."

A moment later Nigel stood among the group of men who had gathered round their captive. It was too dark to see him, and they dare not strike flint and steel.

Simon passed his hand roughly over him and felt a fat clean-shaven face, and a cloth gabardine which hung to the ankles. "Who are you?" he whispered. "Speak the truth and speak it low, if you would ever speak again."

The man's teeth chattered in his head with cold and fright. "I speak no English," he murmured.

"French, then," said Nigel.

"I am a holy priest of God. You court the ban of holy Church when you lay hands upon me. I pray you let me go upon my way, for there are those whom I would shrive and housel. If they should die in sin, their damnation is upon you."

"How are you called then?"

"I am Dom Peter de Cervolles."

"De Cervolles, the arch-priest, he who heated the brazier when they burned out my eyes," cried old Andreas. "Of all the devils in hell there is none fouler than this one. Friends, friends, if I have done aught for you this night, I ask but one reward, that ye let me have my will of this man."

But Nigel pushed the old man back. "There is no time for this," he said. "Now hark you, priest—if priest indeed you be—your gown and tonsure will not save you if you play us false, for we are here of a set purpose and we will go forward with it, come what may. Answer me and answer me truly or it will be an ill night for you. In what part of the Castle does this tunnel enter?"

"In the lower cellar."

"What is at the end?"

"An oaken door."

"Is it barred?"

"Yes, it is barred."

"How would you have entered?"

"I would have given the password."

"Who then would have opened?"

"There is a guard within."

"And beyond him?"

"Beyond him are the prison cells and the jailers."

"Who else would be afoot?"

"No one save a guard at the gate and another on the battlement."

"What then is the password?"

The man was silent.

"The password, fellow!"

The cold points of two daggers pricked his throat; but still he would not speak.

"Where is the blind man?" asked Nigel. "Here, Andreas, you can have him and do what you will with him."

"Nay, nay," the priest whimpered. "Keep him off me. Save me from blind Andreas! I will tell you everything."

"The password then, this instant?"

"It is 'Benedicite!'"

"We have the password, Simon," cried Nigel. "Come then, let us on to the farther end. These peasants will guard the priest, and they will remain here lest we wish to send a message."

"Nay, fair sir, it is in my mind that we can do better," said Simon. "Let us take the priest with us, so that he who is within may know his voice."

"It is well thought of," said Nigel, "and first let us pray together, for indeed this night may well be our last."

He and the three men-at-arms knelt in the rain and sent up their simple orisons, Simon still clutching tight to his prisoner's wrist.

The priest fumbled in his breast and drew something forth. "It is the heart of the blessed confessor Saint Enogat," said he. "It may be that it will ease and assoil your souls if you would wish to handle it."

The four Englishmen passed the flat silver case from hand to hand, each pressing his lips devoutly upon it. Then they rose to their feet. Nigel was the first to lower himself down the hole; then Simon; then the priest, who was instantly seized by the other two. The men-at-arms followed them. They had scarcely moved away from the hole when Nigel stopped.

"Surely some one else came after us," said he.

They listened, but no whisper or rustle came from behind them. For a minute they paused and then resumed their journey through the dark. It seemed a long, long way, though in truth it was but a few hundred yards before they came to a door with a glimmer of yellow light around it, which barred their passage. Nigel struck upon it with his hand.

There was the rasping of a bolt and then a loud voice; "Is that you, priest?"

"Yes, it is I," said the prisoner in a quavering voice. "Open, Arnold!"

The voice was enough. There was no question of passwords. The door swung inward, and in an instant the janitor was cut down by Nigel and Simon. So sudden and so fierce was the attack that save for the thud of his body no sound was heard. A flood of light burst outward into the passage, and the Englishmen stood with blinking eyes in its glare.

In front of them lay a stone-flagged corridor, across which lay the dead body of the janitor. It had doors on either side of it, and another grated door at the farther end. A strange hubbub, a kind of low droning and whining filled the air. The four men were standing listening, full of wonder as to what this might mean, when a sharp cry came from behind them. The priest lay in a shapeless heap upon the ground, and the blood was rushing from his gaping throat. Down the passage, a black shadow in the yellow light, there fled a crouching man, who clattered with a stick as he went.

"It is Andreas," cried West-country Will. "He has slain him."

"Then it was he that I heard behind us," said Nigel. "Doubtless he was at our very heels in the darkness. I fear that the priest's cry has been heard."

"Nay," said Simon, "there are so many cries that one more may well pass. Let us take this lamp from the wall and see what sort of devil's den we have around us."

They opened the door upon the right, and so horrible a smell issued from it that they were driven back from it. The lamp which Simon held forward showed a monkeylike creature mowing and grimacing in the corner, man or woman none could tell, but driven crazy by loneliness and horror. In the other cell was a gray-bearded man fettered to the wall, looking blankly before him, a body without a soul, yet with life still in him, for his dull eyes turned slowly in their direction. But it was from behind the central door at the end of the passage that the chorus of sad cries came which filled the air.

"Simon," said Nigel, "before we go farther we will take this outer door from its hinges. With it we will block this passage so that at the worst we may hold our ground here until help comes. Do you back to the camp as fast as your feet can bear you. The peasants will draw you upward through the hole. Give my greetings to Sir Robert and tell him that the castle is taken without fail if he comes this way with fifty men. Say that we have made a lodgment within the walls. And tell him also, Simon, that I would counsel him to make a stir before the gateway so that the guard may be held there whilst we make good our footing behind them. Go, good Simon, and lose not a moment!"

But the man-at-arms shook his head. "It is I who have brought you here, fair sir, and here I bide through fair and foul. But you speak wisely and well, for Sir Robert should indeed be told what is going forward now that we have gone so far. Harding, do you go with all speed and bear the gentle Nigel's message."

Reluctantly the man-at-arms sped upon his errand. They could hear the racing of his feet and the low jingle of his harness until they died away in the tunnel. Then the three companions approached the door at the end. It was their intention to wait where they were until help should come, but suddenly amid the babel of cries within there broke forth an English voice, shouting in torment.

"My God!" it cried, "I pray you, comrades, for a cup of water, as you hope for Christ's mercy!"

A shout of laughter and the thud of a heavy blow followed the appeal.

All the hot blood rushed to Nigel's head at the sound, buzzing in his ears and throbbing in his temples. There are times when the fiery heart of a man must overbear the cold brain of a soldier. With one bound he was at the door, with another he was through it, the men-at-arms at his heels. So strange was the scene before them that for an instant all three stood motionless with horror and surprise.

It was a great vaulted chamber, brightly lit by many torches. At the farther end roared a great fire. In front of it three naked men were chained to posts in such a way that flinch as they might they could never get beyond the range of its scorching heat. Yet they were so far from it that no actual burn would be inflicted if they could but keep turning and shifting so as continually to present some fresh portion of their flesh to the flames. Hence they danced and whirled in front of the fire, tossing ceaselessly this way and that within the compass of their chains, wearied to death, their protruding tongues cracked and blackened with thirst, but unable for one instant to rest from their writhings and contortions.

Even stranger was the sight at each side of the room, whence came that chorus of groans which had first struck upon the ears of Nigel and his companions. A line of great hogsheads were placed alongside the walls, and within each sat a man, his head protruding from the top. As they moved within there was a constant splashing and washing of water. The white wan faces all turned together as the door flew open, and a cry of amazement and of hope took the place of those long-drawn moans of despair.

At the same instant two fellows clad in black, who had been seated with a flagon of wine between them at a table near the fire, sprang wildly to their feet, staring with blank amazement at this sudden inrush. That instant of delay deprived them of their last chance of safety. Midway down the room was a flight of stone steps which led to the main door.

Swift as a wildcat Nigel bounded toward it and gained the steps a stride or two before the jailers. They turned and made for the other which led to the passage, but Simon and his comrades were nearer to it than they. Two sweeping blows, two dagger thrusts into writhing figures, and the ruffians who worked the will of the Butcher lay dead upon the floor of their slaughter-house.

Oh, the buzz of joy and of prayer from all those white lips! Oh, the light of returning hope in all those sunken weary eyes! One wild shout would have gone up had not Nigel's outstretched hands and warning voice hushed them to silence.

He opened the door behind him. A curving newel staircase wound upward into the darkness. He listened, but no sound came down. There was a key in the outer lock of the iron door. He whipped it out and turned it on the inner side. The ground that they had gained was safe. Now they could turn to the relief of these poor fellows beside them. A few strong blows struck off the irons and freed the three dancers before the fire. With a husky croak of joy, they rushed across to their comrades' water-barrels, plunged their heads in like horses, and drank and drank and drank. Then in turn the poor shivering wretches were taken out of the barrels, their skins bleached and wrinkled with long soaking. Their bonds were torn from them; but, cramped and fixed, their limbs refused to act, and they tumbled and twisted upon the floor in their efforts to reach Nigel and to kiss his hand.

In a corner lay Aylward, dripping from his barrel and exhausted with cold and hunger. Nigel ran to his side and raised his head. The jug of wine from which the two jailers had drunk still stood upon their table. The Squire placed it to the archer's lips and he took a hearty pull at it.

"How is it with you now, Aylward?"

"Better, Squire, better, but may I never touch water again as long as I live! Alas! poor Dicon has gone, and Stephen also—the life chilled out of them. The cold is in the very marrow of my bones. I pray you, let me lean upon your arm as far as the fire, that I may warm the frozen blood and set it running in my veins once more."

A strange sight it was to see these twenty naked men crouching in a half-circle round the fire with their trembling hands extended to the blaze. Soon their tongues at least were thawed, and they poured out the story of their troubles with many a prayer and ejaculation to the saints for their safe delivery. No food had crossed their lips since they had been taken. The Butcher had commanded them to join his garrison and to shoot upon their comrades from the wall. When they refused he had set aside three of them for execution.

The others had been dragged to the cellar, whither the leering tyrant had followed them. Only one question he had asked them, whether they were of a hot-blooded nature or of a cold. Blows were showered upon them until they answered. Three had said cold, and had been condemned to the torment of the fire. The rest who had said hot were delivered up to the torture of the water-cask. Every few hours this man or fiend had come down to exult over their sufferings and to ask them whether they were ready yet to enter his service. Three had consented and were gone. But the others had all of them stood firm, two of them even to their death.

Such was the tale to which Nigel and his comrades listened whilst they waited impatiently for the coming of Knolles and his men. Many an anxious look did they cast down the black tunnel, but no glimmer of light and no clash of steel came from its depths. Suddenly, however, a loud and measured sound broke upon their ears. It was a dull metallic clang, ponderous and slow, growing louder and ever louder—the tread of an armored man. The poor wretches round the fire, all unnerved by hunger and suffering, huddled together with wan, scared faces, their eyes fixed in terror on the door.

"It is he!" they whispered. "It is the Butcher himself!"

Nigel had darted to the door and listened intently. There were no footfalls save those of one man. Once sure of that, he softly turned the key in the lock. At the same instant there came a bull's bellow from without.

"Ives! Bertrand!" cried the voice. "Can you not hear me coming, you drunken varlets? You shall cool your own heads in the water-casks, you lazy rascals! What, not even now! Open, you dogs. Open, I say!"

He had thrust down the latch, and with a kick he flung the door wide and rushed inward. For an instant he stood motionless, a statue of dull yellow metal, his eyes fixed upon the empty casks and the huddle of naked men. Then with the roar of a trapped lion, he turned, but the door had slammed behind him, and Black Simon, with grim figure and sardonic face, stood between.

The Butcher looked round him helplessly, for he was unarmed save for his dagger. Then his eyes fell upon Nigel's roses.

"You are a gentleman of coat-armor," he cried. "I surrender myself to you."

"I will not take your surrender, you black villain," said Nigel. "Draw and defend yourself. Simon, give him your sword."

"Nay, this is madness," said the blunt man-at-arms. "Why should I give the wasp a sting?"

"Give it him, I say. I cannot kill him in cold blood."

"But I can!" yelled Aylward, who had crept up from the fire. "Come, comrades! By these ten finger-bones! has he not taught us how cold blood should be warmed?"

Like a pack of wolves they were on him, and he clanged upon the floor with a dozen frenzied naked figures clutching and clinging above him. In vain Nigel tried to pull them off. They were mad with rage, these tortured starving men, their eyes fixed and glaring, their hair on end, their teeth gnashing with fury, while they tore at the howling, writhing man. Then with a rattle and clatter they pulled him across the room by his two ankles and dragged him into the fire.

Nigel shuddered and turned away his eyes as he saw the brazen figure roll out and stagger to his knees, only to be hurled once more into the heart of the blaze. His prisoners screamed with joy and clapped their hands as they pushed him back with their feet until the armor was too hot for them to touch. Then at last he lay still and glowed darkly red, whilst the naked men danced in a wild half-circle round the fire.

But now at last the supports had come. Lights flashed and armor gleamed down the tunnel. The cellar filled with armed men, while from above came the cries and turmoil of the feigned assault upon the gate. Led by Knolles and Nigel, the storming party rushed upward and seized the courtyard. The guard of the gate taken in the rear threw down their weapons and cried for mercy. The gate was thrown open and the assailants rushed in, with hundreds of furious peasants at their heels. Some of the robbers died in hot blood, many in cold; but all died, for Knolles had vowed to give no quarter. Day was just breaking when the last fugitive had been hunted out and slain. From all sides came the yells and whoops of the soldiers with the rending and riving of doors as they burst into the store-rooms and treasure-chambers. There was a joyous scramble amongst them, for the plunder of eleven years, gold and jewels, satins and velvets, rich plate and noble hangings were all to be had for the taking.

The rescued prisoners, their hunger appeased and their clothes restored, led the search for booty. Nigel, leaning on his sword by the gateway, saw Aylward totter past, a huge bundle under each arm, another slung over his back and a smaller packet hanging from his mouth. He dropped it for a moment as he passed his young master.

"By these ten finger-bones! I am right glad that I came to the war, and no man could ask for a more goodly life," said he. "I have a present here for every girl in Tilford, and my father need never fear the frown of the sacrist of Waverley again. But how of you, Squire Loring? It standeth not aright that we should gather the harvest whilst you, who sowed it, go forth empty-handed. Come, gentle sir, take these things that I have gathered, and I will go back and find more."

THE WHITE COMPANY AND SIR NIGEL

But Nigel smiled and shook his head. "You have gained what your heart desired, and perchance I have done so also," said he.

An instant later Knolles strode up to him with outstretched hand. "I ask your pardon, Nigel," said he. "I have spoken too hotly in my wrath."

"Nay, fair sir, I was at fault."

"If we stand here now within this castle, it is to you that I owe it. The King shall know of it, and Chandos also. Can I do aught else, Nigel, to prove to you the high esteem in which I hold you?"

The Squire flushed with pleasure. "Do you send a messenger home to England, fair sir, with news of these doings?"

"Surely, I must do so. But do not tell me, Nigel, that you would be that messenger. Ask me some other favor, for indeed I cannot let you go."

"Now God forbid!" cried Nigel. "By Saint Paul! I would not be so caitiff and so thrall as to leave you, when some small deed might still be done. But I would fain send a message by your messenger."

"To whom?"

"It is to the Lady Mary, daughter of old Sir John Buttesthorn who dwells near Guildford."

"But you will write the message, Nigel. Such greetings as a cavalier sends to his lady-love should be under seal."

"Nay, he can carry my message by word of mouth."

"Then I shall tell him for he goes this morning. What message, then, shall he say to the lady?"

"He will give her my very humble greeting, and he will say to her that for the second time Saint Catharine has been our friend."

CHAPTER XXII

HOW ROBERT OF BEAUMANOIR
CAME TO PLOERMEL

Sir Robert Knolles and his men passed onward that day, looking
back many a time to see the two dark columns of smoke, one
thicker and one more slender, which arose from the castle and
from the fort of La Brohinière. There was not an archer nor a
man-at-arms who did not bear a great bundle of spoil upon his
back, and Knolles frowned darkly as he looked upon them. Gladly
would he have thrown it all down by the roadside, but he had tried
such matters before, and he knew that it was as safe to tear a half-
gnawed bone from a bear as their blood-won plunder from such
men as these. In any case it was but two days' march to Ploermel,
where he hoped to bring his journey to an end.

That night they camped at Mauron, where a small English
and Breton garrison held the castle. Right glad were the bowmen to see some of their own countrymen once more, and they
spent the night over wine and dice, a crowd of Breton girls assist-
ing, so that next morning their bundles were much lighter, and
most of the plunder of La Brohinière was left with the men and
women of Mauron. Next day their march lay with a fair sluggish
river upon their right, and a great rolling forest upon their left
which covered the whole country. At last toward evening the towers of Ploermel rose before them and they saw against a darkening sky the Red Cross of England waving in the wind. So blue was
the river Duc which skirted the road, and so green its banks, that

they might indeed have been back beside their own homely streams, the Oxford Thames or the Midland Trent, but ever as the darkness deepened there came in wild gusts the howling of wolves from the forest to remind them that they were in a land of war. So busy had men been for many years in hunting one another that the beasts of the chase had grown to a monstrous degree, until the streets of the towns were no longer safe from the wild inroads of the fierce creatures, the wolves and the bears, who swarmed around them.

It was nightfall when the little army entered the outer gate of the Castle of Ploermel and encamped in the broad Bailey yard. Ploermel was at that time the center of British power in Mid-Brittany, as Hennebon was in the West, and it was held by a garrison of five hundred men under an old soldier, Richard of Bambro", a rugged Northumbrian, trained in that great school of warriors, the border wars. He who had ridden the marches of the most troubled frontier in Europe, and served his time against the Liddlesdale and Nithsdale raiders was hardened for a life in the field.

Of late, however, Bambro had been unable to undertake any enterprise, for his reënforcements had failed him, and amid his following he had but three English knights and seventy men. The rest were a mixed crew of Bretons, Hainaulters and a few German mercenary soldiers, brave men individually, as those of that stock have ever been, but lacking interest in the cause, and bound together by no common tie of blood or tradition.

On the other hand, the surrounding castles, and especially that of Josselin, were held by strong forces of enthusiastic Bretons, inflamed by a common patriotism, and full of warlike ardor. Robert of Beaumanoir, the fierce seneschal of the house of Rohan, pushed constant forays and excursions against Ploermel so that town and castle were both in daily dread of being surrounded and besieged. Several small parties of the English faction had been cut off and slain to a man, and so straitened were the others that it was difficult for them to gather provisions from the country round.

Such was the state of Bambro's garrison when on that March evening Knolles and his men streamed into the bailey-yard of his Castle.

In the glare of the torches at the inner gate Bambro was waiting to receive them, a dry, hard, wizened man, small and fierce, with beady black eyes and quick furtive ways. Beside him, a strange contrast, stood his Squire, Croquart, a German, whose name and fame as a man-at-arms were widespread, though like Robert Knolles himself he had begun as a humble page. He was a very tall man, with an enormous spread of shoulders, and a pair of huge hands with which he could crack a horse-shoe. He was slow and lethargic, save in moments of excitement, and his calm blond face, his dreamy blue eyes and his long fair hair gave him so gentle an appearance that none save those who had seen him in his berserk mood, raging, an iron giant, in the forefront of the battle, could ever guess how terrible a warrior he might be. Little knight and huge squire stood together under the arch of the donjon and gave welcome to the newcomers, whilst a swarm of soldiers crowded round to embrace their comrades and to lead them off where they might feed and make merry together.

Supper had been set in the hall of Ploermel wherein the knights and squires assembled. Bambro and Croquart were there with Sir Hugh Calverly, an old friend of Knolles and a fellow-townsman, for both were men of Chester. Sir Hugh was a middle-sized flaxen man, with hard gray eyes and fierce large-nosed face sliced across with the scar of a sword-cut. There too were Geoffrey D'Ardaine, a young Breton seigneur, Sir Thomas Belford, a burly thick-set Midland Englishman, Sir Thomas Walton, whose surcoat of scarlet martlets showed that he was of the Surrey Waltons, James Marshall and John Russell, young English squires, and the two brothers, Richard and Hugh Le Galliard, who were of Gascon blood. Besides these were several squires, unknown to fame, and of the new-comers, Sir Robert Knolles, Sir Thomas Percy, Nigel Loring and two other squires, Allington and Parsons. These were the company who gathered in the torch-light round the table of the Seneschal of Ploermel, and kept high revel with joyous hearts because they thought that much honor and noble deeds lay before them.

But one sad face there was at the board, and that belonged to him at the head of it. Sir Robert Bambro' sat with his chin leaning upon his hand and his eyes downcast upon the cloth, whilst all round him rose the merry clatter of voices, everyone planning some fresh enterprise which might now be attempted. Sir Robert Knolles was for an immediate advance upon Josselin. Calverly thought that a raid might be made into the South where the main French power lay. Others spoke of an attack upon Vannes.

To all these eager opinions Bambro' listened in a moody silence, which he broke at last by a fierce execration which drew a hushed attention from the company. "Say no more, fair sirs," he cried; "for indeed your words are like so many stabs in my heart. All this and more we might indeed have done. But of a truth you are too late."

"Too late?'" cried Knolles. "What mean you, Richard?"

"Alas; that I should have to say it, but you and all these fair soldiers might be back in England once more for all the profit that I am like to have from your coming. Saw you a rider on a white horse ere you reached the Castle?"

"Nay, I saw him not?"

"He came by the western road from Hennebon. Would that he had broken his neck ere he came here. Not an hour ago he left his message and now hath ridden on to warn the garrison of Malestroit. A truce has been proclaimed for a year betwixt the French King and the English, and he who breaks it forfeits life and estate."

"A truce!" Here was an end to all their fine dreams. They looked blankly at each other all round the table, whilst Croquart brought his great fist down upon the board until the glasses rattled again. Knolles sat with clenched hands as if he were a figure of stone, while Nigel's heart turned cold and heavy within him. A truce! Where then was his third deed, and how might he return without it?

Even as they sat in moody silence there was the call of a bugle from somewhere out in the darkness.

Sir Richard looked up with surprise. "We are not wont to be summoned after once the portcullis is up," said he. "Truce or no truce, we must let no man within our walls until we have proved him. Croquart, see to it!"

The huge German left the room. The company were still seated in despondent silence when he returned.

"Sir Richard," said he, "the brave knight Robert of Beaumanoir and his Squire William de Montaubon are without the gate, and would fain have speech with you."

Bambro started in his chair. What could the fierce leader of the Bretons, a man who was red to the elbow with English blood, have to say to them? On what errand had he left his castle of Josselin to pay this visit to his deadly enemies?

"Are they armed?" he asked.

"They are unarmed."

"Then admit them and bring them hither, but double the guards and take all heed against surprise."

Places were set at the farther end of the table for these most unexpected guests. Presently the door was swung open, and Croquart with all form and courtesy announced the two Bretons, who entered with the proud and lofty air of gallant warriors and high-bred gentlemen.

Beaumanoir was a tall dark man with raven hair and long swarthy beard. He was strong and straight as a young oak, with fiery black eyes, and no flaw in his comely features save that his front teeth had been dashed from their sockets. His Squire, William of Montaubon, was also tall, with a thin hatchet face, and two small gray eyes set very close upon either side of a long fierce nose. In Beaumanoir's expression one read only gallantry and frankness; in Montaubon's there was gallantry also, but it was mixed with the cruelty and cunning of the wolf. They bowed as they entered, and the little English seneschal advanced with outstretched hand to meet them.

"Welcome, Robert, so long as you are beneath this roof," said he. "Perhaps the time may come in another place when we may speak to each other in another fashion."

"So I hope, Richard," said Beaumanoir; "but indeed we of Josselin bear you in high esteem and are much beholden to you and to your men for all that you have done for us. We could not wish better neighbors nor any from whom more honor is to be gained. I learn that Sir Robert Knolles and others have joined you, and we are heavy-hearted to think that the orders of our Kings should debar us from attempting a venture." He and his squire sat down at the places set for them, and filling their glasses drank to the company.

"What you say is true, Robert," said Bambro, "and before you came we were discussing the matter among ourselves and grieving that it should be so. When heard you of the truce?"

"Yester-evening a messenger rode from Nantes."

"Our news came to-night from Hennebon. The King's own seal was on the order. So I fear that for a year at least you will bide at Josselin and we at Ploermel, and kill time as we may. Perchance we may hunt the wolf together in the great forest, or fly our hawks on the banks of the Duc."

"Doubtless we shall do all this, Richard," said Beaumanoir; "but by Saint Cadoc it is in my mind that with good-will upon both sides we may please ourselves and yet stand excused before our Kings."

Knights and squires leaned forward in their chairs, their eager eyes, fixed upon him. He broke into a gap-toothed smile as he looked round at the circle, the wizened seneschal, the blond giant, Nigel's fresh young face, the grim features of Knolles, and the yellow hawk-like Calverly, all burning with the same desire.

"I see that I need not doubt the good-will," said he, "and of that I was very certain before I came upon this errand. Bethink you then that this order applies to war but not to challenges, spear-runnings, knightly exchanges or the like. King Edward is too good a knight, and so is King John, that either of them should stand in the way of a gentleman who desires to advance himself or to venture his body for the exaltation of his lady. Is this not so?"

A murmur of eager assent rose from the table.

"If you as the garrison of Ploermel march upon the garrison of Josselin, then it is very plain that we have broken the truce and upon our heads be it. But if there be a private bickering betwixt me, for example, and this young squire whose eyes show that he is very eager for honor, and if thereafter others on each side join in and fight upon the quarrel, it is in no sense war, but rather our own private business which no king can alter."

"Indeed, Robert," said Bambro, "all that you say is very good and fair."

Beaumanoir leaned forward toward Nigel, his brimming glass in his hand. "Your name, squire?" said he.

"My name is Nigel Loring."

"I see that you are young and eager, so I choose you as I would fain have been chosen when I was of your age."

"I thank you, fair sir," said Nigel. "It is great honor that one so famous as yourself should condescend to do some small deed upon me."

"But we must have cause for quarrel, Nigel. Now here I drink to the ladies of Brittany, who of all ladies upon this earth are the most fair and the most virtuous, so that the least worthy-amongst them is far above the best of England. What say you to that, young sir?"

Nigel dipped his finger in his glass and leaning over he placed its wet impress on the Breton's hand. "This in your face!" said he.

Beaumanoir swept off the red drop of moisture and smiled his approval. "It could not have been better done," said he. "Why spoil my velvet paltock as many a hot-headed fool would have done. It is in my mind, young sir, that you will go far. And now, who follows up this quarrel?"

A growl ran round the table.

Beaumanoir ran his eye round and shook his head. "Alas!" said he, "there are but twenty of you here, and I have thirty at Josselin who are so eager to advance themselves that if I return without hope for all of them there will be sore hearts amongst them. I pray you, Richard, since we have been at these pains to arrange matters, that you in turn will do what you may. Can you not find ten more men?"

"But not of gentle blood."

"Nay, it matters not, if they will only fight."

"Of that there can be no doubt, for the castle is full of archers and men-at-arms who would gladly play a part in the matter."

"Then choose ten," said Beaumanoir.

But for the first time the wolf-like squire opened his thin lips. "Surely, my lord, you will not allow archers," said he.

"I fear not any man."

"Nay, fair sir, consider that this is a trial of weapons betwixt us where man faces man. You have seen these English archers, and you know how fast and how strong are their shafts. Bethink you that if ten of them were against us it is likely that half of us would be down before ever we came to handstrokes."

"By Saint Cadoc, William, I think that you are right," cried the Breton. "If we are to have such a fight as will remain in the memories of men, you will bring no archers and we no crossbows. Let it be steel upon steel. How say you then?"

"Surely we can bring ten men-at-arms to make up the thirty that you desire, Robert. It is agreed then that we fight on no quarrel of England and France, but over this matter of the ladies in which you and Squire Loring have fallen out. And now the time?"

"At once."

"Surely at once, or perchance a second messenger may come and this also be forbidden. We will be ready with to-morrow's sunrise."

"Nay, a day later," cried the Breton Squire. "Bethink you, my lord, that the three lances of Radenac would take time to come over."

"They are not of our garrison, and they shall not have a place."

"But, fair sir, of all the lances of Brittany—"

"Nay, William, I will not have it an hour later. To-morrow it shall be, Richard."

"And where?"

"I marked a fitting place even as I rode here this evening. If you cross the river and take the bridle-path through the fields which leads to Josselin you come midway upon a mighty oak standing at the corner of a fair and level meadow. There let us meet at midday to-morrow."

"Agreed!" cried Bambro. "But I pray you not to rise, Robert! The night is still young and the spices and hippocras will soon be served. Bide with us, I pray you, for if you would fain hear the latest songs from England, these gentlemen have doubtless brought them. To some of us perchance it is the last night, so we would make it a full one."

But the gallant Breton shook his head. "It may indeed be the last night for many," said he, "and it is but right that my comrades should know it. I have no need of monk or friar, for I cannot think that harm will ever come beyond the grave to one who has borne himself as a knight should, but others have other thoughts upon these matters and would fain have time for prayer and penitence. Adieu, fair sirs, and I drink a last glass to a happy meeting at the midway oak."

CHAPTER XXIII

HOW THIRTY OF JOSSELIN ENCOUNTERED THIRTY OF PLOERMEL

ALL night the Castle of Ploermel rang with warlike preparations, for the smiths were hammering and filing and riveting, preparing the armor for the champions. In the stable yard hostlers were testing and grooming the great war-horses, whilst in the chapel knights and squires were easing their souls at the knees of old Father Benedict.

Down in the courtyard, meanwhile, the men-at-arms had been assembled, and the volunteers weeded out until the best men had been selected. Black Simon had obtained a place, and great was the joy which shone upon his grim visage. With him were chosen young Nicholas Dagsworth, a gentleman adventurer who was nephew to the famous Sir Thomas, Walter the German, Hulbitée—a huge peasant whose massive frame gave promise which his sluggish spirit failed to fulfil—John Alcock, Robin Adey and Raoul Provost. These with three others made up the required thirty. Great was the grumbling and evil the talk amongst the archers when it was learned that none of them were to be included, but the bow had been forbidden on either side. It is true that many of them were expert fighters both with ax and with sword, but they were unused to carry heavy armor, and a half-armed man would have short shrift in such a hand-to-hand struggle as lay before them.

It was two hours after tierce, or one hour before noon, on the fourth Wednesday of Lent in the year of Christ 1351 that the men of Ploermel rode forth from their castle-gate and crossed the

711

bridge of the Duc. In front was Bambro with his Squire Croquart, the latter on a great roan horse bearing the banner of Ploermel, which was a black rampant lion holding a blue flag upon a field of ermine. Behind him came Robert Knolles and Nigel Loring, with an attendant at their side, who carried the pennon of the black raven. Then rode Sir Thomas Percy with his blue lion flaunting above him, and Sir Hugh Calverly, whose banner bore a silver owl, followed by the massive Belford who carried a huge iron club, weighing sixty pounds, upon his saddlebow, and Sir Thomas Walton the knight of Surrey. Behind them were four brave Anglo-Bretons, Perrot de Commelain, Le Gaillart, d'Aspremont and d'Ardaine, who fought against their own countrymen because they were partisans of the Countess of Montfort. Her engrailed silver cross upon a blue field was carried at their head. In the rear were five German or Hainault mercenaries, the tall Hulbitée, and the men-at-arms. Altogether of these combatants twenty were of English birth, four were Breton and six were of German blood.

So, with glitter of armor and flaunting of pennons, their warhorses tossing and pawing, the champions rode down to the midway oak. Behind them streamed hundreds of archers and men- at-arms whose weapons had been wisely taken from them lest a general battle should ensue. With them also went the townsfolk, men and women, together with wine-sellers, provisions merchants, armorers, grooms and heralds, with surgeons to tend the wounded and priests to shrive the dying. The path was blocked by this throng, but all over the face of the country horsemen and footmen, gentle and simple, men and women, could be seen speeding their way to the scene of the encounter.

The journey was not a long one, for presently, as they threaded their way through the fields, there appeared before them a great gray oak which spread its gnarled leafless branches over the corner of a green and level meadow. The tree was black with the peasants who had climbed into it, and all round it was a huge throng, chattering and calling like a rookery at sunset. A storm of hooting broke out from them at the approach of the English, for

Bambro was hated in the country where he raised money for the Montfort cause by putting every parish to ransom and maltreating those who refused to pay. There was little amenity in the warlike ways which had been learned upon the Scottish border. The champions rode onward without deigning to take notice of the taunts of the rabble, but the archers turned that way and soon beat the mob to silence. Then they resolved themselves into the keepers of the ground, and pressed the people back until they formed a dense line along the edge of the field, leaving the whole space clear for the warriors.

The Breton champions had not yet arrived, so the English tethered their horses at one side of the ground, and then gathered round their leader. Every man had his shield slung round his neck, and had cut his spear to the length of five feet so that it might be more manageable for fighting on foot. Besides the spear a sword or a battle-ax hung at the side of each. They were clad from head to foot in armor, with devices upon the crests and surcoats to distinguish them from their antagonists. At present their visors were still up and they chatted gayly with each other.

"By Saint Dunstan!" cried Percy, slapping his gauntleted hands together and stamping his steel feet. "I shall be right glad to get to work, for my blood is chilled."

"I warrant you will be warm enough ere you get through," said Calverly.

"Or cold forever. Candle shall burn and bell toll at Alnwick Chapel if I leave this ground alive, but come what may, fair sirs, it should be a famous joust and one which will help us forward. Surely each of us will have worshipfully won worship, if we chance to come through."

"You say truth, Thomas," said Knolles, bracing his girdle. "For my own part I have no joy in such encounters when there is warfare to be carried out, for it standeth not aright that a man should think of his own pleasure and advancement rather than of the King's cause and the weal of the army. But in times of truce I can think of no better way in which a day may be profitably spent. Why so silent, Nigel?"

"Indeed, fair sir, I was looking toward Josselin, which lies as I understand beyond those woods. I see no sign of this debonair gentleman and of his following. It would be indeed grievous pity if any cause came to hold them back."

Hugh Calverly laughed at the words. "You need have no fear, young sir," said he. "Such a spirit lies in Robert de Beaumanoir that if he must come alone he would ride against us none the less. I warrant that if he were on a bed of death he would be borne here and die on the green field."

"You say truly, Hugh," said Bambro. "I know him and those who ride behind him. Thirty stouter men or more skilled in arms are not to be found in Christendom. It is in my mind that come what may there will be much honor for all of us this day. Ever in my head I have a rhyme which the wife of a Welsh archer gave me when I crossed her hand with a golden bracelet after the intaking of Bergerac. She was of the old blood of Merlin with the power of sight. Thus she said:

> 'Twixt the oak-tree and the river
> Knightly fame aid brave endeavor
> Make an honored name forever.

Methinks I see the oak-tree, and yonder is the river. Surely this should betide some good to us."

The huge German Squire betrayed some impatience during this speech of his leader. Though his rank was subordinate, no man present had more experience of warfare or was more famous as a fighter than he. He now broke brusquely into the talk. "We should be better employed in ordering our line and making our plans than in talking of the rhymes of Merlin or such old wives' tales," said he. "It is to our own strong arms and good weapons that we must trust this day. And first I would ask you, Sir Richard, what is your will if perchance you should fall in the midst of the fight?"

Bambro turned to the others. "If such should be the case, fair sirs, I desire that my Squire Croquart should command."

There was a pause while the knights looked with some chagrin at each other. The silence was broken by Knolles. "I will do what you say, Richard," said he, "though indeed it is bitter that we who are knights should serve beneath a squire. Yet it is not for us to fall out among ourselves now at this last moment, and I have ever heard that Croquart is a very worthy and valiant man. Therefore, I will pledge you on jeopardy of my soul that I will accept him as leader if you fall."

"So will I also, Richard," said Calverly.

"And I too!" cried Belford. "But surely I hear music, and yonder are their pennons amid the trees."

They all turned, leaning upon their short spears, and watched the advance of the men of Josselin, as their troop wound its way out from the woodlands. In front rode three heralds with tabards of the ermine of Brittany, blowing loudly upon silver trumpets. Behind them a great man upon a white horse bore the banner of Josselin which carries nine golden torteaus upon a scarlet field. Then came the champions riding two and two, fifteen knights and fifteen squires, each with his pennon displayed. Behind them on a litter was borne an aged priest, the Bishop of Rennes, carrying in his hands the viaticum and the holy oils that he might give the last aid and comfort of the Church to those who were dying. The procession was terminated by hundreds of men and women from Josselin, Guegon, and Helleon, and by the entire garrison of the fortress, who came, as the English had done, without their arms. The head of this long column had reached the field before the rear were clear of the wood, but as they arrived the champions picketed their horses on the farther side, behind which their banner was planted and the people lined up until they had inclosed the whole lists with a dense wall of spectators.

With keen eyes the English party had watched the armorial blazonry of their antagonists, for those fluttering pennons and brilliant surcoats carried a language which all men could read. In front was the banner of Beaumanoir, blue with silver frets. His motto *"J'ayme qui m'ayme"* was carried on a second flag by a little page.

"Whose is the shield behind him—silver with scarlet drops?" asked Knolles.

"It is his Squire, William of Montaubon," Calverly answered. "And there are the golden lion of Rochefort and the silver cross of Du Bois the Strong. I would not wish to meet a better company than are before us this day. See, there are the blue rings of young Tintiniac, who slew my Squire Hubert last Lammastide. With the aid of Saint George I will avenge him ere nightfall."

"By the three kings of Almain," growled Croquart, "we will need to fight hard this day, for never have I seen so many good soldiers gathered together. Yonder is Yves Cheruel, whom they call the man of iron, Caro de Bodegat also with whom I have had more than one bickering—that is he with the three ermine circles on the scarlet shield. There too is left-handed Alain de Karanais; bear in mind that his stroke comes on the side where there is no shield."

"Who is the small stout man"—asked Nigel—"he with the black and silver shield? By Saint Paul! he seems a very worthy person and one from whom much might be gained, for he is nigh as broad as he is long."

"It is Sir Robert Raguenel," said Calverly, whose long spell of service in Brittany had made him familiar with the people. It is said that he can lift a horse upon his back. Beware a full stroke of that steel mace, for the armor is not made that can abide it. But here is the good Beaumanoir, and surely it is time that we came to grips."

The Breton leader had marshaled his men in a line opposite to the English, and now he strode forward and shook Bambro by the hand. "By Saint Cadoc! this is a very joyous meeting, Richard," said he, "and we have certainly hit upon a very excellent way of keeping a truce."

"Indeed, Robert," said Bambro, "we owe you much thanks, for I can see that you have been at great pains to bring a worthy company against us this day. Surely if all should chance to perish there will be few noble houses in Brittany who will not mourn."

"Nay, we have none of the highest of Brittany," Beaumanoir answered. "Neither a Blois, nor a Leon, nor a Rohan, nor a Conan, fights in our ranks this day. And yet we are all men of blood and coat-armor, who are ready to venture our persons for the desire of our ladies and the love of the high order of knighthood. And now, Richard, what is your sweet will concerning this fight?"

"That we continue until one or other can endure no longer, for since it is seldom that so many brave men draw together it is fitting that we see as much as is possible of each other."

"Richard, your words are fair and good. It shall be even as you say. For the rest, each shall fight as pleases him best from the time that the herald calls the word. If any man from without shall break in upon us he shall be hanged on yonder oak."

With a salute he drew down his visor and returned to his own men, who were kneeling in a twinkling, many colored group whilst the old bishop gave them his blessing.

The heralds rode round with a warning to the spectators. Then they halted at the side of the two bands of men who now stood in a long line facing each other with fifty yards of grass between. The visors had been closed, and every man was now cased in metal from head to foot, some few glowing in brass, the greater number shining in steel. Only their fierce eyes could be seen smoldering in the dark shadow of their helmets. So for an instant they stood glaring and crouching.

Then with a loud cry of "*Allez!*" the herald dropped his upraised hand, and the two lines of men shuffled as fast as their heavy armor would permit until they met with a sharp clang of metal in the middle of the field. There was a sound as of sixty smiths working upon their anvils. Then the babel of yells and shouts from the spectators, cheering on this party or that, rose and swelled until even the uproar of the combat was drowned in that mighty surge.

So eager were the combatants to engage that in a few moments all order had been lost and the two bands were mixed up in one furious scrambling, clattering throng, each man tossed hither and thither, thrown against one adversary and then against another, beaten and hustled and buffeted, with only the one thought in his mind to thrust with his spear or to beat with his ax against anyone who came within the narrow slit of vision left by his visor.

But alas for Nigel and his hopes of some great deed! His was at least the fate of the brave, for he was the first to fall. With a high heart he had placed himself in the line as nearly opposite to Beaumanoir as he could, and had made straight for the Breton leader, remembering that in the out set the quarrel had been so ordered that it lay between them. But ere he could reach his goal he was caught in the swirl of his own comrades, and being the lighter man was swept aside and dashed into the arms of Alain de Karanais, the left-handed swordsman, with such a crash that the two rolled upon the ground together. Light footed as a cat, Nigel had sprung up first, and was stooping over the Breton Squire when the powerful dwarf Raguenel brought his mace thudding down upon the exposed back of his helmet. With a groan Nigel fell upon his face, blood gushing from his mouth, nose, and ears. There he lay, trampled over by either party, while that great fight for which his fiery soul had panted was swaying back and forward above his unconscious form.

But Nigel was not long unavenged. The huge iron club of Belford struck the dwarf Raguenel to the ground, while Belford in turn was felled by a sweeping blow from Beaumanoir. Sometimes a dozen were on the ground at one time, but so strong was the armor, and so deftly was the force of a blow broken by guard and shield, that the stricken men were often pulled to their feet once more by their comrades, and were able to continue the fight.

Some, however, were beyond all aid. Croquart had cut at a Breton knight named Jean Rousselot and had shorn away his shoulder-piece, exposing his neck and the upper part of his arm. Vainly he tried to cover this vulnerable surface with his shield. It was his right side, and he could not stretch it far enough across, nor could he get away on account of the press of men around him. For a time he held his foemen at bay, but that bare patch of white shoulder was a mark for every weapon, until at last a hatchet sank up to the socket in the knight's chest. Almost at the same moment a second Breton, a young Squire named Geoffrey Mellon, was slain by a thrust from Black Simon which found the weak spot beneath the armpit. Three other Bretons, Evan Cheruel, Caro de Bodegat, and Tristan de Pestivien, the first two knights and the latter a squire, became separated from their comrades, and were beaten to the ground with English all around them, so that they had to choose between instant death and surrender. They handed their swords to Bambro and stood apart, each of them sorely wounded, watching with hot and bitter hearts the mêlée which still surged up and down the field.

But now the combat had lasted half an hour without stint or rest, until the warriors were so exhausted with the burden of their armor, the loss of blood, the shock of blows, and their own furious exertions, that they could scarce totter or raise their weapons. There must be a pause if the combat was to have any decisive end. "*Cessez! Cessez! Retirez!*" cried the heralds, as they spurred their horses between the exhausted men.

Slowly the gallant Beaumanoir led the twenty-five men who were left to their original station, where they opened their visors and threw themselves down upon the grass, panting like weary dogs, and wiping the sweat from their bloodshot eyes. A pitcher of wine of Anjou was carried round by a page, and each in turn drained a cup, save only Beaumanoir who kept his Lent with such strictness that neither food nor drink might pass his lips before sunset. He paced slowly amongst his men, croaking forth encouragement from his parched lips and pointing out to them that among the English there was scarce a man who was not wounded, and some so sorely that they could hardly stand. If the fight so far had gone against them, there were still five hours of daylight, and much might happen before the last of them was laid upon his back.

Varlets had rushed forth to draw away the two dead Bretons, and a brace of English archers had carried Nigel from the field. With his own hands Aylward had unlaced the crushed helmet and had wept to see the bloodless and unconscious face of his young master. He still breathed, however, and stretched upon the grass by the riverside the bowman tended him with rude surgery, until the water upon his brow and the wind upon his face had coaxed back the life into his battered frame. He breathed with heavy gasps, and some tinge of blood crept back into his cheeks, but still he lay unconscious of the roar of the crowd and of that great struggle which his comrades were now waging once again.

The English had lain for a space bleeding and breathless, in no better case than their rivals, save that they were still twenty-nine in number. But of this muster there were not nine who were hale men, and some were so weak from loss of blood that they could scarce keep standing. Yet, when the signal was at last given to reëngage there was not a man upon either side who did not totter to his feet and stagger forward toward his enemies.

But the opening of this second phase of the combat brought one great misfortune and discouragement to the English. Bambro like the others, had undone his visor, but with his mind full of many cares he had neglected to make it fast again. There was an opening an inch broad betwixt it and the beaver. As the two lines met the left-handed Breton squire, Alain de Karanais, caught sight of Bambro's face, and in an instant thrust his short spear through the opening. The English leader gave a cry of pain and fell on his knees, but staggered to his feet again, too weak to raise his shield. As he stood exposed the Breton knight, Geoffrey Dubois the Strong, struck him such a blow with his ax that he beat in the whole breast-plate with the breast behind it. Bambro fell dead upon the ground and for a few minutes a fierce fight raged round his body.

Then the English drew back, sullen and dogged, bearing Bambro with them, and the Bretons, breathing hard, gathered again in their own quarter. At the same instant the three prisoners picked up such weapons as were scattered upon the grass and ran over to join their own party.

"Nay, nay!" cried Knolles, raising his visor and advancing. "This may not be. You have been held to mercy when we might have slain you, and by the Virgin I will hold you dishonored, all three, if you stand not back."

"Say not so, Robert Knolles," Evan Cheruel answered. "Never yet has the word dishonor been breathed with my name, but I should count myself fainéant if I did not fight beside my comrades when chance has made it right and proper that I should do so."

"By Saint Cadoc! he speaks truly," croaked Beaumanoir, advancing in front of his men. "You are well aware, Robert, that it is the law of war and the usage of chivalry that if the knight to whom you have surrendered is himself slain the prisoners thereby become released."

There was no answer to this and Knolles, weary and spent, returned to his comrades. "I would that we had slain them," said he. "We have lost our leader and they have gained three men by the same stroke."

"If any more lay down their arms it is my order that you slay them forthwith," said Croquart, whose bent sword and bloody armor showed how manfully he had borne himself in the fray. "And now, comrades, do not be heavy-hearted because we have lost our leader. Indeed, his rhymes of Merlin have availed him little. By the three kings of Almain! I can teach you what is better than an old woman's prophecies, and that is that you should keep your shoulders together and your shields so close that none can break between them. Then you will know what is on either side of you, and you can fix your eyes upon the front. Also, if any be so weak or wounded that he must sink his hands his comrades on right and left can bear him up. Now advance all together in God's name, for the battle is still ours if we bear ourselves like men."

In a solid line the English advanced, while the Bretons ran forward as before to meet them. The swiftest of these was a certain Squire, Geoffrey Poulart, who bore a helmet which was fashioned as a cock's head, with high comb above, and long pointed beak in front pierced with the breathing-holes. He thrust with his sword at Calverly, but Belford who was the next in the line raised his giant club and struck him a crushing blow from the side. He staggered, and then pushing forth from the crowd, he ran round and round in circles as one whose brain is stricken, the blood dripping from the holes of his brazen beak. So for a long time he ran, the crowd laughing and cock-crowing at the sight, until at last he stumbled and fell stone-dead upon his face. But the fighters had seen nothing of his fate, for desperate and unceasing was the rush of the Bretons and the steady advance of the English line.

For a time it seemed as if nothing would break it, but gap-toothed Beaumanoir was a general as well as a warrior. Whilst his weary, bleeding, hard-breathing men still flung themselves upon the front of the line, he himself with Raguenel, Tentiniac, Alain de Karanais, and Dubois rushed round the flank and attacked the English with fury from behind. There was a long and desperate mêlée until once more the heralds, seeing the combatants stand gasping and unable to strike a blow, rode in and called yet another interval of truce.

But in those few minutes whilst they had been assaulted upon both sides, the losses of the English party had been heavy. The Anglo-Breton D'Ardaine had fallen before Beaumanoir's sword, but not before he had cut deeply into his enemy's shoulder. Sir Thomas Walton, Richard of Ireland one of the Squires, and Hulbitée the big peasant had all fallen before the mace of the dwarf Raguenel or the swords of his companions. Some twenty men were still left standing upon either side, but all were in the last state of exhaustion, gasping, reeling, hardly capable of striking a blow.

It was strange to see them as they staggered with many a lurch and stumble toward each other once again, for they moved like drunken men, and the scales of their neck-armor and joints were as red as fishes' gills when they raised them. They left foul wet footprints behind them on the green grass as they moved forward once more to their endless contest.

Beaumanoir, faint with the drain of his blood and with a tongue of leather, paused as he advanced. "I am fainting, comrades," he cried. "I must drink."

"Drink your own blood, Beaumanoir!" cried Dubois, and the weary men all croaked together in dreadful laughter.

But now the English had learned from experience, and under the guidance of Croquart they fought no longer in a straight line, but in one so bent that at last it became a circle. As the Bretons still pushed and staggered against it they thrust it back on every side, until they had turned it into the most dangerous formation of all, a solid block of men, their faces turned outward, their weapons bristling forth to meet every attack. Thus the English stood, and no assault could move them. They could lean against each other back to back while they waited and allowed their foemen to tire themselves out. Again and again the gallant Bretons tried to make a way through. Again and again they were beaten back by a shower of blows.

Beaumanoir, his head giddy with fatigue, opened his helmet and gazed in despair at this terrible, unbreakable circle. Only too clearly he could see the inevitable result. His men were wearing themselves out. Already many of them could scarce stir hand or foot, and might be dead for any aid which they could give him in winning the fight. Soon all would be in the same plight. Then these cursed English would break their circle to swarm over his helpless men and to strike them down. Do what he might, he could see no way by which such an end might be prevented. He cast his eyes round in his agony, and there was one of his Bretons slinking away to the side of the lists. He could scarce credit his senses when he saw by the scarlet and silver that the deserter was his own well-tried squire, William of Montaubon.

"William! William!" he cried. "Surely you would not leave me?"

But the other's helmet was closed and he could hear nothing. Beaumanoir saw that he was staggering away as swiftly as he could. With a cry of bitter despair, he drew into a knot as many of his braves as could still move, and together they made a last rush upon the English spears. This time he was firmly resolved, deep in his gallant soul, that he would come no foot back, but would find his death there amongst his foemen or carve a path into the heart of their ranks. The fire in his breast spread from man to man of his followers, and amid the crashing of blows they still locked themselves against the English shields and drove hard for an opening in their ranks.

But all was vain! Beaumanoir's head reeled. His senses were leaving him. In another minute he and his men would have been stretched senseless before this terrible circle of steel, when suddenly the whole array fell in pieces before his eyes, his enemies Croquart, Knolles, Calverly, Belford, all were stretched upon the ground together, their weapons dashed from their hands and their bodies too exhausted to rise. The surviving Bretons had but strength to fall upon them dagger in hands, and to wring from them their surrender with the sharp point stabbing through their visors. Then victors and vanquished lay groaning and panting in one helpless and blood-smeared heap.

To Beaumanoir's simple mind it had seemed that at the supreme moment the Saints of Brittany had risen at their country's call. Already, as he lay gasping, his heart was pouring forth its thanks to his patron Saint Cadoc. But the spectators had seen clearly enough the earthly cause of this sudden victory, and a hurricane of applause from one side, with a storm of hooting from the other showed how different was the emotion which it raised in minds which sympathized with the victors or the vanquished.

William of Montaubon, the cunning squire, had made his way across to the spot where the steeds were tethered, and had mounted his own great roussin. At first it was thought that he was about to ride from the field, but the howl of execration from the Breton peasants changed suddenly to a yell of applause and delight as he turned the beast's head for the English circle and thrust his long prick spurs into its side. Those who faced him saw this sudden and unexpected appearance. Time was when both horse and rider must have winced away from the shower of their blows. But now they were in no state to meet such a rush. They could scarce raise their arms. Their blows were too feeble to hurt this mighty creature. In a moment it had plunged through the ranks, and seven of them were on the grass. It turned and rushed through them again, leaving five others helpless beneath its hoofs. No need to do more! Already Beaumanoir and his companions were inside the circle, the prostrate men were helpless, and Josselin had won.

That night a train of crestfallen archers, bearing many a prostrate figure, marched sadly into Ploermel Castle. Behind them rode ten men, all weary, all wounded, and all with burning hearts against William of Montaubon for the foul trick that he had served them.

But over at Josselin, yellow gorse-blossoms in their helmets, the victors were borne in on the shoulders of a shouting mob, amid the fanfare of trumpets and the beating of drums. Such was the combat of the Midway Oak, where brave men met brave men, and such honor was gained that from that day he who had fought in the Battle of the Thirty was ever given the highest place and the post of honor, nor was it easy for any man to pretend to have been there, for it has been said by that great chronicler who knew them all, that not one on either side failed to carry to his grave the marks of that stern encounter.

CHAPTER XXIV

HOW NIGEL WAS CALLED TO HIS MASTER

My sweet ladye," wrote Nigel in a script which it would take the eyes of love to read, "there hath been a most noble meeting in the fourth sennight of Lent betwixt some of our own people and sundry most worthy persons of this country, which ended, by the grace of our Lady, in so fine a joust that no man living can call to mind so fair an occasion. Much honor was gained by the Sieurde Beaumanoir and also by an Almain named Croquart, with whom I hope to have some speech when I am hale again, for he is a most excellent person and very ready to advance himself or to relieve another from a vow. For myself I had hoped, with Godde's help, to venture that third small deed which might set me free to haste to your sweet side, but things have gone awry with me, and I early met with such scathe and was of so small comfort to my friends that my heart is heavy within me, and in sooth I feel that I have lost honour rather than gained it. Here I have lain since the Feast of the Virgin, and here I am like still to be, for I can move no limb, save only my hand; but grieve not, sweet lady, for Saint Catharine hath been our friend since in so short a time I had two such ventures as the Red Ferret and the intaking of the Reaver's fortalice. It needs but one more deed, and sickerly when I am hale once more it will not be long ere I seek it out. Till then, if my eyes may not rest upon you, my heart at least is ever at thy feet."

So he wrote from his sick-room in the Castle of Ploermel late in the summer, but yet another summer had come before his crushed head had mended and his wasted limbs had gained their strength once more. With despair he heard of the breaking of the truce, and of the fight at Mauron in which Sir Robert Knolles and Sir Walter Bentley crushed the rising power of Brittany—a fight in which many of the thirty champions of Josselin met their end. Then, when with renewed strength and high hopes in his heart he went forth to search for the famous Croquart who proclaimed himself ever ready night or day to meet any man with any weapon, it was only to find that in trying the paces of his new horse the German had been cast into a ditch and had broken his neck. In the same ditch perished Nigel's last chance of soon accomplishing that deed which should free him from his vow.

There was truce once more over all Christendom, and mankind was sated with war, so that only in far-off Prussia, where the Teutonic knights waged ceaseless battle with the Lithuanian heathen, could he hope to find his heart's desire. But money and high knightly fame were needed ere a man could go upon the northern crusade, and ten years were yet to pass ere Nigel should look from the battlements of Marienberg on the waters of the Frische Haff, or should endure the torture of the hot plate when bound to the Holy Woden stone of Memel. Meanwhile, he chafed his burning soul out through the long seasons of garrison life in Brittany, broken only by one visit to the chateau of the father of Raoul, when he carried to the Lord of Grosbois the news of how his son had fallen like a gallant gentleman under the gateway of La Brohinière.

And then, then at last, when all hope was well-nigh dead in his heart, there carne one glorious July morning which brought a horseman bearing a letter to the Castle of Vannes, of which Nigel now was seneschal. It contained but few words, short and clear as the call of a war-trumpet. It was Chandos who wrote. He needed his Squire at his side, for his pennon was in the breeze once more. He was at Bordeaux. The Prince was starting at once for Bergerac, whence he would make a great raid into France. It would not end without a battle. They had sent word of their coming, and the good French King had promised to be at great pains to receive them. Let Nigel hasten at once. If the army had left, then let him follow after with all speed. Chandos had three other squires, but would very gladly see his fourth once again, for he had heard much of him since he parted, and nothing which he might not have expected to hear of his father's son. Such was the letter which made the summer sun shine brighter and the blue sky seem of a still fairer blue upon that happy morning in Vannes.

It is a weary way from Vannes to Bordeaux. Coastwise ships are hard to find, and winds blow north when all brave hearts would fain be speeding south. A full month has passed from the day when Nigel received his letter before he stood upon the quay-side of the Garonne amid the stacked barrels of Gascon wine and helped to lead Pommers down the gang-planks. Not Aylward himself had a worse opinion of the sea than the great yellow horse, and he whinnied with joy as he thrust his muzzle into his master's outstretched hand, and stamped his ringing hoofs upon the good firm cobblestones. Beside him, slapping his tawny shoulder in encouragement, was the lean spare form of Back Simon who had remained ever under Nigel's pennon.

But Aylward, where was he? Alas! two years before he and the whole of Knolles' company of archers had been drafted away on the King's service to Guienne, and since he could not write the Squire knew not whether he was alive or dead. Simon, indeed, had thrice heard of him from wandering archers, each time that he was alive and well and newly married, but as the wife in one case was a fair maid, and in another a dark, while in the third she was a French widow, it was hard to know the truth.

Already the army had been gone a month, but news of it came daily to the town, and such news as all men could read, for through the landward gates there rolled one constant stream of wagons, pouring down the Libourne Road, and bearing the booty of Southern France. The town was full of foot-soldiers, for none but mounted men had been taken by the Prince. With sad faces and longing eyes they watched the passing of the train of plunder-laden carts, piled high with rich furniture, silks, velvets, tapestries, carvings, and precious metals, which had been the pride of many a lordly home in fair Auvergne or the wealthy Bourbonnais.

Let no man think that in these wars England alone was face to face with France alone. There is glory and to spare without trifling with the truth. Two Provinces in France, both rich and warlike, had become English through a royal marriage, and these, Guienne and Gascony, furnished many of the most valiant soldiers under the island flag. So poor a country as England could not afford to keep a great force overseas, and so must needs have lost the war with France through want of power to uphold the strug-gle. The feudal system enabled an army to be drawn rapidly together with small expense, but at the end of a few weeks it dis-persed again as swiftly, and only by a well-filled money-chest could it be held together. There was no such chest in England, and the King was forever at his wits' end how to keep his men in the field.

But Guienne and Gascony were full of knights and squires who were always ready to assemble from their isolated castles for a raid into France, and these with the addition of those English cavaliers who fought for honor, and a few thousand of the formidable archers, hired for fourpence a day, made an army with which a short campaign could be carried on. Such were the materials of the Prince's force, some eight thousand strong, who were now rid-ing in a great circle through Southern France, leaving a broad wale of blackened and ruined country behind them.

But France, even with her southwestern corner in English hands, was still a very warlike power, far richer and more populous than her rival. Single Provinces were so great that they were stronger than many a kingdom. Normandy in the north, Burgundy in the east, Brittany in the west and Languedoc in the south were each capable of fitting out a great army of their own. Therefore the brave and spirited John, watching from Paris this insolent raid into his dominions, sent messengers in hot haste to all these great feudatories as well as to Lorraine, Picardy, Auvergne, Hainault, Vermandois, Champagne, and to the German mercenaries over his eastern border, bidding all of them to ride hard, with bloody spur, day and night, until they should gather to a head at Chartres.

There a great army had assembled early in September, whilst the Prince, all unconscious of its presence sacked towns and besieged castles from Bourges to Issodun, passing Romorautin, and so onward to Vierzon and to Tours. From week to week there were merry skirmishes at barriers, brisk assaults of fortresses in which much honor was won, knightly meetings with detached parties of Frenchmen and occasional spear-runnings where noble champions deigned to venture their persons. Houses, too, were to be plundered, while wine and women were in plenty. Never had either knights or archers had so pleasant and profitable an excursion, so that it was with high heart and much hope of pleasant days at Bordeaux with their pockets full of money that the army turned south from the Loire and began to retrace its steps to the seaboard city.

But now its pleasant and martial promenade changed suddenly to very serious work of war. As the Prince moved south he found that all, supplies had been cleared away from in front of him and that there was neither fodder for the horses nor food for the men. Two hundred wagons laden with spoil rolled at the head of the army, but the starving soldiers would soon have gladly changed it all for as many loads of bread and of meat. The light troops of the French had preceded then and burned or destroyed everything that could be of use. Now also for the first time the Prince and his men became aware that a great army was moving upon the eastern side of them, streaming southward in the hope of cutting off their retreat to the sea. The sky glowed with their fires at night, and the autumn sun twinkled and gleamed from one end of the horizon to the other upon the steel caps and flashing weapons of a mighty host.

Anxious to secure his plunder, and conscious that the levies of France were far superior in number to his own force, the Prince redoubled his attempts to escape; but his horses were exhausted and his starving men were hardly to be kept in order. A few more days would unfit them for battle. Therefore, when he found near the village of Maupertuis a position in which a small force might have a chance to hold its own, he gave up the attempt to outmarch his pursuers, and he turned at bay, like a hunted boar, all tusks and eyes of flame.

Whilst these high events had been in progress, Nigel with Black Simon and four other men-at-arms from Bordeaux, was hastening northward to join the army. As far as Bergerac they were in a friendly land, but thence onward they rode over a blackened land-scape with many a roofless house, its two bare gable-ends sticking upward—a "Knolles' miter" as it was afterward called when Sir Robert worked his stern will upon the country. For three days they rode northward, seeing many small parties of French in all directions, but too eager to reach the army to ease their march in the search of adventures.

Then at last after passing Lusignan they began to come in touch with English foragers, mounted bowmen for the most part, who were endeavoring to collect supplies either for the army or for themselves. From them Nigel learned that the Prince, with Chandos ever at his side, was hastening south and might be met within a short day's march. As he still advanced these English stragglers became more and more numerous, until at last he over-took a considerable column of archers moving in the same direction as his own party. These were men whose horses had failed them and who had therefore been left behind on the advance, but were now hastening to be in time for the impending battle. A crowd of peasant girls accompanied them upon their march, and a whole train of laden mules were led beside them.

Nigel and his little troop of men-at-arms were riding past the archers when Black Simon with a sudden exclamation touched his leader upon the arm.

"See yonder, fair sir," he cried, with gleaming eyes, "there where the wastrel walks with the great fardel upon his back! Who is he who marches behind him?"

Nigel looked, and was aware of a stunted peasant who bore upon his rounded back an enormous bundle very much larger than himself. Behind him walked a burly broad-shouldered archer, whose stained jerkin and battered headpiece gave token of long and hard service. His bow was slung over his shoulder, and his arms were round the waists of two buxom Frenchwomen, who tripped along beside him with much laughter and many saucy answers flung back over their shoulders to a score of admirers behind them.

"Aylward!" cried Nigel, spurring forward.

The archer turned his bronzed face, stared for an instant with wild eyes, and then, dropping his two ladies, who were instantly carried off by his comrades, he rushed to seize the hand which his young master held down to him. "Now, by my hilt, Squire Nigel, this is the fairest sight of my lifetime!" he cried. "And you, old leather-face! Nay, Simon, I would put my arms round your dried herring of a body, if I could but reach you. Here is Pommers too, and I read in his eye that he knows me well and is as ready to put his teeth into me as when he stood in my father's stall."

It was like a whiff of the heather-perfumed breezes of Hankley to see his homely face once more. Nigel laughed with sheer joy as he looked at him.

"It was an ill day when the King's service called you from my side," said he, "and by Saint Paul! I am right glad to set eyes upon you once more! I see well that you are in no wise altered, but the same Aylward that I have ever known. But who is this varlet with the great bundle who waits upon your movements?"

"It is no less than a feather-bed, fair sir, which he bears upon his back, for I would fain bring it to Tilford, and yet it is overlarge for me when I take my place with my fellows in the ranks. But indeed this war has been a most excellent one, and I have already sent half a wagonload of my gear back to Bordeaux to await my homecoming. Yet I have my fears when I think of all the rascal foot-archers who are waiting there, for some folk have no grace or honesty in their souls, and cannot keep their hands from that which belongs to another. But if I may throw my leg over yonder spare horse I will come on with you, fair sir, for indeed it would be joy to my heart to know that I was riding under your banner once again."

So Aylward, having given instructions to the bearer of his feather-bed, rode away in spite of shrill protests from his French companions, who speedily consoled themselves with those of his comrades who seemed to have most to give. Nigel's party was soon clear of the column of archers and riding hard in the direction of the Prince's army. They passed by a narrow and winding track, through the great wood of Nouaille, and found before them a marshy valley down which ran a sluggish stream. Along its farther bank hundreds of horses were being watered, and beyond was a dense block of wagons. Through these the comrades passed, and then topped a small mound from which the whole strange scene lay spread before them.

Down the valley the slow stream meandered with marshy meadows on either side. A mile or two lower a huge drove of horses were to be seen assembled upon the bank. They were the steeds of the French cavalry, and the blue haze of a hundred fires showed where King John's men were camping. In front of the mound upon which they stood the English line was drawn, but there were few fires, for indeed, save their horses, there was little for them to cook. Their right rested upon the river, and their array stretched across a mile of ground until the left was in touch with a tangled forest which guarded it from flank attack. In front was a long thick hedge and much broken ground, with a single deeply rutted country road cutting through it in the middle. Under the hedge and along the Whole front of the position lay swarms of archers upon the grass, the greater number slumbering peacefully with sprawling limbs in the warm rays of the September sun. Behind were the quarters of the various knights, and from end to end flew the banners and pennons marked with the devices of the chivalry of England and Guienne.

With a glow in his heart Nigel saw those badges of famous captains and leaders and knew that now at last he also might show his coat-armor in such noble company. There was the flag of Jean

Grailly, the Captal de Buch, five silver shells on a black cross, which marked the presence of the most famous soldier of Gascony, while beside it waved the red lion of the noble Knight of Hainault, Sir Eustace d'Ambreticourt. These two coats Nigel knew, as did every warrior in Europe, but a dense grove of pennoned lances surrounded them, bearing charges which were strange to him, from which he understood that these belonged to the Guienne division of the army. Farther down the line the famous English ensigns floated on the wind, the scarlet and gold of Warwick, the silver star of Oxford, the golden cross of Suffolk, the blue and gold of Willoughby, and the gold-fretted scarlet of Audley. In the very center of them, all was one which caused all others to pass from his mind, for close to the royal banner of England, crossed with the label of the Prince, there waved the war-worn flag with the red wedge upon the golden field which marked the quarters of the noble Chandos.

At the sight Nigel set spurs to his horse, and a few minutes later had reached the spot. Chandos, gaunt from hunger and want of sleep, but with the old fire lurking in his eye, was standing by the Prince's tent, gazing down at what could be seen of the French array, and heavy with thought. Nigel sprang from his horse and was within touch of his master when the silken hanging of the royal tent was torn violently aside and Edward rushed out.

He was without his armor and clad in a sober suit of black, but the high dignity of his bearing and the imperious anger which flushed his face proclaimed the leader and the Prince. At his heels was a little white-haired ecclesiastic in a flowing gown of scarlet sendal, expostulating and arguing in a torrent of words.

"Not another word, my Lord Cardinal," cried the angry prince. "I have listened to you overlong, and by God's dignity! that which you say is neither good nor fair in my ears. Hark you, John, I would have your counsel. What think you is the message which my Lord Cardinal of Perigord has carried from the King of France? He says that of his clemency he will let my army pass back to Bordeaux if we will restore to him all that we have taken, remit all ransoms, and surrender my own person with that of a hundred nobles of England and Guienne to be held as prisoners. What think you, John?"

Chandos smiled. "Things are not done in that fashion," said he.

"But my Lord Chandos," cried the Cardinal, "I have made it clear to the Prince that indeed it is a scandal to all Christendom and a cause of mocking to the heathen, that two great sons of the Church should turn their swords thus upon each other."

"Then bid the King of France keep clear of us," said the Prince.

"Fair son, you are aware that you are in the heart of his country and that it standeth not aright that he should suffer you to go forth as you came. You have but a small army, three thousand bowmen and five thousand men-at-arms at the most, who seem in evil case for want of food and rest. The King has thirty thousand men at his back, of which twenty thousand are expert men-at-arms. It is fitting therefore that you make such terms as you may, lest worse befall."

"Give my greetings to the King of France and tell him that England will never pay ransom for me. But it seems to me, my Lord Cardinal, that you have our numbers and condition very ready upon your tongue, and I would fain know how the eye of a Churchman can read a line of battle so easily. I have seen that these knights of your household have walked freely to and fro within our camp, and I much fear that when I welcomed you as envoys I have in truth given my protection to spies. How say you, my Lord Cardinal?"

"Fair Prince, I know not how you can find it in your heart or conscience to say such evil words."

"There is this red-bearded nephew of thine, Robert de Duras. See where he stands yonder, counting and prying. Hark hither, young sir! I have been saying to your uncle the Cardinal that it is in my mind that you and your comrades have carried news of our dispositions to the French King. How say you?"

The knight turned pale and sank his eyes. "My lord," he murmured, "it may be that I have answered some questions."

"And how will such answers accord with your honor, seeing that we have trusted you since you came in the train of the Cardinal?"

"My lord, it is true that I am in the train of the Cardinal, and yet I am liege man of King John and a knight of France, so I pray you to assuage your wrath against me."

The Prince ground his teeth and his piercing eyes blazed upon the youth. "By my father's soul! I can scarce forbear to strike you to the earth! But this I promise you, that if you show that sign of the Red Griffin in the field and if you be taken alive in to-morrow's battle, your head shall most assuredly be shorn from your shoulders."

"Fair son, indeed you speak wildly," cried the Cardinal. "I pledge you my word that neither my nephew Robert nor any of my train will take part in the battle. And now I leave you, sire, and may God assoil your soul, for indeed in all this world no men stand in greater peril than you and those who are around you, and I rede you that you spend the night in such ghostly exercises as may best prepare you for that which may befall." So saying the Cardinal bowed, and with his household walking behind him set off for the spot where they had left their' horses, whence they rode to the neighboring Abbey.

The angry Prince turned upon his heel and entered his tent once more, whilst Chandos, glancing round, held out a warm welcoming hand to Nigel.

"I have heard much of your noble deeds," said he. "Already your name rises as a squire errant. I stood no higher, nor so high, at your age."

Nigel flushed with pride and pleasure. "Indeed, my dear lord, it is very little that I have done. But now that I am back at your side I hope that in truth I shall learn to bear myself in worthy fashion, for where else should I win honor if it be not under your banner."

"Truly, Nigel, you have come at a very good time for advancement. I cannot see how we can leave this spot without a great battle which will live in men's minds forever. In all our fights in France I cannot call to mind any in which they have been so strong or we so weak as now, so that there will be the more honor to be gained. I would that we had two thousand more archers. But I doubt not that we shall give them much trouble ere they drive us out from amidst these hedges. Have you seen the French?"

"Nay, fair sir, I have but this moment arrived."

"I was about to ride forth myself to coast their army and observe their countenance, so come with me ere the night fall, and we shall see what we can of their order and dispositions."

There was a truce betwixt the two forces for the day, on account of the ill-advised and useless interposition of the Cardinal of Perigord, Hence when Chandos and Nigel had pushed their horses through the long hedge which fronted the position they found that many small parties of the knights of either army were riding up and down on the plain outside. The greater number of these groups were French, since it was very necessary for them to know as much as possible of the English defenses; and many of their scouts had ridden up to within a hundred yards of the hedge, where they were sternly ordered back by the pickets of archers on guard.

Through these scattered knots of horsemen Chandos rode, and as many of them were old antagonists it was "Ha, John!" on the one side, and "Ha, Raoul!" "Ha, Nicholas!" "Ha, Guichard!" upon the other, as they brushed past them. Only one cavalier greeted them amiss, a large, red-faced man, the Lord Clermont, who by some strange chance bore upon his surcoat a blue virgin standing amid golden sunbeams, which was the very device which Chandos had donned for the day. The fiery Frenchman dashed across their path and drew his steed back on to its haunches.

"How long is it, my Lord Chandos," said he hotly, "since you have taken it upon yourself to wear my arms?"

Chandos smiled. "It is surely you who have mine," said he, "since this surcoat was worked for the by the good nuns of Windsor a long year ago."

"If it were not for the truce," said Clermont, "I would soon show you that you have no right to wear it."

"Look for it then in the battle to-morrow, and I also will look for yours," Chandos answered. "There we can very honorably settle the matter."

But the Frenchman was choleric and hard to appease. "You English can invent nothing," said he, "and you take for your own whatever you see handsome belonging to others." So, grumbling and fuming, he rode upon his way, while Chandos, laughing gayly, spurred onward across the plain.

The immediate front of the English line was shrouded with scattered trees and bushes which hid the enemy; but when they had cleared these a fair view of the great French army lay before them. In the center of the huge camp was a long and high pavilion of red silk, with the silver lilies of the King at one end of it, and the golden oriflamme, the battle-flag of old France, at the other. Like the reeds of a pool from side to side of the broad array, and dwindling away as far as their eyes could see, were the banners and pennons of high barons and famous knights, but above them all flew the ducal standards which showed that the feudal muster of all the warlike provinces of France was in the field before them.

With a kindling eye Chandos looked across at the proud ensigns of Normandy, or Burgundy, of Auvergne, of Champagne, of Vermandois, and of Berry, flaunting and gleaming in the rays of the sinking sun. Riding slowly down the line he marked with attentive gaze the camp of the crossbowmen, the muster of the German mercenaries, the numbers of the foot-soldiers, the arms of every proud vassal or vavasor which might give some guide as to the power of each division. From wing to wing and round the flanks he went, keeping ever within crossbow-shot of the army, and then at last having noted all things in his mind he turned his horse's head and rode slowly back, heavy with thought, to the English lines.

CHAPTER XXV

HOW THE KING OF FRANCE HELD
COUNSEL AT MAUPERTUIS

THE morning of Sunday, the nineteenth of September, in the year of our Lord 1356, was cold and fine. A haze which rose from the marshy valley of Muisson covered both camps and set the starving Englishmen shivering, but it cleared slowly away as the sun rose. In the red silken pavilion of the French King—the same which had been viewed by Nigel and Chandos the evening before—a solemn mass was held by the Bishop of Chalons, who prayed for those who were about to die, with little thought in his mind that his own last hour was so near at hand. Then, when communion had been taken by the King and his four young sons the altar was cleared away, and a great red-covered table placed lengthwise down the tent, round which John might assemble his council and determine how best he should proceed. With the silken roof, rich tapestries of Arras round the walls and Eastern rugs beneath the feet, his palace could furnish no fairer chamber.

King John, who sat upon the canopied dais at the upper end, was now in the sixth year of his reign and the thirty-sixth of his life. He was a short burly man, ruddy-faced and deep-chested, with dark kindly eyes and a most noble bearing. It did not need the blue cloak sewed with silver lilies to mark him as the King. Though his reign had been short, his fame was already widespread over all Europe as a kindly gentleman and a fearless soldier—a fit leader for a chivalrous nation. His elder son, the Duke of Normandy, still hardly more than a boy, stood beside him, his hand upon the King's shoulder, and John half turned from time to time to fondle him. On the right, at the same high dais, was the King's younger brother, the Duke of Orleans, a pale heavy-featured man, with a languid manner and intolerant eyes. On the left was the Duke of Bourbon, sad-faced and absorbed, with that gentle melancholy in his eyes and bearing which comes often with the premonition of death. All these were in their armor, save only for their helmets, which lay upon the board before them.

Below, grouped around the long red table, was an assembly of the most famous warriors in Europe. At the end nearest the King was the veteran soldier the Duke of Athens, son of a banished father, and now High Constable of France. On one side of him sat the red-faced and choleric Lord Clermont, with the same blue Virgin in golden rays upon his surcoat which had caused his quarrel with Chandos the night before. On the other was a noble-featured grizzly-haired soldier, Arnold d'Andreghen, who shared with Clermont the honor of being Marshal of France. Next to them sat Lord James of Bourbon, a brave warrior who was afterwards slain by the White Company at Brignais, and beside him a little group of German noblemen, including the Earl of Salzburg and the Earl of Nassau, who had ridden over the frontier with their formidable mercenaries at the bidding of the French King. The ridged armor and the hanging nasals of their bassinets were enough in themselves to tell every soldier that they were from beyond the Rhine. At the other side of the table were a line of proud and warlike Lords, Fiennes, Chatillon, Nesle, de Landas, de Beaujeu, with the fierce knight errant de Chargny, he who had planned the surprise of Calais, and Eustace de Ribeaumont, who had upon the same occasion won the prize of valor from the hands of Edward of England. Such were the chiefs to whom the King now turned for assistance and advice.

"You have already heard, my friends," said he, "that the Prince of Wales has made no answer to the proposal which we sent by the Lord Cardinal of Perigord. Certes this is as it should be, and though I have obeyed the call of Holy Church I had no fears that so excellent a Prince as Edward of England would refuse to meet us in battle. I am now of opinion that we should fall upon them at once, lest perchance the Cardinal's cross should again come betwixt our swords and our enemies."

A buzz of joyful assent arose from the meeting, and even from the attendant men-at-arms who guarded the door. When it had died away the Duke of Orleans rose in his place beside the King.

"Sire," said he, "you speak as we would have you do, and I for one am of opinion that the Cardinal of Perigord has been an ill friend of France, for why should we bargain for a part when we have but to hold out our hand in order to grasp the whole? What need is there for words? Let us spring to horse forthwith and ride over this handful of marauders who have dared to lay waste your fair dominions. If one of them go hence save as our prisoner we are the more to blame."

"By Saint Denis, brother!" said the King, smiling, "if words could slay you would have had them all upon their backs ere ever we left Chartres. You are new to war, but when you have had experience of a stricken field or two you would know that things must be done with forethought and in order or they may go awry. In our father's time we sprang to horse and spurred upon these English at Crécy and elsewhere as you advise, but we had little profit from it, and now we are grown wiser. How say you, Sieur de Ribeaumont? You have coasted their lines and observed their countenance. Would you ride down upon them, as my brother has advised, or how would you order the matter?"

De Ribeaumont, a tall dark-eyed handsome man, paused ere he answered. "Sire," he said at last, "I have indeed ridden along their front and down their flanks, in company with Lord Landas and Lord de Beaujeu, who are here at your council to witness to what I say. Indeed, sire, it is in my mind that though the English are few in number yet they are in such a position amongst these hedges and vines that you would be well-advised if you were to leave them alone, for they have no food and must retreat, so that you will be able to follow them and to fight them to better advantage."

A murmur of disapproval rose from the company, and the Lord Clermont, Marshal of the army, sprang to his feet, his face red with anger.

"Eustace; Eustace," said he, "I bear in mind the days when you were of great heart and high enterprise, but since King Edward gave you yonder chaplet of pearls you have ever been backward against the English!"

"My Lord Clermont," said de Ribeaumont sternly, "it is not for me to brawl at the King's council and in the face of the enemy, but we will go further into this matter at some other time. Meanwhile, the King has asked me for my advice and I have given it as best I might."

"It had been better for your honor, Sir Eustace, had you held your peace," said the Duke of Orleans. "Shall we let them slip from our fingers when we have them here and are fourfold their number? I know not where we should dwell afterwards, for I am very sure that we should be ashamed to ride back to Paris, or to look our ladies in the eyes again."

"Indeed, Eustace, you have done well to say what is in your mind," said the King; "but I have already said that we shall join battle this morning, so that there is no room here for further talk. But I would fain have heard from you how it would be wisest and best that we attack them?"

"I will advise you, sire, to the best of my power. Upon their right is a river with marshes around it, and upon their left a great wood, so that we can advance only upon the center. Along their front is a thick hedge, and behind it I saw the green jerkins of their archers, as thick as the sedges by the river. It is broken by one road where only four horsemen could ride abreast, which leads through the position. It is clear then that if we are to drive them back we must cross the great hedge, and I am very sure that the horses will not face it with such a storm of arrows beating from behind it. Therefore, it is my council that we fight upon foot, as the English did at Crécy, for indeed we may find that our horses will be more hindrance than help to us this day."

"The same thought was in my own mind, sire," said Arnold d'Andreghen the veteran Marshal. "At Crécy the bravest had to turn their backs, for what can a man do with a horse which is mad with pain and fear? If we advance upon foot we are our own masters, and if we stop the shame is ours."

"The counsel is good," said the Duke of Athens, turning his shrewd wizened face to the King; "but one thing only I would add to it. The strength of these people lies in their archers, and if we could throw them into disorder, were it only for a short time, we should win the hedge; else they will shoot so strongly that we must lose many men before we reach it, for indeed we have learned that no armor will keep out their shafts when they are close."

"Your words, fair sir, are both good and wise," said the King, "but I pray you to tell us how you would throw these archers into disorder?"

"I would choose three hundred horsemen, sire, the best and most forward in the army. With these I would ride up the narrow road, and so turn to right and left, falling upon the archers behind the hedge. It may be that the three hundred would suffer sorely, but what are they among so great a host, if a road may be cleared for their companions?"

"I would say a word to that, sire," cried the German Count of Nassau, "I have come here with my comrades to venture our persons in your quarrel; but we claim the right to fight in our own fashion, and we would count it dishonor to dismount from our steeds out of fear of the arrows of the English. Therefore, with your permission, we will ride to the front, as the Duke of Athens has advised, and so clear a path for the rest of you."

"This may not be!" cried the Lord Clermont angrily. "It would be strange indeed if Frenchmen could not be found to clear a path for the army of the King of France. One would think to hear you talk, my Lord Count, that your hardihood was greater than our own, but by our Lady of Rocamadour you will learn before nightfall that it is not so. It is for me, who am a Marshal of France; to lead these three hundred, since it is an honorable venture."

"And I claim the same right for the same reason," said Arnold of Andreghen.

The German Count struck the table with his mailed fist. "Do what you like!" said he. "But this only I can promise you, that neither I nor any of my German riders will descend from our horses so long as they are able to carry us, for in our country it is only people of no consequence who fight upon their feet."

The Lord Clermont was leaning angrily forward with some hot reply when King John intervened. "Enough, enough!" he said. "It is for you to give your opinions, and for me to tell you what you will do. Lord Clermont, and you, Arnold, you will choose three hundred of the bravest cavaliers in the army and you will endeavor to break these archers. As to you and your Germans, my Lord Nassau , you will remain upon horseback, since you desire it, and you will follow the Marshals and support them as best you may. The rest of the army will advance upon foot, in three other divisions as arranged: yours, Charles," and he patted his son, the Duke of Normandy, affectionately upon the hand; "yours, Philip," he glanced at the Duke of Orleans; "and the main battle which is my own. To you, Geoffrey de Chargny, I intrust the oriflamme this day. But who is this knight and what does he desire?"

A young knight, ruddy-bearded and tall, a red griffin upon his surcoat, had appeared in the opening of the tent. His flushed face and disheveled dress showed that he had come in haste. "Sire," said he, "I am Robert de Duras, of the household of the Cardinal de Perigord. I have told you yesterday all that I have learned of the English camp. This morning I was again admitted to it, and I have seen their wagons moving to the rear. Sire, they are in flight for Bordeaux."

"'Fore God, I knew it!" cried the Duke of Orleans in a voice of fury. "Whilst we have been talking they have slipped through our fingers. Did I not warn you?"

"Be silent, Philip!" said the King angrily. "But you, sir, have you seen this with your own eyes?"

THE WHITE COMPANY AND SIR NIGEL

"With my own eyes, sire, and I have ridden straight from their camp."

King John looked at him with a stern gaze. "I know not how it accords with your honor to carry such tidings in such a fashion," said he; "but we cannot choose but take advantage of it. Fear not, brother Philip, it is in my mind that you will see all that you would wish of the Englishmen before nightfall. Should we fall upon them whilst they cross the ford it will be to our advantage. Now, fair sirs, I pray you to hasten to your posts and to carry out all that we have agreed. Advance the oriflamme, Geoffrey, and do you marshal the divisions, Arnold. So may God and Saint Denis have us in their holy keeping this day!"

The Prince of Wales stood upon that little knoll where Nigel had halted the day before. Beside him were Chandos, and a tall sun-burned warrior of middle age, the Gascon Captal de Buch. The three men were all attentively watching the distant French lines, while behind them a column of wagons wound down to the ford of the Muisson.

Close in the rear four knights in full armor with open visors sat their horses and conversed in undertones with each other. A glance at their shields would have given their names to any soldier, for they were all men of fame who had seen much warfare. At present they were awaiting their orders, for each of them commanded the whole or part of a division of the army. The youth upon the left, dark, slim and earnest, was William Montacute, Earl of Salisbury, only twenty-eight years of age and yet a veteran of Crécy. How high he stood in reputation is shown by the fact that the command of the rear, the post of honor in a retreating army, had been given to him by the Prince. He was talking to a grizzled harsh-faced man, somewhat over middle age, with lion features and fierce light-blue eyes which gleamed as they watched the distant enemy. It was the famous Robert de Ufford, Earl of Suffolk, who had fought without a break from Cadsand onward through the whole Continental War. The other tall silent soldier, with the silver star gleaming upon his surcoat, was John de Vere, Earl of Oxford, and he listened to the talk of Thomas Beauchamp, a burly, jovial, ruddy nobleman and a tried soldier, who leaned forward and tapped his mailed hand upon the other's steel-clad thigh. They were old battle-companions, of the same age and in the very prime of life, with equal fame and equal experience of the wars. Such was the group of famous English soldiers who sat their horses behind the Prince and waited for their orders.

"I would that you had laid hands upon him," said the Prince angrily, continuing his conversation with Chandos, "and yet, perchance, it was wiser to play this trick and make them think that we were retreating."

"He has certainly carried the tidings," said Chandos, with a smile. "No sooner had the wagons started than I saw him gallop down the edge of the wood."

"It was well thought of, John," the Prince remarked, "for it would indeed be great comfort if we could turn their own spy against them. Unless they advance upon us, I know not how we can hold out another day, for there is not a loaf left in the army; and yet if we leave this position where shall we hope to find such another?"

"They will stoop, fair sir, they will stoop to our lure. Even now Robert de Duras will be telling them that the wagons are on the move, and they will hasten to overtake us lest we pass the ford. But who is this, who rides so fast? Here perchance may be tidings."

A horseman had spurred up to the knoll. He sprang from the saddle, and sank on one knee before the Prince. "How now, my Lord Audley," said Edward. " What would you have?"

"Sir," said the knight, still kneeling with bowed head before his leader, "I have a boon to ask of you."

"Nay, James, rise! Let me hear what I can do."

The famous knight errant, pattern of chivalry for all time; rose and turned his swarthy face and dark earnest eyes upon his master. "Sir," said he, "I have ever served most loyally my lord your father and yourself, and shall continue so to do so long as I have life.

Dear sir, I must now acquaint you that formerly I made a vow if ever I should be in any battle under your command that I would be foremost or die in the attempt. I beg therefore that you will graciously permit me to honorably quit my place among the others, that I may post myself in such wise as to accomplish my vow."

The Prince smiled, for it was very sure that vow or no vow, permission or no permission, Lord James Audley would still be in the van. "Go, James," said he, shaking his hand, "and God grant that this day you may shine in valor above all knights. But hark, John, what is that?" Chandos cast up his fierce nose like the eagle which smells slaughter afar. "Surely, sir, all is forming even as we had planned it."

From far away there came a thunderous shout. Then another and yet another.

"See, they are moving!" cried the Captal de Buch.

All morning they had watched the gleam of the armed squadrons who were drawn up in front of the French camp. Now whilst a great blare of trumpets was borne to their ears, the distant masses flickered and twinkled in the sunlight.

"Yes, yes, they are moving!" cried the Prince.

"They are moving! They are moving!" Down the line the murmur ran. And then with a sudden impulse the archers at the hedge sprang to their feet and the knights behind them waved their weapons in the air, while one tremendous shout of warlike joy carried their defiance to the approaching enemy. Then there fell such a silence that the pawing of the horses or the jingle of their harness struck loud upon the ear, until amid the hush there rose a low deep roar like the sound of the tide upon the beach, ever growing and deepening as the host of France drew near.

CHAPTER XXVI

HOW NIGEL FOUND HIS THIRD DEED

FOUR archers lay behind a clump of bushes ten yards in front of the thick hedge which shielded their companions. Amid the long line of bowmen those behind them were their own company, and in the main the same who were with Knolles in Brittany. The four in front were their leaders: old Wat of Carlisle, Ned Widdington the red-headed Dalesman, the bald bowyer Bartholomew, and Samkin Alyward, newly rejoined after a week's absence. All four were munching bread and apples, for Aylward had brought in a full haversack and divided them freely amongst his starving comrades. The old Borderer and the Yorkshireman were gaunt and hollow-eyed with privation, while the bowyer's round face had fallen in so that the skin hung in loose pouches under his eyes and beneath his jaws.

Behind them lines of haggard, wolfish men glared through the underwood, silent and watchful save that they burst into a fierce yelp of welcome when Chandos and Nigel galloped up, sprang from their horses and took their station beneath them. All along the green fringe of bowmen might be seen the steel-clad figures of knights and squires who had pushed their way into the front line to share the fortune of the archers.

"I call to mind that I once shot six ends with a Kentish woldsman at Ashford—" began the Bowyer.

"Nay, nay, we have heard that story!" said old Wat impatiently. "Shut thy clap, Bartholomew, for it is no time for redeless gossip! Walk down the line, I pray you, and see if there be no frayed string, nor broken nock nor loosened whipping to be mended."

The stout bowyer passed down the fringe of bowmen, amidst a running fire of rough wit. Here and there a bow was thrust out at him through the hedge for his professional advice.

"Wax your heads!" he kept crying. "Pass down the wax-pot and wax your heads. A waxed arrow will pass where a dry will be held. Tom Beverley, you jack-fool! where is your bracer-guard? Your string will flay your arm ere you reach your up-shot this day. And you, Watkin, draw not to your mouth, as is your wont, but to your shoulder. You are so used to the wine-pot that the string must needs follow it. Nay, stand loose, and give space for your drawing arms, for they will be on us anon."

He ran back and joined his comrades in the front, who had now risen to their feet. Behind them a half-mile of archers stood behind the hedge, each with his great warbow strung, half a dozen shafts loose behind him, and eighteen more in the quiver slung across his front. With arrow on string, their feet firm-planted, their fierce eager faces peering through the branches, they awaited the coming storm.

The broad flood of steel, after oozing slowly forward, had stopped about a mile from the English front. The greater part of the army had then descended from their horses, while a crowd of varlets and hostlers led them to the rear. The French formed themselves now into three great divisions, which shimmered in the sun like silvery pools, reed-capped with many a thousand of banners and pennons. A space of several hundred yards divided each. At the same time two bodies of horsemen formed themselves in front. The first consisted of three hundred men in one thick column, the second of a thousand, riding in a more extended line.

The Prince had ridden up to the line of archers. He was in dark armor, his visor open, and his handsome aquiline face all glowing with spirit and martial fire. The bowmen yelled at him, and he waved his hands to them as a huntsman cheers his hounds.

"Well, John, what think you now?" he asked. "What would my noble father not give to be by our side this day? Have you seen that they have left their horses?"

"Yes, my fair lord, they have learned their lesson," said Chandos. "Because we have had good fortune upon our feet at Crécy and elsewhere they think that they have found the trick of it. But it is in my mind that it is very different to stand when you are assailed, as we have done, and to assail others when you must drag your harness for a mile and come weary to the fray."

"You speak wisely, John. But these horsemen who form in front and ride slowly towards us, what make you of them?"

"Doubtless they hope to cut the strings of our bowmen and so clear a way for the others. But they are indeed a chosen band, for mark you, fair sir, are not those the colors of Clermont upon the left, and of d'Andreghen upon the right, so that both marshals ride with the vanguard?"

"By God's soul, John!" cried the Prince, "it is very sure that you can see more with one eye than any man in this army with two. But it is even as you say. And this larger band behind?"

"They should be Germans, fair sir, by the fashion of their harness."

The two bodies of horsemen had moved slowly over the plain, with a space of nearly a quarter of a mile between them. Now, having come two bowshots from the hostile line, they halted. All that they could see of the English was the long hedge, with an occasional twinkle of steel through its leafy branches, and behind that the spearheads of the men-at-arms rising from amidst the brushwood and the vines. A lovely autumn countryside with changing many-tinted foliage lay stretched before them, all bathed in peaceful sunshine, and nothing save those flickering fitful gleams to tell of the silent and lurking enemy who barred their way. But the bold spirit of the French cavaliers rose the higher to the danger. The clamor of their war-cries filled the air, and they tossed their pennoned spears over their heads in menace and defiance. From the English line it was a noble sight, the gallant, pawing, curveting horses, the many-colored twinkling riders, the swoop and wave and toss of plume and banner.

Then a bugle rang forth. With a sudden yell every spur struck deep, every lance was laid in rest, and the whole gallant squadron flew like a glittering thunderbolt for the center of the English line.

A hundred yards they had crossed, and yet another hundred, but there was no movement in front of them, and no sound save their own hoarse battle-cries and the thunder of their horses. Ever swifter and swifter they flew. From behind the hedge it was a vision of horses, white, bay and black, their necks stretched, their nostrils distended, their bellies to the ground, whilst of the rider one could but see a shield with a plume-tufted visor above it, and a spear-head twinkling in front.

Then of a sudden the Prince raised his hand and gave a cry. Chandos echoed it, it swelled down the line, and with one mighty chorus of twanging strings and hissing shafts the long-pent storm broke at last.

Alas for the noble steeds! Alas for the gallant men. When the lust of battle is over who would not grieve to see that noble squadron break into red ruin before the rain of arrows beating upon the faces and breasts of the horses? The front rank crashed down, and the others piled themselves upon the top of them, unable to check their speed, or to swerve aside from the terrible wall of their shattered comrades which had so suddenly sprung up before them. Fifteen feet high was that blood-spurting mound of screaming, kicking horses and writhing, struggling men. Here and there on the flanks a horseman cleared himself and dashed for the hedge, only to have his steed slain under him and to be hurled from his saddle. Of all the three hundred gallant riders, not one ever reached that fatal hedge.

But now in a long rolling wave of steel the German battalion roared swiftly onward. They opened in the center to pass that terrible mound of death, and then spurred swiftly in upon the archers. They were brave men, well led, and in their open lines they could avoid the clubbing together which had been the ruin of the vanguard; yet they perished singly even as the others had perished together. A few were slain by the arrows. The greater number had their horses killed under them, and were so shaken and shattered by the fall that they could not raise their limbs, over-weighted with iron, from the spot where they lay.

Three men riding together broke through the bushes which sheltered the leaders of the archers, cut down Widdington the Dalesman, spurred onward through the hedge, dashed over the bowmen behind it, and made for the Prince. One fell with an arrow through his head, a second was beaten from his saddle by Chandos, and the third was slain by the Prince's own hand. A second band broke through near the river, but were cut off by Lord Audley and his squires, so that all were slain. A single horseman whose steed was mad with pain, an arrow in its eye and a second in its nostril, sprang over the hedge and clattered through the whole army, disappearing amid whoops and laughter into the woods behind. But none others won as far as the hedge. The whole front of the position was fringed with a litter of German wounded or dead, while one great heap in the center marked the downfall of the gallant French three hundred.

Whilst these two waves of the attack had broken in front of the English position, leaving this blood-stained wreckage behind them, the main divisions had halted and made their last prepara-tions for their own assault. They had not yet begun their advance, and the nearest was still half a mile distant, when the few survivors from the forlorn hope, their maddened horses bristling with arrows, flew past them on either flank.

At the same moment the English archers and men-at-arms dashed through the hedge, and dragged all who were living out of that tangled heap of shattered horses and men. It was a mad wild rush, for in a few minutes the fight must be renewed, and yet there was a rich harvest of wealth for the lucky man who could pick a wealthy prisoner from amid the crowd. The nobler spirits disdained to think of ransoms whilst the fight was still unsettled; but a swarm of needy soldiers, Gascons and English, dragged the wounded out by the leg or the arm, and with daggers at their throats demanded their names, title and means. He who had made a good prize hurried him to the rear where his own servants could guard him, while he who was disappointed too often drove the dagger home and then rushed once more into the tangle in the hope of better luck. Clermont, with an arrow through the sky-blue Virgin on his surcoat, lay dead within ten paces of the hedge; d'Andreghen was dragged by a penniless squire from under a horse and became his prisoner. The Earl of Salzburg and of Nassau were both found helpless on the ground and taken to the rear. Aylward cast his thick arms round Count Otto von Langenbeck, and laid him, helpless from a broken leg, behind his bush. Black Simon had made prize of Bernard, Count of Ventadour, and hurried him through the hedge. Everywhere there was rushing and shouting, brawling and buffeting, while amidst it all a swarm of archers were seeking their shafts, plucking them from the dead, and sometimes even from the wounded. Then there was a sudden cry of warning. In a moment every man was back in his place once more, and the line of the hedge was clear.

It was high time; for already the first division of the French was close upon them. If the charge of the horsemen had been terrible from its rush and its fire, this steady advance of a huge phalanx of armored footmen was even more fearsome to the spectator. They moved very slowly, on account of the weight of their armor, but their progress was the more regular and inexorable. With elbows touching—their shields slung in front, their short five-foot spears carried in their right hands, and their maces or swords ready at their belts, the deep column of men-at-arms moved onward. Again the storm of arrows beat upon them clinking and thudding on the armor. They crouched double behind their shields as they met it. Many fell, but still the slow tide lapped onward. Yelling, they surged up to the hedge, and lined it for half a mile, struggling hard to pierce it.

For five minutes the long straining ranks faced each other with fierce stab of spear on one side and heavy beat of ax or mace upon the other. In many parts the hedge was pierced or leveled to the ground, and the French men-at-arms were raging amongst the archers, hacking and hewing among the lightly armed men. For a moment it seemed as if the battle was on the turn.

But John de Vere, Earl of Oxford, cool, wise and crafty in war, saw and seized, his chance. On the right flank a marshy meadow skirted the river. So soft was it that a heavily-armed man would sink to his knees. At his order a spray of light bowmen was thrown out from the battle line and forming upon the flank of the French poured their arrows into them. At the same moment Chandos, with Audley, Nigel, Bartholomew Burghersh, the Captal de Buch, and a score of other knights sprang upon their horses, and charging down the narrow lane rode over the French line in front of them. Once through it they spurred to left and right, trampling down the dismounted men-at-arms.

A fearsome sight was Pommers that day, his red eyes rolling, his nostrils gaping, his tawny mane tossing, and his savage teeth gnashing in fury, as he tore and smashed and ground beneath his ramping hoofs all that came before him. Fearsome too was the rider, ice-cool; alert, concentrated of purpose, with, heart of fire and muscles of steel. A very angel of battle he seemed as he drove his maddened horse through the thickest of the press, but strive as he would: the tall figure of his master upon his coal-black steed was ever half a length before him.

Already the moment of danger was passed. The French line had given back. Those who had pierced the hedge had fallen like brave men amid the ranks of their foemen. The division of Warwick had hurried up from the vineyards to fill the gaps of Salisbury's battle-line. Back rolled the shining tide, slowly at first, even as it had advanced, but quicker now as the bolder fell and the weaker shredded out and shuffled with ungainly speed for a place of safety. Again there was a rush from behind the hedge. Again there was a reaping of that strange crop of bearded arrows which grew so thick upon the ground, and again the wounded prisoners were seized and dragged in brutal haste to the rear. Then the line was restored, and the English, weary, panting and shaken, awaited the next attack.

But a great good fortune had come to them—so great that as they looked down the valley they could scarce credit their own senses. Behind the division of the Dauphin, which had pressed them so hard, stood a second division hardly less numerous, led by the Duke of Orleans. The fugitives from in front, blood-smeared and bedraggled, blinded with sweat and with fear, rushed amidst its ranks in their flight, and in a moment, without a blow being struck, had carried them off in their wild rout. This vast array, so solid and so martial, thawed suddenly away like a snow-wreath in the sun. It was gone, and in its place thousands of shining dots scattered over the whole plain as each man made his own way to the spot where he could find his horse and bear himself from the field. For a moment it seemed that the battle was won, and a thundershout of joy pealed up from the English line.

But as the curtain of the Duke's division was drawn away it was only to disclose stretching far behind it, and spanning the valley from side to side, the magnificent array of the French King, solid, unshaken, and preparing its ranks for the attack. Its numbers were as great as those of the English army; it was unscathed by all that was past, and it had a valiant monarch to lead it to the charge. With the slow deliberation of the man who means to do or to die, its leader marshaled its ranks for the supreme effort of the day.

Meanwhile during that brief moment of exultation when the battle appeared to be won, a crowd of hot-headed young knights and squires swarmed and clamored round the Prince, beseeching that he would allow them to ride forth.

"See this insolent fellow who bears three martlets upon a field gales!" cried Sir Maurice Berkeley. "He stands betwixt the two armies as though he had no dread of us."

"I pray you, sir, that I may ride out to him, since he seems ready to attempt some small deed," pleaded Nigel. "Nay, fair sirs, it is an evil thing that we should break our line, seeing that we still have much to do," said the Prince. "See! he rides away, and so the matter is settled."

"Nay, fair prince," said the young knight who had spoken first. "My gray horse, Lebryte, could run him down ere he could reach shelter. Never since I left Severn side have I seen steed so fleet as mine. Shall I not show you?" In an instant he had spurred the charger and was speeding across the plain.

The Frenchman, John de Helennes, a squire of Picardy, had waited with a burning heart, his soul sick at the flight of the division in which he had ridden. In the hope of doing some redeeming exploit, or of meeting his own death, he had loitered betwixt the armies, but no movement had come from the English lines. Now he had turned his horse's head to join the King's array, when the low drumming of hoofs sounded behind him, and he turned to find a horseman hard upon his heels. Each had drawn his sword, and the two armies paused to view the fight. In the first bout Sir Maurice Berkeley's lance was struck from his hand, and as he sprang down to recover it the Frenchman ran him through the thigh, dismounted from his horse, and received his surrender. As the unfortunate Englishman hobbled away at the side of his captor a roar of laughter burst from both armies at the spectacle.

"By my ten finger-bones!" cried Aylward, chuckling behind the remains of his bush, "he found more on his distaff that time than he knew how to spin. Who was the knight?"

"By his arms," said old Wat, "he should either be a Berkeley of the West or a Popham of Kent."

"I call to mind that I shot a match of six ends once with a Kentish woldsman—" began the fat Bowyer.

"Nay, nay, stint thy talk, Bartholomew!" cried old Wat. "Here is poor Ned with his head cloven, and it would be more fitting if you were saying aves for his soul, instead of all this bobance and boasting. Now, now, Tom of Beverley?"

"We have suffered sorely in this last bout, Wat. There are forty of our men upon their backs, and the Dean Foresters on the right are in worse case still."

"Talking will not mend it, Tom, and if all but one were on their backs he must still hold his ground."

Whilst the archers were chatting, the leaders of the army were in solemn conclave just behind them. Two divisions of the French had been repulsed, and yet there was many an anxious face as the older knights looked across the plain at the unbroken array of the French King moving slowly toward them. The line of the archers was much thinned and shredded. Many knights and squires had been disabled in the long and fierce combat at the hedge. Others, exhausted by want of food, had no strength left and were stretched panting upon the ground. Some were engaged in carrying the wounded to the rear and laying them under the shelter of the trees, whilst others were replacing their broken swords or lances from the weapons of the slain. The Captal de Buch, brave and experienced as he was, frowned darkly and whispered his misgivings to Chandos.

But the Prince's courage flamed the higher as the shadow fell, while his dark eyes gleamed with a soldier's pride as he glanced round him at his weary comrades, and then at the dense masses of the King's battle which now, with a hundred trumpets blaring and a thousand pennons waving, rolled slowly over the plain. "Come what may, John, this has been a most noble meeting," said he. "They will not be ashamed of us in England. Take heart, my friends, for if we conquer we shall carry the glory ever with us; but if we be slain then we die most worshipfully and in high honor, as we have ever prayed that we might die, and we leave behind us our brothers and kinsmen who will assuredly avenge us. It is but one more effort, and all will be well. Warwick, Oxford, Salisbury, Suffolk, every man to the front! My banner to the front also! Your horses, fair sirs! The archers are spent, and our own good lances must win the field this day. Advance, Walter, and may God and Saint George be with England!"

Sir Walter Woodland, riding a high black horse, took station by the Prince, with the royal banner resting in a socket by his saddle. From all sides the knights and squires crowded in upon it, until they formed a great squadron containing the survivors of the battalions of Warwick and Salisbury as well as those of the Prince. Four hundred men-at-arms who had been held in reserve were brought up and thickened the array, but even so Chandos' face was grave as he scanned it and then turned his eyes upon the masses of the Frenchmen.

"I like it not, fair sir. The weight is overgreat," he whispered to the Prince.

"How would you order it, John? Speak what is in you mind."

"We should attempt something upon their flank whilst we hold them in front. How say you, jean?" He turner to the Captal de Buch, whose dark, resolute face reflected the same misgivings.

"Indeed, John, I think as you do," said he. "The French King is a very valiant man, and so are those who are about him, and I know not how we may drive them back unless we can do as you advise. If you will give me only a hundred men I will attempt it."

"Surely the task is mine, fair sir, since the thought has come from me," said Chandos.

"Nay, John, I would keep you at my side. But you speak well, Jean, and you shall do even as you have said. Go ask the Earl of Oxford for a hundred men-at-arms and as many hobblers, that you may ride round the mound yonder, and so fall upon them unseen. Let all that are left of the archers gather on each side, shoot away their arrows, and then fight as best they may. Wait till they are past yonder thorn-bush and then, Walter, bear my banner straight against that of the King of France. Fair sirs, may God and the thought of your ladies hold high your hearts!"

The French monarch, seeing that his footmen had made no impression upon the English, and also that the hedge had been well-nigh leveled to the ground in the course of the combat, so that it no longer presented an obstacle, had ordered his followers to remount their horses, and it was as a solid mass of cavalry that the chivalry of France advanced to their last supreme effort. The King was in the center of the front line, Geoffrey de Chargny with the golden oriflamme upon his right, and Eustace de Ribeaumont with the royal lilies upon the left. At his elbow was the Duke of Athens, High Constable of France, and round him were the nobles of the court, fiery and furious, yelling their warcries as they waved their weapons over their heads. Six thousand gallant men of the bravest race in Europe, men whose very names are like blasts of a battle-trumpet — Beaujeus and Chatillons, Tancarvilles and Ventadours — pressed hard behind the silver lilies.

Slowly they moved at first, walking their horses that they might be the fresher for the shock. Then they broke into a trot which was quickening into a gallop when the remains of the hedge in front of them was beaten in an instant to the ground and the broad line of the steel-clad chivalry of England swept grandly forth to the final shock. With loose rein and busy spur the two lines of horsemen galloped at the top of their speed straight and hard for each other. An instant later they met with a thunder-crash which was heard by the burghers on the wall of Poitiers, seven good miles away.

Under that frightful impact horses fell dead with broken necks, and many a rider, held in his saddle by the high pommel, fractured his thighs with the shock. Here and there a pair met breast to breast, the horses rearing straight upward and falling back upon their masters. But for the most part the line had opened in the gallop, and the cavaliers, flying through the gaps, buried themselves in the enemy's ranks. Then the flanks shredded out, and the thick press in the center loosened until there was space to swing a sword and to guide a steed. For ten acres there was one wild tumultuous swirl of tossing heads, of gleaming weapons which rose and fell, of upthrown hands, of tossing plumes and of lifted shields, whilst the din of a thousand war-cries and the clash-clash of metal upon metal rose and swelled like the roar and beat of an ocean surge upon a rock-bound coast. Backward and forward swayed the mighty throng, now down the valley and now up, as each side in turn put forth its strength for a fresh rally. Locked in one long deadly grapple, great England and gallant France with iron hearts and souls of fire strove and strove for mastery.

Sir Walter Woodland, riding hard upon his high black horse, had plunged into the swelter and headed for the blue and silver banner of King John. Close at his heels in a solid wedge rode the Prince, Chandos, Nigel, Lord Reginald Cobham, Audley with his four famous squires, and a score of the flower of the English and Gascon knighthood. Holding together and bearing down opposition by a shower of blows and by the weight of their powerful horses, their progress was still very slow, for ever fresh waves of

French cavaliers surged up against them and broke in front only to close in again upon their rear. Sometimes they were swept backward by the rush, sometimes they gained a few paces, sometimes they could but keep their foothold, and yet from minute to minute that blue and silver flag which waved above the press grew ever a little closer. A dozen furious hard-breathing French knights had broken into their ranks, and clutched at Sir Walter Woodland's banner, but Chandos and Nigel guarded it on one side, Audley with his squires on the other, so that no man laid his hand upon it and lived.

But now there was a distant crash and a roar of "Saint George for Guienne!" from behind. The Captal de Buch had charged home. "Saint George for England!" yelled the main attack, and ever the counter-cry came back to them from afar. The ranks opened in front of them. The French were giving way. A small knight with golden scroll-work upon his armor threw himself upon the Prince and was struck dead by his mace. It was the Duke of Athens, Constable of France, but none had time to note it, and the fight rolled on over his body. Looser still were the French ranks. Many were turning their horses, for that ominous roar from the rear had shaken their resolution. The little English wedge poured onward, the Prince, Chandos, Audley and Nigel ever in the van.

A huge warrior in black, bearing a golden banner, appeared suddenly in a gap of the shredding ranks. He tossed his precious burden to a squire, who bore it away. Like a pack of hounds on the very haunch of a deer the English rushed yelling for the oriflamme. But the black warrior flung himself across their path. "Chargny! Chargny *à la recousse!*" he roared with a voice of thunder. Sir Reginald Cobham dropped before his battle-ax, so did the Gascon de Clisson. Nigel was beaten down on to the crupper of his horse by a sweeping blow; but at the same instant Chandos' quick blade passed through the Frenchman's camail and pierced his throat. So died Geoffrey de Chargny; but the oriflamme was saved.

Dazed with the shock, Nigel still kept his saddle, and Pommers, his yellow hide mottled with blood, bore him onward with the others. The French horsemen were now in full flight; but one stern group of knights stood firm, like a rock in a rushing torrent, beating off all, whether friend or foe, who tried to break their ranks. The oriflamme had gone, and so had the blue and silver banner, but here were desperate men ready to fight to the death. In their ranks honor was to be reaped. The Prince and his following hurled themselves upon them, while the rest of the English horsemen swept onward to secure the fugitives and to win their ransoms. But the nobler spirits—Audley, Chandos and the others—would have thought it shame to gain money whilst there was work to be done or honor to be won. Furious was the wild attack, desperate the prolonged defense. Men fell from their saddles for very exhaustion.

Nigel, still at his place near Chandos' elbow, was hotly attacked by a short broad-shouldered warrior upon a stout white cob, but Pommers reared with pawing fore feet and dashed the smaller horse to the ground. The falling rider clutched Nigel's arm and tore him from the saddle, so that the two rolled upon the grass under the stamping hoofs, the English squire on the top, and his shortened sword glimmered before the visor of the gasping, breathless Frenchman.

"*Je me rends! je axe rends!*" he panted.

For a moment a vision of rich ransoms passed through Nigel's brain. That noble palfrey, that gold-flecked armor, meant fortune to the captor. Let others have it! There was work still to be done. How could he desert the Prince and his noble master for the sake of a private gain? Could he lead a prisoner to the rear when honor beckoned him to the van? He staggered to his feet, seized Pommers by the mane, and swung himself into the saddle.

An instant later he was by Chandos' side once more and they were bursting together through the last ranks of the gallant group who had fought so bravely to the end. Behind them was one long swath of the dead and the wounded. In front the whole wide plain was covered with the flying French and their pursuers.

The Prince reined up his steed and opened his visor, whilst his followers crowded round him with waving weapons and frenzied shouts of victory. "What now, John!" cried the smiling Prince, wiping his streaming face with his ungauntleted hand. "How fares it then?"

"I am little hurt, fair lord, save for a crushed hand and a spear-prick in the shoulder. But you, sir? I trust you have no scathe?"

"In truth, John, with you at one elbow and Lord Audley at the other, I know not how I could come to harm. But alas! I fear that Sir James is sorely stricken."

The gallant Lord Audley had dropped upon the ground and the blood oozed from every crevice of his battered armor. His four brave Squires—Dutton of Dutton, Delves of Doddington, Fowlhurst of Crewe and Hawkstone of Wainhill—wounded and weary themselves, but with no thought save for their master, unlaced his helmet and bathed his pallid blood-stained face.

He looked up at the Prince with burning eyes. "I thank you, sir, for deigning to consider so poor a knight as myself," said he in a feeble voice.

The Prince dismounted and bent over him. "I am bound to honor you very much, James," said he, "for by your valor this day you have won glory and renown above us all, and your prowess has proved you to be the bravest knight."

"My Lord," murmured the wounded man, "you have a right to say what you please; but I wish it were as you say."

"James," said the Prince, "from this time onward I make you a knight of my own household, and I settle upon you five hundred marks of yearly income from my own estates in England."

"Sir," the knight answered, "God make me worthy of the good fortune you bestow upon me. Your knight I will ever be, and the money I will divide with your leave amongst these four squires who have brought me whatever glory I have won this day." So saying his head fell back, and he lay white and silent upon the grass.

"Bring water!" said the Prince. "Let the royal leech see to him; for I had rather lose many men than the good Sir James. Ha, Chandos, what have we here?"

A knight lay across the path with his helmet beaten down upon his shoulders. On his surcoat and shield were the arms of a red griffin.

"It is Robert de Duras the spy," said Chandos.

"Well for him that he has met his end," said the angry Prince. "Put him on his shield, Hubert, and let four archers bear him to the monastery. Lay him at the feet of the Cardinal and say that by this sign I greet him. Place my flag on yonder high bush, Walter, and let my tent be raised there, that my friends may know where to seek me."

The flight and pursuit had thundered far away, and the field was deserted save for the numerous groups of weary horsemen who were making their way back, driving their prisoners before them. The archers were scattered over the whole plain, rifling the saddle-bags and gathering the armor of those who had fallen, or searching for their own scattered arrows.

Suddenly, however, as the Prince was turning toward the bush which he had chosen for his headquarters, there broke out from behind him an extraordinary uproar and a group of knights and squires came pouring toward him, all arguing, swearing and abusing each other in French and English at the tops of their voices. In the midst of them limped a stout little man in gold-spangled armor, who appeared to be the object of the contention, for one would drag him one way and one another, as though they would pull him limb from limb. "Nay, fair sirs, gently, gently, I pray you!" he pleaded. "There is enough for all, and no need to treat me so rudely." But ever the hubbub broke out again, and swords gleamed as the angry disputants glared furiously at each other. The Prince's eyes fell upon the small prisoner, and he staggered back with a gasp of astonishment.

"King John!" he cried.

A shout of joy rose from the warriors around him. "The King of France! The King of France a prisoner!" they cried in an ecstasy.

"Nay, nay, fair sirs, let him not hear that we rejoice! Let no word bring pain to his soul!" Running forward the Prince clasped the French King by the two hands.

"Most welcome, sire!" he cried. "Indeed it is good for us that so gallant a knight should stay with us for some short time, since the chance of war has so ordered it. Wine there! Bring wine for the King!"

But John was flushed and angry. His helmet had been roughly torn off, and blood was smeared upon his cheek. His noisy captors stood around him in a circle, eying him hungrily like dogs who have been beaten from their quarry. There were Gascons and English, knights, squires and archers, all pushing and straining.

"I pray you, fair Prince, to get rid of these rude fellows," said King John, "for indeed they have plagued me sorely. By Saint Denis! my arm has been well-nigh pulled from its socket."

"What wish you then?" asked the Prince, turning angrily upon the noisy swarm of his followers.

"We took him, fair lord. He is ours!" cried a score of voices. They closed in, all yelping together like a pack of wolves. "It was I, fair lord!" — "Nay, it was I!" — "You lie, you rascal, it was I!" Again their fierce eyes glared and their blood-stained hands sought the hilts of their weapons.

"Nay, this must be settled here and now!" said the Prince. "I crave your patience, fair and honored sir, for a few brief minutes, since indeed much ill-will may spring from this if it be not set at rest. Who is this tall knight who can scarce keep his hands from the King's shoulder?"

"It is Denis de Morbecque, my lord, a knight of St. Omer, who is in our service, being an outlaw from France."

"I call him to mind. How then, Sir Denis? What say you in this matter?"

"He gave himself to me, fair lord. He had fallen in the press, and I came upon him and seized him. I told him that I was a knight from Artois, and he gave me his glove. See here, I bear it in my hand."

"It is true, fair lord! It is true!" cried a dozen French voices.

"Nay, sir, judge not too soon!" shouted an English squire, pushing his way to the front. "It was I who had him at my mercy, and he is my prisoner, for he spoke to this man only because he could tell by his tongue that he was his own countryman. I took him, and here are a score to prove it."

"It is true, fair lord. We saw it and it was even so," cried a chorus of Englishmen.

At all times there was growling and snapping betwixt the English and their allies of France. The Prince saw how easily this might set a light to such a flame as could not readily be quenched. It must be stamped out now ere it had time to mount.

"Fair and honored lord," he said to the King, "again I pray you for a moment of patience. It is your word and only yours which can tell us what is just and right. To whom were you graciously pleased to commit your royal person?"

King John looked up from the flagon which had been brought to him and wiped his lips with the dawnings of a smile upon his ruddy face.

"It was not this Englishman," he said, and a cheer burst from the Gascons, "nor was it this bastard Frenchman," he added. "To neither of them did I surrender."

There was a hush of surprise.

"To whom then, sir?" asked the Prince.

The King looked slowly round. "There was a devil of a yellow horse," said he. "My poor palfrey went over like a skittle-pin before a ball. Of the rider I know nothing save that he bore red roses on a silver shield. Ah! by Saint Denis, there is the man himself, and there his thrice-accursed horse!"

His head swimming, and moving as if in a dream, Nigel found himself the center of the circle of armed and angry men.

The Prince laid his hand upon his shoulder. "It is the little cock of Tilford Bridge," said he. "On my father's soul, I have ever said that you would win your way. Did you receive the King's surrender?"

"Nay, fair lord, I did not receive it."

"Did you hear him give it?"

"I heard, sir, but I did not know that it was the King. My master Lord Chandos had gone on, and I followed after."

"And left him lying. Then the surrender was not complete, and by the laws of war the ransom goes to Denis de Morbecque, if his story be true."

"It is true," said the King. "He was the second."

"Then the ransom is yours; Denis. But for my part I swear by my father's soul that I had rather have the honor this Squire has gathered than all the richest ransoms of France."

At these words spoken before that circle of noble warriors Nigel's heart gave one great throb, and he dropped upon his knee before the Prince. "Fair lord, how can I thank you?" he murmured. "These words at least are more than any ransom."

"Rise up!" said the smiling Prince, and he smote with his sword upon his shoulder. "England has lost a brave Squire, and has gained a gallant knight. Nay, linger not, I pray! Rise up, Sir Nigel!"

CHAPTER XXVII

HOW THE THIRD MESSENGER
CAME TO COSFORD

Two months have passed, and the long slopes of Hindhead are russet with the faded ferns—the fuzzy brown pelt which wraps the chilling earth. With whoop and scream the wild November wind sweeps over the great rolling downs, tossing the branches of the Cosford beeches, and rattling at the rude latticed windows. The stout old knight of Duplin, grown even a little stouter, with whiter beard to fringe an ever redder face, sits as of yore at the head of his own board. A well-heaped platter flanked by a foaming tankard stands before him. At his right sits the Lady Mary, her dark, plain, queenly face marked deep with those years of weary waiting, but bearing the gentle grace and dignity which only sorrow and restraint can give. On his left is Matthew, the old priest. Long ago the golden-haired beauty had passed from Cosford to Fernhurst, where the young and beautiful Lady Edith Brocas is the belle of all Sussex, a sunbeam of smiles and merriment, save perhaps when her thoughts for an instant fly back to that dread night when she was plucked from under the very talons of the foul hawk of Shalford.

The old knight looked up as a fresh gust of wind with a dash of rain beat against the window behind him. "By Saint Hubert, it is a wild night!" said he. "I had hoped to-morrow to have a flight at a heron of the pool or a mallard in the brook. How fares it with little Katherine the peregrine, Mary?"

"I have joined the wing, father, and I have imped the feathers; but I fear it will be Christmas ere she can fly again."

"This is a hard saying," said Sir John; "for indeed I have seen no bolder better bird. Her wing was broken by a heron's beak last Sabbath sennight, holy father, and Mary has the mending of it."

"I trust, my son, that you had heard mass ere you turned to worldly pleasure upon God's holy day," Father Matthew answered.

"Tut, tut!" said the old knight, laughing. "Shall I make confession at the head of my own table? I can worship the good God amongst his own works, the woods and the fields, better than in yon pile of stone and wood. But I call to mind a charm for a wounded hawk which was taught me by the fowler of Gaston de Foix. How did it run? 'The lion of the Tribe of Judah, the root of David, has conquered.' Yes, those were the words to be said three times as you walk round the perch where the bird is mewed."

The old priest shook his head. "Nay, these charms are tricks of the Devil," said he. "Holy Church lends them no countenance, for they are neither good nor fair. But how is it now with your tapestry, Lady Mary? When last I was beneath this roof you had half done in five fair colors the story of Theseus and Ariadne."

"It is half done still, holy father."

"How is this, my daughter? Have you then so many calls?"

"Nay, holy father, her thoughts are otherwhere," Sir John answered. "She will sit an hour at a time, the needle in her hand and her soul a hundred leagues from Cosford House. Ever since the Prince's battle—"

"Good father, I beg you—"

"Nay, Mary, none can hear me, save your own confessor, Father Matthew. Ever since the Prince's battle, I say, when we heard that young Nigel had won such honor she is brain-wode, and sits ever—well, even as you see her now."

An intent look had come into Mary's eyes; her gaze was fixed upon the dark rain-splashed window. It was a face carved from ivory, white-lipped and rigid, on which the old priest looked.

"What is it, my daughter? What do you see?"

"I see nothing, father."

"What is it then that disturbs you?"

"I hear, father."

"What do you hear?"

"There are horsemen on the road."

The old knight laughed. "So it goes on, father. What day is there that a hundred horsemen do not pass our gate, and yet every clink of hoofs sets her poor heart a-trembling. So strong and stead-fast she has ever been, my Mary, and now no sound too slight to shake her to the soul! Nay, daughter, nay, I pray you!"

She had half-risen from her chair, her hands clenched and her dark, startled eyes still fixed upon the window. "I hear them, father! I hear them amid the wind and the rain! Yes, yes, they are turning—they have turned! My God, they are at our very door!"

"By Saint Hubert, the girl is right!" cried old Sir John, beating his fist upon the board. "Ho, varlets, out with you to the yard! Set the mulled wine on the blaze once more! There are travelers at the gate, and it is no night to keep a dog waiting at our door. Hurry, Hannekin! Hurry, I say, or I will haste you with my cudgel!"

Plainly to the ears of all men could be heard the stamping of the horses. Mary had stood up, quivering in every limb. An eager step at the threshold, the door was flung wide, and there in the opening stood Nigel, the rain gleaming upon his smiling face, his cheeks flushed with the beating of the wind, his blue eyes shining with tenderness and love. Something held her by the throat, the light of the torches danced up and down; but her strong spirit rose at the thought that others should see that inner holy of holies of her soul. There is a heroism of women to which no valor of man can attain. Her eyes only carried him her message as she held out her hand.

"Welcome, Nigel!" said she.

He stooped and kissed it.

"Saint Catharine has brought me home," said he.

A merry supper it was at Cosford Manor that night, with Nigel at the head betwixt the jovial old knight and the Lady Mary, whilst at the farther end Samkin Aylward, wedged between two servant maids, kept his neighbors in alternate laughter and terror as he told his tales of the French Wars. Nigel had to turn his doeskin heels and show his little golden spurs. As he spoke of what was passed Sir John clapped him on the shoulder, while Mary took his strong right hand in hers, and the good old priest smiling blessed them both. Nigel had drawn a little golden ring from his pocket, and it twinkled in the torchlight.

"Did you say that you must go on your way to-morrow, father?" he asked the priest.

"Indeed, fair son, the matter presses."

"But you may bide the morning?"

"It will suffice if I start at noon."

"Much may be done in a morning." He looked at Mary, who blushed and smiled. "By Saint Paul! I have waited long enough."

"Good, good!" chuckled the old knight, with wheezy laughter. "Even so I wooed your mother, Mary. Wooers were brisk in the olden time. To-morrow is Tuesday, and Tuesday is ever a lucky day. Alas! that the good Dame Ermyntrude is no longer with us to see it done! The old hound must run us down, Nigel, and I hear its bay upon my own heels; but my heart will rejoice that before the end I may call you son. Give me your hand, Mary, and yours, Nigel. Now, take an old man's blessing, and may God keep and guard you both, and give you your desert, for I believe on my soul that in all this broad land there dwells no nobler man nor any woman more fitted to be his mate!"

There let us leave them, their hearts full of gentle joy, the golden future of hope and promise stretching out before their youthful eyes. Alas for those green spring dreaming! How often do they fade and wither until they fall and rot, a dreary sight, by the wayside of life! But here, by God's blessing, it was not so, for they burgeoned and they grew, ever fairer and more noble, until the whole wide world might marvel at the beauty of it.

It has been told elsewhere how as the years passed Nigel's name rose higher in honor; but still Mary's would keep pace with it, each helping and sustaining the other upon an ever higher path. In many lands did Nigel carve his fame, and ever as he returned spent and weary from his work he drank fresh strength and fire and craving for honor from her who glorified his home. At Twynham Castle they dwelled for many years, beloved and honored by all. Then in the fullness of time they came back to the Tilford Manor-house and spent their happy, healthy age amid those heather downs where Nigel had passed his first lusty youth, ere ever he turned his face to the wars. Thither also came Aylward when he had left the "Pied Merlin" where for many a year he sold ale to the men of the forest.

But the years pass; the old wheel turns and ever the thread runs out. The wise and the good, the noble and the brave, they come from the darkness, and into the darkness they go, whence, whither and why, who may say? Here is the slope of Hindhead. The fern still glows russet in November, the heather still burns red in July; but where now is the Manor of Cosford? Where is the old house of Tilford? Where, but for a few scattered gray stones, is the mighty pile of Waverley? And yet even gnawing Time has not eaten all things away. Walk with me toward Guildford, reader, upon the busy highway. Here, where the high green mound rises before us, mark yonder roofless shrine which still stands four-square to the winds. It is St. Catharine's, where Nigel and Mary plighted their faith. Below lies the winding river, and over yonder you still see the dark Chantry woods which mount up to the bare summit, on which, roofed and whole, stands that Chapel of the Martyr where the comrades beat off the archers of the crooked Lord of Shalford. Down yonder on the flanks of the long chalk hills one traces the road by which they made their journey to the wars. And now turn hither to the north, down this sunken winding path! It is all unchanged since Nigel's day. Here is the Church of Compton. Pass under the aged and crumbling arch. Before the steps of that ancient altar, unrecorded and unbrassed, lies the dust of Nigel and of Mary. Near them is that of Maude their daughter, and of Alleyne Edricson, whose spouse she was; their children and children's children are lying by their side. Here too, near the old yew in the churchyard, is the little mound which marks where Samkin Aylward went back to that good soil from which he sprang.

So lie the dead leaves; but they and such as they nourish forever that great old trunk of England, which still sheds forth another crop and another, each as strong and as fair as the last. The body may lie in moldering chancel, or in crumbling vault, but the rumor of noble lives, the record of valor and truth, can never die, but lives on in the soul of the people. Our own work lies ready to our hands; and yet our strength may be the greater and our faith the firmer if we spare an hour from present toils to look back upon the women who were gentle and strong, or the men who loved honor more than life, on this green stage of England where for a few short years we play our little part.

THE END

SUGGESTED READING

BARBER, RICHARD. *Edward, Prince of Wales and Aquitaine.* Woodbridge, England: Boydell Press, 1978.

BARBER, RICHARD, AND JULIET BARKER. *Tournaments.* Woodbridge, England: Boydell Press, 1989.

CARR, JOHN DICKSON. *The Life of Sir Arthur Conan Doyle.* London: John Murray, 1949.

CHAUCER, GEOFFREY. *Canterbury Tales.* Trans. A. Kent Hieatt and Constance Hieatt. New York: Bantam Books, 1964.

CONAN DOYLE, ADRIAN, ED. *Sir Arthur Conan Doyle: Centenary 1859–1959.* Garden City: Doubleday & Company, 1959.

CONAN DOYLE, ARTHUR. *The Annotated Lost World.* Ed. Roy Pilot and Alvin Rodin. Indianapolis: Wessex Press, 1996.

---. *The Complete Sherlock Holmes.* New York: Deluxe, 2002.

---. *Memories and Adventures.* London: Hodder & Stoughton, 1924.

---. *Through the Magic Door.* New York: McClure, 1908.

EDWARDS, OWEN DUDLEY. *The Quest for Sherlock Holmes.* Edinburgh: Mainstream Publishing, 1983.

GIES, FRANCES. *The Knight in History.* New York: Harper & Row, 1984.

HOPKINS, ANDREA. *Knights.* New York: Shooting Star Press, 1990.

MCKISACK, MAY. *The Fourteenth Century: 1307–1399.* Oxford: Oxford University Press, 1959.

SLATER, STEPHEN. *The Complete Book of Heraldry.* London: Hermes House, 2003.

STASHOWER, DANIEL. *Teller of Tales: The Life of Arthur Conan Doyle.* New York: Henry Holt, 1999.

SUMPTION, JONATHAN. *Trial by Battle: The Hundred Years War, Volume I.* London: Faber & Faber, 1990.

---. *Trial by Fire: The Hundred Years War, Volume II.* London: Faber & Faber, 1999.

TUCHMAN, BARBARA W. *A Distant Mirror: The Calamitous 14th Century.* New York: Ballantine Books, 1979.

WAUGH, SCOTT L. *England in the Reign of Edward III.* Cambridge: Cambridge University Press, 1991.